ENDGAME

Books by **Kristine Smith**

ENDGAME

The Chronicles of Jani Killian

KRISTINE SMITH

SFBC

SCIENCE
FICTION

CONTACT IMMINENT Copyright © 2003 by Kristine Smith
  Publication History: Avon Eos mass market paperback, November 2003
ENDGAME Copyright © 2007 by Kristine Smith
  Publication History: Eos mass market paperback, November 2007

First SFBC Science Fiction Printing: December 2007

Published by arrangement with
Eos
An Imprint of HarperCollins*Publishers*
10 East 53rd Street
New York, NY 10022-5299

Visit The SFBC online at http://www.sfbc.com

ISBN 978-0-7394-9103-4

Printed in the United States of America.

CONTENTS

Thalassa
Commonwealth Colony of Elyas
Summer, Year One

My name is Torin Clase, and I have been charged with writing the story of Jani Kilian. Who she is, and how she came to be.

A quarter century ago a Vynshà priest named ní Tsecha Egri prophesied that one day his race, the idomeni, and my race, the humanish, would blend in the fullness of time to form a single people. In his quest to promote his vision, Tsecha compelled his people to allow humanish to live on the idomeni homeworld of Shèrá, and to establish a consulate on the outskirts of the dominant city of Rauta Shèràa.

Tsecha also compelled the idomeni to allow humanish into their dominant educational institution, the Academy. That first class of six students learned documents protocols from the race that devised them, as tensions grew between those bornsect idomeni who feared the humanish presence within the Shèráin worldskein and those few who believed that Tsecha's blending prophecies defined the future.

When these tensions erupted into civil war, one of those six humanish graduates, Jani Kilian, had attained the rank of Captain in the Commonwealth Service. As she worked to mediate relations between humanish and idomeni, she learned of illegal dealings between them that would have given victory to the ultraconservative elements of the idomeni and bolstered repressive forces within the humanish government. But when she acted to expose this conspiracy, she was killed, murdered as the transport in which she rode exploded on takeoff outside the hospital-shrine of Knevçet Shèràa.

But killed and dead are two different things. Kilian was saved by a humanish physician named John Shroud, who refashioned her using idomeni genetic material. He believed he had inacti-vated what he considered the undesirable aspects of that material, but he had not.

As the war drew to its bloody conclusion, Kilian escaped with her life. For almost twenty years she lived a fugitive existence in the colonies, on the run from her past, each day growing more aware of the change that had begun to claim her. Last year, she traveled to the Commonwealth homeworld of Earth for the first time, to the capital of Chicago. There she investigated crimes that provided her with the links between her past and her future, and revealed to her the path she was destined to follow as the first of her kind. The first hybrid.

She lives in Chicago still, working with the idomeni embassy and studying the ways of a priest with ní Tsecha, whom she calls "inshah." Teacher. Doing that which she is bound to do, for she is, as ní Tsecha named her, the Kièrshia, the "toxin," the bringer of pain and change. She is also, as I have said before, the first.

And I so wish to meet her . . .

CONTACT IMMINENT

CHAPTER 1

"Chicago is a cold place. In every way."

Clase, *Thalassan Histories, Book I*

"*Coppélia* is a classic tale. In it, a doctor named Coppélius builds a clockwork doll and tries to give her life." Colonel Niall Pierce sat with his booted feet propped on the edge of the portable com–array console, hands folded primly in his lap. "A young couple, Franz and Swanilda, cross his path. Franz falls in love with the doll, named Coppélia, whom he thinks is a real girl. Swanilda becomes determined to find out more about this mysterious beauty who has stolen her lover's heart, and breaks into the doctor's house to find her." He leaned back, the harsh overhead light washing out his bronze Service burr to pale brown and casting his features in sharp relief. Narrow. Angled. The wolf in repose. "And it's a comedy, I'll have you know. Nobody dies."

"Imagine my amazement." Jani Kilian tucked her hands inside the sleeves of her field coat and huddled against the curved wall of the prefab bunker. Outside, freezing rain fell—she could hear it patter on the domed roof. Insets in the polyfoam wall and floor supplied the heat that made the space bearable—she pressed against the hard smoothness, soaking up all the warmth she could. "I thought someone had to keel over every five minutes for an opera to qualify as a classic."

"*Coppélia* is a *ballet*, not an opera." Niall tilted his head back and spread his hands palms up, begging the ceiling for respite. "I told you all about it at lunch last week, but it appears to have slipped your mind." He turned to look toward the figure who sat on the floor next to Jani. "Have you ever attended a ballet, ní Tsecha? Humanish dancing?"

"No, Colonel." Ní Tsecha Egri, the Haárin dominant, shook

his head back and forth, his latest adoption of humanish gesture. "I have seen plays, and holoVee programs. Histories and such. No dancing." He pushed up the edge of his headscarf with one gold-skinned finger and scratched his scalp. "Nìa," he leaned close to Jani, his voice falling to a whisper, "ballet is leaping about to music?"

"Pretty much, inshah."

"I saw a dancing goat once. Is that as ballet?"

"It is quite similar, yes." Jani unfolded to her feet and walked across the shelter to join Niall at the console. She placed a hand on his shoulder, felt his warmth through his blue fatigue shirt, and tried to remember the days when she could feel warm under conditions like this. "Any change?"

Niall glared in injury, the scar that cut his left cheek from his nose to the corner of his mouth deepening as he frowned. "A dancing goat?" His eyes spoke to the frustrated patron of the arts that he was. Honey-brown and long-lashed, his only handsome feature, they were currently laced with aggravation and regret over missed performances and unappreciative students who ignored lunchtime instruction.

Jani offered a rueful grin. "I'm sorry you couldn't attend your ballet. I know you looked forward to it." She dragged a stool from beneath the console and sat next to him, then pointed to the display screen in the center of the flickering communications array. "Doesn't look any different than it did twenty minutes ago."

"Part of that's the fact that the pickup's malfunctioning. Our comtech should be back any minute with the replacement parts." Niall sighed. "The image straightens out every few minutes. From what I can see, they're still clearing snow. Marking out the cordon." He massaged the back of his neck. "Mine clearance is one of those dichotomous activities. Nerve-wracking to perform, but boring as all hell to watch. Especially when no one seems to be doing anything."

"I heard that." A male voice laced with annoyance emerged from the array's speaker system. "If you're both bored in that nice, warm, *dry* bunker, two hundred meters from all the stuff that goes *boom*, I'd be more than happy to trade places with you."

Niall and Jani looked at one another and smiled. "Hey, Pull," Niall said with a laugh. "How's it going?"

"Saturday night at the Haárin enclave—what a rip-roaring place." The irritation in Lieutenant Randal Pullman's voice was palpable.

Jani glanced back at Tsecha, who had risen and now walked across the bunker to join them. He stood taller than she by a head—the top of his headscarf grazed the light fixture as he passed beneath it, sending it swinging back and forth and casting his thin frame in weird shadows on the wall.

"Rip-roaring, nìa?" Tsecha stood over Jani, arms folded and hands tucked in his sleeves, his long face skull-like. "What is rip-roaring?"

No sound emerged from the speaker for a time. Then came a throat-clearing cough. "Is that you, ní Tsecha?"

"Yes, Lieutenant Pullman—glories of the night to you." Tsecha glanced at Jani and bared his teeth, cracked amber eyes bright with humor. "What is rip-roaring?"

"Rip-roaring? It's—it—" A long sigh rattled. "Ah, boy."

"Out with it, Pull." Niall's shoulders shook.

"Rip-roaring means . . . exciting, ní Tsecha. Thrilling." Pullman's voice grew softer with each passing syllable. "Electrifying."

"So you find standing in deep snow late at night an excitement? I learn more of you each day, Lieutenant." Tsecha's air of mischief faded. "What of the mine?"

Pullman's voice emerged more businesslike. "From what I have been able to determine thus far, ní Tsecha, the mine is most likely a remnant from an old field exercise. The Service used to operate training facilities here before the land was leased to the idomeni."

"What sort of mine—have you yet determined such?"

"No. Ní Tsecha. That's still under investigation."

"It is a trainer, as you say? Or a dud? Such objects emit signals particular to their type, do they not? One simply identifies the signal, and thus the type of mine, and removes it accordingly."

"Yes. Ní Tsecha. We have not yet identified the signal."

Jani glanced at Niall to find him regarding her, his face set with concern. They had both sensed Pullman's reluctance to discuss the situation. *They've had two hours to ID that mine, and they haven't yet. What's the problem?*

She reached for the console controls and tapped one of the pads. The flat display shimmered, then the two-dimensional image pushed out from the screen, lengthening and widening to form a three-dimensional layout of the mine site. The casualty radius, centered by a black X and encircled by an orange ring two hundred meters in diameter, stared out like a huge bull's-eye. The image stuttered every few seconds as the relays miscued, but it remained steady enough to discern the movement of personnel and equipment, both human and idomeni. "There's the demolitions tech." Jani pointed out the lone figure standing within the cordon, operating the remote-control 'bot that cleared snow from around the mine. "He's still digging the thing out, but I can already spot it at this scale. Why's he still working?"

"Where is Dathim?" Tsecha leaned over the console and searched the miniaturized scene for the towering figure of his suborn. "I will contact him and learn what he knows." He walked to the far side of the bunker as he dug inside his coat for his handcom.

Niall leaned close to the speaker and dropped his voice. "OK, Tsecha stepped away for a while," he said, the sharp tones of Vynshàrau Haárin serving as background. "What's going on?"

In the three-dimensional image, a figure at the edge of the cordon raised a hand. Pullman, kitted out in grey and white winter camou topped with a layer of body armor. "The disposal tech thinks that some water got into the brain of the mine and is screwing up the thing's ability to respond to signals. I'd never heard of that happening, but your guy confirmed. Faber, your comtech. He's at the supply truck hunting for parts for your console."

Niall edged about in his seat as he studied the scene. "So if the tech doesn't know what kind of mine we're dealing with, how the hell is he setting up?"

"According to Ordnance, it's one of two types. Either a Slager that's live but sans detonator, or a Beekman trainer that's most likely a dummy but could be live as well. The Slager's casualty radius is the greater of the two at one hundred meters, so that's what we've gone with." Pullman-in-miniature paced a tight circuit on the edge of the cordon. "It's getting tense here, sir. The Vynshàrau have already gone nose-to-nose a couple of times with our folks. They're picking apart the fact that one of our demis detected the mine signal in the first place—they want to know why we were flying that far inland over their territory. Diplomats from both sides are weighing in with all kinds of questions and demands, and to top off this shitcream sundae, I don't think this tech could find his ass at high noon in the Hall of Mirrors."

Niall patted the front pocket of his shirt, the usual resting place for his nicstick case. "Who's handling the diplomats from our team?"

"Dubrovna. Problem is, everyone at this level is used to dealing with Cal Burkett. Hard to back down to a major when you're used to dealing with a general."

"So why the hell isn't Burkett there now?"

"He's with the PM, sir, back in Chicago. They're patched in via the same live feed you have. It's my understanding that they're briefing Ambassador Shai."

Niall massaged the back of his neck in earnest. "Tell me about the tech."

Pullman muttered something foul under his breath. "Name's Wode, sir. Lance Corporal Rikki—two k's and an i. Supposed to be good, but you wouldn't know it from the way he's fartin' around out here. He's recalibrated his equipment four times already, and if he digs out any more around that mine, the entire forest floor is going to collapse."

Jani tried to imagine the thoughts going through Wode's mind—surrounded by testy soldiers and bureaucrats of two species, mindful that every move he made, or didn't make, would be examined under a dozen microscopes, each using a different filter. "A Slager would require one type of code to ensure disarm, a Beekman another. A cross-up in signals would precipitate a crisis I don't even want to think about. If the mine brain is malfunctioning and he's unsure about which type he's dealing with anyway, isn't it better that he take his time?"

"He has to make a decision sometime, ma'am, or hand it over to someone who can. We have to clear this thing and get these people and idomeni out of here before a fistfight breaks out." Pullman's image seemed to stride atop the console board from one set of touchpads to another. "Why can't we just clear the area and blow it up? Hell, we could have blown it up from Sheridan."

Niall hung his head. "We have to be able to show the intact device to Ambassador Shai and prove it didn't pose a danger to the Haárin."

"They're not willing to take our word for it?" Pullman asked.

"Over the last three months, four Haárin have been attacked and the enclave itself has twice been the target of vandalism. The newssheets are questioning the presence of the Haárin enclave so close to the Commonwealth capital, and the last time Ambassador Shai's skimmer floated through Chicago unescorted, somebody heaved a brick at it." Jani could sense Niall's stare, and avoided it. Sometimes she felt as though he didn't want her to talk about the worsening relations between the idomeni and humanish, as if doing so made matters worse. "Given that," she continued more quietly, "I don't think they'd take your word for the time of day, do you?"

Pullman-in-miniature kicked at the snow. "No, ma'am."

Jani sensed someone approach from behind, and turned to find Tsecha standing at her shoulder. "Dathim has told me that Shai has sent nìaRauta Elon to see to this matter, along with her suborns, nìRau Ghos and nìRau Feres." Tsecha turned his head to face his left, then brought up his left hand chest-high, palm facing outward. It was a High Vynshàrau gesture of dismay, of the sort he seldom employed since his outcast to Haárin. That he felt compelled to express his consternation in such a definite manner said all that needed to be said about Elon. "I recall her from my time as ambassador. The Council willed her as my security dominant; thus was I forced to tolerate her." He broke off his posture and looked to Niall. "I should attend this matter, Colonel. Your Lieutenant Pullman should not be left alone to deal with such as Elon."

"No, ní Tsecha. Sorry." Niall shook his head. "While your concern is appreciated, your assistance is not required. We have Major Dubrovna to deal with nìaRauta Elon—Lieutenant Pullman is safe." He patted his shirt pocket again, his longing for a dose of nicotine etched in every line of his face.

"You have not dealt with Elon. She is as a mine whose signal you do not know!"

"You stay *here*!" Niall's voice shook the air in the small space. "Ní Tsecha. Please." He sat forward, hands dangling between his knees, his gaze fixed on the floor as he struggled to regain his composure. "To most Chicagoans, you are still the symbol of the idomeni presence on Earth. That presence . . . is being questioned by some humanish at the present time, and because of that, both your dominants and mine feel that you should not be observed involving yourself in this matter."

"OK." Jani stepped between the two, man and idomeni, and felt the current of tension that flowed between them. "That explains why you're keeping Tsecha holed up here." She stared down at Niall until he raised his eyes to meet hers. "Why am I here?"

They studied one another—Jani sensed the time pass just as she discerned Niall's examination, just as she knew how she appeared in his eyes. The strange golden cast to her brown skin. Her long-limbed gangliness. Her eyes, dark green irises surrounded by the paler sea of sclera, eyes unlike those any human being ever possessed.

Niall took a deep breath. "You know damned well why you're here. Everywhere Tsecha goes, you're never far behind. You're as

much associated with the idomeni presence here as he is. You're—"
He reached into his pocket, then yanked out his hand as though it
burned.

"I'm the hybrid. I'm what all those questioning humanish fear
they'll see one day when they look in the mirror." Jani swallowed
a howl of frustration. "I'm not contagious, Niall. It took months of
medical intervention to get me this way."

"I know that."

"So why—" Jani fell silent as a sharp *thunk* sounded from outside. Another.

They all looked to the door of the bunker as the panel slid
open. A young man decked out in Service raingear blew in, escorted by a gust of chill wind.

"I'll have those relays retimed in a minute, sir." He swept back
his hood and undid his coat fasteners as the water dripped and
puddled around him. The cold had bitten his ears and nose—they
flared red against his pale skin and dark hair. "I spoke with the
techs down at the truck—they said the sub-Misty's functioning
normally. What we're seeing up here is what's really happening
down there."

"Thank you, Faber." Niall's face lightened, his relief at the interruption obvious. "What's the mood like down there?"

"Irritable, sir." Faber hung his coat in the gear alcove at the far
end of the bunker. "Everyone's wet. Cold. Waiting for something
to happen." He turned to face them and hesitated, his gaze passing
over Tsecha and Jani before settling on Niall. "At the rate things
are going, they're going to be there awhile."

"And every hour spent here translates to a month's worth of
follow-up investigation." Niall shot Jani a questioning look. "Aren't
you supposed to be going on a trip soon?"

Jani nodded. "Outer Circle. Day after tomorrow."

"Hmm. Looks like you may miss most of the fun." The flatness in his voice gave away nothing. "How long will you be
gone?"

"Six weeks out, same back. Week or two to do what I have to.
Close to four months."

"We'll be well into spring by the time you get back." Niall
stood, then walked across the bunker to the gear alcove. "Probably
about the time the first reports get issued." He dragged on his field
coat. "I'm going to take a walk. See what I can see from out here."
He activated the door panel and pushed through the gap without a
backward glance.

"I do not believe, nìa, that he wants you to leave."

Jani turned back to Tsecha, who had cocked his head to one side, a gesture of curiosity more humanish than Vynshàrau. "He will have to get used to the fact, inshah."

"Yes. As will you."

Jani hesitated. "I'm going outside." She walked over to Faber, who stood bent over the console. "Excuse me."

Faber straightened, then slowly lifted his gaze to look Jani in the face. "Yes, ma'am." The top of his head only reached her shoulder, and the difference in height seemed to rattle him.

Among other things. Lance Corporal Micah Faber of Supreme Command Communication Systems, Jani decided, didn't like her. She'd run into it more and more often as of late, this sense from some humanish that they didn't want her to get too close. *If I kissed him atop his pointy little head, would he run screaming into the rain?* Given the tension around the place, maybe now wasn't the time to experiment. "Could I borrow your coat?" she asked, knowing full well that to him the request might constitute the same sort of invasion. "I need to talk to Colonel Pierce, and my coat isn't keeping me warm as it is."

"Ma'am." Faber led her back to the alcove. He lifted his coat from its hook, shook off the remaining droplets of water, then held it out for her.

Jani took the coat and flung it across her shoulders like a cape. "I promise I'll touch it as little as possible," she said, leaving him to redden like an alarm as she slipped out into the rain.

She found Niall huddled in the shelter of a nearby stand of evergreens. He turned when he heard her approach, but didn't speak.

"You want to go down there, don't you?" Jani wedged into the shelter beside him. The rain fell about them in a steady patter, but the canopy of branches slowed the flow-through to the occasional drop. "Go ahead—we're fine up here."

"I have been ordered to remain with you and Tsecha, and remain with you and Tsecha I will." Niall had already flipped open the top of his nicstick case and removed a long, white cylinder. He bit down on the bulbed end—the tip flared blue-white in the cold wind. "Tell me about this trip of yours." He stuck the other end in his mouth and took a long drag, then released a stream of smoke with a groan of relief.

Jani pulled Faber's coat more tightly around her shoulders. "I told you about it last week, during lunch. It crossed paths with *Coppélia*—they must have cancelled one another out."

"Humor me," Niall replied, not amused.

"I'll be paying a courtesy call on the Haárin at the Karistos enclave on Elyas. Their dominant, ná Feyó Tal, is a favorite of Tsecha's. He wants me to deliver a gift to her." Jani knew how inadequate the explanation sounded, but Tsecha had given her little more to go on.

Feyó requires an assistance, nìa.

"You're leaving at a time like this to deliver a *gift*?" Niall exhaled another cloud of smoke, which the wind sliced to nothing. "Haárin shuttles leave Luna once a week. Let one of them play errand boy."

"You just finished saying that I require protection to continue to work in Chicago. I think my getting away for a few months might be a good idea."

I cannot leave this damned cold place, nìa—Shai will not allow such. But you may go, and go you must.

Niall shook his head. "On the contrary—I think it will make matters worse. You'll be acting as the intermediary between two Haárin enclaves. How is that going to dispel the perception that you're not human anymore?"

"But I'm not human anymore."

"That's news to me."

"Only because you don't listen."

They lapsed into edgy silence. In the distance, dim illumination shown through the trees. Every so often a shout would carry. A flash of light from a piece of equipment.

Yes, it is dangerous here for Haárin. It is dangerous everywhere, nìa. You must go.

The bunker door opened a crack—Faber's head emerged. *"Wode's started to move the mine, sir!"*

"About damned time." Niall extinguished his 'stick against the wet trunk of a tree and shoved the spent cylinder in his pocket.

Jani followed him into the bunker, to find Faber sitting at the console, Tsecha looming over him. She returned Faber's coat to the alcove, then joined them.

"They just got started, sir." Faber glanced over his shoulder at Jani before switching his attention to Niall, who had dropped into the chair next to him. "Wode's decided to use a biobot to hoist it. He must be too worried about signal cross-up to use a standard comwave."

"Jack up the mag on this," Niall replied. "I want to see what's going on."

Faber worked comtech magic on the console. The outer edges of the image disappeared as the area of the cordon itself expanded. As if on cue, Pullman glanced up—Jani could see the droplets of rain that dotted his armor and ran down his face like sweat.

"Drop that face shield, Pull," Niall grumbled.

"Sir." Pullman flipped down the poly barrier. "Wode's ready to lift the thing."

"Will wonders never cease." Niall braced his elbow on the edge of the console and covered his mouth with his hand, his eyes fixed on the scene playing out before them.

Wode looked even younger than Faber. Colder, too. The wind had nipped his cheeks as well as his nose, so that he looked flushed with fever. He stood thirty meters from the exposed mine, his hands gloved with the translucent sensor web that enabled him to control the cylindrical biobot. He stood still, straight, his arms bent at the elbow and hands facing in as though he held a box by the sides. Every few seconds one finger would move, then another. Each time he moved, the biobot would edge closer to the mine.

The mine itself seemed a puny thing. A blank silver oval the size of a man's hand, it vanished like an eclipsed moon as the biobot rolled over it.

"The 'bot's hollow," Niall said, eyes still locked on Wode's every move. "Once it's settled above the mine, it will hoist it up inside."

"Then the bottom of the 'bot will close," Pullman added. "The mine will be encased until it can dry out. Wode figures fifteen minutes with some warm air circ, and he'll be able to identify the signal."

"Why's he standing so close to the mine?" To Jani, Wode appeared like a man entranced, eyes closed, shoulders slumped, fingers twitching. "Can't he do that from outside the cordon?"

"He says that the problem with bio signals is that they're weaker than standard comwaves." Pullman's voice held a skeptical edge. "He says he has no choice."

As they watched, one of the Vynshàrau broke away from the crowd and walked inside the cordon to stand by Wode. A young male, his thin frame padded by armor, his face covered by a shield.

"It is Feres," Tsecha said, "Elon's suborn."

Niall stood and bent over the console. "Pull, what the hell is going on?"

"Feres is a witness, sir. The Vynshàrau don't trust our transmissions. They want one of their own to watch the mine be contained."

"That's bullshit!"

"We tried to block it, sir, but Dubrovna overrode."

"Well, I just trumped her. Stop everything *now*! Get that Vynshàrau out of there *now*!"

"Yes, sir!" Pullman stepped inside the cordon. *"Wode, pull up now!"*

Wode and Feres both turned.

Light travels faster than sound. The flash filled the image space like a miniature sun. Yellow-white. Blinding.

Then came the thunder of the explosion. The bunker shook, the light fixture trembling as though a giant set down his foot.

They had all dropped to the floor. Now Niall bounded to his feet and ran for the door. *"Faber—stay behind and watch them!"* he shouted as he pushed through the gap.

Jani lay on her stomach, the echo of the explosion still sounding in her ears. "Ní Tsecha?"

"I am most well, nìa."

"Good." She boosted to a running crouch and headed for the door, then fell to one knee as a hand gripped her coat sleeve.

"You're not supposed to leave." Faber's eyes were wide. His hands encircled her arm without clamping down, as though the thought of contact repulsed him.

"Stop me." Jani shook him off and bolted.

The rain fell harder now. Jani coursed through it, following the light and the equipment sounds. The cries.

Then she broke through a ring of trees, and the console image filled her eyes. The vehicles. The humanish. The idomeni.

She took one step. Another. Tried to avoid the shattered branches, the flecks of red in the snow. Watched medics hoist Pullman atop a gurney and cover him with a medblanket. *They're taking care with him—hurrying*—That meant he lived. *Please.*

"What the hell are you doing here!"

Jani turned to find Niall bearing down on her from the other side of the cordon.

"Who let her in here!" He waved toward a figure in body armor. "Morton! Get her out of here now! Carry her if you have to!"

"I'm going!" Jani held up her hands like a surrendering prisoner, two steps ahead of the advancing Morton. "I said I'm going!" She broke into a run, didn't stop until she stood amid the
trees again. She looked behind her to find Morton had returned to
the site. Emergency illumins flashed yellow and orange against
the night sky. An ambulance siren wailed.

CHAPTER 2

Jani checked every room and alcove as she walked down the aisle of Service Medical's Trauma Center, keeping one eye toward collision avoidance as doctors and nurses darted around her and orderlies pushed past her with skimgurnies and carts bearing equipment.

She found Niall in a waiting area within sight of the main nurses station. He sat in a darkened corner, hunched over a spent nicstick, the floor in front of his chair wet and mud-streaked from the mess shed by his boots.

He looked up as she entered. A streak of mud coated his left cheek, smoothing over his scar, erasing his sinister air. Indefinable dark stains spotted the coat he'd draped over the back of his chair, as well as the front of his fatigue shirt and trousers. They might have been blood, but it was impossible to tell in the poor lighting. "You made it out of the madhouse."

Jani lowered into the chair next to his. "I saw Tsecha back to the enclave, then hitched a ride on one of the equipment trucks. The last ambulance had just left." She glanced toward the hall in time to see two nurses break into a sprint. "How's Pull?"

Niall started to speak. Stopped. Licked his lips. "Something hit his right side hard. Part of the biobot casing. A piece of Wode or Feres. Medical doesn't know for sure yet, but there may have been a fault in his armor." He patted his left side. "Kidney's gone. Liver's banged up. Even though his augmentation had kicked in, he bled . . . a lot." He exhaled with a shudder. "They got to him in time. They don't need to break out the brain boxes and make sure he's still hitting on all boards."

"So the tally is?"

"Two dead, Feres and that . . . *tech*." Niall slumped back. "Twenty-seven wounded, including two Haárin and three deputy ministers."

"I heard on the way in that Mako just left to see the PM." Jani tried to imagine the mood in that meeting, and found she didn't want to. She despised Admiral-General Hiroshi Mako, and though he preferred to deny it, he felt the same way about her. But a member of his Service had made an error that threatened to kneecap humanish-idomeni relations already crippled by recent tensions, and it fell to him to explain what had happened. Jani almost felt sorry for the man. Almost, but not quite. She ached for Niall, however. He was the A-G's man-on-the-scene, and even though it hadn't been his show to run, she knew he'd blame himself for every error and miscue. "So what went wrong?"

"Where do I fucking start?" Niall held up his closed fist, then raised his index finger. "We should never have let Diplo make the calls." The middle finger. "We shouldn't have allowed all those observers on-site." Ring finger. "Like Pull said, we should have cut all the crap off at the pass by doing a remote disinter-disarm from Sheridan, and told Shai to kiss our collective ass when she howled." He glanced at Jani sidelong. "In so many words." He let his hand drop and lay his head back. "Of course, none of this would have happened if whoever had been in charge of the initial land clearance had done their job. A lot of brass is going to go over the side before this investigation is signed off."

Jani rose and walked across the alcove to the vend machines, digging in her trouser pockets for tokens. "You're using some pretty nasty training mines now compared to what they used in my day." She found the coffee selector and ordered two cups.

"That was no trainer. It was a live and kickin' Slager with an intact detonator sensitive enough to respond to the biobot signal. Once Wode pulled it out of the ground and enclosed it in the 'bot compartment, a heartbeat could have set it off." Niall took the dispo cup of coffee Jani handed him, but instead of drinking it he just stared into the steam rising from the liquid. "I'm going to see his face in my sleep. Looked like a damned twelve-year-old. Should have been operating a remote control skimmer in his parents' backyard, not a mine removal device in the woods in the middle of the night."

"It's not your fault."

"Yeah."

Jani returned to her seat. Sipped her coffee, and winced at the taste of the sour machine brew. "So what was a live and kicking Slager doing buried on the grounds of the Haárin enclave?"

Niall tried his coffee. He swallowed it without a change in expression. Either he was made of hardier stuff than she or he was simply too numb to taste. "You remember the drill. Sometimes the demo techs play it too smart and put the real stuff out there to practice on." He scratched at the dried mud on his face, then stared at the dirt under his nails. "That's against procedure, however, because, well, people can get hurt. So they fudge the records, which then means that they can't always depend on them to tell them what's out there. The old hands know that. But they didn't send an old hand—fresh-out-of-the-box Wode got the call. By the time they got someone out of bed who realized what that could mean, it was too late." He rose and walked to the vend area, still scratching at his muddy cheek. He grabbed a dispo napkin from the dispenser next to the machines, then soaked it in the stream from the water fountain. "Not to change the subject, but what are you doing here?" He leaned against the wall as he cleaned his face. "I thought you'd stay with Tsecha."

"I wanted to find out about Pull." Jani peeled an advertising sticker from her cup, a pass good for two free tickets to a midweek showing at the base Veedrome. "Tsecha and Dathim are administering to the injured Haárin."

"I thought that was the sort of thing he'd been teaching you over the last few months. How to act as a priest."

Jani nodded. "I've learned some of the ceremonies and protocols. But there are a few Haárin who haven't adjusted to me yet. One of them was among the injured—Tsecha and I both figured that the last thing she wanted to see was my face bending over her, muttering prayers."

Niall finished cleaning his face, then checked the results in the smooth metal surface of one of the coolers. "I wouldn't have expected Tsecha to give in like that. He's a great one for shoving things down people's throats."

"He's starting to feel discouraged."

"Welcome to the damned club." Niall tossed back the last of his coffee, then crumpled the cup into a ball and banked it off the wall into the trash. "Not to change the subject again, but how do you feel? My augmentation's activated. People keep backing away when I try to ask them questions."

Jani watched Niall kick at the floor like a restless horse pawing the ground. She couldn't imagine backing away from him for any reason, but she nursed the same Service-made gland in her head that he did, and the synthetic neurotransmitters it pumped out had much the same effect on her as they did on him. "I feel—focused. Like I have things to do, and I can't rest until I get them done. Colors are sharper. Sounds seem louder. Everyone else moves too slowly. The usual."

"Started to come down yet?"

"No." Jani paused and tried to get a sense of herself. "Maybe a little. The hybridization has made it less predictable than it used to be." Or rather, less predictable in its unpredictability. At one time, her augie caused her senses to jumble. Sounds became aromas, while touch and scent sang to her in a range of tones. Now she simply grew tired and jittery as her brain and body said "Enough" and battlefield alert gave way to moody exhaustion.

"Sometimes I think I should take all that medical advice I've received over the years and have the thing taken out. I feel like hell." Niall gathered his coat. "If you contact Special Services, one of them can see you home. I have to check on Pull. Then I need to contact his parents."

Jani watched her friend move with the heavy-footed gait that spoke of exhaustion and the emotional bottoming-out that in his case went along for the ride. "Niall, stop hammering yourself. Pull will be all right."

Niall looked at her and nodded, his predator's face reddened from rough washing, his poet's eyes dull. "Yes. I can tell his folks with complete confidence that the Service is up the spout with the finest medical staff in existence anywhere." He walked out into the hallway in the direction of the nurses station, shoulders bowed. "And idiots aplenty to ensure they keep in practice."

Jani walked out into the night to find the rain had finally stopped. The sky had cleared as well; only some fast-moving clouds remained to obscure Luna, and hide the few stars that could be seen through Fort Sheridan's blaze of outdoor lighting.

"I'm not calling Special Services," she said to herself. She'd never tell Niall, but his regard didn't buy her much in the way of acceptance—except for Pullman, no one else on his staff liked her very much. A silent ride into the city lacked appeal under the best of circumstances. With humanish-idomeni tensions now thick on the ground, the word *best* did not apply.

Instead, she followed the walkways from the hospital to a less-traveled area of the base. On the way, she passed office buildings in the semidark of graveyard shift. Maintenance sheds. Rolling landscape buried beneath melting snow, broken up by stands of bare trees and winter-stripped shrubs.

Before long South Central Bachelor Officers Quarters came into view, a multistory cement block devoted to the housing of male officers in various stages of transition. Jani walked in the front entry, ready to avert her eyes on the off chance she encountered anyone in the halls or the stairwell. *I should have applied film to them.* But her identity as a human-idomeni hybrid was well-known—all of Chicago knew what her eyes looked liked. What good did it do to apply a film to make them appear human, when everyone knew what lay beneath?

She keyed into the stairwell, took the steps two at a time. Stopped at the fifth floor. Negotiated the familiar twist of hallways before coming to a stop in front of the door marked WEST-1, the name L. PASCAL etched into the metal nameplate.

Jani reached for the buzzer, but the panel slid open before she had a chance to press the doorpad.

Lucien Pascal stood in the doorway, a disheveled vision in Service blue pajama bottoms, white-blond burr diffusing the backlight to a pale aura around his head. "I've been trying to track you down for the last hour." He stepped back to allow her to pass. "You have a real talent for falling off the map."

"A talent I worked at for years. Nice to know I'm still in practice." Jani caught the barest whiff of cologne as she entered the spare three-room flat. A peppery scent, lighter than the throaty musk Lucien favored. She looked toward the bedroom. The door was open, the corner of the bed that she could see was rumpled. "How much have you heard?"

"Good morning. It is officially morning now." Lucien stepped in front of her, blocking her view of the bedroom. "I'm fine. I'm not hurt. Tsecha is fine. So is Dathim. Everyone you know is all right. If any of those comments are incorrect, could you tell me now so that I'm not caught by surprise later." He moved closer. The light fell across his neck and chest, accenting scattered red blotches, along with several fresh bruises that formed a characteristic pattern.

Jani touched a red mark near the hollow of Lucien's throat. "I'm fine. Tsecha is fine. Dathim. Everyone you know." She pressed her fingertips against the bruises, gauging them—yes, they had been left by someone who had gripped far harder than they had to. "You, on the other hand, look a little roughed up."

Lucien gripped Jani's wrist and eased her hand away. In contrast to Niall, his face was the poet's, fine-boned and full-lipped, with just enough softness about the jaw to imply a vulnerability that in truth had never existed. Again in contrast to Niall, his eyes were the predator's, chill brown and calculating, windows to a mind that saw life as a gameboard and all others as pawns, to be played, or sacrificed, as the situation demanded.

"You want to know how much I've heard?" He backed away and walked about the sparsely furnished sitting room, picking up clothes, straightening couch cushions. "Demiskimmer on lake patrol flew too close to the Haárin enclave. Picked up a choppy transmission that spelled 'one of our mines.' They informed Ordnance, who said 'oops' and informed the world, who converged on the enclave. The demolitions tech they sent to pull the mine misread the signal, killed himself and a Vynshàrau." He stopped in mid-pillow fluff and looked at Jani. "Anyone you knew?"

"Feres. One of Elon's security suborns."

"One of the hardcore elite. That should play well back on Shèrá." Lucien resumed his housekeeping. "Have I missed any of the high points?"

"Not really. Except that they thought the mine was a trainer, but it turned out to be live and fully armed."

"Ouch."

"Yeah." Jani started her own walkabout, poking through the places Lucien had yet to straighten. "For someone who looks like he just rolled out of bed, you sure do know a lot." She arrived at a chair one step ahead of him, grabbing for the object that lay in a small heap beneath.

"That's not yours." Lucien bumped her and tried to pull the thing from her hand as she reached down for it.

"It's not yours, either." Jani held the article up for inspection. It proved to be a man's Service-issue T-shirt. "Wrong size." She sniffed the neck and detected the same spicy odor she had when she entered the flat. "Wrong scent, too. Besides, you don't fling your clothes around the room."

"Not unless someone asks me to." Lucien plucked the shirt from her grasp and folded it. "He works for the Public Affairs Office. When the first calls came in, his admin tracked him here. It's his job to head up damage control, which in turn means he has to know what damage needs to be controlled." He glanced at her beneath his lashes. "I can be very persuasive when I want to be." He lay the shirt over his arm. "Another memento to add to the others," he said as he smoothed his hand over it. "Are you even a little jealous?"

"Of what? Those lovely bruises?"

"Sometimes you have to give a little to get a lot in return."

Jani patted a chair cushion into place, then slipped off her coat and sat. The standard issue ergoworks braced her back and legs, but not well enough to ease the growing aches that signaled the need for sleep. "You played him. It's a talent you've worked at for years. You're still in practice, too." She tried to stifle a yawn and failed. "If we were both dropped in the middle of a strange city, I daresay we'd manage pretty well. But we're both in Chicago, and the natives know our footprints. We need to take care."

Lucien strolled to the couch and sat. "You're not making much sense, you do realize that?"

"I'm leaving for Elyas the day after tomorrow."

"I know."

"I'll be gone awhile."

"I know that, too." Lucien lay the T-shirt on the cushion beside him and stroked it like a cat.

Jani followed the smooth flow of his muscles, the play of light across his chest and stomach. An hypnotic sight, marred only by the bruises that had blued and darkened in the time since her arrival. *Mr. Public Affairs plays rough.* She toyed with the idea of tracking down the man and giving him a little of what he dished out, except . . . *It's none of my business.* Lucien lived most of his life outside her purview, and he never did anything without a reason. If he felt that what Mr. PA offered was worth the knockabout, the best favor she could do him was to stay out of it.

He does what he feels he has to. Circumstances had compelled Jani to live the same way once. Maybe it was the memory of that time that touched the anger in her now, a vein of hostility that opened more and more frequently as her hybridization advanced and the idomeni aspects of her personality emerged.

So much rage. Jani struggled to focus on the present. *What do I have to work with? Look at the situation as it is, not as I think it should be.* "Seeing as you're in Intelligence, how difficult would it be for you to attach yourself to the mine investigation?"

Lucien's hand stilled atop his souvenir shirt. "Officially, my spec is communications. Weapons interface falls roughly under that header, but there are people in Ordnance who know a lot more about the subject than I do, and they're the ones who will be called in to answer questions."

Jani examined the back of her right hand. She had cut it sometime during her run through the woods—a thin line of dried blood traced along her knuckles. "Unofficially, your spec is killing inconvenient people." She flexed her fingers, felt the wound sting. "Apply yourself in that direction for a bit."

Lucien's hand moved to his thigh, the T-shirt forgotten. "You think that mine was put there deliberately?"

"I heard a whole truckload of reasonable explanations during the return ride across the lake. Now I'd like to hear the unreasonable ones." Jani gazed at the sitting room walls, flat white and as bare as the day they were finished, without even a tacked-up holo to indicate the personality of the man who lived within their bounds. "The Haárin took up residence in the enclave four months ago. At first, things seemed peaceful. The Holland area wasn't populated by humanish, so no one lost their property. The Haárin had less reason to go into Chicago, so they didn't rattle the natives by turning up in odd places, as they had been wont to do when they lived on the embassy grounds."

"Dathim used to enjoy doing that." Lucien grinned. He nursed an infatuation for the Haárin that had led to the development of one of the Commonwealth's stranger friendships.

"Yes, he did. The people who looked up to find two meters worth of long-faced Vynshàrau looming over them didn't find it so enjoyable, however." Jani smiled anyway. The tales of Dathim's exploits had made for an evening's entertainment on more than one occasion. Then she sobered. "As I said, things seemed peaceful at first. The honeymoon lasted for about three weeks. Then one morning an Haárin security suborn found one of the enclave food repositories broken into and humanish excrement smeared over the bins."

"I don't need the recent history lesson." Lucien dragged the T-shirt onto his lap and picked at the hem. "I spend as much time there as you do, if not more. I know all about it."

"Did you know that whoever got in there destroyed kettles containing experimental media? Thanks to some urging by ná Feyó and the other Elyan Haárin, Tsecha had sanctioned research into synthetic foods. When Shai found out . . . my old teacher barely managed to talk himself out of a one-way trip on a fast cruiser back to Shèrá." Jani fought the urge to rest her head on the seatback. If she did that, she'd drift to sleep, Lucien's soft voice serving as lullaby. "Then came that sniper attack. Skimmer sabotage. Add the mine, and we've got people who not only know what they're doing but have access to very nasty things."

Lucien locked his hands behind his head and sprawled back, a pose that displayed his naked torso to its best advantage. No matter how serious a discussion turned, he never forgot what he considered the essential argument. "Do you think the Service is responsible?"

Jani admired the view, however calculated. "The mines and weapons are manufactured by Family companies. They fear the Haárin's economic competition just as the Service fears their impact on Commonwealth security. If you assume the Family supplied the means, then the question becomes whether they do the dirty themselves or hire it out. I'd say the field is pretty wide open."

"Given that, I'm surprised you're still planning on leaving tomorrow."

Jani shrugged. "I have no choice." She felt Lucien's stare, knew he expected her to tell him why she had to leave, and knew just as surely that the less she told him, the better. *That won't be difficult—I don't know much.* "Ná Feyó has told Tsecha very little—she doesn't trust the security of the Haárin communications linkages. All he can determine is that she's enmeshed in some sort of power struggle. An Haárin version of a bornsect fallout. He can help her by throwing his support her way—most Haárin still consider him their religious dominant even though he's no longer Chief Propitiator of the ruling bornsect. The ideal solution would be for him to visit the Elyan enclave himself, but he's afraid to leave Earth. He thinks he'll draw unwelcome attention down on Feyó. He also thinks that once he's left Earth, Oligarch Cèel won't allow him to return."

"So he's sending you as his emissary?" Lucien eyed her skeptically. "I've watched you train in bladework with Dathim. He's told me enough about your religious instruction to know that it will take years to learn all you need to. You've only been at this a few months."

"I know." Jani shifted in her seat. She nursed her own bruises thanks to Dathim's enthusiastic teaching. A sword in his hand worked like a metal-plated fist. "But I didn't come into this wholly unprepared, and I've helped the Elyan Haárin before. If Tsecha tells them, through me, to support Feyó, they will."

"Is she that important?"

"To him, she is." Jani fielded Lucien's smirk. "It's not just that he esteems her. Feyó's a radical by any measure, and she has a revolutionary's personality. She knows how to work idomeni and humanish alike. If she loses her position, there's no one of her caliber to replace her. Considering how thoroughly Haárin shipping lines and trade routes have integrated with their Commonwealth counterparts, her ouster could destabilize the entire Outer Circle."

Lucien lowered his arms and sat up. "If she's so magnetic, why has she lost influence?"

"That's what I have to find out." Jani once more fought the urge to close her eyes. Like Niall, she knew what she'd see when next she dreamed. Pullman's raw-boned vitality, reduced to pools of blood in the snow. Wode's slow fingerings as he maneuvered the biobot over the mine. "I don't want to leave now, but I don't have a choice. That's why I'm asking you to plug yourself into the mine inquiry."

Lucien stood, purloined T-shirt in hand. "Someone is going to wonder why I'm interested." He padded across the carpeted floor and disappeared into the bedroom. "The fact that I'm information-gathering for you isn't going to fly. I'm not supposed to feed classified data to Haárin intermediaries."

Jani listened for the sound of a dresser drawer opening, then closing, the sign that the T-shirt had joined its brethren in their very private display case. "Could you tell people you're doing a favor for an old Family friend?"

"I'm sure I'll think of something. I always do." Lucien stepped into the bedroom doorway. "I found a blue-bordered envelope in my paper mail yesterday. It contained a nice, thick sheaf of documents from the Office of Review, all signed off." He folded his arms and leaned against the jamb. "Effective last month."

Jani smiled, and meant it. "Congratulations, Captain. I know you were starting to feel anxious."

"I'm not sure how long I'll stay a captain if I have to keep the home watch. Things have a tendency to spin out of control when you're involved."

"I won't be here."

"You'll be here in spirit. That should prove sufficient to upset the domestic balance of power." Lucien pretended interest in the condition of his hands. "So, now that's settled, any plans until the sunrise?"

Wariness worked through Jani's growing haze as the many possible replies to Lucien's simple question presented themselves. She'd visited his flat only a handful of times, and had never stayed the night despite his veiled, and not-so-veiled, invitations. As always, she felt that she intruded, that she had entered a place in which she didn't belong, the inner workings of which she didn't want to know. She stood and gathered her coat. "I should go home."

"I hope I haven't offended your delicate sensibilities." Lucien's voice sharpened, the soft French Provincial accent faded to nothing. "I have showered. Unfortunately, the bruises won't be healed before you have to leave—"

"*Lucien.*" Jani stopped in the middle of the room. The hand that held her coat felt gloved in lead. It hung at her side, leaving the garment to drag on the floor. "The psych job. Save it for someone who buys it."

"I would have done anything he wanted in order to find out how you were."

"Rough trade for information. You've done it before. You crave the power. The control. You like it. Your. Choice." Jani fixed on the image of Pullman being lifted from the snow onto the stretcher—the memory touched some deep place within her and released sensations she'd long suppressed, touch and smell and sound. "Well, there were times in my event-filled past when I didn't have a choice. So stop trying to make me feel guilty about all the awful things you've put yourself through on my account, because your primary consideration has always, *always*, been what's best for Lucien Pascal." Her breathing came labored—the sense of weight had moved up her arm and across her chest.

"Post-augie irritability, compounded by fatigue and the effects of hybridization. Aggravated by all those memories that bubble to the surface because you've lost the will to keep them locked down where they belong." Lucien left the doorway and walked to her, shaking his head. "I know the feeling."

Jani opened her hand and let the coat fall to the floor. "You are a liar."

"Yes, but I'm *your* liar." Lucien rested his hand on the open neck of her coverall, then waited to see if she'd pull away. When she didn't, he opened the top fastener, the second, the third, his fingertips brushing her skin with each slow movement. "Your spy. Your whore. Your whatever you happen to need at the time." He bent close, his lips and tongue tracing swirls of heat along her throat and neck as he slipped the garment from her shoulders. "All I want in return is the chance to make us both feel better for a little while. Is that too much to ask?"

Jani took Lucien's hands in hers and held them away from her body. Caught the chill that flashed in his eyes, the anger at a need denied. Pushed down his hands until they hung at his sides, then freed them. Counted the seconds as they stood, still and barely breathing, separated by a few scraps of cloth and a gulf of understanding wider than any sea.

"My choice." She leaned forward and kissed him.

CHAPTER 3

"If the mine *was* deliberately planted, how do you think the idomeni will react?" Lucien exited the Boul just as the early morning traffic slowed to the usual crawl. "Relations are tense now, but when haven't they been?" He steered the Service-issue sedan onto the deceptive quiet of the Parkway, a graceful seclusion of town houses and apartment buildings separated by parks and scattered shops and restaurants. "Besides, we lost one of ours in this mess, too. That must count for something."

"Not really." Jani took what she could from the beauty of the hour—the streaking of the eastern sky into bands of orange and indigo, the illuminated columns of the Chicago skyline that formed the Parkway's backdrop. "Ever since he became Oligarch, Morden nìRau Cèel's goal has been to turn back humanish-idomeni relations fifty years."

"Fifty years ago there were no humanish–idomeni relations." Lucien turned down the first in the succession of tree-lined avenues that led to Jani's house. "Isn't Cèel a little young to be that closed-minded?"

"Age has nothing to do with it. He was just as isolationist twenty years ago at the Rauta Shèràa Academy." Jani thought back to the Cèel she had watched from afar that lifetime ago, the green-eyed, slope-shouldered warrior who turned away whenever a humanish crossed his path. "If we find out that the mine was deliberately planted, I predict a proclamation from Cèel that all bornsect and Haárin must forsake the evils of the humanish Commonwealth and return to the godly confines of the Shèrá worldskein. I then predict that a certain percentage of the Haárin will tell him to go to hell.

After that, things should get really interesting." She paused to yawn. She should have taken the opportunity while at Lucien's flat to grab a couple of hours' sleep. Needless to say, she hadn't availed herself of that particular option.

The trees that lined the narrow streets had been strung with colored illumins. Backlit by twinkling leaves, Lucien cocked his head like a young boy considering what he wanted for Christmas. "You're thinking civil war?"

"No, we enter uncharted territory with that one." Jani sat up straighter as the skimmer rounded onto the street she called home, a cul-de-sac of eight identical three-story houses, each built of tan brick and ringed by metal gates and hybrid greenery. "Civil war is the divinely ordained shedding of bornsect blood that may or may not lead to a regime change. A bornsect offensive against balky Haárin who refuse to toe the line hasn't occurred in recorded idomeni history to my knowledge. Cèel would have to have decided that the Haárin who disobeyed were no longer true Haárin, that proximity to humanish had degraded them to the point that they no longer merited his protection. It would prove an interesting point for the theologians to debate at Temple. I can see arguments for both sides."

"Can you?" Lucien eyed her doubtfully as he turned up the narrow drive that curved behind her house, then waited for the gate to slide open. "All that religious instruction has sunk in, has it?"

Jani tipped her hand in a back and forth motion that spoke more of the humanish bargaining table than it did any idomeni gesture. "It's just rules. Rules and order. I'm a documents examiner by trade, remember. A paper pusher. That's all we know, rules." She glanced at Lucien as he unfastened the top of his shooter holster, his gaze locked on the skimmer's dashboard array. "What's wrong?"

"Readings from the backyard. One skimmer. Two men. One of them is armed." Lucien tapped codes into touchpads—multiple views of the house and yard formed on a small display. "You have company." He relaxed, but only a little. "Your doctors make house calls, I see." He drifted up the drive and around the house, coming to a stop a few meters behind a silver sportster. Safety lighting activated, illuminating the yard and the two men who emerged from the sleek vehicle.

"So much for a little time to ourselves," Lucien muttered.

Jani alit from the skimmer just as John Shroud and Val Parini drew near. Val led the way, his stride clipped and his head high.

"Not that we were worried, mind." He circled around to Jani, high-boned face aging from boyish to middle-aged as he drew closer and the details came into focus. "How are you?" His examination took on a professional sharpness as he looked her up and down. "What happened?" A light brown forelock fell over his eyes, and he pushed it back with a curse.

Jani looked Val over as well. A blue pullover and dark green trousers peeked out beneath his brown coat. Mismatched clothes thrown on in haste. Not his habit at all. "What did you hear?"

"That's my one and only girl—never give an answer when another question will do." Val took a step closer. The safety lighting struck him full in the face, illuminating hazel eyes gone dull and bloodshot from lack of sleep. "Service Medical called our shop. They needed to borrow one of our DeVries shunts. Neuro demanded to know why, and managed to pull a story out with pliers. Blown mine at the enclave. Thirty or so people hurt. People and idomeni, I should say."

"The shunt isn't for Lieutenant Pullman, is it?" John asked as he slipped in behind Val. Unlike his business partner's, his clothing matched—a pearl grey daysuit topped by a coat of the same color. "I understand he was one of the injured." He stopped near the front end of the Service skimmer, not too close yet not too far away, his monkish face a studied blank. Taller and rangier than Val, with the dour countenance of a period painting, he looked imposing even in the harsh lighting.

Snow wraith, Jani thought as she took in his white cap of hair and parchment-pale skin, his eyes filmed the same silvery grey as his garments. *Albino*, her less romantic side reminded her. *The sun is rising, and daylight isn't his time*. "It wasn't for Pull, no. He suffered abdominal injuries, not brain damage. He'll be fine, though."

John nodded. Paused. "Niall's all right?"

Despite the tension in the air, Jani hid a smile. *I know that one was a struggle, so we'll give you full points for effort*. John and Niall did *not* like one another. Niall felt that John had forced Jani's hybridization upon her, which was true, and John felt guilty enough over the situation that the criticism stung. *But he knows Niall and I are friends, so he tries*. It had been a difficult thing to witness as of late, John Shroud's laboring to be flexible. Like watching an oak trying to bend as a willow, with all the creaking and straining the image implied. "Yes, Niall's all right." She walked around Val to John's side. "You wouldn't happen to be carrying a shooter by any chance?"

The quick change in subject caught John by surprise. He blinked. Then the look in his eyes sharpened and the color rose in his cheeks. "We couldn't find out whether you'd been hurt or not, and we didn't know what we'd find here."

"John thought we might arrive to find ministry security stripping the place." Val sauntered past, his hands in his pockets. "He's been taking lessons." He freed one hand and raised it, forefinger extended, miming a weapon.

"And they'd have dropped him before he had a chance to sight down." Lucien paused to refasten his holster. "Speaking as ex–Ministry security, that's what I'd have done."

"And on that note." Jani herded the men toward the house, avoiding John's glower and Lucien's jaundiced glare.

The house was pleasant enough, three floors of white walls, trayed ceilings, and skylights, with enough old wood to imply an age it didn't possess. Niall had chosen it for the location, the stone in a ring of older Family dwellings, set in the geographic middle of the Parkway neighborhoods. He reasoned that with human-idomeni tensions increasing as they were, the security forces of the other houses would guard Jani as well as their own charges, if only to prevent any unpleasantness that might find her from slopping over into their jurisdictions.

Jani keyed her visitors through the rear entry and waited as they doffed their coats. Her own, she kept on. The number of humanish visitors she entertained prevented her from adjusting the temperature of the house to the higher setting her hybrid internal thermostat demanded, and she had resigned herself to feeling chilled until summer.

"You look beat." Val wandered over to her, his trousers and pullover now truly revealed for the mismatched muddle that they were. "I hope you managed to catch some sleep, at least."

"No, I didn't." Jani avoided Lucien's pointed look. She pressed a hand to her stomach, and felt as well as heard the grumble. "Some food would be good."

"I'll take care of it." Lucien strode down the hall toward the kitchen, neat in winterweights, his orange captain's bars bright against the dark grey shirt.

"I'll make coffee," John grumbled as he took off after him.

Jani watched the two men disappear through the kitchen doorway, then turned to Val, who eyed her in tired amusement.

"Lucky you. It's been a long time since I had two men fighting over me." He grabbed her sleeve and pulled her after him, stopping along the way to straighten a holo of a city scene that hung crooked on the wall. "I was afraid something like this might happen if we showed up unannounced. But after we got that first call from Service Medical, John spent hours twisting arms for word about you. No one he called knew anything, which did wonders for his mood. Lucien can say what he likes, but if I had the choice between battling a ministry security team or my business partner, I think I'd take my chances with the nominal professionals."

Jani leaned against Val and lowered her head to his shoulder. "I should have called him, I suppose."

"Yes, you should've." Val slipped an arm around her waist and steered her toward the kitchen. "That was the least you could have done."

"Thank you."

"You're welcome."

By the time they entered the kitchen, the aroma of brewing coffee had already staked its claim to most of the room. The scent of frying onions, however, had taken hold of the area near the stove and seemed destined to beat back any and all comers with the aid of a few more ingredients.

"Omelets, I think." Lucien removed eggs, cheese, and other items from the cooler and set to work mixing and chopping, revealing not only an enviable ease around the kitchen but also the fact that he'd visited Jani often enough to know his way around hers. This in turn wasn't lost on John, who shot Lucien looks of increasing sharpness as he scrabbled through drawers and cupboards in the hunt for coffee accessories.

"If anyone has any particular dislikes," Lucien said, "tell me now because I'm throwing in everything I can find."

"Hold the green pepper, if there's any green pepper to hold." Val held a chair for Jani as she sat at the square, four-person table, then took the seat next to hers. "Can't abide the stuff."

Lucien turned. Val never spoke to him if he could avoid it, and his surprise at the man's response informed his face with a teenage lightness. "No green pepper, it is." He held Val's gaze just a beat too long, then returned to his cooking.

"Christ." Val's face reddened, his voice dropping to a rough whisper. "Doesn't he even bother to hide it when you're around?"

Jani shrugged. "His is a continuing quest to make me jealous—it irks him that I never rise to the bait. Besides, he's going to be on his own for the next few months. He needs to lay groundwork for future conquests."

"I am not interested." Val watched Lucien chop and stir for a time, then shook his head and looked away. "I told you before that avoiding stuff like him has become a second vocation of mine. You sure as hell don't need his brand of trouble, either."

"And John, of course, is no trouble whatsoever."

"So sometimes he sticks his nose in where it doesn't belong."

"Try meddling and controlling."

"He's trying to learn to back off—give him a break. At least I don't see him getting you killed anytime soon. Or trying to hurt you so that he can relish some sense of power." Val paused to reload, but before he could continue his defense, the object of his labors joined them, a tray of cups in hand.

"I hear whispering." John had removed his suit jacket in the interim, revealing the white, band-collared shirt he wore beneath. "What are you two plotting now?"

"The usual mayhem." Jani accepted the steaming mug he handed her. "I should have let you know I was all right. I'm sorry."

"Not a problem." John sat down across from her, concentrating on his coffee as though avoiding her eye. "I daresay you were otherwise occupied."

Jani heard Val mutter "John" under his breath, thought of a score of cutting rejoinders, and voted down them all. Instead, she sipped her coffee, and as usual found it as rich, complex, and overbearing as the man who'd made it.

"Breakfast is served." Lucien carried a plate in each hand and two more nestled in the crooks of his arms, setting them out with the skill of a waiter from Gaetan's before returning to the counter for toast and other side dishes. "You're almost out of these," he said as he set a small tablet dispenser beside Jani's plate.

Jani shook out two of the brown digestive enzyme tablets and tossed them in her mouth, washing them down with coffee. "Should I just give Xenodietetics a call?" she asked, directing her question to Val.

"I'll take care of it." John shoved a forkful of omelet in his mouth, chewing with the stolid determination of a man duty-bound to find something to complain about. He couldn't, though. Cooking was part of Lucien's toolkit, and like everything else in the set, the skill was flawlessly executed. For several minutes the sounds of cutlery clatter were the only ones to be heard.

Jani dredged a last corner of toast through a smear of cheese. "Loathe as I am to eat and run, I need to find out what's going on." She popped the morsel into her mouth, savoring the flavors as well as the final moments of relative peace in what promised to be a whirlwind of a day. "The *Trib-Times* morning edition is out by now, and the news services have had all night to patch together something lucid." She pushed back from the table and stilled, her hands braced on the edge, trying to work up the nerve to stand up and walk to her office.

John wadded his dispo napkin, tossed it atop his plate, then picked it up again. "I didn't realize you put that much stock in public information sources."

"I don't when it comes to fact. But as a gauge of public mood, of what the PM wants people to think, they're hard to beat." Jani watched him twist the corner of the napkin between his fingers until it shredded, then glanced at Val to find him staring down at his plate. "You know, I spent a few months of my life in a basement watching you two take turns not telling me things. This is Mealtime Ploy Number Thirty-Seven—Studiously Disinterested in One Another." She sat back and folded her arms. "What's going on?"

Val tapped his fork against his cup. "Could you spare us a few minutes?"

"Even if this mine incident hadn't occurred, we still would have arrived on your doorstep. We need to talk to you." John's metal stare never left Jani's face. "Alone."

Jani looked at Lucien, who continued to eat as though unaware of the insult, a skill learned through years in Family service. "I've asked Lucien to wangle a place on the mine inquiry team. If you know something that you think can help in that regard, we both need to hear it."

John looked at Val, who held up his hands in a *Who knows?* gesture. "We're not sure if it does or not." He glanced around the small, brightly lit kitchen, then pushed back his chair and stood. "Not in here. Someplace a little less closed in." He circled around the table, plucked his jacket from the drawer pull on which he'd hung it, and headed out the door.

With Val and Lucien at her heels, Jani tracked John to the library. A shrine to paper, to information, the room was her favorite in the

house, a two-story space topped by a skylight of shooter-proof
scanglass and lined from floor to ceiling with filled shelves and
storage niches. When alone, as she usually was, it served as her
office, her dining room and lounge; when work claimed too much
of her time, it served as her bedroom as well. As she followed
John to the semicircular couch that served as the room's centerpiece, she harbored the selfish hope that he didn't intend to deliver
bad news, since she knew it would affect her feelings toward the
place, and make her feel as though she'd lost something dear.

"How secure is it in here?" John had put his jacket back on,
and paced around the couch with his hands shoved in his pockets.

"How secure do you need it to be, Doctor?" Lucien stood with
his back to a bookcase. His voice came sharp, the first sign that
John's animosity had started to grate. "I recognize the position
Jani is in, as well as her penchant for privacy. I have adjusted matters accordingly."

"That's what worries me." John eyed the ceiling as though he
expected a recording holosphere to float past at any moment.

"Before anyone says something I'll regret." Jani walked to her
desk, which was located near the french-windowed rear wall. She
opened a touchlocked drawer and removed a flat metal case.
Opening it, she picked through various discs and cylinders until
she found the object she wanted, a brushed silver tube that chirped
when she twisted it about the middle.

"This is the newest block out there. Covers a fifteen meter radius." She placed the device in the center of the low table that
stood in front of the couch, then fell into a nearby lounge chair.
"What is said here will stay here."

Lucien hurried over to the table, his eyes wide. "Where did
you get that?" He leaned over the device as he spoke, and flinched
as his voice fractured and wobbled.

Jani set about getting comfortable. She slipped off her boots,
then tucked her legs beneath her and covered them with her coat.
"A street vendor on South Wabash." *By the name of Niall Pierce.*
She looked from John to Val and back to John. "So?"

John walked to the couch and sat down, eyeing the block as
though he didn't quite trust it to do its job. "Approximately two
weeks ago I received a shipment of artwork from one of my colonial brokers." He reached into the inside pocket of his jacket and
removed a metal case similar to Jani's. "My senior admin found
this inside." He flipped open the case and removed a cylinder of
his own. It was shorter and thicker than the block, and flared on

one end like a tiny trumpet. "He almost disposed of it, thinking it was a catalogue. I took it from him, to peruse at my leisure. I finally opened it last night." He set the device on the table beside the sound block, then touched a raised dot on its side and sat back.

Light flickered around the device's mouth, then burst forth toward the glass ceiling. An image formed.

A young man—no more than eighteen. Slim. Attractive in a gawky yearling way. Dark brown hair, clipped short. A green pullover that bagged at the neck.

Jani stood. The hologram consisted of the young man's head and torso only, but it displayed at such a height that she could look it in the face. She leaned close and studied the stark bones, the long neck. She looked to Val, who stood off to one side, gaze fixed on the floor. Then she leaned around the image to question John, but he sat on the edge of the couch with his head in his hands and didn't answer when she called.

She returned to the figure, her heart pounding. Green eyes. Humanish eyes. Like hers had been before she changed. Strange, though. Too monotone. Too dark and lifeless. As though someone had painted the irises with a single color.

She felt someone move beside her, and turned to find Lucien at her elbow.

"You don't realize what you're seeing, do you?" He looked to the image and shook his head.

"We had nothing to do with it. Val and I." John's voice sounded far away. "I swear to you, Jani. You have to believe me. We didn't do this."

"We didn't," Val said. "You have our word."

The young man raised his open right hand, palm facing out, lips moving as though he recited something. Jani tried to decipher what he said, but she couldn't—the image chopped in places and his mouthings weren't emphatic enough. So she concentrated instead on his spindly fingers, which were so long that at first glance she thought they contained extra joints. *Arachnodactyly—I know you well.* Jani raised her own right hand and placed it against the image of his, matching his spidery fingers with hers, length for length. She studied his skin and found it gold, studied his wrist and found the bird-boniness she saw every time she dressed or bathed or checked her reflection in a mirror.

"He looks enough like you to be your brother." Lucien looked from Jani to the image, his voice hushed. "He's a hybrid, too."

CHAPTER 4

The library had a bar. They all made use of it. Val took his usual gin over ice, and fixed a double shot of bourbon whiskey for John. Even Lucien, who generally avoided anything that could interfere with his self-control, opted for a shot of vodka.

Only Jani, on whom alcohol had ceased to have much effect, played the teetotaler. She made do with lemon tonic over ice, to which she added several slices of bitter orange as substitute for the ethanolic warmth and bite. "The most obvious question is," she said as she returned to her seat and propped her stockinged feet up on the table, "are you sure this thing is real?"

"I talked to several people—CapNet technicians, an actress friend of mine." Val dragged a wireframe chair beside Jani's and sat heavily. "Yes, these images can be faked rather readily. But even if this one was, why bother? Why make John and me think that someone out there has manufactured another hybrid if they in fact haven't?"

"Bait. To draw you out." Lucien had taken a seat on the couch on the side opposite John. He rested his head back, drink in hand, and surveyed the view through the skylight. "Someone wants one or both of you to visit wherever this thing came from."

Manufactured . . . thing . . . Jani thought of filmed green eyes, and wondered at the clarity beneath. Thought of a youthful face, and wondered how old he'd been when the change took him. *Did you have a choice, whoever you are, or did you have it thrust upon you? Do you even exist, or are you simply a trick of light and technology?* "Where did the image come from, by the way?" She sensed that she knew the answer, but asked the question anyway. "Where is this particular colonial broker located?"

"I wondered when you'd ask that." John had boosted his legs onto the couch and once more removed his jacket, but appeared more rumpled and tired than relaxed. "Amsun, the Outer Circle's most populous world. That's why Val and I would have come to see you regardless of other events. You're on your way to Elyas, another Outer Circle colony. You're acting for Tsecha in some diplomatic capacity. I wondered if there was any chance that your trip and our discovery could be related."

Lucien kept his sights fixed on the skylight. "It's possible."

Jani picked a slice of bitter orange from her drink and bit into it, savoring what to her hybrid palate tasted like pleasant astringency. Judging from John's wince, however, no humanish would have shared her opinion. "Tsecha hasn't been able to learn the whole story. All he's been able to piece together so far is that someone has challenged ná Feyó for dominance of the Elyan Haárin. Our feeling is that whoever the challenger is, they most likely don't possess Feyó's influence with the other Haárin or the colonial humanish. Given that, Feyó's loss could destabilize the region."

"*Our* feeling?" John's brow arched. "Have you adopted the imperial 'our' or are you speaking for Tsecha, too?"

"We speak with one voice. I am his suborn." Jani paused to drink. As she did, she became aware of a quality of silence, a tension that evidenced itself whenever she referred to herself as Tsecha's underling.

This time, Val issued the objection. "I thought your official position was human-Haárin liaison."

"It's hard to liase when one side isn't interested in participating." Jani tried to keep her voice low and even, but over the past months she'd explained herself more times than she could recall, and the idomeni half of her had long ago lost what little patience it possessed. "First the meeting notices stopped. Then I had my ministry security clearances pulled, one by one. If I hadn't turned over my documents business to Steve Forrell and Angevin Wyle, all three of us would have gone broke."

"You could have said something," John muttered into his glass. "I have managed to put a little aside over the years."

"Then you could have been criticized for involving Neoclona in an idomeni-owned business venture."

"You're *not* idomeni!"

"I know that, and you know that, but no one else in this city is interested in the distinction anymore!" Jani hesitated as her heart skipped a beat and a reenergizing warmth pumped through her veins. Her idomeni temper, which took hold lately anytime her blood rose. *Slow down—this isn't the time.* She pulled in a deep breath, another, and waited for her throat to unclench so she could speak normally. "I don't know if you've noticed, John, but your association with me has been coming under some heavy scrutiny lately."

"Is that all it is?" John's voice emerged softer as well, his gaze fixed on nothing. "An association?"

Lucien's head came up. "Could we please keep to the subject? We have an image of a hybrid that may or may not be real. If it isn't real, who faked it and why, and if it is real, how did that boy become a hybrid and who treated him?"

Time passed as the four of them practiced not looking at one another. Then Val raised his hand like an uncertain student in a difficult class.

"John and I have a guess as to who could have provided treatment." He looked at Jani. "You aren't going to like it."

"I don't like any of this so far. So it gets worse?" Jani met Val's bleary-eyed stare, and read his thoughts as though they were her own. "No. Not him."

"I bet I know who you're thinking of, Doctor." Lucien concentrated on the view above his head once again as he tilted his empty glass back and forth. "Eamon DeVries. The third man in the Neoclona triumvirate. He used to be my physician when I worked for Exterior Minister Ulanova. I think he's the one who augmented me, but I was never able to determine it for sure. He's been spending more and more time away from Earth these past few years. Some say he attends to Minister Ulanova when she's in residence at Exterior Main on Amsun, but I know for a fact that she's had another personal physician for the last two years because I ran the woman's security screening myself."

Silence fell once more as everyone pondered Lucien's information. He'd been Anais Ulanova's lover for over ten years, from his early teens up to the previous year, when he met Jani—no one felt inclined to argue with him regarding his knowledge of the Exterior Minister's medical issues.

"So what's Eamon been up to if he hasn't been seeing to Anais?" Jani twisted a length of orange peel into a tight knot, then dropped it back in her glass. "Don't you two check up on him?"

"Of course we do." John massaged his forehead. "We have a contract—call it division of labor—"

"We stay out of the gadget business, Eamon stays out of the gene business." Val got up, glass in hand, and walked across the room to the bar. "We felt it would be better for all concerned if we each stuck to our specialties." He saw to his own refill, then poured out a splash of bourbon and carried it over to John, all the while ignoring Lucien's empty glass.

Jani waited for Val to return to his seat. Waited for a frustrated Lucien to push to his feet and get more vodka for himself. Waited, all the while sensing John's eyes on her as she nursed the feeling that the past never died, but simply bided its time until it saw the chance to insert itself into the present. "There are people out there who felt you should have been imprisoned for the hybridization work you performed on me all those years ago. But if every person who broke the law during the last idomeni civil war was sent to the Lunar shipyards, we wouldn't have anyone left to run the government. Or the NUVA-SCAN business conglomerates. Or the Service. So, after the Commonwealth reopened relations with the Shèrá worldskein, a few deals were made to calm troubled waters. People went away, or went into other lines of work. Was this contract Neoclona's deal? Did Eamon officially take the fall for all of you?"

John tossed back his drink in a single swallow. Val ran his finger along the edge of his glass and stared at the floor.

"Looks like he may have gotten a little of his own back, doesn't it?" Jani stared across the room at John, who eventually raised his eyes to meet hers. "Am I correct in assuming that you'd like me to look into this while I'm in the area?"

"No." John swung his legs off the couch and sat up. "I want to accompany you." He leaned forward, elbows on knees, looking as gangly as the figure in the image. "If Eamon is involved . . . his dispute is with me, not Val. Matters have accrued between us for years. Now's as good a time as any to sort them out once and for all." He rubbed his chin. "And if he isn't involved, he may know who is. He always did have a nose for the nasty."

Jani hoped she didn't look as uncomfortable as she felt. *Just me and John.* In the close confines of a ship. *For the next six weeks.* "I don't see how it can work," she said too quickly. "It was hard enough getting the dispensation for me to travel on an Haárin craft, and you're not me."

"We can always travel on a Neoclona ship. We do have one or

two to spare." John sat back slowly. "It does offer advantages. It's less official-looking—that should serve to keep the Commonwealth off both our backs. There would be more privacy for you—we have private slips at every dock between here and the Outer Circle, so you won't have to worry about being hounded by the press."

Jani had to give John credit. His ability to sustain an attitude of studied innocence had improved over the years. "You've been thinking about this."

"Not at all." John glanced at her, and the light in his eyes flickered, the first crack in the façade. "Well, perhaps just a little."

"It makes sense." Lucien still stood at the bar. He had finished his vodka and moved on to fruit juice, a sign that recess was over and the time for clear-headed thinking had arrived. "Everyone will be so fixed on trying to figure out whether or not you've resumed your relationship, they'll forget about all the other possible reasons for your being together."

Jani sensed John's surprise at an unexpected ally, Val's restlessness as he waited for what would come next. "The ones whose opinions count won't be so easily distracted."

"They will be if Doctor Parini and I drop a few well-placed hints." Lucien looked to Val, his smile brilliant. "I think we can come up with a story acceptable to all, can't we, Doctor?"

Jani stared at Lucien until she drew his attention away from Val. Then she raised her glass. *"Bravo!"* She savored Lucien's discomfort, the sight of his smile slowly fading. "You play the pimp for me and wedge Val into a corner, all in one masterstroke. John and I can't say no, because I need to get to Elyas, he needs to see to Eamon, and we both need to find out about this alleged hybrid. Meanwhile, you stay behind with Val and plan, and oh the planning you need to do. Hours and days and weeks worth, as all the while you work to wear him down."

Lucien had been leaning against the bar. He drew up straighter now, his free hand clenching into a fist. "I'm sure I don't know what you mean." His hand relaxed. "I'm merely suggesting a strategy for getting you off Earth with as little complication as possible." Clench. Relax.

"That would make two of us with an in at Neoclona. You're tallying the ill-gotten gains already, aren't you?"

"I really don't know what you're talking—"

"Hah! *Liar!*"

"Jani?" John rose. He pocketed the imager and the sound

block, then edged toward her in a sideways shuffle, as though approaching an animal he didn't trust. "Did anyone in Service Medical examine you after you left the enclave?"

"No. Why?" Jani grew conscious of her pounding heart, the sing of blood in her veins. Her skin prickled, as though she sensed an approaching storm. "I feel fine."

"I'll get the bags." Val shot out of his seat and headed for the door, waving a dismissive hand at Lucien along the way.

Jani tried to bolt as John closed in, but his hand on her shoulder stopped her before she could rise from her seat. *"I'm all right."*

"Humor me," John said, his grip like a trap.

"Follow the lights." Val held a black cube the size of his head, dotted on one side with an array of pinpoint red illumins. "When I say 'Now.'"

"Do I have to?" Jani sat atop the kitchen counter, pounding out a beat against the cabinet doors with her heels. "It's just my augie experiencing a storm surge. It's been happening off and on for the past month or so." She gave the doors an extra hard kick—one jarred open under the impact, and she pushed it closed with a bang.

"Do what Val says, please." John set up the sound block, then stepped off to the side, arms folded. "If your augmentation is still firing, we may need to bring you down."

"Now," Val said.

Jani struggled to avoid looking at the lightbox Val held, even as she felt herself drawn to the flickering lights like an accident scene. "But I feel . . ." The first pattern splashed across the surface—she followed it like a cat tracking the flight of a bird. "I feel better than I have in months. My joints don't ache anymore. My back—" The patterns continued, irregular jumps and flutters, abrupt changes in speed and direction. "You know, those lights are really irritating."

Val shut down the box and shook his head. "Whatever's going on, it has nothing to do with her augmentation. If it still fired, she'd have gone under by now."

John walked to the table, on which Val had placed two hefty carryalls. "You've felt this way for a month?" He scrabbled through one of the bags, and after a few moments' digging came up with a sensor stylus. "I wish you'd said something before now." He approached Jani, gesturing for her to hold out her hand.

Jani held out her right hand, feeling a tremor of warmth as John enclosed it in his and pressed the vibrating end of the stylus against the tip of her index finger. "The anger comes in a rush, like a drug. Once it surfaces, it needs to discharge somewhere, I guess." John released her—as always, she felt the pressure of his grasp long after the flesh had parted.

"While I couldn't think of a better target for your wrath than Captain Pascal, I can imagine times when it would be better for you to keep your mouth shut." John examined the stylus readout and frowned at Val. "Blood readings are normal, relatively speaking." He tucked the stylus into his trouser pocket. "Tact and diplomacy were never your strong suits, and now that idomeni mood swings have apparently entered the picture, it's only going to go downhill from here."

"Tsecha's idomeni, and he manages all right," Jani muttered.

"No, he doesn't—" John and Val replied as one. Then all three of them grinned.

Val walked to the table, lightbox in hand. "A full Neuro workup would be a good idea." He slipped the device into a padded sack, then zipped the sack closed and tucked it into one of the bags. "If we determine where the changes have occurred and to what extent, we could design an augmentation to act as a moderator."

"We don't have time." John drew up next to the counter and leaned against it, a move that brought him closer to Jani. "I could start the preliminary work on the ship if I took one of our neurologists along."

Jani shook her head. "Drag someone away from home for three months or more on a day's notice? Not on my account, please."

"It's an unwritten part of the job description," Val said as he slung one of the bags over his shoulder. "Neoclona offers classes. If you can't learn to pack for a twelve-week long haul in ten minutes flat, we kick you out to live amongst the heathen." He hefted the other bag and trudged to the door. "If you pass the test, the Commonwealth is yours to command."

"Ten minutes? Why not make it a month?" Jani called after him. "I can do it in less than five."

"Unfair." The sound of Val's steps receded down the hall. "Too much practice!" A muffled curse drifted back as he pushed through the rear door, followed by silence.

Jani stared down at her socks for a time, then looked up to find

John regarding her with an odd mix of amusement and concern that it seemed he reserved lately for her and her alone. "Would a new augmentation help smooth out the mood swings?"

"Possibly." He boosted atop the counter next to her. "The problem is that it would need to function all the time, as opposed to your Service augmentation, which only has to operate at times of extreme duress. You'd experience many of the same issues—misfirings, over- and undercontrol, the risk of chronic bioemotional disorders, which may turn up that much more quickly because of the increased exposure to modified neurotransmitters. Then there's the fact that you possess the only hybrid brain in the Commonwealth. Even with advanced modeling, it would all be guesswork on the part of my Neuro group until we learned more about how your brain functions, and I'm really not anxious to see you become a test subject for every tweak and nudge that comes down the pike."

Jani thought back to the hybrid boy's image. A smile and long, thin hands like hers. "What if I'm not anymore? The only hybrid brain in the Commonwealth."

John smoothed a hand over the front of his jacket, then started fiddling with one of the fasteners. As usual, tension made him fidgety. "Like Val said, holo images can be very readily faked. I'm more concerned with who it is who's trying to attract our attention. And why." He forced a smile. The harsh kitchen lighting accentuated every line on his so-pale face. "I'll let you worry about whether it has anything to do with your little matter."

"I wish it was a little matter." Jani rubbed her stomach, where Lucien's omelet weighed heavily amid the growing churn. "A little matter at this stage in the game would be a positive delight." She held out her hand to John. "Are you still carrying that shooter?"

John's brow arched. Then he reached into his inside jacket pocket and removed a burnished C-curve of dull silver.

Now it was Jani's turn to act surprised. "Fancy." She took the graceful weapon from him and examined it, conscious at every level of the residual warmth the metal held. "A Beecham-Grenoble S-40. Strong enough power source to kick it up into the medium-range class. How long have you been taking shooting lessons?"

"About two months. A club I belong to has a range. One of our new staff members in Orthopedics is ex-Service." John looked down at the floor. "She's been showing me the ins and outs."

Has she? Jani's heart skipped, but not because of a flood of idomeni anger. No, this was more a humanish brand of emotion, unreasonable though it was. *He has every right—I showed up here with Lucien, and he knows we didn't spend the night sitting around talking.* "Just remember that if anyone who knows weapons sees this, they're going to assume you know what you're doing and re-act accordingly." She handed the shooter back to him, taking care not to touch his hand.

"Funny. Marya said the same thing." John's lips curved, an almost-smile that contained enough self-satisfaction to inspire violence.

I won't push him off the counter. What she wanted to do, against all reason, was push her hands through that silky mass of hair and pull him to her, shatter twenty years' separation with a single kiss. Wipe away the smile inspired by another woman and replace it with one inspired by her. *I love you, John Shroud.* She'd admitted the fact long ago, to him as well as to herself, and knew he felt the same. *But it would never work.* No matter how they tried, it always came down to her independence versus his desire to protect her. *There's nothing left to talk about. Nothing left to feel jealous over.* Yet jealous she was, painfully so. That meant it was time to change the subject. Time to stick to business. "Lucien was right, you know. Any ministry guard worth a damn would have dropped you before you'd sighted down."

John's smile died. "I still believe he exaggerated."

Jani shook her head. "Tensions are mounting. The bornsect Vynshàrau think they're losing their souls and their Haárin. The Families know they're losing money and their grip on the Commonwealth frontier. Everyone's trying to figure out a way to keep what they have, and that ozonelike odor you smell is the short, sharp scent of panic in the wind."

John sighed as he slipped the Beecham back inside his jacket pocket. "That misplaced mine didn't help, I'm sure."

"No, it didn't help one bit." Jani slid off the counter and walked to the table. Val had stacked the dirty plates and cutlery to one side in order to deposit his and John's medical gear. She picked them up and carried them to the cleaner. "I need to take a trip back across the lake. Break the news to Tsecha about the ship, find out what transpired at the enclave after I left." She inserted all the tableware into the appropriate slots and holders. "I thought I'd try to catch some sleep first."

"Are you going to tell him about our possible hybrid?" John pushed off the counter, then paused to fuss with his jacket.

Jani closed the cleaner, then activated it. "I have to, especially if it's possible that it may be entangled with Feyó's problem."

"How do you think he'll take it?"

"It's what he prophesied. What he prayed for all these years." Jani yanked a dispo towel from a countertop dispenser and wiped her hands. "On the other hand, considering the current climate, he may wish our young friend had chosen a less tangled time to make his appearance." She crumpled the dispo and tossed it into the trash, followed the flash and the puff of smoke that signaled its demise, then walked with John into the hall.

"I don't know if I'll see you before we leave." He seemed subdued, as though the import of their upcoming journey had just struck home. "Seventeen-up is the usual departure time for an afternoon trip. I'll send a skimmer for you at about sixteen."

"All right." Jani felt his presence beside her, and tried not to think about it. "I should have called. I'm sorry."

John grinned weakly. "You have this knack for putting yourself in the middle of things. When I heard that a mine had exploded at the enclave, I thought the worst."

Jani touched John's arm, pulling away just as a look of surprise crossed his face. "I was in a bunker, 200 meters away, with Niall, Tsecha, and a comtech who didn't like me very much."

"More fool him." John hesitated at the door, as though he wanted to say more. Then he saw Val lower the skimmer boot lid and circle around to the driver's side. "Tomorrow," he said, his businesslike demeanor returned.

Jani took John's coat from the rack and handed it to him, feeling its softness long after she released it. "Tomorrow." She saw him out, watched him get into the skimmer, then watched the vehicle float out of sight.

She then returned to the library to find Lucien standing at the bar sink cleaning the glasses. He looked up when she entered, then quickly away. Jani walked to the couch and lowered onto it, yawning as the cushions swallowed her up. The remains of her augmentation, her idomeni nature, both had retreated, leaving her drained. She hoisted her legs aboard, lay back, and contemplated the square of blue sky visible through the skylight.

"You embarrassed me."

Jani lifted her head. Lucien had finished with the glasses and now wandered the room, straightening and adjusting. *When he's on edge, he needs to move. Just like John. Just like me. We're none of us comfortable enough in our skins to stay in one place.* "It's going to happen more and more often. My brain is changing. My bioemotional balances." She tried to inject some levity into her voice. "If you think you're getting the raw end, look at me. I'm going to wind up even more popular than I am now." Lucien ignored her as he continued his housekeeping promenade, and she decided that in this particular instance, surrender was the better part of valor. "I'm sorry." She tried to think of a bright side. "If it's any consolation, Val had you figured out before I opened my mouth. He doesn't fool easily."

"That's all right. I love a challenge." Lucien gave a chair one last shove-into-place. "I need to get back to Sheridan." He headed for the door, but at the last moment he slowed, then turned and approached the couch. "You want him to be real, don't you?" Sunshine streamed through the skylight, lightening his hair until it looked as white as John's. "The hybrid boy. You want him to be real and you're afraid that he's not."

Jani opened her mouth to protest, but no words emerged. As usual, Lucien got right to the heart of the matter, then grabbed and twisted. "It's a mistake to get one's hopes up," she said after a time. "I learned that the hard way."

"If it's any consolation, two hybrids would upset people twice as much as one." Lucien drew alongside the couch, then leaned over. "Even more than that, considering that one is you." He kissed her, softly at first, then not softly at all, leaving her breathless as he slipped away without another word.

"*Au revoir, mon capitain.*" Jani regarded the closed door as the minutes passed, and gradually another sensation took hold. Less painful than love, less urgent than lust, yet in its own way as implacable, as undeniable.

She held up her hand, imagined the hybrid boy's still hanging in the air before her. Saw them meet, felt warm flesh instead of cool light. Pressed hard, palm against palm, finger against finger, each matching as though they mirrored one another.

"I always wondered what it would have been like to have a brother." She lay there, holding her hand in place until sleep claimed her.

CHAPTER 5

A muddle of images. Wode's face as he turned to the sound of Pullman's shout, melting into that of Feres, the dead Vynshàrau.

A sound. A name. Her name.

Jani.

Feres's face shortening. Widening. The eyes altering from gold to green, sclera paling, whitening, changing—

Jani?

—to a face she knew well though she'd seen it only once. A young face with filmed eyes, humanish films that covered, but not well enough—

"Jani."

Jani opened her eyes.

"Jesus, gel." Niall Pierce released a shaky sigh. "You weren't waking up and you weren't waking up. I thought I'd have to call Shroud." He sat on the edge of the low table, one hand braced on the couch cushion near Jani's head. "I've been jawing at you for five minutes—didn't you hear me?"

"I fell—" Jani stared above her head at the view through the skylight, and saw only dark slate grey where there'd once been sunlit blue. "Oh, damn."

"Oh damn is right." Niall sat back, his expression lightening as he realized she was conscious and aware of her surroundings. "It's a little after nineteen. You slept most of the day away." He offered a fangy grin. "Join the club. I called Pull's folks from the doctors' lounge, then sat back to take a breather. Too many hours later . . ." He shook his head. "One of the neuros ordered them to let me sleep. Damned augie. After I woke up, I shambled to the office. Far North Lakeside was a beehive, of course. Sat through nine meetings in as many hours, then decided the hell with it and bolted."

Jani tossed back her coat, which had served as a coverlet, and slowly sat up. "How's Pull?"

"Awake, but bleary." Niall reached into his shirt pocket and pulled out his nicstick case. "Doesn't remember the blast, which is a good thing, if you ask me."

Jani motioned for Niall to move down the table so she could swing her legs off the couch. "And the meetings?"

"The usual. How, what, when, why, and who can we throw to the dogs?" He pulled a 'stick from the case and crunched down on the tip with intent. "Everyone's poring over field exercise notes going back six years. Pulling in everyone from Spacers First Class to Ordnance chiefs, questioning them on every move they made during this or that night maneuver a year or more ago. If Service Investigative thinks people are hiding things, they're going to break out the truth sera, and won't that be fun for all concerned." He slumped, the smoke curling around his head like a free-form halo. "Mako's still with the PM. Couple of loons burned an idomeni in effigy on the grounds of the Exterior Ministry, which was as close as they could bloody get to the embassy, thank God. Shai's in special session with the Oligarch, or in as much of a special session as she can be via Misty communications. Could be the end of the month before they get all that back and forth sorted out."

Jani tried to imagine Morden nìRau Cèel's response when the news of the mine reached him. *Will you think past the end of your nose for once in your life, you chill bastard, or will you thank the gods for giving you the excuse you need to close the enclave?* "Any word from Tsecha?"

"He gave a short interview on CapNet this morning. Spoke English, and looked right into the cam. Sincere regrets for all lives lost. Said the word 'accident' three times that I counted. Wily old bird, trying to calm the whitecaps. Hope someone listens." Niall stood up and walked to the bar. "You still leaving tomorrow on your gift-giving excursion to Elyas?"

Jani watched Niall pour himself a drink. Scotch and soda, his usual. He'd switched out of his soiled fatigues for civvies, tan trousers, and a cream pullover that seemed too casual a choice for the man who wore them. *Niall doesn't relax well.* At the moment, he didn't appear relaxed at all. "Yes, I'm still leaving tomorrow."

Niall turned to face her, glass in hand. "I stopped by the

kitchen on the way down the hall, thinking you might be in there. Quite a few plates stacked in the cleaner." He didn't look at Jani but at some spot above her head.

"You had to open the cleaner to find that out. Did you think I was hiding inside?" When Niall didn't reply, Jani sat up a little straighter. She'd been questioned in this same offhand manner countless times in her past. The best response was, of course, to tell the truth. At least regarding the facts that could be checked. "I went to see Lucien after I left you. He brought me back here. We found John and Val waiting for me. Service Medical borrowed some equipment from Neoclona, and they found out what happened. They came by to see if I was all right. We all came inside. Lucien made breakfast."

"John and Pretty Boy in the same room. That must have made for some fun." Niall set aside his drink, then wandered to Jani's desk and riffled through a stack of old newssheets. "That's the whole story?"

"Are you asking as my friend, Niall, or as Colonel Niall Pierce, Special Services, hatchet man-in-waiting to Admiral-General Hiroshi Mako?"

"Would the answer be different, depending?"

"You didn't think I was home. You thought I was at the enclave. You came here to search the place."

"Better me than anyone else." Niall circled around to the opposite arm of the couch and sat down across from Jani. "Two hours ago a Neoclona shuttle filed an O'Hare-Luna flight plan. Luna Station reported soon after that a Neoclona cruiser submitted GateWay requests from Mars through to Amsun. Elyas is a four day skip from there. John Shroud's going to take you to deliver your gift himself, isn't he?"

Jani shrugged. "He's rich. He can afford to be generous."

"Jani." Niall sat back and thumped his head against the couch cushions. "You can't shove things down people's throats. Tsecha tried that with his predictions of hybrids and a blending of the human and idomeni races, and where did that get him? He lost his position as religious leader of the ruling bornsect, along with all the power that went with it. The soapbox. The ability to persuade, to change from within. And oh, he's such a charismatic bastard— he could have charmed the birds from the trees, but he blew it." He took a last pull on his 'stick, then pondered the spent cylinder. "And then there's you, taking up where he left off. There's no one I'd rather have at my back with a loaded shooter, but so help me, if there's one person I wouldn't want arguing for my life before a judge and jury, it's you, with your 'my way or go to hell' approach to everything."

"I recall telling you once that I was not political." Jani concentrated on picking through the past, on uncovering the evidence to counter Niall's assertions. On countering the words themselves, without stopping to consider their meaning. "I recall you replying that politics had gotten us into the messes we were in, that the city needed someone with my point of view."

"I have been known to make mistakes." Niall hung his head. "You strong-armed Chicago into opening the doors for an Haárin enclave before they were ready to accept Haárin in their midst. We're paying the price for that now."

"Enclaves have existed in the colonies for close to half a century. Chicago is a tad behind the curve."

"It's the Commonwealth capital. The heart of humanity. It already had an embassy, just like we have our embassy in Rauta Shèràa. It didn't need anything else until it was prepared to accept it. It's a bigger step to take *here*." Niall snapped the 'stick in two and tossed it into a dish set out for the purpose. "It feels threatened. It's overreacting, falling on any hint of trouble and magnifying it a hundredfold."

Jani imagined Niall's speech in a voice other than his Victorian twang. A guttural baritone, Earthbound in accent, educated without sounding cultured. "Thank you, Colonel, for delineating the Admiral-General's point of view so well."

"It's mine also. To an extent." Niall rubbed his eyes. His skin appeared dull and sagged, as though he hadn't slept at all. "I'm a human being, Jan. This is my Service. This is my world."

"I am not a human being." Jani looked down at her hands, the hands that had matched so well those of a boy who odds were didn't exist. "Do you understand that now?"

Niall sniffed, kept his gaze fixed on the floor. "You're—" He took a deep breath and tried again. "You're leaving tomorrow at seventeen-up."

You ought to know. Jani bit back the words. She didn't want her farewell to Niall to consist of a fight. "Yes."

"You need to see Tsecha." Niall stood, worked his shoulders. "I'll take you."

Jani watched him move, his actions controlled and cadenced. *He's conserving his ammo*. Warming up, but not too much. Expending just enough energy to get him where he needed to go. *Oh,*

Niall. You still have another shoe to drop, don't you, me lad? She rose, gathered her coat, and started for the door, then waited for him to join her.

The ride over the lake to the enclave proved more pleasant than Jani expected. Niall stuck to opera, ballet, and general Sheridan gossip. For her part, Jani talked about her parents and her youth on the colony of Acadia, since Niall had been orphaned at an early age and often hinted that he liked hearing tales of family life.

"They've gone back, your folks. To Acadia." Niall swore under his breath as lake chop struck the underside of the skimmer, sending a shudder through the cabin. "I thought things weren't safe there."

"They've improved. The PM installed a new governor, who happens to be someone the Acadians actually like. A few heads rolled in the Legislature. A few undesirables left in their socks." Jani looked out the window to the moon-dappled swell that stretched to blackness beyond. "Papa never admitted it, but he always felt that coming to Chicago was tantamount to running away. Maman didn't want to admit it, but she was homesick. When Oncle Shamus sent up the distress flare late last year that his resort business had grown too big for him to handle alone, I knew it was only a matter of time." She thought back to the day they came to break the news to her, their eyes alight. "Maman knows twelve ways to coax an obsolete dicad battery back to life. Not much call for that in Chicago."

"Aren't they worried about you?"

"Yes. They want me to join them. Shamus has enough work to merit keeping his own documents examiner on staff."

"Seems a ready-made job."

"It's too cold." Jani hunched deeper into her coat. "That's why the Haárin never tried to negotiate an enclave there. The weather's too rough, even for the Oà, and they're the northernmost idomeni. They've experience with harsh winters."

"That's why coats were invented." Niall eyed her askance. "What's the real reason you don't want to go back?"

Jani tried to glare him into submission, but as usual he met her straight on. "Some of those people form my first memories," she said finally. "I know them. I know how some of them would react if they saw me now. They haven't taken it out on my parents because I've been gone so long it's like I never really lived there, but if I showed up now . . ." In the distance, the lights of the enclave burned through the dark, and she bid silent thanks for this conversation's end. "It's my parents' home. They love it. I don't want to ruin it for them."

"You were born there. It's your home, too." Niall looked to her for some response, but before he could argue one out of her, Haárin security cut in with an ID request.

"Not anymore." Jani whispered it under her breath, so he couldn't hear. They veered north and followed the beach. Before long the first enclave outbuildings came into view. She saw Tsecha standing at the head of the dock, Dathim at his side.

Tsecha led Jani onto the glass-walled veranda of the enclave's meeting house. The building had been constructed atop an artificial hillock. The veranda itself faced the lake, and overlooked the rest of the enclave. Nighttime security lighting cast eerie shadows on the short streets that ran below, lined with smooth-walled houses, the business exchanges and other buildings that served the needs of the Chicago Haárin.

"So you travel with Shroud." He lifted his right hand waist high, then curved it in puzzlement. "There is a Neoclona hospital in Karistos for him to visit. Otherwise, what purpose does he serve?"

"Cover, inshah. If it is thought that I travel with him, no one will question closely why I travel to Elyas." Jani fielded Tsecha's bewildered posture. Despite his extensive experience with matters humanish, the ways of the heart left him lost. *Well, that makes two of us.* She waited for more questions, and when she didn't get any, looked to her teacher to find him staring out the window.

"The injured Haárin are well. They walk, and have returned to their homes. The Vynshàrau Feres is most likely dead, but Shai still confers, and Sànalàn informs me of nothing. Such, she said, is of no concern to me, as she is now Chief Propitiator, not I. Yet I knew Feres, and feel the concern I am not allowed." Tsecha started to pace. He wore a typical Haárin color-clash of purple overshirt and yellow trousers. His shirtsleeves billowed over his hands, sweeping back and forth in time to his stride. "If your John treated him, there would be no question of recovery. Feres would be made whole again. New limbs, as were given you nearly twenty of your years ago. New organs. But because he is idomeni, the extent of his injuries are seen to cast doubt upon the wholeness of his soul." He paused in mid-stride and regarded Jani, amber eyes dulled by worry to old gold. "Did you ever question the wholeness of your soul, nìa, after your treatment?"

Jani looked down at her hands, pressing them together as though in prayer. The real right and the animandroid left, outwardly identical, inwardly so different. Red blood flowed through one, dark pink carrier through the other. The same held true for her legs, fake left and true right. *My cobbled-together limbs.* Just one aspect of her cobbled-together body, which if one pushed the point, could serve as an outward manifestation of her hybrid psyche. *Watch your step, Kilian—philosophical waters run deep.* "Quite often, inshah," she admitted, because the faster she admitted to it, the sooner she could stop thinking about it.

"But you knew enough to consider such, which is something that I find most indicating an unchanged state of self." Tsecha nodded at his own response, too wrapped up in thought to notice his pupil's discomfort. "Sànalàn, of course, would deny such. Such an ungodly chief propitiator she is. To her, Feres's destroyed body indicates that his soul is no longer whole. If he has not yet died, I fear he soon will."

Jani spread her hands apart, then lowered them to her sides. "When I see you consider as a priest, I wonder if you wish you still served as ambassador. Politics is easier than religion."

"No longer, nìa. It seems to me, and truly, that Chicago is as Rauta Shèràa was when you schooled at the Academy. The nearness to humanish would destroy us all, so they said in Temple and Council. Six documents students, and a Consulate set behind high walls. So few, to be accused of so much."

Jani stood near the center of the bare room, absorbing the Vynshàrau-level heat through every pore. Wishing she merely paid a social call, and could leave the difficult questions she needed to ask out in the cold where they belonged. "Our nearness helped destroy the Laum."

Tsecha chopped the air with his right hand, a harsh Vynshàrau Haárin negative. "The Laum destroyed themselves. They took the worst of humanish, the greed and the need to control with secrets. If they had taken the best of humanish, the ability to adapt and explore, to change, they might have survived."

Jani took a step nearer the window. "The hell you say?"

Tsecha hung his head. "You are most correct, nìa. The best of humanish is not what I am seeing now."

They stood side by side, watching the occasional Haárin, swaddled in ankle-length coat and trailing scarves, emerge from a building and dash down the street. "Even before I left Acadia to school on Shèrá, before I realized the depth of variation between worlds, I never thought of myself as a citizen of the Common-wealth. I always referred to myself as Acadienne. *Une jeune fille de les Vieux Rouges.*" Jani caught Tsecha raising a curved hand in puzzlement, and smiled. "A young girl of the Old Red. My birth-place, Ville Acadie, is built on red clay. The first colonists chris-tened it 'Le Vieux Rouge.' That's also the name of our football team."

"Ah. The Commonwealth Cup." A little of the confusion cleared from Tsecha's face. "Acadia Central United. They lost the final match to a group from this place."

"Gruppo Helvetica." The name still stuck in Jani's throat, months after the fact. "Acadia tried too hard. They wanted it too badly. Gruppo had its weaknesses—they'd have beaten them-selves if given the chance." She watched a youngish trudge up the street, kicking a stone. "Niall thinks the Haárin tried too hard to force their way in here, that I tried too hard helping you. We set Chicago back on its heels, threatened them. Gave them something to fight."

"Your scarred colonel does not like me. He believes I keep you from what you should do, whatever that is. I most doubt he could tell me, if I asked." Tsecha drummed his fingers against the win-dow. "So little I understand of humanish pairings, even after so many years. You are not with Colonel Pierce as you are with Lu-cien?"

"No, inshah." Jani sighed. *Maybe if I drew a diagram* . . . "We are friends, as you were with Hansen Wyle."

"Angevin's father. My Hansen of the godly hair. He taught me much of humanish ways." Tsecha brightened for a moment, bar-ing his teeth wide. Then the expression faded. "Not enough, most sadly, to understand your colonel. He seemed most as upset when you said you would speak to me alone."

Before Jani could reply, the door to the meeting room opened.

"Glories of this damned cold night to you, Kièrshia!" Dathim Naré, Tsecha's secular suborn, strode in coatless and hatless, his gold-brown skin paled to dun from the cold. "Pierce has returned to his skimmer, to smoke. I remind him of the protocols forbidding open displays of eating on idomeni lands. He tells me that a nic-stick is not food, and I should look the other way. He enjoys argu-ment, that one." Two meters tall, broad-shouldered, a face of shadowed hollows and heavy bone, he seemed suited to chill and wind even though he had been born in a desert and craved heat as much as Jani. "He tried to question me of what you both would speak of. I pretended I did not understand his English." He dragged a wireframe seat from against the wall and set it by the window. "So," he said as he sat in a humanish male sprawl, "do you speak of Kièrshia's bruises, and why I shall always be able to defeat her with blades? Do you speak of Feyó? Of mines? What?"

"We speak of football, and old clay, and old times." Tsecha looked down at his suborn and shook his head in a humanish display of frustration. "Ask your questions, nìa. Dathim grows impatient."

"I played him to a draw the day before yesterday. Only the third time I fought with two blades—I think I surprised us both." Jani caught Tsecha's teeth-baring and Dathim's grimace, then turned back to the window to watch the youngish continue to kick her stone. Another young Haárin had joined her, darting back and forth in front of her in an effort to distract. "How much did Feyó tell you, inshah, about this challenge to her dominance?"

"What I have told you, nìa, is all I know," Tsecha replied. "I have no secrets."

Jani heard the youngish cries through the glass, the stone clatter against a metal post. "John received a shipment from Amsun some days ago. Inside the container he found an imager, a device that displays recorded holo images."

Tsecha sighed. "I do know of such things, nìa."

"The image contained in the device looks just like a male hybrid. Did Feyó tell you anything that might indicate that someone on Elyas engaged in that sort of research?" Jani looked to Dathim, to find him regarding her, back straight, gaze fixed. *This is the first he's heard of this.*

"Another hybrid?" Tsecha raised a hand to gesture surprise, but stopped halfway. He looked Jani in the face, eyes now clear and bright. "Feyó told me that she did not trust the security of our communications. This was why she gave so little information, and made certain she spoke in terms most vague." He made to gesture again, and stalled again. "Another hybrid." He fell silent, left hand curved and resting against his chest, a gesture of great surprise cut off in mid-flourish.

"Holo images may be easily forged, may they not?" Dathim stood and walked to Tsecha's side. He hovered over the elder male, his usually blank posture tensed and curved with worry.

Jani nodded. "Yes, ní Dathim. But if the image is indeed a forgery, it then begs more questions than it answers. Why use a hybrid image as a lure, and what, if anything, does this image have to do with Feyó's problem?" Outside, the youngish had moved on to other distractions, leaving the street empty and quiet.

Tsecha let his hand fall to his side. "Dathim fears that I will take such joy in the discovery of another hybrid that I will forget how to question." He turned away from the window and made a slow promenade of the room, his hands clasped behind his back, half hidden by his shirtcuffs. "He does not know me as well as he believes he does." His tone sharpened, his English harsh with impatience. "What do you believe, nìa?"

"I can speculate until the sun comes up." Jani turned and leaned against the glass, wondering if any of the Haárin could see the three of them from their houses. "I wish I had more facts. John and Val recognize the possibility that the image could be faked, a lure to draw them to Elyas. Add to this the chance that Eamon De-Vries may be involved, and the plot gets murkier and murkier."

"Eamon!" Tsecha threw his head back and emitted a barking laugh. "Always the secrets, with that one. Always *money*." Cruel humor shaved years from his face and posture. "I most envy you, nìa, for you will learn so much strange truth, and I fear you may not trust the security of our communications sufficiently to inform us of your discoveries. Thus will I live for months and months without word." His posture softened. "Do you believe it possible, nìa, that this hybrid exists?"

Jani looked about the room. Dathim had worked his tilemastery on the surfaces, decorating them with interlocking networks of cord and chain that made it seem as though the walls were lashed together. All linked. All inseparable, one from the other. "I exist. Why not another?" She followed the path of one chain, tracking it until it lost itself in a tangle near one corner. "But I refuse to speculate. I will wait for facts."

"Ah." Tsecha clasped his hands. "I know many at Temple who would say that you do not sound much as a priest."

"It is better to wait for facts." Dathim walked to the far wall and traced one length of chain with a discerning hand, frowning at an imperfection only he could see. "We will remain here, and wait for Mako's facts about his mine. Kièrshia will go to Elyas, and search for facts of an image that vanishes when one alters a switch." He rapped the wall with his fist, then walked to the door. "Safe journey, hybrid priest. Do not cut yourself, and glories of the damned cold night to you."

Tsecha watched Dathim leave, then tilted his head and curved his shoulders in a posture of regret. "He and his suborns have spent the time since the incident scanning the enclave for more mines. I have seen in him a fear of humanish that I have never seen before." He straightened. "Do you feel prepared, nìa, for this journey?"

Jani hesitated, caught by the abrupt change in subject. "No," she said finally, "but I've never felt prepared for any journey I've taken. I learn what I can beforehand, and deal with each thing as it comes."

"You depend on your Lord Ganesha to remove all obstacles from your path, as always? Your wise elephant god who sits atop a mouse?" Tsecha offered a close-lipped, humanish smile. "Your Lord must have every room in his house filled, so many obstacles has he cleared over the years."

Jani laughed. "He complains to me that he must build more." She crossed to where Tsecha stood, and as she approached saw him as Feyó, as any of her Haárin would. Reassuring in his age, his lined face a testament to a common history, a common belief, both in their gods and the path down which they led. *When they see me, they must not see* me, *but what I am through him. Tsecha vo Kièrshia. Tsecha's toxin.* She felt a now-familiar inward quaver, and hoped her old teacher couldn't see her fear of failure. As she joined him, they uttered a prayer to Shiou, the goddess of order, and as she did with Niall, Jani concentrated on the words, not their meaning. *I go to help Feyó, and find a hybrid.* Saving souls would have to wait for another time.

"You leave a cold place behind," Tsecha said after they uttered the closing. "I understand Karistos is quite warm."

"That, I look forward to." Jani walked to the door, pausing so Tsecha could catch her up. "It's possible that I may be able to communicate with you via Neoclona—they're known for their security. But if I see any problem, I will not risk it."

"And if you see the hybrid?" Tsecha leaned close, the lack of gesture in his speech betraying his excitement. "I would so wish to know, if possible."

"I'll do my best." Jani gave his arm a tentative pat, felt old muscle like cord beneath her hand. "You will take care? Stay out of trouble?"

Tsecha looked her in the eye. Bornsect idomeni reserved such familiarity for their most intimate moments, but as a whole, their Haárin had adopted the humanish approach. "I will do as I do, nìa."

"One more thing to worry about." Jani sighed. "Glories of this strange night to you, inshah." She took her leave of him, her boots sounding a muted cadence down the empty hall.

She walked down the deserted street, conscious of being watched yet unable to tell by whom. Down one alley, then another, until she came to the bare dunes. Niall waited for her there, huddled inside the skimmer, coat collar pulled up to hide his contraband nicstick. He released the passenger-side door as she drew near; she lowered inside. Niall then banked the vehicle around and they headed back across the lake.

The other shoe. Jani rested her head against the seatback, the soft thrum of the skimmer motor providing counterpoint for her thoughts. *With all that's happened, why is he here?* She glanced at Niall, then away before he sensed her gaze. *All hell's broken loose at Sheridan, Mako's on the hot seat, and where's his right-hand man? Carting one of the root causes of all the trouble back and forth across the lake like a hired driver.* Granted, Niall did see to her security. *But that can't be foremost in his mind right now.*

She yawned. However long she'd slept, it hadn't been enough. "This reminds me of a few nights at Rauta Shèràa Base. I'd get dragged out of bed to answer questions about this or that shipment that the Laumrau claimed we hadn't cleared with them. When I showed them the signed-off paperwork, they pulled out the tweezers and looked for mistakes." She smiled humorless remembrance. "Foodstuffs, mostly, that they couldn't classify under their strict fruit-nut-meat-veg system. Prepack meals drove them crazy."

"I couldn't have handled that crap." Niall shook his head, voice heavy with the man-of-action's disdain for the clerk's side of things.

"Turned me into a stickler where the rules were concerned." Jani ignored Niall's derisive snort. "And it wasn't like a Sheridan transport dexxie's job. The Families still controlled the Service back then, so you found yourself faced with these situations where you knew no one had broken rules, but yet and all they had these cesspit aromas about them. I spent half my time digging for the rest of the story." She laughed. "Chicago at its worst had nothing on a Family member out for their due. They had a way of turning the most simple procedure into a personal mint. Billet privileges were the worst. Chapter and verse, quote, 'Any civilian craft is required to offer any and all assistance to a Service member requiring emergency transport in the course of performance of his duty,' unquote. In my day, the owner of the ship involved could bill the Service for expenses incurred. Service members who were also Family members used it as a way to billet themselves in style on one of their own ships. Then they'd bill the Service for the cost of everything from food to fuel to crew salaries and uniforms. Abascal, the Treasury Minister—his uncle once tried to pass off the cost for a complete refit for a spaceliner. I made a lot of friends shutting that one down."

"That's changed," Niall said quietly. "The reg now states that assistance is to be provided free of any financial consideration."

Jani studied his profile in the half-light. Too sharp to ever be bland, too wary to ever count as unassuming. "Had reason to look it up recently, did you?" She tried to feel angry, but settled for a vague dissonance. The echo of that last shoe hitting the ground. "And your duty is?"

"Observe the situation in Karistos. Report same." Niall held up a hand, let it fall. "Better me than anyone else, like I said before."

"Yet you'll do your duty as you see fit."

"So will you, Jan. So will you."

It was still many hours to sunrise. The wind had picked up, driving spray over the skimmer. They'd left the lights of the enclave behind, and the glow of Chicago had not yet come into view. The only light was the moon through the clouds and the skimmer headlamps shining off the black water.

They pulled into Jani's drive to find two skimmers had beaten them there. Jani recognized Val's sportster, and assumed the nondescript brown four-door as yet another of Lucien's refugees from the vehicle pool.

"Sounds like a reunion," Niall said as they entered the house, voices raised in loud discussion reaching them from the library.

John, Lucien, and Val had staked out separate corners of the room—they rose as one when Jani entered. She tried to catch John's eye, but he had fixed on Niall, his pale skin reddening.

Niall nodded in brusque acknowledgment. "Doctor."

John didn't nod back. "You might have come to me first before sending in the Judge Advocate's rep with a writ."

Niall walked to the bar. He hefted the scotch decanter but set it aside and took a soft drink from the inset cooler instead. Duty called, after all. "I might have." He popped the cap, took a long swallow. "And you would have agreed without any argument whatsoever, wouldn't you have?"

John opened his mouth to dissent but thought better of it and turned to Jani. "Bad weather moving in." His look gentled. "Our departure's been shuffled. We leave before sunrise."

"Doesn't leave a body any time to say good-bye," Lucien said. He stood at the far side of the room, out of range of the trio of male glowers that greeted his veiled comment. "I'll keep an eye on the place."

"Thanks." Jani burned a mental image of the boyish grin she received in reply, to savor as needed. "I can sleep on the shuttle, I guess." She backed out of the room. "I'll get my gear."

She mounted the stairs and entered her bedroom, walked to her closet and opened the door. Pushed aside a rack of Lucien's clothes, revealing the shelf hidden behind. The narrow ledge contained one thing only, a small blue duffel of the sort the Service had issued twenty years before. *Jani's Noah bag*, Lucien had dubbed it. *Contains two of everything, in case of disaster.* Coveralls, underwear, bandbras, socks. Other essentials she'd added as the date of the trip grew closer. One scanpack, however. And one shooter, nestled in the scanproof depths.

She pulled the bag off the shelf and hitched it over her shoulder. Rearranged Lucien's clothing, then slid the door closed. Trotted down the stairs and back to the library. Four examining stares moved from her face to her bag, then back again, none showing the least surprise at the lightness of her load.

"OK," she said. "Let's go."

CHAPTER 6

Micah Faber keyed into his flat, waiting until the door opened completely before stepping inside. A minor point for some, but important to him. His training dictated that door panels were to be rammed aside, punched through, demolished, if necessary, that they were barriers to be breached rather than portals to be entered. His home, he had decided from the start, needed to be treated differently.

The lights came up, revealing a sitting room in disarray from the previous night's panic. Contents yanked from drawers and shelves and strewn across the floor, cushions pulled from the small couch and single armchair and tossed about like playing cards. In the far corner, the holoVee display, an indestructible one-piece panel spot-molded to the wall, flashed and fluttered in silent cacophony. A woman, weeping and gesticulating, the CapNet reporter who stood beside her nodding in professional concern, while behind them bystanders waved, made faces, or yelled as the spirit moved them.

Micah groaned. He'd seen the same story a half-dozen times since returning to the base that morning. The woman spoke for a group that had banded together to protest the proximity of the Vynshàrau Haárin enclave to the city. Only one Spacer had died as a result of this accident, but what if there were more accidents, and what if more humans died? She couldn't sleep at night for the fear. None of her friends could sleep.

Micah walked to the console and shut it off. "Spare me." If the Weeping Madonna, as he'd dubbed her, wished to protest the enclave, there were things she could do, and sobbing to a reporter wasn't one of them.

He turned away from the holoVee and stumbled over one of the chair cushions. He picked them up and rammed them back in their wrought-wire framing, then did the same with those for the couch. Rust-red polycanvas, water and stainproof, identical to the cushions one would find in any of a dozen flats in the wing. The other dozen units lay claim to cushions in a green so moldy looking that it served as the deciding factor when Micah had gone flat-hunting that previous summer. He'd had to cough up a ten percent lease premium for a corner location, but considered the resulting cramp to his financial style an acceptable price to pay for cushions that didn't look like they'd been liberated from a damp cave.

The furniture seen to, Micah moved on, picking up the magazines, training manuals, and other things he'd emptied from the drawers of the storage cabinet. Within a few minutes he'd restored the room to its former order, and celebrated the feat by braving the mayhem of the corner kitchenette to liberate the half-liter of vodka he'd bought a few days earlier. He cracked the seal and took a long, hard pull, the alcohol heat burning down his throat and rattling his sinuses.

"Don't know why the hell I did this." He picked up a few pieces of cutlery, the first things that he'd strewn across the floor after he received Wode's call. Wode should have known better, of course. Flat-to-flat comport calls were a definite thumbs-down. Common sense dictated that Service Investigative couldn't possibly bug every enlisted housing unit at Sheridan, but Wode and Micah had been taught not to take chances. *Use public at all times* had become their mantra since they each learned of the other's existence.

Micah stepped around a scatter of plastic bowls and leaned against the counter, bottle still firmly in hand. The last thirty-six hours had ripped past in a blur—the mine site evac, the return to Sheridan, the report-filing, the interviewing. Qualified personnel had been in such short supply that Micah had set up the recording for his own debrief. He'd been tempted to leave the wafer out of the recorder, but he knew somebody would figure it out eventually, and the next time around they might not go so easy on him. As it was, no one had asked the right questions. Interrogators from the vaunted Service Investigative Bureau, and they missed every clue.

It had all been there for them to see, plain as the sun in the sky. Wode's stupid errors, the too-peaceful look on his face as he worked the biobot. Hell, it had been his idea to have the Vynshàrau witness the actual excavation—Micah had been standing near the tech truck pulling parts for the bunker console when he overheard Wode put the bug in Dubrovna's ear! *Ask the Vynshàrau to appoint a witness, ma'am.* And Micah had remained by the truck, his heart pounding until he thought his chest might burst, and kept his mouth shut for the good of them both.

Fabe?

Micah took another swig of vodka. He hated alcohol, the fact that he poisoned himself, but it was the only thing that seemed to help him sleep lately. Help him work. Get through the day.

Fabe, there's a problem.

Micah closed his eyes, and heard Wode's voice in his ear. Heard it as he had that short day and a half earlier, soft and preternaturally calm.

The mine. Someone screwed up—they found the mine. I switched tags with Ling. I'm taking the call.

That's what staggered Micah—the calm. As though Wode talked of home, his favorite lake for fishing, the girl he thought he loved.

Can't let them find it. Can't blow the Group. I just wanted you to know. They'll probably call you in to run com-arrays and you'll know what's happening and I want you to please, please leave me be. I know what I'm doing.

Another swallow of vodka, even though his gut ached already.

You don't know me. Remember that.

No food since that morning. He knew he asked for trouble.

They'll be there. The frog-eyes. Maybe I'll take some of them with me.

But some things just needed to be washed down as quickly as possible, and this was one of those things.

I wanted you to know that I regard you as the truest of friends, that knowing you has meant the world and all to me.

Another gulp. Another.

Good-bye, Fabe.

Micah leaned against the counter, his breath coming in fits and starts, blood roaring in his ears. His stomach lurched—saliva flooded his mouth. Only a stride away, yet he barely made the sink in time. He vomited until his abdominal muscles cramped. Tried to rinse his mouth from the tap, but the touch of liquid on his tongue set him off again.

After he finished, his nose ran and his eyes teared, a mockery of grief. "That's all the break you get, Faber, *all* the break you get!" If he lived to 150, he'd always despise himself for what he did after Wode disconnected. "Worried about my own cheap ass!" Smashed the comport, then tore his flat from one end to the other, searching for any trace that Wode might have left behind during his infrequent visits, ripping and shattering from kitchenette to sitting room to bedroom and bath in a paranoid rage so fierce he knew that if anyone had come upon him then, he'd have killed them.

"Coward." He filled his hand from the tap, sluiced it over his face. Then put his head down on the cool countertop, sheltering himself with his arms as though the ceiling shook down. Breathed.

Heard the knock eventually. The entry buzzer. The voice.

"Fabe! Hey—open up!"

"Damn." Micah straightened as quickly as he dared. Wiped his face with a dispo cloth. Walked from the kitchenette through the sitting room to the entry, fought for control of his rubbery knees, checked his reflection in the mirror by the door and saw the red-rimmed eyes and blanched face of a ghoul staring back. Opened the door, because the knocking and buzzing rattled his head like artillery and he wanted it to stop. "Yo, Cash," he said, turning his back immediately on his visitor. Of all the people he didn't want to catch him in the middle of a private flameout, that meddling pain-in-the-ass Cashman had to head the list.

"Where the hell you been?" Cashman squirted inside and hurried after him, round-faced and springy of step, bobbing at his shoulder like a balloon. "I heard you leave Saturday night. Figured you got lucky, but then I saw Court at the Veedrome later and she said you switched on-calls with Howie earlier in the week and you got reeled in." He grabbed Micah by the shoulder and spun him around to face him. "You were *there*." He looked Micah in the face, and took a step back. "What happened to you?"

"I was sick." Micah patted his stomach, and almost doubled over again.

"Hey, no disgrace there, my friend, no disgrace at all." Cashman trundled to the chair and flopped down. He wore winter-weights, and had already yanked out his shirttail and undone his collar. "So what happened? All we heard was the official accident report, then that garble on CapNet."

"Afraid I can't add anything." Micah sat on the couch, forcing thoughts of Wode from his mind as he struggled to construct a reply to Cash's question. Nothing too informative, just a tidbit or two sufficient to get the creep off his back and out the door. "I didn't work at the site. I was holed up in a bunker outside the cordon."

Cashman sat forward, all goggle eyes and messy shirt. "Oh, a bunker. Fabe hits the big time. Only VIPs hole up in bunkers—who'd you pull to baby-sit?"

Micah coughed, groaning as a gut muscle cramped. The idea of him, of *anybody*, having to baby-sit Colonel Pierce turned his head inside out. "Scarface, for one."

"The Pierced One?" Cashman winced in sympathy. "Bet that was a party. Who else?"

"Just two others." Micah tried to swallow the names in the hope Cashman wouldn't catch them. "Tsecha. Kilian."

"You were holed up in a bunker with Jani Kilian!" Cashman's mouth gaped. With his round eyes, he looked like a fish. "I saw her once. Last summer, when she was still in. Walking across South Central on the way to the Doc building." His mouth slowly closed, his eyes narrowing.

Micah's throat tightened. He'd seen the same reaction all too many times and it made him sick. The wondering. What she looked like. Felt like. As if any man who called himself "human" would lay a finger on her. *"And?"*

Cashman raised his head, blinking as though he came out of a daze. "Nothing. Just saw her once is all." He sniffed. "Tsecha too, huh. Saw him make a speech once." The thought of the Haárin dominant didn't make him quite as dreamy-eyed. "Aren't you hot?" he asked, pointing to Micah. "You still got your coat on."

Micah looked down, saw the belt ends of his field coat curled in his lap like dead snakes. How could he have forgotten? *Haven't been back here since that night—had to wear it—then I got here, had to clean up first—* "I had just come in when you stopped by. Didn't have a chance to take it off." He shook his shoulders, felt the coat slide down, pulled his arms out. *She wore this.* He tried not to think about it. *I'll get it cleaned.* What he wanted to do was burn it, but then he'd have to pay for a replacement, and his rent was due next week.

I promise I'll touch it as little as possible.

Micah felt the heat rise up his neck at the memory. Kilian standing over him, with her giraffe neck and frog eyes. The disdain in her voice, so matter of fact, as if she talked to everyone that way. *Hero of Knevçet Shèràa*, he'd heard someone call her last week. Another colonial, of course. Figured. They always stuck up for one another.

"Fabe?"

Micah glanced over at Cashman to find the man staring back, his chin propped on his fist.

"You need to get out, my friend. They finally got the latest installment of *Raven's Raiders* at the Veedrome, and Court thinks the gang should see it together." Cashman pointed at him. "And Court has a friend."

Micah groaned inwardly. Court was a civvie clerk at Base Admin. A frustrated general, with more friends than hairs on her head. "Really."

"Yeah, you need to get out. We all need to get out." Cashman leaned over and patted Micah's shoulder. "Nasty deal, man. I wouldn't want to be whoever put that mine there. But we're just a couple of Supreme Command comtechs, and the weight of the world is not ours to carry." He headed for the door. "I need to clean up. Be back in a half."

Micah waited until he heard the door slide closed. Then he slumped forward, his head in his hands, and tried to push all thoughts of Wode from his mind, as he'd been taught. "Some will die. Don't think of their deaths as an end. Don't even think of the sacrifice. Instead, think of what the act accomplished, of the good that resulted." One dead Vynshàrau, or as good as dead, according to CapNet.

He reached around and dragged the field coat onto his lap. Stood and walked to the kitchenette. Picked up a knife from the floor. Held the coat in front of him with one hand, punched the knife into the back seam with the other, and ripped down.

Like gutting an animal, really. Sleeves off. Collar. Separate the back from the sides.

"One little two little dead little frog-eyes." Micah cut and kept cutting, rendering the coat into smaller and smaller scraps. He could wear his duffel coat to the Veedrome, and he'd think of something to cover the rent.

He thought of Kilian standing over him, inserted the knife in a seam and yanked.

"Now if you'd been Raven, would you have trusted the Star Queen when she said she'd cure Foxy's alien virus if you turned over the plans to the Death Cruiser?" Cashman's head popped above the divider that separated his cube from Micah's. "I mean, come on, you haven't been able to believe a damned thing she says for nineteen episodes, all of a sudden you're trusting her with your girlfriend's life?"

Micah adjusted his workstation display to block as much of Cashman's face as possible. "Cash, give it a rest. You've been moaning since we got in this morning."

"I'm going to write a letter to the producer." Cashman's head vanished. A few seconds later the chiming sound that heralded the activation of his workstation rang out.

"Raven had no choice. Foxy's the only one who can activate the Death Cruiser's killcode." Hough, a new addition to the Com-Sys bullpen, kicked his feet back and weighed in. "The virus affected her memory—if she can't remember the code, they'll never be able to stop the Cruiser from destroying the Queen's homeworld."

Cashman's head popped up once more. "But—"

"Good morning."

Cashman fell silent. Hough's feet hit the floor.

Micah stood.

"I need to find the Lakeside One-B conference room, but the one I found has been gutted." A captain stood in the bullpen entry, decked out in dress blue-greys, his brimmed lid tucked under his arm. Tall. Blond. *Famous for all the wrong reasons*, as Lieutenant Bloch, the bullpen wrangler, once said. *They don't give medals for what he's good at.* Lucien Pascal, who sometimes rivaled Raven and Foxy as the topic of bullpen conversation.

No one answered him. They all just stared. Then Micah gave himself a mental kick.

"You need One-B Junior, sir. The interim conference room." He cut through the cubicle maze and past Pascal into the hall. "The directions are a little convoluted. If you'd follow me, please."

"Thank you, Lance Corporal." Pascal fell in behind him. "*Raven's Raiders*. Poor Foxy's virus is the hot topic everywhere, it seems."

"Yes, sir." Micah tried to keep the sharpness out of his voice. He'd bailed out of the bullpen to get away from the endless yammer. Even talking about talking about it made him want to break something.

"Gives them something else to talk about, I suppose."

Instead of the death of a good Spacer? "Yes, sir."

"You're not a fan?"

"No, sir." Micah looked back over his shoulder to find Pascal eyeing him. Pascal, who jumped everything from old ladies to guys to hybrids. *Shit.* He turned around and quickened his step. "Some friends took me to try to cheer me up, but it didn't work very well." *Shut up, shut up, shut up—he couldn't care less and it's none of his business anyway.*

"I saw the first installment. I didn't find it very coherent." Pascal's French Provincial accent broke through with his r's, that peculiar, throaty sound that every female who'd met him seemed to comment on.

Sounds like gargling. Micah rounded one corner, then another. "Just down this hall and make a left, sir. Second door on the right." He stepped to the side so Pascal could pass him.

"Thank you, Faber." He blew past Micah, a pair of majors in his sights, catching them up just as they entered the conference room.

Micah stared at Pascal's back, his heart tripping. Then he looked down at his winterweight shirtfront. "My nameplate reads 'Faber.' He read it. That's what they're for." He flicked the gold rectangle with his finger, then double-timed it back to the bullpen.

"I heard Bloch call him 'the CMO.' Chief of Mattress Operations. He'll do anything once, and most things as often as possible." Cashman leaned forward and kept his voice low so no one at the surrounding tables could hear him.

Micah smashed a cracker inside its packet and poured the resulting crumble atop his chili. Lunch at Far North Enlisted Mess—table after table of chatter in a glass-walled cavern designed to magnify every sound. *Wode's memorial service today.* But he hadn't dared go. Couldn't even send a note to Wode's parents. Members of the Group weren't supposed to know one another. He and Wode should never have even met. It had been happenstance. Accident. Almost a year ago. Cold spring rain, much like today, and a mess filled to bursting. No place to sit but with a stranger.

So they talked, and found they had more in common than they possibly could have imagined. A hatred of the idomeni as fierce as their love for their humanity, deep as marrow, vital as blood. A determination to do whatever they could to drive the alien from their homeworld, their Earth, their Commonwealth. A disgust for the attraction Chicago seemed to feel for the idomeni ambassador, Tsecha.

And as time went on and the trust between them grew, the realization that they both belonged to an organization that until then had seemed like a figment of their imaginations, a wish not quite come true.

Micah grabbed another pack of crackers from the pile on his tray. If he kept mucking about with his food, maybe no one would notice he wasn't eating.

"Bloch's going to get his ass creamed if he doesn't keep his mouth shut." Hough stabbed the air with his soup spoon. He looked like a lecturer—too skinny, with thin hair and pinched features. Someone who loved the sound of his own voice. "Everybody knows Pascal has an in with Old Man Mako."

"Who's everybody?" Cashman singsonged. "You's everybody?" He batted his lashes until Hough chuffed in disgust and started eating again. Then he glanced sidelong at Micah. "Fabe's a somebody, is what he is. Did bunker duty with some pretty special people night before last." He paused. "Well, one of them is people, anyway."

"Who?" someone downtable asked.

"Kitty-eyes Kilian, and Tse-cha-cha-cha." Cashman rocked his shoulders in time. "And Ol' Scarface."

"Pierce is good." Hough shook his head. "Scares the hell out of me, man."

"My mother scares the hell outta you," Cashman muttered, interrupted again and ticked about it.

"Too bad she didn't scare the hell outta your dad," shot the downtable interrogator, to the amusement of some.

Micah took the sugar round from the table service and shook some into his hot tea. His mother had always given him hot tea when he felt bad, with lots of sugar and lemon. He knew it would take more than hot tea to make him feel better now, but anything was worth a try at this point.

"Pierce left this morning on a long haul," Hough said when the laughter died. "I shoved through a billet privilege chit first thing I signed on." He exhaled through his teeth. "He's tighter with Mako than Pascal is, and Pascal's bad enough." He buttered a roll, pressing it so hard that crumbs tumbled to his tray. "Everybody should just learn to shut up."

"Including you, maybe?" Cashman took a too-big bite of his sandwich. "Where were you before you came to ComSys?"

"Finance. Time-reporting." Another chorus of jeers greeted that admission. "Laugh all you want," Hough said, coloring. "All expense reports go through there so we can charge trip time to projects. Pascal traveled more than any looie that wasn't a courier, and all the time got buried in places where you couldn't follow up. No classes, training, meeting minutes. Just billets, meals, and miscellaneous." He looked from face to face to see who listened, but he needn't have bothered. He had everyone's attention now. "His spec's communications matrix design—how best to lay out an array to gather info—but you'd never know it from how he spends his days." He took a bite of his roll, butter shining his lips as though he licked them. "Sometimes specs got nothing to do with what you do, and sometimes rank's got nothing to do with what you are."

"He's in on the mine thing now." That from a full corporal named Chou who did scheduling. "That was the room he asked about—Junior's where they met to talk about how the full-bore Slager got confused for a trainer."

Micah's spoon hit the side of his cup, splashing tea. No one noticed, luckily. They'd all fallen into a Hough-induced funk, eating in silence, their eyes fixed on their food.

He checked the view outside. The rain still fell, needling cold. Craving the solitude, he'd walked to work that morning, and found he'd needed every bit of warmth his duffel coat provided. *Maybe it'll stay cold for the next couple of weeks*. Until he saved enough for a new field coat. After returning home from the Veedrome, he'd stayed up half the night incinerating the hacked remains of his old one in his trashzap. The unit charger had gone dead twice, and toward the end he'd had to make do with charring the scraps, then tearing them apart with this fingers until only fine black fluff remained. And thinking about Kilian as he did so, because for all he loathed the idomeni and their intrusion into his humanity, her medically induced hybridization sickened him even more. Saved her life, he'd heard someone say once. Better she'd died above the sands of Knevçet Shèràa, an honorable Spacer's death.

"So, Fabe?" Cashman gave Life of the Lunchtable one last try. "What's Jani Kilian really like?"

"Tall," Micah replied, to the biggest laugh of the day.

Micah stepped out the side door of the Supreme Command C-wing, one arm of the multilimbed sprawl that comprised Fort

Sheridan's brain. The sky hung low and smoke-hued. The wind had picked up as well, stealing the ends of his muffler from the confines of his coat and whipping them about.

"It's supposed to be spring soon, damn it." But the cold rain still fell, its soft *pat-pat* against his garrison cap interspersed with the occasional icy *tick* of sleet. He broke into a trot, weaving through the end-of-shift crowd that filled the walkway. He thought for a time to catch a shuttle to his flat block, but each shelter he passed was packed with fellow Spacers who'd had the same thought. He'd have to stand and wait in the rain anyway. May as well keep moving.

The crowds thinned as he left the lakeside office buildings and reached the flat expanse of the Quad. Less shelter from the wind now—he hunched his shoulders and wiped a hand over his tearing eyes.

"Good afternoon, Lance Corporal Faber."

Micah slowed, despite the fact that every muscle and bone in his body urged him to run. Run and not stop until he'd put as much distance as possible between himself and the pounding footsteps that drew closer with every stride. "Good afternoon, Captain Pascal, sir." He drew his hand out of his pocket to salute.

"Never mind that. Hands are for pockets today." Pascal drew alongside. He looked as cold as Micah felt, his face half hidden behind the turned-up collar of his field coat. "I hear rumors that it will dry out eventually." Rain dripped from his lid brim, spattered his face like sweat.

Micah swallowed hard. "Yes, sir."

"I didn't realize." Pascal looked down at him, eyes shadowed by his lid and the angle of the walkway lighting. "You'd said this morning that your friends had taken you to the Veedrome to cheer you. You're a comtech. You ran the bunker com-array at the enclave night before last." A flash of white teeth, framed by the dark blue collar. "You were there."

"Yes, sir."

"We went over the site roster during my meeting this morning. I saw your name." Pascal paused. "You met a friend of mine, I'm sure. Jani Kilian."

"Yes. Sir."

"Funny how things go. We all know someone who knows someone. No one ever remains unknown for long." Another flash of teeth. "*Au revoir,* Lance Corporal." Pascal broke into a lope. "That means 'until later.' "

"Good afternoon, sir." Micah slowed and watched the man dart around scattered pedestrians, turn a corner and disappear. His jaw ached from clenching, and he didn't quicken his pace until someone jostled him and told him to wake up.

CHAPTER 7

Elon stood outside the entry to nìaRauta Shai's rooms and awaited the summons that she had expected for two humanish days. Her right hand ached, the healing of her finger and wrist bones not yet complete. Her physician-priest had offered her relief from the pain, but she had denied such. Pain focused the mind, and she had much this day on which to focus.

"Elon?"

She looked in the direction of the voice, tilting her head in regard even as she raised her left hand in question. "Ghos. You have taken leave of the journey room?"

Her suborn moved next to her against the wall, then took a half step forward so that Elon stood behind him, as was seemly. "When there is no journey to take place, it is unseemly to remain. We pray, but to what end? We wait, but to what purpose? We know what the decision must be, yet we delay." He had finally discarded the soiled and torn outdoor uniform he had worn that night at the enclave, and now dressed as Elon had, in the garb of his skein and standing, the pale green trousers and overrobe of embassy security.

Elon contemplated the color, savoring its calming blend with the pale sand of the walls and floor, the metal tones of the ceiling lamps, the pale brown of Ghos's braided hair. "Ní Tsecha believes the decision should be as different."

"Ní Tsecha is no longer Chief Propitiator of the Vynshàrau. If he came to such a decision as Chief Propitiator, he would be made as outcast as he already is." Ghos's shoulders rounded in anger. "Why does Shai allow him here? His place is over the water."

"Shai has asked nìaRauta Sànalàn to prepare an argument and

use such to debate ní Tsecha. Such is Sànalàn's first attempt to define a point of theology. As Chief Propitiator, it is something she must learn, and truly."

"The priests debate, and delay Feres's godly death." Ghos brought up his arms and crossed his wrists so that he hid his face. "Anathema."

"Perhaps." Elon flexed her injured fingers, spread them wide, and savored the throbbing spasms that resulted. A self-punishment for her belief in theology. "But there are those in Council who consider times as they once were, Tsecha as the propitiator and Sànalàn as his suborn. Tsecha is Haárin now, and Sànalàn speaks for us to the gods. Such is as it must be. Such is as they must accept. Therefore, nìaRauta Shai will ensure that they do so."

Ghos slowly lowered his arms. He stood hunched, his wrists still crossed before his chest. "Feres must die."

"Yes." Elon enclosed her right hand in her left. Her physician-priest would berate her for damaging his handiwork, but such could not be helped—she tightened her grip until her heart stuttered and her stomach felt emptied of her soul. "But first, there is theology." She heard the door open behind her, and drew up straight. She felt as though she floated upon water, the coolness of sweat trickling beneath her shirt.

"NìaRauta Elon." Shai's suborn stepped aside, and held the door for her to pass.

"Go to Feres." Elon gestured in departure to Ghos, raising her right hand and turning it palm out, so that it obscured the side of her face. "I will bring word." Shai's suborn stared at her hand, and she hid it within the folds of her overrobe before she entered the room.

NìaRauta Shai's workroom comforted the eye as none other in the embassy. Rectangular in shape, each curved display niche in one long side had been set perfectly opposite a narrow window on the other. The two short sides each contained a doorway, again in perfect opposition. Little furniture marred the fineness of the space: Shai's worktable, a semicircle of chairs in sufficient number to seat those attending, a sculpture stand in one far corner.

"You must sit, Elon. I have heard from many that you sustained injury in the explosion." Shai sat to the left of the midpoint of the semicircle, in the second lowest-level seat, as befitted her penultimate status. She glanced up in Elon's direction, then waved her hand in the vague, unreadable manner that she had adopted for use with humanish and unfortunately employed in her dealings with her own. "Sit, Elon."

"Indeed, sit, Elon." NìaRauta Sànalàn, possessing the highest standing as the guardian of the soul of every Vynshàrau, sat at the midpoint of the semicircle, in the lowest-level seat. As Shai, she wore trousers, shirt, and overrobe in palest sand. Only the red banding that adorned the cuffs of her overrobe served as disruption. Her light brown hair she still wore gathered in the tight nape-knot of an unbred. That would change, though, for an overture had been made by Shai's suborn and the pairing had been deemed seemly. Soon, Sànalàn would wear her hair in the braided fringe of a breeder, as did Shai and Elon.

Elon walked to one end of the semicircle. Because of her lesser standing, her chair stood higher than Shai's or Sànalàn's—the height of her seat required her to brace her feet against a cross-bar and boost up. To do so required two hands to grip the chair arms—she set her right hand atop the cold, hard metal, to use it as guide without putting weight on it. Her pain was her own. There were those in the room with whom she did not wish to share it.

Yet they understood anyway, as was their way.

"I will not ask you to sit, Elon." Tsecha spoke Vynshàrau Haárin, his voice stripped of gesture. "It seems to pain you to do so, and truly." He sat at the end of the semicircle opposite her, in a chair at a level slightly below hers, yet higher than Shai's. Such was a compromise position, since as an Haárin, he had no right to a place of respect behind any bornsect, but as former Chief Propitiator, he had once held the dominance over every idomeni, as Sànalàn now did.

Elon eased into her chair, her hand throbbing with a sharpness that spoke of a bone rebroken. "What pain I feel, Tsecha, is made even greater by the sight of your clothes." Shirt and trousers of differing hues of purple and a headwrap of dull green, discordant as chemical fire against the sand and stone hues of the walls and floor.

"We know you despise one another." Shai sat slightly slumped in her chair, her hands pressed together at the fingertips, another conflicting display of humanish posture and gesture. "The whole of the embassy knows you fought in the circle prior to the war of Vynshàrau ascension, that you each bear scars inflicted by the other. Even nìaRauta Sànalàn, who was as youngish at that time, knows your story. Spare us further, if you would. I have sat these last days amid carping humanish, each blaming one for the existence of the other. I have no patience left." She uncurved, but only a little. "I speak here now as Suborn Oligarch. If we sat now in a meeting room in Temple in Rauta Shèràa, the chief propitiators of all the bornsects would preside over this debate and cast final judgment as to the soundness of argument. But this is damned cold Chicago—they are not here, and the issue is such that we have no time to send a transmission and await their response. Thus will I act as Temple conclave, and decide." She tugged at the edge of her overrobe, straightening a fold. "The technicians record this, Tsecha."

"Yes, Shai." Tsecha sat in a humanish posture, his elbows on the chair arms, his fingers interlaced.

"After I have cast my decision, this meeting will be transmitted to Temple. There, the chief propitiators will determine whether I decided properly."

"Yes, Shai."

"I explain this to you now, so that you have no reason to dissent later."

"I will dissent if I need to, Shai, now or later. Such is my way."

"Then you will look as a fool."

"As is my name. 'Tsecha' is as 'fool' in Sìah Haárin."

"It is as fool in every language." Shai pressed her fingertips against her forehead just above the bridge of her nose and held them there. "I will begin by saying that Admiral-General Mako has informed me that he regrets this incident with his entire heart and soul, for whatever such regret is worth. The fact that Dathim Naré and his facility suborns have uncovered no other weaponry thus far supports the Admiral-General's claim that the mine uncovered two humanish days ago was an aberration, and that his Service left no other weapons behind on the enclave property." She lowered her hand. "Is this not true, Tsecha?"

"It is indeed the case, Shai." Tsecha nodded in an annoyingly humanish manner. "It would be most helpful, of course, if you permitted us to allow Service Ordnance to screen the area with their equipment. It is their weaponry, after all. Who better to scan for it? But we do what we can."

Shai's shoulders rounded. "Such is not the reason for this meeting, Tsecha."

"No." Tsecha raised his right hand, then let it fall, another of his meaningless gestures. "The reason for this meeting is to decide upon a death."

Time passed. Shai may have believed that Tsecha wished to speak further. When he did not, she exhaled heavily and pointed to Elon. "Let us begin."

Sànalàn hesitated. Then she stood, her posture most straight in honor of the gods, and pronounced the opening prayer. An invocation to Shiou, a plea for order.

Elon glanced at Tsecha, and saw that he mouthed the prayer as Sànalàn entoned. She touched a scar on her left forearm, a ridged hack he had given her so long ago, and rejoiced in his downfall.

Sànalàn finished the prayer and lowered to her chair. Shai then gestured to Elon. "Tell us of Feres's injury."

Elon sat up most straight. She had already described the circumstances many times, yet each instance felt as the first. She labored to recall the details, yet could only call up sensation. The cold rain that numbed her. The sound of the wind through the bare trees. The low hum of equipment. "At the time the mine detonated, I stood with Ghos beside the enclave vehicles, just outside the boundary set by the humanish technician. Colonel Dubrovna, General Burkett's suborn, had advised that one of our number act as witness to the removal of the mine from the ground. 'An act of good faith' is how she referred to such. I watched Feres enter within the boundary and approach the humanish technician. The technician spoke to him, and Feres moved closer, until he stood within reach. Then I heard a shout—one of the humanish soldiers sought to halt the excavation. 'Wode,' he shouted. 'Pull up now.' Feres and the humanish technician, Wode, both turned toward the soldier." Elon drew her right hand over her soul and pressed her left hand over it.

"I saw a flash, heard the detonation. I lay on the ground. Ghos lay atop me—he bled from shrapnel that would have struck me. I fell atop my hand, and broke bones." She raised her hands before her, as though to push. "I ordered Ghos to move so I could rise. He did not understand. He could not hear. I could not hear. I pushed him from me and rose, and looked to the center of the boundary circle." All she could recall. Red upon white. The disruption. "I could not see the humanish. I saw Feres. His legs. One arm. Gone. Blood. I pulled Ghos to his feet, behind the Haárin vehicles. I sought to run to Feres, but Dathim Naré blocked my way and said he was for the priests." She lowered her hands. "That is all."

"Feres also received an injury to the forward third of his brain. A fragment of the mine." Sànalàn spoke. Her voice seemed at youngish, as wind through a pipe. "The physician-priests administered to him most quickly. In a physical mode, he lives, but great damage has been done to his processes of thought. I have consulted with them, and determined thus. If Feres recovers as he is, he will be not-Feres. If Feres becomes not-Feres, he cannot continue the journey to the Star, for Feres had no proper death, and not-Feres had no proper birth. They would each be as half-beings, without sequence to their lives, neither with a clear path to the Star. Feres must therefore be allowed to die, to complete his path in the way the gods intended."

Elon listened, each word Sànalàn spoke touching her soul. *He must die . . . his soul is as lost now, for it can no longer think and knows not the path.* She shivered as from cold, imagining its wanderings.

Tsecha still sat with his hands linked. Even during Sànalàn's invocation, he had not altered his position. "When I still dwelled within Temple, before the Vynshà ascended to rau, I knew Feres. As a youngish, he took his place in Temple school, in the classes taught to seculars." He bared his teeth. "Once, he took colored rounds of plastic and hung them from the branches of all the garden trees. When we sought to reprimand him, he climbed to the top of the tallest tree and could not be compelled to lower himself down. Aeri, my then-suborn and Sànalàn's body-father, had to request a skimmer from the warrior base that could rise as high as the treetop. Thus did we bring Feres down." He unlinked his fingers, then spread them wide, yet another unfathomable gesture. "Vynshàrau evaluation of brain function is not of sufficient depth to ensure the proper decision is reached. Many of the parameters for assessment have not altered since the time of my predecessor, Xinfa nìRau Cèel, at a time when Pathenrau ruled and the first colonies had just been founded. John Shroud once calculated the time as over 150 humanish years. Such is stagnation!"

"You now confer with humanish physicians concerning matters of idomeni medicine, Tsecha?" Shai's hand chopped the air in an Haárin gesture of dismissal. "You have conferred also with Feyó of the Elyan Haárin, this I know and truly, one who should be made outcast from outcast if such were possible."

"If you wish to enter this debate, Shai, you must complete the exams you failed when we were both at Temple. Otherwise, it is to Sànalàn that I speak." But even as Tsecha spoke thus, he positioned himself as though he lectured at Temple and spoke to no single idomeni, for it was well-known at the embassy that he despised his former suborn as weak, and disdained any contact with her. "Feres is, possibly, not-Feres now. But if time is allowed, if he heals, he may return to that which he was. Methods of evaluation must be improved. More intensive testing must be performed. It is not enough to say 'the wound is here, therefore the damage must be thus,' for each brain is as different, and at times wounds thought grave may be strangely overcome."

Sànalàn had rounded her shoulders, comprehending her former dominant's insult. "And if Feres does not overcome his wound completely, then what? He is still not as he was, still not-Feres. What then, Tsecha? How then do we treat this incompletion?"

"I maintain that even an incomplete Feres is yet something-of-Feres, and as such still recognizes his particular Way, at least in part." Tsecha sat forward, left hand clenched in a fist. "That part must be allowed to continue Feres's journey until as much as possible has been done to recover all of what he was. Humanish act as thus, preserving as much as possible of what was, conserving, aiding the soul in adapting to the trauma of the loss. Otherwise, you allow to die one that would have lived, and affected, and labored. You mock life by surrendering too readily to death."

Sànalàn's voice deepened as her anger grew. "I have said before, humanish fear death too greatly."

"And Vynshàrau fear it not at all, which leads to waste. Which is the greater sin, Sànalàn, to labor greatly to preserve, or to turn one's back, and do nothing?" Tsecha turned on Shai so quickly that she flinched. "You are not qualified to decide the merits of our arguments, Shai, or questions of theology. I will enter my protests of this mockery to Temple as well. This is not a decision to be made quickly. The physician-priests must research. Arguments must be prepared—"

"As Feres's soul stumbles on some path not his own, on some path inconceivable to any godly idomeni." Elon knew she did not speak aloud, yet she heard her words. As did Tsecha, who looked from her, to Shai, then Sànalàn, and curved his mouth in a humanish smile.

"You reached your decision before you heard any argument, this I know and truly. No matter my reasoning, no matter if Sànalàn remained silent and declined to speak at all, your decision would be the same. Feres must die, so order may be maintained. Feres must die, so that your souls may rest as content. But of Feres himself, you do not know, you will never know, because he will never be allowed to speak." Tsecha stood and walked to the door, his shoulders so bowed it was as though he could never straighten. "Each time we meet for argument, you disgust me more."

Sànalàn rose to her feet, even as Shai sought to pull her down. "You have not been given leave to go by your propitiator, Tsecha!"

Tsecha turned. "Then let me say to you, Sànalàn, whom I reared as a youngish, whom I sought to instruct in the ways of the gods, and so failed. Let me say to you here, so that all may know—I do not recognize you as propitiator. The Chicago Haárin do not recognize you, for you condemn the innocent to death. It is you who are as anathema. You whom the gods disdain!" He strode to the entry and out before the door even swept aside completely, before Shai's suborn could attend him.

Shai took on the same posture as Tsecha's. Time passed before she spoke. "It is most as convenient, is it not, that Tsecha spoke as he did on an official transmission. Thus verification of his words has already been accomplished." She gestured to Elon. "Go, and do as the gods compel. I must confer with Sànalàn."

Elon slid off her chair. Her broken hand had swelled past the wrist, and burned to the touch. She felt as though she ran even as she moved quite as slowly. "Glories of the evening to you, nìa-Rauta Sànalàn," she said as she awaited benediction. But Shai and Sànalàn already conferred, and no longer saw her even as she stood before them.

Elon followed Shai's suborn to the entry, stepped into the hall-way, waited as the door closed behind her. Then she saw the physician-priest's suborn standing at the hallway's end, and followed her without a word.

Elon entered the journey room, then stepped to the left side of the entry. The room held little. A bed in its center, surrounded by the instruments and machines of the physician-priests. A side table, draped with an altar cloth and set with a scroll along with the handhelds and scanning devices used to test response and level of consciousness.

Ghos stood at the foot of the bed, head high, hands raised above his head, his prayer voice a keening that resonated within the bare room.

The physician-priest stood at Feres's swaddled head, from around which the bracing framework had been removed. She held out her hands, palms down and slightly cupped, so that they covered his face as a hovering mask. Then she walked to each monitor, each instrument in turn, and deactivated them.

Elon remained near the door, even though custom required she stand behind Ghos. She feared sickness, as did every idomeni, especially those who traveled beyond the worldskein. Unprotected by a blessed environment, surrounded by tainted air and soil, any occurrence, any accident, infection, fever, could leave them as Feres was now. *Such is what happens when we leave our godly home. Such is what happens when we live in the damned cold places.*

Her thoughts stopped as Feres made a sound. Quiet, almost as nothing, a soft gasp. Ghos ceased his prayers. The priest returned to the head of the bed.

Elon waited for another sound. Any sound. She watched Feres's hand, rested atop the bed covering, still as the sculpture in Shai's room, and listened. Listened. Listened.

And heard nothing more.

The physician-priest brought together her hands so the cupped palms faced one another, still above Feres's face. Then she reached outward and opened them, sending Feres's soul to Ghos, his dominant.

Ghos lowered his hands, crossing them before his chest, capturing Feres's soul and holding it close. Then he turned to Elon, head tilting in question when she delayed drawing near.

With a stride so heavy her boots scraped the floor, Elon stepped deeper into the room, holding out her hands just as Ghos dropped his arms. Feres's soul fled to her for safekeeping, feeling as a weight within her broken hand, stopping her breath in her throat and causing her heart to pound, her own soul to ache. She walked to the side table and stood before the scroll. If she had stood on the godly soil of Rauta Shèràa, she would have walked outside and offered Feres's soul to the sky that in the end would claim them all. In its stead, however, she could only show him this construct of parchment, wood, and gilt from his birth house. Such would he inhabit until the next transport ferried him to the Shèrá homeworld, where a Temple propitiator would release his soul and send it upon its godly way.

Elon placed her hands upon the open scroll until her hand ceased paining, and she knew that Feres's soul had left her. She then closed the cover.

The three of them stood in silence. Then the physician-priest stepped back from the head of the bed, and in doing so pronounced their vigil finished, and Feres's life officially ended.

Elon watched the priest's suborns enter with the floatbed. Muttering prayers, they removed the bed covers and lifted the remains of Feres's body onto the hovering platform. She contemplated the still face for the first time, and found it as pale and smooth as stone, strangely undamaged by the impacts that had destroyed his brain and body and forced him to the end of his journey.

Why? Because Tsecha, whom she had fought, prophesied a joining of races, and because Feres, as a member of the security skein, had pledged to protect the holders of such chaotic opinion whether he believed in such himself or not. Feres, whose soul stumbled in blind pursuit of that which all godly idomeni merited without question, an orderly death.

An orderly death. She followed Ghos from the room, and contemplated such.

CHAPTER 8

Elon sat in the veranda enclosure, cradling her bandaged right hand in her lap. Her physician-priest had berated her about the damage she had inflicted upon herself, as she had expected him to. An assault to the soul, he had said, to rebreak bones that had already been set and mended. Thus had he shielded the hand in a poly case and bound it with strips of altar cloth. Thus, as well, had she come to sit upon the veranda in the middle of the damned cold night, with a command to pray to Shiou to bestow a sense of order upon her soul.

"There is no order." Not in this place. This she now knew, and truly. Even Shai and Sànalàn, whom she trusted, had in the end shown more concern for trapping Tsecha in his admission of heresy than for the state of Feres's soul. From Shai, this might have been expected—she believed that the only way to prevail against humanish was to act as they did. Thus had she prohibited godly disputation in their presence, and altered her own posture and gestures so that even those who knew her since youngish days could no longer determine her thoughts.

But Sànalàn . . . Elon had expected more from the one who had displaced Tsecha. There had been no benediction at meeting's end, and no prayers for Feres. For one who enjoyed the special esteem of both Temple and the Oligarch, Sànalàn had shown herself most unworthy.

Elon lay back her head against the stone, blessedly warm from the heating devices set within. The veranda consisted of a series of enclosures such as the one in which she sat, walled-off spaces furnished with floor mats or low chairs and tables, where Vynshàrau could meditate in solitude or gather to engage in godly disputation. She could overhear one such debate, far off in one corner, a marvel of contention involving some point of Council law. She listened for a time, taking solace in the raised voices as she sometimes took such in the sound of the lake waves striking the shore, or the heat from a flame that reminded her of the blessed warmth of home.

"Elon?"

She flinched at the sound of her name. Such was not her habit to take to the veranda in the middle of the night. None whom she knew would think to look for her here—

"Elon?"

—except one.

"Ghos." Elon strained for some sound of movement. *"I am here."* She waited. *"Ghos!"*

A shadow fell across the enclosure entry. Then a looming figure in shirt and trousers, a boot in each hand.

"What good does it do for you to walk without sound when you shout my name and I must shout yours in return?" Elon pushed the low table to one side with her foot so that Ghos could unroll one of the mats and seat himself. "Your hearing has not yet returned from the night of the mine. You must go to your physician-priest."

"I have had enough of priests." Ghos lowered to a crouch, then fell back onto the mat, a sign that his muscles still ached from that night as well. "Hearing returns with time. This I know, and truly."

"Not at all times, and if the damage is permanent, it must be repaired or you risk injury to your soul!"

"Hearing returns with time." Ghos pulled on one boot, then the other. "Breaker of fingers."

Elon bent one leg to her chest, sheltering her bandages from Ghos's view. "Why are you here?"

"To report of the embassy, which I could not do as we attended Feres." Ghos took up the handheld that hung from a cloth wrap about his waist and activated it. "The border with Interior is active, as always. Their guards have not ceased patrol since the night Minister van Reuter faced arrest, over one of their years ago. Whatever they search for, they have not yet found it." He tapped the display with his knuckle to change the entry. He spoke Vynshàrau Haárin, his voice completely stripped of gesture, as was his way when he reported to Elon. "The border with Exterior is quiet, as always. Interior should send some of their guards to them, I most believe." Another tap. "The lake is as quiet. We detect demis in flight well north of here. Service exercises, one assumes, but we await confirmation." Another tap. "The biodefense trials have been completed. The research dominants fear, and truly, that revised pink is not yet deployable throughout the embassy as a way of protection. It attacks all humanish biodevices evaluated, but it also damaged certain types of medical implants, as the material your physician-priest used to remend your broken bones. It attacks some of our device boards, rendering them useless. The biologics dominants fear contamination. Humanish have walked these halls since this building began its function. Vynshàrau have interacted with humanish, then entered the laboratories."

Elon gestured in disagreement. Most unfortunately, the action required the use of her right hand. She could not curve her fingers properly, and felt the anger rise as Ghos bared his teeth. "The workers are trained in methods to prevent such cross-contamination, and laboratory air systems are configured to remove such as well."

"One might believe." Ghos deactivated the handheld and returned it to his belt. "It is my feeling that embassy systems have not functioned as properly since Dathim Naré's time. He understood them, how to maintain them."

"Dathim Naré now lives over the water, Ghos."

"He should return to this place, where he belongs." Ghos raised his gaze and looked Elon in the face. "It is a matter of security, as the humanish say. We would be more safe if Dathim Naré resided here. Therefore, he must reside here."

Elon regarded Ghos just as openly. "He will not do so, nor will Shai compel him. He is more outcast even than Tsecha, and thus she does not trust him."

"Within the worldskein, such would not matter. He would do as he is bid."

"We are not within the worldskein, Ghos."

"No. We are outcast, beyond all godly bound." Ghos looked away. Then he pulled the low table toward him and reached for his belt once more. "Feres's scroll has departed for the embassy dock at Luna. His remains have been burned and dispersed by Sànalàn's suborn, whose training I most doubt." He removed a small bag, untied the opening, then poured the contents atop the table. Pattern stones, which caught what light there was and reflected it in ever-changing spirals of blue, green, and yellow.

"This is no place for games, Ghos." Despite her displeasure, Elon found herself drawn to the stones, marking the patterns as they changed, watching Ghos align those that matched, then

deducting the points he lost as the patterns changed before he finished.

"No. This is a place of discussion." Ghos gestured frustration
as the spirals altered to lines just as he constructed the final row.
"And what will we discuss, Elon? How little Shai has informed us
of her discussions with the Service humanish concerning the
mine? How humanish reporters speak of Feres as though his error
killed the technician Wode, and not the reverse?" His fingers
played over the stones, never stopping even as he spoke, aligning
them as quickly as the patterns reformed—whorls, sprays, lines—
yet not completing the sets in time. "How much we are hated in
this city, yet we stay? How with each humanish day, we lose more
of our souls as the injury that is this place wounds us, never to
heal? How we are damned?"

Elon picked up one of the stones, ignoring Ghos's mutter that
she interfered with his game. "We are all those. There is nothing
to discuss." She turned the stone over, held it to the light. A yellow
and blue whorl, tightening to a spiral, then swirling into concentric circles. "Is there a remedy? Such is what merits discussion,
Ghos." She bared her teeth as Ghos looked her in the face once
more. She relished his strangeness, his grey eyes against paler
skin than hers, much as his body-mother, who was as Sìah. "Ghos
of the stones."

Ghos did not respond to her humor. He concentrated on his
patterns, as he always had when he contemplated action. "If the
Oà challenge Cèel, we will be called back to Shèrá to fight. Oà
must not succeed. They have never ruled as rau. They have not the
experience to deal with humanish."

"Oà will not challenge without the Haárin, and the Haárin follow Vynshàrau." Elon set the stone back upon the table. "For
now."

Ghos's hand stopped in mid-play. "Explain."

Elon watched the pattern of the stones change. *Ghos has completed only half the lines—he has lost too many points.* Yet she
knew from his attention to her that he no longer cared of stones.
"Tsecha repudiated Sànalàn when his plea to maintain Feres's life
failed. He said he did not recognize her as his propitiator. Cèel
will thus move against him. When the Haárin learn of this, and
they will, some will remove their support from Cèel."

"For what reason?"

"Tsecha is dominant of the Chicago Haárin, and as such is
considered by most Haárin as their dominant as well. Thus will

they turn from Vynshàrau and support the bornsect that Tsecha supports, whether such is Oà, or Pathen, or Sìah." Elon touched her bandaged hand, which had numbed. "We will not know what may happen for some time. First Shai must tell Cèel, then Cèel must confer with Council and Temple. Then the word will spread throughout the worldskein, and all will know . . ." She listened for the sounds from the other side of the veranda and heard nothing. Did they listen to her now as she spoke of Tsecha's heresy? "It becomes most as complicated."

"Politics." Ghos mixed his stones together, then waited for the new pattern to form. "Blood is cleaner."

"—and it should be a pretty good party." Cashman dragged the beer dispenser out of the skimmer boot and lowered it onto the two-wheeler he'd appropriated from the apartment building's utilities chase. "I invited the bullpen crew, and some of the folks from SysAdmin, and Court's bringing a couple of friends."

Micah hoisted the last bag of food out of the boot and set it atop the dispenser. "The exam for Comtech One is in a few weeks. I need to hit the manuals."

"That's my Fabe. They finally give us a day off from all this inquiry crap, and you decide to celebrate by studying." Cashman slammed down the boot hood, then dragged the two-wheeler around in a wide circle and pulled it across the garage toward the lift. "This was the first day in two weeks that we didn't have to record some poor bastard's inventory screw-up or requisition miscalc or scheduling cross-over, and I for one intend to take full and complete advantage of it." Without warning, he yanked the cart into a sharp turn and headed toward the locked cage that housed the building's delivery slots, row after tightly packed row of lockers set aside for packages and other bulky personal mail. "Only take a second. I haven't checked in a few days. Last time I let it go too long, my sister sent me real ice cream. Who the hell sends anybody real ice cream? Stuff melted. Stunk up my box for a week."

"I remember." Micah waited as Cashman keyed into the cage, then followed him in. His heart tripped—he felt a warmth spread through his body that was almost embarrassing. *It's been over three weeks*. He approached his locker as if it were a girl waiting for him, his emotions warring. Eager to the point of euphoria. Terrified enough to turn and run.

"Not even a snack food sample from the exchange." Cashman

slammed his locker door closed. "I need to call my folks and make them feel guilty."

Micah palmed open his locker—his hand sweated so much that he needed to press it down twice. *Please . . . please . . .* He caught sight of the familiar white mailer amid the trashzap chargers and building announcements, small and battered, bearing the mail code of an off-base holoVee store.

"Looks like some of us have friends." Cashman grabbed for the mailer, wresting it from Micah's grip. *"Whoa ho,"* he cried as he read the mail code, "I know what this is!"

Micah froze, his heart still pounding, mind racing. *This place gets too much traffic.* He glanced at the rows of lockers, the narrow aisles that separated them barely wide enough to walk down. *Couldn't hide a body here.* At least, not for very long.

Cashman gave the mailer closure a half-hearted tug, then tossed it back to Micah. *"Studying."* He grabbed the two-wheeler's handle and pulled it out of the cage. " 'Space Vixens from the Planet Clitoris'—that's what you'll be studying."

Micah gripped the mailer so tightly his fingers cramped, and still he held on. He wanted to shout *How dare you! That's what you think! You're wrong!*

But a wilier part of him interrupted. *Let him think that. Let him think whatever he wants, as long as he doesn't guess the truth.* He tucked the mailer under his arm and walked out of the cage. Closed the gate after him. Headed for the lift only to find Cashman waiting, sly grin in place.

He stepped aside so Micah could board, then let the door slide closed. "So." He watched the floor numbers creep upward. "Can I borrow it when you're done?"

Micah sighed. "Sure." That meant he'd have to waste tomorrow's lunch break on a trip to the shop to search for something appropriately smutty. *It's called cover,* the wily part of him said. He thought of Captain Pascal and his miscellaneous accounts. *This is what it feels like.* He pondered it, and found it good.

Micah keyed into his flat, pausing until the door opened completely even as his nerves screamed. Stepped inside, waited for the panel to slide closed, then activated the lock.

"Space vixens." Sometimes he despaired of his fellow Spacers, their lack of imagination. He set the mailer atop the storage cabinet. Then he hung up his coat, activated the kitchenette and bedroom lighting, all the usual first-few-minutes-at-home business that he did every day. He already wore suitable clothes, base casual pants and a heavy knit athletic pullover. To ease his grumbling stomach, he raided his cooler for a dispo of milk and a candy bar. Hunger dulled if not sated, he returned to the cabinet and picked up the mailer.

"Why did they wait so long?" Micah tore open the tough plastic envelope and removed a small white foldover the size of his palm. Opened the flap and removed an ummarked wafer. He held it by the edge, tipping it from side to side, watching the light reflect off the surface in pale curved rainbows and wondering who else had touched it. Had it been a leader of their Group? Someone like the Old Man, who monitored their scattered numbers from some all-seeing vantage point and chose or discarded for the good of humanity? Or had it been a trusted second-in-command, someone like Scarface Pierce, whose job was to take the raw material his master gave him and mold it into a defender worthy of his race?

Micah opened the bottom drawer of the cabinet and removed a headset, along with a pair of earbugs and linked gloves and socks. The usual virtual training gear, used by pilots, surgeons, mechanics, anyone who needed to learn a highly specialized skill.

"If I planned to watch *Space Vixens*, I'd need another linking connection." He frowned. He'd need to get it tomorrow when he stopped at the shop to buy his decoy holo. That way, in case his flat was ever searched, there would be no question in anyone's mind that the only thing Micah Faber was guilty of was an unfortunate predilection for interactive pornography.

"That means I should get more than one holo." If you're going to build a cover, may as well make it shooter-proof. "This is getting expensive." He walked over to his couch and sat, then bunched a couple of cushions against the armrest and lay back. Pulled on the socks. Stuck in the earbugs and donned the headset.

Micah listened to his breathing, magnified to a slow gale within the confines of the face-covering headset. Ambient sound had been blocked. Incident light. He slipped the wafer into a slot in the headset, then dragged on the gloves. Waited.

First came a series of tones. Like chimes, they sounded, first louder, then softer. Repeating. Repeating. The preparative hypnosis, designed to lower the barrier between his conscious mind and the scenario that would soon play before it like a—

—classroom. Chairs in two concentric circles, arranged around a woman dressed in a steel-grey T-shirt and baggy fatigue pants. Razored Service burr, accentuating a face too broad and bony to be feminine. Chrivet. Sergeant. Micah's god-on-earth for the duration of his training. He'd sat before her three times so far, and liked her within certain tight limits. She knew her job—therefore, she was worth listening to. Beyond that . . . he tried not to think of her beyond that.

"The V-790 exoskeletal array is the most advanced exo yet developed by the Service." Chrivet stalked the center of the circle, the focus of all attention and savoring it. "When you wear it, you will be able to run farther and faster, jump higher, and shoot better than any human being who ever lived. You will be damned nigh invincible."

Micah snatched glimpses of his classmates around Chrivet's stalking form, twenty-eight young, fresh faces each evidencing varying degrees of attention. Bevan, narrow and dark, who thought he already knew it all but deigned to listen anyway. Foley, shorter and lighter, who followed Bevan like a starved pup. Manda, pale-skinned and black-haired, who glanced back at Micah across the gulf of Chrivet's circle and smiled.

Micah smiled back. Felt the heat creep up his neck. Down. Knew that Chrivet still spoke, and couldn't have repeated a word she said if his life depended on it.

Don't do this to yourself, man—that isn't even her face. He and Wode had talked about the scenario setup many times after they stumbled upon the fact that they were both members of the Group. How the odds were that since their names had been changed, their faces most likely had as well. That only the downloaded personalities remained the same. Voices, maybe. Enough to train. Enough to bond. Enough to befriend. Not enough to identify.

Those eyes. So blue. It would have been unspeakably cruel of the scenario brain to render Manda's eyes a fiction. *So what does she see when she looks at me?* Micah saw his own face in every reflective surface, but that was because that's what he expected to see. *How different are we?* And would it matter come the day they all finally met?

Without warning, an expanse of darker blue obliterated his view of Manda. He blinked, realized he stared at Chrivet's crotch, and lifted his head as though she'd jerked him under the chin.

"Can't you hear me, Mister Tiebold!" She glared down at him, cheeks reddening. "I asked you a question."

Tiebold. He still hadn't gotten the hang of his scenario name. No one else seemed to have a problem with theirs—why did he with his?

"I didn't . . ." He took the deepest, longest breath in the world. It ended too soon. "I didn't hear you, ma'am."

Chrivet's eyes narrowed. Small, close-set, piggy eyes, dull clay without a glimmer of beauty.

Not like Manda's—Micah gave himself a mental slap. No more Manda. Not now. Not if he wanted to remain with the Group. Learn about the V-790. Avenge Wode, and drive the idomeni from every corner of the Commonwealth.

"You didn't hear me, Mister Tiebold?" Chrivet smiled. Her teeth were square and white with no spaces between, as though they'd been carved from a single block of poly. "You're bored. Nothing here of sufficient interest to hold your attention. You know it all." Her voice, which normally skirted the edges of agitation, emerged dangerously calm. "Well, since you know everything—" She stepped to one side and pointed to a place outside the circle, beyond the double ring of chairs. "—perhaps you'd like to show us all how to suit up."

At first glance it seemed that someone had beaten Micah to it. A helmeted figure stood outside the circle, taller than he and broad-shouldered, tricked out in a tight black coverall with articulated joints. Dull-finish body armor plated across the chest, abdomen, and thighs, while metal framing ran along the outsides of the legs and undersides of the arms.

Micah took one step toward the still, silent figure, then another, conscious as ever of Bevan's sneer, Chrivet's eagerness to pounce on his anticipated screw-up. *It's just an exo, stupid— no one's inside.* He studied the smooth front of the suit, looking for fasteners, clasps, groping for some hint as to how to get into the damned thing. *Shit.* He stopped in front of it—it was taller than he by half a head. *I sat through a presentation once.* His job had been to set up and monitor the imager, but he'd stuck around at the speaker's request and got to listen to the whole thing. *There's a release near the top of the left shoulder*—He reached up, his fingers brushing what felt like a raised seam. He pressed down, and the shoulder sagged open with the sound of cracking ice.

Keep peeling down. He sensed Chrivet move in beside him, and glanced over to find her regarding him with thin-lipped disgruntlement. *Yanked away one chance for you to humiliate me.* He turned back to the exo. *Sadistic bitch.* He opened up the side seam down to the ankle. The metal frame supported the coverall as he worked his way inside, felt the slip of the material over his hands.

Rubbery yet silky, nubby in places from inset connections and sensors.

"Unlike previous exos, the V-790 is designed to allow the wearer to suit-in themselves. But in the interest of time—" Chrivet started at the ankle and worked up, yanking the seams together and sealing them tight. "The suit contains a constrictor array so the wearer can tighten or loosen as needed—"

Micah drowned her out again as he adjusted his helmet, then started fiddling with the controls. The air inside the exo smelled metallic, burnt, as though the suit was brand new and still outgassing.

"A damned manual would be nice," he muttered under his breath. He heard a *ping* in his left ear, followed by a flash of light. Then, as nicely indented and numbered as you please, a series of headers scrolled across the inner surface of the faceplate. "Voice activation—good to know." He scanned the words that flowed before his eyes. Bodily Functions. Weapons. Defensive Equipment. "How about walking?" He looked past the words, through the display, and saw Chrivet and the others eyeing him expectantly. *Oh boy*. He bunched his muscles as though he prepared to leap off a ledge, and legged forward—

"*Shit!*" Micah went airborne, hitting the inner ring of chairs, scattering wireframe in all directions. Shouts filled his ears. A woman's scream. Another stride and he hit the opposite side of the circle, blowing chairs aside like bits of foam. Heard Chrivet yell, "*Stop!*" One more immense stride. Another. The wall came to meet him like a fist in the face—he dropped his weight on his back heel like a pedwheel kick brake, and stopped a hairbreadth in front of the painted brick.

Four strides. His heart pounded, columns of red bobbed on the display. Five meters a stride—had to be. "I ran—" Across a huge cavern of a room in the time it took to shout one word. "Shit." He said it again, softer this time. He felt like the animal he rode had taken off beneath him and run down the face of a cliff, carrying him along for the ride. *But I stopped it*. Could he have gone through the wall? *I'd rather not find out*.

"Turn around, Mister Tiebold," Chrivet called after him, "and take it a little more slowly this time."

Micah lifted his left leg, edged it to the side, and felt it swing out. *Little movements go a long way*. He let the momentum take him, moving into the rotation like a dancer. It worked. He felt as though he drifted into position, like a leaf falling from a tree, but in the end he found himself facing Bevan and the rest, standing straight and tall.

"You certainly know how to walk across a room, Mister Tiebold." Chrivet had moved well out of Micah's direct path, and now stood against the wall to his left. "Now take one step forward. Then peel out and give someone else a turn." She looked around. "Clear the rest of these chairs out of the way."

Micah took the lesson from his turnaround, and edged his leg forward. Felt the low glide. A single step—only a meter or so this time. He raised his right hand beside his head and imagined the muzzle of a mid-range at his right shoulder. According to the presentation, the weapon would be bolted to the rear framing, all charged and ready to go. *Just pull it down and fire.*

"Peel out now, Tiebold."

Micah sighed. Lowered his hand, crossing it over to his other shoulder. Popped the seam. Exited the suit. Took a seat against the wall and watched everyone else. Imagined again and again the thrill of those few strides. Daydreamed of the power inherent in the flick of a finger. The kick of a leg. Lay his head back against the wall and—

—opened his eyes. As always, he felt as though he'd been under for hours. But when he checked his timepiece, he found that only twenty minutes had passed. Not as compressed as a dream, but not real-time, either. In between.

Micah sat up. He removed the wafer from his headset, then pulled off all the gear piece by piece. Rose shakily, his thigh muscles aching from tension, his gut rumbling. When he walked, he felt the exo about him like a shield.

For a time he felt the urge to crash Cashman's party. He wanted to shoulder his way through a room full of people, shout to make himself heard above the din. Drink and laugh.

"Except . . ." He knew what he'd hear as soon as he walked in. *Hey Fabe—what happened to the holo? Hey everybody, meet my buddy, the scholar.* "I'll stay in." Heat up a prepack. Watch the 'Vee. First thing in the morning, he needed to stop by the public comport kiosk at Forrestal Block, two apartment buildings removed from his. Tuck into a booth and punch in the code that had arrived with that very first training wafer, three months before. Then stick his latest wafer into a player, jack the player into the comport, and send the entire transmission on its way to God knew where, this time supplemented by his physical data, his bioemotional scan, his responses to the training scenario. A DI's recruit report, packed into a few seconds of transmission chatter. After that, melt the wafer down in his trashzap. Then wait for the next mailer to arrive.

"How long?" Not three weeks, not if a training regimen had begun. "More often." A couple of times a week, maybe, for weeks and weeks to come.

He relived sensations. The lightness. The power. Then he shut his training gear away in its drawer and walked to the kitchenette to make his supper.

Micah decided later that he hadn't paid sufficient attention to his surroundings. He had risen early, showered and dressed, then transmitted his data in the usual fashion. Caught a shuttle to Far North Lakeside and settled into his cube early enough to catch the tail end of third shift. He took advantage of the downtime to tap into systems and dig up a schematic of the V-790, secure in the knowledge that it would be at least an hour before Cashman peered over the divider and regaled him with details of the party.

He was immersed in the Motion Control section of the manual when he heard a throat-clearing behind him—he spun his chair around, his heart in his throat.

"I didn't mean to alarm you, Lance Corporal." Pascal stood in the cube entry. He still wore his field coat; a black briefbag hung from one shoulder. "Emergency meeting in Lakeside Junior—we're having trouble with the conference calling system."

"Yes, sir." Micah reset his workstation to standby and pushed to his feet, blowing past Pascal more quickly than was mannerly. *Back down—you haven't done anything wrong.*

Pascal quickened his pace and caught him up. "You're interested in exoskeletons, Faber?"

Micah's heart skittered. He hated the fact that Pascal knew his name. "I ran the imager for a V-790 presentation a few weeks ago. It looked interesting."

"The engineers took too many shortcuts in the environmental controls, and diverted power to movement and weapons systems." Pascal's voice sounded tight. "They feel that if you can run away from it or shoot it, you don't need to protect against it. Not sound, in my opinion. But no one asked me."

"No, sir. I mean, yes, sir." Micah ducked into the conference room ahead of Pascal and headed straight for the combooth in the far corner. Flicked the switches he had to, then ran a systems check. Emerged from the booth. "Should be good to go now, sir."

Made for the door, conscious as a hunted beast of the gaze that tracked him until he left the room and emerged into the safety of the hallway.

"Jerk." So no one asked the great captain's advice on the design of the V-790? Well, soon a lowly lance corporal would know more about it than he would, and wouldn't that be a great feeling? The thought made Micah smile, until the memory of those dead brown eyes eyes boring holes in his back wiped it away.

CHAPTER 9

> "Because of the distance from Earth, the
> Outer Circle worlds are the least traditional of
> all the Commonwealth colonies . . ."
>
> Clase, *Thalassan Histories, Book I*

"I'm a colonial, too, Jan, a point you seem all too willing to overlook." Niall walked the edge of the exercise mat as though it were a tightrope, heel-to-toe-to-heel, arms held out to the sides for balance. "And when it comes to the Jewelers Loop gross domestic product rankings, Victoria is the poorest of poor relations. I understand deprivation. I learned all about having to make do with the dregs while others with more clout got the cream." He wore summer base casuals—grey T-shirt, dark blue shorts, and white trainers—and seemed well-met with the ship's small gymnasium. His arms looked hewn from wood, his legs muscular and still faintly tanned despite five weeks spent under ship lighting. "Just because Elyas and the other Outer Circle worlds can't get chocolate sauce for their sponge cake is no reason for them to allow the Haárin to take over their damned shipping networks."

Jani sat on the far end of the mat and watched Niall totter and turn. "The issue that brought all this to a head last fall involved something a little more serious than chocolate sauce. As I recall, the quality of Karistos's water was at stake." She crossed her trousered legs at the ankle. She wore a long-sleeve pullover as well, topped with a heavy crew sweater in a jewel shade of purple, their ship name, DENALI, etched across the front in silver. "You insist on trivializing the fact that the colonies have been chronically undersupplied for decades, at times to the point of crisis."

"I don't trivialize it!" Niall halted in mid-wobble and stepped to the middle of the mat. "The Families screwed up. They didn't think past the ends of their credit balances. A few of them behaved in a remarkably stupid manner. Well guess what? They're finally waking up. The great beast is blinking and looking around and sees reason for concern."

"For its credit balance."

"For its security."

Jani worked to her feet and walked to the games rack, which had been bolted to the far wall. "If Cao and her cronies want to win back the confidence of the Outer Circle Merchants Associations, their task is simple." She took a wooden martial-arts sword from one of the slots and swung it back and forth like one of Dathim's practice blades. "Let them revamp the Commerce and Transportation ministries. They've cleared the wharf rats from a few docks—let them keep going. Let them divest themselves of the shipping companies that they own to eliminate any nasty little conflicts of interest, and let the new owners win business in the competitive arena, not take it as something they're owed." She stilled, then began to shift her weight from side to side, knees bent, guiding the blade in a slow sweep before her.

Niall tracked the end of the blade as if it were the head of a snake. "Dathim teach you that?"

"He told me that my old bones require a gradual progression of movement. In other words, I need to warm up." Jani smiled. "He's older than I am and he needs to warm up even longer, but that's different, of course. He is the teacher and I am the student, and his is a life pure and free from contradiction and pulled muscles."

Niall watched her for a time. Then he walked to a bench set against the far wall, beneath which he'd stashed his gym bag. "I'll say this, you're getting better at changing the subject. You even managed to get the last word in the bargain." He dragged the bag atop the bench and scrabbled through it, removing a short-handled racket and a hand towel. "We've had the same discussion in different forms since we boarded this bucket at Luna. Why don't we call it a draw and be done with it? You won't change my mind, and I won't change yours."

Jani stopped in mid-arc, then drew the blade to a neutral stop against her right shoulder. "You're angry."

"Resigned, more like. Returning to the role of concerned observer with a heavy sigh." Niall began his own warm-up, rotating his wrists, then flicking the racket back and forth. "You talk a very good game. But you play it, as well, and have the scars to prove it. Proof for the doubting Thomases. You possess a hefty share of credibility." He offered a sad half smile, twisted into a smirk by his scar. "And you've got this revolutionary gloss that's difficult for we more boring souls to ignore."

Jani rolled her eyes. "I'm not a revolutionary. I'm not—"

"Jan, if you tell me you're not political, I'm going to clout you across the back of the head." Niall pivoted from side to side. Forehand. Backhand. "You're about as political as they get, whether you choose to believe it or not."

"My political options dwindled to nothing when the ministries shut me out. I'm a priest-in-training now." Jani walked back to the rack and slid the blade back into its niche. "I don't understand how you can defend the Commonwealth as you do. It certainly hasn't treated you much better than it has me."

"I believe in the ideal, if not always the execution. Then there's the colony kid in me—I hate waste. If a system is flawed, you repair it. You don't turn your back on it." Niall's back and forth slowed. "Unless you want it to continue to devolve so that you have a knee-jerk justification for doing something that you know you shouldn't be doing in the first place."

Jani waited for Niall to stop, to shoot a pointed look in her direction, but he continued his warm-up as though she wasn't in the room. *You bastard—you don't even have to check to see if you hit the target, do you?* But then, he'd hit it back in Chicago, where he'd first attached himself to her like a second shadow—it was just a case now of gathering the details. *Which I've managed to keep from him.* But they would dock at Elyas Station the next shipday. At that point all bets were off. He'd find out about the hybrid, real or faked. About Feyó's problems with her Haárin. And he'd transmit it all back to Chicago, for Mako to take to Cao on a silver platter, the peace offering found just in time to save his Admiral-Generalcy.

"Good morning."

Jani turned toward the gym entry to find John standing there, smile fixed in place as he looked from her to Niall and back again. "I've interrupted another political argument. I can tell." He had dressed as Niall had, in shorts, T-shirt, and trainers, but any resemblance ended there. He had chosen white and pale blue for his outfit, colors that matched his skin and the veins that ran beneath. He was taller and lankier than Niall, and looked as though he might break in a stiff wind until you saw how the muscles of his forearm bunched and defined when he clenched the handle of his gym bag.

"You'd think that after five weeks cooped up together, you two would have hashed everything out." He exhaled with a rumble. "I guess not." He strode toward them, the soles of his trainers squeaking on the coated flooring. He skirted the edge of the mat and tossed his bag atop the bench next to Niall's. Then he dug out a racket and a dispo of balls, popping the container lid and shaking one out so it bounced toward Niall. "Odds or evens?"

"Odds." Niall plucked the ball out the air, then turned it so he could read the vendor mark. "Serial number ends in five. My serve."

John swung his racket in a relaxed arc. "It's a little late in the trip to say this, Jan, but I'd appreciate it if you didn't rile the colonel before our matches." He tried to sound humorous, but a warning glint hardened his blue-filmed gaze. "He tends to take it out on me in an annoyingly predictable manner."

"He means that I whip his ass." Niall jerked his chin in the direction of the door that led to the ballcourt. "After you, Doctor."

"Colonel."

Jani lagged behind the two men as they walked to the ballcourt entry, listening to their banter. It sounded good-natured enough on the surface, but she had sensed their mutual dislike bubble to the surface more than once over the course of the trip, especially when John perceived that she and Niall had argued. *John never liked him, and now he doesn't trust him.* If trust stemmed from knowing exactly what a person would do in a given situation, however, Jani trusted Niall completely. *He'll do what he perceives is his duty.* Just as she said he would back in Chicago. *And so will I.* Just as he said she would. *We know one another too well.* Trust, therefore, was absolute on both sides. *Pull the other one, Kilian, it sings "Oh, Acadia."* She settled in front of the observation window and waited for the game to begin.

After a few minutes of warm-up, the men moved into position. Niall bounced the ball off the floor and struck it, his racket hand a blur. Behind him, John lunged for the rebound as best he could, but it sailed past him, striking the window with a solid *thuck*. He took advantage of his location to glare at Jani. She shrugged an apology.

"One to the server," Niall announced, grinning. His good mood vanished, however, when John won the next exchange and claimed serve.

Go, John. Jani pumped a fist below the level of the windowsill and braced for John's serve until a movement in her periphery claimed her attention. She looked to the side and found one of the

Denali comtechs standing there, professionally sharp in a coverall of the same rich purple as her sweater.

"Transmission for you, ma'am," the young woman said. "From Elyas."

"Thanks." Jani settled into the combooth seat, then nodded for the tech to shut her in. As the door closed, the lighting in the booth dimmed to half power. The display, meanwhile, brightened with a series of vendor logos, followed by a warning of the awful fate that would befall any unauthorized viewers of the message about to play.

"How about the authorized viewer?" Jani grew conscious of her sweaty palms, and wiped them against her trouser legs.

The display image stuttered for a few seconds as idomeni and humanish technologies collided. Then a face that had grown more and more familiar since the autumn took shape. A high-boned oval, the paler gold-tan of the Sìah, graced by dark grey eyes softened by silvery sclera.

"Glories of the day to you, ná Kièrshia." Ná Feyó Tal, dominant of the Elyan Haárin, spoke lightly accented English, and appeared as relaxed and comfortable as she usually did during transmissions. She wore her grey-streaked brown hair drawn back in her usual humanish-style horsetail. Her visible clothing was simple in cut and pale in color, an open-necked crossover shirt in the light green shade she favored. "We anticipate your visit. I look forward and truly to news of ní Tsecha." She had angled her face so she would look Jani in the eye if they sat in the same room, an attention to detail that many Haárin overlooked and bornsect eschewed on principle. "I trust your journey proved most pleasant, and that you anticipate our reunion as much as I."

"Glories of the day to you as well, ná Feyó." Jani sat back, folding her arms so she could tuck her hands up the sleeves of her sweater. "Ní Tsecha sends his regards as well, and wishes he could have made this journey himself."

Feyó's lips curved in a vague almost-smile, which on a human female would have been considered enigmatic. "I most wish he could have as well." She lowered her gaze for a time. When she raised it again, the clear-eyed reserve had returned. "Tomorrow, ná Kièrshia. It would be most appropriate, I believe and truly, if one of my shuttles docked with the *Denali*, and if we took you off thusly and I escorted you to Karistos myself. If you could consult with your ship's engineer and tell me if docking arrangements are possible? I may transmit to you all the information needed for this determination."

Jani studied Feyó's image for any sign of tension. The transmission was taking place in real-time, with minimal smoothing of any delays. Was it an instrument hiccup that made for the tightening around the Haárin female's mouth, the furrow between her eyes? Or had the worry that she'd so far managed to hide finally broken the surface? "What's wrong with meeting at Elyas Station?"

"The station is most crowded, the humanish docks especially. Transfer to the Haárin side of the station is not always smooth." Feyó waved a hand in a meaningless gesture. "We would have more of a chance to talk. Of ní Tsecha, and the damned cold winter of which he complains."

Chatter like a couple of old, dear friends? Catch up on old times? Jani waited for Feyó to give her some hint, and knew she could sit there all day. *She wants me under her control as quickly as possible.* "I will get the engineer, ná Feyó." She pressed the alarm touchpad and summoned the comtech.

The next half hour passed in a flurry of discussion and data transmission. Feyó called in one of her technical dominants to speak to the Haárin side of the docking equation. Jani wedged into a corner of the booth and watched the universal language of headshakes, mutters, and mathematics, but in the end the conclusion was what she expected. The designs of the ships were too different, and the time too short. A straightforward junction wasn't possible, and a retrofit inside twenty-four hours out of the question.

"Ná Feyó." Jani returned to her seat after the engineer departed. "What is going on?"

Feyó raised her right hand, palm facing out, and rested it against her left cheek. That fallback to a High Sìah expression of confusion told more about her state of mind than any words could. "I know little. I suspect much."

"You believe someone will try to get to me before you do. At Elyas Station, or on the ground in Karistos."

"We have heard rumors. We have learned over the months of the need to listen to such."

"Ní Tsecha believes that your dominance has been challenged. Is your challenger the one who wants to get hold of me?"

Feyó's hand dropped, the sound of her sharp intake of breath gasping through the speaker system. Then the tension left her like a drawn-out sigh. "When we spoke in Chicago, ní Tsecha told me how necessary it became for him to learn to read between humanish lines. He explained to me how such is to be done." Again, the High Sìah gesture of confusion. "It seems, and truly, that he has learned to read between my lines as well, for I told him nothing of any challenge."

Jani waited for Feyó to continue, but the female remained silent, the back of her hand still pressed against her cheek. "It seems to me," she said finally, "that the Elyan Haárin have taken to subterfuge with a vengeance. Unfortunately, you're still not clear as to which side you're supposed to hold back information *from*." She tapped the display with her fingernail until Feyó looked up. "I'm the one who's the focus of untoward interest. You can talk to *me*."

Feyó nodded, then drew in a deep breath. If she'd been humanish, one could say that she was screwing up her courage. "The one who would challenge me wishes to state her case to you in person, to persuade you to intercede for her with ní Tsecha. She believes that with his support, she will face acceptance."

"You are the acknowledged dominant of the Elyan enclave." A twinge of paranoia compelled Jani to check the seal on the com-booth door, and make sure no one standing outside could overhear. "You enjoy the support of the Outer Circle Haárin, and the confidence of humanish as well. Anyone who would challenge you would have a difficult time arguing their case. And if they tried to kidnap me, or harm me in any way, they would lose any chance of gaining Tsecha's support."

"This one does not understand such. She is arrogant, and believes that she has only to speak to you to convince you of her position."

"What is her name?" Jani asked. "What is her standing?"

Feyó hesitated. "Her name is Gisa. She is an agronomist, as I am. Her beliefs are most as extreme. She attracts the impatient, those who do not understand how an enclave must function if it is to survive alongside humanish!" Feyó's eyes gleamed with anger. "My security will protect you, ná Kièrshia, of that you have my pledge. Gisa will not find hold of you."

Jani experienced a a sickeningly familiar turn of stomach. *It's like I never left Chicago.* The same undercurrents. The same power struggles.

She thought of the single bright spot, the only thing that offered her any sort of reprieve. "Among the rumors you've learned to listen to, ná Feyó, have you heard anything concerning another hybrid? A young male, to be precise?"

"No, ná Kièrshia." Feyó shook her head. "No rumors of young hybrid males." She looked Jani straight in the eye, her gaze unwavering.

Jani reached the gym entrance just as John and Niall emerged, sweaty and silent. John offered a rueful smile. Niall, on the other hand, eyed her with a wariness he normally reserved for strangers.

"Ná Feyó contacted me. She thinks someone may try to kidnap me at Elyas Station." She tried to maneuver to John's side but found her way blocked by Niall's strategically placed foot.

"Kidnap?" He toweled his face, then stuffed the cloth in his bag. "Why?"

Jani backed off, then wandered a semicircle in the middle of the corridor. *"Kidnap" is so strong a word. Should she have said "accost"? "Delay"?* Besides, all Feyó had to go on was rumor and guesswork, and she didn't possess the experience in handling either to make the most reliable of sources. "It isn't definite. But a rival named Gisa has challenged Feyó for the dominance of the Elyan Haárin. Feyó believes Gisa wishes to convince me of the rightness of her cause. She'll try to talk me into supporting her, and ask me to intercede for her with Tsecha."

"We'll be disembarking on the human side of the station." John set his bag down at his feet. He held a towel, too, but instead of wiping his face, he worked it in his hands, first bundling it, then shaking it flat, then bundling it again. "Any Haárin who tried to infiltrate the dock area would stand out."

"Those docks have enough twists and turns for someone to hide in, assuming they decide to try infiltration rather than assault." Niall's grim expression lightened as he focused on their new problem. The wolf on the scent. "What did Feyó tell you?"

"Pretty much what I told you. She couldn't provide specifics. All she has is a feeling."

"A *feeling*?" Niall still held his racket. He tightened his hold on the grip, working the head up and down as though he shook someone's hand. "What's that worth?"

"I don't know." Lacking a racket or a towel to worry, Jani shoved her hands in her pockets and paced. "All I can say is that I've never seen her this angry."

The three of them pondered, expending varying levels of nervous energy as they did.

Niall finally ended the silence by flicking his racket in a sharp backhand, then stuffing it in his bag. "I can start with station security. Fort Karistos should be able to spare me some bodies." He turned to John. "What about Neoclona, Doctor?"

"Whoever you need." John started down the corridor toward the comdeck. "We can light a fire under them right now."

Niall fell in behind, lagging until Jani caught him up. "Did Feyó give you any other information? Anything at all?"

Jani shook her head. "She's promised me her security. If there's anything else to know, they should know it."

Niall kept his attention fixed on John's back. "This political issue—is this what you didn't want to tell me?" He clenched his hand into a fist and pounded his thigh. *"Damn it, Jani."*

Jani thought of a bright smile and badly filmed eyes, and said nothing.

The comdeck get-together lasted well into the ship-afternoon. John bailed first, after tempers flared and it became obvious that there could only be one Chief of Operations and Niall was it. Jani remained behind to act as Haárin translator, but as it turned out, both Feyó's suborns and the Haárin who worked station security all spoke passable English. Not only that, but they seemed to thrive under Niall's blunt direction, which in turn rendered Jani's fears of diplomatic incident moot. When she finally slipped out the door, no one noticed that she left.

She meant to return to her own cabin, but she didn't feel like being alone, and that meant there was only one other place for her to go. *I've done it often enough this trip.* And never stayed longer than a few minutes. *I respect John's privacy, just like he respects mine.* And all in all, they had both done an excellent job of avoiding anything even approaching a delicate situation.

More fool me. She pushed the thought from her mind as she turned down a short, dead-end corridor, stopped before the lone set of doors, and hit the buzzer.

"Come in," sounded the so-familiar bass.

Jani hesitated. Even in the middle of a brightly lit hallway, John's voice inspired thoughts of the dark. She wiped her hand along her trouser leg, then touched the doorpad. The panel slid aside—she crossed the threshold and walked down a short entry that opened into the white and yellow sitting room. "Every time I come in here, I think the same thing." She took in the woodweave chairs and couches, the brightly patterned cushions, and as usual felt as though she'd walked onto the veranda at a sunny resort. "No Neoclona purple? No Persian carpets? No ebony hardwood?"

"Very funny." John rose from his lounge chair, the latest issue of the Karistos *Partisan* in hand. His hair was still wet from the shower, and he'd changed into a more familiar long-sleeve pullover and trousers in shades of tan. "The colonel still whipsawing my security?" He rolled the newssheet into a tight baton and slapped it against his hand. "I don't know how I managed to stay out of harm's way for the last twenty years without having him around to bark at me."

"John, it's his job. He's good at it."

"I've only been shot at *once* that entire time. Guess who I can thank for that?"

Jani held up her hands and backed away. Then she walked to the wall-spanning display case and pretended interest in an aquarium. She heard nothing for a time, then a slow tread of footsteps from behind that set her heart pounding.

John moved in beside her, a relatively safe arm's length away. "Are you frightened?"

Of what? The unknown danger awaiting at Elyas Station, or the more immediate peril standing beside her now? *Take my pick.* Jani wanted to move closer to John and take his hand in hers. Instead, she leaned close to the aquarium and tapped her finger against the glass. One of the fish, a blue and orange swordfin, floated up toward the sound and shadow, bumping the glass with its nose as it tried to draw near. "According to Feyó, Gisa just wants to talk. It doesn't follow that she'd try to hurt me. She'd squander any chance she had to influence Tsecha." She raised her finger higher. The fish followed. "I'm concerned about what this challenge could mean. To the Elyan Haárin. To Outer Circle stability."

"I'm afraid my concerns are more immediate." John pulled open one of the case drawers and removed the same S-40 he'd shown her in her Chicago kitchen over a month before. "Do you still have your shooter?"

"Yes. Stowed safely in the bottom of my bag." Jani reached out and took the weapon from his hand. "You planning a shootout in the middle of the VIP dock area?" She checked the powerpack and was relieved to find it disengaged. *Glad to see Doctor Marya your shooting instructor actually taught you something about shooting.* "Speaking of weapons, how did the match go?" she asked as she handed back the S-40.

John took back the weapon and slipped it back in the drawer. "I played him close the first game. Lost it eight-ten. Then it got ugly. He swept me—four straight." He tapped his finger against the glass to draw the swordfin's attention, but it ignored him, intent upon Jani. "Whatever happened between you two, he needed to take it out on somebody. Lucky me."

Jani pressed her face to the glass and looked more deeply into the aquarium. Toward the rear of the tank a miniature shark swam a lazy circuit, occasionally grazing the bottom and kicking up silt. "He knows I'm hiding something from him. He's known since we left Chicago. For now, he thinks I held back information about Feyó, but once he finds out about the suspected hybrid . . ." She rapped the side of the aquarium with her knuckles, sending fish darting in all directions but for the steadfast swordfin. "John, he's my friend."

"I know." John folded his arms and leaned against the case. "You and Niall are halves of the same whole. Moody. Introspective. Hard on others, but even harder on yourselves. A couple of damaged idealists on a never-ending quest to find something to believe in. He thought he found that thing in you. Now you're moving away from him, and he's angry." The room was too bright for him. Like a moon or a star, darkness defined John Shroud best.

Jani looked up into tired eyes, filmed a pale amber that reminded her of Tsecha's. "You've been thinking about this a lot."

"Val does most of that sort of thinking. I listen and take notes." John smiled, then walked over to a free-standing terrarium and smoothed a hand over a broad green leaf. "I confirmed for the umpteenth time that Eamon DeVries has had no more than a paper relationship with Neoclona-Karistos for the past six months of the Common calendar. His labs are closed. His office is dark."

"Do you believe them?"

"Eamon was never the type to command loyalty. I see no reason for senior staff to lie on his behalf, especially if they know that any illegal action on his part could lead to criminal charges against them all." John walked back to the aquarium and grinned at the swordfin. "Looks like you made a friend."

Jani gave the glass a final tap, sending the fish wriggling in a series of tight circles. "I didn't do anything special. I just tapped the glass and it followed."

"I know how it feels." John sniffed, then turned quickly away. "It was a pleasant trip, overall, considering." He looked back at Jani, his expression expectant but guarded, withholding his reaction until he could gauge her response, then temper his accordingly.

"Too bad it couldn't have been under different circumstances." Jani turned away from him just as he moved toward her. "I wish you'd have given a thought to yourself, though. You're a powerful man, and if you throw that power behind me, my enemies will become yours, and potent enemies they are. You're not untouchable."

"I started you down this path. I swore a long time ago that I'd see you through to the end."

"I don't know where the end is."

John stuffed his hands in his pockets and scuffed his shoe against the carpet. "Probably a good idea to have some company along the way, then, isn't it?"

"Probably." Jani headed for the door before John could answer. The hallway was colder, darker. She kidded herself that she knew where she was going and why.

CHAPTER 10

"Fort Karistos has sent up a welcoming party to meet us at the dock. There's a major named Hamil, with whom I've dealt in the past, and a colonel named Brondt, whom Hamil says is sound." Niall set down his coffee cup. "After we disembark, we'll take a scoot ride over to the shuttle slips in the next concourse. We'll be watched all along the way—the usual precautions. Hour or so later, we'll be on the ground at the fort." He took a long pull on his nicstick. "We've cut Feyó and crew out of the picture completely," he continued through a stream of smoke. "And with them, the mysterious Gisa."

Jani tore flakes of crust from a roll, then dropped them onto her plate. "Feyó must have been upset when you told her I wouldn't ride down to Karistos with her."

"She must understand that she left you no choice." John hefted a carafe and refilled Jani's coffee cup, followed by his own and finally, grudgingly, Niall's. "She told you that you were at risk, but couldn't define what that risk was. You had to deal with the information as you saw fit."

The three of them sat in the passenger dining room, the remains of their final *Denali* lunch spread about them. Jani took in the stark blondwood tables and slat chairs, the ceiling coated to display blue sky complete with scudding clouds, the panel walls that exhibited a continuously shifting array of terrestrial nature scenes. *Picnic's over.* She sensed Niall's sidelong examination, John's more direct scrutiny. "I need to pull my gear together." She stood, waving both men back in their seats as they made to rise with her. "Meet you at the ramp after the docking klaxon sounds the all-clear." She sensed their surprise at her leave-taking, and hurried out the door before one of them could ask her why the rush.

"Plague of conscience." Jani wove down the narrow, bright corridors for the next-to-last time, marking the turns and exits, the alarms and dead ends as she had for every ship she'd ever traveled on. "Nerves." Fear at what might await at the dock despite Niall's efforts at incident aversion, and what she knew awaited her on the Elyan surface.

She passed one of the crew members, nodded a greeting, fielded the polite, professional response. *John's people, and he's trained them well.* Not once during the voyage had she noted even the slightest glimmer of reaction to her green-on-green eyes, her dietary requirements, her extended forays in the gym or the library as she worked with the practice swords or hunted for some obscure tract on bornsect history. "I wonder if John ordered them to baby me, or if they made that decision on their own?" She turned down the short corridor that led to her cabin, keyed her way in, and passed through the green and copper sitting room into the bedroom.

She got down on her knees and reached beneath the bed, dragged her duffel into the light, and pulled out underwear and socks. Tossed everything atop a chair and boosted to her feet, savoring as she often did the smooth workings of her changed body. "No more aches. No more pains. Only rebel Haárin who want to kidnap me. Lord Ganesh giveth, and Lord Ganesh taketh away. Remove this obstacle from my path, oh Lord, I pray." She opened her closet and removed the sole item hanging within, a cream white wrapshirt and trousers she bought during their layover at Padishah, simple and flowing enough to pass even Vynshàrau muster. She tossed it atop the bed. Then she undressed and adjourned to the bathroom to shower.

The first warning klaxon had sounded by the time she emerged, giving notice that Elyas Station had confirmed the *Denali*'s ID and docking privileges and that approach could commence. She dressed with more than usual care, making sure that she tied the wrapshirt sash neatly and gave her brown boots a brisk wipedown.

"Where's Lucien when I need him?" she muttered as she retied the sash. He'd performed cabin steward duties for her during her first trip to Earth, and embedded a sense of doubt concerning her clothes sense that had stayed with her ever since. "No makeup," she added as she dug once more through her duffel. The Haárin didn't paint their faces, and the gold undertones in her brown skin tended to overwhelm any other color she added.

She pulled a small net bag from a side pocket and removed the single object it contained. "Time to show you to company," she said as she held the ring up to the light. The gold band glittered, the clear red stone darkened to burgundy by the chemical illumination. "My ring of office." A long-ago gift from Tsecha that she had only been able to wear in the last year, fashioned as it was not for the human she had been, but for the hybrid she'd become. She slipped it on the third finger of her right hand, then reached back in the bag for her outfit's finishing touch.

"You are going to piss off some folk, I think," she said as she shook out the off-white overrobe. One of Tsecha's long-discarded robes of office, its rough cloth pulled as she drew it on, bunching the sleeves of her wrapshirt and dragging across her shoulders.

It was most as difficult to wear, nìa, and truly. When Sànalàn helped me don it, she was forced to yank it as though she dressed a squirming youngish.

"That's because you are a squirming youngish, inshah," Jani said with a smile. She shot the red-slashed cuffs, then regarded herself in the full-length mirror set into the opposite wall.

She didn't recognize herself at first. The pale color of the clothing threw her black hair and dark skin into sharp relief, making her face and hands seem like holes in the air.

Then, slowly, she slipped into focus, this half-woman she had become, clothed in the vestments of an alien religion she had yet to claim as her own. Her jaw and chin, too long for humanish, too narrow and rounded for an adult Vynshàrau. Taller than most humanish females, yet shorter than most Vynshàrau by half a head or more. In-between neck. In-between eyes. Not quite idomeni, yet no longer human enough.

You believe in order, nìa. Therefore you are of Shiou whether you honor her or not. One of Tsecha's lessons wended through her head. *You are my toxin, my Kièrshia, bringer of pain and change. Therefore you are also of Caith, whether you honor her or not as well. When you act for me, you are of me, as much as though I myself attended.*

Jani studied herself for a moment, then turned back to the chair and hefted her duffel. Looked around the bedroom for the last time, a delicate place in bronze and shades of blue that despite its richness still felt as transitory as every billet she'd ever traded her documents services or language skills for. In the background, the final docking klaxons sounded, first softly, then louder and more strident as the *Denali* drew into its slip and ended its five and a half week journey with a single, barely detectable shudder.

She set the duffel back on the bed, dug into the scanproof pocket, and removed her shooter. She held it up to the light as she had her ring, and examined the casing. Scuffed blue, the metal nicked and gouged. "And now I am of Jani Kilian as well." She drove the powerpack into the grip with the heel of her hand, felt the weapon purr to life. "This I know, and truly." She slipped the shooter into her trouser pocket, shouldered her duffel, and left.

John and Niall waited for her in the ramp enclosure. They had returned to their usual formality, John in a daysuit of light blue, Niall in dress blue-greys. They both started when they saw her walk toward them, their gazes riveted as though they'd never seen her before. John smiled eventually. Niall didn't.

Jani rounded her shoulders as she drew near, and slipped into a croaky, crabbed mutter. "When shall we three meet again, in thunder, lightning, or in rain?"

John's eyes widened. Then he threw back his head, his dark laugh filling the enclosed space.

Niall's reaction proved more subdued, the corner of his mouth turning up slightly as he cleared his throat. "When the hurly-burly's done, when the battle's lost and won." He finally grinned, then shook his head. "Figures you'd read that one."

"The Scottish play—yes, I liked it." Jani slipped in between the two men. "Dathim read it, too. But then, he's drawn to anything with knives in it." She heard a thump from the other side of the door as the first set of seals opened, and her breath caught.

John squared his shoulders. "I buy the first round after we touch down at Fort Karistos."

Niall faced the door and nodded once. "You're on."

Elyas Station's singular decor had been counted among the legends of spaceport architecture from the day rumors of the plans first reached beyond the Outer Circle. The designer, for reasons no one ever fathomed, had ignored the eastern Mediterranean culture that flavored the Elyan colony, instead choosing to indulge her personal fascination with things Gothic, as in stained glass, stone vaults, and the odd gargoyle or two.

"Damned place always reminded me of my worst hangover." Niall led Jani and John into the arched and transepted Service concourse, the clash of voices and background music battering them like artillery. "If I'd been the Elyans, I'd have blown the damned thing to bits before it opened."

"Well, they always did have an odd sense of humor, as I recall." John turned to Jani. "I was last here five years ago, when we opened the Karistos facility. They had dubbed this place 'Our Lady of the White Elephant.' I've forgotten the Elyan Greek translation."

"Should've been 'Our Lady of the Hangover,'" Niall grumbled as he eyed the gargoyle that glared down from atop a nearby shop awning.

"Colonel Pierce, sir. A pleasure to see you again." A mainline major in summerweights broke away from the edge of the concourse bustle and started toward them, followed by a sideline colonel in similar kit. "Major Hamil, Diplomatic Annex." He smiled at Jani, then stepped back to allow the colonel to come to the fore. "This is Colonel Brondt, Office of the Station Liaison."

Niall nodded to Hamil and shook hands with Brondt. "I thought you'd have met us right at the gate, Colonel, considering the gravity of the situation."

"You haven't been out of sight since you disembarked, Colonel." Brondt had the relaxed air of a man who handled at least one major crisis per station-week. He was the same height as Niall, with the stocky build and broad-boned face that betrayed the Hortensian German origins his schooled accent managed to hide, and an indoor pallor that spoke to a career spent in stations like this. "Your shuttle is a five-minute walk down the first starboard transept." He shook John's hand, then turned to Jani. "Ná Kièrshia. *A tún a vrest dinau.*" He tilted his head to the left and brought up his curved left hand, palm up, in a single easy motion, a sound gesture of respect.

"A glorious afternoon to you as well, Colonel." Jani's gesture mirrored his, even though she stuck to English. "My compliments on your Sìah Haárin."

"You learn fast on this job, ná Kièrshia, or you don't have it for long." Brondt stood back and gestured for them all to walk ahead of him. "Now, let's get you out of here."

Niall and John walked ahead, followed by Hamil, who seemed adept at stepping aside and staying out of the way. Jani fell in behind, soaking in the Station ambience for the first time in years. *Ah, the insanity.* She passed a carving of a long-unseated Prime Minister done up with the doun face and robes of a medieval saint, and put her hand over her mouth to hide her smile. No telling the political leanings of her Service hosts, and she didn't want to risk ticking off the very folks charged with seeing her safely out of the station.

"How was your trip?"

Jani glanced to the side to find Brondt walking beside her. "Not bad. Pretty uneventful, really. I worked. Studied. Caught up on my sleep. The usual long-haul pastimes."

"So you're ready to just dive in here and get to the matter at hand?" Brondt's face brightened, the emotion casting an unnatural sheen over his skin. "Whatever that happens to be," he added, the flush rising. "None of my business, of course."

You're absolutely right about that, Colonel. Jani quickened her step as the distance between her and John and Niall grew. "Yes. The matter at hand." Either several troop transports had disgorged at once or all the shops held sales at the same time—Spacers clogged the concourse, veering in front of them, cutting around them, their shouts and laughter bouncing off the hard, nonabsorbing station surfaces.

Jani pressed her hands to her temples to ease the throbbing in her head.

"You could have brought us in to a less busy area of the station, Colonel!" Niall shouted over his shoulder.

"I'm a great believer in hiding in plain sight, Colonel." Brondt smiled at Jani, his manner as unperturbed as if the concourse had been deserted. "Alone's not the same as hidden." He quickened his step so he walked slightly ahead of Jani, bumping her shoulder just as she was about to pass a pair of giggling SFCs and veering her off course.

"Colonel, I was trying to—" Jani turned to Brondt as they passed beneath a round of stained glass—the gold and pink lighting shone on his face, coloring his skin and defining his features. His forehead, so broad and high. His jaw, a shade too full and long for his round face. His eyes, a brown so dark as to be black. Flat. Dead. As blank as those of the young male in the image. As empty as her own eyes had been when she used to film them, when their green-on-green had become so dark that only the most opaque covering would do. When their hybrid nature—

Hybrid—

Hybrid—

Brondt met her gaze, and she knew. He sensed her surmise—his expression brightened for the barest instant, making him look quite young.

Then Jani heard sounds of argument, and looked ahead to find Niall barking at Hamil and pointing at her, John craning to sight her in the crowd. Felt a hand on her arm, and looked down to find Brondt's fingers closed around her wrist.

"There are currently three shooters trained on them." He spoke Sìah Haárin, stripped of gesture and barely audible above the noise. "If you try to get away, we will force the situation. But I don't want that to happen. Please." He shook his head. "The ones helping me—they're rather excitable. They don't understand half measures, and we were told to do whatever was necessary to bring you in." He pointed down a narrow chase that ran between two storefronts. "This way."

Jani rebalanced her weight so he couldn't pull her forward. "Call off your dogs and I'll go with you."

"Not until we have you secured."

"Call them off."

"*I. Can't.*" Brondt pulled her toward the chase. "Your friends are trying to force their way back here—we have five seconds, probably less—please, Kièrshia, *now!*"

Jani looked ahead. Saw Niall shoulder Hamil aside and push back through the crowd toward her. Saw John reach into his pocket, where he'd no doubt stashed his S-40. *No, John—they'll think you know what you're doing!* "I'm going. I'm going."

"Hurry." Brondt pulled her after him through the gap.

Jani felt her head clear as the noise damped to nothing, the only sounds her boots and Brondt's tietops striking the bare flooring. She tried to loosen his hold on her wrist, but he just gripped tighter, glancing back at her as though he sensed her trying to make her move. "I'll remember this."

"We—" Brondt lifted his free hand in pleading. "We have our reasons."

"You don't have any that are good enough." Jani tried to drag back as sounds reached her from behind. Shouts. Running.

Then Brondt pushed against what looked like bare wall. A panel slid open, and he yanked Jani after him into the dark. "Co-operation is the best move now, really." He let her momentum carry her ahead of him, stripping her duffel from her shoulder and tossing it aside, grabbing her free wrist from behind so he trapped them both. Then he moved in close, shoving one of his feet between hers and kicking them wider apart so she couldn't gain the leverage to kick back or pull forward. Then he raised her hand to her own mouth and clapped it over so she couldn't cry out, and held her for the few vital seconds it took for the footsteps pounding down the chase to reach the panel then pass it by.

Jani took in the tight, dusty space lined with array boxes and exposed conduit, inset safety lighting barely sufficient to cut through the gloom.

"The woman who designed this place, bless her, loved her cubbyholes. The shopkeepers here lost merchandise like water until we mapped them all out." Brondt pulled Jani's hand from her mouth. "I'm going to step back and release you. Now."

As soon as Jani felt Brondt's grip loosen, she turned, swinging out her arm and kicking her leg out and around. Unfortunately, she struck empty air—Brondt had leaped clear and stood against the far wall, breathing heavily.

"Your reputation precedes you, Kièrshia. I will admit to feeling concern when ná Gisa told me that I needed to subdue you by myself." He ran a hand over his rumpled shirtfront, then pushed away from the wall. "Now, if you would follow me, please."

Jani freed her shooter from her pocket. "One thing you can say for Service docks—they never scan for weapons because most everyone is armed." She aimed at Brondt and sighted down. "We're going back out to the concourse. Unfasten the top two closures of your shirt and turn around, arms at your sides."

"Ná Kièrshia, *please*." Brondt sighed heavily, then did as she asked. "You don't understand the situation."

"In my experience, no one who took me hostage ever had my best interests at heart. That's the only aspect of the situation I've ever needed to understand." Jani edged close enough to Brondt to grab his shirt by the collar and yank down, dragging it around his elbows and effectively pinning his arms to his sides. "You walk out ahead of me," she said as she patted him down. "Try to strike me, I'll shoot you. Try to run, I'll shoot you."

"I'm not armed," Brondt said.

"You should've been. Kidnapping isn't a gentleman's game." Jani backed off and waved him ahead of her. "We'll wait in the concourse for John and Niall. Then we'll return to your office and have a nice long talk."

"Aren't you even going to ask?" Brondt moved toward the panel while trying to look at her over his shoulder. "I must be the first hybrid you've ever met. I must be. Don't you care?"

"No, she doesn't, boyo," a familiar voice rasped through the murk. "She's too busy thinking about how best to drop you if you try to run." A wet chuckle sounded. "I know where Johnny and the colonel are. They're still under our guns, so to speak. Drop your weapon."

"Doctor DeVries." Jani let her shooter hand fall. "It hasn't been long enough."

"Tell me, Kilian, tell me." Footsteps crunched. A figure cut through the dimness, as short and stocky as Brondt, but bent, with the plod of the terminally desk-bound. "With rings on her fingers and blood on her clothes, she shall sow chaos wherever she goes." Eamon DeVries moved beneath one of the inset lights, which cast a sickly green light across a slack face, a wattled neck. "I take it back. No blood. Only because I got here in time." He raised a shooter, a sister to John's S-40. "As you can see, I'm no gentleman. But we've both always known that, haven't we? Brondt, you damned fool, button yourself up and take her shooter." He jerked his head toward the rear of the space. "There's an opening back there that leads to the shuttle docks. Let's go."

CHAPTER 11

The rear opening of the cubbyhole led to a series of short corridors, the drift in design of doors, the rise in temperature, and the language on identity plates indicating the transition to the Haárin wing of the station. Humanish seldom did business there in person—both Brondt in his Service uniform and Eamon in his Elyan-style overshirt and loose trousers drew attention from the passengers and crew members who walked the concourse. Jani, however, managed to trump them both by virtue of her propitiator's overrobe. The clash between the traditional bornsect garb and her distinctly humanish hairstyle attracted puzzled postures, and more.

"We're being followed." Eamon glanced over his shoulder at the scattered groups that shadowed them. "You should have stripped that damned shirt off her first thing, boyo."

"I couldn't do that," Brondt muttered under his breath. "She's ní Tsecha's suborn. She's Kièrshia."

"She's a gutter-bred git named Jani Moragh Kilian, and she'd have shot you without a second thought." Eamon glared at her sidelong. "You knew this would happen, didn't you?"

"Didn't occur to me, no. Just a happy accident." Jani made a show of sniffing the air. "That's one thing you always notice on the Haárin side of a station—no food odors. Scents as fresh as recycled air can be."

"Belt it." Eamon steered her down a half-lit walkway. "Thank bloody God," he said as they approached a shuttle boarding ramp.

"You're sure it's the right one?" Jani looked around in mock anxiety. "You're sure you didn't pick the wrong ramp in a panic?"

Eamon grabbed her arm above the elbow and yanked her to a

stop, then shoved his shooter in her face. *"I should just shoot you now!"*

Jani looked down at him over the barrel—she stood a full head taller, and could tell from the way his glare flickered that it bothered him. "John would kill you," she said softly, "and I would save you a seat in hell."

Eamon's eyes narrowed at the mention of John, his finger twitching above the shooter charge-through.

"We have to go." Brondt pushed Jani aside until he stood in the shooter's path. *"Now*, Doctor. This is not the place." He stared Eamon down until the man turned away with a huff. Then he prodded them both down the ramp toward the shuttle entry as a crowd of curious Haárin watched from the concourse.

The shuttle appeared half filled by the time they entered the main cabin. "They saved you the throne of honor in the back of the craft." Eamon pointed to an empty seat in the middle of the rearmost row, located at the end of the aisle. "Go there and sit tight and shut up."

Jani headed down the aisle toward her seat, mindful of the rapt gazes that followed her. She tried to study them without seeming to, curiosity warring with anger at her predicament. *One . . . ten . . . seventeen . . .* Seventeen faces, hybrid all, yet . . . *Some of them look humanish. Some look Haárin. And some . . . I can't tell.* Humanish who looked much as Haárin, who wore flowing trousers and overrobes and had arranged their hair in braided fringes and napeknots. Haárin who wore trousers and tunics, shirts with neckpieces, long skirts and wrapdresses, their hair worn long and loose or trimmed close to their heads. *Dathim would howl.* His sheared head, which he thought so daring, wouldn't have earned him a guest pass into this club.

She reached her seat and lowered into it, gripping the arms for support as her knees went wobbly. As one, the hybrids turned back to watch her, their expressions ranging from expectant to eager to, in a few cases, fearful. One of those belonged to the helpful Major Hamil, who sat by a window and seemed intent on ducking behind his seatback whenever Jani looked in his direction.

"Let's get going!" Eamon called out from his seat in the middle of the cabin. "Half the Haárin in the station saw us. Someone must have reported us by now."

"We can't." Brondt paced the aisle and checked his timepiece. "Torin's not—"

A commotion in the front of the shuttle claimed everyone's

attention. At first Jani thought that John and Niall had tracked her down, but the disturbance turned out to be a late arrival, a young hybrid who shot through the cabin door as though someone tossed him. He careened off the wall opposite the opening, then staggered down the aisle as he tried to regain his balance.

"Sorry! Sorry!" He righted himself, all elbows and long legs, and leaned against Brondt for support. "The stationmaster just closed down the connections between the humanish and Haárin sections. If we don't break away in the next five minutes, we'll get caught in a sweep. They've already called out—" His eyes met Jani's and he fell silent.

The face from the image, the hair a little lighter than she recalled, the skin a little darker. *It's summertime in Karistos*. She tried to calibrate her knowledge of the place's seasons against the Commonwealth calendar. *Late summer, edging into autumn*. He must have spent a great deal of time outside. *Torin*.

"They've already called out station security." Torin started toward the rear of the cabin again, his step slower and steadier, eyes still on Jani. "The Haárin are always slow to respond to any alarms from the humanish side. If we're in the breakaway queue, they should let us leave."

"We'll be in the queue as soon as you sit yourself down and strap in." Eamon reached out and pushed Torin toward an empty aisle seat. "Now get to it!"

Jani saw Torin make a sour face at Brondt as he fell into the seat and secured himself, saw Brondt clench his fist close to his body, out of sight of Eamon, and pump it once in encouragement. *The two of them are allies—they sent Torin's image to John.* She adjusted her own safety straps as she pondered what she sensed so far. *Torin and Brondt don't like Eamon, and I'm guessing Eamon doesn't like them either. This would mean that Eamon doesn't know about the image. Assuming he's working closely with Gisa, that means she doesn't know, either.* The cabin lights fluttered, and she felt the telltale vibration of the shuttle engines rattle up through the bottom of her seat. *Threats, kidnappings, hurried exits, and dissension in the ranks.* She sat back. "Chicago, it's as if I never left you."

"Did you say something, ná Kièrshia?"

Jani looked up to find Brondt standing over her, her duffel in his hand. "I prayed, Colonel. Spacecraft make me nervous."

"I can't see much of anything making you nervous." Brondt lowered Jani's bag to the floor at her feet, then bent low to grapple it to the seat support. "I've returned everything but your shooter," he said as he straightened back up.

"Trusting of you." Jani drew in her legs so he could maneuver into the open seat in the row in front of her.

"Personally, I think I could have returned it to you. If you were going to try something, you'd have done so by now. Your history is one of a woman who doesn't hesitate." Brondt sat down and strapped in just as the shuttle accelerated, pushing them both back against their seatbacks. "You're angry, yes, but I also think that you're as struck by us as we are by you. If I'd released you at any time during our gauntlet run here, I'd have bet a year's paychit you wouldn't have made a move to flee. And I'd have won."

"You're sure about that?" Jani stared at the back of Brondt's head, but he didn't turn around or respond, and deep down she knew it was just as well.

Jani eased out of her seat and scooted down to the observation port at the end of her empty row as soon as the shuttle had punched through the Elyan stratosphere. She knew the other hybrids watched her and that they would probably report her interest to Gisa. *I just want to see where I'm going*, she told herself, and almost believed it.

"Have you been to Elyas before, ná Kièrshia?"

Jani turned from the port to find Torin at her elbow. Like Brondt, he'd settled upon a humanish look, filming his eyes the same dead green he wore in the image and dressing in trousers and a short-sleeve pullover in shades of brown. Up close, the gold tone of his skin was more easily defined, the slight elongation of his facial bones more readily discerned. He had a mobile, expressive face and restless hands, the corners of his mouth twitching as he plucked at the seatback in front of him.

"Only the station. Not the surface." Jani looked out the port again as the shuttle banked over a midnight-blue sea, then coursed along a line of steep cliffs.

"The largest settlements are built around the Bay of Siros." Torin pushed an empty seat forward and wedged into the row beside her. "Karistos is on the opposite side. So's the fort. We're on this side."

"The hybrid enclave." Jani repeated the phrase to herself once, then again, wondering at its sound, its meaning. Reminded herself that she had come here for a purpose, and that she was being held against her will. That John and Niall searched for her. That she was a hostage among captors, one of whom would cheerfully shoot her if she gave him any reason at all.

"We've called it Thalassa," Torin said, his eyes fixed on the view outside the port. "We're coming up on it . . . *now*."

The shuttle rounded a cliff bend, and Thalassa appeared. Narrow streets crawled along the cliff edges and partway down the slopes, lined with boxy white and cream structures, single and multistoried, some topped with colored domes of pale blue or yellow, others with flat roofs patched with small gardens. In the center of it all loomed a larger building, four stories of white and cream stone, edges rounded and polished, which seemed to emerge from the layered rock like the nose of a star liner that had crashed into the far side of the mountain and tunneled through to rest near the cliff's edge.

"That's the main house." Brondt had worked his way into the gap behind Torin. "Doctor DeVries lives there, and our dominants. Our meeting rooms are there, and the library, and the clinic." He glanced at Jani, gauging her reaction. "It's quite a settlement."

Paid for with Neoclona money, in direct violation of a Neoclona contract. Jani felt a tingle between her shoulder blades, and turned to find Eamon staring at the three of them. *As soon as John reaches Fort Karistos, he's going to track you down.* She turned back to the port. *And when he sees all this . . .*

"We have to strap in," Brondt said. "We'll be landing soon."

After another bank and turn, the shuttle touched down on a well-maintained runway about 250 meters from the settlement. Everyone stood as the door opened and the exit ramp lowered, except for Brondt, who remained in his seat in front of Jani.

"You'll leave last, of course." He held back as the others streamed out, row after row. "What do you think so far?"

"I think I've seen performances at the Lyric Opera that were less rehearsed." Jani reached down to unstrap her duffel so she wouldn't have to witness the way the color flooded Brondt's face. "I'm not here by choice, but by threat. I'm your prisoner. I'd advise you to not forget that fact, Colonel, because I certainly won't."

"I understand your anger." Brondt smoothed a hand over the arm of his seat, a back and forth action that seemed to calm him. "All we ask is that you watch, and listen, and keep an open mind."

Jani rose. "You're asking a lot."

"I don't think so." He offered a half-smile, then rose and started down the aisle.

Jani waited until he had gone halfway down the aisle before she shouldered her bag and followed. When she reached the ramp, she stood at the top of the stair for a time and let the Elyan sun beat through her clothes and pummel her bones, and watched the other hybrids hurry up the path. Some were met by those who had stayed behind, while some remained alone. Torin, she noticed, hooked up with an older female and another young male and disappeared down one of the winding lanes that led to the smaller houses.

What sort of place is this? Jani stepped down the ramp stair, mindful of the salt-scented breeze that whipped her trouser cuffs around her ankles and floated her overrobe behind her like a cape. *Thalassa was a goddess, a personification of the sea.* She raked through the scant remains of her classical education for anything else concerning sea deities or legends. *I remember lots of monsters, and drownings.* Her boots crunched on the runway. *Ships dashed upon the rocks.* From her vantage point she could see only the top of a few of the domes, the main house jutting above it all like the prow of an ancient watercraft.

It was a stark, desolate landscape. What trees there were grew gnarled and stunted, with silvery-green leaves and thorns as long and thick as fingers. A scattering of knee-high tufts of reddish grass formed the only ground cover; Jani caught sight of tiny rodents darting from beneath them to the more reliable shelter of the rocks as she walked up the path that led to the settlement.

Brondt waited for her at the point where the path graded up toward the house. He had appointed himself her escort—that much was obvious—but whether he did so in his name or Gisa's had yet to be determined. "We had some rain last night," he said, holding up his hand as though waiting for more drops to strike. "That floods the smaller animals out of their holes. Insects come out at dusk that burrow under your skin to lay their eggs. If you have any cuts or sores, better bandage them. You saw some of the rodents. They like to get into the closets and build nests in your shoes—the scent repellents don't seem to work. And you'll hear howling. Those are the feral dogs. Walking alone in the dark isn't advised—the sound fences don't seem to work very well to keep them away. No one's ever been attacked, but a pair of them did follow Torin right up to the entry of the main house once." He'd switched out his tietops for hiking boots on the shuttle, and handled the rocky path as easily as if he walked on pavement. "That remark you made about the opera, and performances." He sighed. "You have a reputation for seeing things as they are. All I'm asking is that you reserve judgment until you see the rest of the play."

"That's the second time you've mentioned my background." Jani quickened her pace to catch Brondt up, only to have him hurry that much faster, to stay one respectful stride ahead of her. "My reputation. My history. My past is not the issue here."

"Your past dictates our present. Our future." Brondt looked back at her. "Don't you understand? You were the *first.*" Before he could say more, the front door of the house opened. Two figures stepped out into the shaded entry, but only one of them continued into the sun. A female in her middle years, dressed in humanish-style trousers and a short-sleeve shirt in the same yellow and blue as the domed roofs.

"Glories of the day to you, Kièrshiarauta!" she called in lightly accented English. She wore her brown hair in a braid that draped over one shoulder, and a series of gold hoops along the edge of one ear. "It is a great and godly thing that you are here. All of Thalassa rejoices, and I, Gisa Pilon, rejoice the most!"

As Jani drew closer, more details of the female's appearance came into focus—her forearms, which bore the scars of multiple challenges, and her Sìah grey eyes, which contained a coolness missing from her voice and her manner. "Ná Gisa." Jani raised her right hand in a simple humanish greeting, a gesture calculated to reveal nothing of her dismay.

Feyó looked me in the face and denied knowing anything about Torin. But how could she acknowledge Gisa as her rival without knowing about Thalassa, and who lived here? *She couldn't.* That meant she lied, as blatantly as any humanish. *But why? What the hell have I walked into?* She blanked her expression as best she could. The time had come to count the cards and play them close to the vest. "Godliness, I most fear, had very little to do with my attendance here."

Gisa's step hitched as she walked down the path. She glanced at Brondt, then quickly away. "All that is fated is godly," she said after a moment, "and your presence here was foretold by ní Tsecha himself."

"Ní Tsecha. Yes." Jani brushed past Gisa and continued up the path. "We must soon speak of ní Tsecha, and truly," she added as she passed into the shadowed entryway.

"Glories of the day to you, ná Kièrshia," Gisa's companion called out in English, sibilant and monotonal.

"Glories of the day—to you." Jani stopped, and hoped the darkness hid her expression.

Gisa's companion was apparently female, judging from the higher pitch of its voice and the narrowness of its shoulders beneath its thin green coverall. "Indeed was your presence foretold, and we have waited for so long." A figure from a dark place, skin a mottle of pale yellow patched with tan and brown, eyes milky blue like dirty snow, dull brown hair close-cropped, the discolored scalp visible beneath.

Jani nodded once in acknowledgment, and hoped that the shock she felt didn't show. She had spent years subsisting in the less traveled reaches of the Commonwealth, and knew that medical conditions that would never have existed in the Jewelers Loop or the Channel Worlds sometimes cropped up in such places. But this female appeared more Haárin than humanish, and even the most radical outcasts kept their illnesses private, for they believed such exposed weakness threatened the welfare of the soul. "What is your name?"

The female bared her teeth, red-brown as the darkest patches of her skin. "I am Bon." She took a step back, then beckoned in humanish invitation with a bandage-swaddled hand. "You must enter, ná Kièrshia, and see the place we have prepared for you!" She keyed the door open and stepped inside the house, waving for Brondt and Gisa to enter before Jani, in keeping with protocol.

Jani waited for the pair to precede her, then stepped inside. She sensed that she was being watched, but she couldn't tell by whom, or where they had hidden themselves.

What she finally saw comforted the eye with its simplicity. The bottom floor of the house formed a graceful U-shaped flow of half-open rooms separated by waist-high barriers and flower-filled planters. In the center was a partially roofed courtyard decorated with fountains and fruit trees, walled at the open end of the U by the mountain and around the curve by walkways that trimmed the three upper floors. The pale earth tones of the stone predominated, accented by the jewel colors of the foliage. Only in Rauta Sheràa had Jani seen houses so well-met with their surroundings.

"Stunned unto silence, she is. A miracle." Eamon walked out of the gloom to join them, a frosted glass in hand. "The last time I saw you this quiet, Johnny and I had just pulled you out of the regen tank. Had to siphon out your mouth with a hose. I told Johnny that was a mistake." He raised his drink in a toast, then tossed it back as though he stood at a Karistos bar, not in the presence of two Haárin.

Jani checked Gisa and Bon for their reactions, and found them regarding her calmly. *They planned this. It's all part of the show.* She looked around, and found that she was indeed being watched—heads poked up over the backs of chairs and around the ends of couches, and took note of her every move.

"You hide your surprise well, ná Kièrshia." Gisa looked toward the assembled hybrids, a glow of pride informing her sharp features with a lightness seldom seen on an idomeni face. "Whatever you believe, ní Tsecha would be most as pleased. This is his blended world. This is what he prophesied so long ago. It is the future as we all know it shall be. Why then must we continue to suborn ourselves to old ways, and those who promote them?"

Jani looked toward the representatives of the blended world, and felt a roomload of bright-eyed expectancy enclose her like a noose. "By 'old ways,' you mean ná Feyó. You would challenge her for dominance of the Elyan Haárin."

"Such is my right, as dominant of the Thalassans."

"Is this place recognized by the Outer Circle Haárin as an enclave? Have members of the Trade Association visited to pay their respects?"

"Such is only a matter of time."

"When that time comes, if it comes, will be the moment to offer challenge, not before." Jani kept her voice low, speaking rapid, ungestured English she hoped most of the hybrids couldn't understand. "You will have to do better than that if you wish to dominate Haárin, and you will have to do better than that if you wish ní Tsecha's support."

Gisa offered an arrogant smile. "That, ná Kièrshia, is why you are here."

"I think I'll take a walk outside." Jani brushed back her overrobe and shoved her hands in her trouser pockets to stop their shaking. "By myself, if I'm allowed."

"But ná Kièrshia," Bon called after her. "We wish to show—"

"A walk. Alone." Jani's boot heels struck the bare tile, the sharp clip echoing throughout the space. The door opened as she approached, and she shouldered through before it opened completely, the whine of the mechanism following her like a siren wail.

CHAPTER 12

Jani walked around to the bay side of the house, veering off the path and through the red-green scrub toward the cliff. The sun pressed down like a physical force, while the breeze brought with it the smell of the sea, but little coolness.

"John, did you get away? Niall?" She toed the cliff edge, kicking a stone over the side and watching it plummet to the waves below. "Are you still at the station? At Fort Karistos? Did you contact ná Feyó?" She squinted out over the water and watched white seabirds with black-tipped wings swoop and drift, answering her questions with screeches. Then she scanned past them toward the cliffs on the opposite side of the bay, straining to catch sight of Karistos, or the fort, searching the skies for the telltale glint of a shuttle coming in for a landing.

"They're trying to sandbag me. Everywhere I turn, I see eyes like mine. Faces. They want me to feel at home, to forget that they brought me here by force, that they threatened my friends." The noise of the seabirds faded into the background as her thoughts turned inward and her perceptions narrowed. Now she saw a rodent skitter across the rocks, heard the rustling hum of insects emerge from the dried grass. Sensed movement behind her even though she couldn't see it, and reached into her duffel for the shooter that wasn't there.

"We mean you no harm, ná Kièrshia."

Jani turned to find Brondt standing behind her, off to one side. He still wore summerweights, but had removed his eyefilms—his irises proved a strange yellow-green that reminded Jani of a cat. *And he moves like one, for all his heft. Now you see him, now you don't.* "Colonel." She nodded. "You'll have to forgive me. Imprisonment makes me jumpy."

Brondt stepped forward as far as he could, so he stood a half a pace or so in front of her. While the position may have been more respectful, it was also dangerous—the tips of his boots extended beyond the cliff edge, and pebbles tumbled and bounced down the steep incline each time he shifted his weight. "You're not imprisoned, ná Kièrshia."

"I'm not?" Jani let her arms hang at her sides, swung them forward so her hands met with a soft clap, then back again. "You mean that if I happened upon one of the enclave skimmers and made to drive out of here, you'd let me go?"

"Yes."

Jani fanned her face with her hand. For the first time since the Chicago summer, she felt sweat trickle down her back. She let her duffel slip to the ground, removed her overrobe, and tied the thin garment around her waist. "You sent Torin's image to John Shroud. Why?"

Brondt stared out over the bay. "I don't know what you're talking about."

Still human enough to lie. Jani picked up her duffel and slung it across her back, a position that left her arms free and allowed her to reach the strap disconnect if she needed to drop the bag in a hurry. "Neither you nor Torin like Eamon DeVries—that's obvious. Do you feel his medical skills have proven inadequate to the task of caring for the hybrids? Do you think he needs help? Don't tell me that he wanted John to come out here—he'll lose his place as Neoclona's third leg when John confirms that he's been engaging in research his contract bars him from performing." She stepped back from the edge, picked up a stone, and flung it into the bay. "Eamon seems fairly well allied with Gisa. Does your disaffection with him extend to her as well?"

Brondt stared back at her, eyes wide, sclera glinting yellow in the bright sun. "Disaffection is too strong a word," he said softly. "Concern, perhaps. Uneasiness."

"Gisa has brought the Outer Circle to the edge of disorder."

"Perhaps she had help."

Jani walked the cliff edge. Then she started down a narrow path that widened as it angled toward a row of houses that had been built on a road cut into the cliff face. "Tell me about Thalassa, Colonel Brondt."

Brondt hesitated, then started after her. "My name's Dieter," he said as he edged past Jani on the path and reasserted his suborn position in front of her. "We've lived here for six months of the Common calendar. Construction is still going on, but we've all the primary structures in, courtesy of Doctor DeVries. Houses. Storage. Community buildings, garages and such." He led her past the first of the houses, a two-floor white structure with rounded corners, its windows shuttered with yellow slating. Like the other houses on the cliff side of the street, it had been built flush against the cliff face, so that the rock served as one of its walls. The houses on the bay side, however, were freestanding, the sun lighting them into brilliant boxes of coated stone.

"Six months?" Jani followed Brondt down the street. "Is that how long you've been hybrids?"

"No—some of us have been receiving treatment for quite some time." Brondt glanced back at Jani and smiled. "You should see the look on your face. So surprised. You've been one of many for several years now."

Jani heard the sounds of opening doors—before long, a small crowd of hybrids lined both sides of the street. Some waved at her, while others bared their teeth. She recognized a few from the shuttle, but other faces were new. The youngest were teenage like Torin, with spindle limbs and faces that brought back memories of the bazaars of Rauta Shèràa, when the sharp scent of *vrel* blossom permeated the air and the rise and fall of a score of idomeni tongues had filled her ears. "Why did you do it?"

"Some of us had no choice." Brondt stopped to pick a dead leaf from a potted shrub set in front of one of the houses. "You've heard the hypothesis that there are environmentally induced diseases that can only be cured by hybridization?" He waited for Jani to nod. "We had a few here. Bone and metabolic disorders. Horrible to suffer, to see. Neoclona Karistos could do nothing. Then Doctor DeVries let it be known that other things could be done." His face lit. "What an incredible experience to bear witness to the healing. Within weeks, in some cases, after the treatments began."

Jani wandered farther down the street. Past the last of the houses a building that was little more than a door was set into the cliff face. "And the rest of you?"

"We believe in change, and the need for a better world." Brondt's quiet, clipped voice infused the words with a sincerity that a more passionate pronouncement would have overshot. "In blending, there is strength."

"You're a Service officer."

"Yes. Hamil and I both."

Jani thought of Niall, tracking Brondt through Fort Karistos systems, closing in. The wolf on the scent. "You're finished."

"We expected to be finished about the time our next physicals rolled around, anyway." Brondt reached up and touched the leaf that studded the corner of one collar tip. "They were good posts while they lasted. We had access to a great deal of intelligence. We knew all about Colonel Pierce's assignment, for example. That allowed us plenty of time to cover tracks and rearrange the furniture." He smiled, this time more coolly. "The man is, in many ways, almost comically obvious in his methods."

Jani felt the blood rise. "He's just as obvious in his temper, his influence, and his dedication."

"And he's your friend." Brondt's smile faded. "Considering the circumstances, I wonder how that can be possible."

Jani paced the street, beating down an idomeni temper that struggled to surge to the surface. "Any significance to the domes?" she asked, because the color drew her fevered eye and she fixed on it for want of anything more calming.

Brondt fell back into his role as tour guide. "In Karistos proper the domes signify places of worship, or the homes of priests or rabbis. Here . . ." He shrugged. "The Haárin picked them, for the most part. They like the color." He pointed to the door in the cliff face. "You should be warned—we do experience some heady storms, as well as the occasional land tremor. Each house has its own emergency gear. We also have stations like this set up throughout the enclave." He led Jani down the incline to the hole in the wall and palmed inside.

The interior lit up as soon as they crossed the threshold, to reveal a single, rock-walled room, the walls lined with carton-stacked shelves. The shelving had been bonded to the floor and ceiling to prevent collapse, with nothing stored above shoulder height.

"This is one of the storm shelters. We have flares, food kettles and water generators, blankets and spare clothing and such." Brondt patted the shelving framework, then walked deeper into the room. "In case of tremor, get off the cliff. Go above to the land around the main house, what we call 'the flat.' We've bolstered the houses with shock-dissipating poly infusions, but I'm an old-fashioned boy in that regard. The land always wins."

As Brondt talked, Jani wandered from shelf to shelf, lifting carton lids and checking the contents. When she came upon the flare pistols, she checked her escort to see if he watched. Then she slipped a pistol into her trouser pocket, adjusting her overrobe so it obscured the bulge. She followed up with a couple of charge cartridges, and set the carton lid back into place just as Brondt rejoined her.

"We should get back to the main house." He walked to the door, then waited for her to join him. "It's almost time for mid-afternoon sacrament."

"Cocktails at fifteen-up?" Either she'd kept her voice low enough that Brondt had not heard, or he decided that ignoring her was the better course. She stepped back out into the glare of the day, and found the hybrids gathered at the end of the street. Several others had joined them from other parts of the enclave. Those in the back rows had leaped atop planters for a better view, while some looked down from verandas or second-floor windows.

"Tell us of ní Tsecha, ná Kièrshia!"

"When will he come here?"

"Does he know of us? What will you tell him?"

Jani walked across the street to a shoulder-high boulder that had been left in place like a free-form monument to the rugged terrain. She set her hands and clambered to the top, then edged forward until she stood at the very tip. *Don't look down.* She did anyway, and watched the waves crash against the rocks a hundred meters below.

Then she reached beneath the overrobe into her pocket and pulled out the flare pistol, keeping her back to the other hybrids so they couldn't see what she did. She shoved the charge cartridge into its slot, raised the pistol above her head and squeezed it off. One—two—three—

The flares lofted upward, contrailing blue smoke. The charges blew one after the other, splaying streaks of yellow-white that fanned over the bay like fronds of starlight, brilliant even against the daylight sky. Visible from Karistos, surely. Visible from the Fort.

"*Ná Kièrshia!*" Brondt tried to climb up the rock after her, but cat-quick though he was, he didn't hoist and scramble well.

—four—five. Jani pressed the charge-through again, heard nothing but a hollow click. "Defective cartridge. That's the problem with flare pistols—you can never be sure what the damned thing will do." She reversed the chamber and ejected the clip, then turned to the hybrids, who muttered among themselves and watched her in puzzlement.

"If you wished to notify Doctor Shroud and Colonel Pierce of your presence, ná Kièrshia, you could use one of our comports. It is more direct, and does not smoke and flame."

Jani turned, and saw Gisa standing in the middle of the road, eyeing her in bemusement.

"You are not a prisoner here. There is no reason for you to re-sort to such actions—you may contact your companions and leave at any time." Gisa cocked her head, her look turning thoughtful. "We all have read of your life." She pointed to Torin, who watched from the upper level of one of the houses. "Torin Clase has drawn together all the records, as is his way and his duty as our histo-rian." She let her hand fall to her side, and took a few steps closer to the rock. "I most understand why you would fear entrapment. Your history is that of one who has been chased. Imprisoned. But much as we despised to do what we did, such was the only way we knew we could talk to you as ourselves. If you had gone with Feyó, she would have never brought you here. You would only have known us through her words, her fears."

Jani felt the tug of Gisa's own words. Her voice. *Feyó domi-nates by simple authority. This one tries to be your friend.* She wasn't sure which method she distrusted more. "You despised to do such, yet you did it. You threatened my friends."

Gisa shook her head. "We would not have harmed them."

"I was led to believe differently." Jani glanced at Brondt, who declined to meet her eye. "The Elyan enclave is well-established, while Thalassa is a young place. Why should Feyó fear you?"

"Because we are not of the old ways!" The shout came from one of the houses, and was soon echoed up and down the street.

Gisa remained quiet until the last murmur died away. "Be-cause we are not of the old ways," she repeated softly, showing an actor's gift for timing. "We treat food in the humanish manner, as is sane. We study all aspects of all our many gods. Yet in order to maintain her place among the conservatives, Feyó would compel us to behave fully as Haárin. To take our meals as solitary once more. To take our rules from her." She drew close enough that Jani could see the hard shine in her eyes. "That is the issue, ná Kièr-shia. Are we of ourselves or are we of the Elyan Haárin? Who will represent our wishes in the meeting rooms of the Outer Circle? Feyó, who has never visited this place for fear of contamination by our new ways, or I, who have taken the first steps down the road of ní Tsecha's prediction?"

"Feyó is esteemed by ní Tsecha." Jani stood on the edge of the rock, the flare pistol dangling from her hand. "To humanish and Haárin outside this place, she represents the solidarity of the Outer Circle. If her power is seen to weaken, others will see it as a chance to attack, and Karistos will be as it was only a short time ago. A lawless place, controlled by those who could not give a damn for Haárin, and even less for Thalassa." She tucked the pistol into her waistband and leaped down from the rock. "You must know this if you know anything. Yet you battle Feyó, and Feyó battles you. What neither of you realize is that by your actions, you have put me in the middle. If you know my history as you claim to, you know this is not a sound thing for either of your strategies." She walked past Gisa and the other hybrids, and trudged up the road toward the main house.

After a few moments, she heard footsteps behind her. She picked up her pace, thinking it might be Gisa trying to catch her, but when she heard the muttered curse in Hortensian German, she slowed. "You lied about the threat to my friends, Colonel."

"No, I didn't." Brondt drew alongside her. "Feyó hasn't endeared herself with her heavy-handedness; there were rumors that she had sent her security to wrest you away from Colonel Pierce and escort you back to the Elyan enclave. Some of our more militant denizens took that rumor to heart." His step slowed as his breathing grew labored—the slope was steep and the heat relentless. "They tend to overreact, and Gisa does us no favors by looking the other way. She believes the occasional skirmish will cause everyone to respect us. She does not understand the fear that such behavior could raise, that hybrids are violent, unstable." He stopped to wipe his sleeve across his brow. "At times I feel as though I'm juggling grenades." Jan paused at the cliff's edge and looked to the other side of the bay, where the white buildings of Karistos shone like snow against the red-brown of the rocks. "Could Feyó see those flares? Are they enough to let her know that I'm here?"

"She knows." Brondt spoke so quietly, one might have thought he hadn't spoken at all.

Jani turned back to him, where he stood amid the rocks and stared down at his hands, a weighty figure with a deceptive ability to maneuver. "I work with a captain back in Chicago who has a lot in common with you." Yes, the pieces fit. Yes, they made the usual sort of messy political sense. "You're a spy for Feyó. You're the one who let her know that Gisa planned to kidnap me, then you turned around and did the deed yourself to keep Gisa's trust."

"Ná Feyó knows you're here. She contacted Doctor Shroud and Colonel Pierce immediately after we left the station. She charged me with keeping you safe." Brondt shot Jani a look of Niall-grade frustration. "As I said, you don't make it easy." He took a deep breath, and started up the incline.

Jani waited for him to draw even with her, then continued toward the main house. Other hybrids passed them now, singly or in groups, their looks filled with confusion, anger, or a warring combination of both. "Why didn't you tell me?"

"How would that knowledge have made you feel toward me, better or worse than you do now?" Brondt eyed Jani sidelong, then looked away as though he guessed the answer. "You must understand, I am not against ná Gisa. I just . . ." He sighed. "I want Thalassa to thrive, to prosper. But ná Gisa is too bold and ná Feyó is too timid. There must be a place that is as we are. Somewhere in between."

As she and Brondt turned onto the walkway that led to the house, Jani caught sight of ná Gisa walking up the road behind them, regarding her with a mixture of expectancy and annoyance. A phalanx of hybrids preceded her, muscular males who had once been humanish, rough-edged and callused. *Behold the more militant denizens of Thalassa.* Unpleasant images coursed before her mind's eye of their reaction if they discovered a double agent in their midst. "You're walking a thin line, Colonel."

"Indeed." Brondt drew ahead of her as they approached the entry, and wrestled his expression into one of bland formality. "Remember, ná Kièrshia," he said as he preceded her through the door, "my future is now in your hands."

They entered the house to find the demirooms lit by inset lighting and floor lamps, the chairs and couches occupied by hybrids, many of whom held glasses or cups. *I'll be damned—it really is the cocktail hour.* Jani veered away from the scattered groups toward the courtyard, where a series of long tables had been assembled into a U-shape. Some of the younger hybrids, Torin among them, finished laying out dishes and cutlery, then set out candle bowls at measured intervals, shallow dishes filled with oil atop which floated sparkling fuel cells.

They all eat together. In one room. At the same time. Even though the incident with Eamon's drink had prepared Jani for the fact, the realization still shook her. *Tsecha still follows the old protocols.* As did Dathim, despite his daring in other areas. *How would they react to this?* She settled into the role of observer, so she could describe the scene to them when she returned to Chicago, and so she could set her feelings aside, to deal with later.

"Ná Kièrshia?" Gisa joined Jani at the opening to the courtyard, her composure regained. "You wish something to drink?"

"Water, please." *Followed by a shower, please.* Jani tugged at the overrobe, which remained twisted around her waist, the flare pistol still hidden beneath. Sweat beaded her face, while grime streaked her trouser suit from her scramble up the rocks. "Alcohol isn't worth the bother anymore, and I'm picky when it comes to coffee."

"Been drinking a lot of Johnny's brew of late, have you?" Eamon wandered over, a lime-garnished glass well in hand. "A proper little couple you've become, so I've heard."

"We see one another once in a while." Jani took a glass from a tray carried by an agitated Torin. He'd removed his films since their arrival—as she expected, his eyes proved the same deep green that she saw each time she looked in the mirror. "It isn't very complicated." She watched as he cut across the courtyard, looks passing between him and Brondt as well as the older female that Jani had seen him with after their arrival. Shorter and rounder than any idomeni, her reddish hair in a scalp-hugging clip, she wore a simple shirt and long skirt, and a worried frown.

"I still do not understand humanish pairings." Gisa stepped aside so that Bon could join them. "Here at Thalassa, I see so much I do not understand—fighting and weeping and sadness—all over something so simple. With the blending comes peace to the soul, this I know and truly. The fighting ends, and pairing is approached with reason." She crossed her right arm on her chest, palm inward, in a gesture of humility, then departed for the opposite leg of the U, Bon preceding her.

She doesn't want to talk to me. Jani tasted the water and winced over its bland processed purity. *I've upset her plans to sweep me off my feet.*

"Lost in the surreality of it all, are you, Kilian?" In the few minutes that had passed, the sweat had soaked through the front of Eamon's white overshirt. "You've got that look about you. Dead-faced and still as stone, just like you were the day Johnny explained all the things he'd done to you when you were too comatose to object."

Jani looked across the room as Bon turned toward Gisa and tilted her head in acknowledgment of something her dominant had said. The afternoon sun shone upon the open courtyard and played across her sheared hair, through which showed patches of scalp as mottled and scarred as her face. "What's wrong with Bon?"

Eamon sniffed, then took a healthy swallow of his drink. "Analogue of Günther's disease. One of the autosomal recessive porphyrias. A cutaneous variety, not the neurologic version that you had. She was already heterozygous for it; I had tried to tweak her heme pathway, and damned if I didn't nail just the right mutation to make her homozygous. A one in a million chance, that, but every so often you hit those." He shrugged. "Anyway, a month or so after her last treatment, we moved here. The day was sunny, like they all are, and we whiled away the hours going in and out, ferrying personal belongings and furniture and such." Bon looked toward them, and he lowered his voice. "The porphyrins accumulate in the tissue, the skin. When sunlight hits them, they give off singlet oxygen. Wreaks hell on things organic. The blistering started almost immediately she walked outside. She looked as though she'd been torched by the time we got her downstairs to the clinic."

Jani looked down at her hands, the real and the fake, imagined the ravaging wrought by the heat of the transport explosion, and wondered what it felt like to watch the destruction unfold. "So why haven't you cured her?"

"Do you think I'm a bloody incompetent then?" Eamon curled his lip. "I repaired the mutation that day, but she wouldn't let me mend the scars. They were *à lérine*, she said. A challenge by the sun, which represented any who would prevent her from hybridizing, from becoming as she was meant to be." He held up his open hand in front of Jani's face, then slowly curled his fingers. "Her hands—they're like claws, twisted with scar tissue. She could lose fingers if she doesn't get treatment, but she doesn't care. Her hands for her enclave. Her life, if needed, for her enclave. Fair trade, she calls it." He leaned close, bringing the soupy stink of humanish sweat with him. "They're all like that. This is a religious experience to them—they're the chosen of the gods. You're going to have your hands full managing this herd, my little tin divinity, and it couldn't happen to a more deserving soul." He straightened. "Any other questions?"

"Just one." Jani gave the tasteless water one more chance, then set the glass on the edge of a planter. "Why?"

Eamon's dissolute face set in cruel lines, his weak mouth firming. He'd always been odd man out among the Neoclona Three. He lacked John's elegance, Val's wit and good looks. But he shared their scientific arrogance, and it emerged now, like a mask of youth. "Because they wanted it. Needed it, some of them, to survive." He smiled. "And because I could. Because old Johnny thought he'd nicked my tendons but good, and I proved him wrong."

"I thought you had a contract." Jani grew conscious of movement around her, and stepped closer to the planter to allow hybrids bearing serving dishes room to walk around her to the table. "John and Val stayed out of gadgets, you stayed out of genetics."

"Contracts were made to be broken." Eamon shook his drained glass so the ice rattled. "We'll see how eager Johnny is to rack me after he gets here and we've had a chance to talk. He gets a chance to see what his castoff has done." He headed for the table, then paused and turned back to Jani. "I did it better than he did, you know, the bonny Bon notwithstanding. None of the problems you had with food, with bone and muscle disorders. And I worked over fifty-seven of them. Johnny only worked you." He took a seat near the top of the U and poured another drink from the bottle one of the hybrids had left beside his plate.

Jani waited, knowing that everyone would seat themselves according to rank and that soon only she and Gisa would be left standing. She sniffed the air, expecting the harsh tang of Sìah herbs and spices, and stilled as a more familiar aroma rattled her sinuses. *Curry?* She sniffed again. *And hot plum sauce?* She looked across the room toward Gisa, who had taken her low seat near the top of the U and now gestured to her and pointed to the chair next to hers, the seat of honor, the lowest seat at the table.

"Anything in a blue-rimmed dish is mine," Eamon said as Jani took her place, his burr hatcheting through the softer voices around him. "I made them work out a code after I damned near lost the lining of my mouth to a veg stew."

Jani examined the server that Gisa handed her, which contained a green bean and potato *toran*. "What does a gold rim mean?"

Eamon raised a hand and rocked it up and down in a so-so gesture. "Medium. Anything in the paisley is about your speed. Death to mucus membranes."

Jani lifted the lid of one of the paisley tureens and inhaled. *"Dahi machi."* She ladled some onto her plate. "Fish curry," she added for the benefit of a bewildered-looking Brondt, who sat several seats uptable and poked through the servers as if they could poke back.

"That was our surprise for you, ná Kièrshia. Your fellow Acadians thought to prepare you a proper welcoming meal." Gisa gestured downtable toward two of the younger hybrids, a male and female who nodded toward Jani, pride battling dismay on their faces and not quite winning the battle.

"It's very good." Jani took a large bite for the benefit of one and all.

"Good, yes." Gisa speared more delicately with a twin-pronged Sìah fork. "And yet you question us. Stand upon rocks and shoot pistols into the air. We who cook so as to honor you, who take so much pride in welcoming you here."

Jani sensed the stillness in the air, the charge of expectation. *You're undercutting my authority.* Hungry as she was, she set her fork aside. *Putting me on the spot in front of your suborns.* "Your interpretation of hospitality is most odd, and truly. You did not behave as seemly, yet you expect me to respond as though nothing untoward has occurred."

"We were so happy—"

"Happiness does not preclude diplomacy, or for that matter, common sense." Jani detected Ambassador Shai's tartness in her speech, and wondered how low she had fallen that she considered the Vynshàrau bornsect a model for anything. "We face a political crisis here of your making, Gisa. If you wish to discuss such over fish and fruit, by all means let us do so. But if you suppose that hunger, fatigue, and the stunned awe I feel at this place will affect my judgment or predispose me in your favor simply because you are as you are, you are most an idiot!" She picked up her fork and resumed eating, conscious of the brittle silence that had fallen, broken only by the sound of Eamon's snuffling gurgle as he laughed into his drink.

"Do you always set the room on its ear like that?" Brondt led Jani up the stairs to her quarters. "I mean, I've listened to idomeni in-your-face for years, but *Christ*."

"She asked for it."

"She has a point."

"But wielding it like a club doesn't help." Jani glanced over the railing, where the clean-up crew cleared dishes and linen and disassembled the table. "I'm sorry, but I have to weigh fifty-seven hurt faces against the stability of the Outer Circle. If you were in my place, what would you pick?" She waited for Brondt to reply, but he kept his thoughts to himself as he led her to a set of double doors at the end of the hallway.

He palmed open one panel and it swept aside, revealing a huge curve of a bedroom, the far wall floor-to-ceiling glass facing the bay. Decorated in blues and greens shot with coral, it included its own sitting room and, upon further examination, a bathroom larger than some flats in which Jani had lived.

"Nice." She tossed her duffel atop the bed, walked to the dresser and noted, with a stab of discomfort, that she looked as worn and battered as she felt. "More than nice. Lovely. Really."

Brondt positioned himself just inside the doorway. "I should have told you everything. I'm sorry. I thought seeing the hybrids, this place, would slow you down for at least a couple of hours. I was wrong." He pressed a hand to the side of his face. "Boy, was I wrong."

"You think I'm not affected?" Jani perched on the edge of the bed. "I'm . . . stunned doesn't begin to cover it. But a situation has developed that needs to be headed off quickly—I don't have time to sit back and marvel at it all."

"Is that the sort of life you lead back in Chicago? Never a chance to breathe?" Brondt jerked his chin toward the view out the window. "It's different here."

"No, it's not. Put two or more bodies in the same room, you get what you've got here now. Same race. Different race. Different species. It doesn't matter."

"Isn't there anything here you like?"

"I'm not cold anymore." Jani dragged her duffel onto her lap. "And the view across the bay is very pretty."

Brondt eyed her with something that struck her as perilously close to pity. "Glories of the evening to you, ná Kièrshia. If you wish to leave in the morning, all you have to do is say so." He reached into his trouser pockets, removing Jani's shooter from one and the disconnected charge packet from the other. He walked to the dresser, set them down, then left.

Jani sat on the bed for a time, staring at nothing. Her anger had receded, leaving edginess and a certain heaviness of limb behind, mood and sensation that reminded her of post-augie letdown.

She finally stood, duffel still in hand. Walked to the dresser and retrieved her shooter. Adjourned to the bathroom, undressed, and showered off the grime and sweat. Dragged on an ancient Service T-shirt and a slightly newer pair of base casual shorts to serve as sleepwear. Returned to the bedroom and lay her trouser suit on a chair atop her duffel. "No need to unpack." She wouldn't be staying.

She opened the window, and felt the warm breeze off the water, touched with the scent of storm. "Rain tonight." She adjusted the pane to close in case water came in, then doused the lights. Tucked her shooter beneath her pillow, then lay atop the bed. If she listened closely enough, she could hear the waves and the occasional cry of a seabird.

CHAPTER 13

"Ná Kièrshia! Ná Kièrshia!"

Jani's eyes snapped open, her heart thudding as the bang of a fist against a door panel shook the air.

"Ná Kièrshia!"

She sat up. Pushed her legs over the side of the bed. Grabbed her shooter from under her pillow and stood.

"Ná Kièrshia!"

She stilled. Felt cool tile beneath her bare feet. Heard the patter of rain outside the window. Her head cleared. "Kièrshia. That's me." She sat back down, one hand over her mouth, and waited for her heart to slow.

"Ná Kièr—!"

Jani dropped her hand. *"Wait a minute!"* She stood once more, tucking her shooter into the waistband of her shorts as she walked to the door.

The panel slid aside to reveal Brondt standing bleary-eyed in the hallway. "Enclave security detected a skimmer headed this way. Two males. Humanish." He wore civvies, a long-sleeve pullover, and baggy trousers, topped off by a shoulder holster complete with shooter. "I thought you'd want to meet them personally."

"I instructed the guards to hold them at the property boundary, and to inform them that you were on your way." Brondt guided the four-seater down the path, then turned onto a wider road paved with crushed stone. "They won't try anything heroic, will they?"

"Depends how convincing your guards are." Jani watched the

road by the light of the skimmer headlamps. "Are they hybrid from the human side, or from the Haárin?"

"Both." Brondt accelerated, sending rain droplets skittering across the coated windscreen. "But one of them is former Service. She should be able to keep the lid on things."

They coursed through the dark, the enclave receding into the distance, its brightness supplanted by the inset illumins in the road itself. It lay before them, like a ribbon of pale gold, the rain changed to silver needles by its light.

Jani hugged her duffel close. She'd dragged on a coverall over her shorts and T-shirt, plunged her bare feet into her boots, and followed Brondt to the skimmer in a daze of movement. Now she battled a lingering sense that the hounds closed in from behind. *That's just memory.* Remembrance of other late night escapes, hangover from her time on the run. *No one's after me anymore.* That didn't hold true, however, for the other occupant of the vehicle. "Speaking of Service," she looked at Brondt, who kept his eyes on the road, "you might have been looking at a medical discharge before you decided to give me a guided tour of the Haárin side of Elyas Station. But at this point I'm thinking desertion of post as well as whatever other minor charges the Judge Advocate can dig out of his desk drawer."

Brondt glanced at her. "Not kidnapping?" When Jani didn't reply, a change came over him, a subtle shift as though some tension left him. Then he twitched one shoulder in a not-quite shrug. "I did what I had to. When the time comes, I'll pay the price."

"You and Hamil both." Jani squinted through the rain, on the lookout for shapes in the distance. "Are you the only active-duty hybrids?"

"It's just the two of us. For now." Brondt decelerated as the outlines of a checkpoint dome shimmered in the distance. "Pierce and Shroud—will you be going with them?"

"I think it may be best." Jani sat up straighter as several figures resolved in the misty half-light. *Everyone seems to be talking calmly. No bodies laid out by the roadside.* She searched for a telltale white head—her breath caught when she saw John look toward their approaching skimmer.

"I wish it had worked out differently." Brondt halted the vehicle in the middle of the road, then slowly rotated it so it faced back toward the enclave. "Pardon me if I don't get out. Pierce won't react kindly to seeing me, and I don't want to give myself over to the

JA just yet." He fingered the steering mech. "Don't cast us aside too quickly. Please."

"I'm not unmoved. No one could see the things I have and remain so." Jani popped her gullwing and pushed it upward. "But ná Gisa has helped put both you and the Elyan Haárin in a difficult position, and she doesn't strike me as someone inclined to back down." She slid out of the skimmer—the warm rain brushed her face and spattered her coverall. "I'll talk to Feyó. That's all I can promise."

"I'll carry that promise to those who think as I do." Brondt lifted one hand from the mech. "Glories of the early morning to you, ná Kièrshia." He accelerated as soon as Jani slammed down the gullwing, and sped back toward the enclave.

Jani waited until the skimmer had dwindled to a slice of shadow against the light of the road. Then she hefted her duffel and headed for the checkpoint dome. *When shall we three meet again?* She looked to the sky. *No thunder. No lightning*. Only the rain.

"We had just left Fort Karistos Command when we saw the flares play out over the bay." Niall broke away from the small group and walked toward her, impeccable in tan desertweights. "I knew it had to be you."

"Are you all right?" John followed close behind. "We tried to contact the enclave using codes Feyó gave us, but no one responded." He looked less natty than usual, in drab grey trousers and short-sleeve shirt, the shine of his hair quenched by the wet.

"I'm fine." Jani gestured a quick *Be quiet* out of sight of the enclave guards, who watched her with the same perplexed agitation as had their brethren back at the house. Either they had witnessed her fits of idomeni temper, or good news traveled fast. "Let's go." She headed for the skimmer, a white four-door with the bland lines of the vehicle pool, popped the gullwing and piled into the rear seat.

Niall slipped in behind the steering mech and yanked his door closed. "Was that Brondt who drove you here?" He twisted around to look back at Jani, the overhead light defining his bloodshot eyes. "He and that bastard Hamil are mine."

Jani held her tongue until John got in and closed his door, then bent over her duffel to hide her face from the guards as Niall kicked the skimmer out of standby and circled around onto the road. Odds were that the hybrids didn't possess a directed pickup or any other sort of long distance monitoring device, but her on-the-run paranoia still rode her shoulder and she couldn't make herself take the chance. "Brondt is Feyó's mole," she said after they moved some distance down the road. "He's the one who told her about Gisa's plan to kidnap me. He also let Feyó know that I had made it to the enclave safe and sound."

"His last year's physical raised some eyebrows at the Service medical facility." John grabbed a dispo cloth from an in-dash compartment and used it to towel his wet hair. "Some of the test results could have been attributed to various metabolic disorders, but to have them all show up in one person at one time captured attention." He lowered the passenger mirror and watched Jani as he checked his eyefilms. "At the time, no one suspected hybridization. They all thought that big white house across the bay was simply home to some Haárin-human experimental living arrangement, and being Elyan, they shrugged and looked the other way. Lately they've been putting two and two together and not liking the answers." He let loose a grumbling sigh. "Needless to say, they think I'm involved. One reason it took us so long to hook up with you is because I've spent most of the evening sitting in a room packed with lawyers and Service investigators."

Jani sat quiet, aware of the stiff way Niall held himself, the stillness of his hands on the steering mech.

"I had to tell him, Jan." John's voice guttered in resignation. "You disappeared, and we had no idea where Brondt had taken you. The dockmaster shut down the human side of the station to keep shuttles from leaving, but she has no authority over the Haárin section, and they ignore her unless she insists with intent. Niall threw the threat of Service intervention into the mix, but by the time we convinced the Haárin to cooperate, your shuttle had already broken away."

Jani slowly raised her gaze until it met Niall's in the rearview.

"I knew you were hiding something from me." His voice came soft, his Victorian twang barely noticeable. "A colony of hybrids, courtesy of Eamon DeVries. Imagine."

"Until—" Jani's face burned. Her throat tightened. "Until I met Brondt, I thought there was only one hybrid."

"Ah well. Only one." Niall shrugged. "That makes all the difference, doesn't it?" He reached into his front shirt pocket and removed his nicstick case. "That would be the young man with the flat green eyes whose image Doctor Shroud was kind enough to finally show me an hour or so ago." He shook out a 'stick and crunched the tip.

"His name's Torin." Jani sat back and rested her head against the seat.

"How many are there?" John's voice held a tension that indicated he didn't really want to hear the answer.

"Fifty-seven." Jani monitored John's reflection in his mirror, watched his eyes close, his mouth set in a thin line. "Eamon's living with them. He built the big white house across the bay. The outbuildings. He's quite pleased with himself."

"Is he?" John folded his arms and slumped in his seat, the darkness of his thoughts reflected in his shadowed face.

"You have a busy day ahead," Niall said, this time ignoring Jani's reflection in the rearview. "First, Feyó wants to see you. Then some members of the Service Investigative Bureau are hoping you can spare them a few minutes of your valuable time." He chewed his 'stick, working it from one side of his mouth to the other, his usual agitated tic.

"You don't need to talk to them." John glanced over his shoulder at her. "The head of Neoclona Legal referred me to a good firm—we can stop by their offices after you speak with Feyó."

Jani felt her gut roil as her temper flared. She tried to fight it down, then wondered why she bothered. Such was as she was now. The hell with pretending otherwise. "I haven't done anything wrong, I don't require legal assistance, and I'll thank you to stop trying to think of new and better ways to lock me down!" She cut off John's protest with a two-fingered Sìah gesture that looked scatologically humanish enough to draw a double take from Niall.

They fell silent, each prey to their own grievances. After a time, they turned off the main road, the vehicle shuddering as it left skimtrack control. They shot across the scrub, the road receding into the distance behind them, thinning to a thread of gold. Ahead, the beam of the skimmer headlamps sliced the darkness, bringing a narrow arc of the scrubland to day-life.

Then Niall banked the vehicle through a short maze of rocks and down a long, winding decline. Shimmering reflection filled their sightline as they neared the bay. The skimmer shook once more as they broke out over the water, and they fast-floated toward the distant lights of Karistos.

Thalassa had taken its architectural lead from its big sister across the water—that struck Jani as soon as she caught sight of the first bright domes of Karistos, backlit by security lighting and dotting the cliff like a scatter of party balloons. Linking them were the same steep, winding streets, only more numerous. Serving as contrast were the same blocky white and tan commercial buildings and houses, only taller and more complex, and separated by parks and plazas instead of rock and scrub.

And Karistos has different trees. Jani leaned forward so she could see them out the window as Niall steered up a steep incline. They were stuck like clusters of onlookers near the intersections of roads, tall and spindly, with stiff, swordlike leaves of the same red-green hue as the Thalassan scrub. They reminded her of the palm trees she'd seen in holoVees, and she watched them drift past until Niall's mutterings broke the silence that had claimed them since she'd snapped at John.

"The streets in this city"— Niall tapped the vehicle directional array with one finger—"would make a plate of spaghetti look organized."

"It's all the one-way streets." John craned his neck as they passed yet another park. "I think I recognize that fountain. Neoclona should be just on the other side. More or less. I say forget the signs and directionals and just turn where you have to. It's still dark. There's no traffic. I'll take the hit if we're stopped."

Minor traffic violations proved the order of the early day. Scant minutes later the three of them trudged across the Neoclona garage, boarded the lift, and floated up ten floors to the penthouse flat.

"Coffee," John said as the door slid aside, revealing a sitting room in cream and blue that complimented Karistos's bayside ambience. "Then a war council." He shouldered into the kitchen, Jani and Niall in close pursuit, and assembled the brewer with a speed born of practice. "But first, I really, really need a shower." He left just as the heady aroma of too much caffeine infused the air, and seemed surprised to find Jani at his heels when he cut down a hallway and stopped before a double-wide door panel.

"I don't want to be alone with Niall just yet." Jani pushed past him into the room, slowing as she took in the large bed that dominated the decor. "Just give me a few minutes." She steered to the opposite side and dropped her duffel atop the dresser. "You wouldn't happen to have a cleaner, would you?" She dragged her grimy trouser suit out of her bag. "I think I should dress for my meeting with Feyó."

"No more 'coverall for every occasion'?" John grinned weakly as he walked to a seemingly blank section of wall and touched it—a panel swung outward, revealing tiered racks of hangered suits and filled shoe racks. "Can't help you with the cleaner, I'm afraid, but you're welcome to root around in here."

Jani peered into the closet, feeling as inadequate to the task as she usually did when it came to the right clothes. "You keep all this stuff here in case you happen to drop by?"

"That's the point of having pieds-à-terre at all our facilities." John stepped inside the closet and jerked his chin toward the racks mounted on the right-hand wall. "Anyway, these aren't all mine—everything on that side is Val's." He cast an assessing eye toward Jani. "You may have more luck with his suits—you're about the same height now. His back is broader than yours, of course, but droopy shoulders are easier to cover up than trousers and jackets that are too long." He took a step back and waved her inside with a broad sweep of his arm. "Have at it."

The suits were arranged by color. Jani bypassed the dark hues that filled the front racks and headed for the cooler pastels and ashy shades in the back. "I feel like I just dropped inside the ultimate lost lambs' bin."

John folded his arms and leaned against a shoe rack. "I doubt you ever found anything like what's in here."

"You'd be surprised at some of the things I managed to snag over the years." Jani pushed past tans and greys to lighter greens and pale blues. "Coats. Boots. Empty diplomatic pouches, which I admit I found rather alarming. Different sorts of devices—those could be hocked or stripped for parts." She took a jacket the color of a new leaf from its hanger and slipped it on. "I always took a pass on the underwear."

"Glad to hear it." John covered his eyes with one hand and shook his head. Then he stilled, seemingly deep in thought. His hand moved lower, to the point of his chin, finally coming to rest on the neck of his pullover. "What would it take for you to get past that mind-set?" He tugged at the already bagged cloth. "The knowledge that it would never happen again? A few years of stability?"

Jani rejected the jacket for length, stripped it off and returned it to its rack. "I don't think I'll ever lose it completely. I'm too much of a fatalist." She gave herself a mental kick as John's shoulders sagged. "It's not your fault. You're not responsible for each and every aspect of my character."

"I know that. I just wonder sometimes whether—" John loosed his grip on his clothing, then filled the fidget void by plucking a shoe from the rack behind him. "Whether all the things you've experienced over the years, including those that I am responsible for"—he turned the polished slip-on over and over as though he'd never seen one before—"if they eliminated whatever chance you had to be happy."

"I'm happy now." Jani held up another jacket, this one a mossy jade piped with brown. "Free clothes." She smiled, stopping just short of an idomeni tooth-baring, then sobered as John responded with a look just short of stricken. "This really isn't the time to worry about the personal." She yanked open the jacket's fasteners, then dragged it on. "I don't know why you've decided that it is."

"Don't you?" John shoved the shoe back in its niche. "Mines. Kidnappings. Cross-species political crises." He stepped away from the rack and paced. "I just want to sweep you away—"

"That's where you get it wrong."

"I know that." John stopped, then kicked at the thick carpet. "I've done a fair job of keeping my nose out of it, in case you haven't noticed. The offer of the lawyers was a lapse. It won't happen again."

Jani checked the fit of the jacket in the mirror that hung on the end wall. "I think this one's an option." She hunted down the trousers and pulled them off the hanger, then unfolded them and checked the waist against hers. "These are going to bag every which way, but the jacket's long enough to cover." She tossed the trousers atop the rack, doffed the jacket, then started peeling back the coverall until she remembered where she was and with whom. "It's not that I don't need anyone's help. *Your* help. But the answer isn't to keep me from doing what needs to be done, it's to help me do it." She ran a finger over the jacket's lasered seaming. "I need clothes more than lawyers. Access to secure communications. Someone to stop the bleeding, if it comes to that. But . . ." She touched the rich cloth once more, then pulled her hand away. "I've said it before. I'll say it again now. Someone is keeping track of every thing you do for me, and it will all come back to haunt you."

John stood with hands in his pockets, gaze fixed on the floor at his feet. "A man doesn't always get to choose his ghosts. That makes me one of the lucky ones." He walked to the rack and pulled out a tunic in an icy shade of melon. "I always thought this color would look good on you. If you need something else in addition to the green." He laid the jacket across the top of the rack. "I'll be outside."

Jani waited until the door closed. Then she hung up the green daysuit and hunted for the trousers that matched the melon tunic.

The cut of the suit was severe enough to pass Feyó's conservative clothing muster, and the trousers fit better than she'd hoped. She considered the fact that as far as she could recall, this was the first time she had donned clothing for no other reason than because John liked it. Then she pushed the thought from her mind, slipped on her boots, raked a hand through her hair, and reentered the bedroom proper to find John sitting on the bed, sorting socks.

Head bent to his task, he looked as he had in the Rauta Shèràa basement. Focused. Serious. *Until* . . . Until the touch of her hand or the brush of her lips over his gave rise to a different brand of concentration.

He looked up when he heard her—a stillness took hold of him when he realized what she wore. "That is your color." He tried to smile, but the attempt died, leaving him wide-eyed and rapt. "It warms you." He looked down at the jumble in his lap, and cleared his throat. "I'll—meet—"

"Outside." Jani grabbed her duffel from the dresser and hurried out of the bedroom, fighting the all-too-familiar heat that set her heart pounding and rattled her nerves.

She entered the sitting room to find Niall perusing the contents of an inset display case, a mug of coffee in hand. He barely glanced at her. Instead, he opened the door of the case and removed a small book bound in burgundy leather leafed with gold.

"There's a certain type of collector who gets under my skin." Niall lifted the cover with his thumb and examined the flyleaf. "Acquiring for the sake of acquiring. Locking beautiful things away, like a miser his money." He closed the book and returned it to its shelf. "Shroud at least reads these, from what I can tell."

"Answered all your test questions correctly, did he?" Jani fell into a chair, sagging more deeply into it as the last of her sexual shakes abated.

Niall walked to a set of glass doors that opened onto a balcony. Outside, the sky had lightened to dawn, streaks of pink and lilac backlit with gold. "So what's the new objective?" He paused to take a swig of coffee. "When we left Chicago, you were to deliver a gift and I was tagging along to fact-find. Shroud was the man with a fast ship, a generous heart, and nothing better to do with his valuable time than cart you all over hell and gone." He rocked back on his heels, then forward, then back again. "Now that's changed. Shroud's partner in all things medical has gone into the hybridization business. Shroud denies all knowledge, but no one believes him. You're trying to figure out how to deal with a hybrid Haárin who wants to bump the acknowledged dominant off her perch, and I'm dealing with security breaches at Elyas Station and Fort Karistos." He finally looked at her, the cool appraisal in his eyes the only outward sign of his anger. "Is there anything you would like to add?"

Jani drummed her fingers against her chair arm. "Off the record?"

"Forget it." Niall moved away from the window and sat in a lounge chair on the side of the room opposite her. "I will now sit back and finish my coffee while you sieve your response through whatever filter you think necessary at this particular moment."

"I can't think of anything to add to your sterling assessment." Jani unfastened the bottom closure of her tunic, then refastened it. "Is Tsecha involved with the hybrids? Did he know about them?"

Jani started to answer, then stopped. *He would have told me if he knew*. She unhooked the closure again. *If he* did *know . . .* It took three tries before she refastened it. *Please Lord, let him stay out of trouble long enough so that I can throttle him.* "You may well speculate in that direction. I prefer not to."

Niall set his mug atop his chairside table with a bang. "*Listen, damn it—*"

"No, *you* listen, damn it." Jani pushed to her feet. "Even better, open your eyes and look at me. Look at me, and see me for what I am."

"I have." Niall's voice held a deadness that struck harder than any slap. "Thank you."

"The lines of communication have opened, I see." John swept in, looking vampirical in Neoclona purple. "Like floodgates." He handed Jani a mug of coffee, then hied to the balcony doors. "Neither of you mean what you said, of course. Just injured feelings on the Service side and delayed reaction to the shock of discovery on the civilian. Well, we can't afford either right now. The complications are dropping litters all over the place and we three need to stick together, however little the prospect pleases." He looked from Jani to Niall, new to the role of peacemaker and clearly uncomfortable with it. "In a few months' time we'll be talking of this over dinner, wondering what the fuss was about."

Jani held the mug to her nose and breathed in the steam. "When the hurly-burly's done."

"My gel." Niall shook his head. "It hasn't even started."

CHAPTER 14

"'Morning, scholar."

Micah looked up from his workstation to find Cashman's moonface looming above the cube divider, then closed his eyes as the rapid movement made his head pound. He'd just signed in—he needed time to get his bearings. He'd awakened with a headache, the trailing ends of a dream playing past his mind's eye. *No, not a dream.* More his other reality, a replay of his twenty minutes a day of Chrivet-driven hell.

We're walkin' in Jesus' footsteps, boys and girls!

At the sound of her imagined voice, he felt his limbs lift, as though he had donned his exo and even now ran through the Sheridan training field, the Wabash tunnels, across Lake Michigan to the enclave, then back again to the embassy, his mechanical stride chewing the kilometers like candy. *I need to stop this now.* With resolution born of a month's practice, he willed his arms and legs heavy, willed them seated, dragged himself back to the present. "What's your problem now, Cash?"

"I've got no problem. It's you with the problem. They want you on Five. The latest in the series of never-ending mine meetings—they need you to run the recorders." Cashman draped himself over the curve of the divider and batted his eyelashes. "You jumped over a few looies to get that gig. What's your secret? Your winning smile? You supplying fun holos for them, too? What?"

Micah locked down his workstation and gathered his gearbag. "If you ever stopped talking, would you turn blue and fall over?"

Cashman puffed out his cheeks. "Regular cupbearer to the

gods, this makes you. You know what the gods did to their cup-bearers, don't you?"

"Kiss my ass."

"Close, scholar. Very close. You must have moved on to the history section. I'm looking forward to watching that one when you're finished with it." Cashman gestured appropriate accompaniment. "One word of advice before you go."

"Only one?"

Cashman pointed to the mirror by the door. "You better brighten up. You look like hell."

Micah turned and studied his reflection. He'd shaved close. His hair was freshly trimmed. Springweights brand new from the package.

Then he looked at his eyes and saw what Cashman saw. Too much white. Stare too fixed. "I had a rough night."

"What was her name?"

"Shut up."

"Come in, Lance Corporal."

Micah stood in the conference room doorway, a chill cramp working through his gut. "I was told I needed to run the recorders for a meeting."

Pascal sat at the head of the table, hands clasped before him, and smiled. "I must not have made myself clear to Lance Corporal Cashman. My apologies." He gestured toward the man sitting next to him. "Come in. Captain Veles and I just want to ask you a few questions."

Micah stepped into the room. His legs felt as they did after a session with the sims. Weightless, yet stiff. Toned and fit, yet aching. "About what, sir?"

"Just have a seat. We need to clarify a few things related to your initial debriefing." Pascal smiled again. As before, the expression began and ended at his mouth. "You recall, surely. The one that took place after the mine explosion."

"Yes, sir." Micah took a seat several places removed from Pascal. Even if the man stood and threw himself across the table, he wouldn't be able to reach him. "That was over a month ago." He glanced at Veles. A stringy man, dark with hooded eyes—he also bore the gold capital *I* on his dress blue-grey tunic collar that marked him as Intelligence. *Intelligence isn't investigating the mine. The SIB is.* For all the good it did them. Meetings from mornings to late at night, work schedules turned on their ears, and damn-all to show for it. It had become comical, really. Unfortunately, he couldn't openly express his appreciation of the joke.

"How well did you know Lance Corporal Rikki Wode?" Pascal asked.

Micah snapped back to the present, raking his memory for any recall of that long-ago interrogation. *But it wasn't an interrogation, just questions.* Informal. Easygoing. No one had suspected him of anything, and had treated him accordingly. "He was the tech who died."

"Did you know him *personally*, Lance Corporal?" This from Veles, in a voice like fine abrasive.

"No, sir." His first lie. He knew that because no one had asked him before if he knew Wode. *I have to remember the lies.* Otherwise, he'd risk giving the wrong answer if they asked him the same question again. *I wish I could take notes.* Maybe he should ask if he could. *Maybe I should just cut my throat now.* That settled it. No notes.

Pascal sat forward and placed several objects on the table. A headset. Earbugs. Gloves and socks. "We found these among Wode's personal effects. Do you know what they are?"

Micah nodded, stopping as his head rocked. "It's a virtual training rig, sir. Pilots use them. Surgeons."

"Other people use them, too." Veles again. "Infantry. Mechanics. Anyone who likes interactives."

Micah tried not to wince at the grate of the man's voice. Why didn't he do something about it, training or something? Better yet, why didn't he keep his mouth shut? "Yes, sir."

"You're called the 'scholar' by several of the other techs." Pascal's voice, on the other hand, sounded too cultured by half. "Why is that?"

Micah gripped the edge of the table. "I'm studying for the Comtech One exam, sir. I've begged off a few parties over the last several weeks as a result." He pulled his hands away, saw the damp prints left by his sweat, and sat forward, crossing his arms over the wet spots. "Just good-natured teasing, sir."

"Is there any other kind?" Pascal smiled again, then looked down at the table in front of him as though consulting something, even though he lacked even a handheld for taking notes. "You weren't originally scheduled for duty the night the mine exploded. You switched on-calls with a Corporal Howard three days earlier."

"Yes, sir." Micah exhaled, heard the shake in his throat and caught his breath.

Pascal's brow arched as the silence lengthened. "Why did you switch?"

Micah swallowed, then coughed as saliva trickled down his airway. Damn it, the switch had nothing to do with anything, and it looked the worst of all the things he'd done. "I did it for a future consideration, sir. Nothing in particular. I work a weekend night for her, maybe sometime in the future, she'll do the same for me. The techs do it all the time."

"They do." Veles frowned. "Plays merry hell with the schedule after a while."

Pascal nodded. "Well, that certainly clears up that issue. I will admit that we wondered about it, and it wasn't covered in your initial debriefing." He appeared as relaxed as Micah had ever seen him, as though he felt the questioning a waste of time but needed to see it through anyway.

Then he ran his index finger over the headset faceplate, and pushed it a little closer to Micah. "Just out of curiosity, do you have one of these?"

Shit. Micah started to chew his lip, then stopped. He'd recorded enough interrogations to know that lip-chewing was bad. It meant you needed time to think about how to phrase your answer, that the simple truth wouldn't serve. That you had something to hide. *He knows why they really call me the "scholar."* Hell with it. "Yes, sir. I do."

Veles glanced at Pascal, but the Chief of Mattress Operations had eyes only for him. "What do you use it for?"

Micah counted to five. His face burned until he felt sure he'd combust. "Interactives, sir."

"Oh." Veles had the sort of thin-lipped smile that begged for a fist.

Pascal barely managed to conceal his own grin. "I imagine you have a . . . library of holos."

Burn . . . burn . . . burn to ash. Even though it was better this way. Even though this was necessary camouflage. "Yes, sir."

Pascal nodded. "See. This is where they've gotten it wrong." He spoke to Veles as though Micah had already been dismissed. "Wode had nothing in his flat. No wafers, either legit, pirate, or homemade. Just the headset and the rest. No one I know just keeps the gear and nothing to play on it. That doesn't make sense." He looked off in the middle distance for a few moments. Then he turned to Micah, blinking as though he'd forgotten he was there. "When is your exam?"

Micah bit back a curse. Every time he thought he knew which direction Pascal would take the questioning, the captain would jerk the steering mech. "Next week, sir."

"Well, good luck to you." Pascal leaned forward to say something to Veles, stopping when he realized Micah still sat there. "Thank you, Lance Corporal. You can go."

"Yes, sir." Micah stood. "Thank you, sir." He brushed his hand as unobtrusively as possible over the sweat spots he had left on the table. Then he walked to the door, all the while expecting to hear that damned voice, that damned accent. *Just one more thing, Lance Corporal . . .* He palmed aside the panel and stepped into the hall, his expression as relaxed as he could manage, ready to turn as soon as Pascal called him back. He kept walking, and waited, kept walking, and waited, and had boarded the lift by the time he realized that the call wouldn't come.

They suspect Wode of something. Micah slipped back into the bullpen, walking on tiptoe to avoid betraying his return to Cashman. *What the hell do they think?* What's more, did it matter? The investigation had yet to turn up anything other than the obvious— a misplaced mine, and an inexperienced tech. *That's all they have.* He sat at his desk and reactivated his workstation. *That's all they'll ever have as long as I keep my mouth shut.*

He sorted through messages for a time. Then the gnawing in his gut got the better of him, and he opened the latest revision of the Service Code. "Rights of the accused." He mouthed his words, determined to avoid Cashman's irritating attention yet too aggravated by the bullpen silence to keep from trying to fill it. He needed to walk off his mood, but who knew who he'd encounter in the halls, or outside? He hadn't seen Pascal for weeks until today, not since the conference call array bung-up. But that didn't mean the man wouldn't turn up in a corridor, or a vend alcove. Appearing out of nowhere seemed a talent of his.

Micah focused on the code. "If they try to talk to me again, I'm going to ask for an advocate." The idea of thwarting Pascal with the request appealed to him. For about a minute. "No one who's innocent asks for an advocate." Besides, they'd just wanted to find out about the duty switch, which even he had to admit appeared suspicious. "And about Wode and his headset." That bothered him. What did they think they knew about Wode?

"Excuse me, Lance Corporal."

Micah straightened as though someone shoved a knee in his back. He knew he did, damned himself for it, and couldn't help himself. Knew who he'd see when he turned around, yet couldn't help for that, either.

"Looking up a point of law, I see," Pascal said as he squinted toward the display. "I hope our little session didn't alarm you."

"No, sir." Micah dug his fingernails into his chair arms. He'd rather have been anyplace on Earth instead of his cube at this moment, and there wasn't a damned thing he could do about that, either. *This is part of the game, too.* To pretend it didn't matter. He wondered if you needed to be someone like Pascal in order to play. If you needed to be someone like Pascal to even take the field.

"We need some help upstairs with one of the imagers." Pascal stepped back to allow Micah room to get by. "I've been advised that it's better to come down personally to request assistance. You folks have been so inundated over the past month and a half that you've turned off your handcoms."

"That's not true, sir." Micah reached into his gear holster and held up his own activated handcom for inspection. "It's the 'how do you turn this thing on' aspect that's getting to us. You'd think that some people had never seen a touchpad before." He pressed a hand to his forehead, then lowered it fast. "Apologies, sir. It's my job." He stood and gathered up his gearbag yet again.

"The joys of Technical Support." Pascal followed him out the bullpen door, then drew alongside as they headed back down the hall toward the lift bank. "I remember it well from my on-call days. You wonder if some people's mothers know they're here." They boarded a car. The doors closed.

"You're from this area, Faber?" Pascal stood to the rear of the car.

Micah nodded. "Yes, sir." He took his place near the front, facing forward so he didn't have to look Pascal in the face. "Small town north of here—Fort Jefferson."

"You must have some opinion about all this trouble with the idomeni."

Micah watched the figures on the floor indicator display increase, and willed them faster. *I thought you were finished with me, Pascal? What are you trying to do?* He thought over his activities, six weeks pondered in a few seconds. *What did I do to attract his attention? Why does he think me suspicious?* "They're odd, sir." Every hate-filled slogan he'd learned from Chrivet scrolled through his head, bubbled to the base of his throat, tickled his tongue like soda. One by one he choked them back down. "I suppose they're all right."

"You suppose they're all right." Pascal snorted. "That has got to be the most tepid assessment I've ever heard." The doors opened and he brushed past Micah into the hall. "We've moved to another conference room." He glanced back over his shoulder. "One of your penmates has been trying to help us set up, but he's not having much luck. Lance Corporal Cashman?"

Oh, hell. "Yes, sir." Micah followed Pascal into one of the larger rooms and found Cashman standing over the pieces of a room-rated imager, fiddling with the mirror array.

"Hey, sch—" Cashman caught himself, eyeing Veles as though he expected the man to pummel him for the infraction. "Hey, Fabe. I've been over every millimeter of this thing and I can't find what's wrong."

Micah took the array from him and examined it. "What's the problem?"

"The thing won't display. Switches work. Signaling checks out. I thought the mirrors were misaligned, but they check out, too." Cashman scratched his head.

"Powerpack charged and loaded?" Micah thought he'd spoken under his breath, but Cashman's dropped jaw and Veles's sharp look indicated that he hadn't. "All right, let's pull apart the image sync."

While he and Cashman worked, Micah sensed the movement around him as Pascal continued to set up for the meeting, removing materials from a coffinlike carrier set against the near wall. The wafer folders containing graphs and figures were expected enough, but the last display piece captured even the dour Veles's attention.

"Excuse me." Pascal set a mid-range shooter the size of a tall man's leg in the middle of the table as though arranging such things atop conference tables was something he did every day. "Show and tell," he said by way of explanation as he pointed the muzzle in the direction opposite the occupants of the room, then returned to the carrier.

We use those. Micah imagined the heft of the weapon in hands, hid a smile as he recalled the excited look on Manda's face when she blasted her first target to dust.

"What the hell?" Cashman backed a half step away from the table. "Keep that thing away from me."

"It's a dummy." Micah tried to keep his attention fixed on the imager, but something about the mid-range bothered him. The loadlight just fore of the grip fluttered like a beating heart, and that meant only one thing with this particular model. *Damned thing's loaded.* His grip on the image sync tightened so that Cashman muttered, and he handed the thing off. *Damned thing's for real.* Powerpack in place and ready to fly, as Chrivet loved to howl at the top of her lungs.

Micah waited for Pascal or Veles to notice, but they had adjourned to the far side of the room to discuss some aspect of the upcoming meeting, conversing in low tones as they checked a handheld display. *Shit.* Meanwhile, the loadlight continued to pulsate, promising all sorts of wall-blowing mayhem to whomever bumped or prodded the thing hard enough to engage the charge through.

Oh hell. Micah reached across the table and hoisted the weapon, taking care to keep it pointed away from everyone. *As if it matters.* As if the damned thing wouldn't blow out two adjoining walls if it let loose. *Damned fools.* He squeezed the grip and jammed back a nearly undetectable lever, discharging the powerpack with a loud click.

"Is there a problem, Lance Corporal?" Pascal gave the handheld to Veles and walked to the table.

"This thing was in firing mode, sir." Micah set the mid-range back on the table, then handed the pack to Pascal. "The power supply was engaged."

"That's the optics light, not the loadlight," Veles muttered.

"Captain Veles is correct." Pascal took the pack from Micah, then lifted the mid-range as though it were a feather and rammed it back into place. "There's a prototype still under development that has the indicators reversed, but the old hands charged with testing the thing are complaining because they're used to reading the loadlight through the sight. That's what this meeting is about." He set the weapon back in its place, shaking his head. "It is a dummy, by the way. This isn't the Haárin enclave." He shot Micah an annoyed glare, then returned to his conversation with Veles.

"How the hell did you know about the prototype?" Cashman removed the first in a series of alignment cartridges from the image sync and held them up to light.

Micah stared at Pascal's back, willing him to turn around, yet fearing what he'd see if he did. *He caught me . . . he caught me . . .* "I saw . . . a presentation."

"That must have been one hell of a presentation." Cashman's face brightened. "Hey, success!" He held up the sync, which now glimmered in activation. "Poles reversed on the left aspect." His brow knit. "I wonder how the hell that happened. No one had any problems with it yesterday."

"I'll bet." Micah waited for Pascal to turn around, to look at him, to drive home with a superior smile the fact that he had won this round. But the man still seemed too involved with the upcoming presentation to care. He didn't even bother to dismiss them, but let them leave without a word.

The day continued free of incident, which meant that Micah didn't see Pascal anymore. He hunted the meeting files for any information concerning mid-range prototypes, any presentation or article that he could point to and say *I learned this here*. But he couldn't find a single reference, including one to the meeting that Pascal claimed to be chairing. *He made it all up. Jazzed the imager and switched weapons, just to trick me.* He wondered what Pascal's next move would be, and if he stood a chance in hell of seeing it coming.

He pondered his situation during his walk home. As he cooked his solitary dinner. As he changed into his casuals, grabbed his sim gear from its drawer, then donned it and lay back on his couch.

The tones sounded. Micah struggled to concentrate on them, and waited. Waited. Waited—

"We're walkin' in Jesus' footsteps, boys and girls! Across the water, one, two, three!"

Micah spotted the back of Chrivet's helmet through the lakespray, and imagined clobbering her with his mid-range. *This is no time for blasphemy, Sergeant.* A swell chopped his ankle, and he barely caught his stumble in time. *If this is the embassy, then we need all the help we can get.*

He tried to imagine what they looked like as they bore down on the shore, larger-than-life figures in full exoskeletal kit, running atop the lake surface as though they splashed through puddles. Superhumans. Metal-framed giants. The first wave in the nightmare war.

Sitting ducks. Micah swallowed, and tasted acid from his overworked stomach. *A fully loaded idomeni lakeskimmer can pick us off from three kees away.* Five, if the exo's emission scramblers malfunctioned, as they had been wont to do lately.

He flicked off his infrared viewer and looked to his right. Bevan ran next to him—he knew that from the position grid on his helmet display—but he couldn't see him. The refractors on the suit surface reflected the color of the water, the nearby shore, the cloud-filled night sky, leaving only the appearance of *something* that might be a shadow of a cloud across the moon, or a breaking wave, or a swooping gull.

But the idomeni will see something. Or they'd believe their instruments instead of their eyes, and shoot.

"Tiebold, where's your infrared!"

"Ma'am!" Micah turned it back on, and watched the dark horizon bloom with shape and color. They passed the last outbuildings of the Exterior Ministry, hazy dull white from trapped heat. *Thermabrick.* He fixed on the view and calibrated. The outlines sharpened.

"Target at eleven, distance zero point two four two kilometers."

Micah looked just off to his left, Chrivet's tinny voice ringing in his ear. *One and a half minutes to landfall.* The first outbuildings of the idomeni embassy came into view, lakeskimmer dry docks and maintenance sheds, cool grey from inactivity.

Or damping. Micah cranked the gain on his comdetect. "Idomeni in the maintenance shed. Three, maybe four."

"O'Shae. Foley." Chrivet gestured toward the shed. "Go!"

The two peeled off and skirted atop the swells, exoclad legs churning. They hit the skimmer ramp at speed, barely missing stride as O'Shae shot a concussion grenade into the shed and Foley ran ahead and sprayed the grounds with deadhead to wreck the biosense.

Micah watched his helmet displays burst into multicolor as the grenade blasted his sound dampers and the deadhead clouds chilled through the air in a purple tumble. *Filters.* He checked the status of his inlets, and breathed a shaky sigh. Deadhead had been manufactured to counter idomeni-made biosensors, but shit happened at the damnedest times and he didn't want to test the limits of his suit systems at this particular moment.

He hit the ramp two strides behind Bevan—any misstep meant collision meant disaster. The grounds swept past, deadhead swirling around them. Twenty meters ahead, Foley bulled through the gardens, spraying brickwork, and hit the entry full-force with his ram. The door blew inward, fileting any idomeni standing within ten meters.

"Lakeskimmers in one minute!"

Micah looked to his right just before he shot through the opening and saw the idomeni vessels ride up over the rocks, mid-range shooters at the ready. One of them fired, then another. A charge cracked over Micah's head, sending his displays into seizure.

Three peeled off to take care of the idomeni. Bevan. Two others. *Too easy, glory boy—the real shit's on the inside.*

Through the hole. Inside the embassy living quarters. No lights. Purple clouds everywhere—Foley, pumping out deadhead, blowing more systems. Micah stayed with O'Shae while the others peeled off down the maze of halls. O'Shae blew the doors, while Micah followed up with blasts into every open room. More concussion grenades. Plaster powdered from the walls and ceiling. A chandelier crashed down.

"Enemy at six five oh!" Manda, one wing over. *"Contact imminent!"*

Six five oh. The main hall. *Through those doors.* Micah dogged O'Shae's heel, advancing another grenade clip just as the displays in his sightline went mad.

"Contact—" A crackle. Nothing.

Manda! Micah checked his display. Blitz of colors. Overload. Through the doors behind O'Shae—purple smoke everywhere. Shouts. Screams. Idomeni, otherworldly giants in exos, fighting hand-to-hand, typed weapons useless, blitzed by deadhead.

Untyped weapons—just fine.

An impact in his right side. A shower of red from below, spraying across his faceplate.

A scream. His.

Micah removed his headset, taking care to wipe away the sweat. He sat up, surprised as always by how drained he felt. Well, maybe not so surprised anymore.

He rose from the couch and checked the clock. *Forty-two minutes.* The actual training exercise still took only fifteen to twenty. *Means the hypno took longer to lull me.* Five minutes more than the last time, and fifteen minutes more overall. *You can build up resistance over time.* What effect that could have on his training, he had no idea.

Micah walked to the kitchenette, working his arms and shoulders along the way. His upper back felt like a board, his legs as stiff as if he'd hiked the Devil's Trail at Fort Aqaba. He filled a cup with cold water and drank it. Refilled, and drank that, too. Then he stood at the sink, cup dangling from his hand, and tried to think about what had happened.

"I should have ramped down my gain before entering the

embassy. That's why my displays kept blitzing—settings too sensitive." Micah lifted the cup, regarded the inside, and poured the few drops of water remaining into the sink. "I shouldn't have burst in after O'Shae. What happened to Manda should have alerted me. Instead of storming the main hall with the rest, I should have searched the halls for more living quarters to blitz." He'd have looked for hostages as well. So far it didn't seem they were being encouraged to take hostages, but if a highly placed Deputy Whatever meant the difference between blood across his faceplate and escaping with his life, it didn't seem such a difficult choice.

"You have the wrong attitude, Lance Corporal." He was supposed to be willing to die for the Cause. "And I have. Fourteen times, so far." Bevan, on the other hand, always seemed to survive, at least longer than he did. That pissed him off. "Why do I keep dying?" What the hell had hit him hard enough to kill him—the exo liners had been built to take grenade-level impacts, and no metal blade in existence could hack through them.

He opened a drawer, removed a flask, and uncapped it. "To the Group. To the Cause." He raised the flask to his lips and threw back his head. Took a pull of whatever the hell it was—gin, vodka? Swallowed fast. Recapped the flask and tossed it back in the drawer, which he kicked closed on his way to the bathroom. "I don't think we should come in off the water." He stepped into the shower, activating it. The spray hit him in the face, jolting him. "Damned Bevan." He muttered over the man's apparent luck. It kept his mind off Manda, and the memory of his own blood coating his faceplate.

CHAPTER 15

Micah expected to find MPs waiting beside his desk when he arrived for work the next morning. Instead he found Cashman, standing vigil with a doughnut and a dispo of vend alcove coffee.

"I have a favor to ask." He followed Micah into his cube and set the office breakfast down on his desk. "It will only take an hour of your time."

Micah stared down at the coffee. He wondered what it would taste like with vodka in it, and if anyone would notice if he hid a flask in his desk. He'd dreamed again the night before. Relived the lake assault from a different angle. Saw what happened to Manda.

"You see, we've got this skimcart that has to be returned to the main receiving dock." Cashman leaned against Micah's desk and dropped his voice to a whisper. "We borrowed it, sort of. I mean, we meant to take it back right after we finished—we used it to help Kirit in SysAdmin move last week and—"

"You stole a cart, and you want me to take it back because someone in Central Receiving knows you took it and they're laying for you." Micah broke off a piece of the doughnut and bit into it. It proved to be coconut, which he hated. But he'd thrown up his breakfast earlier that morning, and his stomach ached from emptiness. "Where is it?"

"In the west stairwell alcove." Cashman patted his shoulder. "And if you ever need anything, anything at all—"

"I'll add it to the list." Micah refastened his coat, then polished off the doughnut, alternating with gulps of coffee. "If anyone stops by for me, tell them whatever you want." He crumpled the cup and tossed it in the trash, then counted his steps as he walked out of his cube to the door, something he hadn't done in years. It was a habit that had taken him through rough times in his youth, one that allowed him to concentrate on the immediate and ignore whatever waited around the corner, forget about whatever he had left behind. . . . *five . . . six . . .*

"Fabe?"

Micah stopped. *Step number seven.* He turned to find Cashman staring after him. "What?"

"You OK?" Cashman shifted from one foot to the other. "You look like somebody died."

Micah smiled, wondering if the expression looked as fake as it felt. Then he faced the door again and resumed his walk. *Eight . . . nine . . . ten . . .*

He found himself watching the faces that passed him on the way to Receiving, on the alert for anyone who looked like he felt. If he did find someone, he decided, he'd swing the cart in front of them, pretend it was an accident, then engage them in conversation. Ask them why they felt the way they did, and if their replies sounded at all likely, whether they belonged to the Group, too.

He needed a friend like Wode again. He needed someone to talk to. His constant dying had gotten under his skin over the weeks, but last night had been the worst of all. He still felt the impact in his side. Saw his blood spatter across every blank surface.

The sun shone warm, but he couldn't feel it. The sky filled his eyes, clear and blue, but he didn't care.

Receiving dominated the Far North region of the base, a five-story whitestone mass set in the middle of a skimway hub jammed with trucks and vans. Micah dragged the cart onto the main platform, told the civilian foreman that he'd found it under a tree in the South Central region of the base, then departed before anyone could ask him any questions. He wasn't in the mood for questions. Answers, yes, he could do with a few of those, but not questions. He trudged back along the main walkway, still watching faces, and counting his steps.

"Good morning, Lance Corporal."

Micah felt the doughnut and coffee meld together into a leaden mass. "Captain Pascal, sir. Good morning."

"Funny seeing you in this area of the base," Pascal said as he drew even. He wore civvies, a blue shirt and darker trousers, a short coat. "Someone who lives in the enlisted housing blocks would come in from the south."

"I needed to drop off a cart in Receiving, as you no doubt saw." Micah gave up on commiserating faces and quickened his step, wondering whether he could lose Pascal in the day shift crowds and knowing just as surely that it would take a bomb to shake the son of a bitch off his tail. "I've already been in the office. But I'm guessing you know that, too."

Pascal watched Micah for a few strides, his face deceptive in its kindness. Then he nudged him toward a snack kiosk, first maneuvering him to a table, then watching him while he purchased two coffees and a couple of breakfast rolls. "If you're ready to talk," he said as he set two dispo trays down on the table, "I'm ready to listen." He sat in the chair opposite Micah and unwrapped his roll, a meat-and-cheese-filled turnover glistening with fat glaze.

Micah watched Pascal bite into the sandwich, the meat juice drip and the cheese string, and quickly looked away. "I'm afraid I don't know what you mean, sir."

Pascal nodded. "All right. Let's back up." He set down his sandwich, wiped his fingers on a napkin, took a swallow of coffee, and sat back. "It's been noted by people you work with that your mood has undergone a gradual but definite change over the past weeks. This change, to the best anyone can determine, first became noticeable shortly after the mine incident at the Haárin enclave." He leaned forward again. The cheap plastic chair creaked under his weight. "Are the two events necessarily related? No, of course not. You may be upset over a family matter, or another personal issue. If this is the case, just say so, and I'll leave you be. But if it's not . . ." He spread his hands wide, then picked up his sandwich and took another bite.

Micah sat, his arms folded across his chest, and tried to concentrate on the people walking past. Uniforms, gym clothes, civvies, all shapes and sizes.

Then a lithe, dark-haired girl caught his eye. She cut through the crowds like a fish around rocks, briefbag jogging against her hip, young face lined with concentration born of stress. *Manda?* He almost boosted to his feet to chase after her, but Pascal's steady stare weighted him down.

"Someone you know?" He finished his sandwich and tossed the tray into a nearby trash receptacle.

"No, sir." Micah sagged back, then picked up the coffee cup and held it for the warmth. "I thought I recognized the eyes."

Pascal watched him, as though waiting for him to say more.

Then he set his elbows on the chair arms and linked his hands, legs stretched out before him as though trying to catch every available ray of sun. "You never showed an aptitude for infantry training while you were in Basic, or an interest, for that matter. All your test scores highlighted your technical abilities." His gaze moved over the passing crowd, then back to Micah. "We all change over time, of course, for varying reasons." He smiled. "Some do so because such is their way. They are always altering, adapting, trying new things. They could no more remain static than I could breathe underwater. For them, change is life." He picked up his napkin, tearing off bits and rolling them between his fingers. "But there are others who change only because they feel they have no choice. They look about them, and see a world they no longer understand. A world they fear. They change because it is the only way they believe they can return things to what they consider normal. They force themselves into situations for which they're ill-suited, ill-trained, in the hope that if they act emphatically enough, their world will revert to the way it was." After he had built a pile of rolled bits of napkin, he started picking them up one at a time and flicking them into his coffee cup.

Micah watched as one piece after another arced into the cup, and prayed for Pascal to miss while knowing as surely as he breathed that his prayer would go unanswered. He broke off a piece of his sandwich, which proved to be the same meat–cheese mishmash as Pascal's, and chewed slowly to keep from getting sick. The morning crowd had thinned, allowing him a clear view of the grounds, the rolling lawns and flowering trees, the bright white buildings beyond. *He's been reading my ServRec.* He swallowed, the food going down like hot cement. *Well, so what? There's nothing there.* Only things that he knew. Nothing he *felt*. Nothing he believed.

"Take the late Lance Corporal Wode." Pascal had stopped flicking napkin nibs, and now tore a long strip and wrapped it around his finger like a ring. "His psych evals revealed a man who felt very strongly that tradition should be maintained, even at the expense of growth, of knowledge. Quite the hidebound individual. You could group him with those people you see on CapNet, the ones who shake their fists at the holocam and shout 'idomeni, go home.'"

Micah set down his cup, then brushed away the coffee droplets that dotted his fieldcoat. He'd flinched at the word "group," but he didn't think Pascal noticed. Hoped he didn't, anyway. *You freak-fucking bastard—you're not fit to speak Rik's name.* He almost blurted his opinion out loud, and barely stopped himself in time. *That's what you want, isn't it? For me to blow up, give myself away. Well, forget it.*

"Some of my superiors feel that Wode took his interest in interactives one step too far, that he obtained the means to engage in some sort of simulated combat training, with an eye toward someday fighting idomeni." Pascal worked the napkin ring from his finger, then started twisting it into a tighter band. "The problem with that was the fact that he skipped the bioemotional pre-conditioning. I've gone a few rounds with the sims over the years, on both sides of the headset. I've seen what it does to people. The hands never get bloody, but the brain can't tell the difference. You kill one too many, or die once too often, and your judgment goes over the side. You lose the ability to think clearly. You hear about conditions like sim synesthesia, sim psychosis, and wonder if they could happen to you." He worked the paper ring from one finger to the next. "At times like that, you need someone who'll listen. Who'll understand."

Micah pressed a hand to his right side, to the ache beneath his ribs that grew sharper and deeper the more Pascal talked. "There's someone in our department who knows all about you. You had an emotional augmentation when you were a teenager, courtesy of Exterior Minister Ulanova. It damps down your emotions, keeps you from feeling." For a mad moment, he wondered if Pascal somehow knew the girl who was Manda. Whether she had fallen for the face and the accent as so many had. Whether Pascal had taken her. "Empathy's only a word to you, so don't even try," he said, rage choking him. "In fact, why don't you just shove it up your ass!"

"I don't understand why you're taking this attitude." Pascal twisted the ring into a figure eight and tossed it into his cup. "I only want to help."

"Yeah, right." Micah forced another bite of the roll. "You know, it's not really the done thing for you and me to be seen together like this. I suggest that given your reputation, a charge of fraternization or even sexual misconduct would give somebody the excuse they needed to bust you right out of here." He stood, brushed the crumbs from the front of his coat. "Thank you for breakfast. Now I really must be going."

"If you believe you have legal recourse, by all means, give it a try. I look forward to answering questions about my interest in you." Pascal stood and performed table-clearing duties, tossing their mess into the trash receptacle. "I'll be watching you, Faber."

Micah started down the walkway. The place between his shoulders burned—he knew Pascal watched him, but would sooner have dropped dead than turn around to confirm. Instead he kept his eyes fixed straight ahead, shoved his hands in his coat pockets to warm them, and counted his steps.

Elon adjusted her headset, struggling to discern anything useful from the burst of voices that battered her ears. Godly though the argument of Vynshàrau might have been, this was not the time.

"I see them, nìaRauta." Ghos steered the skimmer past trees and over logs and rocks, gesturing in anger as branches scraped against the sides of the vehicle with a sound as the claws of demons. "They are . . . *there!*"

In the near distance, the skimmer they pursued became visible, skirting around a stand of evergreens and slicing low-hanging fronds as a blade. A battered thing, its blue color faded from sun and chemical damage. *Humanish.* Elon's shoulders rounded. Only they would allow a vehicle to degrade so.

"They move too quickly for this place!" Ghos slipped into Vynshàrau Haárin, his words as clipped and his voice devoid of gesture. "They will collide with a tree, and the humanish newssheets will say that Vynshàrau are to blame for forcing such." He sped up as well, gaze fixed on the path ahead, hands moving over the controls.

"Humanish blamed us for the mine. For the death of our own. Such would be a change, to blame us for a thing we actually did." Elon removed her shooter from her belt holster and activated it. "This is the fourth such incursion since the mine, Ghos. I tire of such. It must cease."

Ghos slowed as he maneuvered through the forest maze, speaking more than he had since Elon knew him as he declaimed over the madness of the humanish driving. Trees closed in from all sides. A branch thudded against the skimmer roof, sending a frantic fur-tailed animal sliding down the windscreen and off onto the ground.

Ghos half rose from his seat as they careened into a clearing. "We have them, nìaRauta!"

The tree-ringed circle appeared as an animal pit. Four embassy skimmers surrounded the battered two-seater and slowly closed in, backing it toward the trees. Then they moved more closely together, so that they faced it in a line and could fire upon their quarry at Elon's order. As a captured thing, the blue vehicle flitted about the shrinking space, probed for an opening, then stilled as it found none.

Elon activated the skimmer audio array, then paused to beg the gods for calm. She spoke English only when necessary, and as such, did not speak it well—with the prospect of combat, the ability to do such threatened to leave her completely. "You have trespassed upon idomeni land, deeded as such by your dominants." Her words cut through the air as a weapon. "You will throw your weapons from your vehicle to the ground, and disembark." She deactivated the array and gestured to Ghos. "What do you see?"

"Three occupants—two male and a female." Ghos monitored the scan display set in the middle of the control array. "They are all armed—expect four shooters, including a mid-range."

"To activate a mid-range in such a small vehicle—would they be so stupid?" Elon evaluated the distance to the humanish skimmer. "The recoil would send them backward into the trees, and the newssheets would blame us for such as well."

Ghos unholstered his weapon and activated it. "I could leave our vehicle and approach them, compel them to shoot at me, and force them to do such."

"*Ghos!*" Elon slipped into Vynshàrau Haárin, such was her anger. "Feres's soul has just been released—I will not officiate at another Vynshàrau death in this damned cold place!" She gripped her right hand within her left and squeezed. The rebroken bone had long since healed, but if she compressed enough, she could induce some pain, and employ it to focus her mind. "I repeat to you," she said, reactivating the audio array, "throw away your weapons and disembark your vehicle!"

The humanish two-seater hovered low to the ground. Then, as though it awakened from sleep, it elevated slightly, rotating until it faced Elon head-on, until she could discern the vague shapes seated behind the tinted windscreen.

"They are to charge." Ghos reached for his door lever. "They are to—"

Before Ghos could disembark, the humanish skimmer launched toward them, advancing in the beat of a heart, elevating at the last instant, leaping above them so that Elon could see the waves of iridescence the magnetic drives had induced in the metal of the lift array.

Then the audio array screeched, the sound filling her head as a white-hot thing. She screamed and tore the headset away, as around her scan displays blanked, then flooded with light and gibbered signals.

"Their shielding is damaged—they attacked us with such!" Ghos tried to steer the skimmer around, but the magnetic battering had rendered it crippled. The engines whined. The displays showed only fragments of words and histograms.

The other embassy skimmers streamed past them in pursuit of the humanish. Ghos muttered in Vynshàrau Haárin and tried to re-set all systems at one time, while Elon aided him, half deafened, her ears ringing.

At last they reactivated. At last they turned and gave chase. Ghos followed the scan, the trail of broken branches, as Elon contacted her suborns. "They have attacked!" She barely heard her words. *"Take them!"*

They entered another circle of trees, this one nearer the road that led to the humanish skimways. They found four skimmers in a line, facing a wall of brush and stone, and eight Vynshàrau milling in the grass.

Elon disembarked and walked across the circle to her suborns, slowing to allow Ghos time to overtake her and precede her, the cries of birds piercing her deafness.

"They have escaped, nìaRauta." NìaRauta Laur gestured toward the wall. "I witnessed them leap over the barrier as an animal, yet none of our scans detected the disruption of the security array."

"Humanish skimmers do not *leap*." Ghos holstered his shooter and walked to the wall. He climbed to the top, using the brush as handholds, and kicked at loose stones that lay scattered on the surface.

"Scan the grounds," Elon said to Laur. "If these humanish were able to arrive and depart without detection, they most likely spent much time here. It is therefore even more likely, and truly, that they left something behind. Contact the humanish Service and ask them of their mines. Ask them if they ever used this land as a training ground as well." She watched Ghos and another suborn pull at the stones and gesture displeasure. "And contact ní Tsecha. Wherever he is, whatever he does, bring him to me."

Elon returned to the embassy and retired directly to her rooms. Her cook-priest berated her for missing the time of her mid-morning sacrament, then led her to the altar room and stood over her as she begged forgiveness of the gods.

She prayed as she ate, her still-damaged hearing making her voice sound as something far away. Then she removed her grimed coverall, laved, and donned the pale green trousers and shirt, the off-white overrobe more appropriate to hallways and meeting rooms. Sat at her worktable and studied the layout of the embassy, and tried to determine how the humanish gained access to the grounds. Felt the rage build within her as a living thing as she pondered how she had come to be sent to this damned cold place, to watch her suborns die, chase down decrepit skimmers, and remove that which they left behind as a keeper of beasts removed their waste.

Her door chime sounded, though such was its pitch that it took some time before she realized it did so. She rose from her table and walked to her door, forming a fist with her right hand and striking the entryway arch as she passed beneath.

"NiaRauta." Ghos still wore his coverall, and had tucked a documents case under his arm. "You are as deaf."

"Yes, Ghos."

"When the mine deafened me, you compelled me to go to my physician-priest. I will do the same now to you."

"After I speak with Tsecha." Elon cradled her hand, which throbbed and stung when she sought to straighten her fingers. "What is your report?"

"Laur is leading the scanning of the land." Ghos walked inside. He had bound his braided fringe into a single rope of hair to keep it away from his face, which had been scratched in several places by brush and had bled accordingly. "They have already found small amounts of humanish food in storage sheds, in greenhouses and security bunkers."

"No explosives?" Elon waited until Ghos gestured in the negative. "I have read of such things. They wish us to know that they have breached our defenses, that they may do so again as they will. And to do this, they taunt us with their food, for they know that no greater insult to our way exists."

Ghos set the documents case atop Elon's worktable. "I have brought the readouts from the stations confirming no sign of incursion." He removed a sheaf of wafers and set them beside her workstation. "They have overridden our defenses, Elon. What is there to do?"

"Implant our structures with sensors that are not integrated into our systems. Fit those sensors to loud alarms." Elon rubbed one ear. "Drive them as deaf if they invade again." She drew alongside Ghos, tilting her head in puzzlement as she comprehended the condition of his hair. "Ghos, you wear twigs." She

reached up and plucked a thin branch from one of his braids. Half
a finger in length, brown and grey, a hard bud at one end.

Ghos unbound his braids and shook them out with his hands—
three more twigs fell onto the table, along with a strip of leaf. He
picked them up, one by one, then handed them to Elon. "Burn
them. Smear the ash on pieces of scroll and burn them again."

"Such will not serve as enough. Such as this place can never
be purified." Elon rubbed the objects between her hands as though
to grind them to dust, but the wood was too hard and the leaf too
new, and thus did not powder but remained intact. "Yet you would
have left our skimmer and walked before the humanish, drawn
their fire and most surely been injured. Or died."

"You will say that it would be better to die within the
worldskein than here. I maintain that it would not." Ghos rebound
his braids, tying them as tightly as though he prepared for *à lérine*.
"I maintain that we are already damned, all of us damned, so what
difference? Tsecha denies Sànalàn, and should thus face the wrath
of the gods. But time has passed, and what is the decision of Temple? Of Council? Have you read a decision, nìaRauta, for most assuredly I have not. Have you seen him confined, returned to the
worldskein, executed, as he most assuredly should be?" He paced.
"*Politics*. Cèel ponders if he may risk Haárin wrath by doing as he
must to Tsecha, by treating him in the way the gods demand. Thus
do I pronounce him damned, and with him, each of us, for he is as
our Oligarch, and he has failed in his duties, and thus have the
gods rejected us all." He stopped before her, took her damaged
hand in his own and opened it. Took one of the twigs and held it
before her face, looking her in the eye as he did so, as had become
more and more his way. "Each of us to be burned, and the ashes
smeared upon scroll, to be burned again, and even then we will
not be clean."

"*Ghos.*" Elon felt the horror of disputation carried too far.
"You blaspheme."

"Do I, Elon?" Ghos tossed the twig upon her worktable, then
released her hand as though it were a thing of glass. "Yet even so,
this place must burn." He took a step back from her, his eyes still
meeting hers. His pale eyes, so bright against his pallid face,
against which the blood shone like jewel.

Elon looked down at her hand, still felt the departed pressure.
Then she crossed her arm over her chest and tilted her head in
confusion, and even as the entry chime rang out, she did not hear
it until Ghos gestured toward the door.

"NìaRauta?" Laur entered, looked from Elon to Ghos, and stood most straight. "Ní Tsecha attends."

Elon gestured in affirmation, aware of Ghos's anger as a living thing between them. "I will speak with him."

"Politics." Ghos swept a hand across the worktable, sending the twigs and leaf to the floor, and strode to the door, forcing Laur to step aside to allow him to pass.

CHAPTER 16

Elon entered the primary meeting room to find Tsecha standing before one of the low tables that lined the far wall of the sparsely furnished space, contemplating an arrangement of stones. He dressed most as Haárin, as was his habit since his outcast, in a blue that pained the eyes and an orange so near to red as to be ungodly. He looked to the door as she entered, regarding her as he used to at Temple when she argued with him over his blending heresies, his gaze fixed on the floor at her feet, hands clasped behind his back.

"So, Elon. Humanish food in your buildings, and skimmers that leap about as beasts and evade capture." He turned his attention to the stones once more, this time picking one up and stacking it atop another, then removing it and doing the same again. "A grenade of pink could have halted your invader."

"No, Tsecha." Elon's shoulders rounded. Now, as when he served as ambassador, Tsecha felt he knew her duties better than she. "We would have damaged ourselves just as we damaged them. The new pink is not yet ready."

"It was not ready when I served in this place. It takes its time readying itself, and truly." Tsecha picked up another stone, but instead of adding it to his pile, he passed it from hand to hand. "What has Shai said of all this?"

"NìaRauta Shai attends a conclave with Prime Minister Cao. They discuss expansion of GateWay rights, I most believe. As always, Samvasta serves as issue due to its nearness to Shèrá. The humanish wish it so very much, and Cèel has ordered Shai to withhold." Elon stepped across the room to a window that looked out over the gardens. The sky pained the eyes as did Tsecha's shirt, yet such did she esteem, for it lit the hybrid grasses and shrubs to a brilliance that took her to Rauta Shèràa. The time just before first planting, when the leaves greened and the sun burned low in the sky.

Tsecha set down the stone. "You have not told her of this latest incident?"

"No." Elon remained at the window. "I most prefer to examine such matters most completely before I inform nìaRauta Shai. I prefer to understand reasons, and determine that which must be changed." She pressed her hand to the windowpane, imagined heat, but felt only cold. "Humanish did not attack us in this way until the enclave came to be. They did not despise us so until you went out among them. They once enjoyed you, for they believed you only a visitor here. Now they fear you, for they know you mean to stay and force your blending prophecies upon them." She paused, laboring to think of words to describe that which to this point had only been vague impression, the unformed sensation of the soldier who recognized menace she could not define. "Therefore, I would ask you to leave this place, and return to Rauta Shèràa. Today. Tomorrow. As soon as you may."

Tsecha moved down the table, away from the stones and toward a bowl fountain. "And the other Haárin? Dathim and the rest?" He placed his fingers beneath the water stream, and the gurgling softened to a quiet patter.

"They should return with you." Elon stepped back from the window, but remained some distance from Tsecha and his table contemplations. She had never entertained a wish to draw close to him, and now, more than at any time, she wished to remain well away. "I have thought of this a great deal since the time of the mine explosion. Since the time I conveyed Feres's soul to his final place. It is with you that all this began, Tsecha. It is with you that it all will end. It is with you that it all must end."

Tsecha raised his hand from the fountain stream, watched the water drip from his fingers to the tiered bowls beneath. "As always, Elon, your reasoning is flawed. Even at Temple school was it so. When you were required to think as a soldier, you pondered as a student, and when you were required to ponder as a student, you thought of nothing but advance or retreat." He shook the last drops from his hand, then wiped it over the front of his shirt. "My leaving this place will not end these attacks. They would have occurred if I had never lived, for they speak to the weakness of both humanish and idomeni. Humanish, who only know advance and retreat, as the soldier, and idomeni, who withdraw to ponder and suppose, as students until death."

Elon drew back from the window, away from the light that pained her eyes and the color that struck at her soul. Yet she did not want to leave the view, and the need to do so angered her. "We are warriors as well, Tsecha."

Tsecha took a step closer to her, nearer the sun that entered through the window. The brightness accented the water stains of his shirt, the almost-red darkened to blood. "We attack one another within the bounds of our classroom. We argue points of law with blades. But we do not advance. We have built ships of space for as long as have humanish. Yet we have only ten poor colony worlds to show for our labors. They have near to fifty, and bother us as starving youngish for our share." He once more clasped his hands behind his back, and studied a flaw in the ceiling that only he could see. "But as starving youngish, they think only of their own hungers and how to assuage them—if a slap gives them what they wish, they will continue to slap until their target sickens of being struck and slaps back. If I departed, they would most believe, and with reason, that they drove me away. My remaining, all our remaining, serves as a return slap. It is necessary, Elon. It is as it must be. Therefore will I stay."

Elon rubbed her hands together, imagined the twigs between them, the twigs that even now remained scattered across the floor of her rooms. "Allow the humanish to think as they will, but do that which is godly. That which is best for Haárin."

"Such a day it is, Elon, when you think at all of Haárin." Tsecha bared his teeth at the ceiling, then lowered his gaze once more to the place at her feet. "No. Such is my answer. No, and no again." He walked to the other side of the space, toward a cloth-draped pedestal. "I see that Shai maintains sculpture in the meeting rooms." He removed the cloth and poked at the half-formed mound beneath. "During my time at Temple, I never saw her but with a lump of clay in her hand. She required it, so she said, to quell her anger. When she first arrived here, she did not use such. Now I see that she has taken it up again." He studied the sculpture for a time, then shook out its cloth and covered it once more. "Is this why you summoned me here? To beg my return to Shèrá?"

Elon walked to the middle of the room and circled a ring of chairs. Her body ached as it always did after the discord of a pursuit, yet she could not sit. Instead she paced, and pondered what to reply. *As a student*. She gripped the back of a chair, squeezing until her knuckles paled to white. "That is why, Tsecha. Yes."

"Shai will not appreciate this fact. She prefers to know when I am about this place." Tsecha walked to the door, his stride relaxed, as though he had not sentenced a race to despair with his decision. "If you are not occupied with more impossible requests, I would ask and truly that you come with me. Someone is here with whom you as security dominant should speak."

Elon followed Tsecha down the wide corridor that led to the verandas. "I must meet with my suborns most soon to talk of this attack." She had fixed her eyes on her former dominant's narrow shoulders, which had seemed as old when she schooled at Temple and now seemed as those of a youngish, clothed as they were in Haárin blue.

"Then you will want to discuss such here first, I most believe." Tsecha pushed open a hinged door and stepped out onto the walled veranda reserved for humanish.

Elon followed Tsecha out onto the veranda. By the far wall, near a pedestal fountain, stood Pascal, the Service captain, dressed in the clothes of the street. Pale stone colors, she noted, that did not offend the eye, however much their wearer did. Such strangeness. His stunted body, too broad and bulky. His hair, so pale as to be Oà, sheared as close to the skull as Tsecha's and Dathim's, his narrow face and weak jaw. *Ugly beings, are humanish*. How she wished, and truly, that she would never see one again. Next to him stood Dathim, clothed in green and brown, such subdued tones that Elon wondered if he sought mercy from the gods for Tsecha, who dressed as one who could not see that which he wore.

"NìaRauta." Pascal stood as a carving, his back most straight, gaze fixed at a point above Elon's head as a show of respect. "Ní Tsecha has told me of the attacks against the embassy," he continued in adequate High Vynshàrau. "I am most interested, and truly, as to the details, for this is the first I have heard of such."

Elon heard the movement of the door behind her, and turned to find Ghos standing in the entry. He now wore the clothing of the embassy, green and off-white, as she did, and had unbound his braids so they fell freely past his shoulders.

"We have not told humanish of these assaults." He spoke High Vynshàrau. Yet his voice and posture still held his earlier anger, and his intonations came as chopped and truncated as his harshest Vynshàrau Haárin. "What purpose would be served? Feres's soul has already arrived within the worldskein, so long ago did he die, yet humanish know nothing of the source of the mine that killed him. What good, then, to consult with you of this? More time spent, more worthless meetings, more politics, and less knowledge gained for all of that. You are as nothing, and truly."

"Ghos, silence." Elon sensed Pascal's surprise at Ghos's anger, Dathim's and Tsecha's irritation, and took what pleasure she could from the discord. "Even now, nìaRauta Sànalàn labors to purify those places." She stood aside so Ghos could move half a pace ahead of her, as was seemly. "So many are there that she will labor far into the night."

Pascal looked to Tsecha, then away. He drew his hand to his mouth, then recalled where he stood and let it fall. "My High Vynshàrau is adequate to most of my embassy dealings, but it may not prove so if the speech becomes too technical, or too heated. In such instances, I will speak English, and ní Tsecha or ní Dathim will translate. Is such acceptable?" He waited until they all gestured in the affirmative. "Any vehicle that managed to evade your security systems would have to have been specially equipped. Did you obtain any images of this one you saw today? Any scans or other identification?"

"Why should we discuss such with you?" Ghos looked to Pascal. "Strange humanish who befriends Haárin. Suborn of ná Kièrshia, who is anathema to all that is godly. What are you?"

"Ghos!" Elon looked to her suborn, who seemed most as determined to forget her existence, then to Pascal, who gestured again in question. "Yet such is something we would want to know, Pascal. You possess some standing in the humanish Service. Your loyalty is to them. Why, then, would you assist us?"

"Such is a most fair question." Pascal's right hand drew up in hesitation. "I fear the subtleties I must express to explain myself are beyond my grasp of High Vynshàrau, but I will try." His hand lowered. "As nìRau Ghos said, I am indeed suborn to ná Kièrshia. While she is absent from Chicago, I work for her, serving as her eyes and ears."

"But you wear the clothes of the Service, when you remember to." Ghos stepped closer, his hands clenching as his back bowed. "You act as the most ungodly Haárin—all know this who know anything. You serve any and all. You do not comprehend the meaning of order, or loyalty!"

"Ghos! Such is enough." Tsecha's back bowed. "You wish to know more of the humanish who have invaded. I have one with me who can determine such."

"He is disorder!"

"He is between the lines, as he has always been! Such is no surprise to me!" Tsecha pushed up one sleeve. Silvered *à lérine* scars reflected the light, a warning to Ghos.

"He serves only the Kièrshia." Dathim stepped forward, his hands low before him, his weight balanced as a warrior who expected attack. "If you accept nothing else, you must accept that, and if you accept that, you must accept all that follows." He tilted his head, his shaved scalp a glinting mockery of the old ways. "Even a bornsect must comprehend such."

Ghos ignored him, his gaze fixed on Pascal. "Why are you here, humanish? To spy for your anathema, or your Service?"

Pascal raised his left hand chest high, palm out and fingers curved, a gesture of pleading. "I only wish to help. You are being attacked. I wish to find out more of these attacks—I believe I can assist you in preventing them."

"And I should believe you why?" Ghos moved to the side as a fighter trying to find his feet, while Dathim moved with him in an effort to stay between him and Pascal. He moved again, and again Dathim moved with him.

The movements of à lérine. Elon felt her own body sway in response as her fingers closed around the ghost of a blade.

"*Elon.*" Tsecha drew close to her, his voice lowered in a damned humanish whisper. "Ghos is yours—order him to still."

"Why, ní Tsecha?"

"Because my Lucien does not understand what occurs."

"Yet you compel us to understand him? To trust him? Unfair, ní Tsecha. If your humanish does not understand us, then it is time he learned."

"You damn this place with each breath and beg the gods to deliver you, yet when you sense blood, you act as the animals you condemn?" Tsecha stepped around Elon toward Dathim and Ghos, who still moved in strange unison. "*Ghos.* Stand back. My Lucien does not comprehend."

Ghos took a step toward Tsecha. "You brought him here. You, who damned our souls by your outcast."

"You damn your own soul now, Ghos." Tsecha pushed up his other sleeve, revealing another lifetime of scars. "You have not listened. You have not thought. You only attack."

"I attack. Such should be no surprise to you." Ghos punched the air, his fist finding a space past Dathim's shoulder, a handsbreadth from the dodging Pascal.

The action shook Elon from her violent reverie. She stepped forward. "Ghos. Do not waste your honor on such as that. His blood offers nothing but chaos."

Ghos kept moving, foot crossing sideways over foot, a half step ahead of Dathim. "Then I will offer his blood to Caith, and beg her blessing." He dodged in, out, then in again, leaving Dathim still a half step behind. Then his fist shot out. The strike of a beast.

Pascal raised his open palm and met the blow. The crack of flesh and bone against flesh and bone sounded. Another strike. Another defense. Pascal darted away from Dathim so that he could move freely, took his place in the center of the floor. Ghos followed, and the two of them continued to punch one another, landing blows on torsos, shoulders, and arms. The godly moves of the circle of challenge, the only thing missing the blades.

"Ghos!" Tsecha closed in on the male from behind, and barely dodged an elbow in the pit of his soul. "Lucien! Stand behind Dathim. Do so now. End this!"

"There is no end to such as this without blood," Ghos said as he struck Pascal's chest and pushed him back.

Dathim closed in, back bowed. "Do you declare, then?" He closed his hand around Ghos's wrist, stopping him in mid-strike. "Do you declare!" He shook him as a youngish, back and forth, as though he scolded him, his *à lérine* scars flashing pale in the light.

"Dathim! Silence!" Tsecha pushed himself between Ghos and his suborn and grabbed their hands, struggled to pry his suborn's hand from Ghos's wrist. "You have let your anger take you before, and this is not the time for such! Challenge for yourself, if you must, not for Lucien!"

Pascal breathed heavily, sweat coating his face. He straightened slowly, his fists still raised, ready to block Ghos if he struck again. "Dathim, back down."

Dathim turned on him, shoulders rounding. "Ghos has declared against you in every way but the last. You cannot walk away!"

Pascal lowered his fists. "Yes, I can."

"Then." Dathim released Ghos's wrist and backed away. "*Humanish*, who only pretends to learn."

"Ghos." Elon struggled to control her shaking voice. Old scars ached in memory. She longed for the finality of the circle, wished every humanish could leave their blood within its confines, felt her heart pound in response. "Not his blood." *Yes, his blood*, her soul told her, and she closed her mind to its pleas. "It is not godly."

"How godly are the damned?" Ghos flexed his hands, massaged his knuckles, looked toward Tsecha, then away. "I declare."

Pascal looked to Dathim; after a time, Dathim looked to him as well.

In the eye. Elon watched them, uncomprehending. *Most strange.*

Pascal pulled his sweat-darkened shirt from his body. "What do I say?" he asked in English

Dathim responded in English as well. "You say, I accept challenge."

Pascal nodded once. "I accept . . . challenge."

Tsecha pressed a hand to his forehead, a humanish gesture that at times denoted pain. *"Dathim."* He looked to Pascal, then away.

"I don't believe we have a procedure in place for this back at Sheridan." Pascal's voice emerged as dead. "Who contacts who?"

"You are the challenged. Therefore your dominant must contact Ambassador Shai." Tsecha spoke in his English, broad, flat sounds that did not seem to emanate from an idomeni mouth.

"There are—" Pascal paced a tight circle. "There are Service rules prohibiting duels. They're old, and haven't been enforced for a long time, but—" He emitted a harsh sound. "I can think of a few people who might want to try and dust them off."

Tsecha raised a hand, then dropped it, a gesture that for humanish may have meant something but for Vynshàrau meant nothing. "So, it is done." He ran a finger over one of his many scars, then pushed down his sleeves. "My Jani once fought as you will, Lucien, against nìaRauta Hantìa. I will contact General Burkett, who served as her dominant—he may offer advice to yours. He will be most surprised by this, I am sure." His posture altered to one of dismay. "My Jani will be, as well. Is she to be told now, or when she returns?"

"She'll read it in the newssheets, I'm guessing." Pascal looked to Dathim. "I have right of a second."

"I have acted as such before." Dathim nodded once, in an aggravating humanish manner. "I will train you as I trained ná Kièrshia."

"Thus and so." Tsecha pointed toward the entry, then stood most still as Pascal and Dathim walked ahead of him. "Inform Shai, Elon, that if she wishes to berate me, I will not listen." He took his place behind his strange suborn pair and followed them out of the veranda, his step most heavy.

Elon walked to a stone bench set in the veranda wall and sat. "Why, Ghos?"

"Because Pascal is anathema, and he who was Avrèl nìRau Nema brought him here to help us." Ghos seemed most as relaxed now, his shoulders straight, his hands unclenched. "Because it is most fitting for a humanish to bleed here, in this soulless place. Because a cleansing rage is required to burn the cold dead from this place."

"Your hatred is indeed so strong?"

"Yes, nìaRauta. Did you doubt such?"

Elon crossed her right arm over her chest, gripping her left shoulder as hard as she could with her right hand. "I asked ní Tsecha to return to Shèrá, to take the Haárin back into the worldskein with him. To end his damned prophecy."

"Did you truly expect him to agree to such?" Ghos walked to the bench and sat beside her. "Such would be as Dathim rejecting challenge. An inconceivable thing, and truly." He reached for the pouch of pattern stones that always hung from his belt and removed it.

Elon watched him shake the colored ovals onto the bench between them. "Will you kill Pascal, Ghos of the Stones?"

"If I am able," Ghos replied as he worked the lines.

CHAPTER 17

"... for she is the bringer of pain and change ..."

Clase, *Thalassan Histories, Book I*

John steered the skimmer up the narrow two-lane skimway, slowing briefly as one of the momentary pockets of congestion that passed for the Karistos morning rush closed in around them. "Nervous?"

Jani finished smoothing her overrobe, then folded it in her lap and sat back to play passenger for the last few minutes of the drive. "Yes and no. I know Feyó. I like her. I think she likes me." She looked out the window and watched the copper dome of the Haárin Trade Board loom ever larger, its polished roundness at odds with the multistory white and sand blocks that surrounded it. "It's all those nasty unknowns that have me jumpy. How much does she really fear Gisa? How do the Elyan Haárin consider the hybrids? As a curiosity? A threat? Will my presence as a substitute Tsecha help or harm matters?" She stretched a section of overrobe sleeve across her hand and tried to rub out yet another grimy souvenir of her Thalassan rock-climbing exhibition. "I'm not sure nervous is the right word."

"Terrified?" John grinned, his expression made riveting by the black sunshades he'd donned to shield his eyes from the morning dazzle. With the purple daysuit and his blanched skin and white hair, the overall effect was less that of a vampire than Death-takes-a-spin-around-town. "Do you want us to wait?"

Jani shook her head. "You don't have to."

"We'll wait," Niall announced from the rear seat. "I have nothing planned for this morning except to make sure you get to Fort Karistos after we finish here. You, Shroud?"

John's smile wavered. "I wanted to return to the hospital. Drop in on a few folks. See if a personal appearance could jog anyone's memory concerning Eamon." He raised his sunshades, regarding Jani with eyes filmed the same too-dark purple as his suit. "Hence the ensemble. Something about me looking funereal inspires truth-telling in the more impressionable."

"I'll keep that in mind." Jani batted her lashes at him, and they fought a skirmish of weird-eyed stares until a proximity alarm blared, forcing John to steer the skimmer back in their lane and focus on his driving.

Jani sneaked a look at Niall, who occupied the rear seat as if it was a couch, his feet up, Karistos *Partisan* in one hand and a smoking nicstick in the other.

"I can stay behind, then," he said. "Sit vigil in one of these parks." He set down the sheet and took in the view out his window. "Attractive town. Quite classical." He grimaced. "Hotter than hell, though."

John maneuvered the skimmer up to the curb in front of the Trade Board. "I must say, the location of this place surprises me." He leaned forward to catch a better look at the dome through the windscreen. "It's smack in the middle of town. There are outdoor restaurants right down the street."

"Look at the front." Jani pointed to the flat white facade. "No windows. No doors. I'm guessing that the air-handling system filters out all odors, and that any verandas are well sheltered from unseemly views. No Haárin has to tolerate anything they don't feel comfortable with, and the humanish don't have to travel to the enclave for face-to-face meetings." She gathered her duffel and cracked open her gullwing. "Thank Feyó. She opened up the Board to humanish members, making it easier for them to deal with Haárin, which in turn demystified both sides. Some didn't like it, but most saw the advantages. So far, it's working." She pushed out the door, then swung her legs out of the cabin. "Well, wish me luck." She started to boost to her feet, then stopped when she felt the warm press of a hand on her shoulder.

"Luck." John squeezed lightly, then pulled away as though she burned. "When you're finished—"

"I'll be watching for her. I'll call you when she's done." Niall folded the newssheet and tucked it under his arm, then popped his gullwing and got out.

"Thank you, Colonel," John muttered under his breath. "If you lure him in front of the skimmer," he added, leaning close to Jani, "I should be able to at least graze him."

"I don't know—he's pretty fast." Jani straightened the straps of her duffel, conscious to the point of fixation of the memory of John's touch. "I don't blame him for being angry. He'll cool off eventually, I hope. The problem is that in the meantime, he's not going to let me out of his sight." She took a deep, bracing breath— the aroma of grilling meat mingled with the heavy sweetness of flowers and the tangy undercurrent of skimmer battery hyperacid. "Ah well. Onward." She got out, closed the door, and joined Niall, who paced the sidewalk.

"So how do you get in?" He took the half-spent 'stick from his mouth and used it as a pointer. "There's a walkway there." He indicated a pavered path that ran from the sidewalk around the right side of the building.

"That's probably it." Jani dropped her duffel between her feet and pulled on her overrobe. "You could come with me if you wish. Feyó knows you now. I'm sure she wouldn't mind." She glanced back at the traffic in time to see John's skimmer fade around the corner. "You'd have to lose the 'stick, though."

"It's all right. You'd just slip into Sìah Haárin, and leave me behind for lost." Niall looked across the street. "There's a park." He waved his newssheet toward a flower-packed square of green set with benches and tables. "If I get too hot, I'll dive into one of the shops."

"Your choice." Jani hoisted her duffel and headed for the walkway. "See you later."

"Luck."

Jani stopped, then looked back to find Niall regarding her, eyes narrowed by the sun's glare.

"I didn't specify good or bad, mind. We'll let fate decide that." He'd only stood outside for a few minutes, yet the sweat already dotted the front of his desertweight shirt. "I'll be on the lookout for you." The subtle threat of his words hung between them until he broke away, dodging a sudden flurry of skimmers in his dash across the street.

The Trade Board didn't have a lobby, per se. No reception area, no nests of chairs and tables set aside for shooting the breeze. Just a vast open space with a bare tiled floor and plain walls in shades of stone and sand that curved upward to form an arched ceiling, the only decoration a Sìah-style chandelier that resembled a jumble of blades. At the far end, a triple-width door of hammered copper marked the entry to the meeting rooms.

Jani set out toward the doors, her boots sounding muffled echoes. As she drew close, one copper panel swept open. Four Haárin emerged—Feyó, another female, and two males—all attired in shirts, trousers, and overrobes, their hair arranged in the breeder's braided fringe. Jani noted the jewel colors of Pathen on the males, while Feyó and the other female wore the more somber earth shades of Sìah. Feyó stood rearmost, which was to be expected since she possessed the greatest status and wielded the most power.

"Glories of the day to you, ná Kièrshia." Feyó spoke Vynshàrau Haárin in deference to Jani, and through her to Tsecha.

"To you as well, ná Feyó." Jani took in the grey gaze, sharp yet fatigued, that seemed drawn to the red-slashed sleeves of her overrobe.

"Your arrival at Elyas Station was, according to your Colonel Pierce, most as an incident. My apologies."

"You would have been unable to prevent it, I most fear. Some of the hybrids worked at the station. It was what we call in Chicago 'an inside job.' "

"Ah." Feyó cocked her head. "So you have borne witness to Thalassa, ná Kièrshia. You have seen those who live there, who call you 'the first.' You will inform ní Tsecha, of that I am most sure. His dream realized." She raised her cupped right hand in a gesture just short of supplication. "What say you?"

Jani remained silent as the realization of exactly what Feyó feared struck her. *She's afraid of Tsecha. She's afraid of me.* She glanced at the other Haárin, whose expressions and postures held more obvious discomfort. *They all are. They think I'll support Gisa because she's a hybrid, that Tsecha will do the same.* She struggled to quench the anger that flared like flame. Did they think her so simple that she would disregard the stability of an entire network of worlds for such a reason? Did they believe Tsecha, who had survived war, house arrests, and life on the bleeding edge of his stratified culture, would do the same? She stood in place, her face averted, and inhaled deeply and slowly of air that smelled as nothing at all. "It was only by luck that I learned of the existence of a hybrid before I departed Chicago, and even that was not a definite thing. It would have proved most helpful to have been apprised of Thalassa, the fact of which you have known for a very long time."

Feyó drew up straight. "Ní Tsecha will be displeased," she said, her voice pitched high in entreaty.

"He esteems you and values your advice. First with the synthetic foods, then with this, you have led him wrong." Jani struggled with an ire made more profound by the fact that she liked Feyó, and thought she knew her. "Do you comprehend in any way the risks to which you expose him when you do so?"

Feyó's shoulders rounded as anger threatened to supplant any sense of remorse. "I comprehend much that you do not, nà Kièrshia."

She turned and walked through the copper door, and gestured for Jani to follow.

"Ná Gisa had served as suborn to me since her outcast. She had once functioned as a Temple acolyte in the Síah dominant city of Ràlun, and was made Haárin for defending ní Tsecha's prophecies. This was soon after the war of Vynshàrau ascension. Not a wise time to speak of blending." Feyó led Jani to a pair of chairs situated near a window. "From the beginning, she behaved most as difficult, but such is the way of Haárin. And she served the enclave well. She was trained as an agronomist, as was I. Much of our work in synthetic foodstuffs may be credited to her, and truly." She sat, then arranged the drape of the cuffs and hem of her off-white overrobe. "But when ní Tsecha became ambassador, she grew even more as difficult. The time had come, she told me. Soon the blended race would dominate both Commonwealth and worldskein. This is when, I believe, she sought out Doctor DeVries. It took most of a Commonwealth year to build the Thalassan compound. Most of a Commonwealth year until I noticed her change."

Jani sat in the chair next to Feyó's, then sought to settle her nerves by contemplating the room. The sand-toned walls had been painted with representations of grasses and flowers in the corners and where walls and ceiling met, decorations of pale green and light blue accented with the occasional startling purple or pink. Flowering trees, both carved and real, had been placed in copper planters and set throughout the space, adding to the sense of lightness.

Wish it lightened my mood. Jani lowered her duffel to the floor, then nudged it beneath her chair with her heel. "What form has Gisa's challenge taken? Does she wish to meet you within the circle?"

"She sent communications to the dominants of the other Outer Circle enclaves, announcing that she declared my leadership unsound, that she is chosen of Tsecha to lead the Elyan Haárin." Feyó contemplated the view outside the window, a walled garden of native trees and tufts of scrub grass, interspersed with *sanna*, a green and purple striped plant native to the region around Rauta Shèràa. "When one says 'chosen of Tsecha' to Outer Circle Haárin, it can mean more than a single thing. To the more conservative, it means free trader who wishes to expand business. To the more liberal, it means a free thinker who wishes closer dealing with the humanish, as we have in this place. It has not yet come to mean hybrid to either faction, and that is where it all becomes most as confusing."

Jani shifted in her seat. The mantle of negotiator had never fit her well, and she could feel its imaginary collar tighten about her throat. "Have you and ná Gisa ever spoken together? Have you sought to discuss your conflict openly?"

"She is not sound."

"Have you tried?"

"Yes, ná Kièrshia. She will not comprehend sense."

Jani removed her ring and tilted it back and forth. The red stone caught the light and flashed a crimson needle on the wall opposite her chair—the flicker reminded her of a warning signal. "The other Board members will not put Gisa in your place. With or without ní Tsecha's sanction, the simple fact is that she lacks the standing to replace one such as you. Therefore I believe that we may discard that notion right off the bat." She ignored Feyó's look of confusion. Maybe the occasional dose of humanish slang would serve to fix the Haárin's attention on her visitor's words instead of her own arguments. "The underlying issue, from what I could gather, is the status of Thalassa in relation to the enclaves. Could you please clarify your position?"

Feyó remained silent for a time. Then she stood and walked across the room to one of the planters and fussed with an inset illumin attached to the end of a branch. "I offer Thalassa a chance at community, as is necessary for it to function, and to gain esteem from the other Haárin."

"Ná Gisa stated that you sought to treat it as part of the Elyan enclave, that you demanded allegiance to the dietary laws and acceptance of you as dominant."

"Gisa exaggerates."

"Then explain to me what you meant."

Feyó removed a flickering illumin from its holder and examined it. "An idomeni must belong, to a sect, to a skein. We must know how we stand among all others, at all times. Even we the outcast form our enclaves. Rare is the Haárin who survives as one alone, as you have." She glanced back at Jani, catching her eye for a bare instant before turning her attention back to the tree. "But just as important as how we see ourselves is how others see us. The Board members are, as you would say, conservative in their attitudes. Some will perceive Thalassa as disordered no matter what I do. But some will be persuaded that it has a place within the skein, and their opinions must be nurtured if we are to prevent the fracturing of Outer Circle alliances that Gisa's actions invite." She returned the illumin to its holder. It shone more steadily now, the flicker replaced by a faint pulse. "Some Haárin, I most fear, accept ní Tsecha's teachings in the abstract only."

Jani stared down at the ring in her hand, given her a seeming lifetime ago. Not for the first time she wondered if Tsecha realized what he had sucked her into. "You called me 'Haárin' even though I am not truly so and never will be. I am part humanish, as are all the Thalassans. Not only that, but some of us were born humanish. We will therefore always be different. Even as we come to resemble you physically, our minds will never work as yours. What you would perceive as a godly request from a dominant, we might see as an aggression, an untoward domination." She replayed Gisa's walk up the slope toward the main house, the set looks on the faces of her followers. "That is, I most believe, what you see in Thalassa now, the fear that you use the issue with the Board as an excuse to claim Thalassa as part of your enclave."

"It cannot remain alone as it is. The other dominants will not understand."

"Yet it must be allowed something of itself. The other Haárin must understand from the outset that it is as different, so that they do not expect its inhabitants to act in ways of which they are not capable."

Feyó left the planter and walked to a nearby cabinet set in the wall. "The Thalassans must change."

So must you, I think. Jani executed a slow ten-count. "Maybe they must, but not completely. They are a blending of two peoples. Such is the definition of hybrid." She looked down at her ring once more, this time so that she could hide the anger she felt take hold. *Yes, Gisa is out of line.* But Feyó was proving no better, merely less obvious. *Small thanks for little favors.*

"Ná Kièrshia?"

Jani looked up to see Feyó slide aside one of the cabinet doors and remove a hard-sided documents case.

"Three seasons ago, you aided us and the Karistosians in a

matter of water supply." Feyó set the case on a table and opened it, removing a wafer folder and a portable display. "Much has occurred since then. If you attend," she indicated the place by her side, "I will show you."

Jani stared at the display as the last chart faded to nothing. Before her on the table lay stacks of documents, arranged according to language and source, function and content. Dock statistics, transit schedules, metric tonnage moved. What was shipped and who shipped it, to every world in the Outer Circle.

"I had invited Colonel Pierce to participate in our talk." Jani powered down her scanpack. "I am very glad he turned me down." She tucked it back in its case, then returned the case to her duffel. It hadn't been mistrust that had caused her to pull out her dependable device and scan the paper that Feyó had shown her as much as the need to do something—with nerves came the need for motion. "He's concerned that the Haárin control too large a proportion of Outer Circle shipping." She lifted her chin toward the dead display. "He'd send the Service to lock down Elyas Station if he ever saw those numbers."

"We did not behave against humanish law, ná Kièrshia." Feyó gathered a handful of documents folders and tucked them back into the case. "The routes were there. The docks. Humanish had needs that their own did not see to. That being the case, at whom should Colonel Pierce be angry? At Haárin, for doing as they would in a legal manner? Or his own, for neglecting that which they might have taken as their own?"

"Both. He likes to spread it around." Jani lifted the cover of one of the folders and peeked at the topmost document. "Seventy-two point three percent of the transport traffic. Sixty-four point one percent of the shuttle traffic. The total percentage of slips controlled is on the light side—only 58.2—but that's only because whoever ran the tally included private and spaceliner docks. Subtract those, the number jumps to 73.8." She let the cover fall closed. "I'm amazed the Families didn't notice what was happening."

"Haárin suffered lost shipments. Disabled ships. But not so many, and the colonial humanish always seemed most interested in aiding us to recover that which was ours, and capturing those who injured us." Feyó put the last of the folders into the case, then collapsed the display and set it on top. "They preferred us to their own, so it seemed. A strange concept for Haárin, but we adapted, as is our way."

"Apparently." Jani dragged her bag off the table and tossed it atop her chair. "You've heard of the attacks against the Chicago Haárin? You've heard of the mine explosion, and the death of the bornsect security suborn?"

"Yes—ní Tsecha informed me of such." Feyó shut the case back in its recess, her hand lingering upon the door. "Such will not happen here in the Circle. Our enclaves are old and well-established, and humanish have grown used to us."

"That's true for now." Jani walked to the window. The Trade Board building sat atop a hill, and thus commanded a formidable view of Karistos. Roofs of buildings, both flat and brilliantly domed, the palmlike trees popping up in between like strange dandelions. In the background, the blue sweep of the bay, shot through with ripples like liquid silver, backed by the coppery cliffs. *This place . . .* She turned away from the scene, because she wanted nothing more than to contemplate it for the rest of the day. "According to Colonel Pierce, humanish are just learning that those who lived at Thalassa are hybrid. Their . . . esteem for you may change now that they've learned of them. They may blame you for their existence, even though you bear no responsibility."

"We will announce such."

"They may not believe you."

Feyó gestured understanding. "Humanish do so seem to ignore that which is. Ní Tsecha told me of such during our talks in Chicago." When she uttered Tsecha's name, her voice rose in pitch, her back straightening in a posture of respect. "Many of my Haárin have taken to wearing their hair and clothing as humanish, especially since ní Tsecha's outcast. And humanish sometimes wear their hair in a way most as a napeknot. Those who were treated lived in their own places until Doctor DeVries completed the building of Thalassa, and took great care with their appearance so that they could continue to labor in Karistos. But they perhaps need not have done so, for the line, as you might say, had blurred even before DeVries began his work. Such may aid the humanish here to accept that which is."

"Hair and clothing are one thing, blood and bone another." Jani held out her hands, then pressed them together, palm to palm. "And the Thalassans didn't aid their cause by kidnapping me. Even humanish who don't like me—and they are legion—will seize upon that as proof that the hybrids are outlaws, and that animus will transfer to Haárin."

Feyó leaned against the table and crossed her arms in the

humanish manner. "And then there is Gisa, who would lead the Haárin in my place."

Yes, Feyó, and if you continue to push her, this situation may get even more interesting. Jani remained with her hands pressed together, still conscious of the peaceful scene that called to her from behind. "All possible must be done to insure that some sort of concordance is reached, just in case we ever reach the point where it all hits the fan." She paused when Feyó gestured puzzlement. "I mean if humanish–idomeni relations deteriorated past the point of no return."

"You mean war." Feyó pushed away from the table and paced, her braided fringe swinging gently in time to her step. "We do at times speak of such. It is part of our business scheme—who would remain, who would depart, who would control. Would we transport bornsect goods? Humanish? Both?" She stopped and turned to Jani, her head held high, and crossed her right arm over her chest. "I would fight for this place, beside whoever would also fight for this place, Haárin, hybrid, or humanish. I would do so because the worldskein cast me out, and so lost all claim to my loyalty. I would do so because this place is my home."

Jani sensed the weight of Feyó's words, the feeling that she spoke from the same place as Gisa. *Feyó abandoned the Shèrá worldskein when she made this place her home, and Gisa took the rejection one step further.* Now it seemed as though they both sought to reclaim traditions they had left behind. *That must be why they're making such a muddle of it—they're out of practice.* Before she could reply, a series of tones echoed through the room. One of the copper panels slid aside, and one of Feyó's male suborns entered.

"Ná Feyó, there is a transmission from Shèrá." He glanced at Jani, his respectful posture at odds with his obvious desire to speak to his dominant privately. "It arrived by courier. Ná Voln has taken it to the communications room for decode."

"Then I will join ná Voln." Feyó waited for the male to precede her, then started after him toward the door. "And will you join me, ná Kièrshia?" She looked back over her shoulder at Jani. "This transmission, I most sense, will concern you as it does me."

The Haárin communications room, in order to allow for the recording of posture and gesture so necessary to idomeni articulation, was larger than any humanish combooth Jani had ever used. This was offset, however, by the fact that Feyó and her suborn trio apparently made a habit of listening to transmissions together. Jani stood against the back wall of the space, boosting on tiptoe to look around and over the four Haárin to the display at the front.

"I say it is of Temple," one of the males said as the other inserted the wafer into the unit reader. "They have not scolded us for some time now—it is our turn." Before he could say more, the display lightened, which in turn cued the room illumins to lower.

Jani watched the Haárin darken to fluid shapes. The warm air of the booth had grown even warmer in the few minutes since they'd entered. She inhaled the soapy odor of Sìah perspiration, listened to the rustle of cloth and the creak of leather boots.

The display lightened further, and a dour figure, an elderly female in a red-cuffed overrobe, appeared.

"Temple." The talkative male gestured toward the display. "So I said. *Hah.*"

The female began to speak, her High Vynshàrau jam-packed with nuance and loaded phrases. Jani listened. Watched. *A meeting . . . with Shai and Sànalàn . . . over the fate of the bornsect killed at the mine site.* Except the bornsect hadn't died, and Tsecha had argued for his life, repudiating both his propitiator and generations of religious doctrine in the process.

Oh. Damn. Damn. Damn. Jani saw Feyó's growing dismay in the rounding of her shoulders, and felt her own curve in response.

"Ní Tsecha Egri had lived his life in conflict with all that is godly. All that is orderly. He is the first Chief Propitiator to be made outcast, the first to give over his place to his successor while he lived." The female paused, her back bent in anger. "In denying Sànalàn her right as Chief Propitiator, he has displayed once more his disdain for his people, for our gods. We therefore command him to return to Shèrá, so that he may face the discipline of Temple, which should have been his so long ago, yet which he eluded as a beast eludes a trap."

"They will execute him," Feyó said.

"They cannot!" The female suborn turned to her. "They must not!"

"They'll try." Jani leaned against the wall for support. "Cèel has been after him since the end of the war of Vynshàrau ascension. Now he believes he has him. He won't let this opportunity pass." She pushed past Feyó to the door, disregarding the female acolyte's salutation, for the first time since she arrived hoping for cool air to ease the buzzing in her head. She pushed the entry panel aside, leaning against the wall, then crouching low, her head touching her knees.

"You are . . . ill, ná Kièrshia?

Jani looked up to find Feyó standing over her, worry tensing her face like pain. "It occurs to me, ná Feyó, that if you had informed ní Tsecha of the hybrids when you first knew of them, he would have sheltered that knowledge, and behaved accordingly. I'm not claiming that this episode would not have happened, but it might not have." She slowly straightened, her thigh muscles trembling. She recalled her last meeting with Tsecha before her departure, the expression on his face as he told her of Feres, the pain of loss she had never before associated with idomeni. *He's changed.* A hybrid in his way, as she was in hers, and damn the consequences. "We need to stop him."

Feyó cocked her head in puzzlement. "Ní Tsecha?"

"Cèel." Jani started down the hall. "We need to cut him off at the knees." She stopped and turned on her heel, and barely avoided a collision with Feyó. "Do you still stand with ní Tsecha, despite what you learned here today?"

Feyó drew up, raising her chin to appear taller, then looked down at Jani. "What I have learned does not change my thought."

Jani raised her own chin, acknowledging Feyó's response and her own humility. "Will the other Haárin follow you?"

Feyó hesitated. "Most, I do believe."

"Can you make sure?" Jani waited, her heart tripping, until Feyó offered a slow humanish nod. "The other Outer Circle dominants have probably heard the message by now. You need to gauge their reaction, assure them that you're still dominant, persuade the ones who aren't sure. Meanwhile, I need to talk to Gisa." She fell silent as an Haárin female approached. The female wore the battered coverall of an outdoor worker, a brightly patterned scarf wrapped around her head.

"Ná Kièrshia?" Her voice emerged as a high-pitched keening, so great was her regard. "There is a humanish searching for you in the gardens. His name is Pierce. He said something of—" She grabbed her right shoulder with her left hand in a fit of confusion. "—hur-ly bur-ly?"

Jani exited the board building to find Niall pacing the pavered walkway.

"Your boyfriend left the hospital over an hour ago. 'Shot out of here like a bat out of hell' is the term the desk used." He kept patting his shirt pockets, a sure sign that he needed a nicstick. "Three guesses where he went. First two don't count."

CHAPTER 18

"I messaged the fort from a public comport. Told them we might be a little late." Niall steered the borrowed Trade Board skimmer with a light hand, as though he expected it to bolt from under him at any moment. "So? How did it go?"

"Same as usual." Jani's knees banged against the dashboard as they shot down the steep cliff road that led to the Karistos shoreline. "More problems."

"Oh, that's news." Niall glared at the Sìah instrument array, tapping gauges and grumbling. "How the hell do you read these things?"

"I'll tell you if anything goes south." Jani braced for the shudder as the skimmer left the road and took off over the water. "Can you raise Thalassa on the com-array?"

"I can't even tell where the damned com-array is."

"It's here." Jani touched the nearest of the flat-faced indicators, then followed with repeated hail codes in English and Sìah Haárin. "Nobody's responding." She set the com-array to standby, then checked her timepiece. "Either they're all at mid-morning sacrament, or they've made it a practice to ignore contact attempts by Feyó's fleet."

"And I thought Supreme Command infighting was bad." Niall reached into the shirt pocket that held his nicstick case. "Wait a minute." He lowered his hand. "I can't smoke in here, can I?"

"It would be better if you didn't, no." Jani lay her head against the seatback. "If we could, I'd probably ask you for one."

"That good, huh?" Niall pointed the skimmer toward the distant white specks that marked Thalassa. "Did Shroud tell you that he planned to confront Eamon DeVries?"

"No." Jani bit back further commentary. Niall's anger had eased to background noise, and she had no desire to set him off again. "Why would he?"

Despite the fact that he couldn't ignite it, Niall had inserted a nicstick in his mouth anyway. "You're kidding, right?" He worked the cold cylinder from one corner of his mouth to the other. "I figured he told you everything."

"Well, you figured wrong." Jani looked out her window, concentrating on the roll of the water and the occasional swooping seabird, ignoring Niall's pointed looks and the heat that flooded her face.

"He loves you." Niall fiddled with the bank of touchpads and switches until he found the one that controlled the windows. "Much as it pains me to say. I mean, you've apparently narrowed your choices to him and Pretty Boy Pascal, which to me defines rock and hard place. But I stopped trying to figure out women's criteria years ago." He lowered both his and Jani's windows, and the salty green smell of the sea filled the cabin. "But at least Shroud has some feeling beyond his own immediate gratification. He's a man of substance, to say the least. You seem to enjoy one another's company. Judging from that sheep-eyed look you get on your face whenever he comes in a room, I'd guess that you're as over the side about him as he is about you. Then there's all that shared history." He exhaled with a rumble. "I've seen people start out with a lot less and make a go of it."

"I never thought I'd hear you defend him." They were close enough to Thalassa now that Jani could pick out the details of the main house. The windows and balconies. The shadowed overhang of the main entry. *John, what are you doing now?* Arguing his way past Gisa's suborns? Holding Eamon's head under a faucet? "I thought you didn't like him."

"I don't." Niall sensed the tension of the approach as well. His hand hovered for a moment over his holstered shooter. Then he pulled the nicstick from his mouth and shoved it in his pocket. "I just watched you two tiptoe around one another for the last five and a half weeks. It proved quite an education in how far two people will go to avoid the obvious." He backed off the accelerator as they drew near the shore, increasing the vehicle's elevation to avoid the spray of the waves. "Are you worried about this?"

"A little." Jani dug into her duffel, removing her shooter and tucking it into the waistband of her trousers. "Gisa has some overly enthusiastic followers."

"How overly enthusiastic?"

"They had shooters trained on you and John at Elyas Station. Brondt warned me that they'd overreact if I put up a fight."

"Brondt's playing both sides against the middle, and you're a damned fool if you trust a word he says."

"He's all I have."

"Then we're in trouble." Niall reached for his holster again. This time he unfastened the top. "Damn Shroud. Why couldn't he have waited?" He coasted along the beach, weaving to avoid rocks and moorings, until he came to a steep grade. "Is there anyplace on this planet that isn't either straight up or straight down?" He turned up the road, which led to the first of the houses. "Goddamn roller-coastering everywhere you go—" He slowed as a group of hybrids stepped into the road fifty or so meters ahead. Males, humanish and Haárin both. They all wore holsters, though none had drawn their weapons. Yet. *"Oh, give me an excuse."* His foot brushed the accelerator as his hands closed around the steering mech.

"Don't." Jani twisted in her seat so her back abutted the door. "That's all we need is you running hybrids over the edge of the cliff." She grabbed the framing and boosted through the open window so she sat on the ledge. *"I've come to see John Shroud! Is he here?"*

The hybrids looked at one another, their attitudes altering in a blink from threatening to confused. "Yes, he is here. He is with Doctor DeVries." A heavyset male, the apparent ringleader, moved to the front of the group. His comrades helped him along by backing off a stride or three, leaving him standing on his own. He must have felt the sudden breeze at his back, for he held out his hands, palms facing out, to show that he wasn't armed. "Of course, ná Kièrshia, you are welcome, both you and Colonel Pierce."

"Glad to hear it." Jani pulled herself out of the skimmer, then reached through the window for her duffel. "Stay close," she said to Niall.

"Harkens back to the days of me misspent youth, this does." Niall unholstered his shooter and activated it, steering the skimmer with his inside hand. "Ah, the memories."

Jani patted the side of the skimmer, then started up the road. "You expected someone from the enclave," she said to the ringleader. "You typed the signal when I tried to call, and you staked out the road and waited."

The male shifted from one foot to the other, but stood his ground. "Ná Feyó is no friend of ours. She would swallow us into her enclave and subject us to the old ways."

What do you know of the old ways? Jani took in the male's lined face—he had hybridized too late to lose the telltale human-ish softness completely. Then she made note of his fighter's build. *Fighter, not athlete—this one has the look of the docks about him.* What had driven him to hybridize, to turn his back on all he had known and give himself over to Eamon's medical ministrations? "What's your name?"

The male started. Then he stood at attention, as though making a report. "Adam Down, ná Kièrshia."

"Well, ní Down, I am not of the old ways either. I spoke with ná Feyó this morning, met with her at the Trade Board, and I am still not of the old ways. They're not contagious. Besides, you're hybridized humanish, as I am—we couldn't follow the old ways with tracking sensors and holospheres—we're the wrong race. Neither of us would ever be allowed to live in the Elyan enclave, not even if we had a note from ní Tsecha himself. That being the case, listen to me now and spread the word, because I'm only going to say it once. No violence against any of Feyó's, or against Feyó herself. No intimidation. To do so against her or one of hers is to do so against me, and I do not take kindly." When he opened his mouth to protest, Jani raised her hand to silence him. "Do you understand?" She waited for his grudging nod. Then she pointed to his followers and gestured for all of them to start walking.

"Old ways." Jani spoke to Down's back as he trudged ahead of her up the road, as she felt her heart beat, slow and strong. "It's all new ways here—we're making it up as we go. And we had better make damned sure that we think very carefully before we start waving our little tin dickies in the air because we're a spit away from an enclave in which there resides very tall folk with gene-tically short tempers, and we're a spit and a shout away from a fort filled with shorter folk who have more weaponry than either of us have ever dreamed of. Therefore, we are going to try something new here at Thalassa. We're going to try thinking for a change, or so help me Caith I'm going to start kicking butts into the bay, is *that* clear!" She sensed movement out of the corner of her eye, and turned to find Torin pacing her as he entered notes into a handheld.

"I recorded your speech." His eyes shone clear green in the bright sun. "I've entered all your speeches so far into the secret archives. Many of us have already listened to them multiple times."

"I don't give speeches." Jani ignored the laughter that emanated from the shadowing skimmer. "What's it like here?"

"Tense." Torin shrugged. "Gisa announced at mid-morning sacrament that you had left to go to ná Feyó and that you wouldn't be coming back. Now, here you are." He drew in closer, his step still relaxed, a smile on his face. A born actor. "Doctor Shroud arrived about an hour ago. Doctor DeVries was in his room—he lives in the basement clinic, says it's cooler. Bon escorted Doctor Shroud there, then left them. We heard shouting at first, but it died down after a while."

"What's Gisa doing now?"

"Deciding upon the fall planting. But when Doctor Shroud arrived, she said something of preparing for you."

A few of the hybrids waited for them at the top of the road. One female broke away and hurried to Down's side, casting anxious glances at Jani as she did.

"It's the look on your face that's got them jumpy, in case you're wondering," Niall called from behind.

"Thank you."

"I had a Drill like you once."

"Shut up."

"I have just filed your speech," Torin said as he fingered his handheld's touchpad. "I wish I could do so with conversation, but when I asked Doctor Shroud if I could do so as he spoke with Doctor DeVries, his face grew most red." He eyed Jani sheepishly. "I left quietly."

"A nice change of pace on your part." Jani circled to the main house entry, and wasn't overly surprised to find Bon already standing in the open entry.

Niall had parked the skimmer in the pavered circle, and broke into a trot to catch Jani up. "Good God." He stopped when he caught sight of Bon's ravaged face. "Did DeVries do that?"

"Yes and no." Jani grabbed him by the sleeve and maneuvered him ahead of her. "How are you doing on your observing?"

Niall looked back at Down and the other hybrids, who still watched Jani with a blend of trepidation and awe. "They're all like you."

"Down and the male behind him—they were humanish once. The others began as Haárin." Jani looked to Down's . . . Girlfriend? Female? She tilted her head to her left in acknowledgment of Jani's examination. *I wonder what Cèel would have to say about you?* Or even Tsecha, come to that. Jani often wondered if he had ever considered all the ramifications of his blending prophecy.

"Good God." Niall turned back to the house and the myriad faces that watched from the doorway.

"Welcome to Thalassa, Colonel Pierce." Bon bared her mahogany teeth. "Please, enter."

"Doctor Shroud and Doctor DeVries are downstairs in the clinic, which you have not yet seen, ná Kièrshia." Bon gestured like a tour guide toward the lift that led down to the lower level. "We shall take the stairs, one flight only, to the library, wherein ná Gisa awaits."

Niall glanced back at Jani. "Place is a bloody palace." He paused on the landing that overlooked the skylit courtyard, and leaned over the stone railing to take in the whole of the gardens. "Incredible."

"All hybrids come here to study," Bon said, a shine of pride softening her features. "They come to take sacrament, to discuss points of our history and our future."

"Really." Jani waited for Bon to mount the stairs. "I have some things to discuss with Gisa," she said to Niall. "We may slip into Sìah Haárin."

"I daresay I'll understand the gist." Niall couldn't take his eyes from the garden view. "Something to do with how the hybrids fit into the Haárin scheme of things, I'll be bound."

"You might say that, yes." Jani followed Bon to an entry that she saw, was located two floors beneath her own room. *Not my room—I don't live here.* The door moved aside, revealing floor-to-ceiling shelving filled with wafer folders, display cases, a polystone floor with a glasslike finish, and a windowed wall overlooking the bay.

"Oh." Niall stopped and stared. The scholar in him eyed the reading and viewing materials like a starving man poring over a banquet. Then he moved to the view, his rapt gaze marking it as the work of art that it was. He took one slow step inside, then another, as though he entered a church.

"Ná Kièrshia." Gisa sat at a desk at the far end of the room, near the window. "I am most surprised, and truly, that you have returned." She wore the same sort of humanish outfit as the first time Jani met her, this one in shades of yellow and green. "I have been preparing farm plans. We have greenhouses and processed tracts that you have not seen. I hope to show them to you today." She seemed as relaxed and confident as always, so sure of every move she made. "I walked the land and found myself wondering, and truly, what ní Tsecha will say of this place when he finally comes. So many times he fought in the circle to defend the idea of the blending. So many times he bled. The blood of the priest, binding humanish and Haárin. I am filled with awe when I think of it. The blood of the priest that binds."

"We need to talk first," Jani said in Sìah Haárin. "I spoke with ná Feyó earlier this morning."

"I know you did." Gisa answered in English, her eye on Niall, who wandered along the shelves. "You must know then, and truly, that her time is past, and that we who are blended must take charge of Haárin and show them the Way to a new Star." She sat back, her hands folded in her lap, maddening in her calm. "You understand such, this I know. What life have you with humanish now, Kièrshia? They do not think as you do. They do not feel as you do. Their concerns are not yours, for if they were you would not be here. But what life have you with Haárin, who would not even allow you inside their godly houses? Hah!" She raised a hand, gesturing about the library. "This is your place now, among your own. Sit here with me, and take it."

Witch. One who persuaded with feeling, as Feyó did with facts. "During my visit to ná Feyó, she received a message from Rauta Shèràa Temple. Tsecha had denied Sànalàn's authority as Chief Propitiator. Temple decreed that he be called back into the worldskein."

"Hah!" Gisa clasped her hands over her head and shook them. "He is hybrid in all ways but the body!"

"This is not good news." Jani dragged out a chair and sat so she could lean closer to Gisa and lower her voice. Niall might not have been able to understand her words, but he'd be able to understand the music quite well. "Your announcement as to your fitness to take the Elyan Haárin from Feyó has confused the other Outer Circle Haárin. You have said you are Tsecha's choice, but I am here to tell you once and for all that Tsecha supports Feyó—"

"If he knew of this place, if he saw—"

"He would still realize that Feyó is the better choice to lead the Outer Circle Haárin through this crisis, even though he created it himself." Jani rested her hands on the table, spreading her red-trimmed cuffs in the process. "You must back down. You have not the experience to head both hybrid and Haárin. You have put Feyó in the position where she must fight for her survival at a time when the Outer Circle Haárin must project a united front. If Cèel sees you are as one, he may stay his hand regarding Tsecha."

Gisa struck the table with her fist. "We must have a place!"

"This is not the way. This is not the time!"

Gisa wavered. Uncertainty curved her hands further, and softened the hardness of her face. "Then we are as nothing here."

Jani looked into grey eyes gone cold. "That will change. But not this way, and not at this time." She waited for some sign of Gisa's agreement. When none proved forthcoming, she bit back further argument—she had some idea how the female reacted to being cornered, and she didn't want to risk applying too much pressure. "We will speak more of this later."

She pushed back her chair and stood, then turned to find Niall regarding her narrow-eyed over the top of a freestanding display case. Ignoring him, she headed for the door, boots clipping on the glassy floor. She opened the door and stepped out into the walkway, heard the panel slide closed behind her.

Then she heard it open again, followed hard by the crunch of tietops on the tiled walkway.

"I didn't understand a damned word you said back there." Niall quickened his step and fell in beside her. "I did hear Tsecha's name a few times. What trouble is that old bird in now?"

Jani stopped, turning into Niall and halting him with a bump of her shoulder. "If you really want to know, I'll tell you. Communications Ministry techs are bound to plumb it out of the spaceways soon anyway." She waited for his slow nod. "He denounced Sànalàn. The Rauta Shèràa Temple has ordered him back to Shèrá to face disciplinary action. The translation Feyó and I both took from that is that they'll kill him." She waited for him to close his mouth. "We might stand a chance of saving him if a union of Outer Circle Haárin demand he be spared—Cèel's power base is shaky and he needs Haárin support to keep his Oligarchy. But ná Gisa has challenged ná Feyó for the dominance of the Outer Circle Haárin, and if they're hung up with this little episode, they'll be too splintered to compel Cèel to spare Tsecha." She locked her hands behind her back and bent forward at the waist like an instructor teaching a class. "Is that clear?"

"As mud." Niall paced a tight circle, then turned to face her. "I know how you feel about him—"

"Thank you."

"—but how does this affect the Commonwealth? That's my concern. What does an Haárin union that's powerful enough to push around a bornsect Oligarch mean to Chicago?" Niall's beautiful eyes hardened, became one at last with his predator's face. "You see my dilemma? I watched you out there, spouting off like a Drill, ordering everyone around, terrifying them yet drawing them in at the same time. They follow every move you make, as if you were a knife blade catching the sun." He looked off into the middle distance. "Charisma, yes. Mystique. Legend. And as I watch this . . . history unfold before me, I constantly need to remind myself that I'm on the other side. There was a time that I'd have followed you into the maw of hell, Jan, but I can't anymore."

Jani nodded. "I know. I'm not asking you to."

"But you're asking me to stand aside and watch, and I can't do that, either." A shadow found Niall's scar, deepening it to a cruel gash. "I need to inform my superiors of a brewing issue with the Haárin. They'll inform Cabinet Row, who will have to decide what outcome best suits them and push accordingly, and you know as well as I do that a weakened Cèel isn't the worst news for the Commonwealth." He waited for Jani to respond, but had the sense to drop the point when she didn't. "I have to take that skimmer back to the Board. Then I need to check in at Fort Karistos." He stepped around her and headed toward the stairs. "They still want to talk to you."

Jani folded her arms, hunched her shoulders. Idomeni anger, combined with an ache like a punch in the pit of her stomach. "They can go to hell."

"Is that your answer as a Commonwealth citizen?" Niall looked back at her. Raised a pleading hand to her, then let it fall. "Glories of the morning to you, ná Kièrshia. I believe that's the proper phrase." His step sounded once more. "The proper name."

He took the stairs two at a time. Jani looked over the railing and watched him stride across the courtyard to the door, back straight and head held high, like the soldier he was.

CHAPTER 19

Jani wandered the lower level of the house for the first time. It did feel cooler than the upper levels, the white walls and high ceilings allowing a sense of space and light that she had never associated with a basement. Maybe it was the lack of windows that caused her closed-in feeling, the knowledge that the fresh, hot wind never blew through this place. Or maybe it was the memory of Niall walking across the courtyard, on his way to perform his soldier's duty in the way that he saw fit.

She grew conscious of the faces eventually, watching her from the examining room doorways, from around corners, like mice waiting for the feral dog to pass so they could go about their business. She turned to a female who stood in the entry to a laboratory, a hybridized Haárin outfitted in the same medwhite shirt and trousers that had been John's uniform for years, and tried baring her teeth in the interest of good will. When the female backed off a step, however, she realized that at this particular moment, simple questions were probably the better course to take. "Is John Shroud still down here? He came to speak with Eamon DeVries."

"Yes. Ná Kièrshia." The female first pointed down the hall, then stepped out of the room. "The directions . . . too complicated, and truly." She led Jani down one corridor, then another, glancing back at her every few steps as though afraid she might pounce.

Damn it, I'm not a brute. Jani took her shooter from her waistband and tucked it into her duffel to reinforce the opinion, then tried to straighten her back and uncurve her shoulders—the posture of anger came so easily now that she wasn't even aware when it took hold. They came to a stop in front of a plain white door identical to all the others. Only a small plate set off to the side, etched in both humanish and Sìah numbers, marked its identity.

"Thank you." Jani nodded to the female, who bolted as if freed from a prison. *I have got to work on my social skills.* She waited until the corridor was free of traffic, then knocked. "John? It's Jani."

Silence followed for a long beat. Then came the click of a lock being disengaged, the hollow slide of a mechanism. The panel slid open, revealing John, his face set, his suit jacket and sunshades discarded, the sleeves of his white shirt rolled to the elbow. A softening came to his eyes when he looked at her, but he didn't smile. "I wondered when you'd show."

He stood aside, opening Jani's view to the rest of the room. It was an office, air chilled by a space cooler, redolent with the goaty odor of male shut-in and an undercurrent of prepack meals past. A desk filled the middle of the room, surrounded by shelves, file bins, and a worktable set with two workstations. Holos hung from every spare centimeter of wall space—Eamon DeVries with ministers past and present, actors and actresses, sports stars.

The man himself sat on a couch set against the far wall, beshirted and trousered but barefoot still, surrounded by the pillows and rumpled blankets that marked the furniture as his bed. The arrogance that he carried at the station and the bizarre cocktail party had given way to sullenness, his slack face and bagged eyes reflecting the days spent operating on nerve, liquor, and too little sleep.

"Well well." Eamon looked at her, then lay back his head and frowned at the ceiling. "If it isn't the second team."

Jani entered, waiting for John to close the door and find his seat before deciding where to perch. "I doubt I have anything to say to you that John hasn't already covered, and better than I could." She tested the strength of a waist-high bookcase, set her duffel on top, then hoisted aboard, legs dangling.

"He did tell me that you asked him why he did it." John sat at Eamon's desk. "We've spent the last few hours discussing those reasons in greater detail."

"As if they weren't good enough." Eamon jerked his chin toward Jani. "As if they weren't better than the ones you used with *that*. At least Gisa and her crew came to me. At least I had permission!" He yanked his blanket onto his lap and started matching edges and corners. "You're a bloody hypocrite, John—you always have been. Free to do as you will, but God forbid anyone else should presume." He started to fold the mass of cloth, but it overwhelmed him, and he tossed it to the floor in a hail of cursing. "And as for your bloody contract, a decent attorney could hack it to bits. Assuming, of course, that you're looking forward to having Neoclona's laundry basket dumped in full view of the Commonwealth population." He worked to his feet, then knelt on the floor. "Think of all that bad publicity. Just might be the boost that Service Medical and some of those new independent med services are looking for—twenty years of John Joseph Shroud's chicanery, laid open for the public to paw over." He lay flat on his stomach and reached beneath the couch, grunting and muttering imprecations before finally emerging, shoes in hand.

"The problem with taking on Neoclona, Eamon, is that your worth is as tied up in its perceived value as is mine and Val's." John exuded calm edging into boredom. "You could indeed rake us over the public coalpit, but in the end you might find yourself stuck with a portfolio of battered valuations and attorneys' fees based on what you were worth before you opened your mouth." He locked his hands behind his head and hoisted his feet atop the desk. "Then there's the Commonwealth to deal with. I made one"—he cocked his head toward Jani—"you made fifty-seven. The former's a curiosity. The latter's a complication in every future human-idomeni negotiation, and don't think that won't be noted and appreciated by Li Cao and all the highly placed others who will have to grapple with the fallout for years to come."

Eamon remained kneeling, shoes dangling in his grip, eyes fixed on John with a hatred intensified by the smell and clutter and the wall-hung testimony to a life gone by. "You won't win this one, John. You and your deep pockets and your conceit and your Halloween suit." He struggled back atop the couch, then tossed his shoes to the floor and shoved his bare feet inside. "I put as much into this company as you and Val. More, come to that, so don't suppose for a minute that I'll go quietly with a pittance and a scolding as my payment." He tottered to his feet with an unsteadiness that spoke of a hangover as well as overwhelming rage. "I won't be set aside twice." He walked to the door, slowly at first, then faster as he found his balance. "I have rounds now." He grabbed a medcoat from a wall hook next to the door. "Then I'll have my work to do, and I'd prefer it if you were both *out* by the time I return." He pounded the doorframe with his fist until the panel slid aside, then forced through the gap and into the hall.

"That didn't go well." John cocked his head as though listening to the fading pound of Eamon's footsteps, the closing of the door. "I didn't mean to refer to you as a curiosity. Such is the language of negotiation." He lowered his feet to the floor and sat forward, picking through the piles on Eamon's desk like a technician isolating a particularly vile sample. "He'll push. I'll push. In the end we'll work something out, but it won't be pretty. No image for posterity. No handshakes all around." He liberated a wafer folder from the middle of a stack of files, glanced at the cover, then tucked it back in its place, his face reddening. "I see Eamon's taste in entertainment hasn't changed." He leaned on his elbows and cradled his chin in one hand. "And how was your morning?"

"Even better than yours." Jani filled John in on the news from Shèrá, Gisa's and Niall's reactions. "I've asked Feyó to contact the other Outer Circle dominants and rally support. My job was to try to convince Gisa to see sense. I'm giving her time to think before going back for round two."

"For all you know, Tsecha might already be on his way to Shèrá." John poked through the stacks again, freeing a cookie packet and digging out a broken half. "We do it all the time at Neoclona—fix the problem, then announce that we had one." He popped the piece into his mouth and chewed reflectively. "Getting in touch with the home team is, I believe, the order of the day."

Jani drew up her legs and crossed them. The ache in her gut had subsided to a grumble, and she debated asking John if there was any more food to be unearthed from the depths of Eamon's desk. "I don't trust the communications here. There's the Elyan enclave, but I'm not sure that the embassy doesn't tap into enclave-to-enclave communications when it suits them, and they'd be interested in this. Service is the most secure of all, and they are most definitely out."

"There's always Neoclona." John concentrated on smoothing the creases from the cookie packet. "Due to the sensitive nature of some of our data, we've systems in place that would give Niall pause."

Jani thought back to Niall's chill expression, his voice wrung dry of any attempt to argue because he had finally realized it would do neither of them any good. *I'm on the other side*. A malleable phrase, adjustable to fit both of them. "We're edging into a delicate area. The messages Val would be receiving would contain

intelligence that could be considered important to the Commonwealth for both strategic and security reasons. It would concern
Outer Circle dock ownership. Holding companies. Copies of communications with Rauta Shèràa Temple and Council." She looked
across the room at John, met his steady, too-dark eye. "You realize
what I'm asking?"

"Yes."

"Someone with a broad definition of treason might even think
it applies to you."

"Let me worry about that."

"Easier said than done."

"Be that as it may." John clasped his hands together, then
tapped his chin with his doubled fist. "Who would act on the receiving end?"

"Lucien."

"Are you sure?"

"He won't play fast and loose with this. He'd realize that if I
found out, the Commonwealth wouldn't be big enough for him to
hide in." Jani pulled her overrobe around her in an effort to fight
the cold. "I'd like to keep Val out of it."

"I can tell him to have Lucien there at a particular time. The
message never has to pass through his hands. I can tell him that
they're classified Service communications, word it in such a way
that he knows to keep his hands off." He grinned without a trace of
humor. "We're being so careful. It's as though we're already
preparing the story for the lawyers." He stood and gathered his
jacket from the back of Eamon's chair. "Where do we start?"

"I need to dig my report-writing skills out of my duffel and
put together a preliminary something." Jani pushed off the bookcase, then dragged her bag onto her shoulder. "Wait for Feyó's update. Bug her for it, if I can get a message to her."

"I can do that before I go to Neoclona." John rolled down his
sleeves, then dragged on his jacket.

"Then I get to work on Gisa again." The duffel slid from Jani's
shoulder. She caught it just before it hit the floor. "I never thought
this trip would turn out like this. I'm sorry." A weight pressed down
on her from above, bowing her back. Her heart pounded. Panic and
anger, unabated by an augie that couldn't stop it anymore. "Damn
it!" She raised her duffel over her head and slammed it down on
the worktable, scattering data wafers and documents, sending an
old coffee dispo skittering across the floor. *"Damn it!"* She raised
it once more and brought it down. Again. Again.

"Jani?" John rounded the desk and closed in. "Stop it. *Stop it.*"
He wrestled the bag from her hand and let it fall to the floor, then
grabbed her wrists and struggled to force her still. "Stop this. I
said, *stop it!*"

Jani battled the instinct to strike. John stood too close, his
stance too open. So many ways to hit him. So many ways to bring
him down—

Her mind's eye filled with the visions that poured from her
memory, of battles fought and battles feared, past and future joined.
She slowed, then stilled, as the humanish that remained in her
fought the idomeni and slowly gained the upper hand, at least for
now. Who'd have thought she'd find such mercy there? She sagged
against John, shaking free from his grasp as she pressed her face
against his chest, felt his heart beat through his thin shirt. Wrapped
her arms around his waist and pulled him closer and felt it beat
stronger still. Faster.

He touched her hair first, a tentative fingering, as though he'd
never seen such stuff as that before. Then his hands moved down,
over the back of her head, coming to rest on her shoulders.

Jani waited. She could sense his thoughts as though he spoke
aloud, knew he wanted to push her away yet couldn't summon the
will to do so.

"You're not yourself." His bass rumbled as though it came up
through the floor. *The voice of the machine*, Eamon had once
called it.

Not a machine. Oh, didn't she know. She raised her head and
looked into eyes filmed to intimidate, set in a face blanked by the
determination not to care. "Every day, I change a little more. That
means that at this moment I'm as close to myself as I will ever be
again." With that, she reached up and worked her hands through
white hair like shredded silk and pulled him down. His lips hovered near hers, the barest breath apart, allowing them both one last
chance to end it. Then they met, closing a gap of millimeters, of
twenty years' worth of other lives and other lovers and the ever-
present knowledge that all they'd done was mark the time.

Jani savored taste and sense and scent long-lost and long-
imagined. Touched a scar on the back of John's neck, the result of
shatterbox shrapnel from the first wave of Rauta Shèràa bombings. Ran a hand under the neck of his shirt and over his shoulder,
and felt the bump on his collarbone from a youthful fall from a
tree. *I know his body better than mine.* She felt her heat rise, overwhelming the chill of the room. She held John closer, ground

against him and heard the groan rise in his throat, then felt him pull back.

"Now what?" His breathing came rough and his lips had swelled and reddened—his eyes held triumph and lust and joy and love and just the slightest shadow of fear.

"I don't know. The usual, I suppose." Jani looked over John's shoulder to Eamon's rumpled couch. "Just not here, please." She took his hand, held it up to her face, pressed it against her cheek, then kissed it. "I have a room upstairs. I think it's still mine." She felt fully humanish now, suffused and distracted and aching for release. "It'll be a little hot for you, though."

John ran a finger along the line of her jaw. "Somehow, I don't think I'll notice."

Jani picked up her duffel and headed for the door. Her knees had gone to rubber, while her skin had turned into an instrument that sang as the cold air danced over it. The hybrids who stood in the corridors watched her pass but said nothing. She wondered if those who had been humanish noticed the dreamy look she knew must have inhabited her face, saw John walking a discreet distance behind, and added one plus one.

She heard voices behind her and turned. One of the medwhite-clad hybrids had stopped John, asking him a question about some testing protocol. John stared after her as she kept walking. Into the lift, then up to the fourth floor. She strolled along the railing, her eyes on the courtyard, feeling the stares of the hybrids who stood and talked, sat in the adjoining rooms and read. *How can I think about sex at a time like this?* Then she saw John dash out of the basement stairwell and across the courtyard, jacket tails flying, searching for her like the hero in a melodrama.

Then he stilled. Looked up. Saw her, and walked more slowly to the lift. She waited for him in front of the bedroom entry, standing with her back to the door, waiting as he disembarked and headed for her with the determined stride that a long-range shooter couldn't have repelled.

Jani keyed open the door and looked around the bedroom. "Hello?" She walked in, saw the bed still rumpled from her visit a day ago. "All clear."

John walked in after her, taking in the room, the view. Then he turned to her and froze, fixed by the sight of her. "For months I've been playing the 'What if?' game. Would it happen? Where? I thought of the Neoclona flat in Chicago, a clear moonlit night overlooking the lake." He looked around again, then shook his head. "Wrong time of day. Wrong body of water. Wrong . . . circumstances."

"When was it ever easy with us?" Jani tossed her duffel aside, wondering at the condition of the devices it contained, then driving the thought from her mind. "You reach a point when you decide to take things as they are." She laughed, from nerves and fatigue and the call of a love so long denied.

John reached out and pulled her to him. "Are you all right?"

"I will be." Jani could feel the thin layer of sweat that coated his hands. *Good—that makes two of us.* She kicked off her low boots as John swept off her overrobe and jacket. Her back arched as he pushed down her bandbra and cupped her breasts. Then he picked her up as though she weighed nothing, carried her to the bed and lay her down, pulled her trousers down and off, then followed with her underwear, his movements as rapid and ragged as his breathing.

"Day's looking better and better." He pulled off his jacket, then his shirt, revealing wire-frame shoulders and skin like old marble. "At least from where I'm standing." He undid his trousers and let them fall, then fell to his knees beside the bed and leaned over Jani, planting a few quick kisses on her stomach before coming up for air. "Are you going to say anything?"

Jani reached out and pressed her hand against his chest, fixed as she had been years before by the contrast between their skins. Her brown, now tinged with gold. His too-white, blue veins threading beneath. "I love you." She laced her hand through his hair and pulled him close, rising half up to meet him, kissing him as he boosted atop the bed. His hands explored everywhere, every place he'd regrown, rebuilt, reassembled. When she tried to move against him, he held her still and toyed with her, until she thought the build of sensation would make her scream. The clumsy probings of a novice had been replaced by the skilled exploration of a master—her world narrowed to the maze of fire he'd traced over her body, the one place where it burned the hottest. "You bad boy." Her voice emerged drugged. "You've been practicing."

"I had a lot of room for improvement," John said as he pressed atop her. Their breaths caught and they lay, still as death, as between them the wall of two decades of loss and hate and inexorable change faded to nothing.

"I love you," John said as he stirred, and they began to move as one.

Jani caught the play of chemical light across his white hair, flashes of silvery gold that for a discordant moment compelled thoughts of Lucien.

Then John called out her name, and she didn't think of Lucien anymore.

CHAPTER 20

Jani sat at the bedroom window, examining her scanpack under a glaring combination of Karistosian sunlight and the more focused beam of one of the floorlamps. "I think you're OK." She ran a hand over the black poly case, scratched and nicked from years of use. "Didn't mean to shake you up, but I wasn't feeling quite up to speed." She smiled. "I'm feeling a little tired now, but that's OK, too. Not that you care, I'm sure."

"Do you always talk to your scanpack?"

Jani turned in her chair to find John standing in the bathroom entry. "Only when I've been really rough on it. I'm not sure it means anything. There was a paper published about the time I graduated the Academy that posited that since scanpacks did contain brain tissue, they could evidence emotion, feel stress, and respond to sensory stimuli."

John fastened his shirt, frowning every so often and stopping to tug at his cuffs. "Did you believe it?"

"When it's oh-two in the morning and you've got idomeni on one side and Rauta Shèràa Base Command on the other waiting for you to confirm the dating on a handwritten, lubricant-soaked cover page that's all that remains of a fourteen page manifest, you'll believe anything." Jani's smile faded as she watched John continue to fuss with his shirt. "What's wrong?"

"I hate putting clothes back on after I've worn them." He vanished into the bathroom for a moment, then emerged into the bedroom, jacket in hand. "Someone must have a cleaner in this place, but I'm reluctant to go knocking from door to door."

"I have a spare coverall you can borrow." Jani followed his

every move as he walked, bent, straightened. He moved with weighty fluidity, like a man formed of mercury, and she could have watched him until the sun flamed. "Might be a little short in the arms and legs."

"I'll manage." John walked to the table where Jani sat and picked up her shooter. "You had this in your duffel when you were banging it around?"

Jani nodded. "I always disengage the powerpack when I stash it, but still." She took the weapon from him and held it next to her scanpack. "Everything looks all right. Tried all the scanning equipment—everything checks out. I checked the room in the process—we seem to be insect-free."

John paused in his examination of her assorted antimonitoring hardware. "Were you concerned?"

"I'm always concerned." Jani picked up a still-activated monitor and turned it off. "So, no damage to anything but my pride."

"You've no reason to feel that way." John laid a hand on her shoulder and squeezed lightly. "You're still adjusting." He made as if to say more, but stopped, turning abruptly and walking to the bed. "Have you given any thought to coming with me back to Karistos?" he asked after a time.

"I need to stay here." Jani returned her scanpack to her duffel, followed by various other gadgets, then finally by her shooter. "I need to lobby. Seek out like minds. Rally them 'round the banner. Be political, something I'm not necessarily good at." She turned off the lamp, pushed her chair away from the table, and stood. "Call me the minority whip."

"I've wondered once or twice what you'd look like in leather." John's brow arched, as though he managed to surprise himself. "I haven't made a habit of it." He sat on the edge of the bed and started pulling on his socks, then stopped. "I realize how important Tsecha is to you. I know that every move we make now, or don't make, will affect humans and idomeni for years to come." He gave one sock a hard yank. "Pardon my selfishness, but I really don't want to leave now."

"Pardon my selfishness, but I don't want you to go." Jani meant to head across the room to the armoire to store her duffel, but she detoured to the bed and sat next to John. "You must be uncomfortable in this heat."

"The view makes up for it," he replied, giving her the same bewildered look that he had a hundred times in the Rauta Shèràa clinic basement. Then he reached for her.

Jani felt immersed in a sensual wash of soap scent, freshly shaved skin, and a rustle of expensive cloth. *I don't have time for this.* She felt his weight shift as he eased her back, pressed her lips to the place above the pulse in his throat, then held her breath as she felt him still, then loosen his arms around her.

"I hate rushing." John sat up, adjusting his clothes along the way. "I feel like a starving man who has to make do with whatever he can grab from someone else's table." He looked down at her, swallowed hard, then looked away. "Do you think a face-to-face meeting between Feyó and Gisa would do any good?"

Jani worked into a sitting position. "They tried that already. The idomeni aren't much for working past disagreements." The writing implements that she had dug out of various drawers and cupboards beckoned from the desk. "I still need to write that report for transmittal."

"I have some things to wrap up here." John stood and slipped on his shoes, then headed for door. "I'll try to talk to Eamon one more time, now that he's had the chance to ponder his options." He doubled back around and bent to Jani, kissing her hard. "Keep that in mind." This time he walked to the door and didn't stop.

Jani stared at the closed door, then turned back to the brightness of the view with a sigh. Sat on the bed for a time, tapping her boot heels together as she tried to rough out an introduction to her report, and drifted instead to thoughts of love and how she had lived without it for so long.

"Ah, well." She stood up, and carried the sensation of John's embraces with her as she sat at the desk and settled down to work.

Jani left her room, waiting until she heard the lock mech slide into place before continuing down the walkway. Cooking aromas rose from the courtyard and enveloped her, grilled meat and myriad spices and herbs—she peered over the railing, to where the hybrids had gathered to eat, then checked her timepiece.

"Mid-afternoon sacrament." Her stomach grumbled, complaining more loudly the harder she pressed her hand against it to quiet it. She shunned the lift for the stairs and galloped down, inhaling the air in gulps, her mouth watering. "Maybe if they don't let me eat with them, I can strain enough food out of the air." Like John's coffee, the Thalassan cuisine packed a wallop.

Jani reached the bottom of the stairs to find John hovering near the courtyard entry, pacing the short stretch like a tiger in a cage. "It's the smell." His nostrils flared. "I'm so hungry I think I could eat the dishes."

"Eamon said that blue-trimmed dishes hold the mildly spiced foods." Jani squinted toward the table, then ducked down when a couple of the hybrids looked her way. "They've set a few out. No idea what they are, though."

"I don't care." John stilled. "Shall we risk the slings and arrows?" He turned to her and held out his arm.

Jani took it, pulling him close. "All they can do is toss us."

"If they throw food, we'll grab plates and catch what we can." John leaned toward her and spoke out of the side of his mouth. "You head for the door—I'll cover you with one of the lamps." His joking ceased when the hybrids turned toward them as one and watched them enter the courtyard. He sombered and straightened.

"Ná Kièrshia." Gisa raised a glass in a humanish toast. "We are most honored." She took a sip of her drink, then gestured to the empty seat of honor beside her. "Please."

Jani walked around the table to her chair, counting the filled places as she went. *Twenty-five*. Not even a simple majority.

"Looks like most of them work in Karistos during the day." John held Jani's chair, then took the empty place next to her.

"Yes, Doctor Shroud, this is most the case." Gisa offered her hostess smile. "Most work in smaller businesses. Some own their own. The government, not so much, nor the Service. Such places demand a loyalty that we reserve for Thalassa." Her manner was light and practiced, as though all was right between her and Jani, and their argument had never occurred.

Jani scanned the table and caught sight of a familiar face at one end. *Make that two familiar faces.* Torin and Brondt, their chairs angled in such a way that they could see her.

I'm guessing neither you nor Major Hamil can leave the compound, Colonel Brondt. Jani detected a shifting back and forth of Brondt's water glass that she knew counted as his greeting, a whisper compared to Torin's wave of his fork. *I have no idea what Niall has planned for you.* She accepted one of the paisley tureens from Bon and ladled a fish stew potent enough for the rising steam to burn her eyes. *All I can say is that I doubt you'll like it.*

John dished out sliced kettle meat and gravy from one of the blue safety servers. "So far, so good."

Jani took a piece of crisp flatbread from a basket. "They think I've come around to their side." She snapped the bread in two with a decisive turn of wrist. "Which has its advantages."

John glanced at her, his eyes widening. "Oh, I know that look." He seemed about to say more, but before he could, an unfortunately familiar figure took a seat nearby.

"John." Eamon placed a half-empty vodka bottle beside his plate. "I'm amazed that you've managed to stay away from your dear, dear offices this long." He looked from him to Jani, and an instinct honed years before brought a flush of color to his already raddled cheeks. "Oh, Johnny, you let her do it to you again. I remember that sick look on your face, oh how I remember. What was the term I coined? Ah, yes. The overeducated social maladjust wallowing in afterglow."

John stiffened as the decades-old insult hit home. "You haven't changed since Rauta Shèràa, Eamon. Still confusing coarseness with honesty."

"A little coarseness would do you a universe of good, old man. A little of the rough to cut through that gauzy filter you've wrapped 'round your memories."

"Can it, Eamon."

"Damned fool."

"I said, can it."

Eamon fell silent, glaring daggers at Jani between bites of food and gulps of vodka.

Jani took advantage of the silence to monitor Torin and Brondt. They declined to acknowledge her presence further after their first wordless greetings, finishing their meals quickly, then taking their leave a few minutes apart. She noticed others of the group leave abruptly as well—the older female she'd seen with Torin her first day, other solemn faces whose names she had yet to learn.

Jani ate enough to quell the worst of her pangs. Then she reached into the pocket of her coverall and removed the note and message wafer, palming them as she placed her hand on John's thigh. She let them slip onto the seat between his legs, heard the catch of his breath, the flicker of his eye as he tried to glance at her without seeming to.

"I'm off to take a walk—I haven't even seen the beach yet." Jani pushed back from the table, muscles twitching as though gearing up for a run. "Glories of the afternoon to one and all." She stood, acknowledging Gisa's surprised response, the murmurs of the remaining diners, then wandering to the door as though she had nothing but time and a world in which to spend it.

*   *   *

Jani walked down the same road she had climbed in a rage earlier that morning, picking up the details now that she missed before. The nameplates on the houses, fashioned from colored tiles. The occasional glimpse of clutter through an open door, which showed that actual beings lived there, who made actual messes and never quite managed to contain them, like beings everywhere.

The glare of the sun off the water could have served as a weapon. By the time she reached the beach, she wished she'd had the sense to pack sunshades. "The Chicago sun never bothers me." She picked her way through the rocks that poked up through the sand like the shattered teeth of some ancient beast. "But the Elyan sun is brighter, and we're nearer the equator here." She rolled up the sleeves of her coverall to above her elbows, then undid the neck as she felt the sweat bead. Walked past the rocks to where the sand lay wet and smooth, and listened to the slow crash of the waves and the distant screech of seabirds.

"Have you noticed the water?"

Jani turned to find Brondt standing behind her amid the rocks, Torin at his side gripping his ever-present handheld. "I haven't had time."

"Then you should find the time." He walked out to join her. He wore a long-sleeve shirt despite the heat, along with trousers and boots shiny with waterproofing. "If you really look at it, you'll see a purplish tint. Sometimes if there's enough cloud cover and the wind has been blowing in from the islands for a few days, the water looks like molten amethyst, if there is such a thing. Amazing to see. It's an algae, of course. Toxic to humanish—if it touches your skin, you might develop a nasty rash."

Jani took a step back just as the lick of a wave broke over the sand. She'd only brought the one pair of boots, which weren't as well-protected as Brondt's. The last thing she needed was a bout of contact dermatitis. "What about the sea life?"

"The usual fishlike things, some small and brilliantly colored, some dull silver and big as skimmers." Brondt eased into the role of native guide, clasping his hands behind him and rocking back and forth. "A few types are edible, if you sauce them up, but many of us have shown varying degrees of sensitivity. The native life here is just different enough to bother both idomeni and humanish."

"What about—" Jani gasped and slapped at her hand as a pain like an acid spatter stung the skin on the back.

"And then there are the flies. Different from the burrowers I told you about when we first arrived. These just sting like needles pricking." Brondt *tsked*, then fell silent for a time. "You saw ná Feyó." He toed the sand, prodding a shell from its mooring.

Jani looked back at Torin, who straightened as though someone had grabbed the back of his trousers and yanked up. "Don't record this."

"I know. I'm not completely without sense." Torin's air of deference vanished, replaced by the universal sense of injury peculiar to the teenager of any species. "I'll write it down later, when it's over. I have a very good memory."

"He does, you know. Scary, sometimes." Brondt jerked his chin toward a wide, flat rock that sat like a roughed-out table in the middle of the beach. "A few of the hybrid Haárin still maintain contact with the enclave." He sat on a low outcropping that stuck out from the rock's side. "They learned of ní Tsecha's recall. They think Oligarch Cèel will kill him."

"So do I." Jani took a cross-legged seat on the rock's edge. "Gisa needs to step aside. The Outer Circle Haárin need to convince Cèel that they're united, that any action he takes against ní Tsecha could cripple him in event of a challenge from another bornsect." She watched Torin chase a tiny scuttling creature about the sand, touching his toe to it to send it hopping. "Feyó's rounding up her supporters among the other enclaves. I tried to convince Gisa to cease her bid for dominance. Don't know if I made any headway or not."

"So now you're seeking to erode her support from within?" Brondt pulled in his boot just as Torin's creature leaped past, thumb-sized and twin-clawed, with stalked eyes and an iridescent carapace. "That could take some time. Do you think you have it to spend?"

"Probably not." Jani gave a silent cheer as the creature vanished into a gap between some rocks. As always, she felt a kinship with anything that was being chased. "First, I need to find out if ní Tsecha is still in Chicago. Whether or not he still is will dictate my next move. Until then, I'll see to matters here, and . . ."

Brondt nodded. "We shut down quite a few smuggling operations during my time at the station. We always reached a point where we had to sit and wait for something. Information. Confirmation. A noose to tighten. I always found it the most difficult time." He made a show of studying his hands. "Don't look now, but you're about to get your first shot at consensus-building."

Jani looked up the steep enclave road just as the first in a series of scattered groups reached the flat stretch of sand. She recognized most of the hybrids as those who had departed sacrament early, including Torin's older female, who joined him at the place where the hopping crustacean disappeared and probed with him through the rocks.

The others spread out, taking seats on nearby boulders. Then those perches filled, and still they came, some with blankets that they spread over the dry rocky sand, a few with folding chairs. Jani watched as they settled in, expressions guarded yet expectant. Niall's words returned to her . . . *charisma* . . . *mystique* . . . *legend* . . . and still she couldn't accept that they had come here to see her. *I'm Tsecha's representative.* Yes, that was it. A substitute for something else. That, she could understand.

"Ná Kièrshia?" A younger male with the solemn mien of a university student raised his hand. "Are you staying, you and Doctor Shroud?"

"I saw him go to your room." A young female, no more than a teenager, peered at Jani over the young male's shoulder. "And. Not. Come. Out." Her face split in a tooth-baring grin. Then clapped her hand over her mouth and doubled over, stricken by a case of the giggles.

Jani felt her cheeks flame as the humanish hybrids hid their smiles and the Haárin hybrids bared their teeth more openly. "Thank you for noticing."

"But it is just as it was before." Torin's friend had taken a seat atop a rock, while Torin sat on the ground at her feet. "He and you, creator and created. It is fitting."

Jani swallowed. *They know everything about my life. I'm an object of study.* A galling thought for someone who used to pack up and go if she encountered the same face on a street one time too many. "Are you an historian as well?"

"I am Lisse." The female looked more humanish than any of the other hybrids, most likely because she had begun the process so late in life. "I am Torin's home-mother, and an historian as well." She sat forward, eyes like crystal shining with interest. "May I ask—do you mind—your treatments? What do you recall of them?"

"Of the actual insertions?" Jani shook her head. "Nothing. I remember the time just before the explosion. Someone shouted something to the pilot. Half a sentence. 'Hey—' " She felt the pressure of being the center of attention, of multiple pairs of eyes fixed upon her, heard the water and the birds and the nonsound of bated breath. "Month and a half later, I woke up to find John

Shroud sitting in a chair beside my bed." Would she ever forget his solemn white face, or his first words to her? *Hello, creation. My name is John Shroud. Unfortunate name for a physician, don't you think?*

"Did you look as you do now?" That from a humanish-appearing female who shared a blanket with an Haárin male.

Jani held out her arm and rubbed it with her other hand. "They had just taken me out of the immersion tank the day before. My skin was shiny, and very pink." She fingered one of her curls. "I had some sparse black stuff growing out of my head that in theory was hair. My eyebrows were little tufty things. Eyes, a little lighter than they are now. Definitely not humanish-looking." The memories returned, bringing with them the long-forgotten smells of conductive gel and warm plastic. "John and Val Parini prodded me out of bed the next day, made me walk a few steps. After that came therapy—muscle stimulation, mental exercises. Amazing the things you forget when you're in an induced coma for six weeks."

Torin raised his hand. "What do you like most about being a hybrid?"

"Like?" Jani grew as still as the rock on which she sat. Her mind blanked, and she knew the sick feeling she'd had to battle whenever an interrogation had gone too long and cut too close. When the only answer that occurred was the absolute truth, and the absolute truth was the last thing she knew she should say. "I never thought about like or dislike before." She sensed the disappointment in some expressions, and pushed on anyway. If she lied, she might be able to win them for a short time, but the truth always came out, and when it did, she'd lose them forever. "As I changed more and more, as I grew sicker and sicker, I—" She licked her lips and looked everywhere but at the faces around her. "You chose this. I didn't. There will always be a difference in our feelings for that reason. Some of you chose for health reasons, others, because you believe in the blending, but you still made the choice yourselves."

"Isn't there anything about it that you enjoy?" Lisse asked.

"That I can offer my loyalty and regard or withhold them, as I see fit." Jani inhaled shakily—thank Ganesh for the shield of abstractions. "No individual, no system, merits my esteem solely because as a humanish I am bound to follow." She grinned weakly, then shrugged. "That sounds so arrogant. But I've been accused more than once of having a stiff neck." She thought of a few joking replies, but withheld them. These questions deserved serious answers, whether or not she felt comfortable giving them. Whether or not they were the ones her audience wanted to hear.

"My parents are Acadian. They returned there recently, after trying to live in Chicago." Jani imagined the scent of her mother's hair, and closed her eyes for a moment. "Acadia is their home. It calls to them. They carry something of it with them when they leave, and when they return, they bring it back with them, and they have the whole again." Did she make sense? Who would appear more bewildered to a wandering outsider, she or her audience? "I have never been in a place where I felt whole, where when I left, I took something of it with me. Humanish or hybrid, I've never felt that . . . contentment? Is that the word?" She pressed her hand to the rock, felt its warmth, but at the same time, its hardness. "That's how I'd answer you. That the enjoyment you speak of is contentment, and that I've never known it."

Lisse watched her. Did she seem so wise because of her age? Because her gaze never wavered? "I am most sorry."

"I am not," the somber student piped. "Those who are content never strive. Those who are content cannot lead. She is the Kièrshia—she will not be content until all is as it must be!"

The words echoed off the rocks, the cliff face. Jani felt the gazes once more, some pitying, others rapt with an awe that terrified her. *I'm only here because there's no other place for me, because when there are things to be done, I do them—don't look at me like that*!

"We should walk, I think." Brondt stood abruptly. "Show ná Kièrshia this place we call home." He kept his back turned to her as the hybrids gathered their gear. "Meet here in five minutes." He waited until they'd begun their trudge to their houses to turn to Jani.

"Was I that obvious?" She slid down from the rock and bent low, stretching her back.

"I did detect a trapped look, yes." Brondt crossed his arm over his chest in a gesture of uncertainty. "Uneasy lies the head that wears a crown."

"Henry the Fourth, Part Two." Jani fielded his look of surprise. "Too bad you and Niall Pierce started off on the wrong foot. You have a lot in common. A love of the classics." She sniffed. "And an eye that's too sharp by half."

Brondt cast her a sideways glance, then looked out toward the water. "They say that those who wish leadership the least are the ones who merit it the most."

"Are you my conscience, Dieter?"

"Do you need one?" Brondt turned back to face the houses, and watched the hybrids make their empty-handed way back down the road. "No, I don't think you do. A little peace, perhaps, but the two don't seem to go together, do they?"

Jani stared at the man's back, willed him to face her, and knew he wouldn't. Then she looked over the heads of the approaching hybrids and saw John standing on the overhang looking down at her, the sun brilliant off his shirt, his hair. She raised a hand in a small wave—he responded with a barely detectable movement of his fingers. She could feel his eyes on her as she turned and started down the beach. Then the hybrids closed in around her, distracting her, and by the time she turned again, he had gone.

CHAPTER 21

"Haven't seen Pascal around Far North Lakeside as much since the Vynshàrau challenged him to that duel." Cashman stopped in front of a store window and ogled the hologram models that danced through the air in skimpy spring clothes. "I heard he's laying low, hoping it will all blow over."

Micah closed his eyes. He hadn't wanted to join the gang for their weekly day trip into Chicago, but they'd begun remarking about his absences more and more and he'd run out of excuses. *So what happens—we're not off the train five minutes and someone brings up the goddamn—*"It's not a *duel*." He heard his voice tight with anger, and tried to stop himself. But he'd been bottling things up for weeks now. He had to allow the occasional vent or he'd go nuts. "They explained it on *Blue 'n' Grey Today*. It's been in all the 'sheets. It's a *challenge*. They're declaring their mutual animosity to the world. A few cuts on one another's arms, a little blood, and it's all over. It's not like a real fight. Nobody dies." He tried to focus on the dancing models, lose himself in the vision of female breasts and thighs and flouncing hair. But one of them looked too much like Manda, whom he'd seen die three times in the past week alone. He turned away from the window and fixed on the midday traffic instead.

"Jeez, bust me to Spacer First Class. Take my stripes away." Cashman glared at him, then rolled his eyes.

They continued to move en masse down State Street. Micah counted Cashman and Hough, Court and her usual gaggle of hangers-on, a couple of new additions from SysAdmin, all out to enjoy the bright sun and warm breeze, the first hints of summer. Or in his case, to get them all off his back.

But who knows . . . ? Micah took in the buildings and crowds and noise. The vivid colors. The sense of a place as far removed from exos and mid-ranges and Sergeant Chrivet as it was possible to be and still remain on this planet. Maybe, if he was lucky, he'd find one thread of sanity amid the tangle of the past weeks. Maybe he'd forget for a little while, catch his breath, and decompress.

"Fabe's right." Hough shot a questioning look at Micah and cleared his throat, the resident expert determined to reassert himself. "Look at the forearms of any of the idomeni—they're all hacked up. The more scars you bear, the more declared enemies you have, the more honor. Winning isn't the point. Death sure as hell isn't." He paused, his thin little gash of a mouth barely visible. "Pascal's probably spending time training. These fights are very ceremonial, very ritualized. If he gets it wrong, he makes us look bad."

Bullshit. Micah walked to the outside of the group, near the curb, and watched the skimmers course past. *He made us look bad when he accepted the damned fight in the first place*. When he let himself get into the situation where Ghos, the Vynshàrau security officer, challenged him. When he opened up the Service to reporters and Cabinet inquiries and embarrassing questions, and sullied it with alien traditions.

"If it's not a duel, why has the Judge Advocate petitioned Diplo to intervene and get the idomeni to retract the challenge?" Court stood before another store window and watched the clothes flit by. "I mean, they've been digging out laws from the 1800s trying to find an excuse." After a few seconds, the floating images flickered and changed, so that a dozen versions of Court's blond curviness filled the space, each wearing a different outfit. "I don't think it's going to happen, myself."

"Once a challenge has been accepted, neither side can back out." Hough glanced back at Micah, his voice growing louder and more assured when he realized he had no competition for this one. "If Pascal gets hit by a skimtruck, he'll get a postponement. That's the best he can hope for at this point."

"I still don't think it will happen. Too much publicity already, and everyone's locking down. No more statements issued without Mako's OK. Public Affairs is hiring contractors just to man the comports and say 'No comment' to whoever calls for a statement.

It's a nightmare." Court stepped away from the window and headed for a set of double doors that led into the store.

"No!" Cashman bolted after her. "No shopping—we made a deal!"

"I just want to see *one* thing." Court pointed in the vague direction of the dancing images, making it impossible to determine exactly which thing she had in mind. "It will only take a minute."

"Famous last words." Hough hung back to walk with Micah. "I could do with something to drink. You?"

They cut through the store to a noisy arcade, bought frozen sodas at an autokiosk, and found a table amid the press of shoppers catching their breath and store staff taking a break. A minute or so of increasingly edgy silence passed—Micah had been relieved enough to get away from the rest of the gang, but as had become more and more the case lately, he found that he had nothing to say to any of his fellow bullpen denizens. He'd monitored their behavior for some sign that one of them could have belonged to the Group, and once he realized that none of them did, he lost interest. They spent their spare time cruising the Veedrome, rattling on about girlfriends and promotions and upcoming leave. He spent his time killing Vynshàrau in a hundred different ways, then dying himself in a hundred and one. That tended to limit possible topics of conversation.

"Congrats on nailing the Tech One," Hough finally offered, poking the icy slush in his dispo cup with a straw. "They'll probably bump you up to corporal before you know it."

"Thanks." Micah used up a few seconds pulling in a mouthful of strawberry slurry. "They're offering it again next month—thinking of going for it?"

"Thinking about it. Yeah."

"Good luck."

Hough nodded, narrowed eyes fixed on a trio of girls who giggled past. "Guess you must feel pretty relieved about this challenge, huh? Got Pascal out of your hair."

Micah slowly set down his drink. He blanked his mind before any unwelcome ideas invaded, those months-ago thoughts of killing Cashman and hiding him in the delivery cage having taught him a lesson. It bothered him at times, knowing what he could do if he had to. "What do you mean?"

"I saw him a few times, catching you up in the hallways. Making conversation." Hough sucked his teeth. "I never heard anything about him and enlisteds—he's always been pretty careful to toe the regulation line. But there's a first time for everything, I guess."

Micah stared into his drink. Too pink for blood, but if he thought hard enough . . .

"He asked for you a couple of times, on days when you weren't in the pen. Seemed disappointed that you weren't around to handle problems with his . . . equipment." Hough capped his slur with another lick of the teeth.

That's the story going around? Fine. Micah felt his face heat. *Faber supplies porn to anyone who asks. Faber's got the infamous Captain Pascal aching to wipe his stripe.*

"He picked an Haárin second." Hough raised a hand to beckon to Cashman, who had wandered into the arcade looking irritated. "Dathim Naré, Tsecha Egri's suborn. Now he spends most of his time at the Haárin enclave training while Diplo and the JA try to figure out how to fit this challenge into Service protocols."

"They shouldn't have to." Micah braced for the onslaught as the rest of the group departed the store and approached the table.

Hough shrugged. "It was bound to happen sooner or later. Hell, his girlfriend, Kilian, fought a challenge last summer. Not that anyone would call her real Service." He stood, all good manners as a package-laden Court and her friends drew near. "We work with the idomeni. Trade with them. Better we figure out how to handle stuff like this once and for all."

"Once and for all, yeah. By making sure it never happens again." Micah's reply was drowned out by Cashman's loud complaints, Court's rejoinders. *By making sure—* He remained seated as the girls joined them, drawing sharp looks from Hough and Cashman. *By making sure it never—happens.* He swallowed fast as the oversweet slush bubbled up to the back of his throat.

"Let's get going," Cashman muttered. "Before something else catches her eye."

They left the arcade and walked back outside, the bickering over who would help Court carry her bags providing counterpoint to the more usual city noises, the blare of skimmer proximity alarms and the clamor of conversations in a multitude of languages. Micah hung back, anxious to avoid Hough and his innuendoes. Needing to think.

We're going to attack the embassy. Each word rang in his head like a knell. He had no proof, no clue, only the buzz in his head and the ache in his gut, and the mental hangover of a hundred sim sessions. The sure certainty he felt at times that something would happen.

"I say it's time for lunch!" Court announced. Others shouted the names of restaurants—the Interior Ministry public park was chosen, and off they headed. Micah followed well behind, leg muscles tingling with each strike of his shoes upon the walkway, as they turned off State and headed for one of the pedestrian overpasses that led to the lakeside of the Boul Mich.

Micah mounted the overpass steps, stopping when he reached the summit and looking past the sprawling Interior Ministry grounds to the line of trees beyond that marked the southern border of the idomeni embassy compound. *I know that layout better than I know Far North Lakeside's.* Every corridor, utility chase, private chamber and meeting room etched into his brain by the screams of the wounded, the combined stenches of burned flesh, blood, and shit. The shoulder-pounding kicks of his mid-range, so strong that not even his exo's force dissipaters could dampen them completely. The pound of his heart, and the rasp of his breathing as it echoed inside his helmet.

I know that layout. But then, he'd learned many layouts over the course of his training. Shèráin sites like the Temple at Rauta Shèràa. The monument-lined corridor that connected the Academy campus to the Council buildings. Colonial sites like idomeni consulates and Haárin enclaves. And the terrestrial sites, such as the facility in Death Valley, the enclave of the Chicago Haárin, and the embassy.

Combat training for the Cause. He wondered how he could have ever believed it was that simple. *But we always come back to the embassy.* Had anyone else figured it out? Manda? Bevan the Brain? Did Chrivet know, or was she as uninformed as the rest of them, a tool for whoever had chosen them, designed their training, and planned their fate?

"Jeez, scholar, will you move or something?"

Micah turned to find Cashman at his shoulder, one of Court's shopping sacks in each hand. "Just taking in the view."

"You're getting weirder by the day, you know that?" Cashman trudged past him to the opposite end of the overpass, where Hough and the rest waited. "Let's go."

He made it home eventually, sick from a lunch he hadn't wanted to eat, idiot talk he hadn't wanted to listen to. Hough had left him alone, small thanks for little favors, after a few veiled comments about Pascal failed to find their mark.

He'd stopped by the delivery cage, and felt no surprise whatsoever to find the white mailer in his locker. Headed upstairs with sweat-slick hands. Counted his steps down the hall to his flat, and remained in the hallway for some time after his front door had opened completely.

He talked himself into going inside—really, what choice did he have? Locked the door. Went directly to his bathroom and shoved a finger down his throat, eliminating the nasty, not to mention life-threatening, possibility that he'd vomit during the sim and choke in his headset. Cleaned up. Changed clothes. Collected his gear and lay on his couch, ripping open the mailer and inserting the wafer into the slot. Prayed, even though he knew it would do no good. He wanted to be wrong, and he knew he wasn't.

The tones sounded in his ears, over and over and over, until he thought they'd never en—

—Chrivet paced in front of them, an image of the Commonwealth Field of Stars showing on a wall-mounted display behind her. She wore her serious expression, a morose draw-down of the corners of her mouth that took the rest of her face with it. She was lecturing them again, about their fitness as Spacers and the rightness of their cause, something Micah had taken to calling Philosophy 101.

Get on with it. He sat in the rearmost row of seats, alone. Bevan and Foley sat in the front, of course. Manda, her hair gathered in a ponytail that made her look like a prep schooler, sat near the middle and traded whispers with another woman named Patel.

Get on with it. He stared down at his hands. As always, the thoughts that occurred to him when he was conscious intruded now that he'd entered the scenario. He'd stopped wondering whether or not that was normal, and knew he didn't dare ask Chrivet or anyone else about it at this stage of the game. Instead he kept his mouth shut and pondered the same problems that he had when he'd walked the Chicago streets a few hours earlier. Would they attack the embassy? If so, when?

"Mister Tiebold?"

Micah closed his eyes, then opened them and raised his head. "Yes, ma'am."

Chrivet remained silent and watched him, something she did more and more as of late. It was as if she found something lacking in even his simplest responses. Something lacking in him. "Am I boring you again?"

Micah sat up straighter as everyone turned to look at him. Bevan, he noted, had one eye slightly higher than the other, so that he always looked skeptical. Foley pouted, like the brat he was.

Manda, it pained him to note, fixed him with the same puzzled gaze as did most everyone else. Nothing special. Nothing special at all.

Micah's chest tightened as a surge of anger burst through him like a blown grenade. *I'm not bored, ma'am—just wondering how I'm going to die this time is all.* He breathed deep, when all he wanted to do was shout. Tried to sit on every self-destructive impulse he had as well as a few he didn't realize he nursed until now, and then decided the hell with it. *We who are about to die were wondering—* "When are we going to hit the embassy, ma'am? That's what we're working for, isn't it? That's our target." He heard gasps, sensed the tension of breaths held, and watched Chrivet's hands tighten into fists as yet again he jumped the starter gun and offended her sense of Spacer fitness. "I want to hit 'em, ma'am. The idomeni." He entoned the party line, in part because he believed it with all his heart, but mostly because he sensed that if he didn't, he'd be in even more trouble than he already was. "I want to bring them down."

Chrivet's expression shifted, from angry to a pinched annoyance that made her look a prig. "So you want to bring the idomeni down, Mister Tiebold?" She paused for effect. "Well, you're going to get your chance." She reached behind her and touched a pad fixed to the wall beside the display. The Field of Stars vanished.

Micah bit back a curse as images of Pascal bloomed before him, larger than life shots of the man walking around the base, sitting at his desk, making a presentation. *Damn it, can't I get away from him anywhere!*

Then came the shots from the *Tribune-Times*, the cheap gossip sheets. Pascal with the Exterior Minister and other assorted escorts, male and female both, their common thread the fact that they were all older than he, and much, much richer.

Then came the images with Jani Kilian. The social, at a concert, a football game. The professional, as they departed the idomeni embassy, one of the ministries, stood talking to PM Cao.

Micah compared the Kilian he had seen in the bunker with the one he saw here. The same eerie eyes. The same skinny long-boniness, as though she'd shake apart in a high wind. *It doesn't even look human anymore, and he fucks it every chance he gets.*

"I tell you, ladies and gentlemen." Chrivet tapped the display with her finger. "I would like nothing better than to drive a knife through Kilian's mutant eyes for the filth she's inflicted upon this Earth."

"Why is he allowed to remain in the Service?" That from Bevan, his voice thick with revulsion.

"A good question, Mister Bevan, one that many like minds have asked for some time now." Chrivet linked her hands behind her back. She wore a T-shirt, and her arm muscles bunched and flexed with the movement. " 'Friends in high places' is the best excuse any of us could come up with, and where has that laxity led us? To the point where this stain on our collective honor is allowed to go where he will and do what he wishes, and thus drags the Service down to his low level. To the point where he will be taking direction in a circus ring from a bunch of frog-eyed mush-mouths while our oh-so-potent diplomatic officers stand to one side and kneel to traditions that are not ours, that we don't hold with, that are alien to us in every way, shape, and form." She swallowed hard, and shook her head. "Can we tolerate this in a human Service?"

"No! Ma'am!"

"So what are we gonna do!"

"Take 'em down!"

"Take 'em down." Chrivet smiled. "On the day in question, ladies and gentlemen, you have been chosen to show certain interested parties just what true Spacers think of this insult to our great traditions, to our way of life. You have friends in high places, too—they have overseen your training and granted you the honor of showing this Commonwealth what real Spacers are made of." For the first time, she regarded them not with hard-eyed disdain, but with a kindness, a pride, that she hadn't seemed capable of before. "It is indeed the embassy, ladies and gentlemen. You will receive the details soon. Until then, we will do as we have been—we will work through it, and work through it, and work through it again, until each and every one of you could take that place out in your sleep." She straightened up and clapped her hands once. "OK, folks. Let's move!"

They set up a jump point in the thin strip of Exterior wilderness that bordered the embassy. They'd be in trouble if an actual Exterior security patrol showed up, but the ministry ran a skeleton staff when the minister traveled off-planet, as she did now. They didn't expect discovery.

Typical early spring morning, damp and colder for it. A hard wind blew in off the lake. Micah sat in the mud beneath a bare-limbed tree and fiddled with a receiver, trying to pick up any transmissions that emerged from the scattered embassy outbuildings.

Even though his suit liner protected him from the cold and wet, he still knew that he sat in *mud*, heard the damp squelch every time he moved. He adjusted the receiver earsert and upped the gain, straining for any organized sound amid the hum and hiss. The beat of code. The organized gibberish of scrambled voices. Waste of time on his part—the autoreceiver scanned the signals better than he could. But he couldn't convince himself to hand control of his fate over to the mechanicals. Not just yet.

He felt a touch on his shoulder, and looked up to find Manda standing over him, helmet in hand. She'd already donned her balaclava, from which a few stray curls escaped to frame her heart-shaped face.

"It's almost time." Her voice, never sturdy, sounded ready to crack. "I just wanted to say that however this ends—I just wanted to say—" Her lovely eyes filled. One tear spilled over. She locked her hands behind his head and bent down to him, pulling him close, kissing him. She tasted of the rank coffee they had all drunk, but her lips felt silken and she smelled like flowers and those were the sensations Micah took to heart.

Then she was gone, and the jump came to life like a waking beast, donning gear, checking weapons.

Micah rose and stared across the border to the quiet beyond.

A sun obscured by cloud. The lake turned into choppy swell by the wind. Harder to stay upright, and keep from plowing into the person in front of you. Yet still they pounded onward, following the shore, toward their target.

"Let's hit 'em in the gut, boys and girls. Let's kick 'em where they live." Chrivet picked up the pace. "Air all clear, Tiebold? No marble-eyes watching us?"

Micah checked his readouts. "All clear, ma'am."

They burst onto the beach, as they had before. Up the ramp, blowing sheds as they went. Across the gardens and through the walls. Micah applied his lessons learned from past scenarios, holding back when necessary, pushing on when every nerve in his body yelled *No!* Following behind O'Shae, taking out Vynshàrau with every blast of his mid-range, pounding, pounding.

Thorough the doors to the main hall. O'Shae killing the deadhead, then switching to grenades. Joining up with Foley, blasting down every hallway. Smoke. Sparks from blown arrays. Sputtering illumins. Vynshàrau in exos, fighting like demons.

Some fell and rose again. Some fell and remained still. As the meeting room cleared, Micah slipped behind O'Shae again. More halls. Rooms. Bodies. Growing quiet.

"Six five oh, clear."

"Four eight seven, clear."

"Oh nine one—"

Quieter.

"Three four—"

"Eight one—"

"All sectors secure."

Quietest.

O'Shae stopped and turned to him, then raised her faceplate. "Whaddya say, Tieb?"

Micah looked down at his mid-range. For the first time since he'd started the training, he powered it down.

We won.

Micah still sat on his couch, his headgear cradled in his lap. "We cleared the place out. Secured it." Everyone hit their marks, pressed their charge-throughs, came across. He'd even seen Manda at the end of it, hair matted from her helmet, exo streaked with someone else's blood. Something else's blood. Not hers.

He got up. Paced the room, and felt his bones sing with every move. Pulled the wafer from the headset and gathered up his player, then pulled on a jacket and headed for the drop point in Forrestal Block to unload his data. *We did it.* He barely stifled the urge to punch the air. *We did it!*

The air smelled cleaner than Micah had ever known it, as remarkable as if he'd never inhaled it before. He walked as though drunk, barely sensing his feet on the walkway. He tucked the wafer into the inside pocket of his jacket and stopped to mime a baseball pitch. *Strike three—Vynshàrau out!* He set up, went into his windup, and followed through, powering forward into the rough grip of a civvie-clad older man who'd just emerged from the Forrestal One lobby.

"Sorry! Sorry!" Micah straightened the man's rumpled jacket. Then he backed away, giddy and sheepish, and felt the first whisper of doubt as the man stared at him, dark eyes in a dark face, familiar yet out of place.

"Desk jockey has no idea what he's in for." A voice like salt on a wound. "Desk jockey gonna die." Then he hunched his shoulders and strode away, moving a little faster than normal, the way some small men did.

Micah turned and watched the man. *I've seen him before . . . I've seen—* His heart stuttered when the name came back to him. Veles, who'd assisted Pascal during the interrogation-that-wasn't, as well as with the sucker punch with the prototype shooter.

I'll be watching you, Faber. Morning, noon, and night.

Micah wiped a hand over the back of his mouth. He watched Veles until the man disappeared over a rise, then continued on his way with a heavier step. Into the lobby, the comport booth. Sit down. Activate the unit. Breathe. *We won.*

Micah felt his jacket pocket for the wafer. Felt again. Dug deep and rooted around, pulling out a few flecks of thread and nothing else.

He took off after Veles, across the lobby and out the door, dodging pedestrians who seemed to have come out of nowhere. Over the rise, then flat out. Running. Running. Heart in his throat. On the lookout for the small dark man and knowing exactly what he'd do when he found him.

He could run when he had to, but he was no runner. His legs gave out first, oxygen starvation stopping him like a blow. He pulled in great sobs of air, doubled over, then dropped to his knees. Searched for any sign, and found nothing.

CHAPTER 22

"I still maintain that the challenge must be delayed." Tsecha, discordant in green and gold, tore a chunk of clay from the sculpture set against the meeting room wall and worked it between his palms, squeezing it as though it contained something he needed. "There is too much occurring now. Trespassers who leave food about the embassy compound. The mine investigation, which still goes on."

"An Haárin dominant who denies his propitiator and now seeks to avoid the enmity and discipline of Temple." Shai turned from the window opposite Tsecha and his sculpting and bared her teeth. "How many of the acolytes' scars do you bear on your arms, Tsecha? How many of them did you fight in the circle in the time before the war?"

"And now it is their time—is that what you tell me, Shai?" Tsecha pushed the clay chunk back into place, then punched it with his fist. "I did as I most had to, then and now."

"As did Temple, then and now. So you wish to delay matters here in order that your return to Shèrá is set back as well. I have known you too long to suppose otherwise, for I do not recall, and truly, that you were ever overwhelmed by events." Shai pressed a hand to her forehead in a vague, humanish gesture. "This is perhaps, I most think, because you were responsible for those events yourself." She let her hand fall and walked to the center of the oblong space, her sand-colored overrobe a comforting contrast to her diplomatic brown tunic and trousers. "Elon, step farther into this room, please, and prevent this Haárin and I from coming to blows."

Elon moved away from the entry and approached Shai, her

posture as straight as she could manage in Tsecha's presence. *Anathema.* How could she have ever regarded such as he with any sort of respect, even that of an esteemed enemy? "I am here, nìa-Rauta."

"You have not brought Ghos with you?" Shai looked to the entry, her shoulders rounding.

"No, nìaRauta. He works in the practice circle now." As she had when she watched Ghos batter Pascal on the veranda, she felt herself move, a slow drift from side to side, as she imagined her suborn strike and parry with the practice blades. "I advised him to do such, since humanish do not understand the ways of *à lérine* and thus may attack improperly."

"It is good that he is elsewhere. I have no wish to see him now, for he is another with whom I would most happily come to blows." Shai walked to the last in a row of wireframe chairs and sat, drawing her overrobe around her as though the air chilled. "It pains me as sickness to say this, Elon, but the Haárin who stands in this room now is as correct in his opinion of this damned challenge as the gods and circumstance allow him to be."

"The Haárin who stands in this room now rejoices in your esteem, Shai, and truly." Tsecha drove his thumb into the clay and worked a series of grooves across the surface. Two lines down, then two across them, so that together they formed a grid of nine squares. "If he could rejoice in a decision cancelling this damned challenge, he would feel even more as blessed by the gods." He etched a figure in each of the diagonal squares, dragged a forefinger across the entire pattern, then dipped his hand in a nearby container of water and rubbed the clay smooth once more. "My Lucien is not my Jani. He does not understand the circle, and when he does not understand, he strikes as a serpent." He picked up the damp cloth that had served as the sculpture covering and spread it over the clay. "If Ghos had asked Caith's aide in choosing the worst humanish for him to challenge, she would have led him to no other human but to my Lucien."

Shai squinted toward Tsecha's labors, then shook her head and gestured to Elon. "Such was not the time for Ghos to challenge the humanish, Elon. Especially a Service humanish, for it causes Mako and his suborns to wonder if revenge for Feres was his thought."

"It was not, nìaRauta." Elon walked across the room to the table containing the stone formations. "This I know and truly." She stood before one of the arrangements, taking as much strength as she could in their order and beauty as her heart pounded and hers and Ghos's words sounded in her head. *Will you kill Pascal, Ghos of the Stones? If I am able.* But not for revenge, no—Pascal's blood was as that of an animal, and could not serve as fair exchange for that of Feres. *It is enough that he should die for that which he is.* For the disorder he represented, the godlessness that he was.

Elon took up one of the stones, clenching it as she fought the desire to fling it into the rest, to scatter them across the floor. When she sensed motion from the corner of her eye, she half turned, her hand raised, the rounded point of the stone facing out as the edge of a blade—

—and met Tsecha's gaze, ancient gold and arrogant, mocking her as it had in Rauta Shèràa Temple.

"NìRau Ghos, it most seems, wonders at my Lucien's loyalties. He believes him a spy, although for whom he cannot say." Tsecha took the stone from Elon's grasp and tossed it up in the air, then caught it.

"Pascal *is* a spy, Tsecha." Shai gripped the chair next to hers and pushed it back and forth until it aligned with the rest of the row. "Each time he visits here with you and Dathim, I anticipate my dealings with Service Diplomatic, and all the new varieties of requests from General Burkett and his staff, for I know as I know my robes that Pascal goes to them as soon as he finishes here."

"He could do much worse, Shai. This I know, and truly, as do you." Tsecha again tossed the stone in the air, and caught it. "But for every thing he takes, he gives something back, and now he gives us what I tell you now, what I have tried to tell you this entire day. He believes, with reason, that these vehicles that have invaded the embassy grounds are of the Service. He believes, for reasons he has yet to make clear, that there are those in the Service who would attack us here and at the enclave, and see us driven from this city."

"We always knew this, Tsecha," Shai replied. "Even without your Pascal's clarity. The mine they have yet to explain is, I most fear, an illustration of this. It was no accident—this I know and truly. It was meant to be. It was meant to kill Haárin, and took Feres instead, but we will wait unto death for the humanish to admit such."

Tsecha tossed and caught the stone one last time, then held it out to Elon, remaining silent until she took it from his hand. "My Lucien fears something greater, Shai. Greater than a mine, or food in your outbuildings. He fears an assault, against this place or the enclave. An attack by those trained to do such, outfitted with equipment and weaponry as one sees on the battlefield."

Elon placed the stone Tsecha had handed her back within its arrangement, taking care to avoid touching it where he had. "When would this attack occur?" She picked up another stone, this time cradling it between her palms so he could not take it.

"That, my Lucien cannot say." Tsecha watched her as though they stood within the circle, his gaze fixed on her hands as his shoulders rounded in mirror of her posture. "All that he may tell us now is that we must prepare, and keep watch."

Shai stood. "After the explosion of a single mine and the death of Feres, Prime Minister Li Cao and General Burkett and Admiral-General Mako became as my constant companions. I believed and truly that they would never leave my side. I would expect even greater visitation in the case of a supposed assault, Tsecha. Roomfuls of humanish who would remain with me as my shadow from early morning sacrament until the middle of the night." She paced the bare floor, her soft boots sounding against the tile as though she walked through grass. "I do not see them."

Tsecha leaned against the table in a most unseemly way, crossing his arms over his chest and his legs at the ankle, a cramped humanish posture. "My Lucien currently gathers proof. Evidence. When he possesses sufficient, he will go to his dominants, and they will come to you."

"And you must remain here as he gathers this proof, for he will work with you and you only." Shai raised her hands above her head, a plea to the gods. "I understand you, Tsecha, as no one else does. You have constructed a reason to remain here when Temple has ordered you back to the worldskein." She stopped in place and lowered her arms to her sides. "It has therefore fallen to me to enact the wishes of Temple as best I can, and to do this as I determine how much of your story is truth and how much the invention of your spying humanish."

Elon moved into the shaft of sunlight that streamed through the window, closing her eyes for a moment as she took what she could of its sickly warmth. "I most fear, nìaRauta, that very little of what Pascal says may be invented. The humanish who have trespassed on these grounds know our systems. Given the ways in which we protect such information, they could only have learned such through the spying methods the Service uses to monitor that which we do."

Shai turned and looked her near enough in the eye as to be as unseemly. "You agree with Tsecha, Elon?" She folded her arms and tucked her hands within the sleeves of her overrobe. "I struggle to recall when last such occurred." She stood most still. "What state our defenses, then?"

Elon pressed her hands around the stone, drawing the last edges of pain from bones long healed, wondering how much pressure she would need to apply to break them once more. "We may increase lake patrols. We may increase our guards. We may also employ robotic devices as free-float monitors, setting them at our borders. In whatever instance, I most fear, the humanish will know that we have increased our surveillance, and while the lake patrols and guards are allowed by treaty, the devices are not, for humanish fear we would use them to observe that which they do." She relaxed her grip on the stone. "Shall I do as I am allowed, nìaRauta?" she asked Shai. "Or shall I do as I must?"

"Increased patrols may draw fire. We want no more dead." Tsecha still stood against the table, his only movement to straighten his legs, then recross them. "Pink grenades disable weaponry and systems even as they leave the humanish unharmed. Even if the variety we have here now is not fully safe for idomeni systems, such is better than live fire, for such is one thing we cannot take back."

Shai walked to the sculpture that Tsecha had lately attended. "The pink, Tsecha, is even less allowed by treaty than robotic patrols." She raised the damp drapery that covered it, then set it aside and began to work the clay that Tsecha had recently smoothed. "I do not, I most believe, need to tell you of the protests we would hear if such drifted beyond the boundaries of the embassy. Any object containing a bioarray would be disabled, any system touched would be disrupted or destroyed. Li Cao would, as humanish say, never let me forget." Unlike Tsecha, she seemed to savor the feel of the clay—her shoulders slowly uncurved as she worked her hands into the mass. "That being understood, I say to you, Elon, that we should enable the pink systems, for as much as I disdain agreement with the Haárin who leans against the table in an unseemly humanish manner, I cannot help but agree that dead humanish would do us great harm."

"Yes, níaRauta." Elon returned to the table and replaced the stone, taking care to avoid Tsecha's gaze, to avoid drawing too close. "I will begin such today."

"And the challenge, Shai?" Tsecha stood away from the table and let his arms fall to his sides. More humanish deadness.

"That must continue." Shai turned to him, her hands coated to

the wrists in drying clay. "Pascal spends much time at your enclave, Tsecha. He comes here most often as well, and watches us
as though he wishes to learn. Thus and so—we both know and
truly that one cannot learn completely of idomeni until one learns
challenge, and has fought in the circle. Let Pascal learn such then.
I am most sure that Dathim will teach him."

"*Shai.*" Tsecha's shoulders rounded so that he had to tilt his
head to his shoulder to look at her. "You do not know what you do."

"I know exactly." Shai turned from him back to her sculpture.
"You see to your enclave, Tsecha. You are indeed needed here, I
most fear—though Temple may not wait forever to deal with you
as they would, I may convince them to wait a short time." She gestured to Elon. "You, Elon—see to this place. In any way you deem
fit, and truly." She plunged her hands back into the clay, and
worked it so the muscles of her forearms tensed, accenting her *à
lérine* scars. "I most relish the upset this challenge has inflicted
upon the Service. Each day we receive messages from Diplomatic, the Judge Advocate. Even their Medical dominants wonder
over how an emotional augment such as Pascal may behave in the
circle." She nodded in an annoyingly humanish manner. "Disruption is a great thing, and truly."

Tsecha strode to the door, his back still bowed. "You grow disordered, Shai."

"I grow tired of trespass and sacrilege. In exchange, I request
only a little humanish blood." Shai bared her teeth. "See to the
arming of the pink, Elon."

"Yes, nìaRauta." Elon followed Tsecha to the door, pausing at
the entry to allow him time to depart. She did not wish to encounter him alone in any hallway. He watched her as he had at
Temple when he suspected her anger, and knew that a further irritation on his part would spur her to an eruption. "No, Tsecha," she
uttered aloud as she walked the corridors to her rooms. She could
not betray her thoughts to him now—such would wait until a time
that he did not suspect. Only then would he know, when it would
be too late for him to react. Then she would rejoice in his pain.

Elon took mid-afternoon sacrament, her mind as jumbled as the
half-leafed branches she had driven through when she and Ghos had
chased the humanish skimmer. Afterward she sought to rest. But her
thoughts still raced. Her skin tingled as though stung by thorns.

She rose, laved, then donned the rougher clothes she wore to
labor in the damned cold outside, a brown coverall and boots. She

departed the embassy and stalked the outbuildings, moving from utility dome to greenhouse to guard bunker, receiving status reports and giving orders, as all the while her limbs moved as leaden and she ached to the pit of her soul.

She found Ghos eventually, monitoring instrumentation in one of the guard bunkers located at regular intervals along the embassy access road. He worked alongside nìaRauta Laur, but as soon as he realized Elon's presence, he ordered Laur to a task outside.

Elon waited until the suborn female departed before joining Ghos at the console, standing a half stride behind him, as was seemly. At that angle, she could see the dried mud that streaked the back of his coverall, the fragments of twig and leaf that once more sullied his braids, which he had again bound together with a length of cord. "I have met with nìaRauta Shai." She leaned forward and plucked a leaf from his collar. "We are to load the pink into the defense array despite its imperfections. Shai would rather have disabled systems than dead humanish."

"Then she is damned." Ghos turned and looked Elon in the eye, as he had so often of late. "But we know this."

"Yes." Elon reached out again, this time to brush away dirt that shadowed beneath Ghos's eye. When he took her hand and held it, she thought to pull back, but his fingers closed as a vise and she could not have freed herself if she wished to. Her skin burned where his touched, as the sense of weight returned to her limbs. The tension, as though as she had been filled past her ability to contain.

"I have fathered four," Ghos said, first loosening then tightening his hold. "From the first, mothered by Sor nìaRauta Hesai, who maintained security for the hospital shrine at Nen Shèràa, to the fourth, mothered by Ailà nìaRauta Qar, who served as suborn to the Council security dominant."

Elon gestured acceptance of the information with her free hand, even though Ghos's gradual ascension within the security skein was known before she accepted his petition to serve her. If she had approached a male of greater standing, as one of Cèel's security dominants, or one of those who guarded the inner rooms at Temple, she would have spoken of the three she had mothered, each fathered by a male of increasing status over the one before. "I take comfort in your declaration of order, Ghos. So much a haven is it from the chaos of Haárin, the contamination of human joinings."

"This is not a time to think of such." Ghos tilted his head to one side, as though he surprised even himself, for he seldom restrained his thought in deference to the proprieties. "I must complete these settings." He released her abruptly and turned back to the console, examining systems readouts and recalibrating sensors.

Elon drew close behind, until she could sense Ghos's blessed warmth through the chill of the air. "Tsecha sought to petition nìa-Rauta Shai to forbid your challenge of Pascal." She watched his hands move over the console, every flex and curve of his fingers. "Shai denied such. She wishes humanish blood to be shed within the circle."

"Then she shall most certainly have it, and truly." Ghos's voice emerged as gentle as ever it had. "As much as her satisfaction demands, and more besides."

"We will not load the pink."

"No, nìaRauta. Nor will we increase the patrols or release the robot monitors."

"If the humanish invaders come, let them."

"Yes."

"If humanish blood is wanted, let it be shed."

"And ours with it."

"We are most in agreement, Ghos."

"I have always known such, Elon, and truly."

"Yes, as have I." Elon reached out and placed a hand upon Ghos's shoulder, then pulled back when she sensed movement behind her. She turned to find Laur in the entry—the suborn held a disassembled monitor, her posture indicating that she had no sense of how to repair it. Elon left Ghos to aid her. Then she waited outside in the weak humanish sun until he rejoined her, and they returned to the embassy together.

They retired to Elon's rooms, since as dominant the right of place fell to her. First came release, rapid joinings that dispelled the tension that had grown between them as a solid thing. Once, then rest, then again, a meld of unclothed limbs that served to express the oneness of their thoughts, their beliefs. Their fears, and their hatreds. The Way that they planned together. Their mutual Path to their Star.

They lay afterward for some time, savoring the quiet of each other's presence, the serenity that came from two minds that thought as an ordered one. Ghos held Elon by the wrist with one hand as he stroked her arm with the other, from forearm to shoulder, then down, again and again, the rhythm of the motion taking them both to a state approaching trance.

"Ghos of the stones." Elon reached to him and fingered his hair, then gestured in weak dismay as she came away with yet another piece of twig. "Ghos of the forests, who lives in the trees." She took him by the hand and led him to her laving room. There, amid tiled scenes of Rauta Shèràa that one of Dathim Naré's suborns had applied two seasons before, she unbraided his hair and laved it with soap that smelled of the sand and sun, then combdried it, running the nubs over and over Ghos's scalp until he bared his teeth in the pleasure of it. Finally, she rebraided the fine brown lengths, binding them at the ends with jewel-green ties that caught the light as night insects when Ghos shook his head, and clattered like beads.

"So quiet." Ghos stood, his skin as gold beneath the inset illumination, an ordered contrast to the brown of his hair. "I have not known such for so long."

"We have much to do." Elon touched his shoulder one last time, and savored the warmth, the sense of flesh and bone beneath. "But we do not know how much time we have, which means we must act quickly."

They dressed in silence born of shared purpose, then visited Elon's physician-priest, who took the sperm Ghos had deposited and preserved it for blending with one of the eggs that Elon had reserved for such interactions. The embryo would be blended there, then returned to Shèrá for growth and placement with a home-mother.

And in three seasons, a youngish. Elon bared her teeth. A declaration of hers and Ghos's likeness of mind. Another step farther down their Way to the Star, one that would be taken no matter what happened to them.

"I must see to Laur," Ghos said as they departed the physician-priest's workroom. "When she is left alone for too long, she begins to delve too deeply into that which is not her concern." He left Elon without another look or touch, as was the way it was. Their declaration had been made, Ghos' ascension assured. Now came their task, which would serve to bind them as well as any joining, any birth.

Elon walked the corridors that led back to her rooms. The way also led past Shai's rooms—when the panel slid aside and Shai emerged into the passage, Elon wondered if it had been coincidence, or if she had awaited her.

"Elon!" Shai proceeded a half stride behind her. "I have received word from your physician-priest, and rejoice with you. A most ordered pairing, you and Ghos. Such will assure the security of this place, of that I am most sure."

"Yes, nìaRauta." Elon turned and watched Shai return to her rooms, the hallway illuminations casting shadows across her back like spreading stains of blood.

CHAPTER 23

"... a period of such change as shakes one to the depths of their soul ..."

Clase, *Thalassan Histories, Book I*

"The second worst thing about waiting, besides the actual waiting itself, of course, is that you eventually reach a point where you feel the need to do something." Brondt dragged a chair away from the table and spun it around, then sat astraddle. "This is the point that separates your run-of-the-mill poker player from your true gambler. The ability to sit out the lulls when you realize there's nothing you can do. No play to be made."

Jani looked up from the document she and Torin had been examining. She had adjourned to the library after the walk down the beach with the rest of what Brondt called the "like minds," and had spent the last hour or so showing Torin the workings of her scanpack and not—repeat, not—thinking about John, Tsecha, Feyó, Gisa, or Niall. "Dieter." She regarded him as he did her, elbows on the table and chin cradled in hand. "Has anyone ever told you that you're a pain in the ass?"

Torin gasped, then doubled over, his high-pitched laugh bouncing off the walls. Brondt only smiled.

"It's just that I know a coiled spring when I see one." He picked up the empty scanpack case and tipped it upside down, shaking out its nonexistent contents. "I don't think I've ever seen anyone work harder at remaining nonchalant."

Stop reading me. Jani held up the old copy of the *Partisan* that she had used to demonstrate the differences between static and mutable inks, and rolled it into a tight tube. "John should be at Neoclona by now. Assuming Gisa didn't intercept him."

"She wouldn't do that. She's still very idomeni in that regard—her conflict is with Feyó, not you, and not your lover."

Brondt continued to toy with the case, closing the fasteners, then opening them. Then he sighed, the shakiness of his breathing implying that his nerve had limits after all. "If the stories I've heard of ní Tsecha's resolve are true, he's digging himself in back in Chicago. I don't see him giving in without a battle, and you and Feyó are already rallying the strongest bloc of Haárin support that exists. An interesting time will be had by all, but I do believe that in the end, you will save ní Tsecha, and prevail."

"Strong-arm diplomacy over ideology. That's a humanish argument." Jani tossed the newssheet aside, then stood and walked to the window, drawn to the view of the bay, as she had been numerous times over the course of the day. "If Cèel caves in to it, he risks weakening himself in the eyes of his more traditionalist rivals, as we've said a hundred times. If he refrains, he risks losing the Haárin, as we've said a hundred and one. I don't think I'd like to be in his shoes right now, and it's a token flip as to which way he'll finally go." Dusk neared, shading the sky in coral and indigo. Clouds grew, offering the possibility of evening rain. "It's the suicide option that bothers me, the sense that if it all gets too much, he'll just open his shirt and wait for someone to strike him. Who would come after him is anyone's guess. My fear is that they wouldn't wait for Tsecha to decide to return to the worldskein—they'd just send warriors to collect him."

"That's never happened," Torin piped as he made entries into his handheld. "I've read the histories—if Tsecha refuses to return, that alone could tie up the Council in knots. The ideologues don't think on their feet very well—he could stall them just by saying no."

"I've said it before." Jani folded her arms and leaned against the window framing. "No one's gone this way before. We're all making it up as we go, including Cèel. And he was a warrior himself, if you recall. Bornsect battles never experienced the flip-flops that humanish have, but he still needed to possess some flexibility." She looked to Brondt. "Aren't there any comlines here that you trust?"

Brondt shook his head. "No."

"Who can I count on here?"

"To do what, take over the courtyard? Mount an attack on the basement clinic?" Brondt stood and swung a leg over his backward seat, then turned the chair around and shoved it under the table. "You can't do anything worthwhile until you hear from John or Feyó. Until then you'd just be standing on the roof flapping your arms. Might make you feel better, but you're not accomplishing much, are you?" He joined her by the window, his yellow-green eyes reflecting the light like fluorescence. "Rain tonight. We're nearing autumn, which means the storms will become more and more severe." He glanced at her sidelong. "There's nothing you can do without more information, and you've sent out the runners to get it. So, you wait."

"I'm not the most patient of people."

"I'd never have guessed."

The sound of the door opening silenced them. Jani noted that Brondt, for all his talk of calm, flinched at the noise. His hand moved to his trouser pocket as well, which saved her from asking whether he still carried his shooter.

"Ná Kièrshia." Gisa stood in the doorway, less elegant than usual in the coverall and boots she wore when she plied her agronomist trade in the greenhouses and fields. "The time for early evening sacrament approaches and no one sits downstairs. Would you be willing, I wonder, to dine with me?"

Brondt looked to the wall clock. "Midweek in Karistos. End of summer. Outdoor concerts and such . . ." His voice trailed when his eyes met Gisa's, stares locking for a beat beyond casual. "Torin," he said after a moment, "let's batten the hatches—I don't like the looks of those clouds." He glanced at Jani, eyebrow cocked, then walked to the door, pausing at the desk to collect Torin, then departing without any further regard for his dominant.

"Brondt is strange," Gisa said while the subject of her critique was still well within earshot. "Eamon says he looks for a leader as a bee looks for nectar, moving from flower to flower." She bared her teeth, then gestured toward the hall. "Sacrament grows cold. Please."

Jani patted her grumbling stomach, which as usual betrayed her when faced with the prospect of a good meal. "One moment." She walked to the table and collected her scanpack, straightened the newssheets and pushed in the chairs. *So, I wait.* She shouldered her duffel and followed Gisa from the room.

Gisa hadn't been completely truthful concerning her lack of mealtime company. Jani arrived to find that both Bon and Eamon were already eating. Bon nodded to her with the mix of regard and uncertainty to which Jani had grown accustomed, while Eamon grunted in her general direction in between gulps of vodka.

"Another Acadian dish, Kièrshia." Gisa handed Jani a casserole of chickpeas and corn. "Our cooks still seek to please you."

"They must be tearing their hair out over the light turnout." Jani looked around the empty dining area, taking in the neat place settings and filled tureens from which fragrant steam escaped. "How do you plan menus when you never know how many will show up?"

"We begin to adjust." Bon shrugged. "Group meals were planned in the beginning to foster togetherness, and to allow some of those more shaken by change to feel not so displaced." The dimmer evening lighting softened her appearance, shadowing the worst ravages of her skin. "As time goes on, Thalassa will meet as a whole for holidays only. Special occasions."

"Fine with me," Eamon muttered into his glass. "Feel like I'm at bloody day camp half the time." He shoved a forkful of sauced kettle beef into his mouth, his bleary gaze sharpening as it fixed on Jani. "John's in town?"

"Yes." Jani felt Bon's veiled stare, Gisa's more direct examination. "He needed to stop by the facility."

"Better do it while he can." Eamon glared down at his plate for a moment, then shook his head. "Damned fool—" He squinted toward the demirooms, then shielded his eyes with his hand. "Is that you, Niri? What is it?"

Jani turned to see one of the clinic staff hovering at the edge of the courtyard. A young female decked out in medwhites, face set, hands clenched.

"There is a call, sir. From the outbuildings. There has been an accident on the coast road from Karistos—you are needed."

"Accident?" Jani pushed her chair back from the table, the screech of polywood against stone echoing throughout the space. "What sort? Equipment? Skimmer? Did the guards shoot someone? What?"

"Ná Kièrshia?" Bon's voice emerged calm. "We have accidents all the time at this place. The building that goes on. The work."

"In the middle of the evening?" Jani strode toward Niri, holding up her hands in a gesture of surrender and slowing when she realized the young female had backed away and stepped behind a planter. "What happened? *Please.*"

Niri swallowed. "A skimmer—"

"*Shit.*" Jani struggled to lower her voice when every cell in her body begged to scream. "Who was hurt. *Who?*"

"Doesn't matter who—I still need to get out there." Eamon raised his glass, then swore under his breath and set it down with a clatter. "Ah hell." He stood and stepped around the table. "Get Maren and Caris," he said, pointing to Niri. "Tell them to grab the ready bags and meet me in the garage."

"I'm going with you." Jani fell in beside him.

"You don't belong. You'll just get in the way."

"I'm going."

Eamon stopped and turned to her. They had moved under better lighting now—the brightness highlighted the damage that drink and exhaustion had inscribed on his face. "You've done more than enough already." He stood with his hands clenched, his weight balanced, as though he'd strike her given any more provocation.

Then he took a step back, emitting a sigh like a moan of pain. "Fine. Let's see how much worse you can make it." He started for the door, thumping his fist against every piece of furniture he encountered along the way.

Jani followed, pausing as she reached the door. She looked back to the courtyard to find Gisa still seated, Bon standing behind her like a hound guarding its mistress.

"Damn and blast it, stay on the road!" Eamon pounded the dashboard with the flat of his hand. "I should have know better than to let you drive."

Jani steered down the banked path leading from the garage, backing off the accelerator until the up-and-down whine of a straining propulsion array softened to a high-pitched hum. "The shortest distance between two points." She reentered the winding roadway until another scenic curve presented itself, then braced for the shudder as she again steered off-road and out of range of the skimtrack. "It's a straight line—remember?" She punched the accelerator again as a rock formation loomed ahead, coaxing the vehicle up and over as Eamon howled and curled into crash position, his head between his knees, hands locked behind.

"We're clear of the landscaping—you can look up now." Jani sped up as they emerged onto the flat, the road uncurling before them. "It's a straight shot all the way around the horn."

"Damn you to hell." Eamon worked upright, wiping the back of his hand across his mouth. "In a thousand different ways." He looked back over his shoulder just as a rapidly receding flare of red emergency lighting broke through the gloom, blooding his face. The ambulance, bringing up the rear. "I should have ridden with them."

The rain had begun, fat drops that splattered across the windscreen with a hard pellet sound. Jani followed the lighted ribbon of pavement, eyes locked on the darkening distance, on the lookout for flames, flares, safety lighting, or any of a hundred accident signs. "I see something." She banked off the road and veered wide, angling her approach to the distant glow in order to avoid anything that might still lie on the road.

Or anyone. She deflected power to the skimmer headlamps, lighting the landscape for half a kilometer or more. Her heart skipped as the damage revealed itself—three skimmers, two with shattered windscreens. Bodies laid out beside them, sheltered from the rain by plastic sheeting, while humanish and idomeni both ran between them or looked on from a distance.

Then she saw a slender form rise from beside one of the bodies and turn into the glare, hair agleam like molten silver, and muttered choked thanks to her Lord Ganesh.

John loped over to the skimmer as soon as Jani slowed. "There was some kind of explosion, just off the roadway." Jacketless in the rain, blood streaking his white shirt and the side of his face, he gave her the briefest glance before rounding the vehicle to Eamon's side. "Three hurt, all Haárin. Feyó—"

"*Feyó!*" Before Jani could say more, John held up his hand.

"—has a mild concussion, according to the Glasgow Scan. Some disorientation, but she's conscious and can obey commands. One of her suborns has a dislocated shoulder and a broken collarbone, if my human hand scanner can read them properly. The driver's the worst off. The steering array impacted her abdomen . . ." He moved off toward the accident scene, Eamon following close behind, the two of them fixed on what needed to be done.

Jani followed until she came to the nearest prone form. Feyó lay with her eyes closed, head elevated, her body covered by plastic sheeting. John had rigged a barrier against the rain for her, a seat-of-the-pants assembly utilizing a strip of the same sheeting stretched between a tree branch and the skimmer door.

Jani crouched by her side. "Ná Feyó?"

Feyó opened her eyes and looked at her. "Ná Kièrshia." An angry bruise had already bloomed above her right eye, centered by an egglike swelling. "You look as you did at the embassy, on the day we met. So angry, as though you could strike the gods themselves." She tried to sit up, wincing as she shifted her weight to her elbows.

"Please don't move." Jani placed a hand on Feyó's shoulder and eased her back as the surfaces around them altered to flashing red, signaling the arrival of the ambulance. "Forgive the ungodly color of the alarm."

Feyó smiled, but the expression faded quickly. "Others followed me, Kièrshia. Representatives of the dominants from Amsun and Hortensia." She raised a hand and pointed.

Jani followed the line of her hand, and saw a trio of Haárin, two males and a female, dressed in traditional garb, now dirt-smeared and rain-soaked, standing near the other battered skimmer.

"They came to provide support for me." Feyó's voice came faster. "The time had come to confront Gisa—I brought them to Thalassa to see you—"

"That's it—conversation's over." Eamon emerged through the rain and set about dismantling the sheeting. "Go wreak havoc somewhere else," he said to Jani as he helped one of his aides raise Feyó onto a skimgurney.

Jani waited as first Feyó, then her two suborns were loaded into the vehicle. Then she turned to the three visitors, gauging their postures as she approached. *The female's shoulders are rounding—oh, good.* Then one of the males deflected the female's attention and gestured roughly toward Jani, his voice a harsh tumble of Pathen Haárin. The female gave Jani another, more studied look, and slowly straightened.

Make that very slowly. Jani brushed off the knees of her old brown coverall, and wished she'd had the presence of mind to don her overrobe. Unfortunately, it had needed cleaning, and currently hung in drip-dry mode above her bathroom sink. "Can you tell me what happened?" she asked in Sìah Haárin, cutting straight to the chase. Somehow, a more traditional "glories of the evening" greeting didn't seem appropriate, given the circumstances.

"Tripbeam, most likely, and truly." The female raised her arm in gesture, the sleeve of her overrobe sliding back to reveal a hash of *à lérine* scars. "The pale humanish—his skimmer led us. It passed unimpeded. Then followed Feyó. Then came the explosion."

"Tripbeam." Jani looked over the first damaged skimmer. "Keyed to the com frequencies of Feyó's vehicles?" She fell silent—speculations coursed through her brain like comet trails, and she didn't want the Haárin to hear any of them. "Are any of you hurt?" She gestured to the Pathen male, who was attempting to cradle his right arm without seeming to. "You should be seen to, as is seemly."

The appeal to the formalities reawakened something in the two males—taken aback as they seemed by the red flashing lights of the ambulance, they headed for it, their steps quickening as one of the hybrid Haárin walked out to meet them.

The female, however, hung back. She looked Jani in the eye, her brown-gold face a study in emotion barely contained.

"You are the Kièrshia." Her shoulders curved as Jani nodded. "You ask us to enter the place that struck at us? You ask us to take treatment from those who sought to injure us by surprise?" She possessed what the idomeni called "demon eyes," dark brown irises and sclera that in the gloom looked like empty sockets.

"I know who arranged this." Jani shoved her hands in her pockets to keep from gesturing—she didn't know Pathen Haárin very well, and the last thing she needed now was a miscommunication. "I will see to them."

"Hah! Indeed? What remedy?" The female leaned closer. *"Priest. What remedy?"* She glared at Jani as though she expected an answer at that moment. When she didn't receive one, she gestured in angry dismay and resumed her trudge to the ambulance.

Jani watched the female shake off the Haárin aide's offered arm and enter the ambulance on her own. Watched Eamon and one of his assistants secure the vehicle gullwings, then climb inside. Watched the ambulance float away, red light still pulsing through the growing dark. Felt movement behind her, and turned to find John standing there.

"I'm afraid to ask what that was about." He held out his hand—when Jani took it, he reeled her in.

Jani wrapped her arms around his waist and squeezed until she felt him tense under the pressure. "When word came to the house of an accident, all I could think of was you."

"I'm not your problem, from the look of things. Hearing's a little wonky from the shockwave, but beyond that I'm fine." John brushed away raindrops that had beaded on the front of Jani's coverall. "Feel free to hang onto me as long as you wish, though. I'm sure I'm more badly hurt than I can imagine."

Jani leaned back so she could look John in the face. "I think you're right." The rain had washed the blood from his cheek, exposing the raw edges of a jagged gash. "That's deep—it will scar if you don't get it treated quickly."

"I'm not the most important thing going on right now." John gripped her hand and held it away from his face. "I don't think Gisa tried to kill Feyó. The blast wasn't strong enough."

"A warning shot across her bow? I'm afraid I'm not concerned about degree at the moment."

"What are you going to do?"

Jani worked out of John's embrace as the first red flares of idomeni temper stained the outer edges of her vision. "I told them." She paced, her boot soles clogging with the claylike mud. "*I told them.* No violence against any of Feyó's, or against Feyó herself. To do so against her or one of hers is to do so against me, and I do not take kindly." She could have been standing under glass for all she felt the rain. The Pathen female's words echoed inside her head. *Priest, what remedy?*

"Jan . . . ?" John walked to her side and placed a tentative hand on her shoulder.

Jani felt his touch like a growing weight—she shook off his hold, then set off toward his skimmer. "Wait." She stopped. In the distance a low rumble of thunder sounded. "You better drive."

CHAPTER 24

The ground floor was quiet enough that Jani could hear her boots echo on the tile. The demirooms were darkened—no one sat on the chairs and couches and listened to music or watched programs on the 'Vee. No one spoke.

Yet they were there, all the Thalassans. Jani could see them through the interior gloom, standing around the courtyard. Silent. Waiting. They turned at the click of the closing entry, and what sounded like a sigh emerged from them. A collective release.

Jani took a step forward, then paused when she detected movement off to one side, and watched the two familiar forms approach. Torin, her self-appointed historian, gripping his handheld, eyes wide, jaw tight. And Brondt, her self-appointed chamberlain, as outwardly calm as his nature and position demanded.

"Torin and I had just returned from the outbuildings when the ambulance arrived." Only a tightening around his jaw betrayed his unease. "They'd already begun gathering." He looked from Jani to the crowd, then back to her. "What are you going to do?"

"I know what I want to do." Jani held out her hands, then turned them over—they were steady, the palms dry, the fingers curved as though readying to grip the hilt of a blade.

"Jani? What's going on?"

Jani turned to find John standing in the entry, his face shiny with rain but for the dull, dark gash in his cheek. "Have Eamon bring Feyó and the Pathen Haárin up here."

John hesitated, then shook his head. "Feyó is in no condition—"

"She needs to be here." Jani sensed John's uncertainty, his

fear. For her. For what he knew she wanted to do. "Tell Eamon. Bring them here yourself if he refuses to help." She waited, her nerves stretching in impatience as he looked her up and down. A doctor's examination, an evaluation of all the things about her that he no longer understood. "John, *please*."

John pushed a hand through his wet hair, then fixed on Brondt until the other man shuffled his feet and looked away. "I'll do . . . what I can." He stepped around Jani, reached for her as he drew near, and brushed his fingers against hers. "Take care, in every way, for all the good my saying it will do," he said as he skirted the edge of the courtyard and vanished into the shadow.

Jani's shoulders rounded as she headed toward the crowd, the back row parting for her, then closing in behind her as the row in front of them parted. She passed through the innermost circle of the hybrids to find the courtyard stripped of tables and chairs, the planters pushed to the side. Someone had inscribed a circle on the tile with red chalk—Gisa stalked its center, scarred arms bared in her sleeveless shirt, which had been bleached palest dull white to allow the greatest contrast with the blood.

When she saw Jani, she stilled. "This is not your challenge, Kièrshia," she said in English, the beat of the rain against the sky-light a backdrop for her words. "I fight Feyó for the protection of this place."

"Feyó cannot fight now." Jani walked the outer edge of the circle as she fingered the shoulder of her coverall, probing the seam for any gaps in the seal. "Your perimeter defenses saw to that."

"She knew she was not welcome here. Yet she came, so whose fault?" Gisa cut the air with an invisible blade. "I told her that if she came here, she would face challenge. She treats us as hers, and we are not. She acts as dominant, and she is not." Her voice rang out. "She has no place here. No right. This is Thalassa! The place of the hybrid! We live in the new way here!"

Before Jani could reply, a rising murmur drew her attention. She turned to the sound and saw John's white head move through the crowd, the darker braided fringe of the Pathen Haárin representatives following close behind.

Then John emerged and the voices ramped, for he pushed a skimchair in which sat a hunched figure. Feyó, one eye swelled shut, dressed in medwhites. Her shoulders rounded further when she caught sight of Gisa, tensing as though she would push to her feet and enter the circle despite her injuries.

Jani waited until John stilled the chair. Then she walked to it and stood before Feyó. "I am most sorry to ask you to expose yourself in your weakness. But all must see that you cannot fight." She bent low, so that only Feyó could hear. "Gisa told you that you would not be allowed into Thalassa, and that you would face sanction if you sought entry. Yet you came."

Feyó tilted her head to look up at Jani, a posture dictated more by her position than any regard. "To discuss—"

"To discuss what?" Jani backed off a step, so she could look Feyó in the eye, a move that drew some grumbling from the Pathen female. "No, I don't sense an attempt at dialogue gone awry here. What I sense is an attempt at sandbagging that didn't quite work the way you hoped."

"Gisa is chaotic!"

"Gisa is half humanish, and you insist upon treating her as Haárin. She is not fully suborn to you, and you cannot expect her to be so, yet you insist."

"We must have order here."

"Your order, as you see it." Jani glanced around, gauging distances and modulating her voice accordingly. She spoke Síah Haárin, clipped and rapid and devoid of gesture, because the hybrid humanish stood the closest, and with any luck they wouldn't be able to follow what she said. "Gisa insists upon the new ways, you insist upon the old, and neither of you will give a millimeter."

Feyó tried to shake her head. But the motion must have dizzied her—her hands tightened on her chair arms and she sagged forward as though she might go under. "The Elyan Haárin must show unity."

"Your unity, as you see it—Gisa capitulating, and the Elyan enclave swallowing Thalassa." Jani glanced around at hybrid faces suddenly bent on avoiding her eye. "Look around you. How would you expect such as these to blend with your Haárin? I don't agree with Gisa's methods, Feyó, but damn it, you asked for it." *And I'm stuck dealing with it.*

"Are you finding remedy, priest?" The Pathen female leaned close, demon eyes glittering, and jabbed a finger at Jani. "Will you make order from the chaos of this damned odd place?"

"*This damned odd place,*" Jani bit out. "This is *my* place." She pushed the female's finger aside with the flat of her hand. "You forced Feyó to come here, did you not? You make demands as to how things must be, and you do not even know what is here!"

"Ná Wola is a godly Haárin," Feyó said.

"Ná Wola is of Hortensia, and her concerns are not at issue

here and now." Jani held Wola's glare until the Haárin gestured impatience and turned away. Then she slowly straightened, her mind a muddle.

And beneath it all, the overriding concern that Tsecha's future depended upon what happened here in the next few minutes.

Damn it. Human nerves warred with idomeni rage in Jani's heart and mind and soul, neither holding the upper hand for long. The wrong move would fracture the Outer Circle Haárin, alienate the Thalassans forever.

She looked at John, who leaned on Feyó's skimchair as though he needed the support. He still hadn't bandaged his cut cheek—at first glance he reminded her of a battered angel shepherding the survivors of some divine battle to safety.

"I remember a priest in an overrobe striding down the corridor of my ship." John's voice came so low it seemed to rumble up through the ground. "She was all I could see—I couldn't look away." His look grew pointed and a little stunned. "They can't look away either." His voice grew softer, until it barely emerged. "Just do, and it will be right."

Jani shook her head. "No—"

"Yes." He looked away for a beat, then back again, shaking his head. "Trust me—the Pied Piper lives." He jerked his chin toward the circle, where Gisa waited. "Play your tune."

Jani glanced at the nearby faces, and saw expressions ranging from confusion to trepidation, depending, she guessed, on the degree of familiarity with the story John alluded to.

Then she turned back to Gisa. "You claim to honor me because I am the first." She took one step, then another, until she broke the invisible barrier and entered the circle itself. "This you call honor," she said as the mutter of voices around her ramped to a babble, "attacking one esteemed by ní Tsecha, throwing this place into discord?"

Gisa stood her ground. Her chin came up in the humanish manner, her hands clenching as though she already held her blades. "I have said already—my fight is not with you."

"So you have said. Many times." Jani heard Dathim's cadences in her voice, and wondered what he'd say if he saw her now. "Even as you brought me here by force and threat, set a network of five planets on its ear, jeopardized the life of ní Tsecha, whom you claim to esteem above all others, you have yet said repeatedly that your fight is not with me." She felt idomeni anger warm her, and imagined the strength of Thalassa rising up through her from the stones. Sensed John's dark gaze drill her back, and took strength from that as well. "You call me 'the first,' but you do not realize what that means." She caught the reflective flicker on faces as lightning shone through the skylight, saw the fear, and savored it. "I have been a hybrid longer than any of you. As such, I was alone a long time." She flexed her shoulders as the weight of twenty years' wandering bore down upon her. "It is no way to live." She closed her eyes, and saw the colored domes of Karistos, the palms pushing up in between, the slope of the city to the bay. Felt the sun warm her bones, even though it had set hours ago. "I am home now, and it is my home that I defend." She opened her eyes and looked across the circle to Gisa. "I fight for Thalassa. Give me a weapon."

As the voices rose among the crowd, Gisa raised her hand and tilted her head to one side. The posture served as a signal to Bon, who drew to the edge of the circle, a large, flat box balanced in her bandaged hands. Bracing the box against her body, she lifted the lid, revealing two stark curves of Sìah metal. She moved along the circle's edge to Jani and held out the box for her inspection.

Jani lifted one of the blades from its inset, then balanced it on the edge of her hand at the place where the blade itself met the hilt. "Quite fine. Yes." She lifted the blade and pressed the point to the left shoulder seam of her coverall. Her focus tunneled, blinding her to the bodies that pressed as close to the edge of the circle as protocol allowed, narrowing her awareness to the slow pound of her heart and the being who stood opposite her. "Remove this obstacle as you have all others, Lord Ganesh, I plead." With that, she drove the blade through the cloth, slitting the seam. "Allow me the wisdom to understand what must be done." She grabbed the sleeve and yanked down—the material gave with a harsh rip. "Allow me also the courage to do it." She changed hands and drove the blade into the right shoulder seam, slitting it as she had the other, tearing that sleeve away as well, exposing her bare arms to the light.

"Ná Kièrshia?" Gisa paced her side of the circle, blade in hand, her voice lilting in puzzlement. "You have challenged me? You have not said the words."

Jani tossed the sleeves outside the boundary of the circle. "Do you recall our conversation in the library?" Her humanish half took over now—her jaw and throat felt tight as she spoke, and her shoulder muscles ached from tension. "You spoke of your admiration for ní Tsecha. You spoke of the sacrifices he made, his outcast, his many challenges as he defended his teachings. 'The blood of the priest that binds.' Those are your words, Gisa."

The humanish part of Gisa must have sensed the undercurrent that ran through Jani's speech. She backed as far to the edge of the circle as she could, until she teetered so close to breaking the plane that Bon moved in behind her and pushed her back in.

And there Jani waited. She closed in, her blade at the ready, grabbed Gisa by the hair and yanked her face to within a handsbreadth of hers.

"Well, I speak for Tsecha, and I tell you this!" She shook Gisa until she heard her teeth clatter. "You brought me to this warm place, and you showed me these people, *my* people, and then you expected me to stand aside while you and Feyó screwed it up!" She pushed the female away. "It ends here. It ends now. With the blood of the priest." With that, she pressed the point of her blade to her own right wrist and slit her arm to the elbow. The strange warmth came, beginning as heat just under the skin and pouring down. Like water, so thin. The flow, so fast.

"You gave the wanderer a home, Gisa. Then you risked it, and thought she'd stand back and let you do as you would. You need to learn my history better." Jani switched her blade to her right hand, held her left hand to the welling gash until her blood coated it. Then she pressed her bloody hand to Gisa's forehead and swept down, painting half her face.

Gisa raised a hand and touched her blooded cheek, then looked at Jani, eyes wide and glistening. She opened her mouth to speak, but before she could say anything, Jani gripped her by the wrist and dragged her. Across the circle, then outside, toward Feyó and the other Haárin.

Shouts rose in protest, but Jani silenced them with a sweep of her blade. She came to a stop before an alarmed Feyó, Gisa fighting her grasp like a youngish—the strain clenched her arm muscles, forcing even more blood to flow.

"The blood of the priest that binds!" Jani shouted loud enough for the words to echo throughout the courtyard. Then she tossed her blade aside. Still holding Gisa fast, she wiped her left hand over her self-inflicted injury again, then pressed it to the side of Feyó's face.

"You work together, through me." She paused to breathe—her chest felt strangely hollow, her knees as weak. "That which is of Thalassa—" She squeezed Gisa's wrist hard enough for the female to flinch. "—will remain *here*, and that which is of Elyas will remain *here*." She grabbed Feyó's hand and squeezed until the Haárin gasped. "Thalassa will be with Elyas—not *of* Elyas, but *with*. Note the difference." She released both females and stood back. The room rocked as she raised her head; she saw John release Feyó's chair and beckon to one of Eamon's Haárin techs. "There are details, of course. There are always details. The main points are these—Thalassa governs itself regarding internal matters, and defers to Elyas regarding Board matters. Everything else is negotiable."

"This place!" Wola pushed forward, again jabbing her finger at Jani. "I have heard of this place." She gestured about. "I have seen. It is anathema!"

Jani slapped the Haárin's hand away. "*It is not your concern! Ní Tsecha favors this place.*" *Well—he will once he knows about it.* "I represent him and I pronounce it sound. It acknowledges ná Feyó as dominant in matters of business, and matters of business are your only concern." She stopped again to breathe. Inhaling required more effort than it should have. She looked down at her arm to find the bleeding had slowed to seepage. A puddle of red dried at her feet.

"We can finish this later. So says the attending physician." John maneuvered behind Jani and steered her through the courtyard toward one of the demirooms, holding her elbow with one hand and the back of her coverall with the other as he steered her through the press of the crowd.

When they had cleared the last of the hybrids, he leaned forward. "Pied Piper," he whispered in her ear.

"Toot toot," Jani muttered, just as her knees gave way completely.

Breathe . . . breathe . . .

Jani lay on the couch and concentrated on respiration. John had bundled cushions under her legs to elevate them, and applied a coldpack to the back of her neck. The hollow feeling in her chest remained, though it had lessened. Her right arm felt pressured. She tipped up her head and saw that someone had clamped a transfuser around her elbow—the weight of the thing pulled the wound on her arm, which someone had wrapped with loose gauze. The transfuser display array fluttered, red and blue alphanumerics that flashed at just the right frequency to inspire nausea.

Breathe . . .

She lay back her head and studied the ceiling. The edges of the tiles shimmered, like tarmac on a hot day.

Breathe . . .

"Feeling better?"

Jani opened her eyes and found a familiar pale visage regarding her sideways. "I won't be dashing up and down the beach anytime soon."

"Not for a day or two, at least." John raised her shoulders, then sat down and lowered her so she rested on his lap. "You nicked a vein. You only lost a little over half a liter, but you lost it fast, which explains your weakness. Just your body's way of telling you to put your feet up." He plucked one of her curls, then worked his fingers down to her scalp and commenced therapeutic massage. "Then there's your idomeni nature. Funny how your rages drain you as much as your augmentation did."

"Hilarious." Jani yawned. "What's happening out in the land of the fully sanguinated?"

John laughed, sending a pleasant vibration along Jani's shoulders. "Things are bustling. I've ordered everyone to let you rest, otherwise the procession of those wanting to pay their respects would bury you. Wola and friends have departed. Feyó summoned a couple of her suborns to come retrieve them and escort them back to the Elyan enclave. She used the hospital comroom to make the call. Apparently this was seen as some sort of breakthrough in Thalassa-Elyas relations—thought they'd break out the champagne there for a minute."

"If you think it will help, break it out." Jani tilted her head so she could look John in the face. "This house of cards needs all the adhesive it can get."

"Don't underestimate yourself—you always do, you know." John relocated his attention from the top of Jani's head to the back. "I'll have you know that Bon and Torin spent the last hour tearing strips from old table linens and using them to wipe your blood from the courtyard floor. Those strips have become the souvenir of the moment—everyone I've seen has one tied around their right wrist, including Feyó herself." He halted his ministrations long enough to allow Jani a peek at his own band of red-stained cloth.

"You're kidding." Jani reached up and tugged one end of the tie, already stiff with dried blood. "You're not kidding."

"You are well, ná Kièrshia?" Gisa edged within Jani's sightline. She had changed into one of her usual crisp outfits, a trouser suit in pale blue that darkened her grey eyes to gunmetal. "You do not yet appear yourself."

"I feel quite fine, ná Gisa." Apparent ally though the hybrid dominant now was, Jani didn't feel comfortable revealing the extent of her weakness to her. "But my physician compels me to rest, so I must follow his direction."

"I'm writing *that* down," John said.

"There is still much to discuss." Gisa sat in a chair opposite Jani and took care to rest her right hand atop her knee so her strip of blooded cloth was fully exposed. "Details of responsibility. Contingencies. What will happen to us if Feyó loses a challenge—"

Jani held up her hand, then waited for Gisa to lapse into grudging silence. "I'm officially indisposed, and I believe ná Feyó has been battered enough for one day. Tomorrow, ná Gisa, will be time enough. The important thing is that Thalassa now has official standing within the Trade Board, and the cracks in the Outer Circle Haárin's united front have been repaired." She sniffed the air, as much to annoy the impatient Gisa as to confirm that she really did smell what she thought she smelled. "Food?"

"Mid-evening sacrament is at hand, ná Kièrshia." Gisa rose, her attention fixed on the transfuser. "You will sit at table, of course."

"Of course, ná Gisa." Jani pushed her legs off the couch and let their momentum pull her into a sitting position. "I will join you in a moment." She nodded acceptance of the female's gesture of esteem, and watched her cut through the darkened room to the bustling courtyard beyond.

"Do you trust her?" John followed Gisa's progress as well, while he scratched at the dried blood that still stained his cheek. "I sure as hell don't." He turned back to Jani and started disconnecting the transfuser.

"She wants to be Elyan dominant. In a few years, depending on how well Thalassa integrates into the Haárin network and how much the hybrid population grows, she might build sufficient status to have a shot." Jani straightened her arm and rubbed the reddened crook of her elbow where the transfuser injector had attached itself, gasping as her fatigued shoulder cramped.

"You're more qualified to be dominant than she is," John said as he brought his viselike grip to bear on Jani's tightened muscles.

"No, thanks. This priest thing has its advantages." Jani tilted her head to one side and rubbed her cheek against John's hand. "I can do my job without constantly having to worry whether someone's gearing up to knock me off my perch." She savored a final few moments of John's attention, but just as she made ready to work to her feet, the entry chimes sounded.

"If that's the cheery ná Wola come back because she forgot something, the food odors are going to send her screaming into the rain." John stood and turned to the door. "Torin's getting it. Kid's a little lightning bolt—everywhere you look, there he is with a shit-eating grin and that handheld of his."

Jani smiled. "He's my historian."

"He's a pain in the ass. I feel like I've got the *Tribune-Times* tailing me for one of those 'how so-and-so spends his day' stories." John stilled, his eyes narrowing. "Hello. Company."

Jani turned in time to see Torin lead Niall around an obstacle course of furniture. The man wore fresh desertweights, and had a documents case tucked under his arm. He wasn't alone, either. A female captain shadowed him, also in desertweights, documents case also in hand.

"Evenin'." Niall stopped beside Jani's couch and sniffed the air, a picture in studied informality, his Sheridan persona in full force. "Bracing. The aromas alone are enough to make my eyes water. I can imagine the taste."

"You're welcome to join us," Jani replied. "We offer food to please every palate. Even humanish." She hadn't meant the remark as an insult, but if Niall's reddening face served as indication, he chose to take it that way.

"Those are Haárin." The captain looked toward the courtyard at the assembling diners, her eyes widening. "Eating together? In public?"

"They're not full Haárin. They're hybrid, like me." Jani met the young woman's stare head-on, and was treated to the sight of a blond complexion flaring to bright peach. *A blushing bunch, our officers be.* She glanced at Niall just as he reached reflexively for his shirt pocket. "Feel free to light up, Colonel—this is Thalassa." As soon as she spoke, she wished she'd kept her mouth shut— *Colonel* had much the same effect on Niall's complexion as had *humanish.* "Damn it, Niall," she muttered under her breath, "give the A-G's hatchet man gig a rest."

Niall stared down at his shoes for a time. Then he edged around the low table and lowered into the same chair Gisa had recently vacated. "Sit down, Captain," he said to his companion. "If past history is any indication, you're going to need to take good notes." He set his case atop the table, then made a show of looking toward the courtyard. "Are Major Thomas Hamil or Colonel Dieter Brondt here at the enclave currently?"

"I don't know." Jani looked to the collecting diners in time to see Torin dart into the lift. *Off to sound the alarm, I'll be bound.* "I haven't seen them for a while." She looked back at Niall, to find him regarding her with humorless resolve.

"Jan, they're mine." He tilted his head in the direction of his note-taking captain. "I have enough evidence to request a Board of Inquiry as a Friend of the Service. If they decline to talk to me now, it will only get worse for them."

Jani felt John's hand enclose hers. He squeezed—she squeezed back. "This enclave is currently under the jurisdiction of the Elyan Haárin, as are all its inhabitants. If you wish to question either Hamil or Brondt, you will need to submit the appropriate request to ná Feyó Tal's offices at the Trade Board in Karistos." *Where it will be filed appropriately, if I have anything to say about it.*

"Request! They're still Service!"

"Only until their next physicals. At that point they'd have been medicalled out. If I hadn't shown up, that's exactly what would have happened. Why not skip a few steps and dump them now?"

Niall held out a fist as though he meant to shake it in Jani's face, then raised one finger. "Dereliction of duty." He raised a second finger. "Desertion." A third. "Treason, if I can swing it."

"Heavy charges, Colonel."

"Not to mention warranted—Brondt's been feeding the Elyan Haárin information about sealed bid projects and dock restrictions for the past eighteen months, at least."

"Anything detrimental to the Service?"

Niall hesitated. "I'm working on it."

Jani rested her head against the couchback. Her stomach grumbled as the food odors grew stronger and more complex and inviting. "The Service guidelines regarding detriment are fairly malleable, as I recall. A whack of the jeweler's hammer here and there, and they can be reformed to suit the occasion. I need them here, Niall. Brondt especially."

"I am not going to let you rework the Service Code for your own convenience."

"Why not? The Service reworks it for theirs. If they didn't, I wouldn't be alive today." *And neither would you.* Jani kept that to herself, but she could tell from the flicker in Niall's eyes that he heard it anyway. "A good attorney might argue that the bioemotional changes wrought by their hybridization rendered them incapable of proper Service behavior." She looked to John, who eyed her with something dangerously close to cold-blooded admiration.

"That's why you made sure Thalassa fell in under Feyó's control," he said. "To protect them."

"I was thinking of Tsecha, but the same principle applies to them." Jani pondered for a moment. "Do you know any good lawyers?"

John smiled. "A few."

Niall glared at Jani, the hunter's light in his eye returned. "I will say that I expected to have to go to round two on that one." He nodded, and dragged his documents case onto his lap. "Heard much news lately?"

"From Chicago?" Jani shook her head. "I didn't trust the security of the lines for anything important."

"How about public?"

"The 'sheets? Haven't had the chance to dig around much lately." Jani felt her stomach tighten. "Why?"

Niall reached into his documents case and removed a newssheet. "Fort Karistos edition of *Blue and Grey*. Front page." He unrolled the display parchment and handed it to Jani. "One of Elon's security suborns challenged Pretty Boy. Depending on when the details can be worked out, the bout will be scheduled for the end of next month." He reached into his shirt pocket and removed his nicstick case, shook out a cylinder, and bit down on the ignition tip with a decisive crunch. "If we leave now," he said through a haze of smoke, "we just might get to Chicago in time for the show."

CHAPTER 25

"This story isn't very detailed." Jani bit into a piece of flatbread, then brushed the crumbs from the newssheet surface. "Lots of extraneous garbage about Lucien's personal life, but very little about why nìRau Ghos challenged him in the first place."

"Everyone I talk to who knows Pascal thinks the 'general principles' argument covers the 'why' pretty well." Niall set aside a glass of iced tea, then stirred and dredged the contents of his soup bowl. "We're more interested in what he was doing at the Shèráin embassy in the first place. Granted, he does occasionally field for the home team, but most of the time, when he goes there, he goes there for you." He sniffed at the contents of his spoon, then sipped. Paused to roll the broth around in his mouth, then swallowed with a shrug. "Tastes like good old chicken vegetable to me." He picked up a slice of flatbread and crumbled it atop the soup. "He's not talking, and he's been pulling in various markers to avoid being pressed. The thought occurred that this might have something to do with Tsecha's problem. What do you think?"

I think that either you already know, and you want to see if what I say matches, or Lucien is holding something back about the mine investigation. Jani played for time by picking at her food and looking around the half-deserted courtyard. The rain had stopped sometime before, and many of the Thalassans had dispersed to various parts of the enclave to check for storm damage. The few who remained bustled about on various errands, casting not so surreptitious glances at Jani, Niall, and John each time they passed their table. Of the regular residents, only Eamon had yet to show his face. John said that he was still clearing up after the postaccident onslaught, but Jani wondered. Gisa was Eamon's horse, after all, and she had emerged in fine shape from a messy situation. A little gloating on his part wouldn't have been out of character.

"Lucien spends a lot of his off-time at the Haárin enclave. He tends to travel with Dathim and Tsecha as though he's a natural member of the entourage—he doesn't always stop to think about what some humanish and idomeni think of that." Jani pushed aside the newssheet and worked on finishing her supper—the chicken that hadn't wound up in the soup, laced with a hot, dark brown sauce that tasted the way John's voice sounded. "Add to that the fact that, as you say, he isn't universally admired. It's a miracle that something like this didn't happen sooner." She picked up a spice dispenser and shook more ground pepper atop her food. *Lucien, of all the damned times—why now?* "Dathim is training him. That's something, anyway."

"So you're not worried. It's just one of those things, and you see no reason to return to Chicago to check into it." Niall shrugged. "Fine. After I finish this, Captain Eglin and I"—he nodded to his blond cohort, who sat downtable rooting through the bread basket—"will take ourselves off and leave you in peace." He tossed back a swallow of tea, then started back in on his soup, hybrid-watching in between spoonfuls. "What are those things everyone has tied around their wrists?"

"Strips of cloth dipped in my blood." Jani hid her smile at the sound of Captain Eglin's fork hitting her plate. "We had a little excitement here a couple of hours ago."

Niall looked from Jani to John, then back again. "Uh-huh." Alarm warred with irritation on his face—his news about Lucien had been one-upped, and it was obvious from his twitchy expression that the curiosity was killing him. "Cutlery accident?" He raised a butter spreader point up and tipped it back and forth as he eyed the bandage on Jani's arm.

"More a case of pied piper diplomacy." John tossed his napkin atop his plate and pushed back from the table. "And on that note"—" He bent down and kissed Jani. "—I shall hie off to the clinic and see what Eamon's up to."

"Get him to look at your cheek." Jani watched him walk to the lift, his only response to her concern a backhand wave. *Brushing me off already, are you?* The spice residue from his lips had left an enticing sting behind. *Just you wait, Doctor.* She licked it off, then turned back to the table to find Niall eyeing her with annoyance.

"OK, point to you." He pushed away his bowl, then sat back and took his nicstick case from his pocket. "Do you care about this challenge to Pascal or don't you?"

"Of course I care." *Damn it.* Jani scrubbed her hands over her face and stifled a yawn. She needed sleep, and it didn't look like she'd be getting it anytime soon. "Revenge for the Vynshàrau killed in the mine accident crosses one's mind."

"That was the first thing that occurred to us, too, but it's never that simple these days, is it?" Niall took a 'stick from his case, but instead of igniting it, he held it lengthwise and tapped it on the table so it slid through his fingers, then turned it over and started again. "The only direct experience Burkett at Diplo has with challenges was what he picked up with yours last summer. His folks have studied, but you know as well as I do that it's not the same thing. Tsecha's problems have made him persona non grata at his embassy and have also compounded our difficulties in trying to work with him."

"So he's still in Chicago?" Jani hoped the relief in her voice wasn't as obvious as it sounded.

"Yes, he is, for all the good he's doing anyone." Niall took a deep breath. "Not to put too fine a point on it, but we're scrambling here, time is short, and tempers on both sides are just looking for an excuse. We need your help, and I'm authorized to deal to get it." He spoke in a voice so low that even Eglin had to sit forward to hear him. "What do you want?"

Jani sat silent, conscious of Niall's worried glower, Eglin's more goggle-eyed assessment, the fidgeting of a group of younger hybrids who stood off to one side and waited for them to leave so they could clear the table. *All they have to do is ask.* Yes, sometimes it really was that simple. She glanced across the table at Niall, a move sufficient to set him fidgeting. *So that's how a friendship ends.* When what once would have been a request, an appeal, turns to an act of barter. *Fine.* "I note the fact that you made this proposal after you tried to get your hands on Brondt and Hamil."

"I really wanted them, Jan. Brondt especially." Niall shrugged. "Can't blame a man for trying."

"Whyever not?" Jani cradled her right arm—the transfuser site ached and her wound stung every time she moved. "Leave them be. You want them out, medical them. I doubt Mako wants the news of Elyan Haárin dock infiltration to get out, anyway."

Niall tapped the 'stick through his fingers one last time, then stared at it. "Is that all?"

"If I've any consideration left, I'll bank it. If I can." Jani looked to the skylight, the railed walkways, the gardens that surrounded them. Her color-coded dishes and the aromas that fed her just by inhaling. "When were you planning on leaving?" She tried not to think of the view from her bedroom window, the warmth, the sounds of the sea. *I can ask John to come back with me.* That idea, at least, gave her mood a boost.

"Tomorrow early afternoon. I would come here to get you late morning, to allow time for all those last minute complications that always seem to arise." Niall nodded once, a shaky lowering of his chin. "Thank you. I'm gathering the impression that you really don't want to leave right now."

"It's not a good time, no." Jani wondered if despite earlier signs, Feyó's concussion was severe enough to incapacitate her, and if she would still be able to ride herd on the Outer Circle Haárin and maintain the newly mended union. If Gisa would make trouble again. If Niall's word regarding Brondt and Hamil meant anything. "I might ask John to come."

Niall brightened, which indicated how uncomfortable he felt at the prospect of spending over five weeks alone with her. "That would be fine. Whatever you want."

"Yes." Jani dragged her napkin off her lap and tossed it on the table. "Tomorrow, then."

Niall stiffened as the fact of the dismissal soaked in. "Tomorrow." He stood, his chair tottering as he pushed it back with force. "And tomorrow, and tomorrow." He headed for the door, leaving Eglin to hustle to catch him up. "Not an appropriate quote for the moment, but it is still from the Scottish play, and anything with knives in it seems befitting now." The door slid open and he vanished into the night, Eglin closing in behind him like a flustered shadow.

"We confirm Colonel Pierce's information. Ní Tsecha is still in Chicago." Ná Feyó lay atop the scanbed in the clinic's largest examining room, holding a court of sorts, surrounded by suborns and a few of the hybrid Haárin that had come from her enclave. "His movements have been restricted more and more. It is feared and truly that he will simply disappear one day, and that the next we hear of him will be when we learn that Cèel has him." The skin around her eye shone slick with anti-inflammatories, and the swelling had receded enough that she could partially open her eye. "This is not a time I ever believed I would see."

"Ní Tsecha has changed. It's as though he hybridized in the mind instead of the body." Jani sat on a lab chair, which was situated high enough so she could rest her feet atop one of the lab benches. "He's been delving into university libraries, reading of humanish religions and histories. I'm guessing his views would rattle any Haárin, much less a bornsect."

"I wish to meet him, and truly." Gisa sat in the far corner of the room, Bon as usual at her side. "You must bring him back with you, ná Kièrshia, so he may glory in his words come to life."

Jani nodded as the tension ramped. Feyó lay her head back in an attention-getting swoon that drew two of her suborns to her side, an act that brought smiles from Bon and Gisa. *This place is starting to remind me of Cabinet Row.* She huddled in the medcoat one of the techs had given her to cover her bare arms. *Maybe I need a vacation after all.* Not that the trip to Chicago would count. *Please let those damned wristbands keep working after I break orbit, Lord Ganesh, I pray.* "My doctor must see to my injuries—please excuse me, ná Feyó." She slipped off the chair and out the door before anyone had the chance to reply.

Chamberlain, where are you? Jani stalked the halls, shoved aside doors and searched empty labs and offices, on the hunt for Brondt. She had just completed a circuit of the basement and made ready to enter the lift when she sensed a presence behind her and turned.

"Ná Kièrshia." Brondt first bowed in the humanish fashion, then stood as straight as he could in a posture of idomeni regard. A look of uncharacteristic puzzlement suffused his broad features, as though he couldn't decide which protocol stated his feelings better. "I understand I owe you more than I can ever repay." He finally settled for a variation of Service at-ease—feet shoulders-width apart, hands clasped loosely behind his back—which seemed to fit him best of all. "My thanks. Thanks from Hamil as well—he's repairing a leaky roof at one of the greenhouses or he'd tell you himself."

"You're not in the clear yet." Jani stepped away from the lift and started down the hall, pausing to allow Brondt to precede her. "Niall wants your hide—he believes your informing Feyó of station issues constitutes treason against the Commonwealth."

Brondt stopped in mid-stride and looked at Jani over his shoulder. "Do you feel that way?"

"By his standards, I'm a traitor as well. Our friendship kept him from seeing it."

"But you're not friends anymore." Brondt's usually composed gaze softened. "I'm sorry." He hung his head and resumed walking. "I should compliment you on your display this evening." He raised his right hand in a mailfist salute, exposing the strip of bloodstained cloth tied around his wrist. "I knew blood would be shed, but I never thought it would be yours alone."

"I couldn't cut Gisa—that would have signified declaration, which in turn would have led to a permanent schism here." Jani passed a lab and wondered if John worked there, or Eamon. Whether they labored together or kept their distance from one another. "While Haárin are used to dealing with that sort of public animosity, humanish feel the need to escalate. Every drop of blood Gisa shed would have meant a corpse later on, of that I am most sure, and truly." They came upon a small break area, and she herded Brondt inside. "Does Feyó still expect you to provide her information of what goes on here?"

"I believe that now more than ever she will expect such." Brondt waved Jani toward the lone table in the alcove, and poured coffee from the community brewer that dominated one corner of the space. "You've granted Gisa her own power base and ordained it with the blood of the priest." He grinned in memory as he trudged to the table, steaming dispos in hand. "Feyó's not happy with you right now, I'm guessing. She's hoping that if you bring ní Tsecha here, she can work her influence through him to keep you at bay."

"This place is Chicago with palm trees." Jani hunched over her cup. "What are you going to tell her?"

Brondt stared into his coffee. "What do you want me to say?"

Jani leaned forward, elbows on table, and propped her chin in her hands. "We need to strike a balance—if we look too strong, we'll panic the Haárin. If we look too weak, they'll leave us to twist in the wind." She held up three fingers. "I'll be gone three months Common, minimum. Repeated reminders that the one who started it all is coming should keep the lid on the place."

Brondt sipped the coffee and made a face. "So, you are going to try to bring ní Tsecha here?"

"I have to. Chicago's become too inhospitable, and he can never return to the worldskein." Jani tried her own coffee, found it rather good, and felt pity for the soul responsible for making a brew that tasted reasonable to palates at multiple stages of hybridization.

They stood in silence for a time, lost in thought and subdued by fatigue. Then one of Eamon's techs entered, her face brightening when she saw Jani. "Ná Kièrshia!" She held up her right hand, exposing the ubiquitous wristband. "Such a great thing, and truly. It is all we speak of—Doctor Eamon grew quite sick of our talk and bade us all leave his laboratory."

"So Eamon *is* working." Jani finished her coffee and returned to the brewer for more. "The accident took a great deal of his time, I understand.

"The accident?" The tech shrugged, an exaggerated lift of the shoulders that implied she had just learned the gesture. "All who were hurt have been treated. Basic injuries, and truly. Nothing complex." She joined Jani by the brewer. "Doctor Eamon blends skin spray. He must balance the proteins properly, and eliminate those that would cause reaction. Otherwise, mess. Vast mess. Skin like ground meat, he says. So he tests and blends, a different spray for each who is injured."

Jani leaned against the brewer case, enjoying the warmth on her back. "There weren't any hybrids injured tonight, were there? During the storm clean-up?" She looked to Brondt, who shook his head. "John needs to get his cheek fixed, but he's not—" Her mind blanked, and no brewer on Elyas would have been warm enough to ease her sudden chill.

"Ná Kièrshia?" Brondt took a step toward her. "Are you all right?"

"Where is John?" Jani had already left the alcove by the time the tech made it to the exit and called out the room number.

Jani stood before the laboratory door. Hit the entry buzzer. Heard the achingly familiar voice intone, "Come in."

John sat at a desk, bowed over a notebook entry pad. He looked up when she entered, his face lightening. "Hello." He smiled. Sometime after his departure from supper, he had found time to shower and change clothes. He wore medwhites now, the same outfit he had lived in during their Rauta Shèràa basement days, the neckline flecked with damp spots courtesy of his dripping hair.

"I never asked you about the message you sent Val." Jani walked into the room and tried to examine John without seeming to. *Still so pale*. Still a snow wraith, untouched by the sun. *I'm just jumpy*. Letting her nerves get the best of her. *I'm a damned fool*.

"I asked him some business questions, with a few of your carefully worded concerns mixed in. I know it seems like ages, but it was only yesterday. If we're lucky, Val will receive the transmit tomorrow. That's assuming all transfer points are hitting optimally, though, and that's seldom the case." John held a stylus by the ends, and stared at it as though transfixed. "You'll be gone by then, won't you?"

"Yes." Jani lowered into a nearby lab chair, taking care to avoid sitting on the dispenser nestled in her pocket. "You didn't seem concerned upstairs."

"Public air of nonchalance—I've gotten quite good at it over the years." John looked up. "I had to leave the table. I knew Niall was going to ask you to return to Chicago, and you were going to agree, and I'm afraid I just didn't want to hear it."

"I was going to ask you to come along."

"Eamon needs help here. The realization of what he's done has settled around his shoulders over the past few days—his drinking is getting worse and his mood swings are scaring his patients." John sat back and started tossing the stylus into the air. "We all need his brain, but he needs to keep his mouth shut and his hands in his pockets for the next few weeks."

"He's just figured out now what he did?" Jani took a dispo cloth from the bench next to her and started tearing the edge to a fringe. Her mind had turned to a jumble, and she felt the urge to keep her hands busy. "Where the hell has he been?"

"You know us ivory tower types. Heads in the clouds. Refusing to consider the realities of what we do, committed to the art and the art alone." John stopped tossing the stylus and moved on to doodling invisible patterns on a piece of scrap parchment. "It never really hit me what I had done to you until the day we disembarked at Elyas. I had known on an intellectual level, of course. I know your MedRec by heart. But I didn't feel the change in my bones until I saw you walk down that corridor, wearing one of Tsecha's old overrobes." His hands stilled. "Your carriage, your . . . presence, your life, all changed, irrevocably and completely." He hung his head. "Did you ever hate me?"

"Yes." Jani looked away as John's head came up, so that she didn't have to see the pain in his eyes. "I . . . moved on. You used to remind me of the advantages of the situation on a regular basis—I finally started to realize what they were."

"But you hated being the only one. I never knew that."

"I didn't know it either until I saw Torin's image that first time. I've been in a state of befuddlement ever since."

That brought back the smile. "If this is befuddled, I'd hate to have to deal with you when you're on the ball." The expression faded. "When do you leave?"

"Tomorrow morning, late. Niall will meet me here." Jani tore off a corner of the dispo, shredding it to snow that fluttered to the floor at her feet. "Tsecha's troubles were bad enough. Now Lucien. I have to go—I have no choice."

John nodded. "I know."

Jani paused in mid-rip. Then she wadded the remains of the dispo and tossed them atop the bench. "You still haven't fixed that gash." She rose, reaching into her pocket as she approached John's desk. "Hours have passed. You should treat it now."

John sat back, his gaze locked on her hands. "Don't you think a scar would add a certain piratical aspect to the enterprise?"

Jani stopped in front of him and held out the dispenser of humanish skin spray that she'd taken from a first aid tray. "Here. I brought this for you. Humanish skin repair, ready to go."

John took the dispenser from her hand, holding it by the ends as he had the stylus, turning it over and over. "I—" He removed the cover, spritzed some of the solution into the air, then capped it. "Jani—"

"John—"

"Don't look at me like that."

"What the hell do you expect?"

"I—wanted it to be a surprise." He stared at the dispenser as though he read his fortune in it, tipping it at every angle. "Weeks would pass. Then one day you'd look at me, and you'd know."

"You decide to turn your life inside out because you watched me walk down a hallway!" Jani wheeled and paced the perimeter of the room. She usually felt better when she moved, but this time it didn't help. Not at all. "You've just begun." She stopped to swallow, her throat aching. "You can't be that far along yet, no matter how well Eamon's refined the process. Go back."

John's head came up. "To what?" His voice dropped, like a stone into cold, still water. "To what?" He reached out and placed a hand atop his notebook. "I'm recording any changes I feel, as they happen. No one has done this yet—imagine. It will prove an invaluable record." He shifted the notebook back and forth, as though he couldn't find the right position. "I remember what you said, that every day you're as much yourself as you will ever be again. There's another way to look at that, and that is that every day you change a little more. Meanwhile, I stay the same, and watch you move further and further away." His voice darkened.

"You're not the only one who's grown to hate the idea of being alone." He tilted his head to one side, as though the notebook emitted a sound that only he could hear. "Then there's the fact that I love you—do I need to say that again? I've said it so often, but I never did anything about it." He finally looked up at her. "Now I have."

Jani sat transfixed by a gaze that had savored her every expression over the past months, that had just reacquainted itself with her every line and curve. *John* . . . She felt stricken enough to weep, frightened enough to tremble, even as that bastard part of her that had survived almost two decades of a gutter existence sent up a barely detectable murmur of delight. *Friend* . . . *lover* . . . *not alone* . . .

Not alone. Ever again.

"Say something." John forced disinterested lightness into his tone, his usual shield against rejection. "Love you. Bless you. Go away. Go to hell." He exhaled with a rumble. *"Something."*

Jani sat quietly, listening as a laughing group passed close by the door, their voices coming from nowhere, then fading to nothing. She slid off her chair and walked over to John. He drew up straight as she approached, shifting in his chair so he faced her as she circled around, one hand on the edge of the desk, the other on the edge of his chair, braced for whatever he feared she would tell him.

She took his upturned face in her hands and bent close, taking care to avoid his angry wound, savoring the clean scent of soap and the fine roughness of his skin as she brushed her lips over his before pressing down and kissing him harder than she ever had.

They broke apart once to breathe, then joined again. John pulled her onto his lap, holding her hacked arm as lightly as spun glass before snaking his arms around her waist and pulling her close.

"Well," he said, his voice muffled, "if you're not going to speak, I suppose this is an acceptable substitute." He positioned her so he could rest his head upon her shoulder.

"So?" Jani stopped to clear her throat. "That first time I walked in on you and Eamon—"

"I had already proposed the deal. If he hybridized me, I would let him keep his stake in Neoclona." John's face hardened. "Someone like Niall would have appreciated watching him battle through that decision, I think. Very operatic. Greed versus whatever sense of kinship he still felt for me." He looked away, jaw muscles tensed. "Greed won, of course. As if there was ever any doubt."

"I wondered why his disgust with me had moved to a higher level." Jani put her arm around his shoulder. "Does Val know?"

John shook his head eventually. "Not yet. I tried to drop some hints in my message. About how much I enjoyed it here. The fact that you and I were . . . together again." He grinned halfheartedly. "I'll think of something. Val is my best friend. But some things are harder to explain than others."

Jani ruffled John's hair—the air in the office was cool but very dry, and the white strands had already dried. "How do you feel now?"

John shrugged. "Not much different. Yet. Eamon's data show that it takes a few weeks before the mutated enzymes really kick in and the diet needs adjusting." His eyes clouded. "I would have liked one last late supper at Gaetan's. In the rear garden, under the spring stars. Ah, well." He glanced shyly at Jani. "There are stars here, too." He pulled back from her with a sigh. "I need to get dosed." He laced one hand with hers. "Come with me?"

Jani stood and followed him out of the room. "Is it true that doctors make the worst patients?"

"Oh yes—we're big babies. Eamon tells me that I complain about the treatments more than anybody here and nothing's even happened yet." John examined the pale whiteness of the back of his hand. "Not that I can tell, anyway."

They entered one of the busier hallways, then passed through a double-wide panel into a gleaming laboratory. Cushioned scanchairs lined one wall, each one backed by a thin-branched metal tree suitable for hanging drip bags and other insertion devices.

Eamon stood in front of a lab bench, next to the chair farthest from the door. He'd already set out a pair of small metal canisters that contained the gene broth, and now occupied himself with calibrating the injector. When he heard sounds behind him, he turned. His heavy face softened with something like pity when he looked at John, then hardened when he shifted to Jani. "And she shall sow chaos wherever she goes."

"Belt it, Eamon." John took the injector from him, then picked up the cartridges and shoved them into the slotted housing. "So." He held the device out to Jani. "Care to do the honors?"

Jani held her breath as John placed the injector in her hands, then sat in the nearest chair. Avoided his eye as she bent over him and slid the device along his lower arm until it nestled in the crook. The injector was shaped like a scanpack with a curved notch on the end, and had much the same control layout—she intuited the switches for the grips that clasped John's arm just above the elbow, as well as the preinjector that numbed the skin.

"Well well." John examined her handiwork, then lay back his head. "We'll make a medico of you yet."

Jani ran a hand along the injector casing, which grew warm to the touch as the device heated the broth to body temperature. "How long does it take?"

"Ten minutes. Fifteen, if I develop irritation at the site and the thing needs to pump out anti-inflammatory." He watched her as though she undressed, breath quickening, eyes locked on her every move. "Chance to get a little of your own back, isn't it?"

Jani pulled back from the control pad. "Revenge has nothing to do with this."

"Not even a little?" John looked quickly away, his face reddening. "Poetic justice, then. Patient, heal thy physician." He turned back to her. "Whenever you're ready."

Jani placed her hand atop the injector. Behind her, she could hear Eamon curse and stalk off to the other side of the lab. She gazed into John's dark-filmed eyes and tried to imagine what color they'd turn as he hybridized. What shade his hair would darken to. His skin. Whether his voice would alter, and how.

Then she moved her thumb over the injector switch and pressed it.

CHAPTER 26

Jani opened her eyes. She could sense morning through the coated window wall, even though the glass shone dull and the bedroom itself was as dark as a cave. *Niall will be here soon.* She worked out from beneath the covers, moving carefully to avoid waking John.

She showered, dressed in her remaining coverall, then tossed her scanpack, overrobe, and other odds and ends into her duffel and pronounced herself packed. Slung the bag over her shoulder and tiptoed out of the room into the daybright walkway. There, she paused, leaning against the wall and inhaling the flower odors from the gardens below. Orange smells. Red smells. Purple. Yellow. White. She breathed them all in, and filed them away for future reference. *Tomorrow morning at this time I'll be heading out toward Amsun GateWay.* Bound in a diplomatic marriage of convenience to a man she had once called a friend, who was now merely someone she knew well enough to fear more completely than anyone she knew. "Damn." She pushed away from the wall and headed for the lift down to the courtyard.

Early morning sacrament seemed to have caught the Thalassans by surprise—some set out food, plates, and cutlery, while others assembled the table and laid out the linens. They turned as one toward her when she entered the courtyard. Most smiled, waved, or held their wristbands in the air. A few, Jani noted, merely eyed her steadily, as though she were a stranger. *Well well—looks like not everyone buys into my brilliance.* She found that reassuring, in an odd way. After the rough and tumble of life in Chicago, complete and total acceptance would have felt too bizarre for words.

"Glories of this morning to you, ná Kièrshia." Gisa stood near her usual spot at the low head of the table, waiting for her place to be set. She had dressed in uncharacteristically jarring pink and yellow, and had twisted her hair into a loose topknot from which stray strands escaped. "Such a time we have had here."

"Glories of the morning to you, as well, ná Gisa." Jani felt herself slipping into the professional politeness she had employed for her dealings with Cabinet Row. "Everyone seems a little flustered."

"We all stayed awake too long. Hybrid and Haárin who had not spoken since the beginnings of this place spoke together once more. It was a great thing, and truly." Gisa took her seat as the young hybrid who set her place moved on, then motioned for Jani to sit next to her. "And now you must leave. Such sadness."

You are desolation itself, Gisa. Jani concentrated on serving herself, and decided to keep her mouth shut and not explore the idomeni grasp of sarcasm before coffee.

"While you are not here, I will petition Feyó to allow a Thalassan representative to the Trade Board," Gisa continued. "We do not own transports or shuttles." An unspoken *yet* hung in the air. "But many here own businesses or practice skilled trades. They merit one who speaks for them just as do those who own the ships that convey their products."

"That would be a change in Board membership philosophy— they haven't considered that aspect before." Jani glanced up and saw John looking down at her from the walkway. "If this proposal comes from you alone, Feyó may block it. If you go to the other enclaves and find members who wish the same as you, you would stand a better chance of gaining Feyó's approval."

"Such takes time, ná Kièrshia."

"That which is worthwhile often does."

"The Thalassans merit such representation now."

"Do the Thalassans know this?" Jani backtracked as Gisa's puzzled look slowly sharpened. "Which trades are practiced here?" She found herself eating as she always did when she was forced to mix business with mealtime—small bites chewed quickly and swallowed, their taste barely detected.

Gisa thought for a moment, then shook her head. "Too many to name."

"Well, name them as best you are able, then find their counterparts in the other enclaves." Jani felt a hand on her shoulder, and turned in time to catch a wink and a roll of the eyes from John as he sat down beside her. "Feyó will have a more difficult time rejecting a request from multiple enclaves, especially if the larger ones such as Amsun are represented. In addition, it would give you the opportunity to build a reputation as a consensus builder." *Which would be a nice change of pace.*

Gisa poked at her food with her fork, then let the utensil fall with a clatter. "Ná Kièr—"

"Thalassa is an official enclave now, Gisa, and you are an acknowledged dominant. What this means is that you now fall under the rules—you know that as well as I. You cannot act as you will and push these rules aside, and then expect to be treated according to your standing. The conservatives will not stand for it, and at present they are the majority." Jani speared slices of kettle ham onto a slice of soft flatbread. "Unless you want ná Wola poking her finger in your face at every turn, you have to think beyond the boundaries of Thalassa to how you fit into the whole, for this place is too small to act on its own." She stood, makeshift sandwich in hand, and felt a tug on the knee of her pants leg. John, offering encouragement. Or prompting her to quiet down. "In deference to ní Tsecha, the Elyan Haárin gave this place enclave status," she continued, letting the tug go unheeded. "Ponder that. Would any humanish colony have allowed us to declare our sovereignty? Would they even have considered such? What about the worldskein— what part do you imagine Cèel would have allowed us in that?"

Gisa sat still, her head down, shoulders bowed in the age-old posture. *"Gratitude."* She twisted her neck to look up at Jani, her eyes metal. "One tires of gratitude."

"But one must provide it when it is due, or one is as the greedy youngish who knows only to take. Such is not what we want to be." Jani reached behind with her free hand and tugged at John's shirt, then let go. "Now, I am going to take one last walk on this beach. We will have plenty of time in the future, ná Gisa, to argue of gratitude. For today, I think, let us concentrate on deactivating the tripbeam arrays you have set on the Thalassa road." She shouldered her duffel, then circled around the end of the table, making the demirooms in a few easy strides, and was out the door before anyone had the chance to say a word.

"I don't think you can eat this." Jani stood at the water's edge, a fingernail-sized bit of ham in hand. "Wrong proteins—you'll get sick."

The crab-thing she addressed responded by waving its pincers at the toe of her boot. It may or may not have been the same one Torin had chased about the beach the previous day. It seemed more ornery than that one had; on the other hand, there didn't seem to be any others around.

"You probably chased them away." She tossed the fleck of meat onto the sand and watched the crab-thing scuttle over to it and scoop it up, then hop to the solitude of a nearby pile of rocks. "I think I'll name you Gisa." She tossed another bit of ham into the water, followed by the last morsel of bread.

"I've never seen you flee before."

Jani turned to find John standing on the dry region of the beach on the far side of the rocks. "I didn't flee. I just . . ." She bent low to pick up a rock, then flung it into the water. "Gisa wants to build a nation in a day. She won't listen to anyone who tells her that's not how it works." Another bend, another rock, another toss. "We just got over one crisis, and having her push now for a seat on the Trade Board just might precipitate another one."

"You told her what to do." John joined her at the water's edge. He wore light grey trousers and short-sleeve shirt—the sun turned the hair on his arms to silver wire. "She'll gripe, but she'll do it. For one thing, you've already shown her that you're capable of handling whatever ná Wola dishes out. For another, you're the star—she's the understudy. That may grate her, but too damned bad. I didn't see anyone here wearing her blood as a talisman."

"Expert in the ways of the stage, are we?"

"I've known a few actresses. Does that count?" John drew closer and slipped his arm around her. "I'm not used to hearing you argue for the long view. You've mellowed."

"I've seen too much waste. Dealt with too many whose only thought was what they could take." Jani looked to the opposite side of the bay and saw the bright domes of Karistos flicker in the sun like pinpoint gems. "I'm not going to let that happen here."

"Beware the wanderer who decides to stay." John looked out over the water as well, but Jani couldn't tell from his expression how he felt. "What was it about this place that touched you?" He sounded genuinely puzzled.

Jani gave a half shrug. "I don't know. Sometimes, you walk about a place, and everywhere you look says 'home.' This is the first time since my youth that I've felt this way, and I'm not going to let anyone screw that up for me—how's that for mellowing?" She felt a frisson of panic. "You do like it here, don't you?"

"You're here." John smiled, then paused to tug at his shirtfront.

"It's a little too hot for me at the moment." He pondered the view for a time. "It reminds me of the Greek islands. That's a bit of a turnabout for a rain-forest boy like me." He toed an arc in the sand. "I may miss the nightlife more than anything, although Karistos does have an opera company. Two symphony orchestras—wait—make that one symphony orchestra and one chamber music consort. And there's a theater company—"

"When did you find this out?"

"I do talk to people when I'm treating them, you know. The symphony's second violin is a hybrid."

Patron of the arts—yes, I think John may have found a hobby. And the artists of Karistos, a financial wellspring they never dared hope for. Jani nodded, biting the inside of her cheek to avoid smiling. "Not to change the subject," she said, changing the subject, "but should you be exposing your skin like that?"

John held out his free arm in front of him. "I want to see how much I can tolerate. Monitoring the process, remember?" He tilted his arm this way and that, as though he examined a cut of meat at the end of a fork. "A couple more minutes, then I'll have to go in." He let his arm fall. "We're doing a first-rate job of avoiding the issue, aren't we?"

Jani felt his grip around her waist tighten. "I wish I didn't have to go." She put her arm around him and hugged back even harder.

"And I wish I didn't have to stay. Slaves to duty, aren't we?" John seemed to be avoiding her eye now, staring down at the sand while maintaining his hold on her. "I'll have plenty of work to do, at any rate. And if there are any less than attractive aspects to this change, you won't have to see them."

"I don't care about that."

"I do. Some things are better learned about in MedRecs."

They lapsed into silence. John pulled Jani closer, until she had no choice but to turn to face him. He had filmed his eyes pale blue, mismatching his clothes for the first time she could recall, and she wondered whether he guessed what his hybrid eye color might be, and if he did this as some sort of preparation for the future.

Then he bent down and pressed his lips to hers, and she stopped wondering about much of anything.

"Ná Kièrshia!"

Jani pulled back, and felt as well as heard John's muttered *"Damn."* She looked around him toward the cliffside road that led up to the houses, and saw Brondt standing near the bottom, Torin at his side.

"Colonel Pierce is here. So soon." Brondt avoided looking at John as he shrugged.

"Tell him I'm on my way." Jani took one last look at the bay before starting her trudge toward the road.

"I tried to avoid him, but he saw me. I don't believe I am his favorite person at the moment." Brondt stood in place, one hand in his pocket, his demeanor singularly stiff for one usually so unruffled. "I want to—" He stopped, then took a deep breath. "You said that your parents would take something of Acadia with them when they left, then restore it when they returned." He pulled his hand from his pocket and held it out to her. "Take this with you to remember us by. When you return, you may put it back, and make this place whole once more."

Jani held out her hand, and felt the sudden weight as Brondt dropped the stone onto her palm. It was one of the countless water-smoothed shapes she had seen gathered in long sweeps along the shore, a round-edged triangle in banded brown and black.

"Thank you." She coughed to clear her tightening throat, but before she could say more, Brondt turned his back and started up the road, which saved them both. She followed, John at her side, and mounted the incline as hybrids gathered at the top and waited. Then she was among them, and they closed in around her and walked with her to the main house.

Niall stood in the skimmer circle beside a vehicle pool sedan. He had switched out his desertweights for civvies, tan trousers and a white shirt that reflected the sun like a shield, battering the eye like the bright center of a flame. "I know I'm early, but if we make Elyas Station by local noon, we can head out right away." He eyed John, then the rest of her escort, and his demeanor grew formal. "This way, please." He popped the passenger-side gullwing, stood by solemnly as she got in, then slammed the door closed and circled to his side.

Jani lowered her window and held out her hand to John, who stepped forward to take it as he knelt beside the vehicle. "Keep an eye on things."

"Of course."

"Take . . . care of yourself." Jani placed her hand over his, and wondered at the contrast in their skins, as always. *How much darker will he be when I return?* How much closer would they have become?

"I look on it as a great adventure." John exhaled shakily. Then he leaned through the window and kissed her until Niall's not so subtle throat-clearing signaled that it was time to go. He broke away eventually, then glared in Niall's direction. "Pierce."

Niall nodded once. "Shroud," he said, keeping his gaze fixed on the view through the windscreen as he pressed the charge-through.

The skimmer pulled away. At first Jani watched the hybrids recede in her passenger mirror. Brondt. Torin. Bon. Gisa.

Then she fixed on John. When Niall veered the skimmer so she could no longer see him, she lowered the window and boosted herself through, hanging out the door from the waist up, balancing on the frame. The morning air, scented by the sea, flowed around her. She blamed it for the way her eyes stung as she watched John's grey-clad form grow smaller and smaller until they turned the final corner and he disappeared entirely.

Micah sat at his desk and tried to concentrate on his work. A new device. A new manual to read. A new something that he prayed would divert his attention yet never seemed to for long.

Weeks had passed since Veles had picked his pocket outside Forrestal, and his every waking moment since had been consumed by the *waiting*. For the visitors to his flat, the gym where he worked out, the bullpen. *Pairs*. He flipped through one display screen after the other. *They always work in pairs*. That's what he'd heard, at any rate. In case the suspect tried to make a break for it, and they needed to use force to subdue him.

"Hey, scholar?"

Micah closed his eyes. The more things changed, the more Cashman remained the same. "What?"

"I got a call—I can't take it." Cashman's head poked over the cubicle divider. "An *interview* at the Dahlberg Annex. Second floor. Two five five."

Interview. Micah prayed he looked relaxed as his stomach roiled. *Make that interrogation*. He sat back and folded his arms. *No—I don't think so*. Too close to his possible future for comfort. "You don't look busy."

"Not this split second, no." Cashman rolled his eyes. "But I've got to record the insurance talk this afternoon, and I need to be here when the Benefits crew stops by to take them to the room, and before that I need to set up." He held out a soft, fat hand. "Come on, man. I see what's on your display when you don't think anyone is looking. This is right up your alley. All that psych stuff—brain changes during stress and shit."

You noticed. Micah hung his head, then stood and gathered his gearbag. If nothing else, he'd get away from Cashman for the afternoon. That had to be worth something.

"Thinking of changing your spec or something?"

"Yeah." Micah stepped out into the corridor, looking both ways first to make sure it was clear.

The Dahlberg Annex was a three-story white box located just west of the Far North buildings. A poured cement coffin of a place, it contained offices for base auditors and temporary staff. The second floor, windowless and with coded doors throughout, was reserved for miscellaneous "questioning," the sort of discussions that often lead to a date with the counsel of one's choosing and an extended stay at Camp Brigstone.

The rooms are soundshielded. Micah keyed into the stairwell, trudged up the short flight of steps, then keyed out onto the floor itself. *That way, no one can hear the screams.* Not strictly true. He had recorded several interrogations, and in only one had the tension escalated to violence. But they had the guy dead to rights for murder, and he didn't have anything left to lose . . .

Micah walked the corridor and scanned the doorplates. *Two fifty-one . . . 253 . . . 255 . . .* He stopped, keyed in his passcode, pressed his hand to the doorpad. Watched as the door panel slid open, and found himself staring into a damnably familiar face.

"Come in, Faber." Pascal stepped aside and motioned him through. "Always room for one more."

Micah backed away from the door. Then he ran, down the hallway toward the stairwell, only to have one of the doorway shadows move, and change into Veles, who stood at the hallway's end, shooter drawn.

They work in pairs . . . Micah slid to a stop. Held his hands out in front of him to show he wasn't armed. Bit back a howl as Veles grabbed his wrist and spun him against the wall, then kicked at his ankles to spread his legs.

Shit—shit— He felt hands. Yanking his gearbag from his shoulder. Patting down his thighs, his ass, his waist and chest. Knew they didn't belong to Veles, because Veles stood off to one side, shooter aimed at his head. *Keep your goddamn hands off of me, you freak-fucker!* But he pressed his face to the wall and kept his mouth shut because if he said anything like that, well, then they'd have him. If they didn't already.

"Just walk to the room, Micah." Pascal stood too damned close and whispered too damned low.

Micah pushed off the wall and walked, his hands over his head. *They know.* If they didn't know, why Dahlberg? The place was official. It had a reputation. *Why did they set it up through Cashman?* How did they know Cashman was busy, and would bounce the call to him? *Maybe Cashman isn't busy.* Maybe he worked with Pascal and Veles. Maybe he helped with the setup. *Bastard.* He should have killed the loudmouth creep when he had the chance.

He entered the room. White walls and ceiling, cut at regular intervals with inset lighting. Grey floor. All smooth surfaces, suitable for hosing down if necessary. A table and three chairs.

"Have a seat, Micah." Pascal dragged one of the chairs away from the table and sat. He wore dress blue-greys, as did Veles, who declined a seat, preferring to lean against the far wall.

Micah sat. Wiped his hands on his trousers once, then again. Watched Pascal, who pulled his gearbag onto his lap and examined the scuffed exterior.

"This has seen some use." Pascal cracked the fasteners, then began rummaging through the pouches and pockets.

Keep your goddamned hands off my—Micah choked back his silent scream.—*stuff.* He didn't stash anything unofficial in his gearbag anyway—it wasn't as though they'd find anything—

"What do these go with?" Pascal held up a set of earbugs, then placed them on the table.

No. Micah sat back. *They only look like the ones I use for the sims—they* aren't *the ones I use for the sims, so what difference does it make?* "They're all-purpose earbugs, sir. I use them when I need to jack into systems during setups." There. Easy as you please. *I'm supposed to have those, so shove it up your ass, freak-fucker!*

"Air all clear?"

Micah froze. It had to have been Veles who spoke—his voice was unmistakable. *Why does it sound familiar?* Then he remembered. *Chrivet. Something she said.* As they coursed over the water to the embassy, the spray tossing around them.

They cracked the wafer. Well, they must have. Else why was he here? *They know everything.* So why question him here—why wasn't he under arrest and sitting under barred windows at Camp Brigstone? *Because they don't know anything.* But that didn't make sense—

"You have some interesting tastes in pornography, Micah." Pascal looked up from his exploration of the gearbag. *"Tessa's*

Tempting Offer—quite a story. What did you think about the scene in the back of the skimbus?"

Micah swallowed. His head felt as though it might explode. He didn't want to talk, didn't want to answer Pascal's disgusting question. *They searched my flat, found the porn wafer.* But he'd set out traps, flecks of paper and such—he'd have known. *They went to the place where I rented it.* That made sense, too, maybe more sense. Everyone knew what kind of place it was. "Skimbus?" He shook his head. "There's no—no scene like that, sir." He heard Veles's ragged snicker, and imagined his face smashed and bloody.

Pascal shrugged. "Perhaps I'm thinking of another story." He gave one last look through the gearbag, closed the fasteners, and dropped it to the floor beside his chair. Then he reached inside his tunic and removed a small imager. The silver cylinder glinted, the only spot of life in the room.

"I thought you might find this interesting. It's a scene from another wafer." Pascal twisted the imager's activator ring, then set it atop the table. The top of the cylinder flickered. Then the image sprang up, life-size and in full color.

Micah sat, his hands on his knees, his mind a white-hot blank. But he stood astride the table as well, in full exoskeletal kit, midrange in hand, his helmet faceplate a semitransparency that revealed his identity for all to see.

He remembered the moment captured before him, felt the weight of the exo, the heft of his mid-range. The battle had ended, the last regions of the embassy secured. They had won. *We won!*

"Different sort of fantasy, this. Yes?" Pascal cocked his head to one side as he regarded the image.

"We won! We won!" Veles's singsong raked like sandpaper.

Micah looked to the image and wrung the last drop of pride from it. *We won that one.* They hadn't won many since. The room changed as he stared at himself, from white and bare to darker and centered by concentric rings of chairs. Chrivet in the middle, stalking and talking.

Take 'em down!

Micah felt the room shift as part of him stepped atop the table and entered the image while the rest of him remained seated. He turned from his tabletop vantage point, reactivating his mid-range as he swung toward Veles. He rose from his chair as well, raised his arm and sighted down as he took the first room-spanning step—

Then Pascal moved toward him. The bastard should have

fallen, blitzed by the mid-range, but he charged forward, grabbing Micah and spinning him around and down.

Micah yelled as he slammed against the floor. Felt the cold tile—*why!*—the weight of a body atop him—*how!*

Invincible. Invincible! *"We won! We won!"*

"He's hallucinating! Why did you push . . . !" Pascal, angry, yelling in English, then slipping into a language Micah didn't understand. Veles, just as angry, answering in kind.

Micah tried to break loose as Pascal tore open the cuff fastener of his sleeve, then pushed it up past his elbow. Let loose his howl as he felt a sting in the crook of his arm. Felt the cry stop in his throat as the warmth filled him, flowing with his blood to his shoulder, across his chest, into his gut and below.

Quiet. So long since he'd enjoyed . . . quiet. Peace.

"What's your name?" asked a voice in the distance.

"Faber." His lips felt numbed, his tongue thick. Every scrap of pain left him—he felt light enough to lift off the floor and float away. "Micah. Lance Corporal. Cee number—"

"What is today's date?"

Micah told him.

"Tell me about 'we won.' "

Micah told him that, too.

My head. Pounding. *My mouth.* Dry. Infested.

Micah opened his eyes.

Dream? He'd had a number of those lately, each worse than the last. None with Pascal, though. A few with Veles. The same, over and over. Veles had the wafer, and he had chased Veles.

Wafer? Micah turned over on his back. Regarded his room shadows, his dresser and armoire, flush against the wall like—

—*Veles.*

Micah blinked. *We won! We won!* A cry in his head, over and over and over. He turned back on his stomach and buried his head in his pillow.

White room. Bare but for a table and three chairs. Pascal was there. Veles.

"Crappy dream." Micah rose in stages—sat up, pushed his legs off the bed, stood. He didn't recall the walk home from work, yet here he was. He knew he had been at work, because he remembered Cashman hanging over the divider, asking him to cover the interview at—

—Dahlberg.

He stopped halfway to the bathroom. Looked down at himself, naked but for shorts. Worked his arms, and felt a stiff ache everywhere, a soreness in the bend of his right elbow.

A scene flashed. Pascal, dragging him down.

Micah raised his arm and forced himself to examine the spot. Nothing. Walked over to the freestanding lamp, cranked the power to high, and twisted the gooseneck so the source shone full on his arm.

He saw it. Barely, at first, then large and red and pitted after he dug out the microspecs from his gearbag and slapped them on.

A pinprick wound. Like the one an injector would leave behind.

He pushed the lamp away so hard it rattled against the wall. Backpedaled until he hit the bed, then sagged down and clapped his hands over his ears as his brain broke open and the humiliation played again and again. Veles's snicker. The imager. That final takedown, struggling in Pascal's grip.

Pascal.

Micah closed his eyes as other words played through his head, in a soft, accented voice that all the girls loved.

It's quite a game, isn't it? I've played it, too.

Micah bent forward, head between his knees. Covered his head with his hands, and still more words came.

Your story ends after you win, but what comes after? How do you get out? Do they ever tell you how you get out? Seems a bit shortsighted of the designers, don't you think? After all, the game doesn't end when the last shot is fired, but much, much later.

Then came the worst words of all.

If you want to talk about it, you know how to find me.

Micah bounded to his feet. Paced the room. He thought *Flee.* He thought *We're blown.* He thought *They caught us.* "I have to tell—" He needed to warn everyone. In the next wafer. He'd stand up in the middle of class and piss off Chrivet one last time, announce to them all that they needed to run.

Except—

Micah slowed to a walk. Stood still. "Except they might blame me instead." For letting Veles steal the wafer in the first place. For talking to Pascal. For getting caught. *Hough knows Pascal was after me—he'd spill to anyone who asked.* The connection was there, had been for months. *I didn't tell him anything!* Not willingly anyway. *I just—*

"I just let myself be duped, and drugged, and stripped." Of

everything that made him a member of the Group. Of everything that made him a man.

He lowered cross-legged to the floor. Stared at the pattern in the lyno as he imagined the darkness close in around him. He started rocking at some point—didn't remember when. Rocking, as he hugged himself, and stared. *Can't tell—can't—can't—can't tell—can't—can't . . .*

CHAPTER 27

"I wonder what it will be like here tomorrow at this time." Niall looked out the shuttle passenger port as the spacecraft banked for its final approach into O'Hare. "After the challenge."

Jani glanced up from her *Tribune-Times* account of the upcoming "Duel of the Century" just as the city skyline filled the view, backed by cloudless blue. *Vacation's over.* It had proved pleasant, surprisingly enough. Niall's mood had lightened as the distance from Elyas grew, and he had approached Jani with an offer of a truce. By the time they reached Felix, it felt like old times—as long as they avoided any mention of current events, they could almost pretend that nothing had changed between them.

All good things must end. "Chaos, I imagine." She returned to her newssheet. "Bloodsport is, after all, an idomeni invention. Humanish are peace-loving and quite, quite docile."

"Has anyone ever told you that you're sarcastic when you're sarcastic?" Niall tugged at the banded collar of his dress blue-grey tunic, then rested his head against the seatback, his profile blunted to shadow by the brightness outside. "That article you're reading must be great. I can feel the heat from the steam coming out of your ears."

"Echevar, the *Diplomatic Beat* reporter, isn't completely without sense. He understands that it's simply a statement of feeling. No winners. No losers." Jani rolled up the newssheet and tucked it into her duffel, which was secured in the grapple rack at her feet. "The rest make it sound as though a two-being war will be fought, winner take whatever they wish. GateWay rights. Colonial settlements."

Niall tilted his head toward her. "I'd find your sense of outrage more believable if I didn't know for a fact that you're worried sick. On the way here you spent all the time you could in the ship's library gleaning news from every available 'sheet. As soon as we'd dock at a station, you'd disembark and hit every newsstand you could find. You did everything you could to ferret out information except message Pretty Boy himself, which I do confess I found odd. I know you distrust secure lines as much as I do, but I thought nerves would have gotten the better of you eventually."

Jani settled back in her seat. "From what I've pieced together, Ghos is angry with humanish in general—Lucien was just a convenient target." She braced as she felt the shuttle slow into its final descent. "Usually, idomeni anger is more personal, not outrage against an entire race focused on one individual."

Niall pressed his thumb and forefinger to a place above the bridge of his nose, just inside his eye sockets. "Why do I think I'm about to hear something I wish you'd told me earlier." He lowered his hand. "You think Ghos is going to try to kill him, don't you?"

Jani didn't reply, even when Niall's glare threatened to drill a hole in the side of her face. Instead she lay her head back, and counted the minutes to touchdown.

The noise in the Service concourse reached sport stadium proportions, despite the best efforts of the soundshielding. Younger people in civvies made up the bulk of the crowd that filled the glass and metal expanse, along with a smaller proportion of seeming children in dark blue fatigues, duffels large enough to hold bodies slung across their backs.

"Recruits coming in," Niall muttered as he and Jani fled for the quieter reaches of the security wing. "Freshly minted Spacers shipping out. Welcome to Anthill Central." He keyed them through a pair of doors, the silence enveloping them as they passed into a low-ceilinged hallway.

"First and only time I flew in here, I was under arrest." Jani spoke loud enough to draw interested looks from the brace of MPs walking in the opposite direction. "I came in at an off-time—we pretty much had the place to ourselves."

"They try to work it that way." Niall glanced at her over his shoulder. "You've come a long way in a year, my gel." He turned away before Jani could answer, busying himself with the working of another set of doors. "This exit leads outside," he said as he pressed his hand to the touchpad. "Pull should be waiting for us—I got hold of him just before we left Luna." The doormech whined and the panel slid, revealing a short flight of metal-clad stairs that led down to sunlit tarmac.

They clattered down, then stepped out into the face of a cool breeze redolent with machine odors to find Pullman standing beside a dark blue four-door. He looked at Jani, and his somber expression lightened momentarily. "Good to see you, ma'am."

"You, too." Jani thought back to that night months before. Blood in the snow, and a body boosted onto a gurney. "How are you feeling?"

"Everything's been refitted." Pullman patted the spot over his left hip. "Can't complain." He then focused on Niall, nodding toward the silver sportster that floated nearby. "We've got company, sir." He frowned. "Port Security's not happy, but friends in high places made calls, apparently."

Jani set out toward the familiar vehicle just as the gullwings swept upward. Val emerged from the driver's side, natty in a pale blue daysuit. "God, you're a sight for sore eyes, Jan!" He slammed down the door and circled around the front of the vehicle.

The passenger's side door opened more slowly, the passenger emerging with the characteristic stiffness of someone who'd pushed his body further than normal in the very recent past. Dressed in civvies, brown trousers and a long-sleeve cream shirt, Lucien walked toward her, taking care to step in front of Val at just the right time to break the other man's stride and knock him off course.

"Hello." Jani stopped and watched Lucien's careful approach. "Dathim been pushing you, has he?"

"You could say that, yes." He eased to a halt, gazing at her with a fixedness he normally reserved for their times alone. "You look like summer."

Jani felt her face heat. She wore trousers and wrapshirt in pale melon, an acquisition from a Felix Station shop that she had meant to save for John until Niall's mutterings convinced her that she needed to give her coverall a rest. "Thank you."

"Quite a trip, from what I've gathered from Val."

"Yes. You've had quite a time here, too, I believe."

Lucien had the sense to look uncomfortable. For a few seconds, at any rate. "We'll have to bring one another up to speed later," he said with a faint smile.

Before Jani could respond, Val cut between them and threw his arms around her. "Don't. Ask." He spoke in her ear as he hugged her hard enough to hurt. "I've managed to keep body and soul together, but so help me he doesn't make it easy." He backed away, but still held her as though afraid to let go. He looked older, worn by worry that he didn't bother to hide. "You do look like summer. Like a lifeline." He glanced at Niall. "Hello, Colonel—welcome home."

"Parini." Niall nodded. "I was going to take Jani back to her town house. Is there any reason for me to amend that plan?"

"No." Val shook his head in that vague way that could have altered to a nod at any time. "I just wanted to . . . prepare you." He squeezed Jani's shoulders, then let his hands drop. "You have company." He exhaled with a rush. "It's been a time."

Late spring had worked its magic on the town house yard. Bloom-heavy shrubs in rainbow hues lined the front walkway and rear wall, while leafy trees cast shade over the drive. The rest of the street looked much the same, oases of greenery separated by stone walls and wrought metal gates.

Jani remained seated after Pullman switched the skimmer into standby, looking for some exterior hint of the trouble Val had warned her of even as she knew she wouldn't find it. After a few moments, his sportster drifted to a stop alongside—Lucien disembarked first, then walked around to Jani's side of the sedan and popped open her gullwing.

"Let's get going. Faint of heart never won the game," he said as he held his arm out to her.

"They don't get challenged by bornsect security officers, either." Jani shouldered her duffel and climbed out of the skimmer. She caught the discomfort on Lucien's face when she leaned on him too heavily—Dathim must have been knocking the hell out of him during their training sessions. "I've read all the 'sheets. Is what they say reliable?"

"Pretty much." Lucien linked his arm through hers and led her toward the house. "Ghos took exception to my presence at the embassy. He thought I'd come there to spy for the Service. When I tried to explain that I wanted to find out about some hit-and-run raids that had taken place there, he refused to believe me."

"Hit-and-run raids?" Jani tried to extract her arm from Lucien's grip, since Val eyed her strangely, and even Niall arched an eyebrow. Lucien, however, simply placed his hand over hers, encircling her wrist and holding her fast.

"A variation on the attacks that had been occurring at the enclave. Raiders punching through the defenses and leaving tokens of their esteem—food, in these cases—all over the compound."

Lucien led Jani up the short flight of steps, then keyed them through the back door. "That's not the biggest problem they're facing, though."

"What is the biggest problem they're facing?" Niall asked as he closed in from behind.

"Can we get inside first?" Jani let Lucien steer her into the entry, noting the care he took to position her between himself and Niall. "I'd like to see what I'm supposed to have prepared for." Then she looked down the narrow hall that led from the back entry to the main rooms of the ground floor, saw a tall, thin form cut through the darkness toward her, and knew.

"Nìa!" Tsecha, a badly dressed vision in clay yellow and green, clapped his hands in an uneven beat. "I feared Dathim would need to return me to the enclave before I could see you!" He took her face between his hands. "See, Dathim, if I place my fingers beneath her jaw just so, she cannot talk."

Jani shook herself loose from Lucien's hold. Then she gripped Tsecha's wrists and yanked down, breaking his hold as well. "What are you doing here?" She looked around him to Dathim. "Does Shai know he's here?"

"You do not think I can answer such, nìa? You look at Dathim to speak for me?" Tsecha sidestepped until he blocked her view of his suborn. "Shai does not know I am here."

"She believes him at the enclave. I have double-set the security array—I must return him in two hours or all will know he has gone." Dathim folded his arms. One sleeve slid up, allowing a view of a nasty contusion that had the long, thin look of a strike with a practice blade. "He is to stay there until the challenge tomorrow. Then he is to prepare to return to Shèrá."

"My ass." Jani grabbed Tsecha by the collar of his shirt and shook him. "First, I must tell you this. I understand your feelings. I comprehend how all you have learned here has affected your thought. But why are you so determined to make my life a living hell!"

Tsecha grabbed the collar of Jani's wrapshirt and shook her in return. *"Feres should have been allowed to live!"* He stopped abruptly, his auric eyes widening when he realized what he did. He released her, smoothing the folds of cloth around her neck before backing away. "They would not listen. They would not think. They are anathema."

Jani reached out and took her old teacher's bony hand in hers. "You will not return to the worldskien. I will talk to Shai and Cao after the challenge tomorrow. After they hear what I have to say, they will allow me to take you to Elyas." She leaned close. "You will see Thalassa, and you will marvel."

"It is warm. So ná Feyó has always said." Tsecha bared his teeth. "She has told me much. You negated the challenge against her, and repaired her standing among the Outer Circle Haárin." He started down the hall, pulling Jani after him. "Tell me of Thalassa. Feyó has finally admitted to facts. Eamon DeVries's involvement—" He shot a look at Val, who flinched in alarm. "—and the life that is lived there. I confess that Feyó's reluctance to deal frankly with me disappointed. I fear she and her suborns require instruction in how to behave in manners not quite so humanish."

"Do not be too angry." Jani tossed her duffel to the floor inside the entry, then pulled Tsecha after her to the couch, drawing him down beside her. "You will enjoy Thalassa so. It is home. They await your arrival. You are their prophet."

"Prophets are all well." Dathim took a seat on Jani's other side, the ergoworks whining as they struggled to support him. "But we must first live through this challenge." He pointed to Lucien, who had dragged a chair into the shaft of sun that streamed through the skylight. "Tell them what you have told us."

Lucien positioned his chair in the natural spotlight, then sat and waited while Niall and Val staked out seats. "Before Jani left for Elyas, she asked me to pull whatever strings necessary to attach myself to the enclave mine investigation." He sat straight, his back barely touching the chair. His white-blond hair shimmered. "I did so, and as I became more involved, I grew aware of a certain lance corporal named Micah Faber, a tech in Supreme Command ComSys. He was present at the enclave the night of the explosion."

"He was the nervy git in our bunker." Niall nodded toward Jani as he patted his tunic above the place where he usually stashed his nicstick case, then let his hand fall with a sigh.

"Yes, sir." Lucien looked to Jani. "Notice anything about him?"

Jani shrugged. "He didn't like me a bit."

"No, he didn't." Lucien paused to lick his lips. In contrast to his usual air of easy competence, he seemed agitated, off-balance. "For the past few months Micah Faber has been undergoing simulation training in some of our most advanced weapons systems, including the V-790 prototype exoskeleton. He has been taking this training in conjunction with others who share his beliefs, namely that the idomeni should be driven from all places of human habitation. They form an organization called the Group. I believe this Group's members may be found at all levels of the Service, and that Faber and his confederates receive their instructions from superiors who are privy to all inner diplomatic and security workings." He glanced at Jani, and shifted in his seat. "I've obtained evidence that I believe shows that Faber and others intend to mount an assault against the idomeni embassy tomorrow morning, during my challenge with nìRau Ghos, in the hope that this will serve to drive the idomeni from Chicago." He leaned forward slightly, one arm braced on his chair arm, the other resting in a not so relaxed manner on his thigh.

Niall sat with his arms crossed in front of his chest, his hand over his chin. "Where is Faber now?"

Lucien drummed his fingers against his chair arm. "I have him under surveillance."

"So why haven't you locked him up so you can sweat names and details out of him and nip this assault at the bud?"

"*Because it wouldn't do any good.* Sir." Lucien's face darkened. He didn't often lose control, and he had come close. "In the simulation I saw, Faber is referred to as 'Tiebold.' The faces of the other participants change from scene to scene. I believe the trainees are assigned sim names and faces so that no one knows the true identities of the others with whom they're training until the time of the assault."

Jani closed her eyes. *I wonder what John is doing now?* Arguing with Eamon? Discussing music with the hybrid second violin? "How did you find out all this?"

Lucien hesitated again. "During an interrogation of Faber, early last week."

"He spoke freely?"

"No." Lucien hung his head. "Coworkers had commented that Faber had grown moody over the last few weeks. Erratic. I determined that he was buckling under the stress of his training and might prove ready to talk if . . . persuaded." A shadow of anger flickered across his face. "I lured him on a pretext and began to question him. I felt that if I could convince him to think of me as someone he could talk to, he would open up."

Jani glanced at Val and found him staring back, read the same thought in his eyes that she nursed herself. Lucien as brother-confessor. Lucien as friend. The prospect boggled.

If Lucien noticed their silent dismay, he kept it to himself.

"Unfortunately, the officer with whom I was working took a more direct approach. Unbeknownst to me, Faber had been teetering in the edge of a sim-psychotic break and the added pressure pushed him over the edge. I was forced to administer Sera—it functions as a tranquilizer as well as a truth drug. Since he was out anyway, I decided to make the best of a bad business and take what I could from him."

Niall rubbed his chin. Patted his pocket again. "And the name of your partner is . . . ?"

Lucien sighed. "Egon Veles—"

"That bastard should be locked up for life!" Niall opened his hand, then closed it in a fist, over and over. "Sera is damned unreliable when used on those prone to sim psychosis, you know that?"

Lucien nodded sharply. "Yes, sir. Sim psychotics lose track of the difference between reality and the sims. What happens to them in the sims is as much truth as anything they experience in real life. However, need I remind you, sir, that both the embassy and the enclave have been infiltrated over these past several months by people with Service-level equipment, and judging by their actions, Service training as well. These groups apparently exist. Is it unreasonable to entertain the possibility that some of them may be training to carry out more deadly assaults?"

"Let me get this straight." Niall sat forward, elbows on knees, his hands hanging between. "You've arrived at the conclusion that a group of anti-idomeni radicals named, vaguely enough, the Group, will attack the embassy tomorrow during your challenge. You've reached this conclusion based on some suspicious behavior evidenced by a nerve-addled desk jockey, along with a few coincidences thrown in for good measure. You haven't shared your findings with your superiors or anyone else's because you're convinced the Group's strings are pulled by some of them, and you don't know who you can trust."

Lucien touched his forehead, where nature's spotlight had caused sweat to bead. "There's more, sir."

Niall covered his face with his hands. "By all means."

"The ones who engaged in the hit-and-runs were the well-trained assault forces having fun. They know how to get in, and more importantly, they know how to get out." Lucien fingered the edge of his collar. "Micah Faber and his cohorts are another story. These people are not trained combat soldiers. They're receiving repetitive training on one exercise only—the attack on the embassy.

They're not being taught basic skills or even how to maintain their equipment, and they're too ignorant to know what they're not learning. They're one-offs. I'm convinced they're not meant to survive the assault."

Silence settled. Jani felt Tsecha's and Dathim's presence like weights beside her, pressing.

"I most believed, and truly," Tsecha said, "that humanish liked us, in their way."

Niall glanced at Tsecha, then away. "I have heard some crazy things in my life, Pascal, but you just won the prize."

Jani shot a warning look at Lucien, who had opened his mouth to snap back. "Niall, even if you accept only the fact that some anti-idomeni service personnel are self-training for the Great Someday, is it out of line to consider that one or more of them might try something tomorrow, given the significance of the event, and that heightened security measures are therefore called for?" She shivered, and craved heat. "Someone needs to carry the word to the embassy."

Dathim laughed, a hard, low staccato burst. "Elon will trust nothing you say, ná Kièrshia. Nothing ní Tsecha tells her. Nothing I tell her."

"Will she believe what I tell her?" Niall stood and paced. "Or does it need to come from Admiral-General Mako?"

"Mako, I most believe, Colonel, since he is not seen as a friend of my Jani." Tsecha looked to her and gestured helplessness. "Elon is most blind in that regard."

Niall thumped his fist against the wall. "I probably need to go through Burkett. His ears are still ringing from that mine debacle—he's going to love hearing from me."

"Do you want me to talk to him?" Jani recalled Callum Burkett. A long face and an abrupt manner, but a man who listened eventually.

Niall shook his head. "I can handle Cal, but keep your comlines open just in case." He leaned against the wall, then thumped his head against it. "I wasn't planning on sleeping tonight anyway." He glared at Lucien. "I want that sim wafer of yours, and the transcript of your interrogation."

Lucien reached into his shirt pocket and removed a small wafer folder. Rising stiffly, he walked across the room and handed it to Niall, then paced the room instead of returning to his seat.

"Right." Niall tucked the folder inside his tunic, then pointed to Jani. "You're going to be watched tonight. You will not leave this house. I will send Pullman to collect you in the morning. You're to ride with no one else."

Jani barely restrained the urge to salute. "Yes, Niall."

"Yes, Niall—someone make a note of that." Niall turned to Dathim. "You should head back across the lake now. I will provide an escort. Pullman went through OCS with the men I'm thinking of—if any of them are with this Group—" He pushed a hand over his Service burr, confusion aging him. The thought must have occurred that he had known Thomas Hamil, too. "If any—" He stared down at the floor. "Damn."

Val raised his hand. "I think Neoclona security should watch this house, Colonel, if it's all the same to you. In fact, if you require Lieutenant Pullman for other duties, I will see that Jani gets to the idomeni embassy myself."

Lucien quit his pacing. "I can provide escort for ní Dathim and ní Tsecha."

Dathim shook his head. "You must rest. Prepare."

"Ní Dathim's right, Pascal," Niall agreed grudgingly. "You've got enough on your plate. Lieutenant Pullman will escort you across the lake himself, ní Tsecha. I'm going to head back to the base." He eyed Jani, who took the hint and rose to join him.

Niall lowered his voice as they left the library. "If this assault turns out to be a wet fizzle . . ."

"Considering the mood of the city, are the precautions unreasonable?" Jani followed him back down the hall to the rear door. "I don't think so."

"Glad you came back?" Niall tossed her a sad smile.

Jani shrugged. "All I'd be doing in Thalassa is standing on the beach feeding the crab-things." Talking to John. Laughing with John. *Making love with John.* "Doesn't compare, does it?"

"I'll be glad when tomorrow's over." Niall squinched his eyes shut, then opened them, a sign that a headache had come to call. "If I had one of those Kilian-special wristbands, I think I'd tie it on about now."

Jani knew it cruel to push the point, given the circumstances, but she did anyway. "Do you want one?" she asked, rolling up her right sleeve.

Niall started. "I—I'll take the thought and call us even." He touched the doorpad, then pulled his hand away. "I appreciate it, really. I know what it signifies, it's just . . ."

"It's just not your way." Jani opened the door herself, then held it aside for him. "Be careful." She remained there as Tsecha and

Dathim passed, their expressions grim and their steps heavy, then waited until they followed Niall into the Service skimmer before closing the door and setting the lock.

"Not much of a homecoming."

Jani turned to find Val standing in the hallway, a dispo of soft drink in hand.

"I felt so sorry for you and Niall. You both looked like you wanted to flee back to O'Hare and grab the first flight to anywhere." Val moved to Jani's side and slipped his arm around her. "I hate to be selfish at a time like this, but how's John? I've received a few messages. Lots of reassurances, but little information, which isn't like him."

Jani settled in for the first round of what promised to be some pointed questioning. *John, it's up to you to tell him, damn it—he's your best friend.* "Anything lately?"

"Not for two weeks." Val steered her into the kitchen, maneuvering her into a chair, then taking a seat across from her. "What's going on? You're back together." His face lit, shaving years. "Wonderful. He likes Karistos—all right, what does that mean? Is he coming back to Chicago in the near future? Is he coming back *ever*?"

Jani watched Val tap the corners of the dispo against the tabletop, and wished she had something to worry. "He'll be staying on Elyas, at least for a while." She settled for the spice dispenser, opening and closing the slotted lids.

"How are he and Eamon getting along?" Val forced a laugh. "I've been waiting for the legal knives to start slicing and dicing—*Christ,* sorry. I haven't been able to get knives out of my mind for weeks." He begged the ceiling for mercy, then, slowly, his steady gaze moved down until it locked with Jani's. "You were always a good liar. One could never tell from your face or your manner whether you'd just told the truth or the whopper of a lifetime. Give me a break, Jan. Please."

Damn it, John! Jani breathed in once. Twice. "Do you have any messages waiting for you back at your flat?"

"Not that I'm aware of." Val set the drink dispo aside. "Something's happened, and you think I need to hear it from John." He laced his fingers together and tapped his chin, as though he wanted to pray but needed to work up the nerve. "He didn't *kill* Eamon, did he?"

The image of John standing over Eamon's lumpen body brought a laugh from Jani, which told her how bleak her mood. "*No.* Not to worry."

"Not to worry, she says." Val stood and walked around the table. "Easy for her." His eyes held much the same tenderness they always did, but something else had hitched along for the ride. Resignation, an awareness that one of the people he cared about could hold back from him. "Get some rest—you'll need it." He kissed the top of her head, then slipped out the door.

Jani concentrated on the sound of his receding footsteps, then waited. *One still left unaccounted for.* One more colony left to be heard from.

Then she heard movement behind her, so soft it might not have been sound at all. Felt the grip around her arm, dragging her to her feet and spinning her around.

Lucien pulled her close, his grasp tight enough to bruise. "Like summer." He buried his face in her neck. "A warm, warm place." He moved to the hollow of her throat, his lips tracing lines that burned, that left a growing ache behind.

Jani fought every building sensation even as her back arched and her knees went weak. Then she pushed her hands through Lucien's hair, felt the shock of his short stubble instead of John's longer, finger-burying silk, and stopped.

Lucien kept on until it dawned on him that Jani had stopped helping. He lifted his head; clouded eyes met hers. "You're with John now, aren't you?" He shrugged. "Does it make a difference?" When she didn't respond, his gaze slowly sharpened. "I suppose it would with you." He released her gradually, as though she'd change her mind if he lingered. Then he sighed and turned away. "I've been staying here, like a live-in caretaker. I hope you don't mind."

"Not at all." Jani leaned against the table and slowly recovered her bearings. "Thank you again."

" 'Not at all.' 'Thank you.' You're so polite. Makes me wonder what I did wrong." Lucien opened cupboard doors one after the other, then closed them, a mindless circuit of movement.

Jani watched him, sensed his growing agitation, and damned herself for needing to add to it. "I think Ghos might try to kill you."

Lucien wheeled. "You're too late." His voice came too harsh. "Dathim informed me of that right after the bastard challenged me. I'm the focus. The symbol. All idomeni hatred for humanity, done up in one blue and grey bundle. Lucky me, huh?" He laughed as he opened and closed more doors, his movements growing more jerky, the slams louder.

"You're—" Jani thought of her duffel, tossed aside in the library, and of her shooter, nestled in its usual hiding place. "You're welcome to stay, if you don't want to be alone tonight."

"So you'll hold my hand?" Lucien rooted through a drawer, lifting out a bread slicer. "Ice my bruises? Tell me bedtime stories?" He tilted the crimped blade one way, then the other, then tossed it back in its place. "I need something more than that, I'm afraid." He exhaled with a shudder, then turned on his heel and blew through the door into the hallway.

"Lucien?" Jani hurried after him, torn between wanting him to stay and hoping that he'd leave. "Where are you going?"

"None of your business." He pulled a battered field coat out of the entry closet and dragged it on. "Veles might be able to give you a few possibilities, if you need to get hold of me." He keyed open the door and walked outside.

"Don't—" Jani reached the open door to find he had already neared the end of the walkway. *"Lucien."*

He stopped, then slowly turned back to her. Late afternoon had come—the sky had lost its crystal brightness and the first wisp of cloud had formed in the east. He watched her as dogs barked and children ran past, a variation of life that had never touched him. Then he turned away and resumed walking, through the front gate and down the sidewalk, hands in pockets and shoulders hunched, finally disappearing in other houses' shadows.

Jani stood in the open doorway for a time. Then she closed the door and locked it. She worked for a few hours, sorting the paper mail that Lucien had collected, then culling her comport messages. Tried to contact both Prime Minister Cao and Ambassador Shai, and found herself relegated to the same second deputy assistants who dealt with the interview requests from prep school newssheets. Wandered from room to room like a haunt, wondering whether she should toss Niall's caution to the wind and search the city darkside for Lucien, bring him back to this empty house, and meet her growing edge with his.

"Welcome back to Chicago." She stood in front of her bedroom window until the sky darkened and the night took hold.

CHAPTER 28

Elon sat at her worktable and monitored the embassy security array from her display. The function of utilities had always been of little interest to her, but the lines that ferried pink throughout the buildings were closely aligned with those systems, and she needed to acquire Dathim's skill in little time if she was to shut them down prior to the beginning of the challenge.

Her mind felt most godly. Her soul. She had thought they might wait seasons, she and Ghos, to join their paths along the Way. But Admiral-General Mako had scheduled an emergency conclave with the Interior Minister, the Exterior Deputy, and Ambassador Shai, and to Elon's surprise had confirmed all that Pascal had told them weeks before. *Elements in the Service . . . radical . . . intentions to attack . . .* He had requested that the challenge be postponed, and Shai refused to consider such because the humanish Service had already delayed enough, and declaration needed to be made so that one and all could, as she said, *get on with matters*.

"Whatever such meant." Elon's shoulders curved in the first stages of anger. Shai's speech and gestures had grown more humanish since she had come to this damned cold place, though she most strongly denied such when confronted. "It is fitting that she should die here." As she had come to think as humanish, so let her die with them.

Elon continued to scroll through the screens. When she heard her door open, she did not turn to see who visited, for there was only one who it could be at this late time.

"Did you believe him?" Ghos dragged a chair to the side of

Elon's table and sat. "Mako. The small one. Do you believe his tales of upcoming attack?"

"His suborn is the scarred colonel, who knows ná Kièrshia." Elon reached out and plucked a dried grass blade from Ghos's braids—he had spent the day examining border systems, and no matter how well he laved, he never removed all that attached to him. "But Mako himself despises her. He would not act for her." She gestured inconsequence. "Such does not matter. Whether what he says is truth or lie, our systems will still be disabled. The new-form pink will not flow in the lines. And whoever will come, will come."

"So." Ghos's breathing grew heavy as he moved in his chair. He had labored much in recent days to increase his blade skill, and his body ached from the exertion. "But the scarred colonel himself will attend tomorrow. He will demand to know of our preparations."

"Then we lie." Elon looked him in the eye and bared her teeth. Such familiarity was not as seemly since their pairing had accomplished its godly purpose, but the glory of their deaths would surely override such. "Then we lie." She felt a surge of kinship unlike any other she had experienced when Ghos bared his teeth in reply, and she felt the warmth of Rauta Shèràa in her bones as she resumed her disabling of the security array.

The call had come that morning, in Micah's latest wafer. The time, the place, what to bring, what to wear.

Now, twelve hours later, he sat on the floor in the cargo bay of a truck parked in the middle of some unknown woods, cradling his left arm, studying the faces around him as best he could through a haze of pain. *They all look like they did in the sims*. Even though their faces had changed, he'd have known them anywhere. Bevan with his perpetual sneer. O'Shae with her arched eyebrows and startled expression. Manda with her coltish walk, all knees and elbows like a twelve-year-old boy.

Except that now they'd left their sneers and starts and gangly walks behind and sat with him on the floor, their positions mimicking his as the bone-deep pain of blitzed ID chips made them partners in misery.

Micah heard a thud and looked up to find Foley sprawled across the table that centered the bare room. He barely stifled his cry as Chrivet pressed the IDscan to the place on his inside lower arm and activated it. His left arm spasmed just as theirs had. He pressed the side of his face against the cool polywood just as they had, clenching the edge with his free hand, biting his lower lip until the blood came. Chrivet, for her part, displayed a remarkable lack of emotion as she bore down on the device charge-through, delivering that little extra burst of energy that would ensure that Foley's Service ID chip, like the rest, had been rendered untraceable in every way.

Shared agony. One way to bond those for whom the sim exercises hadn't been enough. Micah caught the looks that passed between Manda and Bevan, the way O'Shae scooted along the floor to make room for Foley as he slid down the wall, arms folded, eyes clamped shut. The way she stroked his right arm with her fingertips, sympathy softening the rough planes of her face. O'Shae, who howled for idomeni blood and slaughtered with glee in every scenario.

They all looked up to watch as Patel, the last of their crew to be zapped, walked to the table. Even Foley pried open his lids so that the barest glitter of eyes shown. Fear set Patel's face like stone, but Foley caught her eye and held up a clenched fist. The left one, hand tremoring from the pain. That drew a smile from the stone, a raised fist in return. Then Patel lowered to the tabletop and held out her arm. Got the jolt. Moved to the floor.

Micah studied his compatriots. They all dressed alike, in blue and grey springweights stripped of all designators and badges, anything that identified the clothing as Service. After entering the room, they'd all disrobed to their underwear and submitted to scanning by the focused Chrivet, modesty discarded in the interest of self-preservation, another humiliation designed to bond. *Can't be too careful, boys and girls*, Chrivet had said as she waved the scanning wands over their bodies. *There are a lot of people out there who would like to know who you are*. She had seemed to stare at Micah for an unduly long time when she said it, but she didn't like him, after all. She probably wished someone had found him before he showed up at the truck.

Micah stretched out his arm, slowly worked it back and forth. The pain had eased, but when he tried to pick up a wadded dispo on the floor beside him, he couldn't close his fingers to grip.

"It will take you until morning to regain your strength."

Micah looked up to find Chrivet looming straight above him, her breasts like a ledge she peeked over. "Yes, ma'am." He tried not to stare at her for too long—just as she did on the sims, she unnerved him. As it turned out, she most closely resembled her sim image—the razored hair and downturned face, the muscular build and barking voice. "Looking forward to it."

"Are you?" Chrivet smiled. As always, when she smiled she looked as though she was the only one who got the joke, and it was being played on someone else. "Get some sleep, Tiebold. You're going to need it." Then she walked to the bay controls and lowered the lights.

CHAPTER 29

"Did you get any sleep last night?" Val steered the sedan through the early morning traffic. "I sure as hell didn't."

Jani stifled a yawn. "Neither did I." She caught sight of the *Trib-Times* headline in a kiosk window—TODAY'S THE DAY!—and decided she didn't need to read any further. "Not that it's any of my business, but did Lucien stop by your place last night?"

"*No.*" Val graced her with a fish-eyed stare as he turned onto the Boul artery that would take them to the embassy. "Not that he didn't show up at the occasional odd hour over the course of your absence—that young man doesn't take 'Go to hell' for an answer, does he—but after the challenge, his focus changed. He spent most of his time at the enclave, training. Why?"

Jani folded her arms and hugged herself, shivering despite her long-sleeve tunic and coat. It was a hard sun that shone, highlighting the pedestrians, the other skimmers, the occasional NO BLOODSPORT sign that hung in a store window. "He seemed tense yesterday, is all. Destructive."

"My guess is that he wanted to break John over the head." Val frowned as another No Bloodsport sign came into view. "You were his ticket, Jan. Now you've moved on, and he's angry. Given all the other things that have been going on in his life, I'd say 'destructive' might describe his feelings pretty well." He veered off onto the embassy access road, which was already lined with news vans and buses. "Isn't that how he should feel, considering the circumstances?"

"No. Counterintuitive as it sounds, you really need to go into a challenge with a cool head. Helps prevent accidents." Jani watched as a group of humanish carrying anti-challenge signs trudged up the road. "I'm surprised Niall's letting all these people get this close."

"I doubt he has much choice." Val slowed as he reached the end of the vehicle check-in line. "Face it, Jan, Lucien's story is pretty farfetched. All he has is his gut feeling, some odd wafer recordings, and one name. For all we know, Micah Faber is a one-man fighting force, getting his rocks off killing simulated idomeni on nights and weekends." He let his hands drop to his lap as, up ahead, Vynshàrau and Interior security searched and checked vehicles one by one. "I think we have enough to worry about without throwing a hypothetical attack into the mix."

"Yeah." Jani watched the protestors wave signs, the lettering showing in reverse in her side mirror. "TROPSDOOLB ON." She lay her head back, thought of a black and brown stone nestled in the bottom of her duffel, which she'd left behind at Val's, and muttered a prayer to her Lord Ganesh, as she had so often that morning.

The challenge room was filling by the time Jani and Val entered. A sprawling space, it was furnished at opposing ends with banked rows of seats to accommodate spectators of both species. While some humanish and idomeni still wandered the floor, they stuck with their own for the most part, with little mixing. Jani spotted Tsecha on the idomeni side, gesturing roughly at something Ambassador Shai said while Elon looked on. She caught his eye and raised a hand in greeting; he nodded in return, his expression grim.

Val tugged at his shirtfront. Experience in Rauta Shèràa had taught him the value of cool clothes—he wore a short-sleeve shirt and trousers in white desertweave. "God, this brings back memories, and not all of them happy ones." He took a pale yellow scarf from his pocket and tied it around his forehead to catch the sweat. "My heart's pounding."

"Yours and mine both, Doctor."

Jani turned to find Niall standing behind them, kitted out in desertweights, shooter holster uncapped, an earbug with mouthpiece hugging one side of his head. "What's wrong?"

"No one can find Micah Faber, that's what's wrong." Niall leaned close and lowered his voice. "As soon as I walked out your door yesterday, I called ahead to Sheridan and sent someone to back up Veles. She gets to Faber's building, no Veles, and Faber is nowhere to be found."

Jani surveyed the crowd, which eyed the entry doors in anticipation. "Has Veles shown up?"

"No." Niall brushed his hand over his damp brow. "He was either in on it with Faber, which doesn't make sense, or he's moved
on to more interesting pastures, as he has done in the past. Or . . ."
He hesitated. "Or he's dead." He paced a tight circle, his eyes on
the attendees. "V-790 detection specs have been programmed into
everyone's systems. I've got Exterior security on the north border,
Interior monitoring the south, with my folks mixed in for good
measure. The Vynshàrau are handling the lake and the air—they
were pretty insistent, and Burkett couldn't sway them." His eyes
were bloodshot, his remark about not getting any sleep the night
before seemingly fulfilled. "I didn't like this before, but I really
don't like it now."

"The perimeter of the embassy compound is most closely monitored, and truly." Elon straightened in respect before Shai, then
gestured to one of the many humanish ministers who had come to
attend the challenge. "Admiral-General Mako's suborns have
been most precise with their information. We do not anticipate assault, but we are most prepared for it." She hesitated when she noticed the Kièrshia, who stood beside Colonel Pierce in a far corner
of the room, speaking to another humanish male she did not recognize.

"You are not assisting Ghos in his preparations, Elon?" Shai's
words came rough, so much like Vynshàrau Haárin even when it
was English she spoke. "You have left him to pray alone?"

"It is his right to ready himself in his own way, nìRauta." Elon
felt a surge of anger that Shai would question her in front of the
humanish. So much she spoke of the "united front" they were to
project at all times, yet when it suited her, she ignored her own
dictum most readily. "He requested I depart so that he could contemplate the blade Captain Pascal chose with which to fight."

"The knight marking vigil over his sword." The minister,
Abascal, moved his head up and down. The humanish nod, which
could mean nothing or everything.

"Ghos is not contemplative." Shai jerked her left hand in a
gesture of dismissal. "It is a wonder to me that on this day he di-
vines the meaning of calm. I regret he did not do so on the day he
offered challenge to Pascal."

Elon felt her shoulders curve, and fought them straight. Beneath her overrobe, the weight of three blades provided her the

same calm that Ghos sought with his prayers. "It has always been Pascal's desire to learn of our ways. Did you not say yourself, nìaRanta, that it is thus our place to instruct him?" She offered a gesture of parting, then walked away before Shai gave voice to the anger that bowed her own back.

Elon relaxed as she walked from one side of the meeting room to the other then back, her blades bumping softly against her thigh with every step. According to the perimeter guard, the morning sun offered its usual cold light. She knew that if she walked outside, the wind off the lake would flay her as a hundred knives. *I will never feel that wind again.* The thought filled her with such joy that she wanted to step into the circle and offer thanks to the gods, unsheath one of her blades and bleed herself in their honor. She considered such, striding to the center of the room and stepping up to the painted edge that would soon enclose Ghos and Pascal in combat, ignoring the questioning postures of the Vynshàrau who wondered at her seemliness—

"Elon?"

—but stopping at the sound of the voice. She felt Caith's hand on her heart, as chill as the wind. "Tsecha."

"Such an oddness here. A sense of tension. One would think that neither we nor the humanish understood the concept of fighting." Tsecha's shirt and trousers pained the eye with their colors, the blue of indicator illumins and a yellow seen only if one shone ultraviolet light on certain types of seaweed. "The outer perimeter scan sometimes malfunctioned here. Something to do with the acidity of the soil."

"The soil has been dredged and replaced since you left, ní Tsecha."

"The guardposts near the border with Exterior—the trees impair their ability to sight—"

"Those trees have been cut, ní Tsecha. Exterior Minister Ulanova proved quite accommodating to our request, and truly."

"You are so confident, Elon, and truly." Tsecha positioned the toes of his boots as close to the red-ring edge of the circle as he could without touching. No one expressed surprise at this action, but then, he was Tsecha, was he not, and thus expected to behave as he would, even as the justice of Temple awaited him. "Do you possess such faith in the order of Shiou, or in the quality of your security?"

Elon turned away from the circle and looked her old teacher, her esteemed enemy, in the face. "Security is a most sound thing, and truly. But order is all, nìRau." She gloried in his anger at her use of his former title. It would prove a fitting end to their conflict as the time for their journey to the Star grew closer.

She left Tsecha by the circle and found a quiet corner where she could monitor her scanset in private. She entered the codes for various points about the compound, and received only machine responses. No guards remained in the perimeter—Ghos had ordered them to one of the meeting rooms to watch the challenge via holoremote. He had also reduced the settings of the field arrays to standby status—no autoweaponry would discharge, even if one of the humanish invaders fired at it first. Structural systems announced the same quiet state. The doors of the embassy would open to all who wished to enter.

"Thus and so." Elon deactivated the scanset and returned it to her beltpouch, and offered a prayer to Shiou that the humanish would arrive soon.

"They'll be starting any minute," Jani said as the doors to the challenge room opened and Vynshàrau attendants entered bearing the weapons of choice. "We should choose our seats." She watched Tsecha speak with Elon, the security dominant. Elon ended their conversation abruptly, leaving Tsecha to cut through the crowd on the opposite side of the room and make his way to Shai, whose back bowed as soon as she saw him. "That's my old teacher— sowing disorder wherever he goes."

"Like I said, the memories." Val inhaled deeply as he fell in behind Jani. "The heat. The nerves. The underlying sense of panic."

"They didn't get this fancy when you fought Hantìa last summer." General Callum Burkett, head of Service Diplomatic, followed them to the second row of seats on the humanish side of the room. "If I recall correctly, it was pretty much a case of throwing the blades at you and getting out of the way." He had dressed in the latest Service weapon against Vynshàrau room temperatures, desertweights equipped with cooling cells. His tan shirt still appeared crisp and dry. Sweat already sheened his horsey face, though, and he cast an envious glance at Val's headband as he took his seat.

"The level of formality can vary. Anything from the equivalent of a corner brawl to a three-day event." Jani sat, mindful of the stares, not all of them friendly, that greeted her arrival. "I think the Vynshàrau realize how uncomfortable most of the Service brass feel about this, so they're doing their best to play it up."

As if on cue, the door mechanisms hummed and the panels opened wide. "Remove all obstacles in Lucien's path, my Lord Ganesh, I pray," Jani whispered once, then again.

To an overwhelming press of silence, Dathim and Elon entered. In contrast to his usual attire, Dathim's brown trousers and tan wrapshirt appeared staid—his appearance complemented that of Elon, who wore the dull brown overshirt and trousers favored by diplomatic suborns, topped with an off-white overrobe.

Jani watched as Dathim's amber gaze searched the human side of the room before settling on her. *He's been prowling about his old territory, I bet.* She sensed the question in his stare, noted the tension in his bearing, and felt the long, slow clench of her stomach. *He's found something.* Her legs tensed—she almost stood up, but forced herself still. *He'll tell me when he can.* The challenge had begun—any disruption at this point would be considered unseemly in the extreme.

After a slow ten-count, Lucien and Ghos entered side by side. Lucien looked at home in grey base casual trousers and steel-blue T-shirt; the harsh light thrown by the chandeliers reflected off his muscled arms, accentuating the rough blend of fresh and healing contusions that hashed his skin. He made a quick scan of the crowd as he strode to the place outside the circle that Dathim had chosen, a momentary pause as his eyes met Jani's his only acknowledgment of her presence.

Ghos, for his part, carried with him the odd calm that most idomeni did as they prepared for violence. He moved as though he walked through a garden, eyes fixed straight ahead, snake face in repose. He wore a sleeveless tunic and trousers in off-white, and had bound his fringed braids in a loose napeknot, tying them with a strip of cloth.

Then Dathim bent to Lucien's ear and spoke. Lucien looked to Jani again, then slowly nodded once. Dathim left his side and headed in Jani's direction.

"Ná Kièrshia?" The occupants of the front row scooted in either direction to allow him room. "You must act in my place."

Jani heard the gasps and mutters around her. Everyone had read the 'sheets and learned the challenge drill, and knew what rule Dathim was about to break. "Why?"

"Yes," Niall echoed. "Why?"

Dathim bent close. "I initiated my check of systems, and they did not respond properly." He spoke without gesture, his hands clenched by his sides. "I will go to primary control and evaluate.

When I do this, ná Kièrshia must take my place as Pascal's second."

"I'm sending one of mine with him." Niall started muttering into his earbug mouthpiece, but before he could get out one sentence, Jani silenced him with a tug on his arm.

"You can't send a humanish into the secure heart of the embassy, Niall—you'll stop the challenge—"

"That's not a bad idea."

"—and initiate an incident that will make the Night of the Mine look like a belch at a garden party by comparison." Jani placed a hand on his arm. "Only an idomeni can enter that space, all right?" She waited for Niall's brusque nod before she stood and followed Dathim to the circle. "The neighbors will wonder what happened."

"I do not understand you, Kièrshia."

"Everyone will ask what is going on." The air seemed to press around Jani as the tension in the room ramped. She followed Dathim around the edge of the ring to join Lucien by the weapons rack.

Dathim positioned himself on one side of Lucien and motioned for Jani to stand on the other. "He will attempt to kill you, Pascal. Before I only believed. Now, I know."

Lucien's bland expression never altered. Some of his sangfroid could be explained by his augmentation, but whatever he had indulged in the previous night to ease his tension, it seemed to have worked. "What do I do?"

"Watch his hands. If he strikes at your body, strike at his to let him know that you are aware of what he does. If he cuts you, cut him harder. If the physician-priests protest, let them end it. Otherwise, do as you must to protect your life." The three of them regarded their bornsect opponents on the other side of the circle as Sànalàn uttered an invocation. Ghos, who seemed so serene as to be drugged. Elon, who stood beside him, watching them like a cat sensing movement in the weeds.

"If it goes to hell, I'll be right behind you." Jani picked up one of the short blades from the rack and examined it before returning it to its place. Her temper had risen, spurred by the heat and the shine of metal. The self-inflicted gash on her arm, long healed, tingled. *This is my place—I know my way here.*

Lucien jerked his chin in Elon's direction. "She has a shooter."

"What makes you think I don't?" Jani patted the familiar heft, concealed by her tunic. "I'm Tsecha's suborn—they don't scan me anymore."

"I must go." Agitation surrounded Dathim like an aura—Jani expected him to crackle when he walked.

"Take Fa with you." She looked to the high seats on the idomeni side of the room, where the enclave Haárin had gathered to watch the challenge. "He was your suborn when you worked embassy utilities. He can help you."

"He must stay here and watch. So I have told him. More to worry of here, with so many humanish." Dathim gestured to Lucien. "Fight well, Pascal. Maybe for your next challenge, I will be able to act as I pledged." He straightened and gestured regret to Shai, but before she could beckon him to come and inform her exactly what the hell was going on, he had slipped out the door.

Lucien eyed the silent gathering. "Do we need to announce you as the understudy?"

"Not if no one asks." Jani gestured their readiness to Elon, who responded slowly. "I'd suggest keeping to this side of the circle, and not exposing your back to Elon."

The first crack formed in Lucien's blasé facade, a slight widening of the eyes that spoke of rising temper. "That's going to limit my ability to defend myself against Ghos."

"Not as much as a knife under the ribs." Jani looked to Shai, who gestured wary permission. To Tsecha, who clenched his hand and shook it once. Then, finally, to Sànalàn, who completed her prayer and gestured toward the circle. "It's time."

Lucien walked to the weapons rack and removed his blade of choice, a mid-length curved sword. He entered the circle, back straight, weapon held out to the side. *"We will begin now,"* he said, his High Vynshàrau smooth and free of accent.

"Yes." Ghos collected his blade and entered the circle. *"We will begin now,"* he responded as he lowered into *hain*, the Stance of Welcome.

Lucien bent his knees and started to spread his arms wide in mirror of Ghos, but before he could fully attain the position, Ghos darted forward, sweeping his blade in a wide arc before him. Lucien leapt back, but not before the Vynshàrau's blade raked him, slicing his T-shirt. Blood welled from a gash the width of his torso.

"Ghos!" Tsecha struggled to his feet while Shai tried to drag him back down to his low seat. *"Fight as the gods demand, or I will strike you myself!"*

Ghos ignored him, following his blade in. But Lucien followed Dathim's orders like a physical law, catching Ghos' weapon with the side of his own, pushing it aside, then drawing his sword in and striking the Vynshàrau in the stomach with the point. Ghos gasped and doubled over, his hand pressed to the front of his tunic. He stilled, looking down as he eased his hand away from the wound. Then he bared his teeth and wiped his hand over his tunicfront, smearing the welling red across the off-white cloth in a wide slash. "Only skin, Pascal." Then he raised his sword over his head and strode in.

Lucien's strike should have slowed Ghos, but it didn't. He brought his blade down, his greater height forcing Lucien to hold his blade up higher to block him, force his arm straighter to maintain the distance between them. Lucien's arm shook from the strain, sweat already coursing down his face, his arms. He broke contact and leapt back, dodging Ghos's downward stroke by a handsbreadth.

Jani checked the temperature of the human side of the room. Everyone, civvie and Service alike, sat forward, hands on their knees or the edges of their seats, ready to push to their feet and storm the circle. She caught Niall's eye and held up one hand in a "back down" gesture. Niall nodded, then slowly sat back—some of the Service personnel took his lead, but not all—they watched the battle as if hypnotized by the ring of the blades and the flash of light off polished metal.

Jani felt the same pull, but forced herself to look outside the circle in time to see Elon slip out of the room. *I should follow.* But the challenge already teetered on the brink of collapse, and she had pledged Lucien she'd remain at his back.

Shit. She looked to the idomeni side of the room once more, and motioned to ní Fa once, then again, cursing under her breath when he hesitated.

Then he finally stepped down from his seat, head forward and shoulders rounded in the slump he employed whether angry or not. "Ná Kièrshia?"

Jani backed as far away from the edge of the circle as she dared. "Ní Dathim is in primary control. Go to him."

Fa gestured in the negative. "He said I am to remain here."

"Go to Dathim." Jani lowered her voice when Lucien half turned toward the sound and barely dodged a blow from Ghos. *"Now."* She waited until the door closed after him. Then she reached beneath her tunic and activated her shooter.

"Like Jesus Christ himself, boys and girls!" Chrivet led them in the now familiar charge, lake spray hosing around her with every impact of her exo boots on the water's surface.

Micah declined to rebuke the sergeant this time. *Four minutes to landfall.* He checked his readouts, comparing the heat-emitting rainbow blobs that filled his display with the occasional soft shimmer in the air that marked the location of a sheathed exo. "Walking in Jesus' footsteps." He quickened his pace, his physical params—heartbeat, respiration—edging into orange or red for all categories.

"Slow down, Tiebold." Chrivet's tinny growl filled his head. "Time enough to top out when we hit 'em."

"Ma'am." Micah eased off, trying to shake the wonder that gripped him as he compared the sims to the real thing. The same water beaded on his faceplate in the same perfect spheres, then ran down like weird rain, leaving the same dry surface behind. The same shoreline spanned before him. The same Exterior Ministry lights marked their progress.

Someone should have seen us disembark. But no one had been walking on the private stretch of beach five kees north of the embassy when the truck parked and disgorged them onto the rocky sand. No one spotted them from shore. No one marked them from overhead. They passed through the most heavily patrolled stretch of lakefront bordering the most populous urbanscape on Earth, and no one detected their presence.

The shielding is that good. Micah swallowed a nervous laugh. *All of Chicago belongs to the Group—they know we're here but they're pretending they don't see, pretending they don't realize what we're doing.* He heard the click of his exo intercom, Chrivet's voice again.

"Target at eleven, distance zero point two four two kilometers."

One and a half minutes to landfall. Micah swallowed hard as the first outbuildings of the idomeni embassy came into view.

Elon crept to the entry of the primary utility chase, then paused. She heard nothing for some time, and made ready to turn away and search elsewhere.

Then she heard the scrape of boots on bare concrete, the slow, measured step of someone monitoring the readouts of the embassy systems.

"Ní Dathim?" She stepped inside the chase. "You have no right to work here. You are an Haárin of the enclave now." She squinted into the half-light, and felt the press of systems array structures on either side like a closing in of walls. Saw the blink and flutter of blue and green indicators, the air and water and heat of the embassy.

A motion in front of her, a shadow from behind an array. A head. Dathim, looking around the corner to see who interrupted him. "The embassy defenses have been inactivated." He vanished behind the array once more. "You know your scanset codes, Elon? Enter them, and save me time."

"Why are you not at the challenge?" Elon reached beneath her overrobe, felt the knives, then released them reluctantly and probed for her shooter holster. "Why are you not assisting your Pascal to defend himself?"

Dathim looked around the corner once more. He may have even looked her in the face, but thanks to the gods for the dimness of the light, that she did not need to suffer the knowledge of his unseemliness.

He did not move for a long time. Then he stirred. *"Why did you inactivate the defenses?"*

"This ungodly place must be cleansed with blood." Elon took one step farther down the chase. Another. "Humanish. Bornsect. Haárin. One godly event. The end of this unclean place."

Dathim stepped away from the array that sheltered him. Then he reached to his belt and slipped a blade from its sheath.

Elon's shoulders curved. "No blood here, Dathim." She unholstered her shooter and disengaged the safety in a single smooth motion. "You do not merit a godly death."

CHAPTER 30

Blood streamed from the wounds on Lucien's arms and dripped to the coated floor, smearing and streaking beneath his trainers. He panted as though he'd run kilometers. Sweat soaked his T-shirt and the upper portion of his trousers, flattened his hair, darkening it to yellow. He stood by the edge of the circle now, grabbing a few seconds' respite as he waited for Ghos to initiate the next round.

Ghos didn't look any better. He had settled down since the initial exchange, concentrating on the proper *à lérine* form, confining his cuts to Lucien's arms only. But the need to rein himself in hadn't tempered the fight in him. He moved like the snake he resembled, with no wasted motion, striking after one or two parries before backing away. Lucien had slowed him down by inflicting a deep gash to the outside of his right elbow that hampered his ability to grip his blade. It forced Ghos to switch the weapon to his left hand, but even in that circumstance, his skill and experience showed. For every cut Lucien had managed to inflict on him, he repaid with three.

Lucien's going to sport an impressive set of scars. Jani looked to the human side of the room. *I wonder how Appearances & Standards will fit that into the Officer's Guide.* The officers themselves had been swept up in the tension—they stood, fists clenched, punching the air in silent applause each time Lucien landed a hit. Only Niall stood quietly, muttering occasional comments into his earbug mouthpiece as he monitored the proceedings.

A moment of stasis. Neither challenger breathed. Then Ghos hurtled forward, blade at waist level. Lucien struck it aside, then stepped in with a counterstrike of his own. But he'd had to reach across his body to parry Ghos's attack, and his blow had been weak—the Vynshàrau was able to bring his blade back in, delivering a gash to Lucien's upper thigh.

"Enough!" Jani walked the rim of the circle and considered breaking the plane even though it meant the challenge would end without declaration being made. "This isn't combat. There are no winners and losers. Declaration is made, and the fight ends. You have traded enough blows to declare."

"I have seen challenges that lasted day into night," Shai called out. "So have you, Kièrshia."

"Not when one of the combatants had something else on his mind." Jani pointed at Ghos, goading him by looking him in the eye. *"I know that which you are thinking,"* she said in High Vynshàrau.

Ghos's shoulders rounded as he cocked his head to the side. *"Do you, Kièrshia?"*

Jani looked at Lucien, who eyed her uncertainly. "The purpose of this exercise is to declare your hatred for one another. You've both made your point. Lay down your weapons. Declaration is—"

A sound echoed through the cavernous room, like a distant roll of thunder. Then came a shorter, sharper burst.

Jani looked across the room to Niall—the expression on his face mirrored her thought. *Oh hell—*

"Secure the doors!" Niall pulled out his shooter and jammed home the powerpack. "No one enters or leaves until further orders." He drove the point home by advancing on a gaggle of deputy ministers who tried to push toward the entry. It was anyone's guess what compelled them to return to their seats, the look on his face or the weapon in his hand.

"Ghos?" Shai struggled to her feet, the rest of the idomeni in her row following her lead. "What I hear now—these are our defenses?"

"No." Ghos bared his teeth and held up his sword. "These are our defenses, nìaRauta. Our godly blades. No other are required. Choose one, and fight the humanish as the gods intended."

Another blast. The Sìah chandeliers rattled. Screams and cries sounded.

"We must get to the armory." Tsecha bounded from his seat and across the room, skirting the edge of the circle before stopping at Niall's side. "It is three corridors over." He hesitated as he worked out the translation of directions. "Toward the lake, then left. There is armor there, short and long-range weaponry—"

"Tsecha!" Shai rose and started toward him, two of the security suborns falling in behind. "Silence!"

"We have no choice, Shai!" Tsecha's bowed shoulders stopped the security contingent in its tracks. "The attack Mako warned you of—it has started."

"This challenge is over." Niall stalked across the room to the blade rack. "Everyone with a weapon—a shooter, not a blade—over here. Burkett!" He pointed to the general, who stood and beckoned to a couple of subordinates. "You're handling the home team. Station them by the doors. Keep everyone back." He gestured toward the group of agitated civilians braced against the far wall. "After the away team pulls out, no one gets in without a password." He pointed to two Vynshàrau security and a Service major. "Make it 'crimson'—"

"Not a good word, Niall—the accents." Jani gestured to the three guards. " 'Hana'! *The password is 'Hana'*!" she said once in English, then again in High Vynshàrau. "It's the Pathen dominant city—I doubt any of the Group knows it, and it's easy for everyone to say."

"Hana." Niall nodded. "All right, away team . . ."

While Niall culled the chosen few to storm the armory and hammered out the hallway layouts with Tsecha, Jani kept her eye on Ghos. He had lowered his sword, but he stood on the balls of his feet, ready to move in any direction, the tension radiating from him like scent.

"What have you done, Ghos?" Shai gestured for a pair of Haárin to guard him. "Where is Elon?"

"Dathim knew of the assault Mako told you of. He initiated his own check of embassy systems as a precaution, and did not receive the responses he expected." Jani monitored Ghos's reaction to her words, but saw only the tension. "He's down in the primary control chase evaluating the systems. I do not know if Elon has gone to him, but I sent Fa to check."

"He believes systems are compromised?" Shai's shoulders rounded. "Why did not he tell me this himself?"

"You must ask him such yourself, nìaRauta." Jani still watched Ghos. Their eyes locked once more, and the Vynshàrau's grip on his sword tightened.

"Pierce!" Burkett stepped away from his huddle with the ministers. "Service codes are blocked." He held up an earbug and shook it. "Are Vynshàrau communications blocked as well?" The gestures he received from some of Elon's suborns gave him the answer he needed. "We can't call out. So far, no one's called in."

"All right!" Niall backed away from Tsecha, who walked to the weapons rack and removed a knife and short sword to add to his shooter. "Away team." He waved for the mixed group of Service, Vynshàrau, and Haárin to follow as he headed for the door. "Let's go!"

As Jani headed for the door, she caught movement from the corner of her eye and turned to the circle. *"Lucien!"*

Ghos shook off the two Haárin as they grabbed for him— Lucien turned just as he closed in, blade raised. He brought up his own blade and pushed the Vynshàrau back, then moved in as Ghos swept his blade in a wide, backhand arc that left his body open. Lucien stepped in and plunged his blade into Ghos's abdomen, then tilted it up. Under the rib cage to the heart. Ghos slumped and fell into his arms as blood poured from his mouth, spread across his tunic. Lucien shook him off and let him fall to the floor.

Jani entered the circle and moved to Lucien's side.

"Instinct took over." He stepped closer to her, out of the path of Ghos's streaming blood.

"I know." Jani looked from the gore-drenched front of his T-shirt to his spattered face. "Given the shape you're in, you better stay here."

"How much trouble am I in?"

"I don't think that's our biggest problem right now." Jani took her shooter from beneath her tunic, then grabbed a short blade from the rack and rushed for the door.

Niall moved to block her before she could break through to the hall. "Give someone your shooter and stay put."

"I speak every language you've got here—you need me." Jani pushed past him to the Vynshàrau-Haárin contingent charged with leading them to the armory. Tsecha moved at the head of the group, coding into doors, then covering as his people secured the rooms.

"The old bird has teeth," Niall rasped as he shoved a serrated-edge blade into his belt. "Elon and Ghos lowered the building defenses, didn't they?" He swore under his breath when Jani nodded. "I hope humans can use whatever the hell they've got in that armory." A rumble sounded from behind, and he exhaled with a growl. "That's one exterior wall gone."

Micah blew through the gap in the outer wall that O'Shae had punched. *Where are the fuckin' screamers?* The boundary alarms,

notifying the idomeni of the breach in their defenses. "Breach?"
He laughed, acid searing his throat. "Fuckin' canyon!" He pounded
up the hallway behind O'Shae as he had so many times, swinging
his mid-range into place as she blew the first door. Pulled back on
his charge-through, braced for the kick, and spun back on one heel
as it smacked him. *"Ha-hah!"*

The chatter sounded in his ears, whoops and shouts of laughter from the rest of the Group as the reality of the moment drove
home, backed by the incessant batter and rumble of disintegrating
structure.

"Who's out there! Who's out there!" A lilting female voice,
breathless with glee.

Micah slipstreamed behind O'Shae as she blew another door.
"Patel!"

"Tiebold, is that you? This is for real! This is—"

A crazed flash shot across Micah's display. He unloaded into
another room, then fell in behind O'Shae again. "Patel?" Not her
signals going down, couldn't have been. The noise from the mid-
range must have drowned her out. Must have. "Patel!" Must have.
"Patel!"

O'Shae blew another door. Micah unloaded. Felt the recoil,
but not as much. Stride made a difference. Stride, and how he set.
He hadn't noticed that as much in the sims.

Patel?

They neared an open area—the first of the large meeting rooms.

"Let's go!" O'Shae blew through the double-wide panels like
paper, then—

Micah's display blitzed as the floor shook. The walls. Plaster
rained down as blue flame licked through the gap O'Shae had
punched in the doors.

Micah braked, slamming against the wall in his effort to stop.
His display came up—suit sensors, smelling . . . what did they
smell? Burned—burned—

Stronger than in the sims. Did they realize? It was all
stronger—the recoils, the emotions.

The display histogram of the stink of charred flesh.

"O'Shae?" No response, only a distant rumble, which grew
louder.

Patel's words. Her last words.

This is for real.

"Where is everybody?" He raised his display, looking for signals.

Instead he got flashes. More than one. A dozen. More. Different signals. Live bodies, but not the Group's.

Micah upped his sensor. Heard the sound. The steady *whoosh whoosh* of exo legs pumping. Coming from behind.

He turned and looked down the hall.

Elon raised her shooter just as Dathim ducked back behind the array—

—and staggered forward as a blow shook the back of her head. Black fog closed in. She dropped to her knees, fell to her side, and turned behind her in time to see Fa, Dathim's suborn, lurch toward her, a length of sheathing in his hand.

"*Fa!* She is armed!" Dathim's voice. Hated English.

Elon propped her elbow against the floor, felt the cold through her overrobe, the black fog ebb and flow. Squeezed her hand. Fell back as the force of the shot shook through her.

"*Fa!*" Dathim's voice as an echo in a cave. The caves of Rauta Shèràa, that opened onto the sea. The sound of booted footsteps. First distant, then near her head.

Elon forced open her eyes. Saw an orb of gold amid the black that sharpened to a face. Dathim, daring to look her in the eye.

"Fa is dead," he said.

English. That hated sound. "Speak your own language, Dathim." She heard her voice, her beloved High Vynshàrau, rise and fall within the chamber of her skull.

"I am, Elon," Dathim replied in English as he placed a hand over her face.

Tsecha stood still as the armory array scanned his biometrics. Mechanics hissed and clicked, then the door opened.

Niall stood against the wall, monitoring the rumbles as he tried to raise a signal on his earbug. "Funny they didn't wipe him from the system when he made outcast."

"They did." Jani checked the view down the hall, then fell in line to enter the armory. "Dathim kept reloading him."

"I thought they wiped Dathim from the system."

"They tried."

"Good old Dathim." Niall tapped his mouthpiece with his thumb, then frowned. "The occasional hiss or part of a word, then nothing."

The armory contained all the equipment necessary to outfit embassy security and then some—Tsecha took charge of rooting through all the shelves and cabinets and doling out the minimum required gear. Armor. Helmets. Short-range shooters.

"There's a whole line of exos here," someone called out from the back.

"You cannot use them—they are not typed to humanish."

"Keep it simple, folks—body armor and small arms." Niall had already kitted out in upper body armor and leg shields. "If Dathim gets the pink flowing, all these pretty toys are so much ballast."

"I thought the idomeni had fine-tuned their latest pink so it didn't attack their systems." That came from another of the Service officers. "We won't mention that they shouldn't have it here in the first place."

"And we will not discuss the fact that humanish are exploding holes in my embassy!" Tsecha shoved a helmet under the man's nose. As if in counterpoint, more bursts and rumbles sounded in the distance.

Jani fastened her armor, then added another shooter to her weapon belt. She felt as she did when her augmentation functioned—dry hands, slow heartbeat. Only the undercurrent of anger seemed as different. A desire to break and shatter that she had never known before. *Control yourself, Kilian.*

"Work in teams of three." Niall donned his helmet, faceplate up. "Clear rooms, keep pushing out. You run into something you can't handle, fall back fast. Keep your comlines open—when the works come back on, I want to know where you are." He lowered his faceplate. "Let's go."

"Oh boy, we're having fun now," someone said as they streamed back into the hall.

Pinlights through the dust and smoke. Red needle eyes. Growing bigger. Bigger.

Whoosh whoosh.

Micah looked ahead of him, toward the hole O'Shae disappeared through. Noise came from there as well. Thuds. Crackles.

"Which way?" He didn't realize he'd spoken until his display fired up. Hallways, marked and mapped. The one he stood in now, capped at both ends by moving blobs converging on him.

Whoosh whoosh.

"Shit!" Micah pushed off the wall. Headed for O'Shae's last hole. "There's an offshoot hallway here." Didn't know where it led. Not a dead end—all he cared about. *Move!* He swung down his mid-range and barreled ahead. Fired.

Smoke. A waist-level cloud. Sense display—chemical fire. Toxic. Filters working.

Micah held to the wall, edged forward, hit something with the tip of his boot. Waved smoke away. Looked down.

O'Shae. Part of her, anyway.

"What the hell hit her?" Micah kept moving. Not like the sims—no Vynshàrau, pieces of bodies out of nowhere and *whoosh whoosh* getting louder and louder from behind—

—walls shook. Floor. Blast. Blitzed display.

Micah ran, bouncing off walls as the exo took him farther than the hallway allowed. His mid-range swung like a crazy third arm, jerking up then down, banging the walls, whacking the side of his helmet.

He broke around a corner. Fresh hallway. No smoke, no shatter, no bodies. "Display." He pulled up the hallway, saw the blinking close from all around.

Micah ran as new sounds converged from all directions. High-pitched whines. The unmistakable static crack of shooters.

He ran faster, careened around a corner, bounced off walls like a bead in a box, pushing straight on as a hiss filled his ears and a—

—sea of pink flooded around him. Found openings he shouldn't have had and poured into his exo, like feathered silk against his skin. Shot down his arms and legs, rattling them until they shook like seizure.

"What the fu—" Ragged chirps stung Micah's ears as his sensors went mad, flashes of red and blue zinging before his eyes. The pink—mist—gas—*what!*—flowed around his face. He inhaled, tasted it sweet in the back of his throat—

"Aghhhh!"

—then dragged himself into the shelter of a doorway as something huge and dark spun like a dervish down the center of the hall. The sleek lines of the V-790, encasing a thing gone mad, loose mid-range swinging back and forth, flashes of white light bursting through the joints of the exo.

Then came . . . the scream. Low at first, then thinning and rising in pitch like a siren as the flares grew brighter and brighter and thick strands of grey smoke emerged from the exo and intertwined with the pink.

Micah held his breath and watched as the jerking and twisting slowed, the wail ceased. Then the exo turned, a graceful heel-toe spin, arms floating away from its sides, weaving like a dancer's, shreds of pink mist streaming from gaps in the exo and dancing around its hands.

The mid-range ceased its yardarm swing, its standby hum ramping in pitch.

"Oh shit." Micah bolted down the hall in the direction opposite the singing exo. Cooked like a spud in its skin. Whoever they were. He choked back a laugh that veered to a sob and kept running, legs pumping in an exo that didn't want to go where he told it, its joints stiffening, whiffs of that fucking weird mist puffing out of the gaps with every stride. Dove around a corner into another hall as the heavy whine hit its peak. Tripped over his boots. Somersaulted and spun to a stop against a wall and prayed he'd run far enough—

—and buried his face in his arms just as the explosion ripped. Saw the flash through the pink-eaten gaps in his exo sleeves. Felt the rumble through the floor, the walls, heard the crash of the ceiling as it collapsed.

He looked up as the sound died away, in time to see the last whispers of pink mist flame to blue and vanish. Fragments of ceiling fell atop him. Cracked, buckled wall bowed over him.

Micah stared out at the clear quiet. Then he scooted to his knees and tore at his exo, battling jammed fasteners and tremoring limbs. Unlatched his helmet and flung it away. Tore at the coverall, the boots. Safety joints came apart in his hands—he tossed piece after piece of his suit after the helmet, as far as he could, trying to decoy the last wisps of pink fog that dogged every move of his hands and flurried before his eyes like dust devils.

He checked every flap and fold of his T-shirt, his pull-on trousers. Worked to his feet, testing his every move. "Not gonna take me over—not—no—no—no—" He danced in place, kicked out, did a jumping jack, his overhand clap ringing through the still air.

"All me." He ran down the hall, turned and headed in the direction opposite the dervish's scant remains. Found himself in a hallway still flooded with pink, held his breath as he cut through it, thought *Hell with it* and breathed, then hugged the wall as another rumbling blast sounded.

"Oh—God." Who had cooked in their suit this time? Who? "Manda?" He ran, the layout of the embassy unfurling in his head.

CHAPTER 31

"Hey hey!" Niall gave Jani a thumbs-up sign. "Pull, talk to me!"

Jani smiled as Pullman's dry tones filled her helmet.

"—embassy systems coming up in fits and starts." A pause. Thumps and whines in the background. "Still piecing together what happened. Damned Exterior missed 'em coming in, apparently, and then they blew right through the embassy shields."

"That's because the embassy shields weren't up." Niall's helmet moved in a slow headshake.

"Well, that explains that." More thumps. "We're pulling out bodies. Fifteen in V-790s, so far. Give or take. Hartman's crew is clearing out the south wing. Some of Vynshàrau security were holed up in a meeting room there—bunch of them took it when the roof came down."

Jani glanced to her right, where the third member of their team, a Vynshàrau security suborn named Pashé, stood straight as a statue against the wall.

"Bessard's gang has the west and the outbuildings," Pullman continued. "They're reporting all clear. Jamil's crew has north and east. I don't hear a thing but she's not happy and they're going through again to make sure. She doesn't like that we don't know how many of these people we're dealing with. Any ideas?"

"No." Niall sighed. "Burkett's holding down the challenge room—I've got a team pushing out from there right now. Nothing so far but empty rooms."

A pause. "Jamil just called in, sir. They're at the challenge room. Some Haárin won't let them in without the password."

"I'll go." Jani headed back down the hall. "The sooner we get them out of there, the better."

"We'll all go back." Niall fell in behind Jani. "Pull, I'm calling my team back to the challenge room—I want Jamil's crew to take over."

"Yes, sir. We've got a few Vynshàrau out here now—they said that once they get their systems back up, we'll be able to run a heat scan and nail down the stragglers." More thumps, then a muttered "damn." "Sir, the PM's holed up in the Exterior Annex. She wants a report."

"Tell her to put on a goddamned headset!" Niall quickened his pace. "This place is not yet nailed down."

"No, sir."

"Damn it." Niall moved ahead of Jani and around the corner. "Ministers . . ."

Jani slowed, then looked back to find Pashé still standing in place. "NìaRauta?" She moved back toward her. *"We are going back,"* she said in High Vynshàrau. *"Others will take over."*

"Speak your own language," Pashé replied in English. Then she turned and started walking in the direction opposite, vanishing around a corner in a few long strides.

"Shit!" Jani took one last look in the direction Niall had gone, then hurried after the Vynshàrau. "Can't have gone far—" She rounded the corner and found the female getting ready to boost over a pile of rubble that blocked an entry to another wing. *"Nìa-Rauta! We are going back!"*

"You go back! Humanish!" Pashé flipped up her faceplate—she shared Ghos's stark, snakelike features, and radiated the same tension he had. "Not even humanish. Worse. You go back. Back, and farther back. This is a Vynshàrau place!" She raised her shooter over her head, then set her free hand on the pile of rubble and clambered over the top.

"NìaRauta!" Jani sprinted down the hall toward the blocked entry. "Hate me later—we have to move now!" She boosted atop the rubble and tried to see into the semidarkness beyond. Cracked and buckled walls. Shattered columns. The flow from ruptured plumbing dripped from ceilings, pooled in corners. She strained to discern any movement, but saw only half-dark and shadows, heard only the drip and trickle of running water.

Then a sound reached her. A sharp intake of breath on the cusp of a cry.

She strained to hear more, heard nothing but water, and with a swallowed curse clambered over the rubble pile to the other side.

The air on the closed side of the barrier already felt chilled compared to that on the side that had been secured, its former warmth victim to disrupted air handling and the initial impacts that had broken through from the outside. "Pashé?" Jani reached the end of the hallway and debated her next move. "Right? Left?" She looked down the quiet, broken passages, back over her shoulder to the comparative comfort of the rubble boundary, then started down the corridor. Shooter in hand, creeping with her back to the wall.

First room. The safety illumins in the walls had lighted, revealing a sparse arrangement of soaked furniture and nothing else. *Second room.* Across the corridor. A tricky L-shaped entry with shadows in all the wrong places.

"Hell with this." Jani backed away to return to the safe side, and caught sight of the mound of darkness in the corner of the room. She ducked inside, shooter at the ready, and found Pashé.

Jani knelt beside the Vynshàrau. Cracked the faceplate of her helmet, and caught a whiff of the choking stench of burned flesh. Turned her over, and saw what was left of her face.

The hissing started then, from points along the ceiling. The slow billow of pink. The candy cloud, tumbling through the room.

"Oh, hell!" Jani straightened, turned, pushed through the thickening rose fog toward the door. Lifted her head in time to see a darker form appear in the doorway, blocking her.

An older woman. Broad-shouldered and muscular with a Service burr. Burned face and arms, charred to black in places. One ear was gone. She strode forward, shooter at the ready. She didn't speak—her eyes said it all.

Jani raised her shooter, made to fire, then felt the room shift as her left knee buckled, animandroid muscles cramping. The woman fired at where she had been, the shot grazing her helmet. The display flared in multicolor chaos, then blanked.

Jani tried to boost to her feet, to see what had tripped her even as she kept her eyes on the woman. *I don't see anything . . .* The pink continued its slow-motion tumble throughout the room. She inhaled through her mouth and felt its sweet taste on her lips. She tried once more to rise, almost straightened, tried to sight down once more through the fog—

—and fell again, left leg cramping, the pain like fire, left arm tremoring. Tried to sight down once more. Fired. Saw her shot go wide as both left siders spasmed at once.

"Having a problem?" The woman lowered her shooter and stepped closer. "Whatever you are." She kicked out, caught Jani's shooter with her booted foot, sent it flying.

Damn! Jani tried to tuck and roll as she reached for the blade in her weapon belt, but her left side fought her every move.

The woman tossed her shooter aside and fell on Jani, left hand gripping her right wrist and holding her blade back as she pushed up the faceplate of her helmet.

"Do my eyes deceive me?" She crimped Jani's right wrist until the pain sang, plucked the knife from her grasp.

Jani smelled the woman's scorched flesh as a blistered smile filled her field of vision.

"Cat eyes." The woman held her knife so the point dangled above Jani's left eye. "Mutant eyes." Her voice came thick, smoke-damaged and raw. "Glass eyes—watch them shatter."

Jani tried to will her left limbs steady. Felt them twitch instead, refuse to respond. "You have the look of a sergeant about you. I'll bet you were involved in the training." She watched the woman's smile freeze. "They told you they'd get you out, didn't they? They lied."

The smile vanished. The knife dangled.

Micah edged out of the blasted room, strained for any sound. He thought he'd heard the *whoosh whoosh* of exos again, but the noise had come from reactivated airflow pushing its way through a crumpled outlet grating.

"Walkin' in Jesus' footsteps." This part of the embassy had been hit the hardest—Micah stepped over rubble, fallen sections of wall, pieces of furniture. Splashed through the flooding caused by damaged pipes. He'd found an idomeni clock in one of the blown rooms and tried to figure out how long he'd been inside the embassy, but he couldn't make heads or tails of the display and smashed it as the anger took him.

Walkin' . . . one, two, three. . . . Counting his steps.

"Fifteen minutes? Twenty?" Had it been that long since he'd sent the lakespray flying? Felt that first gorgeous recoil of his mid-range?

He turned the corner, pausing first to look around and check if anyone was in the hall. He hadn't seen anyone for a time, but that didn't mean they weren't there. He heard them through the walls, with their whines, hisses, tremors. They'd find him eventually, since no one had taught him how to get out. It was like Pascal said, damn him.

Walkin'. . . . Four . . . five . . . six. . . .

He walked past one empty, blasted room. Another. Then he heard voices as he neared the third, and his step slowed.

"They promised they'd take care of you." Jani tried to will her limbs calm. The pink had dissipated, and she sensed that the twitching had lessened. The spasms. "Train these nonessentials, give them just enough skill to be dangerous, but not enough to do the job right. We don't want to make it look like the real Service wants the idomeni out, after all. But an offshoot? A submerged couple of percent? We can explain that away to Cabinet Row. Not our fault. Nothing we could control."

The knife shook. "Filth. You should have died years ago."

I did, in theory. Jani tried to bend her leg, jam her right knee into the woman's side. But she couldn't find the leverage, and the woman's body weighted her like stone. "You may as well talk, because they aren't going to help you. They'll probably kill you, in fact, when they find out you lived through the assault."

The woman's eyes were small, mud brown, bright as if with fever. They clouded momentarily, as though she actually heard what Jani told her. But it didn't last. She hadn't come to the embassy to talk.

She raised the knife and her upper body at the same time. Pushed off Jani's helmet, then grabbed a fistful of hair and forced her head still.

"'Night, kitty." The woman's smile widened as she brought her blade up.

Jani felt her left arm still for just long enough. Curled her fingers and brought up the heel of her hand, jamming it against the woman's chin, pushing her head back, pushing, pushing. The woman struck, the blade came down—once—twice—hitting Jani's left wrist, slipping between skin and the edge of armor. Pink carrier spattered—the more that flowed, the more the arm steadied.

Jani kept pushing up, until she felt the weight atop her ease. Brought up her right leg, then kicked out, pushing the woman off. *"Niall!"* She tried to roll over to her hands and knees, tried to stand, but her animandroid limbs still betrayed. They trembled as she put weight on them. Buckled. She fell back to the floor, made slick with rose-pink carrier.

The woman careened backwards, then rolled into a crouch like a cat. She still held the blade. "No one can hear you." She tensed as she made to spring.

"Walkin' in Jesus' footsteps."

They both stilled, and looked to the entry.

"That's what you said." A young man walked into the room. He wore base casuals, sweat-stained and torn, and held the woman's discarded shooter in a loose grip.

Jani fixed on the pointed, pale face. *I've seen him before.* The lance from the bunker, whose coat she'd worn. Faber.

"That's what you said, Sergeant." Faber's voice came quiet, like he spoke to a child. "You trained us and drilled us and told us how special we were, and every time we stormed the embassy in the sims, you said the same thing. Walkin'." His eyes, in contrast to his voice, looked stone-carved. There was a disconnect between how he looked and sounded, what he said and the way he said it. "Well, where is he?"

The woman's breathing had gone shaky, as though she tried to hoist a weight that was too heavy for her. She held out a hand to Faber. "At ease, Tiebold. Stand down."

"That's not my name," Faber responded, "just like Chrivet isn't yours." He raised the shooter, and sighted down. *"Where is he?"*

"I said—" The woman's voice stopped in her throat as the shooter crack sounded. The impact knocked her backwards, sending her sprawling, her limbs jerking as the pulse packet dissipated throughout her body.

"Lance Corporal." Jani had worked into a sitting position, left limbs still twitching. "Stand down."

Faber paused to look at her. Then he turned back to Chrivet, and sighted down once more.

"Drop the shooter, then raise your arms. Above your head. Slowly." Niall entered, shooter fixed on Faber. *"Now!"* The young man slowly lowered the weapon—Niall stepped forward and plucked it from his grasp. *"Pull! Get the hell in here!"* He powered down the shooter and holstered it, then flipped up his faceplate and looked to Jani. "You're bleeding."

"It's just carrier—I'm all right." Jani watched Faber, who still stood in front of Chrivet's body, his eyes fixed on nothing.

Pullman blew in, followed by a mixed bag of human and idomeni equipped with scanners and gurneys. Niall stepped out of the way of a pair of humanish medics who headed toward Chrivet, and came to a halt next to Faber. "Pull, this is Lance Corporal Micah Faber. It was his late buddy made mincemeat out your left kidney."

"Is that a fact, sir?" Pullman flipped up his faceplate. "I'll bear that in mind." He closed in behind Faber, yanking back his arms and binding his wrists with restraints he'd pulled from his weapons belt.

"All right." Niall walked to Jani's side, and crouched down. "What happened?"

Jani raised her shaky left hand. "The pink blitzed my animan-droid limbs—"

"*Before that.*" Niall reached down and detached the armor plate that covered her left forearm, then examined her wound. "I order you back to the challenge room, look around two seconds later and find you gone."

Jani jerked her chin toward the place where two physician-priests administered to Pashé's corpse. "She was on our team. When you ordered us to pull back, she didn't want to go. She didn't want anything to do with humanish."

"So you went after her?" Niall dragged off his helmet, revealing sweat-flattened hair and a reddened groove across his forehead where the stabilizer band had rested. "You want to play on my team, you follow my rules. Stick that in your documents case for future reference." He straightened, then turned back to Pull. "Get him out of here," he said, pointing at Faber.

Pullman took Faber by the elbow and steered him toward the entry, only to stop as they reached the door. "Sir."

Jani looked up in time to see Lucien walk in. He still wore the slashed and bloody casuals from his challenge, to which he'd added a stripped-down assortment of body armor and a packed weapons holster. He looked around the room, gaze fixing first on the two teams of medics before coming to rest on Jani. "You're hurt?"

Jani shook her head. "The pink took out my left side."

Niall grimaced. "I told you to report to Medical, Pascal."

"I'm afraid you were superceded, sir." Lucien approached Faber, a change coming over him as he drew close to the young man. His voice lightened. He even managed a smile. "Good morning, Lance Corporal."

"Good morning, sir." Faber drew up straight, his shoulders working as though he tried to salute. "You were right. You said they didn't show us how to get out. You were right." He fell silent. "You said—" His expression lightened again. It did so only when he spoke, fading to blankness as he quieted. "You said that any-time I wanted to talk, I'd be able to find you."

Lucien moved in front of him. Someone had wrapped his *à lérine* wounds in light gauze through which the blood had managed to seep. "Yes, Faber. You are correct."

"You're not—" Faber hesitated. "You're not the Jesus Sergeant Chrivet told us about."

Niall emitted a harsh laugh. "Not even close, boyo."

Faber looked down at the floor. "Maybe . . ." This time when he spoke, his face remained blank. "Maybe you're the only one I get."

Lucien looked to Niall—the two men fought a stare-down until Niall gave in with a grumble and a sharp nod. Lucien motioned for Pullman to back away, then took his place at Faber's side. "Let's go, Micah. Anything you want to talk about, I'm ready to listen." He ushered the young man into the hallway, Pullman bringing up the rear. Then the medics departed, gurneys in tow— first the humanish, then the Vynshàrau, leaving Jani and Niall alone.

"Let's get you out of here." Niall dragged a gurney over to Jani, shaking his head as he stepped into a wet patch of carrier. "Now I know for a fact that both John and Val have been after you for months to trade in those half-mechanical limbs of yours for full-tissue replacements, but you always put them off." He glared down at her. "This is what you get for sticking with outdated technology."

Jani felt the anger rise, then bit back her retort when she caught the light flash in Niall's eyes. She smiled—he grinned back. Then the laughter took them both, and wouldn't let go.

"*Niall.*" Jani finally gasped, her stomach aching. "They're going to come in here and see the blood and us laughing and lock us both up."

Niall wiped his eyes with the back of his hand. "They tried that. More than once. Never worked, did it? Never did, and never will." He straightened slowly. "We're immune in that regard."

Jani held her good hand out to him. "Please get me out of here."

"As my Captain wishes." Niall bent to her, positioning himself so she could drape her right arm around his neck for balance, and lifted her up.

"Bird bones." He lay her atop the gurney like and infant, then escorted her out of the room.

CHAPTER 32

Jani sat silent as Niall drove them past the shattered midsection of the embassy. He'd seconded a wheeled scoot from one of the damage survey teams, but could only approach within a few meters before the shrub-strewn rubble that had been the walled garden made further exploration impossible.

"They came in off the lake, sheathed to the gills thanks to the latest masking technology, and punched through here." He pointed to the gaping hole where there'd once been a set of triple-width doors. "Exterior scan picked up something big coursing over the water's surface, but before they could analyze the image, it vanished. They chalked it up to an artifact. Morons." He shook his head, then glanced at Jani. "You feeling better?"

"Fine." She forced a smile.

"Fine." Niall reversed the scoot, jerking it into a tight turn. They rumbled over the churned-up lawns and past the smoking outbuildings into the stretch of wilderness that marked the boundary between the idomeni and Exterior lands.

As soon as they passed through the eyescan and were cleared to cross the border into humanish territory, Niall reached into his shirt pocket and pulled out his nicstick case. He shook out a 'stick and with careful one-handed maneuvering bit the bulbed ignition tip, then turned it around, leaning forward so he could put it in his mouth.

He steered across the Exterior lawns and rimmed the edge of the main charge-lot, on the lookout for an empty space amid the triple-lengths of a dozen ministries. "They're all inside," he said. "Cao, every other minister on the block, Shai, Mako."

"Tsecha?" Jani had been on the lookout for her old teacher since Niall floated her out of the blasted office, but she hadn't seen him anywhere.

"They dragged him over first of all," Niall said through a haze of smoke. "Some of the ministers would still rather deal with him than Shai, especially under the circumstances, and don't think that didn't go over like a lead balloon."

They trundled around the ministry building to the lakeside enclosed terrace, which, judging from the various medblanket-covered shapes that filled the area, had been designated the temporary morgue. As they drew close, Jani caught sight of Val sitting on the terrace outer railing, head hanging, hands braced in his knees. He glanced up when he heard their approach, but he didn't smile.

"Doctor Parini." Niall braked to a stop. "So far . . . ?"

"Forty-four dead. Ten Vynshàrau, the rest humanish." Val jerked his chin toward Niall's nicstick. "Can you spare one of those?" Niall tossed him the case; he shook out a stick and ignited it, then drew on it as though it was his last breath.

Jani watched her friend raise the 'stick to his lips. Did his hand shake or was it simply a trick of the breeze? "When was the last time you smoked?"

"The last time I saw something like this." Val glanced at Niall. "Inform your weapons designers, Colonel, that the V-790 leaves something to be desired. After we cracked the third charred corpse out of the remains of their smoking exo, we christened it the 'Lobster.'" He took another drag. "I'll be fine, it's just been a while is all." He looked at Jani again, and something of the old kindness returned to his face. "How are you?"

"The new-gen pink took out my left side." Jani raised her shaking left hand. "Walking is quite the adventure."

"New limbs coming up. As soon as I see whether they need me anymore here." Val stood. "Vehicles . . . ?"

"You can't get into the embassy lot." Niall struggled out of the scoot's tight cabin. "Stake out a spot here, and I'll find you something."

As he strode off, Val walked to the scoot and inserted himself as replacement driver. "I never imagined this." He took a last pull on the 'stick, then tossed it. "Not in a hundred years could I have."

"Not even after that last night in Rauta Shèràa?" Jani watched two orderlies bear another blanketed form onto the terrace. "The Night of the Blade?" She studied her hands, then flexed her fingers, the steady and the trembling. She looked toward the lake and imagined a line of exo-clad forms coursing toward her over the chop, a pale, pointed face among them. Walking. Walking.

Jani and Val arrived at Neoclona Chicago to find the level of tension ramped to warning levels. Jani sensed the looks that followed her as they navigated the hospital halls. Some held curiosity, others concern. But there were enough hostile glares scattered about to drive the two of them to use the stairs instead of lifts when possible, and to avoid telling anyone where they went. They arrived at Orthopedics to find a pair of doctors standing by. Val dismissed them and switched out Jani's animandroid limbs himself, running through the post-installation examination in record time. They then departed the hospital by a different, circuitous route.

"Think the lid will stay on for a week?" Val steered his Service loaner out of the underground garage and blended into the evening traffic.

"I think I'm glad my parents aren't here to see this." Jani saw a group of people standing around a storefront, watching a holoVee display. As the skimmer passed, she could see what they watched—the sweep of the embassy grounds, the shattered main building, the gurneys laden with blanketed mounds that it seemed couldn't possibly be entire bodies but were.

"The idomeni are going to leave." Val edged around a disabled skimmer and drove on. "My prediction. Their embassy is a shambles—they can't stay there. The Haárin are no longer safe at the enclave. Cèel wants them back in the worldskein, so back in the worldskein they will go."

"Except for Tsecha," Jani said, "And the other Haárin. They're going to Elyas."

"How the hell are you going to swing that?" Val slowed as they approached his apartment building, then floated down the ramp to the parking garage. "I remember Cèel—I dealt with him often enough. He was bad enough when he was younger, and by all accounts he's gotten worse." As he approached his private bay, he stiffened, then struck the steering mech with the flat of his hand. "I'll be—"

Jani followed his gaze and felt her own flavor of wonderment when she saw Lucien sitting atop a skimmer charge station console, his duffel on the floor beside him. "I've been ordered to remain under medical supervision, so I thought . . . ?" He tried to shrug, but injury forced him to settle for a borderline flinch. "I'll leave, if you want me to."

Jani felt Val's stare, willing her to look in his direction. "Of course you can stay." She heard him sigh, and pretended she didn't.

"Sheridan's a war zone." Lucien broke eggs into a bowl, then whisked in various spices. "I had to get the hell out. Medical put me on two weeks' leave, so I thought, why not decamp to someplace sane?"

Val sat up and craned his neck as he tried to see what Lucien mixed. "Omelets again?"

"Crepes." Lucien smiled. "There are plenty of fillers in your cooler—fresh fruit, whipping cream, mushrooms. Your kitchen's much better stocked than Jani's."

"You're too cruel." Jani took a lemon slice from a garni plate and bit one end. "You mentioned a war zone?"

Lucien nodded as he ladled batter onto a flat pan. "The wafer Veles lifted from Micah Faber contained a lot more than the training scenarios. There was some background coding that revealed where some of the scenarios were constructed. The first round of arrests took place about three hours ago."

What timing. Jani chewed the lemon slice to the rind. "What happened to Veles?"

Lucien hesitated. "He's dead. They found his body in the garage of Faber's building. A professional kill—Faber wasn't capable. Someone simply wanted to make sure that he got to his outfit."

Val sat back and crossed his arms. "Now, I'm no expert in these sorts of assaults—I've only lived through a few. But the question that occurs is, why? I'm trying to follow all the convolutions, and I just don't get it."

Jani cradled her chin in her hand and regarded him solemnly. "I'm more cynical than you are—correct?" She waited until he shrugged agreement. "Assume the Service wants the idomeni out, even the factions that claim to want to get along. Now look at what happened today." She held up her hand, index finger extended, and earned a matching response from Val. "One, the idomeni will be off Earth within the month, at the latest." Second finger. "Two, the Service learned more about Vynshàrau weapons systems and building defenses in the space of a couple of hours than they could have in months or years of hunt and peck spying." She glanced at Lucien, who had the sense to keep his eyes on his crepe pan, then extended her ring finger. "Three, they've tested a prototype exo in the field against the enemy that they designed it for, and found it wanting. Is that enough, or do you need more?"

Val exhaled with a shudder. "Quite a few people died, some horribly."

Jani studied the plate of mushroom crepes Lucien set before her, and reached for the spice dispenser. "Quite a few of them hated beings like me. They would have to a person cheerfully cut my throat given half a chance." Food aromas filled her nose—she swallowed hard as her throat tightened. "Any man's death diminishes me . . . but be that as it may."

"Micah Faber didn't hurt you." Lucien reached across the table to set out Val's plate—the long sleeve of his pullover rode up his arm, revealing a fresh gauze dressing. "He had more than half a chance, too."

"I think he hated Chrivet more than he hated me. She lied to him." Jani picked up a knife to slice her crepes, then set it down with a clatter as the room light flashed off the glinting point. "Where is he now?"

"Neuro Isolation." Lucien sat down at the table. Up close, the strain of the day showed in his drawn face and ashen skin. "Under guard. He's the only survivor who could do some talking anytime soon."

Jani tried to pick up the knife again, then set it aside for good and settled for slicing her food with the side of her fork. "What are they worried about more, suicide or murder?"

Before Lucien could respond, the kitchen door swung aside. One of Val's admins entered carrying a documents pouch in Neoclona's trademark purple. Val took the packet with a shaky hand, taking a deep breath before opening the flap. "Misty." He pulled a small wafer folder out of the bag. "From John." He flipped open the cover and removed the silvery disc. "Clean up first. I'll be waiting in the view room.

Jani showered and dressed in some of Val's castoffs, a sweater and pull-on trousers in his favorite dark green. She met Lucien by the kitchen, and together they adjourned to Val's viewing room, a plush alcove furnished with lounge seats and a portable bar. Jani sat next to Val, while Lucien hedged his bets by choosing a seat in the row behind theirs that was staggered directly between them. Val, she noted, had availed himself of the bar's contents— a half-filled tumbler of something clear and frosty sat at his elbow.

"And so we begin." Val raised his glass to the display, then fingered the control pad set in his chair arm.

The room darkened, the display lightening in turn. The Neoclona *N* unfurled across the panel, followed by a security warning. Then an emptiness, followed by a face.

"John." Val sank back in his seat. "Oh God."

Lucien just stared.

Jani felt her heart catch, and smiled.

John sat at a desk, most likely his office at Neoclona Karistos, judging from the security flags that continued to scroll along the bottom of the display. He'd forsaken medwhites for a dark blue shirt, to which he'd added a gold and blue length of cloth looped and draped like a scarf.

Almost two months had passed since he'd begun the hybridization process. His skin, once milk tinged with blue, had darkened to the cream-gold of the palest Oà. His eyes, once pink, had changed to dull silver centered with clear grey.

"Hello, Val. I'm guessing words are a waste at this point, aren't they?" His voice rumbled as ever, changes in inflection and phrasing not yet apparent. "Before you fall on anyone here, the first they knew of it was when I walked through the entry ten minutes ago. They seemed . . . shocked, but not altogether surprised. This is Karistos, after all. They look at things differently here."

Jani savored the sight and sound of him, and wondered at the touch. His hair was now the same palest wheat shade as his skin. Did it still feel like silk? Would she have been able to feel it at all, considering that he had cut it into a Service burr so sheared as to make Niall's short back and sides appear mussed?

"I know." John passed a hand over his scalp, as if he had predicted her response. "Too damned short, and I'm too tall for it. So help me, from a distance, I look like a pin. But when it started growing out . . . the half-white just looked too strange. So I let Brondt go at it with the clippers. I told him this wasn't the second day of Boot Camp, but as soon as the first few hairs hit the floor, he became a man possessed. Or should I say 'hybrid possessed'?" He tilted his head to the side. "Brondt. Right. You don't know who he is." His eyes softened, from metal to the underside of a cloud. "Is Jani there? She can explain it to you. The short form is that he's her suborn. He's managing the place while she's away." A smile teased a corner of his mouth, brightened his argent eyes. "I'm the staff physician of the Thalassan enclave. Physician-priest, really—I've been undergoing some training. It's a new universe, Val. A life so different I could never have imagined it. Part of me thinks I should have taken the plunge years ago. But then again, perhaps it was better that I waited until now."

Jani glanced to the side to find that Val had drained his glass and now stared at the display over the rim.

"I'll be staying here. For a while, at any rate." John continued to talk easily, as though he sat across the desk from them instead of five GateWays distant. "I've gone over matters with our legal team here—they're sending the usual stuff and nonsense your way. I've also sent along another Misty that's more official. I'm afraid you're stuck on Earth as long as both Eamon and I remain here. Eamon would like to flee immediately, frankly, but he's too afraid of you to risk returning to Chicago even though he misses the place. He's still in, by the way. I've explained it in the other Misty." He rested his elbow atop the desk and propped his chin atop his fist. "I don't miss Earth at all—isn't that odd? I thought Seattle might be calling my name by now, but I haven't heard a thing. Not even a whisper." He looked into the display. "I miss you, though, old friend. The decent thing would have been to tell you in person, but I couldn't leave, and . . . I thought if you saw me before I was too far along, you might try to talk me out of it." He hung his head. "Perhaps that was a mistake."

Then his head came up. "Is Jani there? Tell her that I miss her. In ways I can't begin to express." His look grew weighty. "And in ways I can express quite well. Tell her I love her." He sighed. "So long, Val. We will talk in person, as soon as we can." The image stilled, then faded. The display darkened.

Val remained motionless, even as the lights came up, fingers laced around the empty glass. "He loves you," he said finally, setting the glass down with a clatter, then boosting to his feet and leaving the room.

Jani found Val in a chair by the window, his head in his hands. He looked up when he heard her approach. His cheeks were flushed, either from alcohol or because he fought back anger, or maybe a combination of both.

"Why didn't you tell me?" His voice emerged rough, as though his throat ached. "You knew. You knew!"

Jani walked to the window. "I believed that it should come from him. You two have been friends for so long . . . I thought he'd tell you in the way he felt best." Out of seeming nowhere, rain had come. Drops spattered the window, then tracked downward like tears. "If it helps at all, he didn't tell me, either. Not until after he'd started. He wanted to surprise me. Boy, did he ever."

A trace of a smile crossed Val's face. "How did Eamon take it?"

"Outraged that John had lowered himself to research subject. Scared, in case someone decided to arrest him. The usual Eamonesque self-interest."

"I hate to break this to you, but I can see his point." Val scrubbed a hand through his hair and sat up. "Once this news gets out, Neoclona is going to quake to its core."

"Don't you think you're exaggerating a little?"

"Do you think Earth's ready for a human-idomeni hybrid heading up the largest single business entity in the Commonwealth? Especially after what happened today?" Val stood and started to pace. "It's going to take every arm I can twist to keep Li Cao and friends from stripping John of everything he owns." His pace quickened. "He's already talked to the lawyers, which means they're working on it, I hope. Not that it will matter much when your anti-idomeni friends start bombing our facilities." He stopped in front of Jani, his face set with a sternness that wasn't entirely an act. "You do like to complicate a man's life, don't you?" He reached out and touched her arm. "Then there's the fact . . ." He raised his hand to the line of her jaw. "Not to sound like a whiner, but do you have any idea how lonely I feel right now?"

Jani looked into Val's hazel eyes, glassy with pent-up anguish. She reached for him and pulled him close—he held her as though she was the last person he would ever embrace, and released her reluctantly.

"When do you think you'll be leaving?" he asked.

Jani shook her head. "Depending on when I get in to sęe Shai and Cao, sometime in the next few days. Assuming I'm not arrested or shot in the street by then."

Val turned away from her, staking out his own place at the window. "Back in Rauta Shèràa, John used to refer to the two of you as Pygmalion and Galatea. The sculptor who carved a woman so beautiful he begged the gods to give her life. In the official story they answer his prayers. One day, she steps down from the pedestal into his arms." He turned to her. "You've given the story a new ending. In this one, Galatea lifts up Pygmalion to join her." His eyes widened. "And how the gods will react, one cannot begin to imagine."

* * *

Jani left Val in the sitting room and set out to find a spot in the vast penthouse where she could find refuge, at least for a little while. After a search, she came upon a small bedroom decorated in the same blues and corals as her room in Thalassa. She hunted through drawers until she found a sheet of parchment and a stylus. Then she sat at the narrow desk and composed a letter to Prime Minister Cao. *I am not political . . . unless I have to be.* She affixed her signature to the bottom, tucked the missive into a documents pouch, then summoned one of Val's admins and asked them to deliver it. That task completed, she walked to the narrow window, took in the view of the rainswept lake, and tried to imagine bare rock cliffs, the palms, and the sun.

"You're really leaving?"

Jani turned to find Lucien standing in the doorway, looked into a face drawn with pain and exhaustion, eyes deadened by a devil's marriage of nature and technology. "I prefer to call it, 'going home.'"

"What about me?" He stepped inside far enough for the door to sweep closed. "If you leave, what happens?"

"At the rate you're going, you may find yourself with a place here, if only as a cook." Jani set her hand on the sill. The wood was coated white, a blued shade that brought out the yellow in her skin by contrast. "We both knew it would come to this eventually. You're incapable of love, and I'm incapable of loving you. We . . . enjoyed one another. Took what the other offered. It's the sort of thing that's nice while it lasts, but it never lasts. Not for long enough."

Lucien cocked his head to one side, as though he couldn't hear her, or didn't understand what he heard. He walked to her, let his hands slip down her arms until he held her hands in his, and traced his fingers over hers.

Then he unfastened the cuff of her right sleeve and pushed it to her elbow, revealing the long, wealed scar she'd inflicted upon herself at Thalassa. "Tsecha told me about this." He ran the edge of his thumb from one end of the scar to the other and back again. "He said you always inflict the worst wounds upon yourself." He rolled up his right sleeve. "I could argue that." Slipping his thumbnail beneath the edges of the gauze, he peeled it away, revealing the fresh wounds that crisscrossed his forearm, some scabbed, some glistening as though fresh. "My first time. It's been a while since I could say that about anything."

He took Jani's right arm in his left hand, cradling it near the elbow. Then he took his right arm and rested it atop hers so their scars overlaid.

Jani flinched as the warmth of his blood touched her skin, felt his grip tighten to keep her close.

"You lead, I follow. You show the way, I walk in your footsteps. That's the way it is." He looked over her shoulder, his eyes locked on some middle distance. "Today, you acted as my second. You backed me up. You warned me when Ghos tried to strike. You were there." His eyes met hers, unfocused. Then he looked down at their arms. "I don't remember my dreams. Everyone dreams, you dream or you go mad. Well, I don't remember mine." He shook his head slowly, then he stilled. "After takedowns, something disconnects for a while. I come the closest to feeling like I'm in an imagined place." His voice had fallen to a murmur. "When I arrived here this afternoon, I entered through the garage. It was dark. I walked to the foot of that short flight of stairs and looked up into the darkness. My sightline closed in—all I could see was a long, empty tunnel of black. And I knew there was no one at the other end. I was completely alone, and I knew it. I always would be, and I knew that, too." He looked at her again, eyes no longer dead but clouded by something that for him marked a place worse than any he had ever been. "That's the way I feel now."

Jani reached up with her free hand and touched Lucien's face. *Liar.* She brushed her fingers over his lips. *Broken boy, who'll say anything to get what he needs.* Hers to see through to the end, because no one else could. "You'll never be alone as long as I'm alive."

"And you're going to live a good, long time, right?" Lucien's face brightened with a smile. You had to look hard to see that it didn't reach his eyes. "Hybrids are supposed to live a long time. That means I will, too." He rested his head on her shoulder, his skin hot as fever. "Although doing what, I have no idea. I always assumed I'd make it to full colonel. Find some general who needed a second right hand, put in my twenty years—"

"Then retire to the country and keep bees?" Jani tried to edge her arm away from Lucien's, stopping when he raised his head to look at her.

"Retire with you." The deadness had left his eyes, replaced by the usual cold, jewel light.

This time, Jani couldn't hold back. "Liar."

"If it makes you feel better to think that," Lucien said as he kissed her.

Jani lay atop the bed as Lucien undressed her—when she reached for his shirt, he pushed her hands away. This was his night to manage, his to prove she needed him as much as he needed her, no matter how she tried to deny it. She could feel it in the way he held her, the way he concentrated on every part of her as though no one else had ever entered this strange land before and only he knew the way. She sensed his desperation, tried to slow him, and felt his need overpower them both. She realized then that he was trying to change her mind, trying to convince her to stay in the only way he could, and told herself that if she was focused enough to think about it at a time like this, he had lost whatever hold he had on her, and their only connection now was the hold she had on him.

Then his hair caught the light, the pale washed gold of it, and she saw John's sheared head and heard his laugh. Felt his wiry weight on top of her and the insistent rhythm inside her, and closed her eyes, and used that sweetest memory to guide her home.

She slept. She dreamed. Unlike Lucien, she remembered. The point of a blade. A charred smile.

"Jani. Jani, wake up."

She opened her eyes to find Lucien leaning over her, steaming cup of coffee in hand.

"The PM's aide called. She's sending a skimmer. It will be here in thirty minutes. You need to get out of bed, shower, and dress. I've laid out clothes. I'm going to the kitchen to make breakfast. Val says to tell you he's got his fingers crossed."

Jani took the cup and struggled into a sitting position. "Do I look that helpless that I need step by step instructions?"

Lucien folded down the bedclothes. "You look like I do. We need downtime, and we won't get it." He headed for the door. "If you're not dressed and in the kitchen in fifteen minutes, I'm sending in Val."

Jani watched him leave. It broke through the daze that he'd donned his dress blue-greys.

She stumbled out of bed and made for the bathroom, cup in hand.

CHAPTER 33

Prime Minister Li Cao's Family estate cut an enviable swath through the Bluffs. Bordered on one side by the lake and on the other three sides by ravine-sliced woodland, it rolled for square kilometer after square kilometer.

The house itself lacked the immensity of the land that surrounded it. A single story built of stone and wood, flat expanses and arches in grey and brown. A house built for the needs of those who lived there, not to impress those who didn't.

Jani followed Cao's aide down a long white hallway as stripped-down as a Vynshàrau corridor, capped at the end by a set of hinged double doors. The aide turned the knob on one side and pushed the panel open, revealing a long, narrow sunroom framed by glass and wood beams. Jani took a deep breath and stepped inside.

The Prime Minister stood at the far end of the room, wearing a floor-length skirt and pullover in the signature cream color of her ministry. "Good morning." She held a cup by its underside like a bowl. "I trust you have recovered from yesterday's . . . episode." The contents of the cup steamed—she held the vessel to her nose to sniff, but didn't drink.

"I am quite well, Your Excellency. Thank you for inquiring." Jani paused just inside the doorway, shifting her weight from real leg to animandroid. She hadn't yet adjusted to her new limb's quirks, and she didn't want to risk a stumble at such a delicate time.

"I admit that I am not sure what to call you." Cao smiled. "Jani or Kilian or Kièrshia. To which name are you answering today?"

Jani walked slowly to the middle of the room. Lucien had chosen a trouser suit in dark green that he always said matched her eyes—she felt like a tree compared to the more diminutive Cao. "Jani or Kilian, Your Excellency, if you don't mind. You're mangling Kièrshia."

Cao had been ferrying the cup-bowl to her nose for another sniff—it stopped in mid-transit. "You never change. Even when you have no room to maneuver, that neck doesn't bend, does it? Kilian?" She walked toward the far windowed wall, where a pair of chairs bracketed a low, round table. "However, in this particular instance, you do have some room. But you knew that, didn't you?" She gestured for Jani to join her. "I decided it would be better if we discussed this matter in private." She sat, the cup still cradled in her hand. "Shai becomes too difficult to deal with when you're present—you bring out her stubbornness. As for ní Tsecha . . ." She shook her head. "I can only take so much torment with my morning tea. Even without you, he's problem enough. Many thought his outcast would eliminate his powerbase, and it did to a point. He lost the bornsect, but they don't count for much anymore next to the Haárin, do they, and he hasn't lost a one of them." She graced Jani with a look of quiet accusation. "You made sure of that." She sat back, and once more held the cup to her nose. "Jasmine. The scent reminds me that summer will come, even though now it is still too cold to enjoy my garden. Tell me about Thalassa."

Read Niall's report. Jani swallowed that response and counted a long pause. When the aide returned with a beverage tray, she asked for coffee, and remained silent until the young woman prepared her cup and departed. "Thalassa is a community of fifty-seven hybrids." *Fifty-nine, after John and I settle in.* "The number is fairly equally distributed between those who were Haárin originally and those who were—"

"I know all that." Cao reached into a pocket in her skirt and removed a data wafer. "Courtesy of Niall Pierce, whose . . . regard for you tended to color some of his more politically significant conclusions." She paused to drink, taking a long draught that betrayed how much she needed the energy and the comfort the tea provided. "Let me rephrase the question. Tell me about Thalassa's influence."

"That's a more difficult quantity to define at present." Jani looked through the window to the garden beyond, arrangements of stone set amid hybrid shrubs blooming yellow and orange. *If I make us appear too strong, she'll hold back whatever she is offer-*

ing out of fear, and if I make us appear too weak, she'll hold back because there's no need to give anything up. "We are the physical manifestation of ní Tsecha's beliefs. There is a fervor about the place you could describe as religious." She flashed back to the day she met Gisa in the circle, and the sight of cloths dipped in her blood. "Our official status at the moment is as a subsidiary off-shoot of the Elyan Haárin, who already possess a formidable power base in their own right. We are a responsibility to them more than an asset at this point."

"You say subsidiary, not suborn."

You would catch that, wouldn't you? "When I left Thalassa, Your Excellency, we were still laying down plumbing in the houses. We are still finding our place."

"Which means you are open to influence, suasion, lobbying, and all the other sins that politics is heir to?" Cao concentrated on the garden view as well. "Or that you are waiting to see which way the wind blows." She glanced at Jani out of the corner of her eye. "You've learned to keep your mouth shut at least part of the time, Kilian. Yet another thing for the rest of us to worry about."

Jani finished her coffee and set down the cup. "I'm sure I don't know what you mean, Your Excellency."

"Of course you don't." Cao sighed. "The bornsect have once more been shaken by life outside their worldskein, and like an injured crab into its shell, they will retreat. The word came today, from Shai, the embassy to be razed, and the enclave as well. They could extract so much more from us if they cared to, but they have lost their resolve. I doubt seriously that they will emerge again under the current regime."

"Cèel will have to if he wants to keep open any lines of communication with the colonial Haárin."

"Cèel, for all his talk of modernity, is still too much of an ideologue. He will die before he changes. I expect another bornsect to ascend to *rau* before too long, as I'm sure you do." Cao ran a finger along the rim of her cup. "I hear other names bandied about by my idomeni-watchers. Doches, the Oà's Chief Propitiator. The Pathen dominant, Aolun. Do either of them strike a responsive chord?"

"I have heard both names mentioned, Your Excellency, but I don't know enough about either to hazard a guess."

"Indeed." Cao tapped an enameled fingernail against the arm of her chair. "John Shroud. Yet another unknown quantity. If I could toss both him and Eamon DeVries into a Luna prison and lose the code, I would do so and gladly." Her tone hardened. "He's backing you financially. Shroud."

"The houses in which the hybrids live as well as the surrounding property are part of Eamon DeVries's personal holdings. John didn't know what Eamon had done until he arrived on site almost two months ago."

"But he didn't respond by kicking DeVries out of Neoclona, as their contract demands, and evicting the hybrids, did he? DeVries is still a member of Neoclona, and the hybrids live there still." Cao's voice held petulance, as though she considered his decision a personal affront. "Why did he decide to hybridize?"

Jani smiled—she couldn't help herself. "He loves me." She looked up to find Cao regarding her with narrow-eyed annoyance, and felt the heat flood her face.

"Love is a marvelous thing, and in and of itself, not as complicating an issue as one might think. Adjustments can be made regarding love." Cao set her cup down, then stood and walked to the window. "It's the money and power that one or the other parties brings to the table that confound matters. John Shroud's personal fortune dwarfs the Gross Domestic Product of any number of colonies. If he chooses to use it in support of the Thalassans, and through them the Elyan Haárin, he will upset the balance of power for the entire Outer Circle."

"The balance of power is already upset. The Outer Circle Haárin control transportation and shipping for the region. At this point, John's money doesn't make a great deal of difference."

"At this point." Cao placed a hand on the window. "The medical aspects of the issue also concern me. The control of Neoclona—"

"You need to discuss that with Val Parini."

"He has scheduled an appointment for this afternoon." The hand dropped. "I had hoped it a social call, but I fear now it will be a negotiating session." Cao remained at the window, gaze fixed on a trio of yard workers digging around the browned skeleton of a shrub.

"The pressing issue at the moment is keeping the Outer Circle Haárin settled." Jani felt her idomeni anger rise. She was hungry and tired. She missed John with a physical ache, and the half-emerged buds in the trees outside the window would emerge into full leaf by the time she saw him again. "The accompanying issues are distance, perceived reliability of the native population, and the military and financial clubs you can wield. At this point, neither you nor Cèel have all those issues weighted in your favor. Therefore, you have to deal."

Cao's shoulders shook in soundless mirth. "The Kilian Tongue of Lead wins out after all." She stilled. "This aborted challenge-cum-murder involving Captain Pascal and the security suborn, Ghos—it complicates matters."

"Ghos and his dominant Elon lowered the embassy defenses to permit attack. Humans died as a result." Jani tried to project a calm she didn't feel. "I've seen the 'Vee reports. Shai has no recourse where that's concerned."

"Except ideology, which is the one great unknown." Cao tapped the window one last time, then returned to her seat. "If the Outer Circle Haárin are placated, what can they offer in return?"

"I cannot speak for them. The Thalassan hybrids are beholden to the Elyan Haárin for protection; in turn, we owe them obedience *to a point*. I can speak *to* them regarding matters of mutual interest." Jani looked out toward the garden—the workers had hacked down the shrub with cutters in preparation for digging out the root remains. "We have the right to protect ourselves—that is paramount. But I can pledge that I will do my utmost to prevent the Elyan Haárin from taking aggressive actions against the humanish colonists."

Cao's voice perked. "Aggressive, militarily speaking? Politically? Economically?"

"Militarily. Politically."

"In other words, you won't persuade the Elyan Haárin away from my docks?"

"They are not your docks, Cao. Your representatives signed contracts in your name. We've dealt with the matter of Sìah Haárin and contracts before—do you really want to revisit such?"

Cao's brow arched—her expression turned thoughtful. "Your speech changes when you become emotional. It becomes harsher, more idomeni-like. I also hear Shai's stubbornness. Is it a Vyn-shàrau trait, I wonder?" She sat forward, hands folded. The light from the window highlighted the fine lines that grooved the corners of her eyes. When she first took office, the power of the Commonwealth seemed bound to rise ever higher. Now, she seemed to be contemplating the opposite trajectory. "I will lend my support to your request that ní Tsecha Egri and the other Chicago Haárin be allowed to resettle on Elyas." She reached into a pocket hidden in the folds of her skirt, and removed Jani's letter, setting it on the table in front of her. "I cannot guarantee that Shai will agree, but she has shown herself more willing to listen to the hard realities than has Cèel." She regarded her hands, heavy with rings. "You should leave tomorrow, I think. That will most likely force Shai to acquiesce to the decision, then explain it to Cèel. She works better under pressure."

Jani waited for Cao to say more, but the woman simply poured herself another cup of tea. *That's it?* She wondered at what they had discussed, and what little had been decided. So what was the point of the exercise? To feel her out? Impress upon her the possibility of alliance? Roust her out of bed in the early morning?

I got what I wanted. Barring any exercise in stubbornness on Shai's part. *Maybe I shouldn't complain too loudly.*

Then she realized the silence. Like suborns of every species, she knew a dismissal when she didn't hear it. "Thank you, Your Excellency." She rose and headed for the door.

Cao remained seated, her gaze fixed on the workers. "Farewell, Captain Jani Moragh Kilian. Kièrshia nìaRauta Haárin. Tsecha vo Kièrshia. Tsecha's toxin come to life, to plague us forever." She paused to hold the cup to her nose. "We will meet again, I am sure. Across one bargaining table or another."

Jani left the room to find a different aide waiting to escort her to the skimmer. The ride back to Val's seemed shorter than had the drive to Cao's house, as was usual with those sorts of visits. When the vehicle drifted to a stop in front of Val's building, Lucien clipped down the steps to meet her.

"We leave tomorrow," she said as soon as they moved out of earshot of the driver.

The barest shadow crossed his perfect face. "I'll alert the enclave."

Micah lay still, listening for any sounds from the hallway outside. When anyone looked through the narrow window, he faked sleep, or talked to himself *with intent*, as though he actually held a conversation with voices in his head. *This isn't going to work forever.* Eventually, they'd drag him out of bed and subject him to a neuroscan. He knew they suspected trauma disorder, along with a laundry list of other problems. He knew that if he told them that he felt sure someone wanted to kill him, they'd add that problem to the list.

"I've seen people in the hall, you understand. Men, mostly, although they sent a woman this morning who could have been Chrivet's twin." He wished he'd had the wit to demand Chrivet tell him her real name before he shot her. He would have liked to know, to compare it with that of the woman who had stood outside his door, staring at him through the window until the day nurse spooked her.

He would have liked to know Manda's real name as well, but he tried not to think about that.

He fell asleep. Dreamed quiet dreams for a change. Awoke with a lighter heart, and had his hopes dashed as soon as he opened his eyes.

"Hello, Micah." Pascal had dragged a visitor's chair to the bedside and sat. He wore civvies, which was surprising, a blue shirt and tan trousers. An outpatient ID bracelet encircled one bandaged wrist. "How are you feeling?" He waited for an answer, then shrugged when one didn't prove forthcoming. "I was in the area—" He raised his braceleted wrist. "—thought I'd stop by to see how you're doing." He smiled. "Veles is dead—did you kill him?"

Micah gripped a handful of sheet as the remembered voice rasped in his ear. He tried to imagine the man's face, but the effort made his head swim. "No."

"You're sure? Didn't have another one of your moments, like you did during our last meeting?"

Micah closed his eyes, then opened them. Unfortunately, Pascal didn't prove a moment. "No. I didn't kill him."

Pascal studied him as though he was a not particularly interesting piece of furniture. "You're the only one left—did they tell you that? They couldn't save Chrivet."

Micah replayed a curtain of brown hair. A coffee-flavored kiss. "No. They didn't tell me."

"And now they have you locked away. No press, no interviews, no lawyers. May as well have fallen down a hole—"

"What do you want!" Micah pushed himself into a sitting position hugging the bed's guardrails as the room tilted. "What the hell do you want?"

"To fix you in my mind." Pascal cocked his head. "In case someone changes your face, your build, your coloring. Mannerisms are the hardest thing to unlearn, and you have a few interesting ones. I won't tell you what they are, of course, because . . . well, then you'd know."

"My face?" Micah leaned forward slowly, and tried to stretch. His muscles felt stiff from inactivity. Flabby. He knew that if he could only work out that ache, his head would clear. He'd stop thinking about advocates and courts martial and prison cells, what the Service wanted to do to him and how quickly they planned to do it. Stop thinking about goddamned Pascal, sitting in his room as though he owned it, all arrogance and alien scars.

He pressed his hands to his head. With all the watchers who had monitored him since his arrival, he'd have thought someone would check on him now. Intervene. Ask Pascal to leave. "I don't know what you're talking about."

"No, I don't think you do." Pascal raised a hand to his forehead, revealing a thin line of blood that marred his shirtsleeve. "If you consider cities as beasts, Chicago qualifies as a predator of sorts. Dangerous, yes, but also shrewd. Adaptable. It moves quickly when it senses the hunter close in." He sat back, hands folded in his lap. "Change is the hunter, in this case. Fear of what the future holds." He smiled. "You are in for an interesting next few months, I expect. I advise you to relax and observe. Take good notes. Remember what is said and who says it. You will witness feats of denial, chicanery, and outright criminality the likes of which you'll never see again. I'd look forward to it if I were you."

"You're crazy." Micah leaned forward and hugged his aching stomach. "Chrivet's dead. I killed her." He relived the scene at times. Dreamed it. Saw the fear in Chrivet's eyes as she faced her own shooter. Heard Kilian call to him to stand down. Wondered if he should have listened. "They're going to execute me."

Pascal shook his head. "No. Not if they want to maintain the support of the ultraconservative anti-idomeni factions, which I think they do. They're scared, you see. They know she won't rest until they're nailed." He looked down at his hands, then fingered his bloodstained sleeve.

"You'll be medicalled out, I'm guessing. That's how the Service usually buries their mistakes." He brushed some imaginary blemish from his trousers, then stood. "I shall follow your career with interest, Micah, whatever it happens to be. I'm quite confident that we shall meet again." He left the room as quietly as he'd entered, the door closing behind him with a sigh.

CHAPTER 34

It was possible to arrange the transport of an enclave's worth of Haárin from a standing start in a day's time, Jani found, if one went without sleep and had the entire Prime Ministry at one's beck and call in the bargain.

And if one has Lucien. She tried not to notice that his labors to that end contained the same undercurrents of desperation as had his lovemaking. *See what I can do*, his every action whispered. *You don't want to leave me behind.*

"I'll handle the cancellation of the town-house lease." He sat beside her in the isolated corner of the idomeni shuttleport that was open to humanish. "The office supply company will pick up the combooth equipment and workstation this afternoon."

"Wipe the boards first." Jani pressed her palms against the sides of her throbbing head. "Erase all the inputs."

"I did that this morning while you were in the shower, after I made breakfast and packed your luggage, such as it was." Lucien stifled a yawn. "It's good to know that I'm still officially on leave and under orders to take it easy." He lay his head against the seat-back and closed his eyes.

Jani turned to study his resting profile, as she had so many times that morning. "Thank you."

One side of Lucien's mouth twitched. "I'm being completely self-serving, of course. That's always the reason behind everything I do."

"I know." Jani lay her head back and closed her eyes as well. The old Service rule—sleep whenever the opportunity presented itself, because you never knew when you'd get the chance again.

She felt herself relax, heard Lucien emit a barely audible snore—

"*Nìa!*"

—until that familiar voice rattled around in her skull and jerked her upright.

Lucien groaned and struggled to his feet. "I knew the silence was too good to last."

"Shai is mad, I have decided." Tsecha swept through the concourse behind Dathim, his coat flapping around his ankles. "To agree to my leaving with you. Cèel will recall her, of this I have no doubt. Kill her, most likely." He stepped to the edge of the barrier that separated the concourse from the humanish section, then shrugged, hoisted his coat to his knees and stepped over it. "We leave in less than an hour. Every Haárin finds that they now have more to pack than they ever brought with them. All is madness." He slumped into a seat.

Jani glanced over at Dathim. "You can arrange to have things shipped."

"Pascal and I have already done such. We are the only two sane ones left." Dathim turned to Lucien. "You will come to Elyas. From what I hear, there is much to organize there as well."

Lucien opened his mouth to speak, then closed it. He looked to each of them in turn, his eyes finally coming to rest on the strapping Haárin. "When I can." He wiped a hand across his mouth. "Excuse me." He hurried from the waiting area, pushing through the entry door before it had a chance to open completely.

Tsecha watched Lucien depart. "Humanish leave-taking. If you have never experienced such, Dathim, you must prepare." He turned back to Jani. "All that will meet again, will meet again. All that will separate, will separate. Such is as it is." He gestured uncertainty. "And yet, I understand . . ." He turned back to look out through the windows to the rolling spring green outside. "Such dreams I had for this damned cold place."

Dathim walked to his side and placed a hand on his shoulder. "Then we should go outside, ní Tsecha, and bid this damned cold place a proper good-bye."

"Yes." Tsecha rose and followed Dathim outside.

Jani looked around the empty area. The other Haárin waited in a separate wing of the port. The shuttles had all arrived, and were being loaded even now. "Nothing to do but wait." She sat down and wondered if she had time to grab a nap.

"Jan?"

She turned.

Lucien stood in the entry. He pressed his thumb and first two fingers together and held them to his lips, as if he held a nicstick. "You have a visitor."

Jani cut across the front of the port and around to the charge lot reserved for humanish skimmers, to find Niall standing beside a dark blue sedan. He couldn't smoke on the premises, so he made do with tapping an irregular beat on the skimmer roof.

"Niall." Jani stopped short of the lot's edge.

Niall stopped in mid-tap, then stepped back from the skimmer. "Hello." He looked up at the sky. "Clear. Not much crosswind. PM kept the reporters away. Good day to fly." He turned to her. "What time do you leave?"

Jani checked her timepiece. "The shuttle dominant wants us aboard in a half hour."

"Can't the idomeni even call their pilots 'pilots'?" Niall paused for a time over that bit of annoyance. "So, I understand the PM herself is providing the ships."

Jani nodded. "They've been in emergency drydock at Luna Station getting retrofitted to transport idomeni. Amazing how quickly things can get done when a Prime Minister wants you out of the way." She sighed, which precipitated a yawn. "It's all gotten very complicated."

"Well, you're involved. Stands to reason." Niall grinned, then scuffed his feet. "Faber's going to be medicalled out. That's the latest buzz, at any rate. Someone in Service Investigative started a death pool—pick the day we find his body washed up on the lakeshore."

Jani recalled the slight figure Lucien led away. Lost. Broken. "I thought I had no pity left, but I pity him. He didn't belong in that sort of operation—he didn't have the mind-set for it. Now all he has left are memories of the dead and a shattered career."

"There but for the grace of God . . . ?" Niall shook his head. "I don't buy it, sorry. It's very simple—there are people who have what it takes and people who don't, and whether you're one or the other is determined at birth." He pushed his hands into his pockets, then pulled them out immediately. "For example, I'd trust you at my back anytime, even when you don't follow orders. But then, you're worth any number of Micah Fabers."

"Don't let any of your friends at Supreme Command hear you say that." Jani smiled. "What about Lucien?"

"You're worth any number of him as well. But I'm not in Intelligence, so I have no say in the matter." Niall shrugged. "What time is it?"

Jani glanced at her timepiece. "Twenty minutes."

"Right." Niall cleared his throat. "I'm . . . going to miss you, now the hurly-burly's done."

Jani's eyes stung. She looked around to see if Tsecha and Dathim were in sight, then walked up to Niall. "I'm going to miss you, too." She slipped her arms around his waist and hugged him.

Niall stiffened at first. Then he hugged back, his hands tentative on her shoulders, as if he never expected to touch her and didn't know what to do.

"Farewell, too little and too lately known, whom I began to think and call my own." His tunic felt rough against Jani's cheek, the cloth scented with fresh air and the sharp undercurrent of smoke. " 'For sure our souls were near allied, and thine cast in the same poetic mould with mine.' " He stopped, inhaled shakily. " 'One common note on either lyre did strike, and knaves and fools we both abhorred alike—' " His voice cracked. He released her abruptly and stepped back, eyes fixed on the ground. "John Dryden. Poet. Critic. Playwright. Restoration period, old England." He turned away, took a long, slow step toward his skimmer, then stopped. "He wrote the poem for a friend who died. 'To the Memory of Mr. Oldham.' John Oldham, a satirist and poet . . ." His voice dwindled once more. He reached into his trouser pocket and removed a folded sheet of parchment. "I've written the rest out, in case you want to read it later. I know how much you love when I give you things to read." He walked back to Jani and handed her the sheet, pale blue with charcoal trim, courtesy of Supreme Command HQ. "Speaking of men named John." He still didn't raise his eyes to look her in the face. "You love him. He loves you. You're happy."

"Yes." Jani nodded carefully. A sudden move on her part and the tears would spill, and once they started, she doubted they'd stop.

"Good. You deserve to be." Niall nodded, then pointed to the sheet of parchment. "It's not that I believe this to be an epitaph or a eulogy, or that we've reached the end of our friendship. I know things have changed between us, and will continue to change, and that . . . a time may come when we find ourselves on opposite sides. But whatever happens, whatever events transpire, I just wanted you to know that . . . I consider you my best and closest friend."

Jani closed her eyes and stood as still as she could. "I feel the same way." She breathed, concentrated on the air pulling in and pushing out. "I have to go." She turned and hurried back to the terminal.

"I may be out your way in the autumn," Niall called after her. "Possibly earlier. Sorting out Fort Karistos."

Jani stopped and turned around. "Mako's sending the right man."

"Yeah." Niall patted his pockets again, then stilled. "Think there's any neutral ground where we can meet for dinner?"

"I'm sure something can be arranged."

"You can still eat in a restaurant?"

"I still eat in a restaurant." Jani regarded Niall for a time. Then she drew to attention and snapped a salute. "Colonel."

Niall saluted back. "Captain."

Jani turned and walked back into the terminal. The place was deserted now—her footsteps echoed within the space, the dull rasp of boot soles against rough tile.

She returned to the humanish side of the concourse and took a seat by the window, waiting for the final call to board. Three shuttles had already departed for Luna, leaving the runways bare and her sightlines clear. She could see Tsecha and Dathim strolling toward the far end of the tarmac, as well as the shuttle dominant who paced around the remaining craft that abutted the concourse's Haárin gangway, executing her preflight walk-around.

Not shuttle dominant. Pilot. Jani replayed Niall's grumble, and smiled.

"And the time dwindles down."

Jani looked around to find Lucien standing at the end of the row of seats. *It's just the two of us.* She'd had a feeling that when the time came for good-byes, his would be the last. Unfortunately, that hadn't helped her prepare. Forewarned and forearmed never did much good when it came to Lucien Pascal. "I was just thinking of something Niall said." She stifled a cough. She loved John more than her life, saw aspects of him in the sun-bright surface of a cloud or the sweep of a shuttle's wing, had only to close her eyes to imagine his smile, his touch.

And yet . . .

"Dathim says I'm not allowed on the tarmac." Lucien walked to the window and watched the pilot circle. "Anything we say needs to be said here."

Jani's hand went to the neck of her coverall, which felt constricting despite its usual baggy fit. "Such as?"

Lucien stood up straight and clasped his hands behind his back. He wore civvies, shirt and trousers in shades of blue that managed to look like a uniform. "I've put in for a spot on Pierce's Karistos audit team. He doesn't know it yet, of course. I can't wait to hear the howls of agony."

Jani grinned. "I'll just bet you can't." She tugged at her cuffs. Checked her timepiece. Then she looked up to find Lucien had turned his back to the window, and watched her.

"You'll miss me, won't you?" He smiled his brilliant smile.

Jani nodded. "Yes, I think I will."

"You think." Lucien stood still for a time. Then he started toward her, walking so slowly, as though he knew she'd wait forever.

Jani's heart pounded as he pulled her to her feet, his hands roaming over her body before locking around her waist. He drew her in slowly, his lips tracing heat over her face, her neck and throat before finally settling over hers. She savored his taste for what she told herself would be the last time. Pepper with a hint of bitter orange, flavors he knew she enjoyed.

He released her just as gradually, hands drifting along her neck, her shoulders, over her breasts before finally falling away. He backed off, fingers curled as though he held onto her still, his eyes locked with hers. Then he turned on his heel and walked to the entry, through the doors and away.

Jani watched the space where Lucien had been as the last sense of him faded. Then she detected motion out of the corner of her eye, and looked out the window in time to see Dathim and Tsecha hurrying toward the terminal.

"It is time, nìa," Tsecha called as he bustled through the entry, his step slowing as he drew close. "Time to leave this damned cold place." He stopped and looked around the terminal as though lost. "So strange. I thought, and truly, that I would die here."

"You might have." Dathim cut in front of Tsecha, then waved him and Jani both toward the gangway. "As we all might have. Now we shall go someplace else, and live." He looked to the window, then away. In his way, he had wanted to live on Earth as much as had Tsecha, but if he felt any regret at leaving, he kept it to himself. "Now we shall go," he said again.

They boarded the shuttle. Jani strapped herself into her seat, then sat back. Studied the other Haárin who had already boarded. Wondered at how far she had come in a year and a half, and where she still needed to go.

Then came the rumble of the engines. The acceleration. The lift and bank of flight.

"Nìa?" Tsecha loosened his seat brake and spun around to face her. "What is that on the water?"

Jani loosened her safety harness and edged closer to the port-hole until she could see the lake below.

The skimmers flitted side by side over the water like low-flying seabirds, their rings of emergency lights blazing yellow-white. At first they darted to the left, then to the right, like glowing waterbugs. Then their paths straightened as they sped up to race the shuttle, their lights flashing on then off in flickering patterns.

"Humanish leave-taking, nìRau." Jani leaned close to the window and watched the display until the shuttle banked and the skimmers disappeared from view.

EPILOGUE

"Who is that youngish, nìa?" Tsecha leaned forward so he could look around Jani, but not so far that he couldn't pretend he looked somewhere else in case someone caught him.

Jani glanced back toward the enclave road, saw the familiar figure sitting atop a nearby rock, and hid a smile. "You did meet him, inshah. Torin Clase—he's the historian."

"Ah." Tsecha nodded as he drew up straight. "He appears most as different when he writes."

"He does get a rather pointed look, yes."

"He is *everywhere*, nìa."

"He believes that recording the history of Thalassa is his born duty. He believes it must be done at the time things happen so that the facts don't get muddled."

"So." Tsecha sniffed. "Can he hear us if we whisper?"

"*No.*" Jani fought to stifle a laugh. "But then he'll try to get you to commit to once-a-week interviews."

"He has done such already, nìa—everywhere I turn—" Tsecha shook his head. "The price I must pay, I most suppose, for this blessed sun."

Jani closed her eyes and felt the heat on her face. Winter was almost upon them, and she could still walk about without a coat in the afternoons. Yet still, at times, she thought about what had been. "I am sorry that Chicago didn't work out. I know how much it meant to you." She hesitated. "It meant a lot to me as well."

"The gods did not mean for me to die in such a cold place." Tsecha bared his teeth. "They meant for us to labor where we were wanted in the first place, where we did not have to spend so much energy asserting our right to *be*." He glanced at Jani, then away. "I speak as one of you. I am not, however—this I know and truly. I do not presume."

Since when? "If you wanted to hybridize, all you'd have to do is go to John and say the word."

"He would enjoy it too much, I believe."

"There would be something rather circular about it, yes." Jani watched a sailracer's rainbow-hued craft swoop in the distance. "It is a good place."

"It is." Tsecha nodded. "It is *warm*, which is a wonder. I did not believe that I would ever enjoy such again." He started down the beach. "Come, nìa. We must speak of ná Gisa again. I fear and truly that she will drive me most as mad."

"In a minute, inshah." Jani stretched her arms over her head, as though she could reach the few wisps of cloud that coursed the sky if she tried hard enough. After a few moments she let them fall to her sides. Rocked back and forth, heel to toe to heel, inhaling the sea air and listening to the birds screech. Then . . .

. . . *she reached into her pocket and removed a stone, one of the banded triangles that are so numerous here. She looked out over the water, as she has done so often since her return. Bending low, she tossed the stone atop the curved mass of them that had washed up over the years past. Then she started down the beach after ní Tsecha, running until she caught up to him, and they talked until sunset.*

ENDGAME

For my Mom and Dad

ACKNOWLEDGMENTS

The list of people who have helped me over the course of this book, and this series, began long and over the years has grown ever longer. In particular, many thanks are due Katharine Eliska Kimbriel, who started as a teacher and became a friend. Elizabeth Moon, who took me under her wing at my very first science fiction convention—Intersection '95 Glasgow (yes, I know—first con was a Worldcon—what was I thinking?)—and made me feel welcome. Joshua Bilmes, who believed in the series and sold it. First readers Dave Godwin and Dave Klecha, for their input and expertise. Berry Kercheval, Melanie Miller Fletcher, Julia Blackshear Kosatka, Tom Hise, and Doranna Durgin, and the rest of my online gang, for support online and in emails, for listening to my wails. Julie Czerneda, for reading the *Endgame* draft and for that one phone call that helped so much. Diana Gill, my editor since the beginning, for her patience, and because she always asked the deceptively simple question that turned the tale on its ear and helped make it better.

And finally, to Mom and Dad, who I know are watching.

CHAPTER 1

The altar room in the Haárin transept of Elyas Station proved much more suitable than Imea nìaRauta Rilas had feared, warm and quiet as any in Rauta Shèràa. A place of clean, white stone, dark woods, and polished silver metal. A place of preparation, and acceptance of the will of the gods.

She had spent half the station-morning in prayer, as was proper for a godly bornsect. She had stood with her back straight, arms raised above her head, and intoned supplications to her favored goddess until the dry air rasped her throat and she grew light-headed from having stood so still for so long. Now, she lowered her arms in a smooth downward sweep, the cramps in her muscles and pain in her joints blending to form yet another prayer.

As her hands fell to her sides, Rilas felt the cuffs of her shirt tumble over her wrists. How she hated this shirt, its blue as blinding as that of an alarm illumin. How she hated her trousers, as purple as her shirt was blue. She thought of her usual clothing, her flowing trousers and overrobe in subtle shades of sand and stone. Her soft tan boots, so much more appropriate than the stiff black things she wore now. She imagined her hair as it should have been, arranged in the braided fringe of a breeder instead of as it was now, loose as a mane, its only binding a leather coil. *A horse-tail.* Such was what the Haárin called the style, in imitation of the humanish.

Anathema.

Rilas turned and walked to the narrow bench next to the entry, where she had set her slingbag. She hoisted it to her shoulder, felt its comforting heft bump her hip. So many things did it contain. And still a few more did she need to add. *Such I must do, and quickly.* Before it came time for her to board her shuttle to the city of Karistos.

Yet as much as she wished to depart, still she hesitated. She felt agitated, angered, as she had so often over the course of her journey from her blessed homeworld of Shèrá to this most ungodly of destinations. So much planning and preparation. *And now I am here.* At that point where planning and preparation transmuted into action and realization. Completion. Triumph.

And yet . . .

Rilas let the bag slide down her shoulder onto the top of the bench. She opened the flap and hunted, through the clothes and the tile samples and all those other objects of no importance. Once she reached the bottom support panel, she touched first one corner, then the one diagonally opposite. The panel separated from the bag frame with a soft *click*. She pushed it to one side and reached into the shielded compartment beneath, felt the tension leave her as soon as she put her hand on the shooter.

She lifted the weapon from its hiding place, confirmed its standby setting by pure reflex, then turned to a bare wall and sighted down. The case fit the curve of her hand, the weight filling an emptiness she had not realized she felt until now. Yet she knew she should not have felt surprise, for such was as it had always been. She possessed metal in her soul, nìRau Cèel had once told her, and as always he spoke truth.

Rilas bared her teeth. *Such is as I am.* Joy filled her as the air she breathed. Even her godless apparel no longer angered her. She always felt most as herself when she held a weapon in her hand.

She stood for some moments, arm extended, imagining targets past, targets yet to come. Then she lowered her arm, this time more slowly. Turned back to her slingbag and returned the shooter to its hiding place. Refastened the bag, raised it again to her shoulder, and departed.

The Elyas Station passenger concourse battered Rilas to the pit of her soul. Voices, humanish and Haárin, combined to a cacophony that pierced the brain. Corridors as long tunnels, walls colored red and blue and purple, lined with darkened rooms—the interiors of which she could not see, marked by signs she did not understand. Smells, ungodly and sickening, a mingling of hot foods and brewed drinks and bodies that had not entered a laving room for days. Tension, as those stenches enveloped her and those bodies passed close enough to touch.

She glanced at an idomeni timeform that hung from a purple-tinged wall, and her step slowed. Her shuttle had not yet arrived at its dock. Once more she had miscalculated, rushed when she did not need to do so. Once more she had time.

More time than I need. Her usual problem, and also, she knew, the cause of her anger. For that time needed to be spent somewhere, and as she traveled on public spacecraft, that meant she spent it in places such as these. Mongrel places, tainted by humanish, and by Haárin who had lost their Way. She watched them walk with one another, converse with one another, these misbegottens. Humanish, their hair braided in breeder's fringes whether they had bred or not, their clothes the flowing overrobes of the most strict bornsect. Haárin, hair clipped skull-close or left unbound, the females in wraps of cloth that clasped their forms or fluttered about them as though torn by winds, the females and males both in blinding patterns and colors avoided by even the most unruly outcast.

Yet I appear as one with them. Rilas pressed a hand to her stomach, and felt her soul rumble. *Elyas is a godless place,* Cèel had warned her, *more so than any of the others you have visited. There, you will witness such as you never imagined possible.* She remembered the weariness in his posture as he spoke, the anger in his bowed shoulders and the turn of his head.

"Soon, nìRau," Rilas whispered to herself. "Soon it will be as it was." As the gods meant it to be, before all had been sundered and defiled. Before the ungodly had put it wrong. "I shall put it most right, and truly." She lowered her hand from her stomach and clenched it. "Soon."

She stood in place and uttered another prayer to her favored goddess, and felt herself calm. So often had she called upon Caith in her times of uncertainty, and just as often had Caith heard her pleas and brought her peace. *In your blessed chaos, goddess, allow me to find my Way.* She kept her head bowed as she prayed, and pretended to read the covers of an array of newssheets displayed in a shop window. In a godly place, she would stand most straight, as she had in the altar room. Then she would raise her hands above her head and plead to Caith in the keening voice of an abject suborn. *But such would call attention, and I am about on secret business.* Business such as that which she had performed on Amsun, and before that on Padishah and so many other humanish places. She bared her teeth for a moment only, savoring the pleasure of her task. *I perform as I must in the midst of my enemies, and it is their methods that I use.* From her names, to her clothes, to the information in the documents she carried, she was as a liar, and when she lied, she became as one with her goddess. *I am of Caith now.* She raised her head to stare at her blurred reflection in the glass, and the warmth of peace filled her. *I am as chaos—*

She sensed a shape out of the corner of her eye, a shadow she had not detected before. Her heart slowed, its beat strengthening. She turned, her hands raised to chest level. Made ready to strike, as she had so many times before—

—but saw no enemy, only a misshapen thing perched atop a pedestal, grey as old stone, tongue lolling and teeth bared. She stepped closer and examined a face as long as a beast's. Then she moved on to its clawed hands, reaching out and touching the cold, smooth surface.

"It's called a gargoyle."

Rilas turned to find a humanish standing at her shoulder. A male, dark-skinned as a Pathen. He wore his black hair clipped short, as was proper for his kind. But he dressed in a most outrageous Haárin style, his shirt and trousers assaulting the eye in clashing shades of green and orange. He looked her in the eye as he spoke, as was the humanish way. A most unseemly familiarity.

"They're the guardians of this place. They watch over the pilots, the mechanics." He edged closer to Rilas, until his shoulder grazed hers. "We've never had an accident with fatalities at this port. We're the only station in the Commonwealth that can make that claim."

Rilas took a full step back, as she had been taught. *You must be most direct and obvious when you repel humanish males,* one instructor had told her most long ago, *otherwise they do not understand.* Many found the long limbs and gold-toned skins of idomeni females attractive, and the efforts of some of them to convince the idomeni females of such had led to unseemly incidents. *I can allow no unseemly incidents now.* Thus would her trained hands remain at her sides, and her yen for the shedding of blood remain unsatisfied.

"I have never seen one of these gargoyles before." Rilas kept all inflection from her voice, and did not look the male in the face. His sort found idomeni eyes most attractive as well, a fact beyond understanding. *Cat eyes,* they called them. *Fool,* Rilas thought, *and blind besides.* She had studied many images of cats, and none of their eyes appeared as hers. Her pupils were as round, not slitted, her iris and sclera dark and pale gold, not a single color. Not as a cat's at all.

"You've never visited our famous station before?" The male bared his teeth. "The architect wanted to construct a Gothic cathedral in the outer reaches of the Commonwealth. There were plenty who said we should have stopped her, but scratch an Elyan and you'll find two things—a unique sense of humor, and bred-in-the-bone pissiness about being told what to do." He pointed toward the wall at the far end of the tunnel-like concourse. "We're particularly proud of our Rose Window."

Rilas looked to the immense circle of glass that filled the space, whorls of blue and yellow separated by translucent red. Blessed red. The holiest of colors. The privilege of priests, used to tint an artificial window that spread artificial light over this most blasted and soulless of places. "A godless thing, and truly," she said, turning away from the sight that even her love of chaos could not make as right.

The male tilted his head and tried to draw her gaze. "I admit this place isn't to everyone's taste." He waited, as though expecting Rilas to respond. When she did not do so, he backed away from her. "There is an area in the east corridor set aside for the more orthodox idomeni." He jerked his head downward, a rough humanish bow. "My apologies for bothering you."

Rilas watched him go, remaining still until his garish form disappeared among the crowd and she felt sure that he would not return. Only then did she walk across the concourse and enter the locker area where Haárin passengers stored their belongings between flights. She encountered several as she made her way down the narrow corridor, and noted that she appeared most as they did. She looked as her name now, ná Nahin Sela, the oddity with which nìRau Cèel had christened her before she left behind the warmth of her native Rauta Shèràa and departed her blessed homeworld of Shèrá. Her dominant had never before chosen the name under which she would perform her assigned tasks, but in this instance they had both felt it appropriate. Most seemly, and truly.

"Nahin." She walked the narrow aisles separating the rows of lockers, repeating her name as some did their gate numbers and departure times. When she came to her locker, she acted the tired traveler in case she encountered any other Haárin, fumbling with the touchlock and struggling to remove the bags as she had seen others do. This was not difficult, as the handle of one bag was not long enough to loop over her shoulder and the other felt as though it had been filled with bricks.

Fools! When next she spoke with those who had rented this locker and left the bags for her, she would berate them. Her travel documents listed her vocation as "tile broker." Did those who assembled that which she needed think she meant to carry tiles on her person! She hefted her clumsy burden of purchases and baggage and hunted for a laving room.

By the time she found an empty laving cubicle, the first call for her shuttle sounded throughout the locker area. She opened the cubicle door with a vend token and edged inside, the weighty bags banging against her shins. She hefted them atop the narrow counter, then began her preparations.

First, she removed cleansing materials and washed her face and hands, tucking strands of hair behind her ears and studying herself in the small mirror. *Most as humanish, and truly.* She wrote a symbol in the air as a gesture against demons, then resumed her search through the smaller of her bags, rooting past shoes and a tightly folded weatherall until she came to the thing she sought.

The small case looked as something that would hold earrings or hair ornaments. Indeed, when she opened it, such was what she found. She fingered past the fine gold loops and tangles of braided cord and beads until she found that for which she searched. A ring, alternating bands of gold and silver set with a scattering of small stones.

Using her thumbnail, Rilas worked one of the stones loose from its setting. The colorless disc appeared smooth and featureless to her eye. She held it to the cubicle light and tilted it back and forth, in search of any scratch or crack. Satisfied that none existed, she held the disc under the faucet and rinsed it under a stream of warm water, working it between her fingers as she did. Just as it flexed and began to soften, she positioned it on the tip of her index finger and bent low over the sink, using the thumb and index finger of her free hand to hold open her right eye.

She flinched as the warmed plastic touched the surface of her eye. The disc adhered and spread, squeezing her cornea—tears dripped into the sink as she fought the urge to sneeze, forced herself still, and quiet. She had performed the same action on Amsun, on Padishah, and numerous other places, yet every time, it felt as a surprise. She blinked once, slowly, and felt the lens settle into place. Blinked again. Then she raised her head and looked into the mirror.

Her right eye looked much as it always did. Shinier due to the tears, but not injured. She leaned toward the mirror and looked more closely, until she was satisfied that the edges of the lens were as invisible. She waited until it absorbed its weight in water and the squeezing feeling subsided, then picked up the small case once more and resumed her exploration.

The second thing for which she searched, she found stuck to the end of a hair clasp. She pried this clear disc from its setting as she had the lens, then warmed it under running water, massaging it until it, too, softened. Then she held it to the opening of her right ear, shivering as she felt it adhere and spread. "Fourteen," she whispered, knowing from experience that the sensor that had attached itself within her ear canal would replay her voice as though she spoke aloud. "Fourteen times have I performed these acts as my dominant has bidden me." She would speak her thoughts aloud from now on, and use exact numbers, dates, hours. The time had come to be precise in all things.

"I am Imea nìaRauta Rilas, and this is my book." She spoke to the mirror, and imagined the lens recording her reflection, her expression, as she knew it did. "I speak from laving cubicle number ten, locker area seven-oh-four, level fourteen, east transept, Elyas Station." She paused, then uttered the date, the time. "My purpose in coming here is to kill ní Tsecha Egri, at the bidding of my most godly dominant, Morden nìRau Cèel."

Rilas tensed as the second call for her shuttle echoed. Outside her cubicle door, up and down the aisle, voices rose. Doors clicked open. Footsteps sounded. She closed the jewelry case, returned it to the small bag, and resumed her search. *If I miss this shuttle, I will forfeit my billet.* Purchasing another would be simple enough, but it would be best, she decided, if she left this mongrel place as quickly as she could. Too many dangers awaited out in the concourse. Too many friendly humanish males. Too many chances to be remembered.

She paused, and willed herself calm. There was still one more thing she needed to find, and if she could not do so, there would be no point in continuing. She set aside the small bag and opened the larger one. The things she had thought felt like bricks proved to be embossed metal cases of the type that opened to form displays. "Displays for ná Nahin, a broker in tile." She opened one case, then another, feeling her calm ebb as the seconds passed and she flipped open cases then slammed them shut as prayers turned to curses and her temper rose—

She found it in the last case, on the bottom of the bag, as was usual. A flat container the size of her hand, greyed blue in color and cold to the touch. She scraped a fingernail over the surface and watched as a thin layer of frost curled, then evaporated. She held the container gingerly, using her fingertips only, so as not to warm it too much, and opened the lid.

The cold that emerged caused condensate to form in the air above—Rilas waved it away with one hand to prevent the moisture from settling on the most special objects within. Her prizes, so carefully designed and produced.

The projectiles filled both sides of the container, arranged lengthwise and nestled in molded depressions in the inner liner. Three on each side for a total of six—two less than she had wanted, but those who made them had told her that she was lucky to get as many as this. *So they said. So they claimed.* She never knew when to believe scientists. They shied away from her, and avoided telling her all they knew unless ordered by nìRau Cèel. *And even then . . .* She wondered about them, even as she knew that they had no choice but to aid her.

She lifted one of the projectiles from its niche and held it up as she had the lens. Muted silver—as long as her small finger, tapered at one end and flattened on the other—the small missile caught the cubicle light and split it as a prism would, sending a shard of rainbow shimmering across the ceiling. Rilas tilted it one way, then the other, looking for seaming or an opening, an inner darkness or shape that revealed that which it contained. Then she returned it to its place and closed the case. Tucked the case back in the bag and closed that as well. Tossed shop wrappings in the trash bin and gathered her baggage. She had all she needed now. It was well and truly time to leave.

The rasp of her boot soles against the bare floor filled the cubicle area. She met no one until she made her way through the narrow, winding aisles and reentered the concourse. The racket of voices battered her for an instant only, receding to nothing as the calm overtook her. Such was a familiar sensation, one she esteemed as she did her dominant and her goddess. She and her task had become one, and would remain as such until she discharged it.

As Rilas approached her gate, she passed a news kiosk. It was a humanish-looking thing, rounded as a hive, covered from floor to top with signs advertising concourse shops and with bright images from the covers of magazines. She quickened her step as she approached the garish thing—such subject matter held no interest for her.

Then one image among the many caught her eye. Her step slowed, then stopped. She approached the kiosk and with a cautious hand removed the latest copy of an Elyan publication from its rack.

The face that stared back at her, she had seen too many times before. In reports from her dominant, compiled by his spies who labored throughout the humanish Commonwealth. In holoVee displays, when important events of the past months replayed. In her mind's eye, as she considered her task and all that might prevent its completion. The face, brown-gold as some Pathen. The eyes, green as Sìah. The hair, black and clipped as short as that of the most ungodly Haárin.

Kilian. The name choked Rilas. Jani Kilian. The Kièrshia. The Toxin. The bringer of pain and change. Rilas felt her calm depart as she thought of her, living a damned life in a damned place on the world around which Elyas Station orbited. Once, Kilian had worn the uniform of her soldierly Service and committed crimes that it pained any godly idomeni to recall. Now, twenty humanish years later, she served as a priest at the bidding of godless Tsecha, a mockery of all in which any godly idomeni believed. Ruled over a mongrel enclave that had no right to exist, a place of infamy and broken faith, of false teachers and the lies they spread to promote their own power.

"Toxin." Rilas touched a finger to the middle of Jani Kilian's forehead and traced a small circle once, then again. As the final call for her shuttle sounded, she paid for the magazine with a vend token. Then she rolled it so as to hide Kilian's face and hurried to her gate.

CHAPTER 2

> . . . for these reasons, the wholeness of a soul is not
> dependent upon the health or condition of the physical
> body in which it resides, and those who espouse such
> are ignorant of the will of the gods. Therefore, to allow
> the death of a body for the stated purpose of preserving
> the integrity of its soul is as sacrilege, and those who
> defend and perform such acts are as anathema . . .

Jani Kilian read the passage once, then again. Then she closed the
leather-bound scroll and backed away from the pedestal on which
it rested for the first few steps, reluctant to turn around. *It won't
bite.* Well, not yet anyway. "When will you publish it?"

Ní Tsecha Egri stood in front of the workroom's narrow window and looked out over the Bay of Siros. His orange shirt rivaled
the rising Elyan sun in brilliance, his bright blue trousers sedate
by comparison. He wore his hair in the idomeni equivalent of a
Service burr, and the blaze of backlight through the glass rendered
the short, pale brown strands nearly invisible, accentuating the
outline of his skull.

He cracked open the pane seals, allowing the smells of sea and
sun into the workroom. "I already have, nìa." He didn't look at her
as he spoke. "Ná Meva sent the transmission to Rauta Shèràa
Temple yesterday evening."

Ná Meva. Jani imagined the elder female bearing down on the
enclave com room, the wafer containing Tsecha's treatise gripped
like a ward against demons, grey-streaked horsetail flicking with
each stride. *Yet another exiled propitiator.* At the Elyan enclave only
a few weeks, and already Tsecha's invaluable sounding board in
matters of theology. *They're two peas in a pod.* Meva as eager to disseminate her dominant's seditious essays as he was to write them.

Unlike some of us. Jani slumped against the wall and tugged at
the front of her grey wrapshirt, a near perfect match for her grey

trousers. She never felt comfortable in the clashing bright colors that most Haárin and Thalassans wore, preferring to stay with drab and somber despite the ribbing she occasionally took. "If you already sent it, why pretend to ask my advice?"

"I do not *pretend*, nìa." Tsecha's shoulders rounded in anger. "I esteem your advice." He straightened slowly. "I did consider my arguments with care. I spent much time reevaluating bornsect histories. I could find no flaw. I then gave a draft to ná Meva, and she could find nothing to dispute."

"You showed it to her before you sent it." Jani heard her own voice, soft and steady, and wondered at her calm. "But not to your religious suborn. Not to the one you're training to take your place. Not to me."

Tsecha stilled, his hesitation obvious. Weighing his words— another humanish habit he had adopted. "You have learned much these past months, but not enough to contribute to this level of discourse." He looked across the room at Jani, the backlight casting his face in shadow, obscuring his expression. "Not yet. In time, yes, I will discuss these matters with you in the same depth as I do with Meva, but until that time . . ." His voice had grown quieter, the usual booming baritone thinned and drained. "I must be sure of the logic of my arguments. Rauta Shèràa Temple will take any error and use it to render the entire treatise as nothing, and I cannot allow that to occur."

Jani pushed away from the wall and paced the workroom. It was the largest and most well-appointed space in the small house, which was located in the heart of the Thalassan enclave. Tsecha had claimed it as his own despite the objections of ná Feyó Tal, the dominant of the Elyan Haárin and his nominal superior, who felt he should reside within her enclave. But bowing to authority had never been one of Tsecha's traits. *Neither is listening, come to that.* "You've called the entire concept of Wholeness of Soul into question. One of the cornerstones of Vynshàrau faith."

"Most other bornsects believe in the concept as well, to their great detriment." Tsecha once more turned his face to the window. "It is an argument that needs to be made."

But do you have to make it now? Jani kept her comment to herself. She'd never held back her own actions for the sake of anyone, family or lover or friend. Maybe this was just life's way of paying back with interest. "The new meeting room's not ready. Dathim told me he'll have to work through the night."

"You change the subject, nìa. Have I angered you that much?" Tsecha shut the pane, then turned and walked to his worktable, a V-shaped stone slab that took up almost a quarter of the room. "So he will work. So he will complain. And still the room will be completed on schedule, and the visit will take place tomorrow, as is planned." He fussed with a stack of wafer folders. "It is a social visit, nìa. So Governor Markos has told us. A courtesy call. I do not know why you worry so."

Jani stopped in front of the table and studied her old teacher. Read their shared history in his stark, high-boned face, the mutiny, and the subterfuge, and the lies. "Governor Stanislaw Markos of the Commonwealth colony of Elyas is coming here to ask you to act as go-between for him with Wuntoi and the other anti-Cèel bornsect dominants. He's bringing with him the governors of Amsun and Hortensia."

Tsecha rolled his eyes, but the gold on gold shading of his sclera and irises blunted his attempted display of humanish irritation. "I know all this, nìa. I do not know why you are telling—"

"Secession. Elyas wants to secede from the Commonwealth, and Amsun and Hortensia and the rest of the Outer Circle want to go with her. They believe Cèel is on the way out, and the Vynshàrau with him, and they want to make nice with Wuntoi and his Pathen because they're the likeliest successors. That's why they need you. They know they'll need the support of the Outer Circle Haárin to have any hope of pulling this off, and the Haárin support Wuntoi as the next Oligarch." Jani planted her hands atop the table, spread her fingers, pondered her gold-brown skin. "This could blow up fast. You should be keeping your head down now, for the sake of Markos and the others, if not for your own, and instead you're attracting attention—"

"The danger is the governors', nìa. They are the ones who wish to secede." Tsecha leaned against the table, his voice deceptively light. "If their attempt fails, it does not affect the Elyan Haárin."

Jani fought the urge to grab Tsecha by the shoulders and shake him. "Thalassa, in case you've forgotten, is in a different situation than the Haárin enclave. You'll dodge the spray when it hits the fan. You'll be able to leave. You'll have a place to go. But what the hell do you think will happen to Thalassa? We're hybrids, in a diplomatic no-man's-land—" She stopped when she heard her voice ring in her ears and saw Tsecha's shoulders start to curve. "You could have waited," she said after her heart slowed and her hands unclenched. "Your treatises. You could have published them some other time."

"They are necessary now, nìa." Tsecha averted his gaze as he spoke, something he seldom did when they stood so close together. "To alter thinking. To persuade, and enrage."

"I think you have the 'enrage' part covered." Jani turned and walked to the other side of the room. "I'm not too sure about 'alter' and 'persuade.'" She stopped in front of a display niche and plucked a small stone ovoid from its base. "It's hard to get anyone to listen once tempers overheat," she said as she hefted the stone. "I should know."

"I must speak. I must protest—"

"But why now?"

"You do not—"

"I don't mean to interrupt."

Jani and Tsecha both fell silent and looked toward the entryway.

"Ní Tsecha. Jan." Colonel Niall Pierce doffed his brimmed white lid and stepped just inside the room. "Just came from the new meeting house. Checking on preparations for tomorrow." He wore semiformal kit of dress desertweights, the white tunic and gold-trimmed headgear startling against his tan trousers and sunbaked face. "Dodging flying tile shards." He grinned, the scar that cut his face from his nose to the corner of his mouth twisting the expression into something sinister. "Ní Dathim Naré is not happy."

"Dathim is never happy." Tsecha gestured impatience, the edge of his hand cutting through the air like a blade. "Always he complains of schedules, of lack of supplies, of . . ."

Jani watched Niall, who seemed transfixed by Tsecha's rant. *He knows we're meeting the governors, but he can't figure out why.* She had tried to keep him from getting involved in the security arrangements for the get-together, but he was Admiral General Hiroshi Mako's man on the spot, and the presence of three high-level colonial officials dictated his participation. *He'll escort them here and wait outside while we talk to them. He won't be able to find out a thing.* She hoped. She prayed.

". . . and still, he is not satisfied!" Tsecha stepped around the table and strode to the door. "I will go and speak with him." He brushed past Niall, barreling through the foyer and into the street. "Ridiculous, and truly . . ."

Jani stepped outside in time to see the brightly garbed figure vanish down an alley between two houses. Sensed Niall draw alongside, and felt his stare etch the side of her face. "Go ahead and say it."

"I never thought I'd see Tsecha grasping for an excuse to get the hell away from you." Niall set his lid back atop his head, then squared it by running the thumbs and forefingers of both hands back and forth along the brim. "I debated whether to go in. Then your voices began carrying and folks stuck their heads out to listen. Decided I had better throw myself on the grenade before they started selling tickets."

Jani glanced toward a nearby house in time to see a head duck back inside a doorway. "We weren't that loud."

"The sound-shielding doesn't exist that can filter out ní Tsecha Egri once he boils over." Niall stared up at a seabird that swooped overhead. "Anything you can talk about?"

Jani gauged the man out of the corner of her eye. With his skin, uniform, and bronze Service burr, he appeared as grave as she, a study in brown and white. He stood a little shorter than she did, his frame lean and muscled, his narrow, wolfish face hardened further by the cheek-cleaving scar. Only his eyes, honey brown and long-lashed, offered a sense of his humor, his well-schooled intellect, his warmth.

His nosiness. Jani pretended interest in the blooms that filled a streetside planter. "What's the word?"

Niall studied her for a moment, then shrugged. "Avelos and the Amsun gang just arrived and are currently ensconced in Markos's villa. Wallach and the Hortensian contingent won't arrive until dawn. Cutting it close, in my opinion, but they didn't ask my advice regarding travel arrangements." He drew closer and lowered his voice as a trio of Thalassans emerged from a house across the way. "Jan? We may be on different sides of the fence, but I can still listen to whatever you can afford to tell me."

It's your skill at filling in blanks that worries me, Colonel. Jani watched as more Thalassans wandered into the street. "Do you want to take a walk?"

Niall exhaled with a grumble. "You want to walk, we'll walk."

They set off along the narrow lane, past the low, white houses with their arched doorways and passages and domed roofs in shades of blue and yellow. While a few Thalassans had brought plants from their home colonies to display in window boxes and planters, native flora dominated the landscaping. Instead of hybrid lawn, creepers in blue and red-dappled green carpeted the spaces between houses, their low tangle broken up with clusters of the same brilliantly flowered shrubs that dotted the hillsides. Like Karistos, Thalassa hugged the cliff line, and the creepers had been trained to stream over the edge, fringing the rock face with variegated ropes of leaves. Views of the Bay of Siros filled the eye from three directions, and the buildings closest to the brink had been trimmed with terraces so Thalassans could enjoy them whenever they wished.

"I still can't get used to this scenery. Been here six months Common and it still takes my breath away." Niall leaned against a guardrail and pulled his nicstick case from his trouser pocket. "So." He removed a silvery cylinder and crunched the ignition tip, then stuck the filter end in his mouth and took a pull. "You two having another difference of opinion?"

Now it was Jani's turn to shrug. "It happens."

"More and more, seems like. What was it this time?"

Jani rolled up her shirtsleeves and held out her arms so the sun could warm them. "I thought that Thalassa would take the place of Rauta Shèràa for him, that he'd come to consider it home. Now I think it reminds him of what he lost. He spent his entire adult life up to his chin in worldskein politics. He was one of the most influential idomeni who ever lived."

"He still is, gel." Niall tugged at his tunic's banded collar, then wiped a few beads of sweat from his brow. Even with cooling cell-equipped clothing, Elyan heat battered non-native humanish with ovenlike intensity. "Just because Cèel stripped him of a title and made him Haárin? Doesn't mean a damned thing to anyone I talk to. Call him by his bornsect name, Avrèl nìRau Nema. Or call him Egri nìRau Tsecha or ní Tsecha Egri or a sack of laundry. He's still a power to be reckoned with." He stepped back from the rail until the shade of one of the Karistos region's weird palm trees fell across him. "Cèel thought that if he made him Haárin, he'd neuter him. All it did was give him the freedom to rebuild his power base, surround himself with like minds." He took a last drag on his 'stick, then flicked the spent cylinder into a trash bin.

"He never needed moral support, or an audience." Jani pushed down her sleeves and refastened the cuffs. "He believes that which he believes. Fine. It's not just duty that compels him to speak out, it's something more. It's in his blood and bone, the air he breathes. He could no more keep quiet about what he feels is wrong with Vynshàrau religious doctrine than I could flap my arms and fly across the bay."

She paced along the rail. "But what he doesn't realize, or *want* to realize, is that every time he shoots off his mouth, I'm the one who gets hit with the flak. Questions about where *I* stand. Rumors that Thalassa is a training ground for anti-Commonwealth extremists. And when I try to tell him that Thalassa doesn't have a diplomatic leg to stand on, that Chicago is afraid of us and *his* radicalism is assumed to be *our* radicalism, he tells me that I do not know of that which I speak." She stopped and glared out at the sun-seared water until her eyes teared from the brightness. "So on he flames. I put out one fire, and a week or two later another pops up to take its place." She turned to Niall to find him leaning on the rail and watching her, his head cocked. "What?" She caught the bare twitch of his lip, and felt her face heat. "Shut up."

"I'm not saying a word." Niall straightened, then pulled a linen square from his trouser pocket. "And I'm not taking one iota of cold pleasure in this at all, even though any sort of chill would feel like heaven at the moment." He ran the cloth over his face, then folded it into a tight square and tucked it up his sleeve. " 'How does it feel?' will never cross my—"

"*Niall.*"

Niall raised his hands in mock surrender. Let them fall, and walked toward the stand of weird palms. "You and I . . ." He lowered onto a rickety chair someone had left beneath. Braced his hands on his knees and looked out at nothing. "We had to build walls around parts of our lives. It's not always easy. I know you well enough to pick up when you're holding back, and I'd guess you could say the same about me. It's difficult, dealing with the conflicts and the suspicion. But when you've a friend . . ." He switched his gaze to the flagstone at his feet. "It's worth it." He sat still and silent for a time, then shook his head as though awakening from a daze. "Tsecha's a strategist, a thinker. You're more a tactician, a field man. I always thought you complimented one another well."

"That depends on whether we're fighting the same battle, doesn't it?" Jani kicked at a loose flake of flagstone, sending it skittering across the terrace. "If we start to fight one another, who do you think has the advantage?"

Niall sat back and folded his arms. "The strategist. They would take the long view, have backup plans in place. But sometimes they get wrapped up in theory and miss details . . ." Again, a shake of the head. Harder, this time. "Tsecha would sooner die than fall out with you. I think it would break his heart." His eyes widened. "*Christ, Jan.*" A scrabble for another nicstick. The sharp *crunch*, followed by the cloud of smoke. "Growing pains. This place has exploded since you arrived here a year ago, and you're still shaking things out. He's adjusting to life in the enclave. You're adjusting to duties as a priest-in-training and the dominance of Thalassa. Stands to reason you'd fight. If you didn't, I'd ask John to check your vitals."

Jani looked toward the settlement, the newest homes that stood on what a month ago had been open land. "There are those here who have no place else to go. Their families disowned them when they hybridized, and their governments don't trust them because they don't know whose side they're on. If Chicago decides that there's some sort of militant hotbed developing here, what action do you think they'll take? Hell, Niall, you get the memos. You have the list of who to pick up first." *And I bet I know whose name is at the top.*

Niall looked everywhere but at her. "I take from this that we have another theological essay to look forward to." He glanced at her sidelong, then turned his attention to his nicstick, working his thumbnail between the filter and the body and prying them apart. "I've read the previous offerings, in translation, of course. He does tend toward the carpet bomb approach when it comes to stating his case."

"He's idomeni. Carpet bombing is standard operating procedure." Jani tapped a beat atop the rail. "He will make his point, regardless of the cost to himself. Or anyone else."

"And you won't?" Niall stared at the dismembered 'stick as though he'd never seen it before, then tossed it into the trash bin. "Parts of Chicago still bear the scorch marks, Jan. You're as radical as he is."

"Would you believe I'm learning circumspection?"

"Not without witnesses."

Jani grinned, but the expression soon faded. "We're here on sufferance, we Thalassans. Beggars, being allowed a place to squat because we're quiet and don't bother anyone." She motioned to Niall, then started walking across the terrace back to the house-lined street. "That can change so quickly, and then what?"

"You're worried that Stash Markos will kick you off Elyas. *You?*" Niall rose and fell in beside her. "He never struck me as the type to harbor a death wish. You're talking nonsense, gel." He glanced overhead and sighed. "I blame this damned sun." He fell silent, fixed on the uphill climb. Then he drew a deep breath. "So, I expect that Markos and the others are coming here to consult with Tsecha about that bombing at the Haárin docks on Amsun."

Not up to your usual standard, Colonel. Jani struggled to keep her face blank. *You're usually so much more subtle when you pry.*

"Yes. They want to make sure the word gets out that they support the Amsun Haárin, and that they'll not rest until they apprehend the parties responsible." And there was her reply, just as stilted. But as good a tale as any, and even more so for being partly true.

Niall studied her, the brim of his lid shading his eyes, hiding them from her gaze. Then he gripped her elbow and pulled her to a stop. "Whatever happens, whatever—" He looked up the street, now filled with hybrids working, talking, and lowered his voice to a rough whisper. "You'll get some warning. I know people. I'll get you out."

"What about John and the others?" Jani nodded toward the bustle. "I wouldn't leave without them." She watched Niall look up the street again. Saw his shoulders sag, and knew his thoughts as though he spoke them aloud. *It's a town now, Niall, with schools and shops, a Net station and a shuttleport. How do you evacuate it without anyone knowing?* She resumed walking, then paused until Niall caught her up. "Mako still give you a hard time about hanging around with me?"

Niall shook his head. "Not as much as he used to."

Meaning he's happy to have a spy in the midst of this brew. Jani pressed a hand to the back of her neck and tried to massage away the growing tightness. "Did you want to check out the meeting house again? Maybe the shards have stopped fly—"

The siren cut the air like a scream, stopping everyone in mid-word, mid-stride. Blessed silence fell for an instant, then another howl. A youngster cried for her home-parent. A few hybrids headed for doorways.

"Shuttle's coming!" a male shouted as he started trotting up the street. "That's the new signal."

Jani looked at Niall, to find that he had pulled his shooter, his knuckles blanched against tanned skin.

"*Jesus.* Maybe you could tell your crew to lower the pitch a little." He powered down the weapon and holstered it. "Damned thing sounds like a shatterbox just before it hits. Bloody banshee wail—"

"I'll tell them." Jani pulled in a deep breath in a futile bid to slow her fluttering heart. "Looks like we have a visitor." She started to walk, one slow step after another. *Breathe. Breathe.*

"Wallach? His crew is scheduled to touch down at Karistos. That's where my team is." Niall quickened his pace and brushed past her, funneling his panic into motion and anger. "Flying fuck governors with their flying fuck timelines and their flying fuck—"

He touched his ear, activating the comlink to whichever subordinate was unlucky enough to be first in the queue. "Beck! What the hell—"

Jani held back until Niall had moved well out of earshot. Inhaled, and felt her heart trip, then slow. Continued to walk up the road, lined with low white houses . . . felt the sun . . . the heat . . .

. . . *the slip of sand beneath her boots . . . a sensation of sliding . . .*

. . . *the hum of a shooter, the pound of her heart . . .*

. . . *the line of tents.*

She closed her eyes. *Please, Lord. Not now,* she prayed. *Not now.*

CHAPTER 3

By the time Jani reached the landing field, the rest of the enclave had already gathered along the runway. She scanned the crowd and spotted a cluster of medcoat-clad Thalassans crowded around a tall, slim figure, like children around a parent.

John Shroud surveyed the scene like a landowner regarding his domain. He smiled when he spotted Jani, and freed himself from the confines of his laboratory tribe. As always, he wore formal clothes beneath his medcoat, a daysuit in palest grey undertoned with blue. His wheat-blond hair had been freshly clipped into a Caesar fringe, which framed and accentuated his monkish visage.

Hello, Doctor. Jani held out her hand, felt her disquiet ease as John's long, strong fingers encircled her own.

"I just spoke with Niall. He's trying to find out who it is." John put his arm around her shoulders and pulled her close. "Governor Wallach's shuttle just touched down at Karistos, so that's off the list. No one's requested permission to make an emergency landing." He looked toward the runway and shrugged. "It's a mystery." He rested his chin atop her head. "Niall seemed a little shaken."

"It was the new approach alarm. It took us both by surprise." Jani backed away so she could look John in the face. "Maybe they could ramp it down just a little bit."

"You're the boss. Tell them. It will be done." John shrugged lightly, a problem easily solved. Then he looked at her, and his gaze altered from affection to professional assessment. "Are you all right?" He moved back so he could see her face more easily. "Niall's not the only one who looks like he's seen a ghost."

"I'm fine." Jani pressed her face against his medcoat, in part so she could take in his scent, but mostly to keep him from questioning her anymore. "There's too much going on is all."

"That's news." John gave her shoulders a squeeze. "I wish Niall would get a move on. Some of us have work to do."

"*I see it!*" someone shouted. "They're coming in over the bay!"

Conversation ceased. Everyone turned toward the water just as a black dot broke through the clouds. It grew rapidly, wings becoming visible, sunlight flashing off the metalloceramic skin.

Jani raised her head and squinted at the approaching shuttle. The underside looked dark, as though the craft had made a bad landing and scraped the hell out of the thermal coating. Then the mess of lines and shading resolved into an all too familiar pattern, two snakes twining around a winged staff. Her stomach tightened. "John? Is that what I think it is?"

"It's a caduceus." John's voice emerged a puzzled rumble. "What the . . . ?"

"It's a Neoclona shuttle, Doctor." Niall shouldered through the crowd to join them. "Expecting any visitors?"

"*No.*" John released Jani and moved closer to the runway's edge as the shuttle passed overhead, then banked for the last time and settled into its final approach, wings flexing and reshaping to compensate for the crosswinds. Then it touched down, dust billowing behind it like a windblown veil, its engines cut back to near silence.

Jani moved in beside John. Took his hand in hers, and felt the barest hint of sweat on his palm.

The shuttle slowed until it drew even with them. As soon as it stopped, the door to the passenger cabin swept upward while the exit stairway emerged and unfolded to the ground.

Valentin Parini stepped up to the threshold before the stairway extended completely. He wore a daysuit in somber greyed green, the severe lines disturbed by the briefbag that hung from one shoulder.

John shook loose Jani's hand, then straightened the already flawless lines of his medcoat.

"I thought he was never supposed to embark on a long haul unless he told you?" Jani watched Val as he let his foot dangle over the first step, waiting for the stairway to stabilize.

"He's not." John's voice sounded like the rumble from the depths of a cave. "It was an agreement he, Eamon, and I made at the beginning, that we would each know where the others were at all times."

"Eamon broke that rule." Jani waited for an answer, and looked over at John to find him watching Val with narrowed eyes.

"Val and I never did." He fell silent, his face a professional mask.

Val collected himself as he started down the stair, disdaining the handholds that ran along both sides. As soon as he hit the ground, he hit his stride, a saunter that had over the years made fists itch and teeth grind from one end of the Commonwealth to the other.

John waited until Val had crossed the invisible halfway point before walking out to meet him. His step was weightier, but just as fluid, with the deceptive quickness of molten metal flow.

Then came the hitch in Val's step, the slowdown as he drew nearer to John. When no more than a couple of meters separated them, he stopped, the shock that filled his eyes at war with the unperturbed attitude he struggled to convey. He shifted his weight from one foot to the other, glancing at Jani without seeing her before returning to John.

It's the first time he's seen John in person since he hybridized. Jani looked at her lover and tried to see him as his best friend did, comparing the albino presence that Val had known so well with the pale blond, gold-skinned figure that stood before him now. *And let's not forget the eyes.* The same silvered blue as John's day-suit, as glittery as jewels when he smiled.

Val fought to appear detached, but his face kept betraying him, dismay and shock and affection jockeying for the lead, with professional curiosity bringing up the rear. His jaw slackened as his eyes widened, the only sound emerging from his mouth a strangled, "I—"

John smiled, stopping just short of a full-blown idomeni teeth-baring. "It really is me, Val."

"Your voice hasn't changed. It still"—Val gestured at waist height—"sounds like it's coming up through the ground." His pronounced widow's peak and arched brows giving his high-boned face a catlike cast. "The Mistys you sent didn't do the transformation justice. My God." He held out his hand. John took it, and they shook. Then the grins broke through and John pulled Val close.

"Any idea what he's doing here?" Niall muttered.

"None." Jani watched man and male hug, Val thumping John's shoulder while John mumbled something that made them both laugh. "I'd like to believe that it's purely a social call, but some-how I doubt it."

Val broke away, wiping his eyes with his sleeve. Then he turned to Jani. "You, my pensive beauty. My one and only girl." He moved in and embraced her, wrapping her in an odd combina-tion of herbal cologne and the ozone sharpness of freshly cleaned cloth. After a moment, he released her and stepped back, lips twitching as though he wanted to say something else but couldn't find the words. His eyes were bloodshot, their deep hazel dulled by spent nerve. He raked a hand through his ash-brown hair, dis-turbing its structured style and looking even more as though he'd just awakened from restless sleep.

Jani struggled with her own conflicting emotions, relishing the sight of her old friend while at the same time wondering why he'd come. "You look tired."

Val shrugged. "Long hauls always wear me down. If the cabin fever doesn't get you, the monotony will." He started to say more, then stopped and hung his head. "There's something else—something I—oh, *hell*." He turned back to the shuttle, one hand pressed to his forehead as though a headache had come to call.

Jani followed his pained gaze, and saw that the passenger cabin door still gaped open, as though someone else still needed to disembark. Then the name formed in her mind just as the all-too-familiar figure stepped into the doorway, white-blond Service burr shining in the sun.

"What in bloody hell . . . ?" Niall's hand went to his sidearm.

Captain Lucien Pascal paused at the top of the stair, looking first toward the bay and the cliffs beyond, then scanning the crowd. He wore desertweights, the sand-toned short-sleeve shirt highlighting his pale hair and tanned skin. As soon as he spotted Jani, he pulled his garrison cap out of his waistband and set it atop his head, then started down the stairs at an easy lope.

"Val?" John's voice was tight, his relaxed air vanished.

"I can explain." Val licked his lips. "It's a *long* story, though."

"I have all the time you need." John drew closer when he real-ized they stood surrounded by perked ears and curious glances. "*Dammit*. Of all the people you could have carted here—"

"Pascal." Niall stepped in front of Jani just as Lucien drew near, blocking him as well as any wall.

"Colonel Pierce, *sir*." Lucien came to attention and snapped a salute, then removed a documents slipcase from his trouser pocket and held it out to Niall. "Captain Lucien Pascal reporting for duty as ordered."

"What?" Niall took the slipcase, ripping open the seals and yanking out the contents, while off to one side John and Val argued in low tones.

Lucien, meanwhile, offered nods and the occasional smile to the Thalassans who had crowded closer. He looked as always like a Service recruitment poster, desertweights fresh, shoes polished to mirror brightness. His orange rank tabs, ribbons, and designators had been perfectly aligned, and his garrison cap set at the optimum angle to imply just enough jaunt with a minimum of cocky. Add to that a frame graced with just the right amount of muscle to flesh out his ranginess, the face of a fallen angel, and chocolate brown eyes that reflected soulless depths, and what you had was the stuff of dreams.

Or in my case, the odd nightmare. Jani surveyed the Thalassans who crowded around them, and to her surprise noted that it was Lucien's forearms and not his looks that attracted the bulk of the attention. Crosshatched by raised scars that had healed white, they served as souvenirs of, judging from the mutterings, one of the more famous battles ever fought by a member of the Commonwealth Service.

"He fought one of Cèel's security dominants within the challenge circle—"

"He killed him."

"He had no choice—"

As usual, Lucien seemed oblivious to the upset he'd caused. He leaned as close to Jani as he dared while Niall continued to pore over his orders. *"Speaking of taking my breath away,"* he whispered in French.

"And he shall spread discord wherever he goes," Jani replied in English. "What the hell are you doing here?"

"Now, is that any way to—"

"Pascal."

Lucien shot Jani a pointed look before drawing up straight and turning to Niall. "Sir."

"I haven't had a chance to check my inbox for my copy of these orders." Niall flicked a corner of the documents sheaf with his fingernail. "Signed by Supreme Command, as I'd have expected." He chose his words with care, loath to even hint at the fact that his revered commander might have inflicted Pascal on him without so much as a "Do you mind?"

"Yessir. Arrangements were made in haste." Lucien's voice came light, imbued with innocence and a sincere desire to help. "Due to the scheduling, I needed to impose upon Doctor Parini and invoke billet privileges in order to arrive in good time." He turned to John. "Please let me know, Doctor Shroud, if Neoclona wishes to pursue remunerations."

"I intend to." John shot another glare at Val, who swallowed hard and fixed on his shoes.

Jani glanced at Niall, who looked ready to smoke the entire contents of his nicstick case at one go.

"We should get inside." Niall folded Lucien's orders and stuffed them back in the slipcase, then turned to Jani. "I would like to use your comroom, if I could."

"Going to shoot Mako a missive?" Jani turned and followed John, who must have decided that they had provided the rest of the enclave with enough gossip fodder for one day and started the up-hill trudge to the Main House.

"You could say that," Niall spoke in a rough whisper, mindful that Lucien had fallen in just a few paces behind. "Assigning that sonofa—to *my* staff." His face flared. "What the *fuck* is he thinking?"

"Are you sure the orders aren't forged?"

"Could you check?" Niall's face lightened for an instant, then the storm clouds gathered anew. "Don't bother. That professional piece of ass knows damn well that if he took Roshi's name in vain, he'd take up permanent residence in the brig within a week. Even he's not that reckless." He smacked the slipcase against his thigh. "God*damn* it."

"Why?" Jani tried to catch Val's eye, but he avoided hers, feigning interest in every stone and shrub he passed. She stared at the top of his head, willing him to look at her, but he remained fix-ated on the rocks and scrub as though they were the most fascinat-ing things he'd ever seen.

"Tell me and we'll both bloody know." Niall jerked a thumb back over his shoulder at Lucien. "Go collect your gear, Captain. And hang onto it. You may need to move at a moment's notice." He exhaled with a growl. "Right back to Earth, if I have anything to say about it."

Jani glanced back at Lucien, who gave her a smile that might have counted as ingenuous as long as she didn't look at his eyes. They shone, alight with the simple joy he always derived from making a difficult situation even worse. He pursed his lips and mimed a kiss, then turned and trotted back to the shuttle. "I don't like this."

"*You* don't like it?" Niall glared at the slipcase as though it held his death warrant. "It's Roshi's signature—I'd know that any-where. His personal parchment." He folded the case in half and shoved it in his trouser pocket. "Bloody fucking hell."

They continued the hike to the House. The wind picked up, blowing sand with abrasive force, as though hurrying them on their way.

The sand around Knevçet Shèràa is darker. The sands of light's weeping, that holiest of idomeni shrines. *Until I desecrated it.* Jani quickened her pace as grains struck her face and neck, a stinging cloud, as though she walked through an insect swarm. *The sand stains.* She remembered the smears on boots and fa-tigues. *Rust red, like clay.* Not like the color of blood. Not like that at all.

"You all right, gel?" Niall trotted up to meet her. "You took off like a rocket back there."

"Fine. I'm fine." Jani walked on up the hill, holding her head up despite the stinging, so she wouldn't have to look at the sand.

A hasty lunch was assembled from the remains of Thalassa's communal mid-morning sacrament and set up in one of the Main House's private dining rooms that overlooked the bay. Niall de-murred, claiming prep for the next day's meeting as an excuse, then headed for the basement comroom, Jani's access codes in hand. Lucien arrived a few minutes after his new commander de-parted, and was about to be sent to the kitchen by John to scrounge what he could until Val intervened. The meal proceeded in awk-ward fits and starts until Val delved into the contents of the liquor cabinet and settled into his oft-assumed role as the unofficial en-tertainment.

". . . and so Eamon stands up before the entire banquet hall and holds up the biggest brassiere I have ever seen." Val paused to take a sip of port, then eased back, glass in hand. " 'A contest,' he announces, in that overwrought burr of his. 'To the woman who can fill this goes the honor of spending the night with me.' So I dig into the centerpiece, pull out two huge cantaloupes, and toss them across the table to him. 'Eamon,' I said, 'just fill it with these. You'll never know the difference, and you can name the first little blossom after me!' "

Jani laughed while eyeing John, who grinned sheepishly.

"Our annual conferences were once the stuff of legend." His grin twitched. "They grew more sedate as we aged."

"Yeah, like the time you tr—" Val stopped, his mouth hanging open in mid-word. He closed it slowly, then silently dropped the subject by taking another sip of wine before turning his attention to the cheese platter.

"Someone's been holding out on me." Jani smiled at John, who winked in reply. That elicited a restive grumble from Lucien, who had spent the entire meal listening to such reminiscences and had grown more irritated with each passing tale.

All this shared history, and you're not part of any of it. Jani glanced at Lucien to find him sitting slumped, fingers interlaced around the base of his brandy snifter, eyes fixed on Val.

Val looked at him once, then again. Then, with a sigh, he set his glass on the table and slid back his chair. "This luncheon was extraordinary." He patted his board-flat stomach. "And filling. If I don't move around, I'll fall right asleep." He wadded his napkin and tossed it atop his plate. "I've been dying to see this place. Mind giving me the grand tour?"

John looked at Jani, then at Lucien. Then he shrugged, placed his own napkin atop the table, and stood. "Why not?" He turned to Jani. "Just give a shout." He shot a glare in Lucien's direction, his jaw working, then nodded to Val. "Let's go."

Jani watched them walk to the French doors, then bobble the "Who leaves first?" with the overwrought courtesy of new acquaintances. They sorted it out after a few moments, John standing on ceremony as host by stepping aside until Val exited ahead of him with a tight smile. She waited until the doors closed and the two had disappeared from view. "What did you do to Val?"

"Nothing he didn't ask me to." Lucien swirled the scant remains of his brandy. "God, talk about beyond the call of duty. Eamon and the melons—how many times did I hear *that* story? Five. Six." His lip curled. "They all sounded the same after the first week. And everyone calls Val Parini a raconteur. It was enough to make me look forward to Pierce's babbling about opera." He raised his snifter toward the door in a solitary toast. "Thanks for the lift, Doc." He lowered the glass and drained it, tilting his head back in order to extract every drop.

"You poor, tortured creature." Jani plucked a lemon wedge from her leftover garnish and bit into it, taking what pleasure she could in Lucien's wince. "You didn't answer my question."

"Mako wanted someone familiar with all the players to look

over Pierce's shoulder." Lucien regarded his empty snifter for a time, then hefted the brandy decanter from the trolley alongside the table. "I mean, Pierce is his dog and all, but sometimes he wonders whether he's as forthcoming as he should be, seeing as you're involved."

Jani watched as he filled the snifter halfway, then added another splash for good measure. "I didn't realize he trusted you that far."

"Some people appreciate my capabilities."

"No accounting for taste, I guess." Jani stood and circled the table. The temperature of the room had been lowered in deference to humanish comfort levels, and the jacket she had donned failed to keep out the chill. "I need some air." She pushed through the doors that led out to the balcony, felt the heat welcome her like an old friend, the bay breeze ruffle her hair. She leaned against the stone railing and spent a few quiet minutes watching bayskimmers from the Karistos Yacht Club fast-float across the water.

When she heard the doors open again, she clenched her fists.

"The scenery reminds me of the Greek Islands." Lucien drew alongside, snifter still in hand, the fill level depleted by half. "Anais took me on a cruise to celebrate my appointment to East Point." He leaned against the railing, and smiled for the first time since lunch began and the stories started. "And a good time was had by all, including a few she never knew about." He paused to take yet another swallow of brandy, glanced at Jani over the rim of the snifter and stopped. "What?"

"I'm not used to seeing you toss down the liquor." Jani slowly opened her hands and pressed them to the warm stone. "Alcohol dulls the senses, you always said, and you needed to keep yours sharp."

Lucien lowered his drink, then set it atop the railing. "Chicago's not the same since you left."

"Lucien, this is me you're talking to, remember?"

"I haven't forgotten." He stared at the snifter. Then he grabbed it, drained it in a single swallow, turned and flung it at the stone arch bordering the doorway. The glass shattered with a sound like a shooter crack, the shards flashing back sunlight as they flew apart and scattered across the tiled floor.

One piece skittered in front of Lucien's foot. He stepped on it, twisting his shoe into it, then pulled back and looked at the powder he'd left behind. His breathing came rough, as though he'd been running. "I haven't forgotten a thing."

Jani remained silent. Every so often a fissure developed in Lucien's carefully maintained veneer, a hint of what he could do if he ever threw off the restraints he'd imposed upon himself, ever said "Hell with it" and let fly. *And he feels that way now.* Which meant she had something else to worry about in addition to the reason for Val's visit and tomorrow's meeting with the governors.

"You were always willing to believe anything about me." Lucien paced along the railing, back and forth, like a caged animal. "Anything but the truth." He stopped, eyes fixed on the water. "I had to see you. I was going crazy in Chicago—I would have said or done anything to pull an assignment here. So, I went to see Mako. I had done a few favors for him in the past. He owed me."

"You're trying to drive a wedge between Roshi Mako and his colonel." Jani stepped away from the railing and pretended to examine blooms on a potted shrub. "Don't think Niall will forget that."

Lucien turned slowly. "I know what Pierce thinks of me. I know what he'll put me through. I'm willing to deal with it." His eyes met hers, bottomless wells of brown. "I love you."

Oh Lord—anything but this. Jani pressed her hands to her temples and squeezed. "*Lucien.*"

"I mean it."

"Lucien, it's a one hundred twenty-five meter drop into the bay from this balcony. Don't bloody tempt me."

Lucien stared at her, his expression blank. Then, as though some internal valve finally released, he smiled and sagged back against the railing. "We both just need to relax." He patted his trouser pocket, then reached into it. Pulled out something, and held it out for Jani to see. "Remember this?"

She caught a glimpse of dull coral shine, the color silvered by the sunlight. A small sphere, a centimeter or so in diameter. *Oh. Hell.* Her face burned.

"I showed it to Val on the way here. He offered to buy it. How's that for tacky?" Lucien rolled the pearl between his fingers. "He kept commenting on the color. Pink or peach—he couldn't make up his mind. What would you call it?" When Jani failed to reply, he shrugged, his smile altering from simple and open to something with an edge. "I didn't tell him how I came to acquire it, of course. Did you even realize that the string had broken? I know I was focused on other matters." He held the pearl up to the light. Then he raised his other hand, pressed the tip of the index finger to the bottom of the pearl and massaged it. "Do you know what this reminds me of?" He watched her face as he slid his finger against the pearl from tip to base once, then again, and again. "It's just like—"

"Please keep it to yourself." Jani looked down and found she held the crumpled remains of a half-opened bloom, its stem snapped at the neck. "You're never this coarse. You are drunk, aren't you?"

Lucien pouted. "I keep souvenirs. You know that. I've got one of Val's—"

"What is the real reason you came here?"

Lucien took a deep breath. Pocketed the pearl and stood, brow furrowed, as though trying to recall something. An Angel of Death, at a loss as to what to destroy next. "The usual. Spread wrack and ruin. Doom, death, disease, and despair."

"Mission accomplished." Jani tossed the remains of the flower over the railing. "Does that mean you can go home?"

"Mako sent me to observe the general situation and report back. A second pair of eyes. Sometimes I do tell the truth the first time." Lucien passed a hand over his face. "I have missed you, you know, disinclined as you are to believe it. I won't ask if you missed me. Judging by the expression on your face, I know your answer." He glanced over the railing. "Hundred twenty-five meters. I'll have to remember that." He turned and headed for the doors. "If you'll excuse me, I really need to find a bathroom."

"Lucien?" Jani waited until he stopped. "Whatever shit you're thinking of pulling, reconsider."

Lucien tried to turn, but caught the side of one shoe on the edge of a tile and stumbled. "God, I am drunk, aren't I?" He righted himself slowly, shaking his head at the wonder of it all. "You have enough to worry about without looking for trouble from me. Val's visit is not social, in case you haven't guessed. The PM ordered him to buy out Shroud's share of Neoclona. A single digit percentage of what that share is worth, and that number's a hell of a lot closer to zero than it is to ten. No more research. No more consulting. He's to find other things to do."

What lunch Jani had managed to eat congealed in her gut. "Why?"

"As a warning to other bad little captains of Commonwealth industry who might consider hybridizing. Or working so closely with the Haárin." Lucien paused to breathe. The alcohol had him by the throat now. "Things are tense, in case you haven't noticed. Human separatists are bombing Haárin docks, Cèel wants to sever diplomatic relations with the Commonwealth, and—the first shots—in any war would likely be fired—in a place like Elyas." Sweat soaked his shirt and slicked his face, making him look as though he'd been caught in the rain. "Now, two percent of Neoclona is still more money than any normal person might expect to see in a lifetime, but it isn't just the money. It's the power, and the influence, and let's not forget the medical research capabilities." He pulled a linen square from his pocket and wiped his face, his neck. "With your principal means of support gutted, where does that leave Thalassa? Where does that—leave you?" He grimaced. "I need— Excuse me." He turned and double-timed through the dining room and out the door.

Jani leaned against the railing as soon as Lucien disappeared from sight. Her gut ached. Her legs felt weak.

Two percent. She imagined John's expression as Val broke the news. The sun still warmed, but she couldn't feel it. The bayskimmers still floated, but she didn't see them.

CHAPTER 4

Rilas steered the skimmer as close to the cliff edge as the directionals allowed. The vehicle's wake sent dried brush tumbling over the rocks, while its high-pitched hum and the shadow it cast as it coursed over the ground drove small animals to the shelter of shrubs and burrows.

In the rearview, she watched the domes and painted rooftops of Karistos recede, replaced by rocky summits that jutted into the cloudless sky. After driving for a time, she stopped the skimmer beside a tumbled mass of stone, hoisted her slingbag from behind her seat, and disembarked. She walked to the edge of the cliff, then along it, looking out to the bay every few strides.

In the short time she spent walking, three skimmers passed her. All carried humanish, who drove too slowly and watched her as though they had never before seen an Haárin. The cliffs of Karistos and the Bay of Siros had become popular places for tourists, and Rilas knew the traffic would grow as the day proceeded. "Most unfortunate. This would have been a good place." She drew a small scope from one of the slingbag's many pockets, held it to her eye, looked toward the bay and the line of cliffs beyond. In the scope's viewer, she at last caught sight of Thalassa, a scatter of glistening rooftops, blue and yellow in the sun.

Rilas touched a pad on the side of the scope, activating the device so it could read and measure. Distances. Heights. Angles. Depths of rooms and thicknesses of walls. After completing the task, she returned the device to her bag and strode back to her skimmer. Already half the day had been spent searching, as had the entire day before. She did not like to take so long to make preparations, but

Karistos had proved a strange place, much worse than nìRau Cèel had described.

She stood beside the skimmer, one hand on the door control, until a humanish male driving alone slowed and asked if she required assistance. She gestured that she could not understand him, then entered her vehicle and drove away. Too quickly—she knew she moved too quickly. She could see the male in her rearview, watching her. Would he remember her? Or did all female idomeni look alike to him, as nìRau Cèel said?

Damned godless place. Never again would she act as a tile broker. As ná Nahin Sela, she had wasted hours at the Trade Board displaying samples and discussing colors and glazes, meeting with prospective customers. *NìRau Cèel told me that I must act as that which I am supposed to be.* Such was the nature of cover. *If I did not act as a merchant among the Elyan Haárin, I would be noticed.* But the training she had received in Rauta Shèràa had not prepared her for these Haárin, who ate and drank in the streets as animals, who looked her in the eye even though they were unknown to her.

Then there were . . . those other. The anathema. The hybrids. She had seen two of them at the Trade Board, a male and female, so much as demons in their misshapen strangeness. Thick limbs. Pale eyes and skin. They had once been as humanish. As humanish, they should have remained.

Rilas drove and studied each passage, each summit. Prayed to her goddess for guidance, and for strength. *This place is of your doing, Tsecha.* Soon, he would pay the cost of his sacrilege.

The sun passed prime. As it began its downward arc, Rilas passed a rocky slope crowded at its base with rubble and dying scrub. She drove past it as she had so many others, and had traveled quite far along the cliff road before she realized what she had seen.

She turned around and drove back to the place, alert to humanish tourists, or shuttles making their final approach to the distant Karistos port or the Service field. Alert to any sign that someone, somewhere, might see her. She fought the desire to reach into the slingbag and remove and activate the devices that could scan the skies as she could not. Monitor the roads. Watch her back, as a humanish would say.

But she dare not. All around Karistos, craft from the humanish Service traveled, scanned, searched. Her devices, while most useful, were also most illegal, and she could not risk their detection now, while she still prepared. In a day or two, when she completed her task and had gone, let the Service find what they would. *Some of it will look most as familiar, as we stole it from them.* Rilas bared her teeth at the thought. Humanish did not believe Haárin capable of stealing, just as they did not believe them capable of subterfuge or sabotage. Most foolish of them, and truly.

She approached the pile of rubble, her joy fading. She slowed the skimmer, hunting for the signs that had attracted her attention and compelled her return. At first she could not detect them, and wondered if she had erred.

Then, finally, one by one, she saw them. A glimpse of masonry colored the same browns and whites as the surrounding stone, barely visible through tangled branches. Straight lines where none should exist, the broken edges of a wall smashed to ruins by the rockslide.

She steered her skimmer behind the rockslide so it was hidden from the road. This time, she activated her shooter. Then she powered down the vehicle, hoisted her slingbag, and disembarked.

Rilas savored the heat, the one welcome surprise that Elyas offered. Wondered at the stone, the sparse vegetation, so much as Rauta Shèràa that she felt as though she tracked quarry on her homeworld. The thought upset her, and she struggled to push it from her mind. When nìRau Cèel counseled her, he had been adamant. Assassination or sabotage, what acts she performed could not be committed on Shèrá. Too much risk of discovery, he had told her. Too much danger, for both of them.

She held her shooter at the ready as she approached the house, circling the place once before pushing a rock aside with her foot and passing through the partly collapsed doorway. She stepped around a pile of rubble and into what had once been a room. Remains of furniture, sticks of polywood and scraps of weave, littered the space. Some lay scattered across the floor, the rest wadded in corners, where it served as bedding for the animals whose claws Rilas heard skittering against the cracked and stained tile. She sniffed the air, grimacing at the tang of waste and rotted flesh, the stench of the things which lived in this place mingled with that of the things which had died. An unseemly place, and truly. None would look for even the lowest Haárin in such as this.

Only when her eyes had better adjusted to the half-dark did Rilas explore further. Grit and dried leaves crunched beneath her feet. Sunlight streamed in through a lone window, highlighting dust motes that leapt and fell like sparks from a fire, disturbed by her passage.

She set her slingbag on the floor. A short time spent pushing aside rock and clutter left her with a space through which she could maneuver as well as a path to the window. She hoped that it would look out over the bay, and was pleased to find that it did. "I can just see the water." And beyond that, the curve of land that held her target.

Rilas recovered her bag from its resting place and carried it to the window, set it on the dusty floor and opened it. She removed wrapped tubes, a small box, a roll of heavy cloth. First she removed the wrapping from the tubes, then laid out the smooth plastic on the floor to serve as a barrier. Lay the tubes atop it, followed by the box and the cloth roll.

She knelt. Picked up the tubes, one short and one long, fitted them together, then set them aside. Unrolled the cloth and removed three items. First, two curves of metal, one large and one much smaller, the stock and the discharge mech. Last, her prize, her most valued thing. A clear glassy cylinder shot through with lines and discs of color. Her sight mech.

She worked with a speed born of practice. Attached barrel to stock. Fastened discharge mech to the underside of barrel, sight mech to the top. Removed the sighting device from her pocket, attached it to the sight mech, and activated data transfer.

Rilas watched the colors in the sight mech brighten and dull, flash and fade. As the last burst of color faded, she detached the sighting device and tucked it back in her pocket. Only then did she rise, turn to the window and raise the rifle. Bracing the stock against her shoulder, she poked the barrel through a gap in the shattered pane and lowered her eye to the sight mech.

Fully assembled, the rifle felt weighty, but balanced, like a finely crafted shooter. She paused to run her hand over the barrel, savoring the smooth chill of the dull black metalloceramic. She then resumed her check, studying the bay and the cliffs beyond through the sight mech.

It is as though I stand there. After all this time, after completing so many such tasks for nìRau Cèel, she still marveled at how the mech magnified the distant view, how the microlenses moved in concert to sharpen, brighten, provide contrast, expose detail no idomeni eye could detect unaided.

Rilas scanned a road that diagonaled along the cliff face and wound past structures before vanishing at the summit. She moved on to a larger structure, one of the largest she had seen on Elyas, which jutted from the cliff face as though part of the stone.

Through windows, she could see figures. The accursed hybrids whose existence pained nìRau Cèel so.

Click—click—click. Her finger twitched on the discharge mech—with each faint *whirr* of the mechs, she imagined bodies falling, souls destroyed, lives extinguished. She scanned other areas of the enclave—

Click.

Walkways. Verandas. Open spaces.

Click.

Killing, killing. Taking life that had no right to exist.

Click. Click. Click.

A small balcony.

Rilas stilled. Eased the pressure on the discharge mech. Watched.

Jani Kilian. The Kièrshia. The cursed thing. Standing, alone on the balcony. She wore a wrapshirt and trousers in grey, plain and free of adornment save for a thick cording of silver woven into the shirt cuffs.

Rilas released the charge-through and looked away from the scope. Her heart beat strongly—she could feel it pound. Her hands were as dry, her mind, as clear. Such was as they were during the best of times, when Caith blessed her and bade her act as her talents demanded.

She set aside the rifle, then knelt upon the rubble-strewn floor and rummaged through her bag. Small stones dug into her knees; she used the pain as a spur, a sign of favor from Caith that it was right for her to act. She removed the frosty flat container. Opened it. Took out one of the chilled projectiles, inserted it into the rifle magazine, clicked the chamber closed. Heard the cylinder slide into place, the rifle hum in activation.

The payload is typed to Tsecha. Even as the technician's words echoed in her head, Rilas lifted the rifle to her shoulder and sighted down, capturing the dark head. Edged the weapon one way, then the other, until the scope signaled TARGET CENTERED with a single yellow flash, and she fixed on the face. Skin dark as Pathen, eyes green as Sìah, combined with weak human bones. The face of an overgrown youngish, a mutant, a made thing.

The payload is typed to Tsecha.

"But it might work with her. The idomeni part of her is of Vynshàrau. There could be enough—"

The payload is typed to Tsecha.

Rilas forced herself to breathe. The Kièrshia stood, unmoving as stone, eyes fixed. A target as she had never had, still and quiet and alone. If this one fell, no one would know for hours.

Then Kièrshia shifted her stare until it seemed to Rilas as though she saw her and studied her in turn.

You should die. Rilas's finger tightened on the charge-through. *You must—*

Tsecha.

Rilas stilled. Cursed the name that filled her head even as she knew it had been sent by her goddess. Relaxed, drawing in one slow inhalation of stagnant air, followed by another. Another.

"Fool." Rilas stood still until she calmed, until she could no longer see the strange green eyes in her mind. Then she broke down the rifle and repacked the components.

I will return to Karistos. I will make sacrifice, and pray, and prepare. Then tomorrow she would return to the ruin and kill the one for whom the weapon had been designed. Avrèl nìRau Nema. A name that had once been and was now no more. Ní Tsecha Egri. A life that was now, and would soon not be.

Rilas shouldered her bag and, with careful steps, departed the ruin. No humanish males lurked in wait outside. No tourists. No movement but branches and leaves in the wind, no sound but animals.

CHAPTER 5

Jani heard the French doors open, but didn't turn to see who her visitor was. She already knew. "It's so nice and quiet out here."

Footsteps from behind, soft on the tile. "Ní Tsecha's over at the never-ending project that is the new meeting house." Dieter Brondt, her secular suborn and resident spy, drew up next to her. "He's arguing with ní Dathim about the tilework."

"Again? And what does he want me to do about that?"

"Make ní Dathim see things his way." Dieter grinned, the expression lighting his round face. "Because we all know how well ní Dathim listens to you."

"About as well as he listens to anyone." Jani paused to rub her eyes. Her head ached from the brightness of the sun off the water, yet the last thing she wanted to do was leave the balcony.

Dieter bent and picked up one of the crystal shards. "I ran into Captain Pascal on the walkway, and immediately directed him to a bathroom." He examined the fragment, then looked around at the other pieces scattered across the balcony floor. "It didn't sound as though lunch agreed with him."

"Heat and brandy."

Dieter winced. "He's on his way to Fort Karistos. Got a com from Pierce to report immediately. 'Scarface blinked,' was how he put it." He gave the shard a last look, then tossed it aside. "Is everything all right?"

"John and Val." Jani beat a cadence on the railing with her fists. "Where are they?"

"The clinic." Dieter planted his feet and folded his arms. He wore a wrapshirt and loose trousers in patterned orange and white.

Hybridization had claimed him late and done little to lengthen his bones or slim his stocky frame, leaving him resembling a fitter than average Buddha with cat-yellow eyes. "Doctor Shroud took Doctor Parini on a tour." He cocked his head. Concerned Buddha. "Is something wrong?"

"Captain Pascal gave me some news before he went to lose his lunch. I don't know whether to believe it or not."

"Would the fact that the good doctors have been holed up in Doctor Shroud's office for the whole of their tour help you decide?"

Jani shot the male a hard look. "Does anything happen around here that you don't know about?" She fielded his blank stare and shook her head. "Val's been sent here to cut John's heart out." She stopped, as though speaking the words would give them a reality they didn't otherwise possess. *But they are real, dammit.* When it came to digging out the nasty, Lucien gave Dieter a run for anyone's money. "He's to buy out John's share of Neoclona. At two cents on the Common dollar."

Dieter's brows twitched skyward. "That's . . . a kick in the teeth." He stroked his chin. "But is it a surprise?"

"Maybe not. Cut off the money, and the Thalassan beast will sicken and die." Jani turned her back to the water and studied the stark white facade of the Main House. "Maybe the surprise is that they waited this long to do it." She pushed off the railing and started for the dining room. "I'm going to stop off at John's office before I go to the meeting house."

"Jani?" Dieter hurried after her, soles crunching on bits of scattered glass. "There are solutions, surely?"

"They should've been put in place already. Assets transfers take time. So do setups of dummy corporations." Jani stepped out onto the walkway that ringed the third floor of the office-laboratory-apartment complex that was the administrative, social, and medical focus of the Thalassan enclave. "That's why Val didn't let John know he was coming. Whoever sent him didn't want to give John the time to adjust." She looked over the railing and down to the ground level central courtyard, where the kitchen crew were setting up for mid-afternoon sacrament, jamming and angling mess tables as best they could amid the planters and fountains. "First rule of auditing. Never call ahead."

"I wouldn't have." A little of the old Colonel Brondt, Elyas Station Service liaison and spotter of smugglers and other illicit life-forms, flashed in Dieter's eyes. "Neither would you."

"Maybe." Jani caught a whiff of curry from the dining area below. She'd have savored the aroma normally, but nerves had claimed her gut as their own and she felt the acid rise in her throat instead. "Bit different when you're on the other end, though." She headed around the walkway to the lift, nodding to the hybrids she passed along the way while at the same time keeping an eye out for any sign of Lucien.

"Doctor Parini can be made to listen?" Dieter followed after her, a misshapen shadow. "He and Doctor Shroud have been friends for so long."

"Depends who has Val by the short hairs." Jani thumped the lift call pad with her fist. The cabin opened—she stepped inside, then turned to face her suborn. "He didn't come here because he wanted to, he came because he was forced, and by someone who knew just how hard to yank. Pretty select list, don't you think?" She raised a hand in farewell as the lift door closed in Dieter's worried face.

The basement laboratory-clinic proved the same low-key madhouse as always, technicians and medicos bustling along the maze of corridors like the white-coated ants they were. Jani negotiated the twisty trail to John's office, then paused and pressed her ear to the door to check if any yelling could be detected through the combination of sound-shielding and the vibration-dampening door panel. She sensed nothing. Took a deep breath and hit the door pad.

John and Val fell silent as she entered, just-spoken words charging the air like static. John sat at his desk, working a small exercise ball with one hand, rolling it over and over again between his long fingers. Val sat on a short couch set against the wall, arms folded and shoulders hunched.

"Jani." John glanced at Val, then away. "We've just been catching up on old—"

"Two percent." Jani dragged a visitors' chair to the side of the desk opposite John and sat. "No more practicing medicine. No more research."

Val's mouth dropped open. "How . . . ?" Then his face flamed and he covered his eyes with one hand.

Yes, Lucien ratted you out. What the hell did you expect? Jani looked across the polished ebony desk at John, who stared back as though she'd just plucked a rabbit out of thin air. "I have my sources."

"Without a doubt." John shook his head, then bounced the ball atop the desk, caught it, and bounced it again. "Val is here at the PM's request. Given the deteriorating relationship between the humanish and idomeni, Li Cao feels that a hybrid at the head of one of the largest commercial entities in the Commonwealth is too great a security risk to tolerate." He gave the ball one final bounce, then stashed it in a drawer and stood. "Anyone want coffee?" Without waiting to see whether anyone actually did, he walked to a lowboy at the far end of the room and started assembling the brewer.

"I'm just the messenger." Val glanced at Jani sidelong, as though reluctant to meet her eye. "The real negotiations will go on in Karistos between lawyers from the Justice Ministry and our—" He shot a look at John, then concentrated on his hands. "—and Neoclona's legal team." He shrugged. "And whoever John hires to represent his interests."

"These negotiations began last week, apparently." John offered Jani a chill smile. "I'm left to scramble. I've already contacted a firm in Karistos that I believe can hold its own." He set out cups, cream, and sugar on a tray while the weighty aroma of his coffee filled the office.

"Why now?" Jani edged away from the desk so John could set down the tray. "John's been here a year. It took Cao that long to decide he was a threat to Commonwealth security?"

Val rose and walked to the desk. "She called me in one day, about two months ago. Oh, it had been busy. Tsecha had just let loose one of his theological broadsides, a story about you had appeared in a scandal sheet, and one of the more conservative ministers questioned John's loyalty during public debate." He spooned sugar into a cup, then waited while John filled it to the brim. "That's when I screwed up." He paused to sip. "She asked if I felt whether the idomeni could win John's loyalty." He looked at John and shook his head. "I told her that the only two things that had won John Shroud's loyalty were his work"—he closed his eyes—"and Jani Kilian."

John set down the carafe. "Very dramatic, Val, but not the wisest choice of words." He hoisted his own cup, then set it down with a clatter, sending scalding brew in all directions. *"Dammit!"* He grabbed a dispo tissue from the dispenser on his desk and wiped hot coffee off his hand. "What is she afraid of, that I'll start working for Rauta Shèràa? Even if I wanted to, Cèel wouldn't take my help on a plate—it would be a repudiation of everything he believes. Or does she think I'll infect the entire Commonwealth with a hybridization bug?" He crumpled the dispo into a tight ball and hurled it into a deskside trash bin. "It doesn't work that way, Val—didn't you tell her? Hybridization is still a slow, labor-intensive process tailored to the individual, and that's not likely to change anytime soon. If she's worried about hybrids by the millions overrunning her government, she's an idiot!"

"She wants to take out the financial underpinnings of this place." Jani gripped her cup in both hands. John had lowered the office temperature in deference to Val, leaving it much too cold for her comfort. "Something happened, and she thinks shutting down Thalassa will help solve the problem." *Something to do with secession. Cao must have heard the rumors.* She picked over one possibility in her mind, then another, until she sensed the stares. Val's unspoken prayer that something she'd say could get him off the hook. John's, that she could give him something to pry Cao's grip from his throat. "I don't know what that could be."

"Well, so much for that." John doffed his medcoat and draped it over the back of his chair. "I have an appointment with my new legal team in an hour. I need to get ready." He looked at Jani. "I'd like you to be there. I know they'll have questions for you. I'm hoping you can at least answer those." He brushed past her and out the door without waiting for a reply.

The door closed. Silence settled. Jani touched her cheek. The sense of having been struck, but without the blow.

Val walked to the wall opposite and focused on one of the framed hangings. "He still has that one." A shade of a smile, soon vanished. "It's hitting him now. It takes a while, with the big things. He got angry when I told him, yeah, but now it's sinking its roots." He hung his head. "I'm just letting you know. I don't think you've seen it. It can get rough."

"Thanks for the warning." Jani turned to look at the image. It must have dated from Val's and John's medical school days. Two gangly young men with toothy grins standing on the steps of a building. Val's hair flopped over his forehead, while John wore a wide-brimmed hat that he'd angled to shade his eyes from the sun. "Is there anything you can do?"

"My influence with Li Cao doesn't extend beyond the tip of my nose." Val's shoulder twitched. "She's declared this a matter of Commonwealth security. If I fight her, she'll take away both our shares and hand them over to Eamon, which would be pretty much the same as her taking over the company." He walked back to the desk and set down his cup. "But there's the election in three months. Yevgeny Scriabin is standing against her, and he's a reasonable man. Most of the pundits are predicting he'll beat her."

"That's three months. A hell of a lot can happen between now and then." Jani swallowed hard as John's coffee took up where the aroma of the curry had left off. She set down her cup, then rose and headed for the door. "I need to see Tsecha before I meet with John's lawyers."

"I'll go with you." Val hurried after her. "At least part of the way. I need to walk. Cooped up on a ship for six weeks with—" He stood aside so Jani could precede him through the door, then hesitated. "This isn't like I thought it would be, to say the least." He stepped out into the corridor, glancing up as though he feared the ceiling might fall on him. "I envisioned a nice, relaxed visit. Dinners in little out-of-the-way places, capped off by dancing and plate smashing. Maybe some sailracing during the day. Then one day, Li Cao calls me, and it all falls apart, bit by bit." He quieted until they entered the lift and the door closed. "I have . . . some explaining to do." He tried for a weak grin, but managed only a wince. "I tried to work up the nerve after lunch, but His Highness sent me out of the room."

Jani shook her head. "Not now, Val."

"If I don't tell you now, I'll lose my nerve." He stepped aside so she could exit the lift first, then fell behind her as they cut across the central courtyard and through a series of demirooms separated by aquaria and low screens.

Jani waited until they departed the Main House and rounded the vast rear yard. "Val?"

"I think I'm losing it. My nerve." He dragged off his suit jacket and slung it over his shoulder. "Dammit." He stopped at the top of the cliff road and looked out over the water. "It's so beautiful here. Hotter than fucking hell, but—" He ran a hand across his brow, already dotted with sweat. "But everything beautiful has a price, doesn't it?" His eyes brimmed. "I'm sorry."

Jani waited until Val cleared his throat and wiped his eyes. "Want me to tell you what happened? You can nod or shake your head at suitable intervals, and it will be like you never really said anything at all."

"You think you know all the words to this one, do you?" Val started down the road, his step slowing as the soles of his dress shoes slid on the gravel.

"In several languages." Jani tried to study him without seeming to. He kept his eyes fixed on the road, braced for the words he didn't want to hear. "First verse—Lucien started hanging around your flat after I left Chicago to return to John. His pretexts were feeble at best. Some bit of news from one of the ministries, or a rumor he'd heard at Sheridan. Being a man of the world, you saw through his act immediately, even felt irritated by his lack of subtlety. But even though you knew he was trying to play you, you just couldn't make yourself send him on his way. He had a connection to me, and he offered all the right responses when you railed against John, which I'm sure you did at least a few times or you wouldn't count as a living, breathing being." She looked away as Val's face reddened, allowing him an illusion of privacy. "Besides, he's just so damned decorative. You did once tell me that you could watch him all day."

Val snorted, denying the inevitable even as he worked closer to admitting to it. "He's not the first good-looking boy to stake me out."

"No, but he's the best-trained. He's an assassin, Val. Gauging the victim is what he does." Jani held up two fingers. "Second verse—after you got used to his coming around regularly, he pulled back. Stayed away for a week or two at a time, then turned up with weak excuses. Just to see how hooked you were." They came upon a small sitting area wedged between two houses, and she stopped and sat on a stone bench.

"I passed that test." Val unfastened his shirt collar, then bent over a tiny fountain and let the water spray over his face. "I wasn't a complete idiot."

Jani nodded. "He figured that out. So when you told him that you were leaving to visit John, his request to accompany you was completely businesslike. Being under orders from Mako himself, he claimed billet privileges, then left you to mull it over. He knew he had you backed in a corner—what could you do but agree? You already suspected that Cao didn't trust you, that her summons was a warning to you as well as to John. It worried you what might happen if you added to your troubles by tossing out Mako's chosen rep on his perfectly formed ear."

Val dragged a linen square out of his trouser pocket and wiped his face. Then he sat beside her and sighed. "Jani—"

"Pressure points, Val. Weakness. Like I said before, he has a talent for spotting them."

"He's not the only one," Val said through his teeth.

Jani hesitated. "Now, the chorus. He had set you up so you had to cart him here or risk appearing disloyal. So, cart him here you did. He should have been content, you'd think, but this is Lucien we're talking about. You had rejected his advances up to that point, and that was a situation that could not be allowed to continue. Even engineered sociopaths have their pride."

"There are only so many places to hide on a ship, and none of them works for long." Val spoke low, as though to himself. "Every damned time I turned around, there he was. His favorite trick was to catch me in the gym locker room or sauna, wander in stark naked and pretend to be surprised to see me. 'I'm *so* sorry, Doctor Parini—I didn't realize you were here.' Yeah, right."

Jani grinned in remembrance. "A bit obvious, but a tried and true method with some history of success."

Val returned her grin, but the expression withered. "After a few quiet days, I thought he had finally gotten the message. Then one ship-morning, about three weeks out, he showed up at my cabin door with a copy of whatever newssheet had been transmitted that day. He was fully clothed, believe it or not. A little rough around the edges, actually. Tired. Distracted. As though he'd given up." He paused, his eyes clouding.

"He handed me the newssheet," he said after a time. "I took it. I said 'Thank you, Captain Pascal,' and he replied, 'You're welcome, Doctor Parini.' We—" He stopped again, inhaling with a shudder. "We just stared at one another. Might have been for a minute or so. Might have been an hour for all I could tell. Neither of us said a word, we just . . ." He swallowed hard. "Then he stepped inside, let the door close behind him. Took the newssheet from my hand, folded it, and set it atop a nearby table. Then he—" He closed his eyes, lips parting ever so slightly. His breathing quickened as his hands clenched and flexed, twisted the linen until it tore.

Then his eyes snapped open. He shook his head as though emerging from a daze and sat forward, elbows on knees, hands dangling between. "You're going to tell me it was an act." He examined the damage he'd wrought upon the linen square, then wadded it and shoved it in his trouser pocket.

"It's *all* an act." Jani put a hand on his shoulder. "Trust me, it's better when you accept it. It makes him a known quantity, with no surprises. A certain brand of simple comfort when the real world becomes too complex to deal with."

Val's lip curled. "Aren't you the understanding one?" He fell silent for a few moments, then sat up and eyed her expectantly. "Your turn."

Jani considered a display of innocence, but decided confusion more believable. "My turn for what?"

"I'm not the only one laying bare my soul here, am I? Be fair."

"What do you want to know?"

"The story behind that pearl. He showed it to me on the way here. Told me he bought it, but we both know that's a joke. He never paid for anything in his life." Val straightened his legs and examined his dust-covered shoes. "I read his MedRec once, remember? I know he keeps souvenirs of events in his life he considers memorable."

Crap. Now it was her turn to shudder, to hem and haw. "What makes you think the pearl's mine?"

"I have my reasons, which I will explain after you tell me the story behind it."

Jani felt the heat creep up her neck. "It's from my dowry." She fielded Val's surprised look. "My parents turned over my dowry to me when they first came to Chicago, and one of the pieces was a pearl necklace." She paused. "One . . . night, I wore it during . . ."

"During . . . ?" Val leaned toward her. "During a fire drill? During charades? What?"

Jani tried closing her eyes, but images flashed that she didn't want to see at that moment. Instead, she concentrated on a scatter of stones at her feet. "I wore it to bed. I had worn it that evening, and didn't take it off. During a particularly active moment, Lucien . . . yanked on it, and the string broke. Pearls everywhere. If I'd known they hadn't been tied properly, I never would have worn them. Those damned things turned up under the furniture for months." She shrugged, forced herself to look Val in the face. "See? No big revelatory episode. Just something I'm sure he saved to embarrass me."

"Probably." Val sighed. His mood seemed lighter, as though her confession had bought him some degree of dispensation. "Why did we let him get under our skin? We're grown-ups. We should have known better."

"They tell you everything you want to hear, and they know how to show you the face you want to see. Even when you know in your bones that you can't trust them, you still try, because you can't accept the fact that they can't feel and that there's nothing they won't do to ensure their survival." Jani rocked to the side until she bumped against him. "Guess who told me that?"

"Dirty pool, Jan."

"I'd just let him into my home when I knew he had set me up to be killed. You tried to warn me."

"But I was wrong. You figured out later that he had blocked the attempt. He pushed you out of the way, took the shot himself. He saved your life." Val frowned. "Granted, he was the one who got you into trouble in the first place." He raked a hand through his hair, then sat forward and buried his face in his hands. "Oh, *crap*."

"He leaves behind wreckage wherever he goes—compared to some, you got off easy. You're here, in one piece. No one shot at you. You're a bit chastened, but you'll get over it." Jani held out her hand. "You survived. Congratulations and welcome to the club."

"Hip, hip, hooray." Val sat up. "Remember when I said that I knew the pearl had to have belonged to you?" He took her hand and squeezed it, then continued to hold it. "About four days out, he started pulling away. Moved his things out of my cabin. He said that he needed to prepare for Niall, but I knew that was bullshit. As if any amount of prep in that regard would do him any good."

Jani tried to reclaim her hand, but Val had it locked up tight. "I wonder how Mako was able to shove him down Niall's throat considering—"

"Don't change the subject." Val glowered a warning. "By the time we were two days out, *he'd* started avoiding *me*. Last night, as we were getting ready to dock at Elyas, I lay in bed, *alone*, stewing in my own juice, when it hit me how much of our time together had been spent talking about you. Your accomplishments. Your background. Things you and he had done together. I even recalled a rather spirited discussion concerning the exact color of your eyes." He regarded her with something akin to pity, mixed with something else that looked a lot like fear. "I'm not very happy being me at the moment, but the one thing I can take comfort in is the fact that I'm not you. I was just something to help pass the time, I know that now. But you, you're his obsession." He smiled sadly, then held her hand to his lips and kissed it. "I need to get back. I want to talk to John before he meets with his lawyers." He released her hand and stood, then circled around the bench and headed back up the road to the Main House.

Jani massaged the spot on her hand that Val had kissed. "Welcome to the club." Problem was, after you paid the initiation fee, you kept paying and paying and paying . . .

I should have guessed that Lucien would keep a souvenir of that night. Like most of their eventful evenings, it hadn't been planned. Lucien had finessed them an invitation to a dinner at one of the ministries, but she hadn't wanted to attend. When she tried to beg off, however, he listed the reasons why she needed to go, all sound business-related incentives of the sort he could recite in his sleep. The issue settled, he had arrived to collect her, passing the time in her sitting room while she finished dressing.

What the hell got into me? She had donned the requisite undergarments and ridiculous shoes. A conservative gown in dark blue. Removed the jewelry satchel from her armoire and opened it, revealing her dowry, the trays filled with gems, gold, and platinum. Picked through the necklaces, bracelets, and earrings.

Then she removed the gown, the ridiculous shoes and undergarments, and dressed herself in as much of the glittery stuff as she could hang from her neck, loop around her waist, hips, and ankles, and wrap around her arms. Out of fifteen kilos of chains, links, and set gems her parents had brought her from Acadia, she managed to don at least five. Gold, topaz, and emerald. Strings of diamond beads. And the pearls.

Lucien had turned as soon as the bedroom door opened. Started to say something, then stopped and stared as she posed in the bedroom entry, still and stylized as one of her mother's statues. She didn't speak and neither did he—adaptable animal that he was, he never asked a single question. He simply walked toward her, peeling off his dress uniform along the way until, by the time he reached her, he was as naked as she was.

He called me a goddess. Among other things he murmured. Whispered. Shouted. So enraptured had they been with one another that they hadn't even noticed the necklace had broken until the morning.

"That was some night." And now the time had come to pay the price for it. "What have you come to collect, Lucien?" She stood and continued on her way to the meeting house. "And who have you come to collect it for?"

CHAPTER 6

"It does not make sense." Tsecha pointed to the half-tiled wall, a mélange of delicate colorings and sketched detail. "What is this? I have never seen anything such as this before."

Ní Dathim Naré, Tsecha's secular suborn, stood beside his dominant with the ill-concealed irritation of an artist coping with the criticism of a wealthy but tasteless client. "Through the middle is the line of the cliffs. Drawn there are the houses of Thalassa. If you stood on a craft, out on the bay, you would see this place as such." Judging from the increasing curve of his shoulders and the stiff set of his jaw, aboard a craft out on the bay was exactly where he wished Tsecha was at that moment.

Tsecha stepped close to the wall. "It does not look like a cliff."

"It does from here." Jani leaned against the wall directly across from the mural. "I think you need to stand at least five or six meters away for it to all fall into place."

Dathim nodded. "At least five or six meters."

Tsecha took a single step back from the work, shoulders curving in irritation. "It does not help."

"Five or six meters." Jani and Dathim spoke in unison. Then Dathim took the bull by the horns, or in this case the propitiator by the elbow, and dragged him backward, marking off the distance with measured strides.

"Here." Dathim released his dominant, then stepped back and waited, arms folded, feet planted shoulders' length apart, like a djinn from one of Niall's operas. Tall and broad, dressed in dusty white workclothes that contrasted sharply with his gold-brown Vynshàrau coloring, he seemed a construct of wood and stone, as one with the buildings surrounding them. "Do you see it now?" His voice, a deadpan rival of John's, rumbled like a seismic shift.

Tsecha stared at the wall, tilting his head to one side, then the other. "I am not sure. Perhaps, nìa, we should request Doctor Parini's assistance?"

Jani shrugged. "John's the art collector. He knows more."

"But John has already seen this wall many times. Doctor Parini provides a fresh eye." Tsecha looked back over his shoulder at Jani and bared his teeth.

Fresh eye, my . . . Jani had to smile back. "You didn't ask me here to talk about the wall. I should have guessed."

"It will not be completed in time for tomorrow's meeting. Such is as it is." Dathim picked up a square of tile with a glaze like the clear aquamarine of shallow water and walked to his worktable. "I thus have time to seek out the opinions of others." He inserted the square into one of his array of tile cutters, then bent low over the device and adjusted the settings. "Others, who know more," he added, not quite under his breath.

Tsecha ignored his suborn's mutterings. He clasped his hands behind his back and walked over to Jani, light mood dissipating with each step. "Of what did Doctor Parini speak? The damned cold of Chicago? His boredom now that his friends have left him?" He paced back and forth in front of her, an older, wiser, more patient djinn.

"Li Cao sent Val here to inform John that he's being bought out. John's opinion on the subject is not being considered. He'll be paid two percent of what his share in Neoclona is worth." Jani remembered Lucien as he broke the news. Drunk, angry, the information he imparted a payback for her rejection. "Val made matters that much worse by bringing Lucien with him." *And I hope he heaved his guts out.*

"Ah, Captain Pascal." Tsecha walked a tight circle. "He grew bored in Chicago as well, without you to torment."

Jani kicked a tile shard across the floor as another scene from the balcony flitted through her brain. *I love you.* Oh, for the days of myth, when djinn walked the land and gods smote liars with thunderbolts. "He says he's here to act as a fresh eye for Admiral General Mako. I don't believe that."

"Nor would I." Tsecha touched Jani's arm, then gestured toward the patio located in the rear of the meeting house. "For Mako despises him. This we know, and truly."

As they entered the patio, the heat hit them full force, untempered by the breeze off the bay. Tsecha inhaled deeply as soon as the sun fell on him, as though he could breathe in the light. "Cao fears John will become an Haárin, and will use his money to support Haárin enclaves, and Haárin companies. That he will rebuild Haárin docks destroyed by humanish bombs. This, I most believe." He sat atop a pallet of floor tile. "Such shows her lack of understanding. John would never be accepted as Haárin. It would be an impossibility."

"Haárin would take his money, though. If he offered it. Which he hasn't." Jani leaned against a stone wall, then slid down to the patio floor. *And so it begins.* The back and forth. The sifting of data until a conclusion could be reached. The hardest process, but in the end, the most educational. *Politics.* The glib, inadequate word that described the many faceted relationship between Commonwealth and worldskein. "Lucien said that John was being made an example. 'If we can destroy one of the most powerful men in the Commonwealth, what could we do to you?'" She slipped off the jacket that she'd donned back at the Main House, then leaned back against the wall and let the heat absorbed by the stone seep into her shoulders. "My concern is that she's heard rumblings about Elyas' desire to secede."

Tsecha shifted as though he sat on a sharp edge of tile. "Talk of colonial secession. I heard such even when I served as ambassador in damned cold Chicago."

"But here we have an actual plot, with names attached." Jani picked at a jacket seam, stopping when she yanked too hard and the material split. "John is so far removed from all that. All he's done since he arrived here is perform research and hybridize the willing." She imagined faces seen every day at the Main House, on the cliff road and the other enclave streets. Eager, hopeful faces. "Some of them will die if he can't treat them anymore, if he can only use the technology he's already developed. We're all moving targets, constantly changing. A treatment that will work on us one day could kill us the next."

Tsecha nodded, an exaggerated up-and-down. "So, he is needed to keep Thalassans alive. Such is an ethical issue. If Li Cao destroys him, she destroys others as well. Innocents." He brightened. "Would you like me to write a treatise on the subject, nìa?"

Jani ignored the question, and instead dreamt of thunderbolts striking far-off prime ministers. "How can she do this? We aren't

Commonwealth citizens anymore. We can't vote. Half of us started life as idomeni. It's not—"

"You have not answered my question about the treatise, nìa."

"Let's not do that right away. Your treatises tend to shear off the tops of heads. It's bad enough when you take on idomeni. Your style may backfire with humanish."

"Ah." Tsecha ran his finger across his forehead and bared his teeth. Then he stood and strolled across the patio, eyes fixed on the sunburst murals with which Dathim had covered the floor. "So. John will no longer be able to treat hybrids. The hybrids of Thalassa, whom I esteem greatly, even when my nìa claims I do not." He glanced across at Jani. "My nìa, whom I also esteem greatly." He stopped and raised a hand, index finger pointing upward. "Li Cao deems this. Tomorrow, we meet with those who work against her. It is most simple. If Markos and his other secessionists wish my support, they will see that John can continue to do that which he does. Even now, they will support him by telling Cao that she cannot do that which she plans."

Jani worked to her feet. "They'd be taking a risk."

"They take risks now." Tsecha shrugged. "One more will not make their chance of death any greater. They must agree to support Thalassa, which means that they must work now to help John. Or they may swing."

"Swing?"

Tsecha mimed looping a rope and putting it around his neck. "Swing." He yanked his arm upward and stuck out his tongue.

"Thank you for that visual." Jani managed a laugh. "Can you give John your support even if Markos and the others can't? Can the Elyan Haárin do anything to compel Li Cao to back down?"

Tsecha raised a hand to chest level, then curved it in question. "She would demand, I think, that the Haárin leave the Outer Circle, which is something that would most please Cèel as well. He starves his colonies, allows them no supply or repair. Samvasta, Nèae, Zela, with their broken GateWays and half-empty enclaves. He drives the Haárin who live there to the humanish, and now Li Cao would drive them back to him."

"What if you pledged to sink your teeth deeper? Take over more businesses, more docks?" Jani sighed. "That might scare her, which will cause more problems than it solves." She tied the sleeves of the jacket around her waist, then walked to the entry that led back into the house proper, boots scuffing against the inlay with a sound like sandpaper. "God, this is a mess."

"We will think of something, nìa." Tsecha moved in beside her, his soft boots silent on the stone.

"Why do we have to?" Jani paused at the entry. "Ná Feyó is your secular dominant. Ná Gisa is mine. Technically. When she sticks her head out of whichever greenhouse she's working in long enough to give me the time of day."

Tsecha regarded her calmly, as though they discussed the weather, not political subterfuge and rebellion. "I most esteem Feyó, but she worries too much of authority, and the opinions of the other enclaves. Power has made her cautious, and this is, I most believe, a time to be daring."

Jani leaned against the entry so that she stood half in and half out of the house, one side in shade, the other in sun. "You want daring, you should bring Gisa with you to tomorrow's meeting."

"Nìa."

"OK, she's irritating, but she merits some regard. She helped create Thalassa."

"She did that of which she was capable. Now her time is past." Tsecha stood in the comparative darkness of the entry. "Rebellion requires focus if it is to be worth anything, and Gisa lacks focus." He leaned forward, the edges of sunlight striking him, highlighting the lines on his face. "If you say black, she will argue white simply to argue. Such is not an attitude that is needed. Not now."

"So you and I can continue to do all the diplomatic dirty work, then hand off all the pretty decisions to our dominants, wrapped up and ready to go."

Tsecha nodded. "Yes. Such is what we do." He reached out and tapped the top of her hand with his fingertips. "As we did in Rauta Shèràa, and in Chicago. As we will always do."

"Something to look forward to." Jani reached up and struck her fist against the top of the doorway as she passed through into the cool of the entry. "Any feedback yet on your latest broadside?"

Tsecha hesitated, hand once more curving in question. Then he bared his teeth. "Wholeness of Soul." He walked farther into the meeting room, stopping to study the floor, a room-spanning blue and white whirlpool. "It is too soon. I would not expect even an acknowledgment of receipt until tomorrow or even the next day." He dragged the toe of his boot along one of the blue-white borders. "Does it still worry you?"

"Everything worries me." Jani lowered her voice as two coverall-clad hybrids entered the house and began carrying stacks of tile to the table where Dathim worked. "Niall doesn't think it will be a problem."

"Colonel Pierce." Tsecha offered a more humanish-looking, close-lipped smile. "To whom you tell everything."

"Not really." Jani felt the heat rise up her neck as she thought of all the things she would never think of telling Niall. "I tell you more than I do anyone. Including some things I hope you don't understand."

Tsecha did a decent imitation of a humanish throat-clearing. "I understand more than you believe, nìa."

"Great." Jani covered her eyes, then let her hands fall. "All my idiocies exposed." She felt more welcome laughter bubble up, until an all-too-familiar figure entered the room and stopped it dead. "Ná Meva."

"Ná Kièrshia. Glories of the day." Ná Meva Tan bustled in, a headmistress on a mission, the long tail of her bright green wrap-shirt flaring in her wake. "Ní Tsecha. Glories of the day to you as well." Her grey-streaked horsetail swung out as she spun around to survey the entry. "More than yesterday, but not yet complete, ní Dathim!"

"Everyone is a critic." Dathim turned to face them. "But I see no one picking up a cutter." Tile dust streaked his face like paint. "Until they do, they can shut up." He gestured to one of his hybrid helpers to bring another stack of tile, then turned back to his table.

"Hah." Meva bared her teeth as the hum of the tile cutter filled the room. "Ní Dathim is as he always is."

Aren't we all? Jani stepped back as Meva and Tsecha fell into a discussion of the patterns Dathim had chosen for the meeting house floors. Meva stood as tall as her religious dominant, her face as stark, her eyes as gold. Like Tsecha, she projected implacability, the inevitable progression of a wave. Rauta Shèràa Temple had cast her out just before Morden nìRau Cèel locked her up, and Tsecha had offered her a place without first confirming with ná Feyó that such would be acceptable. *Meva treads on toes.* Such was her way. *I do like her . . . for the most part.* But she provided Tsecha the opportunity for theological debate that he had lacked for years, and like a desert plant after the first rain of the season, he had flourished.

Then came the first treatise. The second. *And now this one.* The rhetoric escalating as the subject matter cut closer and closer to the heart of what it meant to be idomeni.

"The significance of this—" Meva gestured toward the spiraling whirlpool, then turned to Jani. "You recall such, from your instruction?"

Damn. Jani left the refuge of her corner and joined the two elders near the middle of the floor. "The twinned spiral." She racked her brain. "Blue for water, white for air. The connectedness of life elements, separate yet united, traveling in the same direction until oneness is achieved." She glanced at Tsecha, who continued to study the floor. At Rauta Shèràa Academy, students could find themselves subjected to testing at any time, and as one of the past masters of that particular art, he would see no reason to interrupt what he saw as valid examination.

Meva nodded. "Shiou oversees this progression, of course, for she is of order."

"No." Jani bit back the word *inshah*. Teacher. That title, she reserved for one and one only. "The progression is overseen by Anèth, the guardian of passage, migration, transition—"

"He is body-son of Caith."

"No, he—" Jani caught Tsecha's flinch, and knew she'd failed this particular test the instant before Meva bared her teeth and let out a derisive bark of laughter.

"Anèth *is* body-son of Caith, for chaos and transition are also separate but united. In any transition is the potential for chaotic progression." Meva stepped out to the whirlpool's center and paced around it. "This is a representation of Anèth's guardianship, for the elements remain united to the end. If such represented his relation with Caith, the whorls would diverge along the way, and form eddies, and curve back on themselves. Such as the representation on the secondary floor of Rauta Shèràa Temple—Tsecha, do you recall such?"

"Yes, ná Meva, I recall it most well." Tsecha finally turned to look at Jani, his hands clasped behind his back, his gaze fixed at a point over her left shoulder. The formality of the Academy returned. "The colors of divergence are more similar. Darker gold and lighter, in depiction of the relation of body-mother and body-child. The game of pattern stones evolved from this. The changing patterns represent the interruption of the journey as chaos enters, for the pattern change is unexpected, unbidden." His Vynshàrau Haárin acquired High Vynshàrau inflections as his manner grew more detached. "You should study more, Jani Kilian. You should know this by now."

Words from the past, driven home with the softest yet most direct of blows. "Yes, *inshah*. I will do so." *I will add it to my goddamned list.* She stood up straight, left arm crossed over her chest, a student's posture of respect. Tsecha raised his left hand in dismissal, the barest flick of a finger, before falling in behind Meva and following her into the adjoining room.

So much for that. Jani walked to the door, face aflame. *At least the hybrids are outside.* Otherwise the news of Tsecha's reprimand would have coursed through the enclave by the time she reached the top of the street.

"Ná Meva speaks of you to ní Tsecha."

Jani stopped and turned back to the worktable, where Dathim smoothed the edge of a tile triangle.

"She does not believe you should act as a propitiator." The Haárin's attention remained focused on the cutter, his fingers flicking over the controller. "She does not believe it is that which you are."

Jani shivered as chill anger drove out the heat of embarrassment. *I never spoke against her to him. I knew he esteemed her, and I kept my mouth shut.* Proof once again that no good deed ever went unpunished. "And what does she think I am?"

Dathim shrugged. "She never says." He glanced at her through a haze of white powder. "Ní Tsecha defends you."

Then he stands back and lets Meva test me. And has the doubt she instilled confirmed. "I have to get back to the Main House." Jani hurried into the street, where the sun shone and the air tasted of the sea instead of the chalk of tile dust, the gall of softly spoken words.

The first dream had been simple enough. Half walking, half sliding down a dune in her drop-dead whites, the most formal of the Service dress uniforms, trying to reach the tents, just visible in the distance. The Laumrau tents.

But she never reached them. The slide down the dune never ended, and the tents never drew closer.

"That one's not bad." Jani had heard worse. From Niall. From others, over the years. Seen worse, during a time when her unmonitored hybridization warred with her Service augmentation, and old friends and enemies returned from the dead to say hello.

But she had never dreamed of Knevçet Shèràa. Until these last few weeks . . .

"Stress." Jani perched on the rock formation just outside the

Main House's rear entry. "Fear." Worry about Thalassa. *And now this.* She tried to work up the nerve to get up, to go inside and meet John's lawyers. What if she hurt John's case? What if she said the wrong thing?

Hello, my name is Jani Kilian, and I have blood on my hands.

Twenty-six Laumrau, taking sacrament in their tents.

Twenty-six faces. Each so different, yet wearing the same look of surprise when she raised her shooter and fired.

"I did what I had to." Jani picked up a stone and skipped it across the scrubby ground. "I'd do it again."

She had just gotten used to the everlasting slide down the dune when, last night, a new dream took its place. She wore desertweights this time. Stood at the opening of the first tent. Tried to rip open the flap, only to find that there wasn't one. Kept trying, and kept trying, grabbing for something that wasn't there—

—until she heard the noise behind her, the hum of a shooter in active mode, and knew if she moved, she would die . . .

. . . but that if she stood still, she would die anyway.

"Decisions, decisions." Jani forced a laugh, then fell silent. Then she eased to her feet, walked to the door, and keyed inside.

CHAPTER 7

Jani heard the raised voices as soon as she entered the courtyard. Two daysuited men stood nose-to-nose in the middle of the largest demiroom, while around them other daysuits watched in grim silence. Meanwhile, another group stood in the foyer, three men and two women with handcarts, their attention fixed as well on the escalating argument.

Then a familiar figure moved from the shadow of a planter and hurried toward her.

"Where the hell have you been?" John's voice shook.

"I was with Tsecha." Jani looked past John to the arguing men. "What happened?"

"Officials from Justice arrived fifteen minutes ago with a warrant." John led her back across the courtyard toward the demiroom. "They want everything—records, data. Anything related to research and treatment."

Jani looked toward the group with the handcarts. The *empty* handcarts. "What have they taken?"

"Nothing. Yet." John stuck his clenched fist against his thigh with every stride. "If Quino thinks—"

Quino? As Jani approached, the arguing men fell silent. Then the shorter of the two turned and planted himself in her path.

"Ms. Kilian." He was a small-boned hawk of a man, attired in darkest blue. "I will have to ask you to—"

Quino. "We've met." Jani pressed close, crowding him, forcing him back. "Joaquin Loiaza. You once stood between me and a ComPol arrest warrant. At John's behest, if I recall."

Loiaza stiffened. "Yes, I do remember." He recovered smoothly, his smile a cool, social curve of lip. "Such a long time ago—"

"Less than two years, but I can understand why you might prefer to forget it considering you're now playing for the other team." It was Jani's turn to smile as Loiaza's face darkened. "Explain your presence here."

Loiaza's eyes widened as he took in the full-bore hybrid turnout—the gold-toned skin, the green-on-green eyes. The top of his head barely reached Jani's shoulder, and like most every other man faced with that height difference, he countered by standing as tall as his spinal column would allow and raising his voice. "We are here by the authority of the Commonwealth—"

"Which means nothing to me." Jani paused to breathe, then let the words flow. "This is not an Elyan settlement, Mister Loiaza. This is Thalassa, an autonomous enclave. The Commonwealth has no jurisdiction here." Out of the corner of her eye Jani saw the man with whom Loiaza had argued scrabble in his jacket pocket. He removed a handheld, then turned and started whispering to another man who stood nearby. "As secular suborn to the enclave dominant, ná Gisa Pilon, I am the authority here—"

"Indeed?" Loiaza glanced back at the group behind him, who had broken out the handhelds as well. "I do not recall Thalassa ever having been recognized by the Commonwealth government."

"His Excellency, Stanislaw Markos, Governor of Elyas, has seen fit to recognize our autonomy by treating the Thalassan boundaries as borders, and in other ways. I will leave it to you to explain to him the irrelevancy of that decision." Jani detected the flicker in Loiaza's eyes, and knew she'd scored a hit. *You didn't inform Markos you were coming here, did you? Bad Quino.* Nothing like pissing off your host by invading enclaves and issuing warrants without telling him first. "In any case, there are protocols that should have been followed prior to this . . . invasion, which were not. For example, we did not receive a formal request from the Commonwealth government to speak with Doctor Shroud concerning their wish to speak with him concerning his Neoclona holdings."

"Is this the imperial 'we,' ná Kièrshia? Do you speak for the absent ná Gisa as well, or is the act of obstruction of justice yours alone?" Loiaza's mud-brown eyes had hardened to stone. "No matter. Allow me to formally request now that we be allowed to discuss the matter of divestiture of Neoclona holdings with your suborn—"

"Denied." Jani glanced at the other lawyers. All handhelds had been set aside—she had their undivided attention now. "The conversations that have already occurred will be considered to have never taken place. Any documents or other materials that were taken will be returned to Doctor Shroud immediately. You will depart Thalassa now and reapply formally for permission to speak with him."

Loiaza kicked the last shred of social pretense out the window. "This is ridiculous." His voice emerged as a hiss. "You and your Thalassans are medical mishaps, Kilian, not a sovereign entity."

"We're both, actually, which means that Doctor Shroud's skills as a physician as well as his researches are vital to our continued health and well-being. To deny him the right and ability—not to mention the wherewithal—to practice his profession threatens the lives of all members of this enclave. Innocent members. I think the appropriate term for what might follow if you succeed in your efforts to prevent him from continuing his work is 'humanitarian crisis.' " Jani turned her back on Loiaza and held out her hand to the man with whom he'd argued. "I'm assuming you're one of the good guys? Hello. We haven't met."

The man took her hand lightly, as though he feared a shock. "Rudo Sikara, Ms. Kili—ná Kièrshia." His skin was so black it seemed tinged with blue, the reddened whites of his eyes the only outward betrayal of the current stressful interlude. "This is my colleague, James Cossa." He nodded toward the other man, who was younger, lighter of complexion, and even more battered looking.

Jani hesitated as her backbrain sent out a warning barrage. "Sikara and Cossa. I've heard of you." Her gut tightened. "John said he'd hired an experienced firm. He didn't mention it was the most famous in the Outer Circle."

"I am flattered." Sikara's smile was tight. "I wish we could have met before this. That we could have spoken." His voice matched his smile. "Do you have *any* justification for the claims of sovereignty you've just made?"

"I believe I do." Jani lowered her voice as Loiaza and his team strained to overhear. "Last year, the Commonwealth Service ceased efforts to press charges of treason and desertion against two officers because they had begun the process of hybridization. As hybrids, they were no longer considered eligible for the Service. In the end it was decided that they came under the jurisdiction of the Elyan Haárin dominant, ná Feyó Tal, who at the time was considered

Thalassa's secular dominant. Since that time, she has ceded the governance of Thalassa to ná Gisa Pilon."

"That should not necessarily be construed as an acknowledgment of sovereignty," Loiaza's nasal voice sounded. "A colonial base may find itself in a situation where acquiescing to local practice is preferable to pursuing a course of action that might jeopardize its future dealings with the native population."

Jani turned on him, once more forcing him to backpedal. "Li Cao would do well to follow the Fort Karistos example."

"This is not a matter of local interest only," Loiaza bit out. "The decisions reached here will have far-reaching implications."

Jani stared at the man until a small vein in his temple started to throb. "John's your test case. You'll destroy him to keep the rest of the Commonwealth in line. Think you want to hybridize? Remember what we did to the head of Neoclona, and think again."

"Indeed." Sikara stepped up beside Jani. He wore the simplest of black suits and a white shirt, accented by a yellow and green striped neckpiece. "Nasty precedent, Counselor." He arched one graying eyebrow.

Loiaza licked his lips. "Doctor Shroud is a special case."

"So any decisions reached as a result of this 'special case' will never be cited as precedent in support of any other action against another hybrid?" Cossa proved the more expressive of the two, from his more fashionable brown suit to his continued gesturing as he spoke. "Pull the other one, Quino—it whistles the Commonwealth anthem!"

Silence settled like a layer of ash. Then Loiaza turned to Sikara. "Since we have been evicted pending clarification of Jani Kilian's status as godhead—" He glared at her. "We will return tomorrow, Counselor."

"Pending clarification of Thalassa's status, Counselor." Sikara reactivated his handheld and began jotting. "I, meanwhile, will contact Governor Markos. And ná Feyó Tal as well, whose acquaintance I have enjoyed for several years."

Loiaza started to speak, then closed his mouth and beckoned to the other lawyers. They followed him from the room single file, like nestlings trailing after a pissed-off mother duck, dragging the other Justice Ministry staffers and their empty handcarts along in their wake.

"Well," Sikara said as the door closed. "That took a turn I did not expect." He sat on the U-shaped sofa that dominated the space and regarded Jani with tired eyes. "As I said, it would have been nice if we could have spoken prior to this. You compelled us to reveal aspects of our defense that I wanted to keep close to the vest until we had all the facts."

Jani glanced at John, who perched on the edge of an end table, arms folded, staring at the floor. "What difference does it make whether they know this or not? They did what they did—they can't cover it up. They invaded a sovereign state, and they didn't inform Markos before they tramped through his flower bed to do it. They're in trouble."

"Only if Governor Markos's decision concerning Thalassa's status stands up to challenge." Cossa picked up a long-forgotten glass of iced tea, which dripped condensation on his trousers as he drank. "He serves at Li Cao's pleasure. She can pressure him to change his mind."

"And Feyó can pressure him not to." Jani massaged the base of her neck and felt the knot. "We're a long way from Chicago. The clout flows in both directions out here."

"Li Cao will fight—she has too much to lose." Cossa paused to take a napkin that Sikara thrust at him, and wrapped it around the glass. "If she can destroy John, other humans will be dissuaded from hybridizing by the threat of loss of profession and property." His eyes lit. "I foresee a battle the first time a Family member decides to seek treatment."

"Unfortunately, none of them have yet taken the plunge." Sikara gazed over at John. "That we know of."

"I shouldn't have to remind you, of all people, of the concept of confidentiality." John spoke without raising his head. "It's their secret to keep until they start to show." He worked his fingers as he spoke, like a musician warming up. Then he stilled and fell silent.

When it became obvious that his client had no more to say, Sikara stood. "I have known Quino for years. The best way to handle him is to let him think he's winning from the start. He grows smug, and with that smugness comes complacency. And with that complacency comes the tendency to make mistakes." His expression grew wistful. "Ah well. Still a great deal of room for arrogance." He glanced at Jani. "A great deal." He hefted the briefbag that had rested on the floor at his feet. "In any event, this will be a precedent-setting case."

"To the office!" Cossa slung his briefbag over his shoulder and clapped his hands. "Let's go put on the mud clothes."

"My colleague has such a colorful way of expressing himself." Sikara shook his head with mock gravitas. "John, we will be speaking later." He bowed to Jani. "Ná Kièrshia. We should talk soon." The light in his eye sharpened for an instant, as though *soon* meant *before you speak to anyone else about anything at all.* Then he was gone, and his partner after him.

Jani waited until the men left, until the door closed and the silence settled once more. "I'm sorry I was late." She untied the jacket from around her waist, then walked to the sofa and sat. "I was held up at the meeting house and—"

"Do you know what you're doing?" John's voice emerged like a shudder, cold and deep in the bone. "When you open your mouth, do you have any idea what will fall out? Or are you just making it up as you go?"

Jani stilled. *Is this more of what Val warned me about?* She glanced around the demirooms, the courtyard, on the lookout for a familiar head ducking behind shrubbery. *No wonder he made himself scarce.* "I got them out of here, didn't I? It gave you some room to maneuver." She spread the jacket across her legs and stroked it like a pet. "I believe there's enough precedent to support the concept of our sovereignty—"

"Which reinforces the idea that I'm no longer human enough to run my own goddamned company." John stood, slowly, as though movement pained him. "There's a reason why men like Sikara and Cossa are paid a great deal of money to dig poor bastards like me out of holes. It's because they know what to say and when to say it. They don't just blurt. They don't give the game away."

Jani's hands stalled in mid-stroke. "I'm sorry I upset Mr. Sikara. I will apologize the next time I see—"

"You humiliated Joaquin Loiaza. Do you think he's just going to sit back and take it?" John looked toward the courtyard, where a couple of Thalassans fussed over a flowering shrub and pretended not to be eavesdropping. "We were prepared to give up some things," he continued with lowered voice. "We were prepared to let them think they'd won this round. It made me sick to do it, but I had no choice." He started to pace. "It's a dance. I've led all my life, and now I have to follow, because the steps are everything and if I put a foot wrong, I lose everything."

Jani looked toward the courtyard, where more Thalassans had gathered. Yes, some carried trays of condiments and others table linens, but set-up for late afternoon sacrament usually didn't begin for another half-hour. *But today, there's a floor show.* "Why didn't you just tell me—"

"*I'm telling you now.*" John stopped in front of her. "I should have told you sooner. That was my mistake, and I will pay for it, assuming I haven't already." He bent closer, mindful of their audience. "Some things are not your job. Some things, you leave to those who know what the hell they're doing. Do you really believe you said anything that Sikara and Cossa didn't already know? They were going to wait until they spoke with Markos and prepared him for the onslaught, until they had everything in place. The concept of Thalassan autonomy is a smoke screen. The idea that someone who decides to hybridize risks losing their livelihood, their life's work . . ." His eyes clouded. "That's the more important point." He bit a thumbnail. That was a new tic, one that the angle of his hand revealed had already claimed the index and middle fingers. "Quino's sharp, but as Sikara said, he makes mistakes. This dramatic raid of his was a mistake. You've given him a chance to recover."

Jani sat back, fighting the invisible weight that pressed down on her shoulders. "They won't have time. This isn't Chicago—they're out of their element here."

"They have what they need. A few Service officers. A few colonial officials. If Stash Markos isn't placed under house arrest by sunset, we'll be very lucky." John laughed, a humorless bark. "Of course, they won't call it that. They'll invent a reason to place him in protective custody. A newly discovered assassination plot, or something."

More Thalassans appeared, and the setup for the afternoon meal that Jani always thought of as "fourses" began in earnest. Her stomach growled as aromas of baking bread and various tangy sauces reached her. The animal, demanding her feeding, even as the higher being's gut twisted and she wished she could crawl in a cave and hide. "But if they took your records—"

"That's the documents examiner in you, fixed on paper." John's voice defrosted, a little. "I do keep copies. And the most important things . . . let's just say they're safe, and leave it at that." He quieted. Then he circled around the sofa and strode to the lift. "I'll be downstairs, working. While I still have work to do, and time in which to do it." He nodded curtly to the few Thalassans who offered greetings. Waited by the lift for a few moments, then struck the wall with the flat of his hand and headed for the stairs.

Jani lay back her head and closed her eyes. The hum of courtyard conversation, the clatter of plates and the beeps of cookers,
formed a pleasant background noise. Enough to clear her racing
mind and quiet her rumbling stomach, purge Meva's laugh and
Tsecha's dismissal and John's doubt. But not lulling enough to
bring sleep. That escape route had closed to her, provided no
respite at all. Instead, she just breathed slowly, in and out, and
tried not to think of what tomorrow's meeting might bring.

"Where did you get this ham?"

Jani opened one eye to find Val standing in front of her, holding a filled plate.

"It can't be Virginia, can it? I didn't think Earth would trade
with you." He sat on the edge of the low table and plucked strips
of baked ham from a pile that included sliced hybrid mango and
bean salad.

"It's Hortensian, I think." Jani forced open the other eye and
sat up. "Glad you like it." She watched Val shovel in food with the
focused abandon of a starving teenager. "Should you be here, considering?"

Val stopped his fork halfway to his mouth, then lowered it. "I
begged your excellent Mister Brondt to let me layover. He found
me a room, and I showered. Took a nap. Pretended I was at a resort, far away from everything, waiting for the love of my life to
show up." He tried another bite of ham, then set his plate on the
table. "I have a reservation at some place in Karistos, but as soon
as I'd show up, Quino would lock me down. I'd be a prisoner.
Who needs that shit? I hid as soon as I saw the skimmers in the
driveway." He sighed. "I wanted to see John. I wanted to at least
try to make it . . . not seem so . . ."

"Horrible?" Jani leaned forward, hands clenched between her
knees to keep from reaching out for Val's neck. "Rotten? Insert your
adjective of choice here. If you run out of English, there's Elyan
Greek, my Acadian French—"

"*All right.*" Val pressed his hands to his temples, then locked
his fingers behind his neck. "How is he?"

"How do you think?" Jani forced a smile at two Thalassans
who wandered past. "He went downstairs to work."

"That's John for you. It was the same at Rauta Shèràa. 'John,
that last bomb hit right next door!' 'It missed us? Great! Time
enough for one more assay.'" Val laughed, a sound softened by
memory. "Sikara and Cossa." His brow arched. "John picked the
right man. Rudo hates Quino's guts." His eyes closed halfway as

he accessed long-buried gossip. "Fight over a girl, back in the Pleistocene. Don't know who won. Can't have been over Quino's wife. He wouldn't cross the street for her." He sniffed, then grinned, one marriage dissected and all was right with the world. "So what happened? With Quino and that?"

"It went—" Jani stopped, then studied Val's handsome face. Close enough to reach out and touch, yet so far, far away. "They came for some documents. Both sides worked it out."

"But didn't Rudo—?" Val's brow furrowed. Then his face reddened. "Oh." He looked toward the courtyard, where fourses had hit its stride, a hundred different conversations bouncing off every hard surface. "I guess—" He coughed. "Yeah." He braced his hands on the table's edge, then pushed to his feet and grabbed his plate. "I have to go." He didn't look back as he maneuvered around the planters and the maze of tables and vanished into the shadows.

Well, I finally kept my mouth shut. "And that didn't help, either." Jani girded herself, then rose and walked into the midst of the mealtime melee. Filled a plate and found a seat away from everyone, the transient on the run, with no time to talk.

Then she went to the library. Dragged a favorite chair out onto the balcony. Found a recording board and a stylus and made notes for the next day's meeting.

CHAPTER 8

Jani wandered upstairs eventually, after the Main House had gone dark but for the graveyard crew. A determinedly nonchalant question to the night nurse awarded her the news that John had retired an hour earlier. Now she stood before the door to their suite, hand on the control, and pondered. *He should be asleep by now.* Years of hospital training had left him a light sleeper, but if she undressed in the sitting room and slept on the couch . . .

The door whispered open and she crept inside. Stepped inside the bedroom just long enough to pull a T-shirt out of her armoire, and stilled when she heard the rustle of bedclothes, the voice.

"Where've you been?"

Jani activated a table lamp, since there was no longer any reason to risk her shins in collision with the furniture. "Library."

"I should've guessed." John worked into a sitting position and activated the bedside light. "I ran into Val in the clinic. He was wandering around, trying to make himself useful. He sounded quite hurt. Said you'd given him the boot."

"He asked what had happened with Quino. I didn't tell him." Jani boosted atop the low dresser. Under normal circumstances, she would have sat at the foot of the bed, then edged closer toward the inevitable, but normal was a day ago. A lifetime ago. "I was practicing keeping my mouth shut."

John hung his head. "I'm sorry for that."

Jani smoothed the T-shirt over her knees, stretching out creases. "I can't do anything. I can't make it stop. Every time I open my mouth, I say the wrong thing. Every time I don't open my mouth . . . same difference." She folded the shirt in half lengthwise, then rolled it from the bottom up into a tight tube. When she finished, she stared at it. In another life she'd have tossed it in her duffel and continued packing, but she wasn't going anywhere. Now when things got tough, she had to stay put. "Every time I do something, it's exactly the thing you don't want done."

John's head snapped up. *"I don't need you to do anything."* He flinched as his own volume battered him, then sagged against the headboard. "I just need you to be there. It means a great deal. To be able to look across a table, across a room, and see you." His face lightened in grim wonder. "I can't recall ever feeling so alone. Even in Rauta Shèràa, after you left the first time. The way I felt then was nothing like the way I felt this afternoon. It hit me like a broadside that I was going to lose it. All of it. That Val would do what he could, but in the end he'd save the company . . . even if that meant shunting me aside." His eyes widened, flashing silver in the half-light.

"He wouldn't have . . ." Jani hesitated. Then she shook out the T-shirt and started rolling it anew.

"Even you doubt him." John looked around the room as though searching for something. Then he fixed on her, waiting until her gaze met his. "This year has been the best of my life. I worked. I changed. I learned so much." A bare hint of a smile. "And you were always there, somewhere. Not side by side with me every moment, but still. Always together, working toward the same goal. It was the way Rauta Shèràa should have been. The way my entire life should have—" His voice cracked, and he smoothed his hands over the sheet again and again.

"You think I'll leave you if you lose Neoclona?" Jani looked around the bedroom and saw . . . a room. It possessed a beautiful view and held all she had never wanted or needed, and yet . . . *You leave rooms. You close doors, and never open them again.* They were places you passed through, not places you remained. "I once lived out of a Guernsey Station storage closet for two months. I'm adaptable."

"I'm not. Not anymore." John pushed a hand through his hair, the wheaten strands capturing all available illumination and holding it like a miser. "I won't be the same, after they take it away."

Jani set the shirt aside and slid off the dresser. "You'll be what you've always been." She approached the bed slowly, ready to veer toward a nearby chair at the first hint of rejection. "You were a controlling, arrogant, brilliant, driven pain in the ass in Rauta Shèràa. Before you'd built your empire. Before anyone had heard of Neoclona." She paused at the footboard. "You're still control-ling, still arrogant, still driven. Still brilliant. Still a pain. In these essentials, you will never change. You'll take what's available and remake it as you always have. You are what you've always been, and will continue to be whilst you breathe."

John managed a grin. "That sounds like something your father would say."

"He does." Jani lowered to the edge of the bed, just within arm's reach. "Mostly to my mother."

"A handful, is she?" John pushed down the sheet, then pulled up his legs so he sat cross-legged. "He and I should get together some-time and compare notes on the Kilian women. I think he'd talk to me. He seems to like me a little more than does your mother." His brow twitched. "Brilliant?"

Jani rolled her eyes. "I thought you'd pick that out of the list first."

"But also controlling, arrogant, driven, and a pain in the ass." John wiped a hand over his face. The first hint of beard glinted across his cheeks, combining with ruffled hair and skewed T-shirt to make him appear agreeably rumpled. "And yet you love me anyway."

"I've been told more than once that I possess my own endearing qualities." Jani shrugged. "One of the reasons we're together is be-cause we can't find anyone else who'll put up with us." She looked over at John, to find him staring her down, lips slightly parted.

"We could've found worse places to land." He reached out and grabbed her by the shoulders, pulling her to him, applying rough kisses to her face and neck and lower still as he peeled away first her clothes, then his. He drove into her almost immediately, going off on his own for most of the journey, not waiting for her to catch up. Too intent this time on finding solace to offer any.

Jani held him until he finished, and cradled him as he slept. So much simpler, sex, even though it only served to delay. Even though it was only half the song, the melody sans the words. But she'd set-tle for half, accept it and never argue. For her, the words had always been the difficult part.

All was still and quiet, but for John's breathing and the tumult in her own head. She slept eventually.

And she dreamed.

The sunrise horizon glowed orange as Rilas parked her skimmer behind a rock formation, then gathered dried scrub and branches and spread them across it, obscuring it further. Even the smallest risk could not be allowed, for there were dangers enough at times such as this, when the moment had come to act. When the planning ended and the action began.

Once she had hidden the skimmer, she uttered a prayer to Caith and strode to the house. Her slingbag hung from her shoulder, bumping her hip with every stride. Animals fled before her, scuttling beneath rocks as she passed.

The dawn air felt cool, which she did not expect. So much did this place resemble Rauta Shèràa that she anticipated the same warmth, longed for it. *Soon.* Soon her task would be completed, and she would be free to leave this godless world. Her berths had been purchased, as had her new name, her new possessions. All rested in a locker at Elyas Station, assembled in pieces by those who did not know that which they did, and left in their hiding place by another. So eager, humanish and idomeni both, to perform tasks for payment. So disinterested, humanish and idomeni both, in the reasons for that which they did.

Such is the way of humanish, which the idomeni have taken as theirs. So said nìRau Cèel, who knew all there was to know of these matters.

Rilas surveyed the area around the house, both visually and with a handheld scanner. She compared the signaling to that she had compiled on the day she first visited the place, took note of the minor variations. More small animals had entered and departed, leaving their food remnants and their waste. Leaves had blown in through one of the broken windows, piling in one corner of the area she had chosen for staging. *But no being has entered.* The inevitable disturbances created by a large form walking through a rubble-strewn, dusty space did not reveal themselves. Since the day she first examined this house, no one else had visited.

She walked through the shattered entry, then across the rubble-strewn room to the window. Took one last look at the grounds, the distant cliffs and the sliver of bay beyond. Then lowered her slingbag to the floor and knelt beside it. Opened the flap and set to work, hands moving with speed born of practice as her mind pondered the details of the task ahead.

She removed the pieces of the rifle strut, assembled it and balanced it atop the sill. Assembled the rifle itself. Activated the sight mech, then tossed its satellite into the air to find its way to the area above the target. Removed one of the cylinders from its chill encasement and inserted it into the chamber. Locked it within.

She eased into a half-sitting, half-reclining position atop the wide sill, edging onto her side so she could lie beside the rifle. Brought it close and curled around it. Felt the sharp chill of the rocks through her thin clothing, the edges like blades digging into her skin, and offered the pain to Caith as sacrifice, as always.

Pressed the rifle to her shoulder and lowered her eye to the sight mech. Waited for the secondary to activate, calibrate, and send back the first of the signals.

Nothing for a time but blurred images of portions of the house yard. Then came color. Clarity. The image of the distant road. The houses that lined it. The meeting house around which workers had gathered and commenced their labors.

Rilas settled in. She was at her most vulnerable now, this she knew and truly, so fixed on her target that she could miss any warning signal from her secondary. *But such is as it is.* Such risk was the tribute she paid Tsecha, the fact that at some point she left herself as open, as exposed, as he was.

She breathed the fetid air, let it fill her, became one with the blasted house.

Watched.

Waited.

CHAPTER 9

"Are you worried, nìa?"

Jani looked back over her shoulder at Tsecha. He stood in the middle of the meeting room, hands clasped before him like a headmaster greeting the first class of the term. He wore a tunic and trousers in shades of tan and off-white, topped off by his propitiator's overrobe. The garment's red-slashed sleeves proved the brightest thing in the room, drawing Jani's eye despite her growing nervousness. She tried to recall the last time she'd seen Tsecha wear it. Weeks, possibly months.

Dressed to kill. "I'm waiting for Markos. John and his lawyers think that Li Cao could have him arrested." Jani turned back to the window, which overlooked the street at the point where it angled down toward the beach, on the watch for a flash of reflected sun off a skimmer chassis.

"I would have something to say about that, I think." Tsecha drew up beside her. "I have heard that he did leave his house near to sunrise."

Let's hear it for the Elyan Haárin spy network. "Then he should have been here an hour ago." Jani gripped the window ledge, massaging the rough stone with her thumb until the pain stopped her. "Even if he took the roundabout route and came in from the south, the trip would take an hour, tops." She yawned, then rubbed grainy eyes. John had slept through the night, but she hadn't quite managed. *New dreams for old.* But in this one, the shooter fired.

"Nìa." Tsecha tapped her shoulder. "I see a skimmer."

Jani ran out of the room and through the entry, pausing in the doorway just as the dark blue double-length drifted to a stop a few doors down from the meeting house. Reached beneath her shirt-jacket and undid the clasp of her shooter holster, just in case.

The skimmer's passenger side gullwing swung upward, and Governor Stanislaw Markos emerged into the morning. He looked down the street in the direction he'd come, as if he feared he'd been followed. Then he turned to Jani and blew out a long breath. "Jesus Christ." He seemed at first glance the sort of man one saw on Family fringes, a door opener and holder of the coats, all slicked silver hair and expensive tailoring. But he was Phillipan by birth and colonial to the core, and his lack of affection for Chicago had blossomed over the years into mutual enmity.

"Good morning, Excellency." Jani adjusted her shirt to hide the shooter holster, then walked out into the street. "You look like you've had an interesting morning."

"It was a near thing." Markos's voice emerged guttural, raked by anger and more than a little fear. "Two officials from the Justice annex visited me last night. 'A plot to overthrow your government,' they said. 'You must remain in your home, under guard.' Bullshit. The only plots those idiots know of are those they hatch themselves." He smoothed the front of his cream daysuit and eyed Jani expectantly.

"I think it has to do with John." Jani tried to see who else sat inside the skimmer, but Markos's bulk blocked her view. "And the concept of Thalassan sovereignty."

A corner of Markos's mouth twitched. "I wondered when that would come back to bite me." Then he smiled. "Thank God for friends in high places." He smacked the skimmer roof, and the rear door of the double-length opened. "Come out, Zhenya. We're the first ones here."

The man who emerged paused to stretch, then muttered something to Markos in Elyan Greek that made them both laugh. He stood shorter than average and stockier than was fashionable. His hair had been trimmed in a haphazard bowl that accentuated his broad face, its blond more an absence of color than a brilliant statement, dull as it was and streaked with grey. He wore a loose-fitting outfit in off-white, some new style of tunic and trousers with an open collar and tucks and seaming that betrayed the presence of ventilation panels.

Yevgeny Scriabin. Deputy Commerce minister, and the greatest threat in a decade to Li Cao's hammerlock on the prime ministry. Jani watched him approach, her trepidation an undercurrent, like the first rumblings of food poisoning. *Anais Ulanova's nephew.*

The *S* in the Commonwealth-spanning NUVA-SCAN business conglomerate. *Not the sort I'd turn to at a time like this.* "Your Excellency." She extended her hand as he closed in.

"Ná Kièrshia." Scriabin's hand enveloped hers. "I hope that's the correct appellation. I tore through every idomeni language guide I could put my hands on, but didn't find much that proved helpful." His voice was a rough baritone, his accent a mélange of Michigan Provincial seasoned with Old Russian. "Finally, I broke down and asked my driver. He proved surprisingly helpful."

Jani looked past Scriabin to the skimmer just as his helpful driver emerged.

"Mornin', gel!" Niall smoothed the front of his dress desert-weight tunic, then set his brimmed lid. "Not used to all this subterfuge and evasive maneuvering so early in the morning. Felt like I was sixteen again, running the White Line in the Wodonga Mountains."

Markos laughed. "A Victorian boy, are you, Colonel?"

"Born and bred, Your Excellency." Niall circled around the vehicle toward them, eyes bright with the thrill of the chase. "Shaped and baked to a crusty turn."

Scriabin cocked his head. "The white line?"

Niall slowed. "The White River, Your Excellency," he piped a bit too brightly. "Loops around the northern half of the city of Wodonga. My school chums and I enjoyed many a summer rafting trip." His grin at Jani held a touch of friendly malice. "You look surprised to see me." He herded her into the doorway, leaving Scriabin and Markos standing by the skimmer.

"Rafting with school chums." Jani kept her eye on the two officials, who leaned against the skimmer and waited for the other governors. "Make that running stolen goods from the Wodonga shuttleport to where the hell ever."

"We used rafts sometimes." Niall pulled out his case and plucked out a 'stick. "When the jungle got too dense and the skimtrucks couldn't hold the track." He cracked the tip and took a long pull as he slumped against the polished stone. "I know enough about John to fill in the rest. Cao wants him out at Neoclona. I'm surprised it took her this long. What's Parini's role?"

"Stunned bystander." Jani stifled another yawn. "They let him come here to inform John only after the legal surgery had already started. Now he's hiding out in the Main House, trying to pretend he's just visiting and not having much luck."

"If he fights to defend John, he's out, and Cao hands the whole Easter egg over to Eamon DeVries, third in line and incipient gutter sot." Niall sneered, his scarred lip curling to reveal a pointed canine. "Here's your choice, boy. We destroy you a little or we destroy you a lot." Another pull, a drift of smoke. "Smuggling was cleaner. When you overstepped, they just shot you."

"Who shoots, Colonel?" Tsecha poked his head between them and bared his teeth.

"Figure of speech, ní Tsecha." Niall pulled the 'stick from his mouth and hid it cradled in his hand like a schoolboy caught out during recess.

"*Hah.*" Tsecha turned and vanished back into the comparative dark of the meeting house. "Smoke your nicstick, Colonel, before you choke."

"*Dammit.*" Niall stuck the 'stick back in his mouth, then examined his palm for burns. "Look, gel, I know Markos isn't here just to admire ní Dathim's tilework. I've been here for nigh on six months, and I'm not fuckin' blind. Or deaf." He took one last drag, then tossed the spent 'stick into a nearby planter. "I am, in point of fact, the Service representative at this little discussion, as ordered by Admiral General Hiroshi Mako himself."

It's too early in the morning and I'm too tired to be surprised. Jani looked out toward the street, where another skimmer had joined the governor's. "Any danger of Lucien turning up?"

"He's blogged down with transfer paperwork," Niall said as he headed toward the skimmers. "Should keep him busy for the day."

Scriabin hurried to the new skimmer just as the passenger gullwing drifted upward. "You finally made it."

Jani heard an all-too-familiar voice emerge from the vehicle and froze.

"—not since Rauta Shèràa, when we all feared for our lives every moment." Exterior Minister Anais Ulanova, dressed in cool blue, as ever the elegant hatchet, disembarked the skimmer and immediately latched onto her nephew's arm. "Zhenya, you left Karistos too quickly. We lost you—" She stopped when she saw Jani, mouth stalled in mid-word as though caught in the midst of a scream.

Jani heard Niall emit a low, tuneless whistle.

"Tyotya Ani." Scriabin patted his aunt's hand. "I believe you and ná Kièrshia know one another."

Jani bowed as low as her sensibility allowed, which wasn't much. "Excellency."

Anais Ulanova said nothing, even when her nephew touched her arm and spoke in her ear. She simply stared, eyes dark as space and just as cold.

"Minister Ulanova." Tsecha glared Sìah daggers over the top of Ulanova's head at her nephew. "Minister Scriabin should have informed us."

"Ní Tsecha." If Ulanova noticed the tension in Tsecha's manner, she ignored it. "I trust my nephew implicitly, of course, but given the sensitive nature of this discussion, we felt that the presence of a first-level minister would lend more credence to any agreement reached."

"I know what you're thinking," Niall said as he joined Jani at one end of the long table.

"If you did, you wouldn't sit next to me." Jani continued to watch Ulanova, who still hung onto Scriabin's arm then laughed too loudly at something Tsecha said. "Who was the genius who pulled her into this?"

They had adjourned to the largest meeting room, which opened out onto a small garden complete with bubbling fountain. Jani concentrated on the trickling burble in the hope that the sound would calm her, and knew from the roil in her gut that she hoped in vain.

"She's been Exterior Minister for a long time." Niall lowered his voice as the governors from Amsun and Hortensia, Avelos and Wallach, took seats nearby. "She does know the lay of the land out here."

"The first hint of trouble, she'll sell you out to Cao."

"Not as long as her nephew's involved. He's our insurance. If he falls, she tumbles with him."

Ulanova took a seat near the head of the table, next to Scriabin. Since the initial shock of recognition, she had ignored Jani, and seemed determined to carry that standard throughout the balance of the meeting. She greeted Avelos and Wallach like the old friends they likely were, and complimented Markos's neckpiece before directing her attention to the recording board set before her by an aide.

"Looks like I don't rate a personal greeting." Niall sniffed. "I'm crushed."

"That's what you get for sitting next to me." Jani pulled a folded sheet of parchment from the inner pocket of her shirt-jacket and spread it flat on the table. "Feel free to move if you'd rather sit with the popular kids."

"Nah. I've always been a back-of-the-room type." Niall grinned, the expression altering to a formal smile when Avelos pointed at him.

"So, your Mako's hip-deep in anti-Cao factionitis." Avelos was an angular woman with a voice to match, the light bouncing off her lofty cheekbones and casting deep shadows under her eyes. "Doesn't surprise me—those two never got on. They've been trying to cut one another off at the knees for years."

Niall shook his head. "It's much deeper than that, Your Excellency. There's a fundamental difference in how we view the state of the Commonwealth and her relations with the worldskein. With her colonies."

"The Service is stretched to the brink out here." Wallach, a skinny whip of a man with an unfashionable receding hairline, doodled in the margins of his recording board display. "No one's gotten to the bottom of the dock attacks, and Cèel is threatening to call the Haárin back into the worldskein if any more of their facilities are hit."

"Cèel can call all he wishes." Tsecha had seated himself at the head of the table, hands clasped lightly in front of him, no note-taking device to be seen. "The Haárin will not go."

"Then he'll send his warrior skein to come and get them." Wallach shook his head as a series of interlaced loops appeared on his board. "And who will save our sorry asses from a colonial version of the Night of the Blade?" He glanced across the table at Niall, then resumed his doodling.

"I thank you for raising the subject of defense, Your Excellency." Niall adopted his instructor's voice, world-weary and wise. "His Excellency Minister Scriabin and I, along with those we represent, are also examining this matter from that point of view." He stifled a cough. "Six Common months ago, I was charged with the task of evaluating the situation at Fort Karistos. Over the last two weeks, I have collated my findings. I've concluded that thanks to years of neglect by Chicago, the Service personnel stationed there have evolved in sensibility to the point that they feel more loyalty to their base colony and the mixture of races surrounding it than to their nominal homeworld."

"It's taken you long enough to figure it out." Jani paused as another yawn threatened. *Not now, dammit.* "It's been that way out here for a generation, at least."

Niall nodded agreement. "The decision we're faced with is, do we clean the place out, restaff it with more traditionally loyal forces we can't spare, and alienate the local populations?" He took a stylus from the holder in the middle of the table and rolled it between his fingers. "Or do we work with the situation as it stands, maybe even help it to . . . evolve, then concentrate on developing a close relationship with whoever happens to wind up in charge."

Avelos and Wallach stared across the table at one another, while Markos folded his arms and nodded. "The Service supports secession."

Niall glanced downtable at Scriabin, who nodded almost imperceptibly. "The Outer Circle would remain allied with the Commonwealth—that would be one of the conditions of the separation. But the colonial governments would be granted their autonomy. The forces stationed both here and at Amsun Base would be theirs, to command as they would. To man as they would, be it with humans"—he gestured toward Jani—"hybrids . . . even Haárin." He spoke slowly, his Victorian twang all but buried in careful intonation. "All indications are that Cèel and his Vynshàrau will face a challenge from the Pathen by year's end. Aden nìRau Wuntoi, the Pathen dominant, is ready—he has Oà and Sìah backing, and would be anyone's first pick to assume the Oligarchy. The Pathen and Sìah Haárin are well settled here in the Circle, and we want them on our side *now*. We want friendlies in place so if Rauta Shèràa implodes and civil war spreads throughout the worldskein, our border colonies don't get chewed up in the process." He placed the stylus back in its holder, then worked off his nerves by flexing his fingers. "One war at a time. We can't fight to keep the Outer Circle in check and at the same time take on whatever Cèel throws at us. For that reason, we don't want to risk losing the support of either the resident humans or the Haárin. Or any combination thereof."

Jani made to speak, then paused and pressed her fingertips to the middle of her forehead. She could feel the tightening, and knew it would only get worse. Tracking the Thalassan ball through the diplomatic maze had that effect on her. "You would support the Pathen alliance against the Vynshàrau, knowing Cèel would see this as a threat to his authority, maybe even an act of war." She waited for Niall to nod. He didn't. He didn't look at her, either, which made the sweat bloom along her back. "You'd commit Service troops to this?"

Scriabin nodded. "Yes."

"Troops that you and Mako have no right to commit?" Jani recalled Niall's words during one long ago lunch. *Do you believe in ghosts?* Maybe the bigger question was, did the ghosts believe in you? "The Service taking sides in an idomeni civil war. Am I the only one who's seeing history gearing up for an encore performance here?"

"It would be different this time." Niall's lips barely moved, as though he feared to say the words aloud.

"You, of all people, can sit there and say that to me? We're Exhibits A and B, for crying out—" Jani stopped when she felt the stares from the rest of the table. Took a deep breath. "What happens," she finally said, "when Cao figures out that you're snaking her?"

"She's preoccupied with the upcoming election." Niall sat forward, braced his elbows on the table's edge and gestured toward his ally. "Yevgeny's going to clean her out. He's playing Cao even in most polls, and all his numbers are trending up. In between now and then, we just need to keep Cao out of the loop."

"Thank you for the vote of confidence, Niall, but I take ná Kièrshia's point." Scriabin ignored his aunt's irritated muttering. "The number of like minds on Cabinet Row is significant, and most are not seen to be supporters of mine. Even if I should lose the election—and despite what the good colonel says, odds that I win are even at best—I feel that there will be sufficient push in place to ram the secession bill through."

"Many a slip twixt cup and lip," said Wallach, the resident realist.

"The word's treason." Jani looked around the table, and saw that even Ulanova had grown thoughtful. "Much as I care for some of you, my concerns are other. If Mako gets rousted out of bed in the middle of the night and disappears into some Cabinet Row cellar with the rest of his buddies, what happens to Thalassa? If it becomes known that I aided and abetted a treasonous cause, and with John Shroud stripped of all influence and ability to pull strings due to his expulsion from Neoclona, what happens?" She took note of the lack of surprise at that particular bit of news. *Great Ganesh—did everyone know it was coming but us?* "You'll all be arrested." She clenched a fist and tapped the table. "Meanwhile, Fort Karistos will be restocked with hardcore Earthbound. Thalassans would be split into Haárin or humanish regardless of their level of hybridization—the Haárin would be shipped back to their former enclaves, and the humanish would be jailed. Without medical care, some of them would die. The ones who didn't could be exiled or executed, rejected by their families, or simply stoned in the street like lepers. Thalassa isn't just the only home they have. For some, it's the only home they *can* have."

Scriabin studied Jani for a long moment, then glanced sidelong at Tsecha. "What does Thalassa want?"

"I think the more important question is, why should we care?" Ulanova didn't look at Jani but instead concentrated on her hands, running a fingertip over the edge of one scarlet talon. "What can they offer that makes sustaining them worth the effort?" The single word reply, *Nothing*, hung unspoken in the air.

Jani stared down at her single page of notes. Despite the hours spent on the library balcony, she'd sketched out only a few words, arranged in a list, written in a mongrel Acadian French-Vynshàrau scrawl that no one could read but she. Then she glanced at Tsecha, who studied her in turn with narrowed eyes. *So, nìa?* his look said. Academy examination, but on a different scale, the results the altering of lives rather than student assessments. *Teacher and student, in the class that never ends.* She bit back a nervous laugh, and began.

"Thalassa's bargaining power is that it's the chosen home of a male who is acknowledged to possess one of the foremost medical minds in a generation." Jani traced the first word on the list. *John.* "With some initial support, and a base from which to operate, he can continue to provide the area with a level of economic stability that it otherwise wouldn't possess."

Ulanova raised a hand. "Eamon DeVries—"

"Will wreck Neoclona inside of a year." Jani dug a thumbnail across a word farther down the list, grooving the parchment. *Jackass.* "No one can deny that he's a good device man, but when it comes to the complex dynamics of running a Commonwealth-spanning entity like Neoclona . . ." She took note of the stricken expression on Scriabin's face, and knew she'd struck the right chord. *Or nerve.* "John Shroud, working on the colonial side. Val Parini, on the Commonwealth. A measure of stability during what may turn out to be a tumultuous time." *Friend.* The last word on the list.

"Our Neoclona facility serves the entire colony and provides about one-quarter of the jobs in Unter den Linden and the surrounding area." Wallach sketched something that resembled a tombstone. "I don't want to see that end."

"Neither do I." Avelos shook her head. "I think we can speak for our colleague on Whalen and the heads of the satellites and stations. We need Neoclona as it is today, a strong, *stable* medical care provider and employer."

"This is good." Tsecha bared his teeth. "The Outer Circle Haárin value the opportunity they find here, and wish that John Shroud may continue to thrive so that all remains as it is. We will support your cleaving of the Outer Circle colonies from your Commonwealth."

And we will keep our businesses with you, and continue to run your most profitable ports, and promote the stability of your colonial governments. Jani read between those lines as though they'd been scrawled on the wall in letters a meter high. So did Markos and his colleagues, judging from their soft sighs of relief.

"No one I've spoken with thinks breaking up Neoclona's a good idea. I think a reversal of that particular decision should be easy enough to shove through." Scriabin's shoulders sagged, the first and only sign that he'd felt any tension at all. "Well. It appears we're all in agreement." He looked to Tsecha, who nodded. As one, they pushed back from the table and fell into light conversation while those who used recording boards fingered pads and tapped displays, erasing the contents and purging memories.

What you say here, what you see here, let it stay here when you leave here. Words to keep living by. Jani folded her own notes and tucked them back in her pocket, then looked at Niall to find him grinning at her.

"That was too goddamned easy, wasn't it?" He leaned his head back and stared at the ceiling. "Sad day, when you can't trust common sense."

"It was too easy, but we're all like minds here. The fight comes when Scriabin takes this to Chicago." Jani stood, stretched. Her stomach rumbled, this time from hunger.

"—sabotage." Markos's voice carried from the other end of the table. "Cèel scares me. He's spent the last decade building a network of spies throughout the Commonwealth. He'll find out about this and—"

"Stash." Scriabin closed his eyes for a long moment, then opened them slowly, like a beast roused from slumber. "Cèel's attempts at spy networks have gone and will continue to go the way of all the other humanish practices he has sought to adopt. Subtlety is not his strong suit. I remember when . . ." He circled the table and draped a thick arm around the man's shoulders and steered him to the door.

Jani followed the others outside, sneezing as the sun hit her in the face. "I'm numb."

"Nìa?" Tsecha drew alongside her, arching his brow in a humanish display of puzzlement. "You have that which you wish."

"For now." Niall set his lid, then patted his trouser pocket as the nicotine yearning surfaced. "Keeping it won't be easy."

"It will be a busy time." Tsecha looked out over the bay and bared his teeth. Then he clapped his hands and started after Scriabin. "Minister, I must ask you—"

"Lunch?" Niall glanced at his timepiece. "Make that breakfast."

"Let's go." Jani patted her stomach, then started up the road toward the Main House.

Rilas's heart beat harder as Tsecha moved into her vision field. She willed her breathing to slow, and sighted down until the cross hairs of her sight mech centered on the shorn head and downloaded the target position from the satellite.

Edged the stock away from her chest so the beat of her heart would not jostle the rifle.

Held her breath.

Pressed the charge-through.

CHAPTER 10

"Are you going to tell John right away?" Niall glanced back at Tsecha and the other officials, then unfastened the top clasp of his tunic and dug into his trouser pocket for his 'sticks. "I can't imagine you'd want to keep him hanging."

"I'm torn between blurting everything and holding back. I don't want to get his hopes up." The morning breeze off the water still held a chill, and Jani hugged herself.

"He's a big boy, Jan. He knows how the game is played." Niall puffed out a smoke ring. "Better to give him all the ammo so he can figure it out him—"

"*Ná Kièrshia!*"

Jani turned to find Avelos running up the incline toward them, dress boots skidding on the gravel.

"Ní Tsecha—" The woman stopped, chest heaving as she pulled in air. "He's ill."

Jani rushed past her and down the incline. Saw Scriabin, Markos, and the others standing clustered near the front of one skimmer.

Scriabin broke away and trotted out to meet her. "He leaned against the skimmer. Said he felt dizzy. We helped him to the ground. He said he wanted to sit."

"*Nìa!*" Tsecha leaned to the side to peer at her through a jungle of legs. "I am better now. Help me rise."

Jani turned to Niall, who stood at her shoulder and had already pulled out his handcom. "Call John." Then she pushed past the others and knelt beside Tsecha. "*Inshah*, you should sit here until John comes."

"I can stand." Tsecha gripped her shoulder with a hand like

cage wire. "I am well—I am—well." He pushed himself into a crouch, then slowly straightened.

Jani moved close so she could support him, then struggled to maintain her balance as he sagged against her. "He's too weak to walk—we need one of the skimmers."

Niall moved to Tsecha's other side and took his arm. "I'll drive, but someone needs to help us get him inside."

"I can—not—" Tsecha pressed a hand to his left ear. "Something—" He worked his jaw, then shook his head once more. "—in—my—ear—" He paused, the look in his eyes altering from puzzlement to alarm. "Nìa?" He tried to take a step forward. "I do not—" His knees buckled and he became dead weight, dragging Jani and Niall to their knees with him.

"I see John." Ulanova's voice emerged tight. "Both him and Val."

Jani counted the seconds as John and Val raced down the road toward them in one of the clinic's skimcarts. Another cart followed close behind, carrying a tech and more doctors.

John leapt off the cart while it still moved. "What happened?" He knelt in front of Tsecha, scanner in hand, and pressed the probe against the idomeni's forehead as he checked his eyes. "Ní Tsecha? What happened?"

Jani tried to shift her weight as gravel pierced her knees like nails. "He felt dizzy. We tried to get him into the skimmer, and he collapsed."

"I—cannot—" Tsecha's voice emerged hushed, hoarse, as though his throat had been coated with dust. "The sky spins—"

Val unfastened a gurney from the back of the cart and lowered it to the ground beside Tsecha. "Ní Tsecha, you're going to feel movement under your legs—we're sliding the gurney underneath." He touched a pad on the side of the floating platform and it vibrated, then thinned. He took hold of one end while the tech took the other, and together they worked it under Tsecha's knees. "Now John's going to help you lie back."

"Relax, ní Tsecha." John placed an arm around Tsecha's shoulders and with Jani and Niall's help eased him onto his back. He detached a larger scanner from the side of the gurney and activated it—the relay to the Main House clinic opened immediately, the green illumin fluttering. "Eccles—stand by for signal."

While John talked to the clinic, Val loosened Tsecha's clothing, then plucked scanner probes from a bag he'd pulled off the skimcart and attached them to the idomeni's chest and scalp. "Eccles, are you receiving?"

"Yes, sir," came the tinny response. Illumins flickered over the surface of the scanner as data was relayed and retrieved. "Visualizing a small hole in the left tympanum—"

"I see some bloody discharge." John inserted a probe into Tsecha's left ear, then checked the scanner display. "Does your ear hurt, ní Tsecha?"

"It feels as though something—" Tsecha tried to touch his ear, but John blocked him, taking his hand and gently lowering it to his side.

"Do you hear ringing, ní Tsecha?"

Tsecha grew agitated and tried to pull his hand from John's grasp. *"I cannot hear."*

"Pronounced deafness in left ear." John tried to speak into the scanner while keeping Tsecha still. "Possible inner ear involvement."

"Perforation due to ear infection?" A few beats of silence. Then Eccles's voice, more hesitant this time. "There's no sign of inflammation or fluid buildup."

"There could have been trauma." John lowered until he spoke into Tsecha's right ear. "Ní Tsecha?"

Tsecha licked his lips before replying. "Yes, John?"

"Apologies for imposing upon your privacy, but did you lave your ears this morning? Did your physician-priest administer any treatment?"

Tsecha tried to shake his head, then winced and gripped the edge of the gurney. "No."

"Could be a tumor," Eccles offered.

"Then why aren't you seeing it?" John rose, his facade of professional detachment showing cracks. "Ní Tsecha, we're going to take you to the clinic for further evaluation and treatment."

"Where is—nìa?"

"I'm here." Jani crouched beside the gurney and took Tsecha's hand. "Not going anywhere."

"The clinic." Tsecha blinked as though dazed. "I do so enjoy visiting . . ." He sighed, then finally stilled and closed his eyes.

Jani kept hold of Tsecha's hand as Val and Niall maneuvered the skimcart alongside the gurney, then hoisted the gurney onto the back of the cart and locked it in place. Then she crawled atop the platform beside him.

"Nìa." Tsecha tried to touch his ear again, then let his hand fall. "I want to talk to John."

John wedged himself atop the platform next to Jani, then

waited for Val to pile into the driver's seat and the cart to acceler-
ate before touching Tsecha's arm. "I'm here, ní Tsecha."

"John?" Tsecha reached out to him. "Come where I can hear
you."

John moved so he crouched closer to Tsecha's right side.
"We're almost at the clinic."

"You will treat me as you did my nìa?" Tsecha tugged on
John's sleeve.

Jani tried to read something in John's eyes, his expression. But
his self-control had returned en force—she might as well have
tried to read a wall.

"I will, ní Tsecha." He nodded, his voice a dark blank.

"You will not allow the worldskein control of me?"

John shot a look at Aris, the idomeni hybrid who served as the
xenomedical specialist and currently rode shotgun while monitoring the scanner outputs. "Except for the damage to his ear, all
readings are within normal variation and stable," the male replied,
answering his unspoken question.

"*John Shroud.*" Tsecha's voice held a divine rage. "Promise
me—you will not allow—"

"I won't allow them near you." John squeezed his hand. "But
ná Via, your physician-priest—"

"Not her! Not any of them!" Tsecha struggled to sit up, but the
restraints that held him onto the gurney stopped him. "John—you
must—" He fell back against the gurney pad, his labored breathing
drawing worried looks and hurried scanner evaluations from Aris.

John took a dispo cloth from a dispenser on the gurney foot-
guard and wiped it over Tsecha's brow. "Everything I did for Jani,
all the effort I expended . . ." His hand slowed. "All the care—"

"All the *protection.*" Tsecha kept moving his head to better
hear. "*John.*"

John looked at Jani, then at Aris. "Are you sure—"

"*John!*"

"I swear. By all in which I believe." John shifted so he could
keep an eye on both his patient and the scanner that Aris held. "I
will take care of you."

By the time the skimcarts reached the Main House, Thalassans had already gathered near the entry. Niall worked crowd control, then helped open doors and push planters and furniture out of
the carts' path. "*Please keep clear,*" he called to the hybrids who
hurried across the foyer to meet them. "Wait on the other side of
the courtyard, please."

"There's something—" Aris studied his hand scanner. "I see a small mass in the left internal auditory canal."

"A neuroma?" John leaned forward to look at the display. "Why the hell didn't you spot it before?"

"Because it wasn't there before." Aris stared at his scanner, then muttered something and gestured for Val to stop the cart. "It's growing."

"How—?" John grabbed Jani's wrist. "You have to let go."

Jani gripped Tsecha's hand harder, felt him squeeze back. "No."

Niall took her by her shoulders and eased her off the platform. "Let him do his job, gel."

"Son of a bitch." Aris leapt out of the cart and circled to the gurney. "John, it—"

As he closed in, Tsecha's back arched, his body twisting against the restraints. Other doctors joined John and Aris, moving in rapid concert, one-word orders sounding. As they worked over Tsecha, he continued to writhe and shake, his breath coming in gasps, his skin paling to clay.

Then he shivered. Twitched.

Grew still.

"Oh, God." Aris checked one scanner, then another.

Jani tried to follow as the cart with its motionless cargo was driven to the lift, but once more Niall held her back. She watched the doors open, John and Val unfasten the gurney and carry it inside. The doors closed.

Jani sat in the visitors' alcove, repositioning her chair until she had the best possible view of the door to Tsecha's room. The clinic was quiet, seemingly deserted. John had restricted access to medical personnel only, but when Jani snuck down the stairs and through the corridor, she encountered no guards, only a red-eyed nurse who at first seemed about to ask her to leave, then waved her toward the alcove and disappeared into the room.

She flinched when she heard the *click* of the stairwell door, the clip of hard soles on lyno. Relaxed, a little, when she heard the rough Victorian mutter.

"Where the hell . . . ?" Niall stopped in the alcove entry. "There you are, gel. Kid said he saw you come down here." He dragged a chair beside Jani's and sat, balancing his brimmed lid on his thigh. "You know, the kid who's always writing things down and imaging?"

"Torin." Jani paused to rub her eyes. "Torin Clase."

"Torin—that's his name. Nuisance in the making, he is." Niall drummed his fingers on the arm of his chair. "I turned Yevgeny and the others over to Brondt. They needed to call their offices, settle down their staffs." He sniffed. "Head off any press inquiries at the pass." He glanced toward the door and swallowed hard. "Anything?"

Jani shook her head. "Ná Via, his physician-priest, went in about a half hour ago. No one's come out. I contacted Dathim. He was going to tell Meva and Feyó."

Niall nodded. "Bloody hell, Jan." He sat forward, lid still in hand, working his fingers back and forth along the brim. "It's the not knowing that makes it worse."

"Tell me what you don't know, Niall." Jani waited for him to respond, and took his silence for the surrender she knew it to be.

They both started at the distant *hiss* of the lift door. Soft footsteps followed, played out in double time.

"Jani? Jani?" The voice, as rapid as the steps.

Jani's head started to pound. "In here, ná Meva."

The female appeared in the alcove entry. She had dragged on her propitiator's overrobe over a bright purple shirt and orange trousers, and tucked her hair into a messy knot. "Feyó will be brought by Dathim. I am by myself." She looked toward the door to Tsecha's room, then back to Jani. "You saw?"

"I didn't see him fall ill." Jani rose and walked past Meva into the corridor. "When Niall and I reached him, he was already on the ground. He said he felt dizzy." She paced, heart tripping each time she passed close to the room. "His eardrum had perforated. John ordered him brought here for evaluation. Everything seemed under control. Then scanning revealed a tumor. Then he suffered a seizure, or . . . something." She stopped, closing her eyes as the images flashed. The arching back. The shuddering. The stillness.

"Haárin have gathered in the meeting house, and in the temples. They wait." Meva adjusted her overrobe sleeves, her shoulders slowly rounding. "You are not dressed as is seemly."

Jani looked down at her blue shirt-jacket and trousers, now rumpled and dusty. "I haven't had time—"

"He is your dominant." Meva stepped in front of Jani. "You are to be a priest, and I have never seen you wear your overrobe." She had never displayed the idomeni reluctance to look others in the eye, and her auric glare drilled even more deeply than Tsecha's. *"You do not know your gods, and you do not know your clothes."*

Jani clenched her hands, felt her heartbeat strengthen, then slow. "I am not leaving."

"You must wear that which—"

"I am not leaving to change clothes. Not now."

Niall wedged between them, nudging Jani back. "Tell me where it is, gel."

"Right side of the closet." Jani turned away, listened to Niall's footsteps recede, the door to the lift whisper open, then closed.

"You must prepare." Meva's voice at her shoulder. "For whatever is to be."

Shut up. Jani stuffed her fists in her pockets. Sometimes the anger built, a rank combination of the remnants of her augmentation and typical idomeni temper, but taking a swing at Meva would just make a horrible situation worse. "We still haven't heard from John. We still don't know—" She heard the lift door open again, and turned to find Dathim striding toward them, followed closely by ná Feyó Tal.

"Ná Meva." Feyó's voice emerged tight, her shoulders rounding. She didn't like the propitiator any more than did Jani. "I wished you to travel with me."

Meva waved a hand, an imitation of a humanish *Don't bother me.* "I needed to be here. You delayed for too much time."

"There are prayers to be said. This is a place of sickness."

"It is a place of Tsecha. That is why I am here." Dathim leaned against the wall opposite the door to Tsecha's room. He still wore his workclothes, the brown cloth streaked with white tile dust.

Feyó crossed her left arm over her chest as she drew up very straight, a posture of supplication. Like most of the other Haárin, she had never set foot in the clinic. Her medical matters were still handled by a physician-priest, who labored to keep her soul intact by the usual idomeni blend of modern methods together with prayers and wards against demons, all based on the premise that the injury or illness of one threatened the soul of any other who came in contact with them. Wholeness of Soul, a concept that Tsecha had called "anathema," still formed one of the cornerstones of Feyó's world. "It is not godly."

"You are an idiot, Feyó." Meva turned her back on Jani and fixed on her secular dominant. "Tsecha is here—he fell sick here and needed to be treated *here.* Thus did Via come, *here.* Thus do we all come, *here.*"

"My soul—"

"Would suffer greater damage if you did not come here, to be with him whom you claim to esteem." Meva closed in on Feyó as her own shoulders hunched.

Feyó lowered her arm as her shoulders rounded in a crippling curve. "You dare—"

"Quiet!" Jani pressed a hand to her ear as the sound rattled her aching head, then let it fall when she remembered that Tsecha had done the same thing before those last terrible moments. *I'm going to collapse—I'm going to die.* She gave herself a mental kick. *Don't be a jackass.* "Let's wait for what John and Via have to say." She leaned against the wall beside the preternaturally calm Dathim. *When the tilemaster is the only one controlling his temper, we're in trouble.* She looked across the corridor to the door to Tsecha's room. *John, where are you?*

As if on cue, the door opened and John emerged. He wore a medcoat over his daysuit, shoe covers over his boots. "I—" He looked around as though lost. "We did . . ." He hung his head. ". . . everything. We did everything we could possibly . . ."

From behind him, no sounds. Only silence.

Jani walked to him, sensed his warmth through the chill air, and stepped past him into the quiet.

CHAPTER 11

The air felt cool, weighty, the lights as bright as sunlight reflecting off ice. Val stood over an analyzer—he looked up as she entered. Like John, he had donned a medcoat. Like him, he failed to meet her eye.

Via sat in a chair by the far wall, her head lowered. Aris fed samples into another analyzer, stopping every so often to wipe his eyes.

And finally, in the room's center, a bed, surrounded by blinking plastic boxes, instruments and machines, the body it contained prone, unmoving, another aspect of the silence.

Jani walked closer, each step a labor, the urge to howl like a stab in her throat. Tsecha lay centered like a figure atop a sarcophagus, his face obscured by tubing and sensors, legs straight, arms at his side, the thin bed cover folded down to expose his bare, sensor-dotted chest. His torso, once home to an idomeni's wiry strength, seemed whittled down to faded skin and bone, all muscle, as well as the will and fire that drove them, spent. Extinguished. He looked desiccated now, as though he'd become one with the desert from which he came.

Then she heard the soft pad of footsteps. John's voice filling her head.

"Jani, come over here, please."

She turned and followed him to the door, where Feyó, Meva, and Dathim stood, their stares drawn to the still figure.

"Ná Via?" John gestured to the physician-priest, who rose slowly and joined them. "There is no easy way to say this." He stopped, passed a hand over his face. "He's gone. He cannot breathe on his own. His heart cannot beat on its own. He has no detectable brain function." A shaky sigh, the first hint of the tears to come. "He had a tumor in his left inner auditory canal that we didn't visualize immediately. By the time we did, it had already bulged out into the brain case." He stared down at the floor. "There was blood vessel rupture, and the pressure . . ." He raised his head, eventually. "The damage was catastrophic and irreversible."

"We must do that which must be done." Via's voice emerged soft, its usual strength seeped away.

"He did not believe in it." Meva's eyes never left the bed. "That which you must do. He no longer believed it mattered."

Via sighed, as though she had heard the words from Meva before and expected at some point to hear them again. "I have contacted my suborns, Meva. They have gone to the enclave vaults and broken the seals of Tsecha's chamber. They bring his reliquary. If he had not wished it to be used, would he have preserved it? Think of what you know of Tsecha, who always did that which he would, and answer me."

Meva remained still for a time, before twitching one shoulder in her version of a humanish shrug. "We must ask his suborn." She raised a hand in question. "Ná Kièrshia?"

Jani turned her back on the questioning priest and walked to the side of the bed. An edge of the bed cover had rumpled. As she reached out to straighten it, her hand brushed Tsecha's arm—she jerked back at the touch of soft, warm skin.

"His blood is being warmed by the circulator." John moved opposite her. "His internal thermostat no longer functions."

"He is dead." Feyó smacked the top of an analyzer. "Why can you not say the words, Doctor? Are they not your words to say? Tsecha is dead. Not gone. Not irreversibly damaged. Dead." She pointed to the door. "Ná Via's suborns will soon arrive. We must proceed."

Jani looked at John, who looked away. "John?" She struggled to find the words, to form the question. "Isn't there . . . ?"

Feyó stepped between Jani and John. "We must proceed. To wait longer is anathema."

Val had been sitting with his head in his hands. Now his head came up, eyes glistening. "*What's the rush!* That's the anathema, Feyó. That you're in such a goddamn rush!"

"Val." Jani stared at him until he got up and strode to the farthest corner of the room to pace. "A soul in an artificially sustained body realizes that the body is dead, and tries to depart. But it's trapped, and as the length of captivity increases, it degrades, fragments. The Vynshàrau believe it. Most of the major sects." She stepped around Feyó, dodging the female when she grabbed for her sleeve. "Tsecha, however, had his doubts, and those doubts must be respected."

"He doubted when it came to injury, to sickness." Feyó set herself in Jani's path, stopping her. "But he is *dead*. Life has left him. I look at him, and I see . . ." Her voice faded, the first hint of blankness crossing her face. The first suggestion of loss.

Jani stepped closer to the female. "Where is the urgency? Is it for his sake?" She twitched her head in the direction of the bed. "Or because you fear what the other Haárin will say? That you mishandled him. That you botched it."

"*Yes!*" Feyó's shoulders bowed so that her neck twisted. "Idiot humanish—do you truly believe such does not matter? He is *Tsecha*. Before he was Tsecha, he was Avrèl nìRau Nema, Chief Propitiator of the Vynshàrau. The guide to the gods for all Haárin. If his soul loses its Way, so do all of ours. If he is lost, so are we all."

Jani felt her scalp tighten, and worked a hand through her hair to ease the ache. "NìaRauta Sànalàn is your Chief Propitiator now."

"She is as nothing. He repudiated her, again and again." Feyó's voice emerged in a hiss. "He trained you. You learned from him, and you do not understand that which he was?"

I know what he was to me. Jani stood still. "John?"

John cleared his throat. "It's over, Jan." He gestured toward one of the analyzers. "I can show you the scans, the test results—"

"I have seen the scans, and the test results." Via walked to the bedside, her voice lowered to a whisper. "All is nothing. All the physicians could attempt has been tried. Now is the time for the priests." She rested a hand on Jani's arm, a humanish gesture she seldom employed. "His soul is at great risk. The souls of all Haárin are at great risk. We have to proceed."

Jani nodded. Then she shook off Feyó's hand and walked to Tsecha's bedside. Ignored the muttered Sìah curses that followed her, and waited for a more familiar touch. It came, eventually, a light hand on her shoulder. "It's moving too quickly."

"It's a nightmare." John moved in, close enough to lean on. "I keep telling myself to wake up, but I'm not listening."

"Didn't Via see this coming?"

"I asked her. She'd seen no signs of anything like this."

Jani watched the bare chest rise and fall, and knew John had made a mistake. Knew that Tsecha would open his eyes, tear out the intratracheal insert, the sensors, and demand to know why he'd been treated in such a manner, why everyone had been so stupid. "He didn't seem ill at the meeting house. Did I miss something? Should I have—"

"Stop it." John squeezed her shoulder. "Sometimes you just don't see it coming, and when it hits, there's nothing you can do."

Jani nodded. Her head felt as though it floated, her feet as though they didn't touch the floor. Shock, or hangover from her augmentation, or a little of both. "There's nothing—"

"No."

"He's gone."

". . . Yes."

"Then . . ." Jani turned to Feyó, who had moved to the foot of the bed. "Bring it." She saw the relief in the female's bearing, understood the reasoning behind it, the millennia of religious belief, yet hated her anyway.

"Are you sure?" John's voice in her ear, like a guilty conscience.

"No." Jani shook her head, then closed her eyes to stop the motion. "So many Haárin still consider him their propitiator, even though he isn't. If we don't treat him properly now, the backlash . . ." She looked down at her hands, at the rings she wore, and fought the urge to yank them off and return them to the hands on which they belonged. "He deserves all honor. All ceremony due a chief propitiator. I'll see to it."

"I know." John embraced her, rested his head atop hers. "What do you want me to do?"

"Check the corridor. See if Niall is there. He went to get my overrobe." A voice she didn't recognize, saying things she never thought she'd say.

John opened the door and walked out into the corridor, returning a few moments later with Jani's overrobe in hand. "Can anyone else attend?"

"Come in, Niall." Jani took the overrobe from John and dragged it on. Arranged the sleeves, straightened the hem, and knew herself for the imposter she was. The fake priest, preparing to send the true one upon his Way. "He liked you."

"I—liked him, too." Niall slipped inside and took a place against the wall, straightening gradually until he stood at attention.

"I'll show everyone else out." John released her and headed for the door.

"No." Jani turned to him. "You and Val—you both battled him for so long. His esteemed enemies. He'd want you to stay." She scanned the ceiling. "Does this room have imaging capability?"

John nodded. "Yes, but—"

"Activate it, if you haven't already. It's history. What's more, it's important." Jani looked at John, who stared wide-eyed. "I don't want there to be any questions, ever. No argument that we didn't do this or we didn't do that. I want them to see. I want them all to see." With that, she walked to the foot of the bed and waited.

A few moments later the door opened. Feyó and Via entered silently, bearing the reliquary between them like a pall. It proved to be a simple wooden box, a half meter high and a meter or so long. The wood itself had the ebony hue and tight grain of one of Shèrá's northern varieties, which grew in the mountains and was fed by snow and rain. Strange, that Tsecha had chosen such a wood to hold his scroll, rather than the sandstone of his native Rauta Shèràa.

The two females carried the reliquary over to an empty table on the far side of the room and hefted it on top. Via then left Feyó and beckoned for John to join her in front of the main instrument console, where they had a hasty consultation punctuated by the evaluation of screens filled with data. Then she walked to the bed, her step slowing as she took in the still figure that lay before her. *"É ne lona, Tsecha. É neà lonai . . ."* Her voice lowered to a murmur as she circled to each piece of equipment in turn and evaluated the readouts.

For your journey, Tsecha. For your journey to come . . . A Vynshàrau prayer, a wish that his journey to the First Star would be swift and uneventful. Jani breathed in once, then again. *"É se te lon à kavai,"* she uttered in a priestly singsong. *"É sei te kavao à volai."* She drew a sharp look from Via for the half-humanish imposter that she was, but she didn't care. *For to journey is to know. For to know is to understand.* Those words, Tsecha believed, for all his doubt and argument. Those words, he had the right to hear because of what he'd been. Those words, she had the right to speak because of what he'd been to her.

"Jani?"

She turned to find Feyó standing behind her, her eyes averted.

"Go to your place." Feyó pointed toward the reliquary.

Jani walked to the bench on which the reliquary stood. She lifted the flat lid, suppressed a gasp at its weight, and maneuvered it carefully to keep it from bumping anything. She sensed stares.

Meva's judgment. Via's disapproval. Feyó's more benign concern. She set the lid upon the bench, then looked inside the reliquary. Nestled within lay Tsecha's scroll, the construct that had been made soon after his birth to house his soul after his death.

Idomeni live to die. Jani reached into the reliquary and opened the cover of the bound volume nestled in the padded lining. To her surprise, it felt cold to the touch, rough and weighty. This was the sandstone of Rauta Shèràa, dull umber and gritty, its surface carved with swirling traceries that were the favored imagery of the Vynshàrau. Beneath it lay a face page, blank but for symbols denoting the names of the major gods. Jani looked them over, stopping when she came to a clenched fist, fingers gripping some unidentifiable object. *Caith.* Goddess of chaos, of annihilation. She who destroyed for the sake of destruction.

Bitch. Jani wiped her thumb across the image in an effort to smear it, erase it, give order a little of its own back. But idomeni inks were the finest and this image had been in place for a long time. It remained sharp, bright black against the cream of the parchment. *This round to you, then.* She smoothed her hand over the page, then turned around just as Via took her place at the head of the bed.

The physician-priest paused. Then, leaning forward, she cupped her hands and positioned them above Tsecha's face. After a few moments she straightened and circled the bed once more, this time touching each control pad, shutting down each instrument in turn. When she came to the heart-lung array, she hesitated, then reached out slowly, clenching her hand once before touching the control. What little sound had filled the room ceased. Red indicator lights fluttered across the unit's surface, then faded. Tsecha's chest stalled in mid-rise.

Time stopped, the tick into the next second hanging on some cosmic balance. Jani looked to Tsecha, strained to see some movement, some sign that analysis and instruments had erred and hope had won the day.

But Tsecha remained still and time started again, leaving hope in its wake.

She looked at John. He stood in the far corner of the room, against the wall, shoulders hunched and arms folded. He met her eye for the barest moment before fixing on the floor at his feet. Val stood beside him, as hunched and cramped as his partner.

Then she looked to the entry, and saw Dathim and Meva, tall and still, arms raised above their heads in supplication.

Via resumed her position at the head of the bed, then waited for

Feyó to take her position at the foot. She peeled away the sensors from Tsecha's scalp and chest. Removed the intratracheal insert, sliding it out with a sure hand. After setting it aside, she once more brought her hands together over Tsecha's face, this time cupped together, palms facing one another. According to all she believed, she now held his soul in her grasp, and she moved slowly, as though jostling might damage it. Straightening, she reached out toward Feyó and opened her hands. As she did so, Feyó held open her arms. Via then closed her hands and let them fall, dispatching Tsecha's soul to the protection of his secular dominant.

Feyó crossed her arms, hollow thumps sounding as her hands struck her chest. The seconds passed as she stood in place, eyes closed, hands gripping her shoulders, lips moving in some silent prayer. Then, slowly, she turned to face Jani, and lowered her arms.

Jani held out her hands in time with Feyó's action. All the teachings she had read over the months stated that she would know when she had grasped the soul of the deceased. She would feel its weight, its presence, sense the pain it had suffered over the course of its bodily habitation, the joys it had experienced. She would cross her arms over her chest, and know that she sheltered something most delicate, something that would journey across the bridge to the paradise of the First Star, along the Way meeting its gods. Along the Way achieving peace.

So she gauged every sensation, every thought bidden and unbidden, and felt . . . nothing. Waited for Tsecha's voice to sound in her mind, commanding her to pay attention, and heard only the thudding of her own blood in her ears. She turned to face the reliquary and lowered her arms, reaching inside the box and placing her hands over the scroll. Counted to four because it seemed a good number. Not too large, yet not too small. Four seconds—plenty of time for a soul she couldn't sense to nestle itself within the recesses of a book whose contents she didn't believe. *Thus sayeth the priest.* She closed the cover of the scroll and, with hands that felt as they always had, hoisted the reliquary lid and slid it back into place. As she bent close to the wood, she caught its faint scent, a blend of dry herbs and fresh cuttings, tinged with cinnamon. The *vrel* blossom Tsecha spoke of so often. A tear spilled, spattering the wood, and she wiped it away.

She placed her hands atop the reliquary, the only finishing gesture she could think of. *Ason ea lon, niRau. Good journey, wherever you are.* With that, she let her hands fall, and turned to face the others.

Silence dragged on for one beat. Two. Then Via gestured. "We must go now, and prepare—"

"I'd like some time, please." Jani flinched at the sound of her own voice. "Alone with him. I'd like some time. To say good-bye."

"Good-bye?" Via gestured in question. "Farewells have been made. It is at an end, ná Kièrshia. We must take him out of this place."

"His soul rests in safe harbor. As far as you're concerned, he's secure. No evil can befall him." Jani looked down at her hands, the redstone ring Tsecha had given her more than twenty years before. She tilted her hand back and forth, and watched the scarlet flashes. "A few minutes, Via. That's all. Allow the humanish in me some time."

Via gestured a strong negative. "It is not—"

"A few minutes." Jani saw John push off the wall and start toward her, but when their eyes met, he stopped. "I knuckled under to your traditions. You can damn well knuckle under to mine."

Via sliced the air with her hand. "It is not godly. I cannot—"

"Via." Feyó's voice sounded tired, the bowing of her shoulders a result of exhaustion as much as irritation. "We must assemble your staff to take ní Tsecha's body back to the enclave. Such will take time. During that time, it will be watched by a priest."

"She is no—" Via fell silent as Feyó's shoulders curved further. She glanced at Jani, then away, the struggle to contain her own anger evident in the stiff way she held herself.

"His soul is intact, Via. Your duty is discharged." Feyó nodded to Jani. She then ushered the physician-priest out the door, their under-their-breath back and forth audible until they left the room.

"I will . . . go upstairs." John gestured vaguely in the direction of the entry. "Everyone's waiting." He turned to Aris, then jerked his thumb toward the door. He hurried into the hallway, followed by John, Val, and Niall. The door closed.

Dathim and Meva had lowered their arms at the conclusion of the rite, but remained still. When the door closed, Dathim edged toward the bed. "If all is finished, why do you remain?"

Jani dragged a chair to the side of the bed and sat. "What place for the student but with her teacher?" She looked up at the male, who like Feyó appeared drained, expression blank and shoulders bowing. "Why do you remain?"

"To see what you will do." Dathim finally looked at her. "You will pray?"

Jani hesitated, then shook her head. "I'll sit here, and wish that the last few hours hadn't happened. I'll wish that I could turn back time."

"You will wish in vain," Meva said.

Jani nodded. "But I'll wish anyway." She tugged at another crease in the bed cover. Reached out a finger and grazed Tsecha's arm, felt the cooling even though only a short time had passed.

"Humanish are strange." Some animation returned to Meva's face, a flare of impatience in her downward curve of lip. "And you are still most humanish."

Jani raised a hand in surrender, let it fall. Sat quietly as the minutes passed and Meva and Dathim continued to watch her before giving up and leaving the room.

"With idomeni, the soul is the important thing. The body is as nothing. They'll burn it down to a scraping of ash, and won't even collect it. Lave the crematory with blessed cloths, and rinse it all away." Jani tried to think of something else to say, to find the words that defined what she knew in her heart to be indefinable.

Finally, she gave up, and did the humanish thing, and wept.

CHAPTER 12

Rilas replayed the memory of the cart bearing Tsecha surging up the hill and vanishing around a curve of stone. She had seen him gesture, watched as Shroud bent over him, as the hated Kilian held his hand. He had spoken, yes, but what had he said? Had his words been lucid, or, as she most hoped, only the last ramblings of a dissolving mind?

Not that it mattered. She had performed the act she had come to this damned place to execute. It troubled her that Tsecha had not died within moments after the vector found him and transferred its cargo to his brain, but did the timing matter? Dead was dead.

She should not have stayed in the house for as long as she had, watching Tsecha's transport up the hill. She had worked quickly, breaking down the rifle and packing it away. As she left the house, she set off a protein bomb, obliterating all traces of her presence.

I have succeeded.

As soon as she entered the Karistos shuttleport, Rilas stopped before a news display and read the scrolling headlines.

He must be dead. She waited for the words to appear on the screen, for the bustle around her to cease. For the silence.

Stock market values . . . weather . . . a new holoVee detective series . . .

He must be— Someone jostled her and she stumbled forward, grabbed the back of a bench to keep from falling. She straightened slowly, imagined burying a blade in the heart of that clumsy fool. Then she continued down the concourse toward the Haárin wing, and the locker area where her new documents had been hidden.

No more Nahin Sela. No more damned tiles. She muttered thanks to her blessed Caith.

She hoisted her slingbag, which was nearly empty now. The rifle, the cartridges, the beautiful sight mech, she had coated with protein digester and buried in a remote place off the shuttleport road. Even if discovered, they would prove useless, the biobased mechanics obliterated, only their metal shells remaining. The secondary—

Rilas stopped in mid-stride. *The secondary.* It still hovered above the Thalassan enclave—she imagined its path growing more and more erratic as the signals it sent to the destroyed primary went unanswered. *It does not matter.* Soon its power supply would deplete and it would tumble into the bay. It signaled as biological—no scanning device would track it.

She started to walk again, one step following the next, her feet tingling as though she walked across a high ledge, a sheer drop on either side. *A mistake.* She did not make mistakes—such was why nìRau Cèel had chosen her for this greatest of tasks. *I can make no more mistakes.* Such were an insult to Caith, a temptation to godly wrath.

Rilas hurried down the concourse, then turned down the corridor that led to the locker area. She passed first one Haárin worker, then another. Saw gaps in the ceiling, holes in the walls on either side.

Stopped in front of the entry to the locker area, and found only the hacked-out remains of a doorway, and barrier tape, and an empty expanse where the lockers had stood.

"What is this?" Rilas looked to the workers' dominant, who stood off to one side performing calculations on a handheld.

"Ná." The male nodded to her, a meaningless gesture. "These rooms are being repaired. The plumbing was not as adequate."

"Repaired?" Rilas tried to step past the barrier tape, but stopped as the polymer sensed her presence and beeped a warning. "There is something I must recover."

"All contents have been taken from the lockers and moved to Lost and Found." The male turned his back to her, gaze still fixed on the handheld display. "You go there and present your identification, and you may recover that which is yours."

"Lost and Found?"

"At the end of this concourse, next to the security offices."

Rilas remained in place. Her heart beat harder now. *Identification.* She would display her documents naming her as ná Nahin

Sela and recover a bag containing documents for another, for a name she did not even know. *If they searched the bag—scanned it—* They would ask her why she recovered documents belonging to another. They would demand explanations.

I cannot attempt to claim this bag. Nor could she remain on Elyas long enough to purchase new documents, assuming there were Haárin here who produced such. *I have to remain as ná Nahin Sela.* For the first time, she would depart a place with the same name she bore when she arrived. *Such is not seemly.* Even more important, such was dangerous. Too many here knew her as ná Nahin. Those who worked or lived at the enclave in which she stayed. Those she had spoken with at the Trade Board.

But still . . .

Rilas turned and walked back up the hall toward the concourse. Sensed Caith's laughter as she approached the outgoing passenger gates and scanned the displays for the first Haárin shuttle to Elyas Station. As she walked up to the billet counter and presented her identification.

"Ná Nahin Sela." The female clerk looked her in the eye, baring her teeth as she scanned the identification wafer and processed the billet request. "Glories of the day to you."

"Glories," Rilas replied, even as Caith's glee settled as an ache in her soul.

It started on the shuttle. One Haárin with a handheld, and soon the entire craft knew.

Then the news spread, like the voices of the gods.

As a humanish cathedral. If the designer of Elyas Station had ever wished to observe godly quiet in the place she caused to have made, such desire would have been fulfilled this day. Rilas could track the movement of silence through the Haárin concourse as the news of the death of ní Tsecha Egri revealed itself on wall-mounted displays and announced itself from handhelds. Haárin did not yell or cry out as they comprehended the news. Such was not their way, and even years of godless exposure to humanish had not degraded their response.

Silence.

Rilas pondered the quiet along the Haárin concourse of Elyas Station. Relished it. *Tsecha's hold over the colonial Haárin is as an iron band,* nìRau Cèel had told her. *When it first shatters, they will be as lost.* He had bared his teeth at that moment. *Then they will conclude that the humanish in whom they have trusted have betrayed them. At that moment, they will look back toward the worldskein.*

At that moment . . . Rilas stopped before one of the displays, a humanish broadcast that offered a Sìah translation.

". . . cerebral hemorrhage . . . tumor . . . undiagnosed . . . unusual . . ."

"Hemorrhage?" Rilas stepped closer to the display. "They think it a hem—" She fell silent as the other Haárin gestured her to be quiet, their hands slicing the air, the harsh movements of emotion, distress.

Rilas's heart pounded. *It is not illness—I killed him! I, Imea nìaRauta Rilas, as my Oligarch bade me!* She wondered for a moment at the reaction if she announced such. *They would strike me down, as years ago we struck down the Laum.* They did not yet understand the goodness that had been done for them.

Let them think it illness for now. Rilas stepped away from the group and resumed her walk toward her departure dock, slowing to ponder the displays in shop windows, and to think of the future. *Soon, they will learn it was not a hemorrhage.* Then, the accusations would begin. Against Chicago. Against humanish separatists. The same groups that had been accused of bombing Haárin docks would stand accused once more, would argue for and against the blame, embracing or denying it in proportion to how weak they were, how eager they were to appear strong.

And as humanish argue, idomeni will listen, and realize their errors, and return—

"Hello, again."

Rilas stopped. Turned first toward the concourse, then toward the entry of the shop near which she stood. Saw no one.

"I'm back here."

Humanish male. Rilas clenched a fist. "I do not—"

"You remember me. The other day. The Rose Window." A face emerged from the shadowed recess beside the shop. The dark skin and darker hair, clipped short. Another too bright shirt, this in a yellow that pained the eyes. "I remember you. I never forget a face."

I do not, either. Rilas felt the heat of her soul rise up her throat. *The male who explained gargoyles.*

"I was just hanging around, watching the passing parade." The male looked out toward the concourse crowds, his eyes bleared as though with sleep. "Well, not doing much passing today. Mostly standing around, because of what happened and all. Tragic, just tragic." He shook his head, then leaned against the wall, one hand gripping the brickwork as though he struggled for balance. "Then who do I see window shopping?" He bared his teeth. " 'Oh, look,' I thought, 'a familiar face.' "

Ethanol poisoning. Rilas had been trained to deal with human-ish who degraded themselves in that way, but dreaded such. The chemical slowed their reflexes, yes, but the pits of their souls were as tainted as their brains, and such led to messy outcomes. *If I strike him in the abdomen, he may vomit. I would then need to lave. To change my clothes.* Rilas glanced at a timeform. Her flight departed soon. She would not have the time.

"A little friendly advice? You'd look better with your hair un-braided, loose—but then, most females would." The male leaned closer. His breath stank of harsh sweetness. "My name's Neason, by the way." He held out his hand.

Rilas took a step back. "I will inform your dominant that you are drunk."

The male drew back his hand and stood away from the wall. "You do that." His voice altered, from high and light to low, a voice of threat. "Go right ahead and inform that bitch about any-thing you want. Add your name to the goddamn list." His head moved back and forth as though palsied. Then it stilled. "Did you report me? Were you the one who—"

Rilas raised her right hand and curved it upward in question. "Report?" She tilted her head to accentuate her false dismay. "I said nothing. To anyone."

"Improving relations between the races. That's all I was do-ing." The male's voice rose. "I told her that, the bitch, but did she listen? Did any of them listen?" He shouted now, spittle arcing from his mouth. "I am a diplomat. Do you hear me—*a diplomat!*"

Rilas turned toward the concourse. A few Haárin had turned from the displays and now looked in her direction.

"A fuckin' diplomat!"

"Silence." Rilas pushed the male back into the darkness. "You attract attention."

"Oh yeah?" He grabbed at her hands, missing his grip as the poisoning slowed his reactions. "Think you know how to keep me quiet, do you?" He laughed, filling the dark recess with the stench of his breath. "You come back here and keep me quiet, then."

Rilas had stepped into the recess. As her eyes accommodated to the darkness, she saw the drink receptacles piled in one corner, the door that she knew led to the station interiors and from there to the humanish section.

"If you come back here, you can keep me real quiet." The male opened the interior door. "Come back here with me and I won't make a sound." He shifted his weight from one foot to the other as he sought to maintain his balance. "That's what you want, isn't it? To keep me quiet." He curved his lips without baring his teeth, that strange humanish expression. "I can tell. You don't want me to say a thing."

Rilas felt her heartbeat slow and strengthen. Her hands clenched. "I do not know what you speak of."

"I'll bet you don't." The male backed through the door opening, beckoning to her with a crooked finger. "Liar. I know all your secrets."

"What secrets?" Rilas studied him now. His build. His weight. The way he moved. *A soft thing. Unfit. Untrained.* "I do not know what you are telling me."

"All you idomeni are so mysterious, but you're no mystery to me." The male looked her up and down. "All I have to do is look at you, and I know all about you. What you want. What you need." He made a sweeping motion with his hand. "Come in here, and I'll tell you everything."

"I must go to my dock."

"I know a shortcut." He tried to grip her arm, and swore as she dodged his hand. "Come on now—be nice."

Rilas watched him, even as the strength of her goddess coursed through her. *He knows secrets.* Had he matched the identity she had used to enter the station with that of Nahin Sela? Had he somehow followed her to Karistos without her seeing him? "I will come with you."

The male bared his teeth. "That's more like it." He stepped aside so she could enter the interior walkway, then turned his back so he could close the door.

As he did that, Rilas let her slingbag slide off her shoulder to the floor. She moved in behind him, her gaze fixed on his rumpled shirt collar, the place where neck and shoulder joined.

Raised her hand edge on.

"Now this is how—"

Brought it down.

The male made no sound. He dropped to his knees, pitched forward so that he struck the wall. Slid to the floor, twitched, then lay still.

Rilas watched him, even as panic touched her and every instinct bade her to flee. Waited, until she saw the liquid puddle around his hip, smelled the stench of urine, and knew him to be dead. What he knew of her, he could never tell.

She picked up her slingbag and shouldered it. Turned the door mechanism and felt the finger of Caith touch her soul as the panel failed to open. She studied the mechanism for a moment, determined the two-handed grip and pull necessary to release the catch, and did so.

Rilas entered the concourse, walking past the groups that still gathered around the displays. The boarding alarm for her ship sounded, and she quickened her pace, thanking her goddess that she would soon leave this most damned of places behind.

CHAPTER 13

"Jan?"

Jani looked up to find Niall standing in the entry. "Via and her suborns . . ." She waved toward the bed, which now lay empty, the covers stripped. "About—I don't know—a half hour ago."

"I saw them leave." Niall's voice emerged scratchy, as though his throat ached. "Yevgeny wondered how you were holding up?"

Yevgeny? Jani struggled to place the name. Then the token dropped. "Scriabin's still here?"

"They all are." Niall managed a weak smile. "It's only just afternoon." The expression faded. "All lifetime in a day." He fell silent. Coughed. "Anyway, he asked how you were doing, and if you could see your way clear to stopping by the library when you're up to it."

"Which in minister-speak means now." Jani tried to rise, and found her limbs had gone to lead. "Give me a minute."

"Of course." Niall stepped inside and let the door close, then dragged a chair next to hers. "Take all the time you need."

There isn't that much time. She plucked a dispo cloth from the dispenser on a nearby cart and wiped her eyes. "What's it like upstairs?"

"Quiet." Niall brushed some nonexistent lint from his trousers. "Everyone had gathered in the courtyard. John talked to them a little while ago. He did well, I think."

Jani imagined John's solemn mien, his voice. Not a combination one would choose to lighten the mood, but in this case they probably struck the right note. "What did he say?"

"That Tsecha died as the result of a brain hemorrhage." Niall exhaled with a *whoosh*. "He didn't mention the undiagnosed tumor—let Via field that one."

Jani thought back to the scene in the room a few short hours before, John showing Via analyzer readouts and instrument displays while she dogged his shoulder, like a stranger at a party sticking to the only person she knew. Did she feel lost amid the brightly lit bustle of a humanish-style hospital room? Did John even try to bring her up to speed, or did he barrel along as he always did, and assume she'd keep pace? "Idomeni often don't treat diseases until they fall visibly ill. But I thought Tsecha had gotten past that."

"Maybe Via didn't." Niall shrugged. "And it backfired."

You will not allow the worldskein control of me?

Jani pondered Tsecha's words. He had included Via in his plea—he hadn't wanted her to take charge of him, either. She shivered, and blamed her chill on the temperature of the room. "Willful negligence?"

"I never thought I'd get to be the one to say this, but now you're thinking like a human." Niall pointed an accusing finger. "I will never claim to understand the idomeni mind-set, but I'm not an idiot. Tsecha was *Tsecha*. A former Chief Propitiator, and, for want of a better term, a defining personality. He grew, but not all of his followers kept up. Not all of them thought as he did. If some of them felt that they still needed to treat him as an old-line idomeni because of what he'd been . . . ? They'd ignore a developing problem until it became a problem, then get caught flat-footed when it blew up in their faces."

Jani hugged herself. As she did, the rough weave of her over-robe grabbed onto that of her shirt-jacket, pulling it so that she felt wrapped in restraints.

Then she looked toward the bed, and her eyes filled.

"Jan." Niall touched her arm. "You need to get out of this room." He took her by the elbow and supported her as she stood, then guided her to the door.

"It won't help."

"Humor me."

They navigated the twist of corridors. Heard voices, and followed them until they came upon John and Scriabin sitting in the clinic foyer. Their conversation was low volume, but animated, the sort of discussion one saw in hospitals.

John looked around when he heard footsteps. "Jani?" He stood and started toward her. "I thought you'd gone upstairs."

"I was with Niall." She leaned against him as soon as he embraced her. "He told me that His Excellency wished to see me."

Scriabin stood. "I appreciate Niall's sense of urgency, but there is no rush." He had changed clothes at some point, and now wore shirt and trousers in drab tan that looked like they'd been liberated from Dieter Brondt's own closet. "Anais has departed for Karistos, where press and staff await. I will be following her shortly. Stash and the others are conferring with ná Feyó. Colonial impact will be felt most immediately, of course."

"I imagine it's begun." Jani eased away from John, who ran his fingers down her back, then took hold of her hand.

Scriabin eyed her, then tilted his head toward John. "I told John of our discussion this morning, and the outcome. You have lost an inestimable ally, but that does not change the economic reality. We would prefer that the situation here remain as it is. We will do what we can to ensure that." He looked down at his clothes and sighed. "I dread leaving, to tell the truth. Stash's decision to treat Thalassa as a sovereign state reaped unforeseen benefits. You have borders, and your own com system. No one has to talk to the press because you haven't cleared it, and no one can report back to Cao while they're here because your secure system and Chicago's secure system can't talk to one another." He sighed. "I think I could live here."

"Just say the word, Zhenya." John gestured down the hall toward the labs.

Scriabin's eyes widened. "Perhaps not quite yet." He grinned, then hung his head. "Jani." He looked at her, all professional seriousness. "Words cannot express. He was one of the greatest, most influential beings who ever lived, and you called him friend for over twenty years."

"Among other things." Jani fielded Scriabin's startled look. "If you'd known Tsecha for a quarter-century, you would have, too." Her eyes stung, and she inhaled slowly, exhaled, struggled to maintain control. "Thank you."

"Now it's important that we preserve his legacy. This place—" Scriabin gestured around the foyer. "—and sound relations between humans and idomeni." He squeezed Jani's hand, then nodded to John and Niall and walked to the lift.

Jani waited until the farewells had been said and the lift door closed. "I thought we'd have things to discuss." She let go of John's hand and paced around the foyer.

"They're not machines, Jan, and they know you're not, either. They're giving you time. They know what you're going through."

John stepped in front of her, forcing her to stop. "I have to go." He took her face in his hands and kissed her hard. "I'll see you later." He nodded to Niall, then headed down the corridor into the clinic proper, disappearing around a corner.

Jani remained in the middle of the foyer. Eventually, she stared down at the patterned lyno, then at the gleaming walls. "I'm going to make some coffee."

Niall fell in behind her as she headed for the break room, which was located just off the foyer. "We could go upstairs. Your mess crew has hot and cold running everything up there."

"I need to do something with my hands." Jani scanned the break room for bodies before entering, and was relieved to find it empty. She walked over to the coffee table and started to assemble the brewer. "Want some?"

As usual, Niall chose a table by the wall, with a clear view of the entry. "Sure," he said as he dug for his nicsticks.

For a few minutes the only sounds were the clatter of metal parts and glassware, the gravel tumble of beans, a metal gnashing, and the gurgle of water. Then came the aroma, like dark brown velvet, swamping out the odor of Niall's clove smoke.

Jani rummaged for cups in the community cupboard. She filled them to the brim, forgoing flavorings or any other additives that might dilute the caffeine. Sat down. Took a sip of coffee, tried to savor the flavor, and tasted only heat and bitterness.

Niall took a swallow, then reached for the creamer. "There's awake, and then there's orbit, gel." He poured half the contents of the small pitcher into his cup. "John would be proud."

Jani sat back, cradling her cup. "I'm wondering if I should change." She tugged at the front of her overrobe. "I know this is priestly garb and should be correct no matter the situation. My mother would consider it appropriate, but to her, white is a color for funerals."

Niall tipped back his chair, 'stick in one hand, coffee in the other. "I see your father in black. With a red rose in his button-hole."

"Close." Jani took another sip, felt her head clear. "He preferred sprigs of lavender. He said the scent reminded him of his grandmama." She laid back her head. "The looks I got from Via's suborns when they came in for his body. As though I'd committed some grave sin. Spread out dinner on the edge of the bed." The patterned ceiling reminded her of the beach, the swirls of the tile coating like sprays of sand. "My father would've demanded more time. A proper wake, with stories and whiskey and laughter. We'd have had a chance to say good-bye. We wouldn't have felt like roadblocks in the way of those gods I'm supposed to intercede with even though I don't believe in them." She looked across the table to find Niall watching her, eyes dark with worry.

"Why don't you get some sleep?" He extinguished his spent 'stick, then immediately ignited another. "I'll hold off everyone, tell him that you had things you needed to see to."

"Can't sleep."

"Let John give you something."

"It's not the getting-to-sleep that's the problem." Jani's eye fell on the image someone had tacked up on the wall opposite. A forest scene, all green and leafy and shadowed. Quiet. Peaceful. "It's what happens after I arrive."

Niall stared at the smoke as it drifted upward, then he shook his head. "How long?"

"Three months. Maybe a little longer." Jani set down her cup. Plucked sugar packets from the dispenser, and stacked them one atop the other. "You don't have to listen to—"

"You've listened to me enough over the last couple of years." Niall took a long drag. "How many versions have you heard? A dozen? Two? 'What did you do during the War of Vynshàrau Ascension, young Niall?' 'Night of the Blade, sir. Laum blood running in the streets and shatterboxes shredding the air like tissue. Botched an arrest during evac, blew the commander of Rauta Shèràa Base and two of her cronies to bits, then spent the next twenty or so years covering it up.' " He stared straight ahead, the room's soft lighting making his battered face look very young. " 'And why is that a problem, young Niall?' 'Because, sir, the man people think I am and the man I know I am are quite different. Because the honors I have since received are as dust upon my tongue. Because I'm living a lie.' " His head tilted toward Jani. " 'But I have a friend who tells me that the man I am now is the one who matters.' " He cleared his throat. "Out with it."

"I never . . . even after it happened, I didn't . . ." Jani struggled for the words, wondered if the right ones existed. "The years went by. Nothing. I came here, and I was fine for months. Then . . ." She studied the forest scene again, and wondered at the feel of cool, damp air. "I don't know if it's the heat, or the scenery. Or the fact that this is so much an idomeni place, despite the humanish presence. The voices, that soft rise and fall. The gestures, and the smells, and the colors of the clothes." She paused, debated continuing, and felt the pull of Niall's patient gaze. "The first one. I'm walking down a dune. I can't find my footing, and I keep sliding. There are tents in the distance. The Laumrau tents. I'm wearing drop-dead whites instead of desertweights. I never get to the tents. I never even get to the base of the dune. I just keep walking, and sliding."

Niall remained silent, and waited.

"The second one . . ." Jani tugged at the red-slashed cuff of her overrobe. "I'm wearing desertweights. I have my shooter drawn." She raised a hand, index finger extended. "I'm standing at the first tent and pulling at the flap, but it won't open. It's like the fabric's all one piece—I can't find a gap. Then I freeze, because I know someone's behind me, and if I make any move to turn around, they'll kill me." She felt her heart pound and waited until it slowed. "Then I hear a shooter hum, and it isn't mine, and I know they'll kill me anyway." She flicked the pile of sugar packets, sending them splaying across the table. "Last night, they finally did." She waited for Niall to say something, then looked across the table to find him sitting with a fist pressed to his mouth, his eyes closed.

He lowered his hand eventually and opened his eyes. "Have you told John?"

Jani shook her head. "He'd get Neuro right on it. And who knows what else they'd take out along with the memories? They tend to overcompensate where I'm concerned." She picked up her coffee, then set it back down. "I wish I could drink."

"It doesn't help." Niall's voice emerged quiet, almost a whisper. "You dodged it for all those years. It was one of the things I held onto. Not that it did me any good. But just knowing . . . that if you never had them, maybe eventually I wouldn't have them, either." A twitch of a shoulder. "Doesn't make sense, but not much does. Can you talk to Parini?"

"Val tells John everything. They'd gang up on me like always, tell me it's for my own good." Jani looked at the forest again, but she'd lost the sense of it. Instead, she felt the heat and the dust, and smelled the bay, and saw the body on the gurney. "It happened so fast. He was there, and we were talking, and five minutes later he's on the ground, and ten minutes later he's—"

Niall stood. "I'm getting John."

"*No.*" Jani rose, cup in hand, and walked to the sink. "I'll be all right." She poured the dregs down the drain, rinsed the cup with cold water, held her hand beneath the flow until her fingers ached.

"I need to get back." Niall set his cup on the drainboard. "I sent off a quick missive to Roshi, but I need to prep the one with all the details."

They encountered several clinic staffers in the corridor. Jani fielded words and gestures, meeting sympathy with sadness, and tears with a touch or handshake. And all the while, something roiled within. Restlessness. And anger, looking for a place to land.

Niall ushered her into the lift, then waited for the doors to close. "I'm guessing Pascal sent something to Roshi as well. Maybe I'll intercept it and see what he has to say about me."

Jani forced a smile. "Would anything surprise you?"

"I can think of a few things that would piss me off." Niall flipped his lid from one hand to the other, then ran his sleeve over the smudged brim.

The ground floor proved to be the clinic writ large. Thalassans came from the demirooms, the courtyard, and the offices. Then word traveled, and they hurried down from the three upper levels. The line formed in orderly silence, and Jani walked along it and accepted the words and the hugs and wondered if there was any way to trade all that grief to Tsecha's gods for five more minutes. For a chance to say good-bye. To say anything at all.

Niall hung by her shoulder the entire time, monitoring her every move. When the impromptu receiving line petered out, he herded her to a table, then filled a plate for her from one of buffets.

"I will call later. I'll go through the office so that I don't wake you in case you're sleeping." He set the food in front of Jani, then unwrapped some cutlery from its napkin wrap and handed it to her. " 'His life was gentle, and the elements so mixed in him that Nature might stand up and say to all the world, "This was a man." ' " He spread the napkin across her lap. "The end of *Julius Caesar.* Not completely appropriate, but it says what I mean it to say." He kissed the top of her head, then turned and clipped across the courtyard.

Jani ate a little, then passed the time tearing a roll into tiny bits and feeding the lizards that had taken autumn refuge in the courtyard. Eventually, she heard distant thunder, then the rain spatter against the skylight roof. Looked overhead, and watched the roiling dark through the glass.

"You'd think it would be cold, but it's not."

She tore her attention from the rain just as Lucien emerged from the garden shadows. He wore civvies, brown trousers tucked into low boots and a tan shirt with the sleeves rolled up. A sling-bag hung from one shoulder, and he had tied a weatherall around his waist. "I thought you'd be back at the base."

Lucien shrugged. "I showed up for an emergency staff meeting. But I couldn't get into the room—my coding hadn't been entered into base systems, and according to regs, I cannot attend certain types of meetings unless I have been entered into base systems."

Jani tossed a bit of bread on the floor, where it vanished amid a rustle of leaves and a flick of green and red striped tail. "You have the right security clearances?"

"Yes," Lucien said with a sigh, "but I am not officially in systems. Pierce's admin told me that initialization can take up to a week. She was smiling when she said it." Another shrug. "I could bitch to Mako, but what would be the point? He's in Chicago—any communication he sends Pierce ordering him to give me access would be lost or garbled. They're experts over there at losing and garbling. It's the Elyan way."

"What did you expect? You know he can't stand you, and you forced yourself down his throat."

"Doesn't matter. I've been keeping myself busy." Lucien studied her through narrowed eyes. "I thought you'd have meetings of your own to attend."

Jani looked around the courtyard, then up toward the walkways, where Thalassans milled, chatted. It could have passed for a normal enclave evening but for the pall that hung in the air. "I've been allowed time to grieve."

"How considerate of everyone." Lucien met her low tone with his own. "I have a skimmer parked out on the beach. If you have some time, I'd like to show you something."

Jani eyed his face, rain-damp and drawn. His clothes and boots, mud-streaked and spattered. He'd been looking for something. Would he have come looking for her unless he'd found it? "I have time." She fingered the edge of one red cuff. "Give me a chance to change clothes."

CHAPTER 14

The Service two-seater coursed over the water like a seabird. Whitecaps swelled close enough to touch, spray mixing with rain to spatter across the vehicle's windscreen. Lucien had shut down all lighting both exterior and interior, leaving as the sole illumination the sickly green safety string that ran along the bottom of the dashboard.

Jani huddled against the heated cushions, fixing on the distant lights of Karistos, their yellow-white flicker like stars against the churning dark. "Does Niall know you're here?"

"I don't think he gives a rat's ass." Lucien's voice emerged measured, his native French provincial accent muted to nothing, a sign that anger and humiliation simmered into stew just below the surface. "I spent part of the day filling out forms. Then we heard the news. I tried to get into the staff meeting, like I said before. When that fell through, I pulled some strings at the Communications center, which for some strange reason *did* have me in systems. Poked around. Intercepted some chatter. Changed clothes, gathered gear, signed out the skimmer, and went to have a look around."

Jani rode the silence for a time, listening to the dull hum of the motor and the occasional splash of water against the hull. "What sort of chatter?"

"Details about Tsecha's death."

Jani's heart tripped as Lucien maneuvered the skimmer off the water and along a narrow strip of rock-strewn shoreline, held onto the armrests and squeezed as the vehicle shuddered and bounced. "What bothered you?"

Lucien remained silent until he had steered the skimmer onto the comparative smoothness of a steep incline. "The speed." He paused as he executed a hairpin turn. "I heard folks mention stroke. Hemorrhage. Aneurysm." He shook his head. "I didn't think that Tsecha would allow any condition he developed to advance until the point of crisis." He tore his attention from the narrow snake of a road to look at her. "John didn't discuss this with you?"

"Not in any detail." Jani folded her arms and concentrated on the road ahead. "We were right in the middle of it. John had to focus on treating him." She felt her face heat as Lucien's deceptively gentle laugh filled the cabin.

"Did he really think you wouldn't find out?" He steered around the final turn and up over the edge of the cliff, his voice shaking as the skimmer fought to stabilize over a stretch of rocky scrub.

"Find out what?" Jani closed her eyes and waited. *They were just giving me time to adjust.* Her gut ached. *They were being kind.* She opened her eyes. *Since when?* She saw the lights of Karistos, brightening the horizon like sunrise. *They wanted to talk to me.* And then they didn't.

The sounds of argument remembered . . .
Why the hell didn't you spot it before?
Because it wasn't there before.
It's growing.

"He was killed." Jani heard her voice echo in her head. A barely detectable sound, like the first pebble in the landslide.

"I think the word is 'assassinated.' " Lucien clucked his tongue. "How much time did it buy John? A few hours, at most. Now here you are, hot on the trail." His lips curved in the barest trace of a smile. "You're very angry with him now."

"That's none of your goddamn business."

"If you say so." Lucien fell silent, half smile fixed in place, and steered the skimmer over rock formations and across ravines with practiced ease.

Still several kilometers from the Karistos outskirts, there was little to see besides bare land. Jani took note of the odd house that broke up the monotony, but these appeared uninhabited and, judging from their ruined appearance, uninhabitable.

"This area's prone to quakes," Lucien said, as though reading her thoughts. "The land around here has shifted over the years, and some people didn't choose their building sites very carefully." He pointed out a one-story white stone box that had collapsed in the center as though a giant had stepped on it. "A two-meter crevasse opens up beneath your sitting room—there goes the couch."

Jani heard the skimmer motor hum lower in pitch as the vehicle slowed. "You didn't bring me out here to show me wrecked houses, did you?"

"Just one wrecked house in particular." Lucien slowed to a stop near yet another one-story white box, this one half buried thanks to the collapse of a sheltering overhang. "Although I checked out every abandoned homestead in this general area."

Jani popped her gullwing and disembarked the skimmer. Despite having lived the last two years in the thick of Commonwealth society, she still saw things through the eyes of the fugitive she had been. *Secluded, but half the view blocked by rocks . . . couldn't see someone approaching from the direction of Karistos . . . the outcropping offers too good a hiding place for an intruder.* She would have struck the place from her list, but knew she wasn't looking at it the right way. *Look at the place through the eyes of a killer.* The blocked views still bothered her, but the seclusion seemed more desirable now. "Where did they park their skimmer?"

"Up the road a little. There's a niche with some overhanging shrubbery. They broke off branches and used them for coverage." Lucien drew his shooter and activated it. The high-pitched hum sliced the air, highlighting the quiet. "There are a few sets of footprints around the place. Some bits of trash." He stopped in the doorway, examined the interior, then stepped inside. "Careful what you touch. It's been wiped with a protein bomb, and there's still some of the residue about." He drew a lightstick from inside his weatherall and activated it. Soft illumination rose slowly, casting weird shadows on the walls and ceiling.

Jani trailed him into the house. The interior proved even less inviting than the outside. Cracked walls. Rubble-strewn floors.

But at the far end, a window that allowed an expansive view of the bay and the curve of cliffs beyond, trimmed by a wide, rock-strewn sill.

Jani walked to the spot, on the lookout for disturbances in the dust, anything that could serve to confirm her surmise. "They stood here." She stepped around to gauge the view through the window. "Not the best angle."

"The only alternative is the sill," Lucien said as he stashed his shooter. "They would have had to clear the rubble, though, and beyond some smearing of dust, it shows no signs of having been disturbed. It seems the better choice—more stability for the weapon. But standing allowed more mobility, not to mention a better view of the doorway." He reached into his slingbag, removing a fist-sized ball that looked like crumpled metal foil. "Secondary spotter courses overhead, relaying information on the target back to the primary sight in the weapon's eyepiece." He tossed the ball out the window. It hovered for a few seconds, then shot upward like a shooting star in reverse, vanishing into the dark.

"We'll give it a chance to reach altitude." Lucien reached into his bag once more, this time removing a flat, hand-sized display. "A few hundred meters is usually high enough." He flipped open the display lid and motioned for Jani to join him, holding out the device to her so that she could see the screen.

She found herself looking at an aerial view of the Main House, centered on the balcony outside her and John's bedroom.

"I can zoom in and out at will. I can even record sound." Lucien touched a spot on the display pad and the secondary zoomed in. In a blink, the bedroom window filled the screen, the image sharp enough to discern the outline of Jani's desk and chair through the gauzy curtains.

"As I mentioned," Lucien said as he deactivated the display and closed the case, "the secondary relays images to the weapon sight. In addition, the assassin wore an audiovisual array much like the ones reporters use to record events. In either case, it serves as an archive. Snipers call them their 'books.' They record what is seen through the weapons sight, and it serves as proof of the kill." He tucked the display back into his bag, then walked to the window and waited. Within seconds the secondary flitted through the opening and settled into his hands.

Jani touched the rough globe. "Why didn't enclave security systems pick up on this?"

"It scans as an organism. Systems would identify it as a small bird, or a very large bug." Lucien tossed the device into the air, caught it, then stuck it back in his bag. "Security's a fiction that dissuades only the laziest killers. If someone really wants to get to you, there's nothing you can do to stop them."

Jani looked out the window, imagining the scene beyond the water and the cliffs. Tsecha emerging from the meeting house and walking across the street. The secondary monitoring him, relaying his image to his killer, who lay watching, waiting for the perfect time to strike. "You know it was a sniper. Do you have a name or two that you can offer?"

Lucien hung his head and put his hands in his pockets. Time passed. One minute. Two.

Jani stepped away from the window and walked around the room, pretending interest in examining the rubble. She had known since their days together in Chicago that Lucien's Service career served as cover for his true profession. He had once arranged it so she found his souvenirs, the items he took from his victims and kept as mementos. A casino chip. A scarf. A whiskey glass. Fifteen items in all, each resting atop a clean, folded cloth inside a dresser drawer. How many had he added to the collection since then?

Lucien raised his head. Cleared his throat. "You know what I do."

Jani leaned against the remains of a smashed couch frame. "I've known for a long time."

"And you love me anyway." He glanced at her beneath his lashes, but his heart wasn't in it—he straightened and started to pace. "What's said here, stays here."

Jani shrugged. "Likewise."

"I'm serious."

"And I never am."

Lucien stopped. Looked about the room, focusing on nothing. "I've never talked about this before, with anyone. What I tell you may not seem important, or vital, or secret, but that's not the point. It's talking out of school." He stopped fidgeting and fixed on her. "We don't do that."

Now it was Jani's turn to remain silent. She listened to the wind whistle through the cracks in the roof, branches scrape against the rough stone exterior. "You know what I am, how I think."

Any other time, Lucien might have offered a flirtatious response, or rolled his eyes in irritation. Not this time. This time, he watched her hands, the way she held herself, as though unsure of what she might do. "I've known for a long time."

"Then you know my answer." Jani patted her trouser pocket, and wished she had taken the time to dig her shooter out from its place in the bottom drawer of her dresser. In this house that had apparently sheltered one assassin, in which she conversed with another, she would have taken some comfort in its presence. "I don't care about your assassins' code of silence, or your fears for your future, or your friends in high places. If you know who killed Tsecha, I expect you to tell me. If you know how to find them, I expect you to help me. If you know and you don't help me, be prepared to deal with the consequences. Do you understand what I'm telling you?"

"The definitions of 'rock' and 'hard place.' " Lucien walked to the window. "I don't know who killed Tsecha. I know the type." He turned and leaned against the wall. The half-light conspired with the layout of the room to shadow his face in a way that obscured his age and left him looking too young. "We all have our specialty. Mine is accidents. Mechanical and systems malfunctions. Vehicle crashes. These are the neatest killings, in my opinion. If executed properly, they don't attract undue attention. They look like tragic mishaps to most people. The only ones who know otherwise are those who know how to read the signs." He looked up, eyes fixed on some middle distance, some event in his past. Some target made. "Some of us specialize in explosives. A few prefer poison." He shook his head. "God knows why." He folded his arms, flexing his hands every so often, as though they pained him. "Then there are some who will only employ projectile weaponry, blades, strangulation, a method that requires them to remain in contact with or close proximity to their target." He straightened, then moved to the side, let his bag slide down his arm to the floor, and perched on the edge of the sill. "That's the sort of killer I believe we're dealing with here."

Jani watched Lucien continue to flex his hands. *He's never been one to fidget.* The last time he showed such restlessness, he had just learned that the Haárin he would meet in the circle the next morning planned to kill him. *He was in danger then—is he in danger now?* Was what he told her that important, or had the mere fact of telling it put him at risk? *Do I care?* "Close proximity to the victim. Close-in weapons. You've just described a Service infantryman."

"Infantry's a *job.*" Lucien nudged a small chunk of rubble with the toe of his boot, then kicked it across the floor. "The ones I'm telling you about . . . they consider assassination a calling, like medicine, or the clergy. Every aspect of preparation is ritualized, from the researching of the target to the choosing of the weapon." His eyes narrowed. "The kill . . . needs to be personal." He let his arms fall to his sides, then hunched his shoulders and shoved his hands in his pockets. "Most of us work for money, for position. Tangible rewards, if not always material. It's a job, like any other, for which we receive payment for services rendered. But with them . . ." Again the hesitation, the sense of words being pulled out with pliers. "They see beauty in the act, an affirmation of whatever it is they believe in. I'd be more inclined to believe that one of them killed Tsecha rather than someone with a more commercial bent."

"Why?"

"The risk. Tsecha is the highest visibility target to be hit in decades. The scrutiny will be intense. The investigations. The repercussions." Lucien again glanced at her beneath his lashes, but judging from the edge in his eyes, flirtation was the furthest thing from his mind. "Say that I had been offered the commission to assassinate Tsecha. I know that given your closeness to him, you would become involved in the investigation. If you discovered that I was responsible, you would kill me." His head came up slowly, a trace of the old challenge showing itself in the set of his jaw. "Don't tell me it didn't cross your mind." He cocked his head. "Not even once?"

Not until now. Jani wished again that she'd brought her shooter. "It might have."

"That's my girl. Trust is for other people."

"I'm not people."

"You never were." Lucien looked back down at the floor. "Like I said, I know how you'd react, and that would be taken into account as I considered whether or not to accept the commission."

Jani felt the silence envelop them, the tension crystallize. Even the wind had paused as if to listen. "Was it offered?"

Lucien hesitated. One could almost hear the rattle of an ancient scale as he weighed his options. "No. The fact that it wasn't eliminates a number of possible customers. I'm on their preferred list when it comes to jobs like this."

Questions surfaced in the document examiner part of Jani's mind. Was there a paper list? If so, who kept it and how did they classify it? Who had access? What sorts of accounts did they set up to bury the payments, the expenses? *Just give me a chance to hunt. A chance to dig.* She focused on the emptiness of a niche cut into the wall opposite, the shadows that defined it. Anything to keep her mind from racing until she could find time alone to ponder. "Wouldn't they think twice about sending you on this job, knowing your connection to me?"

Lucien shook his head. "Our past relationship would provide me a legitimate reason to be here. Ex-lover seeking to rekindle an old flame." The winning smile broke through, only to vanish as quickly as it came. "I had nothing to do with his death."

Jani shrugged. "I appreciate the reassurance."

"You look impressed." Lucien bent over and plucked another fragment of rubble from the floor. He straightened, then started rolling the bit of debris between his palms. "He didn't like me."

"He liked you just fine. He just didn't trust you." *That was one thing he and I had in common.* Jani pushed away from the wall and wiped her hands on her trousers to remove the grit. "So, we're looking for a sniper-type killer who considered murdering Tsecha to be a religious experience. Do you have any names?" She waited for an answer. As time passed and none proved forthcoming, she looked up to find Lucien still seated on the sill, watching her.

"Let me take care of it. Send a killer to catch a killer." He continued to roll the rubble fragment between his hands, the movement growing ever slower until it stopped completely. "It might take some time. Years, perhaps. But I would find them and handle them and no one would ever be able to trace it back to you."

Jani studied his face for some indication of his thoughts. She would have expected him to try to cut her off. *Instead, he goes and surprises me by offering to help.* Not that it mattered. "No, thank you. I want to find them myself."

"Why?" Lucien closed one hand around the stone fragment. "I'm not making this offer because I like working with you. I'm a survivor of too many rides on the Kilian express, and I have the scars to prove it." He opened his hand and tipped it to one side—the fragment slid off and hit the floor, bouncing once before coming to rest amid the dust. "This situation needs to be approached with caution, and when it comes to killing . . ." He sighed. "With you, it's always personal."

"We've had this discussion before." Jani felt the stomach-rumbling irritation that always accompanied one of their arguments. "I have only ever killed for reasons of defense, mine or someone else's."

"Only after you went out and looked for it. Met it. Stared it in the face. Challenged it." Lucien rose abruptly and strode across the room, raising dust with every step. "You think you know killing. You're a fucking amateur. You always lead with your emotions, and there is no place for emotion in this. No place for vengeance." He stopped in front of the shadowed wall niche and braced his hands on either side. "I know what you want. You want to watch them die. You want to look into their eyes and watch the light go out—"

Jani moved for the doorway just as Lucien pushed off the wall. He met her in the middle of the room, grabbing her arm and spinning her around to face him.

"—feel their blood flow over your hands. Savor the look on their face when they realize it was you who struck the blow—"

Jani took hold of Lucien's thumb and bent it back. He released her arm with a muttered curse—as he took a step back, she moved in. Brought her fist around. The raised dome of one of her rings caught Lucien square in the mouth—she felt the shock of a solid punch jar her hand, rattle up her arm. As soon she connected, she backed off, raising both hands and opening them wide. He'd grabbed her first—that entitled her to one shot. Anything beyond that would take them both to a place they'd never been, a place they could never depart once they'd entered.

Lucien must have understood that as well. He remained in the middle of the room, bent at the waist, hands on knees, his breathing ragged.

Jani watched as a single red drop fell from his mouth to the dust below. Then another. Another. She looked down at her hand and saw the brilliant crimson of the stone faded by the dull wash of his blood.

"Well." Lucien touched his battered lower lip and flinched. "That had something behind it." He drew back his hand and studied the red that smeared across his fingertips. Then he straightened, one slow move at a time, like a clockwork figure. "I can't comprehend how you felt about Tsecha. Even if I could remember what that depth of regard felt like, I've never known anyone worth the effort." He reached into his trouser pocket and pulled out a crumpled dispo, which he pressed to the seeping wound. "But I've seen strong emotion take over before, and I know where it leads. You'll get yourself killed. You'll get others around you killed. Because you won't back down. Because you want the blood of Tsecha's assassin on your hands."

"Stop pretending to read my mind!" Jani wedged between a broken chair and a fallen portion of the ceiling. Anything to block her path to Lucien. Anything to keep her from going after him again. "You don't know me—"

"I know you better than he—*Ow!*" Lucien winced and pressed the dispo to his torn lip. "I know you better than he does," he continued, his voice muffled by the cloth. "He thought he could get away without telling you anything, like he did in Rauta Shèràa." He pulled the dispo away from the wound and glared at the staining, then crumpled it and shoved it back in his pocket. "I'm trying to get you to do now what I've always tried to get you to do in Chicago. Understand the situation for what it is. See reason." He stood in place for a time, the angle of the lightstick illumination accentuating the rawness around his mouth, the first hints of swelling. Then he turned and walked to the sill, recovering his slingbag from its resting place and hoisting it to his shoulder.

Jani massaged the back of the broken chair, squeezing harder even as she felt the ground-in grit abrade her skin. "Did you ever manage to do it? Get me to see reason, as you understood it to be?"

Lucien stilled. Looked at her and said nothing.

Jani let go of the chair, brushed the ground stone from her hands. "Well, then . . ." She paused as the screech of branch against rock filled the room, a signal of the storm's growing intensity. "Are you going to help me?" She awaited the answer she knew would never come. "This takes me back. Yes, to my Rauta Shèràa days. I've been stonewalled by experts, Lucien."

"And you remember how that ended." His voice came soft, barely audible above the wind. "A bomb on a transport. All aboard killed."

Storm sounds receded. Now Jani heard nothing but the beat of her heart. "You're saying that was my fault?" She tried to swallow, but her mouth had gone dry. "No one was meant to survive Knevçet Shèràa. We were dead no matter what."

"Not as long as Rikart Neumann remained alive. He was one of the masterminds—if you'd played him right, you could have gotten your people out." Lucien looked in her direction. He even met her eye. "Instead, you shot him."

"That was self-defense."

"Only after you confronted him. Stared him in the face. Challenged him." Lucien pressed the back of his hand to his lip, examined it, then shook his head. "When your parents lived in Chicago, I used to visit them."

Jani nodded. "Mama told me that you liked her cooking. You liked being able to converse in French. Papa knew better. He said that you were too nosy, wanted to know too much about me."

"Yes, you inherited your trusting nature from him, I think." Lucien started for the door, then stopped and looked her full in the face. "You were never any different, even as a kid. Always a punch in the mouth when a touch would do just as well." His lower lip had swelled in earnest now, the gash red and glistening. "And now here you are. Decades have past, the scenery's different, but you haven't changed a bit." He watched her, dead brown eyes unreadable, then walked to the door. On the way, he grabbed the lightstick from the place where he'd set it, shook it to extinguish it, then stuffed it in his bag.

Jani let her eyes adjust to the dark. Then she stepped out from between the chair and the rubble and walked to the window. Examined the rock-strewn sill, then the view through the window, imagining as she did a tiny object descending through the air toward its target. How did Tsecha's assassin feel when they saw him touch his left ear, saw the first hint of confusion cross his face? Satisfied? Ecstatic? Righteous?

"Hold that feeling tight," Jani whispered. "You won't enjoy it for long." With that, she turned, looked over the room one last time, and headed for the door.

The force of the wind hit her as soon as she stepped outside, forcing her to turn her back on it so she could breathe. She climbed into the skimmer to find Lucien checking weather reports on the vehicle's display. He ignored her, putting the vehicle in motion before she had fully closed her door.

They rode back to the Thalassan side of the bay in silence. The rain had eased to the odd spatter by the time the shore came into view.

Lucien steered the skimmer up onto the beach and up the cliff road to the Main House. Stopped on the edge of the drive circle near the entry and powered down. "I'll say it one last time. Stay out of it."

Jani didn't reply. She disembarked and walked across the pavered circle to the house, gusts of wind whipping the hem of her weatherall as though hurrying her along. Felt Lucien's stare drill the place between her shoulders, but didn't turn around.

CHAPTER 15

Jani entered the Main House to find a confab going on in the middle of the courtyard. Dieter, Val, and John, standing amid the empty tables and sundered buffets of late evening sacrament, voices rising.

Then John spotted her. "Where the hell have you been?" He started toward her, more relieved than angry, the first hints of a smile lightening his face.

Then something he saw behind her caused him to slow. Stop. Clench his fists.

Jani heard the entry door close. Footsteps.

"Stormy." Lucien removed his weatherall and shook it, sending water spraying. "I'm guessing it'll last the night." He hung the garment on one of the wall hooks near the door, but kept his slingbag with him. "Good evening, Mr. Brondt." He nodded to Dieter, while pointedly ignoring Val. "Could I trouble you to let me use your comroom?"

Dieter's brow arched as he took in the state of Lucien's lip. He glanced at Jani, on the alert for any hint of an objection. ". . . Of course, Captain," he said eventually. "Follow me, please." He cast a last, questioning look in her direction, then headed for the lift, Lucien at his heels.

John waited until the lift doors closed. "Where were you?" He ignored Val's muttered caution. "We were ready to send out Security."

Jani remained still and silent as John drew closer, watching his expression grow more and more grim as he took in her rough clothes, the wet sand that coated her boots. "Why?"

"What do you mean, why?" Val pressed a hand to his forehead. "We were worried sick. We didn't know if you—"

"That's not the question she's asking, Val." John stood hands on hips, and studied the floor. "Not here." He turned and headed across the courtyard toward the enclave offices.

Jani followed, brushing past Val, ignoring his whispered "Please, Jan—" She felt focused, alive, as though she could run for kilometers, go for days without sleep or food. Idomeni rage, a pure distillation of emotion, a force that had built cities and transformed governments and destroyed them just as surely.

She waited in the doorway of an unoccupied office while John checked for squatters, not entering until he gave the all-clear. Waited longer to speak, because so much of what she had to say had already been said, in a clinic basement twenty years before. *Some essentials never change.* Only the circumstances surrounding them.

She walked to a desk on the far side of the room and leaned against it. "When did you know?"

John turned to her. He hadn't looked her in the eye since Lucien's appearance, and he avoided doing so now. "You don't understand—"

"Answer the goddamned question."

John walked over to a chair set against the wall opposite Jani and sat. "The sudden appearance of the mass in his auditory canal. We scanned the area within minutes of his collapse and we saw nothing. We wouldn't have missed it—it was the sort of thing we were looking for." His gaze shifted to some middle distance, memories of the morning playing across his face, mirrored in his clouded stare. "We initially felt it was a neuroma, but those grow very slowly, and this thing grew while Aris watched."

Jani revisited her own memories, carved in her heart and soul with the force of a knife through flesh. John's angry question. Aris's frantic reply. *Why the hell didn't you spot it before? Because it wasn't there before.* She tried to erase the images, the voices, even as she knew that any respite would prove only temporary. "What was it?"

"Preliminary indications are that it was a weaponized prionic. It entered Tsecha through his left tympanum. After it warmed to body temperature, it began to grow." John fell back on his lecture voice, a measured narration devoid of emotion. "It rapidly extruded into his brain cavity and continued to increase in size until it pressed against his brain stem. This led to seizure, followed by unconsciousness, respiratory collapse, and death."

Death. Jani saw the still figure in the bed. Ná Via circling, shutting down the life support systems one by one. "Did he feel any pain?"

"He—" John hesitated, then shook his head. "Once growth began, it was over within seconds. I don't believe he did, no."

"But you don't know?"

"It's unknowable."

Jani brushed away a tear. There were times when she wished John would lie, but those were the times when he never did. "Who else knows the truth?"

"Val. Yevgeny."

"Markos?" Jani's throat tightened. "Ulanova?"

John nodded, after a time. "Yes."

"Niall?" Jani waited as John didn't respond at first, then shook his head. *Because you knew he'd tell me.* "Via?" She waited again, as John stilled and remained silent and slowly averted his gaze. "She's going to figure out that she didn't miss anything, that if it had been a neuroma, she would have seen it long before Tsecha became ill." She recalled the female, normally as aggressive as ná Meva, following John from display to display. Stricken. Confused. "You lied to her. You let her think she screwed up, that she killed him." Then another figure replaced the physician-priest's in her mind's eye. "What about Feyó?"

"What do you think her reaction will be if she learns that Tsecha was assassinated? That one of his beloved humanish brought him down? Do you think she'll listen to anything that any of us have to say?" John looked Jani in the eye now, leaned forward with hands on knees as he let fly the facts. "She'll look at us and see humanish and the dialogue will stop there." He sat back, the lecture winding down. "The truth will come out. When we're ready. When we've prepared."

"When will that be?" Jani felt the subtle shift in the air around her. "Tomorrow? Next month? Five years? Ten?" She could have been in any of a score of offices in the old Rauta Shèràa consulate, arguing the same points, fighting the same old battles, and losing every one. "Or maybe you and your new friend Yevgeny went behind everyone's back and worked your own deal. You cover up the assassination, and he guarantees you keep your share of Neoclona."

John's face darkened. "You believe me capable of that level of deceit?"

"In your sleep. You'll have all your reasons lined up, and they'll all be very sound. To preserve the Outer Circle alliance with the Haárin. To preserve Neoclona, and the stability it provides. To help ensure that Yevgeny wins the election." Jani stood and paced, anger driving her to move. "And on the other hand, we have what? You lied to Feyó, who is the foundation of the alliance. If she ever discovers that you misled her, you'll lose her. Maybe you're assuming that you'll be well enough established by that point that you won't need her. That's one hell of an assumption, but you're in a risk-taking mood." Her step slowed. "Then you lied to me. But, you've done that before."

John stood and started toward her. "Jani—"

"I could have struck you. When I realized that you knew Tsecha had been murdered and you didn't tell me." Jani saw the look in John's eye as he drew closer, as he gauged her expression. Read the tension as he stopped in his tracks, as reluctant to approach her as she was to have him within arm's reach. "Who did it? Do you know? Is anyone looking for them?"

"You know better than that. Exterior is turning over every rock—"

"Including the ones they put in place themselves?"

John begged the ceiling for respite. "We know of several separatist organizations whose goal is to drive a wedge between Chicago and Rauta Shèràa. Yevgeny is maneuvering Anais into pushing all the right buttons." His eyes chilled. Frost on silver. "We aren't letting it slide, if that's what you're thinking."

You keep saying "we," John. It's like you're already back in the game. Jani felt her fingers curl, the sense memory of a hand squeezing hers. "He knew. That he wasn't right. That he'd been injured, infected. And in his last few lucid moments, he begged you to take care of him." She laughed. "You're taking care of him, all right."

"It needs to be done quietly. Carefully, so that—"

"So that Yevgeny can dig for any connections to Li Cao, and use them to drive her from office. So that everything can be positioned to derive the greatest political benefit possible."

"I know it's not your way of doing things." John put his hands in his pockets, shuffled his feet. The frost melting, a little. "Yevgeny told me about the meeting this morning. He told me how concerned you were about Thalassa, about what would happen to everyone here if relations between Chicago and Rauta Shèràa fell apart. If we're careful, you won't have to worry about that. You can just—"

"Go back to being your pet lab experiment?" Jani touched her hand, outlining where Tsecha's fingers had locked with hers.

"Don't worry about anything—John took care of it. He also won back all his marbles in the process—wasn't that bright of him?" She let her hands fall. "Except that you lied to Feyó. That wasn't so bright."

"Any step you take to inform her will destroy everything we've put in place so far." John maneuvered until he stood in front of her. "It's a cracked egg, Jan. A touch could smash it. Think past Feyó to Morden nìRau Cèel. How do you think he'd play Tsecha's assassination? He'd sever diplomatic relations with Chicago and call all Haárin back into the worldskein. Given the circumstances, Feyó would obey. Then Cèel would have what he needs to hold off his enemies and hang onto power, an external enemy at which he can point his warriors." His eyes dulled. "Do you remember the Vynshàrau warriors? I do. Never a shooter when a blade will do the job. Most of what I know about idomeni anatomy and physiology I learned from helping clean up after them."

Jani turned her back and took a slow walk around the room. She had to be careful now, because John had a knack for sounding sensible, for deflecting her every argument and turning her emotion against her. The trick was to avoid looking at his eyes, his hands, his smile. To concentrate on another time, twenty years before, when he'd talked sense and told her not to worry. "If Feyó considered humanish a monolithic entity with a single fixed mindset, she would never have become a follower of Tsecha. She never would have worked to establish her enclave here. She's capable of discerning shades of grey." She heard her voice, so quiet. So sensible. "Every hour you delay informing her adds months, years, to the time it will take to win back her trust, assuming it's even possible to do so." She checked the wall clock, and the investigator she'd once been sent up a howl. "She has networks of informants in place at Elyas Station. Throughout the Outer Circle. They could provide us information about suspects. Names."

John sighed. "Jan, I really don't think—"

"No, of course you don't. You assume, because it's easier and it's faster and it gets you what you want." She looked at the wall clock again. So many hours lost. So many chances. "We've had this argument more times than I can remember. And every time, I've knuckled under. Not always immediately, but eventually. Not because I came to agree with you, but because I loved you and because in the end that always outweighed everything else." She looked at John only long enough to see the first glimmer of realization cross his face. "Not this time."

"Jani?" John stared, brow furrowed, as though she'd said something in a language he didn't understand. "What are you saying? What—"

Before he could finish, she walked out the door. Thought she heard his words follow her as the panel slid closed—

I love you.

—and kept walking. Grabbed an empty dish cart that one of the kitchen crew had left in the corridor and dragged it over to the lift. Boarded, pulling the cart after her, turning in time to spot John stride across the courtyard into the nearest demiroom, where Val waited.

The lift door opened on the fourth floor. She disembarked, cart in tow. Keyed into her suite. Hers and John's suite.

John's suite.

She dragged the cart through the sitting room into the bedroom, through the bedroom into the closet, and started pulling clothes off hangers. Trousersuits, coveralls. Left the gowns behind because she wore them for John. Grabbed boots and trainers from the shoe rack and tossed them atop the clothes. Rummaged along a top shelf until she found her old Service duffel, and added that to the mix, then turned and ran headlong into a flustered Dieter.

"Jani, is something wr—" He looked down at the cart, then at the empty hangers, then at her, eyes widening. "I'm sorry."

"Is there a spare bedroom?" Jani exited the closet. "Preferably on another floor?"

"There are a few guest rooms on the second." Dieter hurried after her. "But they're very *small*."

"I'm nothing if not adaptable." Jani pushed the cart in front of her armoire and dumped in armfuls of T-shirts, underwear, and socks. "You know?"

"Yes." Dieter's eyes glistened. "First I saw—" He looked down at the mess of clothing. "I overheard Doctor Shroud and Minister Scriabin. Then I overheard some of the discussion in the library."

"That's my Dieter. Eavesdropper extraordinaire." Jani uncovered an old Neoclona pullover in a pile of shirts and tossed it aside. "Would your old connections at Elyas Station be amenable to providing passenger manifests and information on persons of interest?" She waited. "I don't like the sound of that silence."

"They've been ordered not to talk to me." Dieter freed a coverall sleeve that had gotten twisted in one of the cart's wheels. "All that Fred in Docks Management would tell me was that the word came from the main office. He wouldn't tell me which ministry."

Jani nodded. *And so it begins.* The stonewalling, leavened with outright lies. "I need to talk to Feyó."

"Actually, she's on her way." Dieter picked up a bandbra that had missed the cart and landed on the floor. "Ná Meva is bringing her." He set it atop the pile, his face reddening. "They apparently have something to ask you."

Knowing Meva, it's more telling than asking. Jani headed for her desk. "Great." She freed her scanpack, a parts bag. "Scriabin needs to be here as well."

Dieter caught a stack of T-shirts just before they tumbled to the floor. "I will contact his offices, but—"

Jani added a favorite stylus to the pile. "What?"

"I have spoken with Doctor Shroud. Many things have already been decided." Dieter took a deep breath. "Minister Scriabin may not come."

"Tell him I'm meeting with ná Feyó." Jani pulled out a drawer and emptied the assorted tools atop the clothes. "He'll come."

Dieter grabbed the back of the cart and helped her steer it toward the door. "I left Captain Pascal in the comroom. Betty is watching him to make sure he doesn't get into anything he shouldn't." He cleared his throat. "What happened to his lip?"

"I belted him."

"He said he fell."

"Captain Diplomacy." Jani stopped in front the door and keyed it open—

—just as John did the same from the other side. His face lightened until he spotted the laden cart. Then the brightness died. "What are you doing?"

Jani dragged the cart past him into the corridor. There, she found her way blocked by Val, who tried to take hold of her arm. "Get out of my way," she said as she shook him off.

"Jan, please let us—"

"Get out of my way, you self-serving son of a bitch."

Val's face flushed. "You don't—understand."

"I understand all I have to." She veered close as she pushed past him, forcing him against the wall. "You, me, and John in the basement of the Rauta Shèràa clinic. And the goal for the day is keep Jani in the dark and pile on that manure. Mushroom, mushroom. The more things change." She waited for Dieter to catch her up, and together they pushed the cart down the corridor toward the lift.

Dieter helped Jani organize her suits and coveralls in her new room's narrow closet, but fled when they reached what he referred to as her "small clothes."

"Coward." She rolled and folded as best she could, but found that for the first time in her memory, she had more clothes than places in which to store them. She concentrated on sorting out anything faded or frayed, letting her hands work while her mind raced. *Ná Feyó, forgive us—I need your help to catch a killer.*

"Well, this is cozy."

Jani turned to find Lucien standing in the doorway. "I obviously need to get that lock recoded."

"It's still set to the factory default. Which means no one has used this room yet." Lucien looked around the small, sparsely furnished bed-sit and sniffed his disapproval. "Can't imagine why." He wandered by the bed and gave the mattress an exploratory prod. "You'd find out more if you stayed with him. Have you thought of that?"

"He's a past master at keeping things from me." Jani closed the door of her tiny clothes cupboard before Lucien could make any comments about her underwear.

"Yet you always manage to find those things out." He dragged a frame chair away from the wall and sat, dropping his slingbag to the floor beside him. "He loves you. He thinks he's doing what's best for you, but he's insecure enough to want to explain his reasons to you in great detail. That gives you leverage." He stretched his legs until the soles of his boots grazed the cuff of her trousers. "If you played it right, you could have him financing your investigation by tomorrow morning." He glanced at his timepiece. "Make that this morning." He scrubbed a hand through his hair and yawned.

Jani walked to the room's slit-like window and listened to the patter of the rain. "I'll play him, you play Val, and we'll take it as far as it goes?"

Lucien rolled his eyes. "In case you hadn't noticed, Val's not talking to me."

"When did you ever let moral revulsion and self-disgust stop you?" Jani tried to gauge her view, but could discern only a few dim lights through the dark and the rain. "Did you find out anything at Base Communications besides how quickly Tsecha died?"

"You mean like names of possible agents of change? Sorry, no." Lucien folded his arms and hunched. He had circles under his eyes and yawned with increasing frequency.

"Who did you contact downstairs? Mako?"

"I needed to send him an update." Lucien rubbed a hand across his cheek, which was starred with blond stubble. "The first messages should hit Chicago in the next day or two, after which the shit will hit the fan and proceed in our direction at speed." Before he could say more, the door buzzer interrupted.

"Jani." Dieter slid the door open halfway and poked his head through the gap. "Ná Feyó and ná Meva have been delayed." His face colored when he spotted Lucien. "I suspect an attempted intervention."

"I wonder if John bothered to contact Yevgeny first, or went over his head and blocked Feyó himself?" Jani picked up a sock that had gone astray and stuffed it into a drawer. "They're going to have fun roping him in. That gang is all generals and no Spacers."

"I'll let you know as soon as anything changes." Dieter shot a last hard look at Lucien, then let the panel slide closed.

Lucien stood. "Come sunrise, I'll be AWOL. I need to get back." He stretched, twisting at the waist, then stilling like an artist's model in mid-pose, allowing a view of flat stomach and line of shoulder that even his bulky clothing couldn't obscure. "What are you going to do?"

Jani waited until he finished his display and turned to face her. "I don't know. I could go into Karistos myself and poke around, but I have a feeling I won't be allowed to leave the enclave." She yawned, felt fatigue press down, draining whatever shock and grief had left behind. "Feyó is my best bet. I need to wait and see whether she can get past John."

"Waiting was never a talent, as I recall." Lucien took one step closer, then another. He'd applied something to his lip that reduced the swelling but not the redness, making it look winestained and wet. "Many were the times I wanted to grab a rope and tie you to the bedpost."

"That's garden variety, as your kinks go." Jani stood her ground as he closed in. "I'm surprised you never tried." She felt the hard edge of his hip as he pressed against her, the warmth of his skin through his clothes and the growing firmness between his legs.

"I wanted to. So many times, I wanted—" Lucien pressed close as flesh would allow, eyes closed, lips a breath away. Then he stilled, eyes snapping open. "Are you playing *me* now?" He backed away. "I can't—" He raised a pleading hand. "When Pierce isn't locking me out of meetings, he's watching me like a hawk. I don't have the latitude here that I did at Sheridan."

"You'll think of something." Jani ignored his grumbling reply. "Who manufactures weaponized prionics?"

"Government labs. Service labs. A few commercial."

"Could Neoclona pull it off?"

Lucien's brow arched. "You are angry with John, aren't you?" He hoisted his slingbag to his shoulder. "Can I sleep first?"

"If you must." Jani stepped out of his way as he headed for the door. "Think you can free up information on any persons of interest who've passed through Elyas Station today? Dieter's been declared *hybrid non grata*. His old connections won't connect."

"You don't ask for much, do you?" Lucien paced like a trapped beast. "No one knows me here—I'm still feeling my way. I can't promise *anything*." He stopped and leaned close, but this time kissing was the furthest thing from his mind. "Are you listening? I'll do—"

"Just do what you can." She leaned against the wall, just beyond reach.

"Whatever I can. Yeah. Move the fucking world while I'm at it, and after I do that—" Lucien struck the doorpad hard enough to make it squeal, and blew out of the room.

Jani remained against the wall, listening to the receding *clip* of Lucien's boots. Then she crossed to the bed, prodding the mattress as he had before sitting on the edge. Her eyes burned as tears sprang unbidden.

"I don't want to sleep. I don't want to sleep." She lay across the bare pad. Begged Tsecha to forgive her for every question incorrectly answered, every task left uncompleted, each lesson gone unlearned. Prayed to Ganesh for mercy. Closed her eyes.

Heat. The sharp spice of *vrel* blossom.

Vrel *can't grow here—it's desert*. She wore drop-deads again. Stood atop a hill some distance from the tents. Made ready to walk down when she saw the curtain of sand close in and felt the lash of the wind.

Before she could take another step, the storm struck. Sand sprayed over her, coating her hands, her face. Filling her mouth, her nose. She fell to the ground and spread herself flat, buried her face in rubble, felt the knife edges of rocks cut through her clothes into her skin. The warmth of her blood as it flowed.

The wind buffeted, hard enough to rock her as the sand swept over her like a blanket—

Jani?

—blowing—

Jani? Wake up.

—burying—

"Jani!"

She struck out, connecting with soft hands that enveloped her fist, absorbing the blow. Opened her eyes.

"Jani? Are you all right?" Dieter's moon face filled her view, brow knit, eyes dark with concern. "Ná Feyó and ná Meva have arrived."

CHAPTER 16

Jani changed clothes. Used what makeup she had to erase the effects of the day from her face. Then she followed Dieter out to the courtyard, and felt the pounding in her head start as soon as she heard the voice bounce off the stone and glass.

"*—and I will speak with her.*" Meva loomed over Scriabin like a specter in a horror 'Vee, waving John silent every time he tried to get a word in edgewise. "She was his chosen religious suborn, most against the wishes of many, but such was as he was. And now she has duties to perform, and she must see to them or his soul will be in peril." She paused to draw breath and spotted Jani. "Ah, there you are." She swept toward her, the hem of her overrobe flapping around her knees. "Damned business. They sought to stop us at the border, your damned security, but I drove past. Let them shoot at us—hah! Let them worry over their souls if they do so."

Jani looked past Meva to the nearby demiroom, where Feyó sat on a couch while Dathim stood sentinel over her. From the corner of her eye she could see John raise a hand in an effort to draw her attention, and ignored him. "Ná Meva, I need to explain something to ná Feyó."

"Then explain it."

"It's difficult."

"Ah. Something she will not wish to hear." Meva looked back at her dominant, voice ripe with sadistic gloat.

Jani stepped closer, lowering her voice as Scriabin tried to stare her silent. "Ní Tsecha was assassinated."

Meva turned and looked her in the face. Her amber eyes were a darker version of Tsecha's, and bright as shattered glass. "No.

This she will not wish to hear now, or at any time." She pondered for a moment, then headed for the demiroom, beckoning Jani to follow.

"Jani." Scriabin bowed as she approached, his ministerial air at odds with his stance, feet wide apart, shoulders rounded like a brawler's. "Please reconsider your decision—"

"Save it, Zhenya." John glared at her, looking away just as their eyes met. "She's not buying."

Jani walked past Scriabin and lowered into the empty chair across from Feyó. *"May you take what glory you can from this godless day,"* she said in her most formal Sìah Haárin. She looked to the skylight above. The night's storm had passed, leaving behind scattered cloud shimmering in coral and indigo, reflections of the rising sun. *His first missed sunrise.*

"Did we set the ground rules regarding language?" John hovered behind her seat. "I don't believe it's fair to use one that half the room can't understand."

"Deal with it." Jani sat up straight, so the top of her head was higher than Feyó's, as idomeni protocols demanded and Thalassan habit seldom allowed. "Ná Feyó." She took a deep breath, felt Meva's stare like a stick prodding her forward. "John Shroud determined that ní Tsecha did not die as the result of a tumor. He was—"

Scriabin moved in behind Feyó and glared, fists clenched.

"—assassinated." Jani stared back, until he closed his eyes and dropped his hands.

Feyó raised a hand and curved it in question. "Killed?"

"Secret killing, ná Feyó. From a distance, by one unknown." Dathim's voice emerged surprisingly soft. "The humanish scroll I gave you to read, many days ago. *Ministerial Histories.* The last Scriabin Prime Minister was assassinated, as was an Exterior minister over fifty humanish years ago."

"Secret killing." Feyó repeated the words in English as she turned to look up at Scriabin. "Is this true, Minister?"

"Yes, ná Feyó." Scriabin shot Jani a look that should have killed her where she sat. "I am saddened to admit—"

"A humanish killed him?" Feyó's hand fell to her lap. "He esteemed humanish most completely."

"Unfortunately, not all humanish felt the same about him." Scriabin moved to the end of the couch so Feyó could see him more easily. "They misunderstood his desire for closer relations with humanish. They—"

"I understand the beliefs of your separatists, Minister." Feyó's voice emerged stronger and lower pitched, the first hints of anger revealed. "I spoke with ná Via for much of the past day. She showed me ná Tsecha's medical scrolls, the results of all his scans and examinations." The female looked up at John, her grey Sìah eyes chill as old ice. "There was no tumor, Doctor Shroud. Not a cell of one existed. Ná Via is most thorough. Such a mistake she would not have made, and it most pains me that you would lie of such."

Jani waited for John to speak, but he only looked down at the floor, his face darkening in humiliation. "They feared your reaction if you learned the truth."

"Yet I learned the truth anyway, but only because I hunted for such."

"Ná Feyó." Jani fought the urge to lean forward, knew that any humanish posture or gesture now would give offense. "We must find who did this. I debase myself in the service of those who lied, and beg your assistance."

"We have been searching since yesterday, when we first learned . . ." Scriabin's voice trailed.

That's right, idiot. Let Feyó know exactly how long you kept her in the dark. Jani slashed the air with the edge of her hand, the idomeni gesture of denial. "Not even Exterior has the reach in the Outer Circle that the Haárin do. We need their help."

"I do not wish to help you." Feyó's shoulders and back curved until her chin grazed her thigh and she had to contort herself to look in Jani's direction. "My security suborns will act for themselves, and search on their own."

"Ná Feyó." Jani felt her own shoulders start to buckle, and forced them back. "He was my teacher—"

"You are of them."

"He was my teacher, and my friend. I esteemed and feared him. He charged me with much, and if you prevent me from acting as he deemed me to act, you will be as damned as the one who killed him."

Feyó straightened a little. Her belief in Tsecha and his teachings had lost her a position at Rauta Shèràa Academy and resulted in her being made Haárin. As much as she hated humanish at the moment, she still felt the pull of her late religious dominant's authority.

"And you wish what, Jani Kilian?" Her voice emerged a tone lighter.

"To find who killed him." Jani held out both hands to Feyó, palms facing up, a gesture of supplication. "And show them the meaning of that which they did."

Feyó uncurved her back and shoulders until she sat upright. "My security knows much of the separatists. Where they find funding, and the devices they use to destroy our docks."

"Your security cannot go into the humanish places to find them, Feyó." Meva lowered beside her dominant. As she did, one sleeve of her overrobe rode up, revealing a web of ragged scarring, souvenirs of multiple challenges. "You need humanish to do such. And such will they do, out of guilt for killing Tsecha, and for holding back from you."

"Such is true." Dathim gazed toward the courtyard, where preparations for early morning sacrament were well along. "Humanish often ponder that which they do. They worry it, like a pack animal the mouthbar, even though that which is done is done and to ponder it does no good." He glanced down at Jani, then back toward the courtyard. "Will you stay here, ná Feyó? They prepare sacrament."

"We could go to the library." Jani teetered on the brink, sensed the possibility of winning and wondered how much harder she dare push. "It was ní Tsecha's favored room, because of the view of the cliffs, and the bay." She glanced at Meva to find her staring back, nodding slightly as though encouraging her to continue. *Desperation makes for the strangest allies.* "It would be a good place for your investigators to work with Minister Scriabin's. It is clean and—"

"I met with ní Tsecha in the library, many times." Feyó grew quiet once more, repose revealing the fatigue that grooved the skin under her eyes and alongside her mouth, the dullness that had replaced the dynamism, which not even rage could completely restore.

The idomeni in grief. Jani looked again at Meva, who stood and gestured to Dathim. "You will return to the enclave with ná Feyó, then bring ní Galas back here with you." She stepped aside so Dathim could help Feyó rise and lead her out of the Main House before the food odors could drift over from the courtyard. "I will stay to ensure that all is prepared properly."

Great. Jani swallowed a groan as Dieter appeared with two comtechs in tow.

"If you wish to come with us, ná Meva, you can aid us in the preparations." He nodded in acknowledgment of Jani's eye roll of gratitude, and hustled the female away before she could argue.

John lowered to the arm of the couch and started massaging the back of his neck. "Well," he said after Meva had moved out of earshot, "that went better than any of us had a right to expect."

"Get this through your damned head." Jani stood and planted herself in front of him. "You may have hitched your wagon to Scriabin's rising star, but as far as the Elyan Haárin are concerned, you are part of Thalassa. As you go, so it goes, and you almost dragged it right into the toilet!"

John's gaze flicked over her face before settling on some point north of her left ear. "I am more sorry than I can say that I caused ná Via to question her judgment, but don't go and—"

"No. Hybrid or not, you act as humanish, you fall into the humanish camp, and given Feyó's sensitivity right now, that's not where you want to be."

"Thanks." Scriabin thrust a thick finger at her. "We are busting our asses—"

"To clean up after something one of yours did. To the idomeni, the act of one is the act of all, and everyone pays. You don't believe me, ask a Laum, assuming you can find one. Any left alive after the Night of the Blade decamped to the far edges of the worldskein, and those colonies are a little hard to get to—" Jani stopped when the entry door swept open and two all too familiar figures strode in.

"Mornin'." Niall dragged off his garrison cap and tucked it into his belt. He wore desertweights, as did Lucien, who followed close behind, slingbag in hand. They both looked dusty and tired, but to that Niall added an almost palpable anger that revealed itself in his coiled-spring walk and the bite in his voice.

Scriabin read the signs as well. He held up both hands in a gesture of surrender. "Niall, I—"

"Save it, Your Excellency." Niall set himself in front of the man, hands on hips. "I've had an educational morning. I *hate* educational mornings. Being awakened at oh-hell-thirty by a concerned party bent on educating me just fucks up my entire day." He lowered his voice as a few Thalassans in the courtyard paused to observe, but what he lost in volume he made up for in snarl. "So Tsecha was assassinated. Did it occur to anyone that it might have been a good idea to inform the individual responsible for hauling their asses off a rooftop when—not *if*, but *when*—the news gets out and the Haárin decide to retaliate?"

Scriabin's face reddened. "We always have contingency plans in place, Ni—"

"Not here, you don't. This is Elyas, where if you don't dot the
i's and cross the t's just right, you get shit. Elyas, where they've
decided they don't want to play with Chicago anymore, and where
the same Haárin that you are about to piss off royally control
eighty-three point four percent of the dock traffic. It's taken me
over six months to work out the systems around here, and you
think you're going to snap your Family fingers and make shuttles
fly while all hell is breaking loose? Well, allow me to be the one to
inform you that if the Haárin do go ballistic, the first ones the locals are going to go after are Family with a big F, and that F stands
for 'fucked,' so go right ahead and tell me how much you don't
need any help getting off-world in case of a political meltdown."
He backed off a stride and stood, eyes fixed on nothing, struggling
for control and only winning by a hair. "Does Roshi know?" He
turned and looked from Scriabin to John and back again, and offered the barest of nods. "We're going to straighten out something
right now. Everything that gets sent to Sheridan comes to me first.
Everything you tell Roshi, you tell me first. Is that clear?"

Scriabin took a deep, shaky breath before answering. "Perfectly, Colonel."

"Good." Niall brushed past the man and pulled up in front of
Jani. "And how was your morning?"

Jani looked past him toward Lucien, who had finished watching the show and now sat in one of the demirooms and hunted for
something in his slingbag. "Lucien filled you in?"

"Yeah. You can imagine my joy when I opened the door to find
him standing there." Niall took her elbow and steered her toward
the courtyard, from whence the aromas of a board-busting Thalassan breakfast emanated. "He figures they didn't tell me because
they knew I'd tell you."

"That's what I thought." Jani headed for the beverage table,
grabbing a mug from the stack and filling it from the brewer. "He
took me to the place he thinks—"

"Yeah, I know. We just came from there." Niall filled two
mugs to the brim with coffee and set them on a tray. Then he
moved down the line and filled a plate with eggs, bacon, and a tea
party's worth of toast and pastry. "We scanned the place fore and
aft, incorporated the analyses he ran yesterday. The fact that the
place was protein-wiped is about the only red flag we have, but
depending on the weapon the killer used, it could've served as the
nest. One has to take into account his experience in these matters,
I suppose." He led Jani to an empty table well away from the other

diners. *"Jesus Christ."* He set down the tray hard, sending coffee splashing. "If I'd known it was assassination yesterday, I could have kicked Station Liaison into overdrive. We could have shut down the private fields and seized passenger manifests for the last fortnight *and* sifted out the probables by now." He sank into his chair. "Now I'm stuck playing catch-up, and I really hate that." He shoved a slice of bacon in his mouth and chewed with intent.

"You can pick Exterior Security's brain." Jani crumbled crisp bread into her vegetable soup. "Scriabin said they've been working since yesterday."

"Exterior Security couldn't find their dicks with both hands." Niall shoveled eggs and bacon between two slices of toast, then spooned chutney over the mess. "I saw Dathim and Feyó leaving as we pulled in." He took a bite of his sandwich, eyeing Jani as he chewed.

Jani tasted her soup, which was bland but filling. She never noticed taste at times like these, a leftover of days spent cadging meals at low-end kiosks, when food was something to quiet the rumble in her gut and keep her going. "I told her. Up until now, she thought it was a tumor."

"You just told her *now*?" Niall covered his mouth with his napkin just in time. "How did that shake out?"

"Things are touchy. She doesn't want to help humanish. Meva helped persuade her, which surprised me." Jani flinched when she felt a finger stroke her upper back, and looked around to find Lucien standing behind her, tray in hand.

Niall nodded toward an empty chair. "Have a seat, Captain. Eat up. We've got a day ahead of us."

"Thank you, sir." Lucien remained standing for a few beats longer, which was enough time to give the hybrids at the surrounding tables a chance to admire him in all his disheveled glory. "Equipment's arriving," he said as he finally took his seat. "Communications arrays. Data scanners. Mister Brondt is directing it be taken to the library."

"It's the designated command center." Jani felt the pressure of Lucien's boot against hers, and responded by pulling away her foot and tucking it behind the leg of her chair. "Neutral territory."

"For now." Niall looked over at the other tables. "What will happen when they find out? Or worse, when an enclave full of Dathims finds out."

"Dathim knows." Jani finished her soup and pushed the empty bowl aside to make room for her coffee. "He's proven remarkably steady through all this." She grabbed a piece of pastry from the top of Niall's pile and dunked it.

"I would think he would," said Lucien, who nursed a crush on the male that had apparently withstood time, distance, and logic.

"Dathim is different." Niall crumpled his napkin and tossed it atop his plate. "What about when the other tilemasters and stevedores and facilities suborns find out? The ones who think with their hands and not their heads?" He glanced at his timepiece. "I need to check in with the base." He shot a look at Lucien that almost qualified as civil. "Ten minutes, Captain."

"Yes, sir." Lucien waited until Niall exited the courtyard. "I had to tell him. I'm the new transfer from Sheridan, which means I have zero pull and no connections."

"You don't have to apologize." Jani wiped crumbs from her fingers, then cradled her cup, savoring the heat. "He needed to know."

"Speaking of needing to know." Lucien tilted his head in the direction of the other Thalassans. "When are you going to tell them? They need to hear it from you before they pick up any rumors."

Jani glanced at a neighboring table in time to catch the occupants avert their eyes. "I'll tell them."

"When?"

Jani took a sip of coffee and pretended not to hear.

CHAPTER 17

By late morning assorted underlings, uniformed and civilian, hybrid, humanish, and Haárin, populated the far side of the library, hard at work in hastily assembled office areas and communications centers, and separated from their superiors by an array of portable soundshields

Jani hunched in her corner chair and took roll. The triumvirate of John, Val, and Scriabin, sitting atop a scrollcase like the three monkeys. *Hear no truth, see no truth, speak no truth.* The unlikely pairing of Niall and Lucien, precipitated by Niall's need to stay informed and Lucien's desperate bid to breach the inner circle.

And then there's Meva. Jani watched the female ride herd on the other side of the barrier, the gist of her words obvious from the unhappy postures of the group of Haárin comtechs who were the focus of her displeasure. Beside her stood Dathim, as silent and watchful as he had been with Feyó.

I'm not used to quiet Dathim. Jani watched the male stare stolidly into space. *Like a lion watching flowers grow.*

At last Meva finished with the beleaguered technicians and passed through the barrier. "All is as prepared as it may be." She dragged her chair next to a display case that contained some of Tsecha's writings, then motioned to Dathim to set his seat next to hers.

Niall waited until the pair had settled in before speaking. "The shuttleports, both public and private, may already be a lost cause, unfortunately, given the time lag." His voice emerged subdued. He sat by the library window, the bright sun accentuating the shadows under his eyes. "I doubt we'll have any more luck at Elyas Station for the same reason, but we have set a safety emergency in motion just in case. Lockdown of all docks while they check passengers and scan all luggage and cargo. We've also seized all passenger manifests generated since the time of Tsecha's death." Bone and tissue crackled audibly as he worked his neck. "And we've contacted the other stations in this part of the Gateway network so they can initiate their own investigations."

Scriabin looked to John. "Does the weapon give any clue as to where it originated?"

"The vector was an engineered variant of Sussex A, a prionic that infects facility and communications biosystems on long haul vessels." John nodded toward Val, who took the baton.

"It's not a common infection, but it isn't rare, either. It pops up sporadically, usually in older systems that have been stressed over a period of years. In the case of boards, it's transmitted when poorly filtered system waste products are recycled and mixed with nutrient broth, which is then used to feed the system." Val slid off the case and walked about, hands in pockets. Only the fact that he kept his back to Lucien offered the barest hint that all was not as fraternal as it seemed. "A reverse-phase filtration step was added to all ship systems a few years ago in order to extract it from the stream. If someone wanted it, all they'd have to do is infiltrate a ship during a layover and get hold of a used filter."

"Sussex A usually takes months to incubate, spread, and destroy an array." John sat arms folded, eyes fixed on nothing. "You see the occasional drip under a console, and think it's a leaky nutrient cylinder. Suffer through the occasional glitchy communication. Catastrophic systems failure doesn't occur until the disease is well progressed." His voice deadened, made lifeless by too-recent memory. "Whoever designed this variant ramped the virulence exponentially, compressed the cycle from months to minutes, and designed it to specifically target Tsecha's brain tissue. Cranial insertion via the left auditory canal, followed by the apparent formation of a neuroma, a slow-growing benign tumor. This was in fact the payload, an aliquot of Tsecha's blood infested with the rogue protein. Once it reached body temperature . . . well, you all witnessed the result." He paused and glanced at Jani, but looked away when he saw that she watched him. "Ruthlessly elegant work. A weapon coded to Tsecha, indistinguishable from his own tissue until it was too late. Even if we'd realized what it was immediately, we could not have halted the cascade in time."

"We've compiled a list of the labs capable of developing this type of entity." Scriabin blew out a long breath. "Unfortunately, it's quite long."

Jani suppressed a yawn. She longed for coffee. Or better yet, sleep without dreams. "Who benefits? Tsecha's death—who benefits the most?"

Scriabin knocked his heels against the side of the case. "The more radical separatists always blamed Tsecha for doing more than any idomeni to initiate and maintain human-idomeni relations."

Jani shrugged. "Have any of them claimed responsibility?"

Niall shook his head. "The fact of assassination has not yet been made public."

"So the group that engineered this Killing of the Century is going to sit back and wait for us to make an announcement before they pipe up?" Jani didn't wait for a reply. Instead, she wrote invisible notes on her thigh, and sorted through the questions that tumbled in her brain. "Boards are farmed from humanish or idomeni brain tissue. Wouldn't a bug that had been altered for use on Tsecha have come from an idomeni board?"

Before John or Val could reply, Niall interjected. "If the Outer Circle is any indication . . . let's just say that the access to docks and ships undergoing repair isn't as well controlled as it should be. Could a human obtain material from an idomeni ship? Most certainly."

Jani wrote another note. "Could a humanish lab have obtained a tissue sample from Tsecha sufficient to build this weapon?"

"It wouldn't take much, unfortunately." Val frowned. "A few skin cells. A single strand of hair with the bulb attached." He sat on the floor against the wall, a position that let him watch Lucien without Lucien seeing him. "And with access to even a lousy booster device, they'd be able to copy and manufacture sufficient genetic material within hours." Before he could say more, one of Feyó's brown-clad security suborns crossed over to their side of the barrier.

"Ex-cuse, pl-ease." Her voice shuddered as she passed through the sound shield, pushing one of the office chairs ahead of her like an orderly maneuvering a seated patient. "We must bring ní Galas a proper chair, ná Meva. He cannot concentrate in a soft thing such as *this*." She kicked the chair with her booted foot, sending it careening the last few meters until it bounced off the wall. "This one." She grabbed the sole idomeni-style chair, a rigid, twisted thing, out of a darkened corner where it had languished since its delivery, and pushed it toward the shield. "I think he is crazy, and truly, but he is the one to sit in it so what do I care?" She launched the chair through the shield with another kick, the sound-canceling field swallowing the last of her mutterings as she followed after.

Val winced. "He's really going to sit in that?" He looked to the other side of the room, where an older male took charge of the chair and sat on it, pressing against the ridged and bumpy seat-back. "I guess he is."

"The mind-focusing properties of pain." Scriabin sniffed and stared into the distance, a professor imparting arcane knowledge. "Strange for an Haárin to persist in the habit. They usually leave that to the bornsects."

"Ní Galas enjoys to be different." Meva looked Scriabin in the face. "And to show off before his suborns." She bared her teeth as the man's face flushed.

The joys of interacting with the idomeni. Jani glanced at John and Val, who had suffered similarly over the years, and who now eyed their compatriot with a combination of pity and *better you than me.*

"There will be some time lag as we let the investigators do their jobs." Scriabin watched Meva as though fearing another embarrassing interruption, relaxing only a little when none appeared forthcoming. "But in the meantime, distasteful as it may seem, we need to consider how to handle the fallout when word gets out that ní Tsecha was assassinated."

"Cèel will enjoy your fallout." Meva pulled a wafer folio from a shelf near her chair and examined the leather binding. "He hated Tsecha, yes, but he hates humanish more. He would not fight for Tsecha when he lived, but he will claim a great loss now that he is dead." She traced her finger over the gold leaf flower that adorned the binding. "You made a great mistake, and truly, when you hid the fact of Tsecha's killing. You should have announced it as soon as it was known. To hide such is to imply that there is reason to hide. Such does not appear as caution to idomeni, but as treachery."

"We certainly esteem your point of view, ná Meva," Scriabin said, in a tone that indicated he believed anything but.

"You should, Minister. I know the idomeni point of view most well, as I am idomeni." Meva reached out with the binder and tapped Jani on the knee. "You knew better, priest-in-training, but you did not go far enough." She sat forward, gripping the binder in both hands like a threat. "Think as Tsecha. Think as he trained you to think, ná Kièrshia. Toxin. The bringer of pain and change, whom your *inshah* declared his suborn for reasons known only to himself."

Jani felt her skin tingle as all eyes focused on her. "He would not have hidden a murder."

"Good, priest-in-training. You repeat that which I said back to me. Such is what four cycles of Academy training gave you."

Jani heard Scriabin cough, Niall mutter a curse. Felt the anger grow, even more than it had with John. "He would declare it. He would face anyone who questioned his motives, and challenge them if they disputed him."

"Indeed, Tsecha would do such." Meva cocked her head. "But Tsecha is dead." Again she bared her teeth, the idomeni's death's head rectos. "And you are his suborn."

Jani's heart skipped. "I should . . ." She tried to lick her lips, to summon saliva in a mouth gone dry. "I should go to Cèel and tell him of murder." Behind her, she could sense Niall's stillness, his held breath. "To his face. I should tell him—to his face."

"*Yes.*" Meva waved the folio at Jani edge on, like a hatchet. "You wake up eventually. This is most reassuring, and truly."

Jani gripped the arms of her chair. She felt as though the room rocked, as though her world shifted beneath her. "I should return to Rauta Shèràa and explain Tsecha's death to Council."

"And to Temple." Meva sat up, then shoved the folio back into its slot. "Idiot—what else can be done?" She looked to Dathim, who embraced his role as the mummers' chorus and simply nodded. "Tsecha and I talked often of his death. We did not talk of murder, no, but simply of death. Of what should be done after." Her voice quieted. "It is fitting that he return. He was Chief Propitiator of the Vynshàrau, and the souls of all Chief Propitiators since the first have been released on Shèrá." She sat up straighter, in honor of the one she esteemed. "I fear for his soul. It began its journey in this damned strange place, and may not find its Way without guidance." She glared at Jani, her shoulders rounding. "Your guidance, priest. That for which you trained."

Jani ran a hand along the arm of her chair, imagined sand beneath her fingers. "I'm not sure I'd be particularly welcome."

"Knevçet Shèràa—I know of it. We all know of it. Twenty-six Laumrau, killed by you." Meva sat back. "Do you regret such? Do you wish you could return them their lives so that they could take yours?"

Jani felt the stares, and held back her answer. Sometimes, she had to remind herself. That her actions at Knevçet Shèràa, defined her. That in the minds of many, idomeni and humanish, Knevçet Shèràa was what they thought of when they heard her name. "No," she said finally. "Given the same circumstances, I would do it again."

"Kill idomeni at sacrament, as they prayed to their gods?"

"Yes."

"And now you would return to Shèrá the soul of the greatest propitiator. You, the killer of Knevçet Shèràa? Tsecha's toxin." Meva's voice emerged a little less impatient, a little more wondering. "You, who declare knowledge of idomeni, do you question that such is what idomeni would expect from you?"

Silence claimed them. For a minute. Forever. Jani glanced at Val to find him staring back at her, his face gone ten years older.

Scriabin cleared his throat. "We'd be at Cèel's mercy as soon as we crossed over into the worldskein."

"You'll be at his mercy as soon as the news of the assassination gets out." Jani looked back at Scriabin, at John and Niall, and saw them looking at her as Val did. Only Lucien maintained his detachment, his eyes holding curiosity rather than empathy. "If you face him, you have the chance to salvage some seemliness."

"A funeral delegation?" Scriabin studied the ceiling. "I assume Li Cao will be sending one, out of fear if not respect for Tsecha. I assume my aunt can append herself. I'm a little low on the diplomatic totem pole to claim a right to attend in my own name, but I can possibly justify my attendance as a male relative, an escort. Given that I'm Cao's opponent, I'll look like I'm grandstanding, but that can't be helped." He shot an uneasy look at Meva, uncomfortable with discussing the Commonwealth's political weakness in front of her. "I can possibly meet with some of the other bornsect dominants, get the lay of the Shèráin land."

"You may meet with Aden nìRau Wuntoi, and assure him that you will support him against Cèel." Meva fussed with the cuffs of her overrobe. "In exchange, he may receive you in the Pathen meeting house, and his acceptance may compel Cèel to receive you whether he wishes or not. Cèel fears Wuntoi—do not think he does not. The Pathen have always offered the greatest threat to Vynshàrau. It will prove, I think, a most interesting problem for Cèel." She studied the display case next to her chair, Tsecha's writings, one by one. Then, with obvious reluctance, she returned her attention to Scriabin. "You look at me oddly, Minister."

Scriabin smiled weakly. "I am used to dealing with the directness of idomeni, not the duplicity."

"We are most as straightforward, compared to you humanish. What is not as straightforward, when compared to humanish?" Meva laughed, the idomeni's monotonal *heh heh heh* sounding like someone trying to cough quietly. "But now you wish to feel more sure, because you have erred, and are uncertain of your standing. In such a case, our intrigue is enough to upset you."

The silence that fell now was the sort that got under the skin and nettled. Jani tried to force thoughts of her imminent return to Shèrá from her mind, concentrating instead on the work being done on the other side of the barrier, the fact that each analysis, each message sent and message received, brought them one step closer to finding Tsecha's killer. After a time, she glanced at Niall, who had taken his nicstick case from his pocket and now massaged it as though trying to absorb the nicotine through the engraved metal.

"If you would smoke, Colonel, please do so." Meva bared her teeth at the surprised looks that greeted her dispensation. "I have entered this place so many times. Any godly bornsect would consider me as damned. I only consider myself as ná Meva Tan. What difference?"

Niall didn't have to be told twice. "Thank you, ná Meva." He pulled his case from his pocket and flipped it open. Removed a gold-striped cylinder, crunched the tip—

—and stalled in mid-inhalation as on the other side of the sound barrier cases emerged from bags and pockets, and tips crunched in filtered silence. About a quarter of the hybrids lit up, by Jani's quick count, along with a lone Haárin who ignored the alarmed postures of her fellows and took a pull with the skill of one who'd had a lot of practice.

Niall shifted in his seat. "Well. Nice to have the company." He expelled smoke in a series of distracted puffs. "So, when would this journey be expected to get under way? The transporting of Cabinet ministers over long distances is not a trivial undertaking."

"Does 'as soon as possible' make your blood run cold, Colonel?" Scriabin's voice emerged strong, his Family-caliber composure returned. "I think ná Meva has made it clear that any delay will only make us look worse."

"Can anyone attend this?" Val raised a hand. "If I'm not part of an official delegation, am I out of luck?"

John leaned forward to get a better look at his embattled partner. "What are you asking?"

"I'm asking if we . . . or if I . . ." Val tapped the floor with his fist. "Well, dammit, John, we fought him for years. Then you wind up here, a hybrid, one of the blended race he started talking about during the war. It's all so damned . . . ironic." He stilled, then scooted forward and gestured to Niall, who tossed him his nicstick case. "And I liked the son of a bitch—pardon the language, but what else would you call him?—and I think that we should attend this ceremony." He shook out a 'stick, then tossed the case back to Niall. "Assuming we can." He crunched the tip, then took a long, shaky drag.

Niall examined the case absently, then shoved it back in his pocket. "What usually happens at these things?"

Meva leaned forward and prodded Jani's knee. "Priest-in-training?"

Jani gritted her teeth. Counted to three. "The most sacred place in Rauta Shèràa is the site of the Temple. The dome rotates, and there's an observation port that allows a view of the region of sky where the First Star is located. I would release Tsecha's soul there so it could see the star, and follow it." She recalled a forbidden daytime visit to the dome, the view through the port of the milk-blue skies of Rauta Shèràa. The uproar at the Consulate when her intrusion was discovered. "I think there is some question as to whether they would let me in, despite what you say."

Meva clapped her hands. "It will be a great confusion. Caith will laugh."

Niall looked to Jani and sighed. "Now which one is Caith?"

"The goddess of chaos. She fights a never-ending battle with Shiou, the goddess of order." In her mind's eye Jani saw the page from Tsecha's scroll. The clenched fist. *Second round soon to come, bitch.*

"I wouldn't mind seeing the old bird wing it to home." Niall's voice sounded deceptively light. "Besides, with all these ministers dancing attendance, I don't have much choice, do I?"

Jani studied him for some sign he joked, even as she knew that this was the last thing he would ever joke about. "You'd go? To Rauta Shèràa?"

"Wouldn't miss it, gel." Niall forced a grin, then sealed the deal by blowing a smoke ring. "God knows why. The variety of ways in which this can go south boggles the mind."

"Then you had better enjoy those while you can." Scriabin shot him a grin laced with cool commiseration, their earlier blow-up, if not forgotten, at least set aside for the time being. "They don't allow you the good ones in the brig."

"But they are required to provide you any brand you want as part of your last meal." Niall's grin proved a little wider, a little colder. "And the one they give you after they tie on the blindfold tastes best of all."

Val rolled his half-spent 'stick between his fingers. "Now isn't that a cheery thought? I wonder if we get our pick, like with our last me—" Before he could finish, Dieter swept through the barrier.

"We've just intercepted a communication from Elyas Station." His eyes met Jani's. "There's been a murder."

CHAPTER 18

Dieter brought up a face on his display. A younger man. Bandan or Phillipan or Earthbound Asian.

"His name was Neason Ch'un." The image flickered, and Dieter eyed the fragrant cloud of board-corroding nicstick smoke that hung just overhead. "His body was found in the interface, the utilities chase-slash-walkway that divides the humanish and Haárin wings of the station. Cause of death was determined to be asphyxiation, resulting from severe trauma to the area between the third and fifth cervical vertebrae." He paused, giving the words one last chew before spitting them out. "Station security believes a drifter responsible."

Lucien leaned against a nearby desk. "That's not the sort of blow you'd expect from a drifter."

"Depends where they drifted in from." Dieter stared at the display. He seemed to have backslid into his former role as station liaison, taken on the look of a mason faced with a crumbling wall and unsure which hole to patch first. "He died yesterday, around station noon. Since the blow was such that death occurred within minutes—"

"Add in the time it takes a shuttle to reach Elyas Station," Jani said, edging closer to the display, "and you have the time Tsecha collapsed."

"At this time, there's no evidence that links this death with Tsecha's assassination." Dieter drummed his fingers against his thigh, then segued into picking his nails. "Ch'un worked for the station as a mid-level vendor liaison. He'd visit shops, talk to the managers, make sure they were satisfied with systems hookups and whatnot." He shuffled his feet. "But the timing bothers me. And as Captain Pascal said, this type of injury is usually indicative of a certain type of killer. A certain type of training." He seemed determined to look everywhere but at the faces surrounding him. "We are still gathering information, of course. We could find out that he argued with a coworker earlier in the day and the matter escalated. We could . . ." He let the sentence fade. Then in the next breath, he straightened, pulled himself together, the professional once more. "Until the matter is resolved, I've requested that the Haárin station dominant keep us informed of developments in this investigation." He turned to Scriabin. "We could use some grease from a ministry, sir, either verbal or written communication to the station chief."

"I'll have my office draw up something within the hour." Scriabin pulled a handheld from his pocket and made a note. "In the meantime, we have ships to outfit, stories to get straight, and a funeral delegation to prepare."

Meva, who stood off to one side, seemed in no hurry to depart. "Feyó will provide all necessary technical and dock support."

"I shall stay here with ná Meva," said Dathim. "I can prepare to depart within minutes. I have no stories to straighten." He glanced at a nearby table, and with the deliberation of a gourmet, plucked a single grape from the bunch some daring soul had sneaked into the area and popped it into his mouth.

Scriabin tore his attention from the placidly chewing Dathim. "My guess is that we'll leave within twelve to eighteen hours. Details tend to sort themselves out rather quickly when Tyotya Ani gets involved." He started toward the shield, then stopped and looked back at Dieter. "Mister Brondt." He stared at the male for a long moment. "You have the look of someone with more to say."

Dieter pretended puzzlement at first. Then he started to drum his fingers against his thigh again. "The late Mr. Ch'un apparently found it difficult to keep his mind on his job. He had a . . . *thing* for Haárin females. He'd spot one he liked on the security monitors, arrange to accidentally run into them, try to chat them up. A few complained to their dominants, who in turn complained to the Station Liaison office. He'd been disciplined a couple of times. Threatened with suspension. Nothing seemed to stop him. So, today they fired him." He resumed his nail picking. "Idomeni are very strong. Ch'un wasn't particularly fit, and testing indicates that he was drunk at time of death. If he tried to force himself on any Haárin female, he'd be bound to get into troub—" He flinched, then pulled a dispo from a nearby dispenser and wrapped it around his finger. "My apologies for suggesting such without proof, ná Meva." He lifted the dispo, glanced at his wounded finger, and swore.

"Haárin have murdered. For some, it is the reason they are Haárin." Meva never averted her gaze from the image of the late Neason Ch'un. "Your comment would not upset anyone who is sensible."

Jani fixed on Ch'un's image as well, desperate for distraction. *People are murdered at stations every day.* Stations were small cities populated by transients, not all of whom were upstanding citizens. *On the other hand, the postmortem could be wrong. Maybe he just passed out and hit his head.* Maybe. "Did anyone notice anything strange around the time of Ch'un's death? Anyone running out of the chase, acting strangely?"

Dieter had liberated a piece of adhesive from one of the desk drawers and seemed intent on securing the dispo around his finger. "No one reported anything."

"On either the humanish side or the Haárin?"

Dieter glanced up from his self-ministrations. "The Haárin were never particularly forthcoming concerning matters in their side of the chase. Since the dock attacks started, they've become even more reluctant to share."

"With reason, ní Dieter." The speaker was the elder male who had requested the bornsect chair. Along with his penchant for pain-inducing furniture, ní Galas Linai shared Jani's affection for bitter lemon over ice. He sat back, drink in hand, while the others sorted seating arrangements out as best they could. Under John's abrupt direction, techs were routed and relocated and the two desks thus liberated shoved together to form one long table. Dathim found chairs while Val and Scriabin sniffed out a bottle of single malt and assorted finger foods from yet another hidden stash.

Only Lucien and Niall remained off to one side, talking in low and surprisingly civil tones. Niall's responses sounded as abrupt as one would have expected, but those grew fewer the longer Lucien talked.

Meanwhile, ní Galas sliced an Elyan lemon in half, then squeezed the juice into a fresh glass of iced water and slid the drink across the desk to Jani. "It is not unheard of for an Haárin to murder another Haárin. But a humanish? Even with the feeling between us as it is, such would be extreme." He shook his head, then bit into the drained remains of the lemon half, chewing the fruit with evident relish. "Ní Defa Roen is my investigative sub-orn." He gestured toward a male seated at the next desk. "He has been in communication with the Trade Board offices on Elyas Station."

"The lockdown of Elyas Station has affected only the human-ish sections, ná Kièrshia, as would be expected." Ní Defa consulted a recording board. "Trade Board Security monitors all entries and exits of the Haárin transept." He was older, lantern-jawed and conservative of dress, with the pale coloring of an Oà. "Station Liaison has uncovered little information," he added, in a voice that proved a surprisingly pleasant rumble. "They provided us names of the Haárin females who complained against Neason Ch'un, but none of these are of the type who would commit this sort of act."

"We're looking for someone unexceptional—an average pas-senger with average luggage traveling to an average destination." Jani met Defa's eye. Like his dominant, he didn't flinch—both had lived on Elyas for a long time. "It is possible that the assassin im-personated an Haárin to avoid humanish security and escaped Elyas Station using Haárin transport."

Ní Galas bared his teeth. "An impersonation as one you de-scribe would not last for long."

Jani's eyes stung as memories surfaced. "Ní Tsecha imperson-ated humanish in Rauta Shèràa twenty years ago." She reached up to wipe away a brimming tear, only to have Niall's silent appraisal stop her. She scratched her ear instead.

"He pulled that in Chicago, too." Lucien had scavenged a hand-ful of nuts from the liberated trove, then returned to his place beside his commanding officer and new best friend. "Two years ago."

"An idomeni would pass more easily as humanish than the re-verse. You tolerate strangeness more readily." Ní Galas stirred his drink, dredging up lemon pulp from the bottom. "I maintain that no humanish could remain undetected for long, no matter how well they trained."

Jani counted to three again. For all his openness, Galas exuded an air of patronizing superiority that begged argument. "If Ch'un's murder had happened last week, or even today, I doubt we'd be talking about it. But it happened at about the time Tsecha's killer would have arrived at Elyas Station."

"That's assuming they had departed Karistos within an hour or so of Tsecha's death." Niall activated another 'stick, which led to a second general round of lighting up. "Even with prep in place, that's cutting it a little close."

"If you had just killed ní Tsecha Egri, would you hang around?" Jani sensed the change in the air as soon as she spoke. The stilling of some Haárin, and the hard rap ní Defa gave his touchboard when a command went awry. *If ná Meva weren't here now, what sort of reception would we have received?* She wasn't sure she wanted to know.

Galas pondered, then motioned to Defa, who in turn gestured to a female suborn. She joined them at their table, flipping open a portable workstation and starting to key.

"Transferring now," she said, her voice a brittle rasp that did little to lessen the tension. "We will first examine all images recorded after the time of the humanish male's death, in the section where he was killed." She made one last series of entries, then twisted the workstation display so it faced the middle of the table. A diffuse beam flashed from the panel, then refocused to form a cylinder of white light. The cylinder in turn unrolled like an ancient scroll, the resulting pane of light thickening until it formed a milky cube.

The milkiness soon cleared, replaced by the image of a crowded concourse. Miniature Haárin, their every expression and movement detectable, their voices a background rise and fall.

Jani rose and circled the table until she faced the concourse image head-on.

"Why isn't anyone moving?" Val sat back, double shot of whiskey in hand. "They're all crowded around the—" His face flushed. "They're all watching the holoVee displays."

"Ní Tsecha's death had just been announced." Ní Galas sat up straight and raised his glass above his head, a combination of a humanish toast and an idomeni gesture of respect.

"This one," Defa said, leaning forward and pointing first to one Haárin who moved too quickly from one display to the next, then another who gestured in anger while talking to a security suborn. Another. Another. As he took note of a figure, the female suborn would stop the image action and home in on it, touchboarding entries as a series of flickers played across the subject's face and frame.

Jani watched, trying to pick up the cadence of the search, to see the crowds through Defa's eyes. *I'm looking for waves. He's looking for eddies. Bare ripples.* She took one step back from the cube, then another, struggling to see the single star in the nebula.

Then she saw. And it turned out to be a wave, after all.

Defa spotted it as well. "This one." He pointed to a conservatively dressed female who appeared as if from nowhere and walked along one side of the concourse for a time before veering toward the middle. "She does not stop at any of the displays."

"She is not humanish. She is idomeni. She is Vynshàrau." The suborn paused, waiting for another request.

Jani watched the female move along the concourse, passing the clustered Haárin like an iceskimmer moving past floes and bergs. Never once pausing to talk to anyone. Never once glancing at any of the displays. She wore a wrapshirt and trousers in sand and pale grey, topped by a darker grey overrobe. Her brown hair had been gathered into a messy horsetail that on closer inspection seemed at odds with her neat clothing. "Show her again."

Defa looked up at her. "She is not humanish, ná Kièrshia." He gestured toward the workstation. "Proportional evaluation and chroma show her as Vynshàrau." He shrugged. "Darker-skinned Sìah is also possible. Or a blended sect. But idomeni, yes, and truly." He squinted as he leaned closer to the cube and watched their latest subject continue down the concourse until she turned down a gangway. "Vynshàrau, most likely."

Jani fought the urge to wrest the touchboard from Defa's suborn and mash pads until she found the reverse feature. "Why doesn't she stop at any of the displays? She doesn't even slow down to glance at them."

Defa twisted around to look her in the face. "She does not stop—" He turned back around to stare at the image. "She does not . . ."

"Maybe none of them transmitted in her language." Niall now sported a glass of whiskey to go with his 'stick. "Maybe she couldn't understand any of the broadcasts."

"Vynshàrau Haárin is the dominant language, Colonel Pierce." Ní Galas had started in on the second half of the lemon. "All Haárin understand it."

Defa folded his arms and cocked his head to the side, the cross-species attitude for *show me*. "Why does she behave as this? She should know and truly that she is being imaged at all times."

Jani walked to the window. The sun had risen to mid-morning, a molten gold ball that bleached the sky. "Could we talk to her?"

Defa's suborn tapped her workstation touchboard, shutting down the concourse image. She flipped the display back around, her hands moving over the board with a musician's dexterity. "She

is ná Nahin Sela." A few more taps. "A trader in decorative tile.
She travels within the fifth cruiser built by Pathen during their last
fallow season, and blessed by Shiou. She travels to the worldskein
by the usual route, then on to Shèrá."

"We will bid security at Guernsey Station to hold her until we
arrive." Ní Galas gestured to another suborn, who opened yet another portable workstation.

"What reason will you give for holding her?" Jani held up a hand
in apology as the Haárin stared. "She might refuse to remain behind.
She may request her dominant's aide in obtaining her release."

"Order is our reason, ná Kièrshia. A reason acceptable to all
godly idomeni, Haárin or bornsect, suborn or dominant." Galas
bared his teeth. He radiated contentment now, like a cat that had
locked up his quarry and could now torture it at his leisure. "Ná
Nahin will remain in place until we arrive at Guernsey Station to
question her. Such is her obligation—she will not refuse such." He
rubbed his hands together, a profoundly humanish gesture. "She is
as ours."

The library huddle broke up an hour later. Galas and his crew fingered four other Haárin for questioning, but none of them interested Jani as much as Nahin Sela and her single-minded walk
through the concourse.

Then the scatter began. Meva and Dathim returned to the enclave to inform Feyó. Val and John hied off to prepare the clinic
staff.

"And the panic is on." Niall tossed a few under-his-breath orders to Lucien, who shot Jani a last loaded look before departing.
"I should have a minimum two weeks to prep for this voyage. Instead I have a grand total of—" He checked his timepiece and
winced. "—nine and one-half hours."

Scriabin gave a silent chuckle. "Sit back, Colonel." He clapped
Niall on the shoulder. "Witness the effect that Family finger-
snapping can have."

"I'm off the hook, then?" Niall offered a crocodile grin. "You
won't want an escort to the shuttleport or coverage on your way to
the station? No escort to Guernsey, either. And oh, when you
reach the worldskein and realize that the news has gotten there
ahead of you that it was assassination instead of a brain tumor and
a substantial proportion of the idomeni population wants to nail
your hide to the nearest surface? I'm guessing your ministry security can handle it."

Scriabin rolled his eyes. "Niall, I was just—"

Niall held up a hand. "Another thing we should get straight right now, Your Excellency, is that this is not a game. You want to play 'my daddy's bigger,' feel free, but you'll be playing with yourself." The chill cast in his eye indicated that he knew exactly what he'd said, that he meant every nasty little double entendre, and would be happy to clarify matters if pushed. "Now, I have a long haul to plan coverage for. By your leave." He turned to Jani, and light in his eyes softened. "I'll check in later." He yanked his garrison cap out of his belt and set it in place as he strode to the door.

Scriabin muttered under his breath as he watched Niall leave. "Arrogant bastard . . ."

"Pot, kettle, black." Jani stood her ground when Scriabin turned on her, eyes wide and face reddening. "He's the AG's colonel for a reason, and he's worried. So am I. We've both lived through idomeni political strife and the Commonwealth's bungling attempts to turn it to their advantage." She waited until the man backed off, until his breathing slowed. "I think he trusts you. In any event, he's thrown in with you for good or ill because he believes it's better for his Commonwealth. It's your job to show that you merit his confidence. Announcing every five minutes that you're the *S* in NUVA-SCAN isn't quite good enough."

Scriabin studied her through narrowed eyes. On close inspection, the sense of the brawler held true, from his wide, broadnosed face to his blocky build and dockworker's hands. "Anais has filled my ears about you ever since we learned you were involved in this. You helped drive the wedge between her and Li Cao. She's been scrambling to keep a claw in ever since, and not having much luck." He jerked his head toward the door. "Then to add insult to injury, you went and stole her bauble. I should thank you for that. Expensive bastard, our blond captain, and from what I've observed, not worth the cost." His voice held the same quality of question as did every heterosexual male's when they pondered the survival skills of Lucien Pascal. "I would have figured you for smarter."

Jani shrugged. This wasn't the time to discuss the matter of Lucien, and even if it were, Scriabin would never be the man she'd choose to discuss it with. "For all his complicating ways, he possesses a uniquely uncomplicated view of life. Sometimes, that can be a refuge."

"And other times, it can be a trap."

"I could say the same about Family loyalty. Capital F."

Scriabin's head snapped back, in the manner of those who commonly questioned others' choices but never their own. "Tyotya Ani has her uses. She quiets the fears of the hardliners who worry that the Commonwealth is disintegrating. Before they realize what's happening, we'll be in." His voice quieted. "Only an idiot would allow her any real power."

Jani considered the Anais Ulanova she had dealt with in Chicago and couldn't help but smile. "Does she know that?"

"By the time it dawns on her, she will be too committed to back out. She will have nowhere else to go." Scriabin leaned close. His breath held the bare hint of whiskey. "Stakes, yes, I understand the meaning of the word. Risk."

"You won't face a firing squad if it goes to hell."

"Are you sure?" Scriabin glanced up at the sun, which had just become visible through the glass roof of the courtyard. "We must continue this discussion at another time. Perhaps your captain can keep score." He snorted. "Assuming he can count that high." He offered a curt nod in farewell and headed for the foyer, only to be intercepted by Dieter bearing a clothes bag containing his outfit from the previous day. He grabbed the bag without a word and left.

Dieter stood still for a moment, then turned to Jani. "You're welcome, Your Excellency. Wear it in good health." He tried to grin and failed, his face showing all the fatigue and sadness and worry that marked the mood of the Main House, which was quiet as a church even as noon sacrament approached. "You'll need help preparing. I can have Gena help you pack, and—"

"I think we have more pressing matters to settle." Jani beckoned him to follow her into the maze of demirooms.

CHAPTER 19

Just track the voices. Especially a certain weighty bass, dark as clouded midnight.

John rose when he spotted her, then sank back into the couch when she ignored him. "We're discussing how to handle matters in my absence." He nodded toward Sikara and Cossa, both dressed in staid black.

"Ms. Kilian." Sikara rose and bowed low. "Our deepest sympathies for the loss of your friend."

"Indeed." Cossa matched his partner's bow even as he eyed Dieter, who stood just outside the bounds of the room.

"Thank you." Jani sat on the end of the couch as far as possible from John, a move that drew a raised eyebrow from Sikara. "I don't mean to sound unappreciative, but as John no doubt told you, we will be departing for Shèrá later this evening." She motioned for Dieter to join them. "This is Dieter Brondt, my suborn. He will act for me in my absence, and I would like him to take part in this conversation." She sensed John's glare, his desire to interrupt trumped by his reluctance to anger her more than he had already. *Yes, I've just hijacked your legal team. Try and stop me.* "I assume John told you that ní Tsecha was assassinated?"

Sikara nodded. "He informed us yesterday afternoon, yes."

Jani looked at John, only to find him intent on his hands. *You told your lawyers before you told me.* She tried to speak, but a rise of anger choked her. *You told your goddamn lawyers!*

"We actually did want to consult with you concerning your assessment of the current situation." Cossa removed a recording board from the briefbag at his feet and activated it.

You mean you want to know whether John's back-door arrangement with Yevgeny Scriabin is still viable? Jani took one deep breath, then another. "If things remain unsettled—" She stopped, then tried again. "That may work in John's favor. A solid source of money in a troubled region does wonders to calm shaky nerves." She watched Cossa transcribe her every word, and wondered if he really hadn't already considered the point. "If there's war, all bets are off. Feyó may take her Haárin and go home, or she may stay, and Cèel would send warriors to collect her. Or Li Cao could send Service troops to drive her out." She shot a look at Dieter, who had dragged a chair into their circle and now sat and watched her expectantly. "I'm glad you brought up the subject, Mister Cossa. Are you still taking clients?"

The two lawyers looked at one another. Then Sikara took over. "We represent cases involving matters of business. Bankruptcies. Dissolutions. Mergers."

Jani nodded. "I admit that Thalassa isn't a business. More a medical condition wrapped around a state of mind. It consists of this house, some surrounding homes and outbuildings, a few criss-crossing roads. A lot of land—the original surveys are stored here in our offices. Governor Markos allows us some autonomy. I think the operative word is 'allows.' " She paused, and heard only the intermittent *click* of Cossa's stylus. "I will be gone for several months. I need to leave some bastards in place to make sure that my home is still here when I get back."

Cossa stopped writing and slumped back. "Thanks. A lot."

"Settle down, James." Sikara sat back more easily and folded his hands, the pose of a man prepared to listen. "I think we've just been paid quite the compliment."

Jani nodded. "When we numbered only fifty or so, I once spent a few days making up sets of fake documents for everyone. A safety net, in case of disaster. Birth certs. ID cards. I even reconfigured inset chips, though I don't think they would stand up to full-bore ministry-level analysis. Now the place has grown too large, and I no longer believe that scattering the inhabitants to the four winds is a viable strategy." Her jaw cracked as she swallowed a yawn. "Thalassa is in a grey zone. In case of war, I want it to be protected. I don't want Thalassans to wind up in prison, or be forced to revert to their original humanish or Haárin state if they don't want to."

Sikara's eyes half closed, as though he listened to music. "The issue I see is one of jurisdiction. Mister Cossa is human, and a Commonwealth citizen, as am I."

"Isn't it our decision?" Jani looked from the senior partner to the junior, searched for any hint of encouragement, and saw only professional blandness. "Can't Thalassa grant you the right to represent us?"

"Perhaps." Cossa studied the tip of his stylus. "How have legal matters been handled in the past?"

Jani looked at Dieter, who shrugged. "We haven't really had any legal matters that required special handling. Internal disputes are handled . . . well, internally. Discussion between the parties, sometimes heated." She leaned against the arm of the couch and propped up her head with her hand. Ached for sleep, even as she dreaded the prospect. "Externally—"

"Externally, all major dealings, including purchases of land, goods, and services, have been handled by Neoclona attorneys working on my behalf." John's voice emerged warm, patient. He didn't look at Jani. He didn't have to. *Go ahead and kick me out of bed,* his tone implied, in a wavelength she had come to know all too well. *I still own you.*

Cossa once more took notes. "So your primary source of wherewithal is Neoclona?"

"Over the last several months we've actually started to develop into something more than an extension of John Shroud's ego." Jani paused until Cossa cleared the large smudge he'd scratched across his board and Dieter stopped coughing. "We're leasing a couple of docks from the Elyan Haárin, and one from a Karistos holding company. We've leased ships, and have begun exporting our food culturing technologies to other colonies. Ná Gisa Pilon, our dominant emeritus, is heading that project." She hesitated, pondered wording, ignored John's mouthing of *dominant emeritus.* "And we've entertained the odd inquiry regarding our willingness to house large amounts of cash."

Sikara's eyes opened wide. "Funds laundering?"

"That, too." Jani rocked her hand in a so-so gesture. "Numbered accounts, mostly. Since we're outside Commonwealth jurisdiction here, I can understand the appeal."

"We are considering the numbered accounts," Dieter added, eyes still watering.

"Conservative projections are that these nonmedical ventures will earn sufficient to support this enclave, even allowing for an explosion in population, within four to five years—" Jani stopped when Sikara held up a hand.

"In event of war . . ."

"In event of war, there are no guarantees about anything." Jani sniffed the air as the aromas of noon sacrament wafted. "But people will still need to eat, and some will still want places to park their funds that the Commonwealth can't touch."

John started to laugh. "This is ridiculous, pie-in-the-sky—"

"If Misters Sikara and Cossa can tie up matters in the Commonwealth courts long enough, we'll have enough money to buy you out." Jani avoided looking John in the eye. "Hell, Elyas already considers us an autonomous entity. We could just declare that the Commonwealth has no jurisdiction and nationalize you now."

Cossa's stylus stopped in mid-word. "That's actually . . ." His brow arched. "It's a ballsy move—"

"That would get quashed by any—" Sikara tapped his chin with his fist. "The decision concerning jurisdiction would likely end up in the Commonwealth Court."

"If a procolonial autonomy figure like Yevgeny Scriabin won the prime ministry and packed the bench with like minds?" Jani finally looked at John, to find him glaring at her, gripping his couch cushion in a white-knuckled clench.

"Not often the patients wind up buying the hospital," said Cossa, driving in the knife just a little deeper.

Sikara looked from John to Jani, and cleared his throat. "I won't ask. It's none of my business *yet*. I will only say that I do not handle divorces and have no intention of starting now." He grew quiet, his lawyer brain already mulling the possibilities. "That being said, my partner and I will evaluate your overall situation. Whatever our decision, Mister Brondt may feel free to call on us at any time during your absence."

Jani looked at Dieter, who nodded. "We have the wherewithal to retain you."

John thumped his thigh with his fist. "Does the term 'conflict of interest' enter into this anywhere?"

Sikara's chin came up. "We are looking after your interests, John, in a manner that isn't so dependent on the outcome of a Chicago-run general election. If your share of Neoclona was successfully nationalized, you'd retain control of all research and medical facilities, and Thalassa would begin to acquire some sort of . . . national identity, for want of a better term." He looked to Jani for confirmation, and frowned when she took her time nodding her reply. "You would likely lose some control of operations and decisions concerning expansion and whatnot, but it would beat the hell out of two percent, give us your ball, and go home. If I were you, I wouldn't dismiss it out of hand."

Dieter stood and clapped his hands silently, a *let's go* gesture that implied how eager he was to flee the room. "I can give you a quick tour of our offices on your way out. We have a retired attorney and a paralegal organizing matters."

"Yes, I'd like that." Cossa stood, stuffing his board in his bag as he nodded to John and Jani, then hurried along, as eager as Dieter to exit stage left.

"I'll catch you up in a moment, James." Sikara stood. "Safe journey to you both." He held out his hand to John, who shook it eventually, then bowed to Jani. "As I stated before, what's going on between you isn't yet my business. I would prefer it remain that way. Remember that you're on the same side. We will be blazing new legal trails here, and Chicago will throw every mud-coated roadblock in our path that they can devise. A united front is essential if we are to succeed." He straightened his jacket, adjusted the fan fold of his pocket square. "It is about control, in my experience. The money loses meaning—a fight over seashells could prove as deadly." He started after Dieter and Cossa. "When in doubt, try acting as adults. And remember what you're working toward."

John waited until the man was out of earshot. "And I thought Val was a sandbagger."

"I want this place protected. These people." Jani heard the rise of voices behind her, and turned to the courtyard to find it filling. Those who sat at tables stood and looked toward the demiroom, while the overflow filled the perimeter of the space. "If it's a choice between your pride and their lives, it's not really a choice, is it?"

"I am not going to let you steal my life's work."

"Who's stealing? You'll still have it. You'll still be able to work, but you'll working for Thalassa, not Neoclona. Does the name change matter that much to you?" She started toward the courtyard, then stopped and looked back to John. "If it does, what the hell are you doing here?" She left him smoldering and entered the courtyard to find that someone had already set out an empty crate for her to use as a dais. She stepped atop it and faced the crowd. Sensed their confusion and the questions and, most strongly, their fear.

"I'm guessing from the looks on your faces that you've heard a little and inferred a lot." Jani paused, tried to grab words out of the air, and decided the hell with it. Words were not her gift. All she could think of to say was the bare truth, and bare truth stabbed like blades. "Ní Tsecha was assassinated. We don't know who did it. No group or individual has yet claimed responsibility. We'll find them. That's all I can say." She felt the pressure of shocked stares, unspoken questions, the first glimmers of anger. *Stay with me, please.* She put her hands in her pockets, then took them out. Looked toward the upper floors and saw more Thalassans standing at the walkway railings, watching her.

"Tonight, Doctor Shroud and I will be leaving for Shèrá as part of a funeral delegation. We will be taking ní Tsecha's soul home." Jani pulled in a shaky breath. "The fact of the assassination is not yet common knowledge. It will disseminate over the next few days, and the reaction will be swift and profound. Only humanish assassinate. The worldskein will blame the Commonwealth, and even though Morden nìRau Cèel cast out ní Tsecha and declared him Haárin, he will still proclaim grievous injury. He—" She stopped herself. Now wasn't the time for a history lesson, even though part of the history was hers. "What I'm trying to say is that things will become very difficult. Elyans may pull away from us. The Haárin may, as well. Sides will be taken, and we straddle the line here." She sensed the further quieting as the realization settled over them. The silencing of the silence.

"Questions?" Jani fielded shock, the loss for words she knew all too well. "Talk to me, to Doctor Shroud. To Dieter Brondt, who will serve in my absence. Talk to one another." She started to step down from the crate, then stopped. Every speech needed an ending, and she'd never possessed the knack for those. "We have sustained a great loss. But we will survive it, and grow, and thrive. We will do it in Tsecha's name, and in spite of those who would stop us." She stepped down, and soon found herself surrounded, the questions battering like shot. *How? What?*

Why?

She answered as best she could. Tried to comfort, although she had never possessed the knack for that, either. Looked past the bodies that crowded her, and saw John doing the same on the other side of the courtyard.

Then someone handed her coffee, and someone else led her to a seat, and they sat and talked some more and tried to eat and she wondered if maybe, just maybe, they would be able to—

"Hey!"

—get through this without a—

"Fight!" Dieter hurtled past her, dodging around tables toward the shadowed far end of the courtyard.

Five minutes. Jani pushed back from the table, sending her chair flying, and took off after him. *We lasted five fucking minutes!* She slid to a stop behind him as he struggled to push into the scrum. Three bodies, maybe four, a punching, kicking, biting mass of bright clothes and fists and elbows.

"Knock it off!" Dieter deflected a blow to his chin, grabbed the back of a collar and yanked. *"Break it up now!"*

Jani circled to the other side. Grabbed the back of a shirt, a handful of hair. Took a wild punch to the breast and struck back hard, heard the howl and rode it, felt the sensations rise. The cold burn of the flesh. The song in the blood. Brought back her fist again and—

"Jani?" Dieter shouted from the other side of the pile. "Jani!"

—lashed out, connected, felt the blessed warmth spatter across her skin. Caught hold of cloth and hair and pulled, lifted a body clean and slammed it against the stone wall. Heard the *hmph* of expelled air, the wheezing intake of breath, a curse. Caught a fist with the flat of her hand.

Recognized the face through the rage and the red.

"Do you want to fight me, Jemmie?" She saw the answer in the young male's widening eyes. That she was the Kilian of Knevçet Shèràa, and of other things whispered of, but not known for sure. That she leaned against him with all her weight, one arm braced across his shoulders, a knee against his leg and a fist in front of his balls, and that whatever advantage he'd enjoyed due to age or anger or strength, he'd just lost it.

Jemmie shook his head as he tried to wriggle out from under. "You said—humanish assassinate. Humanish killed ní Tsecha!" He struggled to point with an arm immobilized by her pressure on his shoulder. "He's humanish!" He twitched his hand toward another young male who Dieter worked to free from the mess.

"That's *Bryan*." Jani paused, put her head back, breathed. "Are you saying that Bryan killed ní Tsecha?" She watched the two look at one another, then away. *Bryan and Jemmie.* They'd arrived at about the same time, did the program together. Worked in the greenhouses. Together. "You've both been here three months. At this point, he's only a little more humanish than you. You're practically the same." She edged back, let Jemmie step away from the wall. "If you're thinking of telling me that it makes a difference that he began as humanish and you began as Haárin, I would beg you to reconsider your argument. You both chose to be made Thalassan, and you did so for a reason. Have you forgotten what it was?" She gave Jemmie's bright blue shirt and aqua trousers a once-over. "Or did you just do it for the clothes?" She watched Jemmie's face redden as the nervous laughter spread through the crowd of onlookers. *Humanish enough to be embarrassed.* Well, that was a start.

"You'll do nothing."

Jani looked around to find the third member of the scrum looking up at her from the floor. One eye had already swelled closed and his lip glistened raw red. *Owen.* He'd come with his father. They'd been there from the start.

"You're up against the Commonwealth, and their Families, and their money." Owen coughed, spit blood and phlegm. "They'll hide whoever did it, and if you fight them, they'll crush you."

Jani stood over him silently, staring him down until he broke contact and hung his head. Then she held out her hand, waited until he took it, and pulled him to his feet. "Humanish or Haárin— it's all the same in this. We will be questioning Haárin who were in the vicinity at the time we believe the assassin passed through Elyas Station. To see if they saw *anything,* if they know *anything.*" She looked at each of the fighters in turn, then at the rest of the crowd.

"We are working together in this, ná Feyó and ná Meva and I. Colonel Pierce. Governor Markos. The colony of Elyas, the Haárin enclave and Thalassa." She shook her head. "If ní Tsecha could see you now, what would he say? You know what he would say, and he'd be a hell of a lot less diplomatic than I am." She stepped over blood-smeared flagstones on her way back to the central courtyard. "Why are we here? Because some of us were ill, and the blending saved us. Because some of us believe that the blending is the future. Because we want to live longer and watch the changes and become that which we are meant to be." She turned back to the three chastened brawlers, stopping them in their tracks. "Don't ever do this again!" Then she walked back to her table and her cold coffee. Sat down and breathed slowly and tried to silence the pounding in her head.

"You're the one who did the number on Owen's lip. That's two in less than a day. Thanks for the assistance, but from now on, let me break up the fights." Dieter sat across from her, a mug of tea in hand. "I left them in the care of angry home-parents." He slid back the lid of a sugar bowl and plucked a couple of cubes, dropping them into his tea. "And so it begins."

"Might be a good idea to introduce *à lérine*. It'll help release the steam." Jani drank her coffee, and wondered if it would keep her awake until she boarded the shuttle. "We were bound to need it eventually."

"Let them challenge one another?" Dieter slumped and stared at her. "We'll spend the next three weeks hosing the blood out of here."

"I don't see an alternative." Jani picked out a roll from the breadbasket, tore off a chunk and dredged it through a dish of herbed oil. "The idomeni in them will crave the structure. And it will prepare them in case any of the Elyan Haárin decide to express their opinion and start offering challenges." She tasted mild grassiness and wished it would burn, blister, keep her awake. "Talk to Dathim. He can recommend some friendly Haárin who can serve as trainers. I guarantee they won't put up with any crap."

Dieter drummed his fingers along the side of his cup. "Someone could die."

"Not likely, given we're right atop a damned clinic." Jani fielded Dieter's stare. "I doubt anyone is going to assassinate one of them." Another chunk of bread. More oil. "We've reached the one-day-at-a-time stage. Start with some organized violence, and see how it goes." She looked up at the skylight, the sun already grazing the edge as departure time grew closer. "Forgive me for leaving you with this, but I have no choice."

Dieter sipped. Shrugged. "There will be washouts, as in any trial by fire. Some may need to return for medical reasons, and maybe they'll eventually see sense. The rest of us should come through stronger, more united." He forced a smile. "Your home will be here when you return." Then he looked past Jani and the smile wavered. "Pierce."

"Brondt." Niall dragged a chair next to Jani and sat. "I seem to have walked into the middle of something." He looked across the courtyard to the scene of the fight, where the guilty parties mopped the floor under the watchful eye of Owen's father. "I wanted to let you know the details so far."

"Snapping Family fingers?" Jani managed a grin.

"Shut up." Niall staged his own raid of the breadbasket. "Shuttle services to Elyas Station are being provided by Exterior, but you'll travel as far as Guernsey on a Commerce cruiser, the *Madelaine*. Pascal and I and a few other of my staff will be claiming billet privileges on both your shuttle and your ship. After we hit Guernsey, it will be our turn. We'll be giving you a ride as far as treaty allows. Then it's back to the *Madelaine* for the balance of the journey to Rauta Shèràa."

"A Service vessel?" Dieter's brow arched.

"A carrier. The CSS *Viktor Ulanov*, who history indicates wasn't the worst Prime Minister we ever had, and who was less of a bastard than others of his family, small *f*." Niall smeared butter on black bread, then swiped a cup from a nearby place setting and filled it from a carafe. "Roshi's orders."

Jani calculated message central transmit times in her head. "He can't have received your messages already."

"He can when he's already halfway here." Niall grabbed another slice of bread, then offered a grinning "thank you" to a young female who slipped him a plate of ham. "He was already on his way out here to assess the Fort Karistos situation personally. He'll reach Guernsey about a week before we do." He folded the meat into the bread and dredged it all through a dish of hot mustard. "It's the general feeling that it's the best way to protect the embassy. Let Cèel see a little of what we have." He took a bite of his sandwich, nodding as he chewed.

Dieter tossed back the last of his tea, then stood. "Your gear won't pack itself." He circled the table and headed for the stairway.

"Don't forget the small clothes." Jani smiled as he turned and shook his finger at her.

"Think you're up to it?" Niall refilled his cup, then scanned the table for something else to eat.

Jani didn't have to ask what he referred to. *Rauta Shèràa in our sights.* She twitched a shoulder. "You?"

"We'll find out, won't we?" The filtered sunlight struck the side of his face, highlighting a throbbing vein and a bunched jaw muscle. "Sleeping well?" He didn't wait for an answer. "Might've been better for your overall health if you'd avoided the spat with your medical team."

"It was more than a spat." Jani broke off crumbs of bread and tossed them into the oil dish.

"I know. Pascal filled me in. I'm having a hard time adjusting to receiving my updates from him." Niall touched his lower lip. "I did notice a spot of imperfection on that face you seem to think so much of." He paused. "So why'd you hit him?"

Jani dropped the last chunk of bread into the oil. "Can I just say that he got on my nerves and leave it at that?"

"Much as I'd like to believe you've finally come to your senses where he's concerned, no." Niall gave up the hunt for further sustenance and dug out his 'sticks. "Like I said before, he thinks they didn't tell me that Tsecha was assassinated because they thought I'd tell you. Why would that worry them?" He exhaled twin streams of smoke, watched it drift upward. "Of course you'd be upset. And you'd want to find out who did it. Not really a stretch. Did they think you'd try to take over the investigation? I thought you were remarkably well-behaved in the library." He set his nicstick case spinning on the tabletop, and it flashed back sunlight like a beacon. "Pascal said he told you to let a pro handle it."

Jani laid back her head. Sleep called again, and she struggled to ignore it. "Handle what?"

Niall swept his case off the table and back into his pocket. "It's bad enough adjusting to working with Pretty Boy. What's bothering me even more is that I find myself agreeing with him. Half the Outer Circle is on this case, Jan. Leave them to it. Let the courts, or a discreet professional, take care of the killer." His timepiece beeped and he grumbled. "Can I use your comroom? I need to send Roshi an update. Take what I said to heart, please?" He made as if to rise, then sat back slowly. "Please?"

Jani watched him slump, the energy seep away, until he looked as tired as she felt. "Niall?"

He dropped his spent 'stick in a refuse dish and watched the last curls of smoke. "You first."

Jani waited, while around her Thalassans talked and tried to laugh. "I'm caught in a sandstorm. It buries me."

Niall nodded. "My long-range misfires, blows a hole in my chest. I look down, and I can see my heart beating. Then it stops." He stood. "First one in months. Maybe I'm not so sorry that Pretty Boy woke me up early this morning after all."

"You don't have to go."

"You're going."

"I don't have a choice."

"Neither do I, gel. If we need to pick embassy personnel off the rooftops, I have to be there." Niall put a hand on her shoulder and squeezed. "Do things right this time." He released her. "See you on the tarmac."

"Yeah." Jani watched him maneuver across the courtyard to the lift and step aboard the cabin. Watched the doors close. "This time." She finished her coffee and headed for her room.

Packing went quickly. Anything that she had left behind in John's suite was retrieved by a solemn Dieter, who considered all the diplomatic possibilities and made sure that the trouser suits outnumbered the coveralls, then added a few gowns to the mix as well. That task completed, they adjourned to the offices, where Jani affixed signatures, discussed contingencies, and wrote the letter formally requesting that the firm of Sikara and Cossa act on the enclave's behalf "in any and all legal matters."

The sun had begun its downward trek as she walked out to the beach. Imprinted the view in her mind in case she never saw it again. After a time, she heard the footfall behind her. The weighty quiet. "He loved it here."

Dathim drew up beside her. "We have put him aboard our shuttle. We leave at sunset. Feyó says little, so Meva speaks for both. She does that well." He wore brilliant green and yellow, his ears arrayed with small hoops of gold, his brown hair freshly shorn. "You said you would show his killer the meaning of that which they did." He looked down at her, eyes gleaming in the fading light. "You will kill them."

"Yes." Jani saw a glimmer in the distance, growing larger with the passing seconds. The Exterior shuttle, approaching at speed. "Are you going to try to talk me out of it, too?"

Dathim looked back out to the water. The lion, ever quiet, ever watchful. "No."

CHAPTER 20

"Glories of the ship's day to you."

Rilas looked up from her solitary game of pattern stones to find another of the passengers standing before her table. A female, attired in the most seemly manner. Hair braided in a breeder's fringe. Trousers, shirt, and overrobe in shades of palest green and sand.

The female bared her teeth, and kept her eyes averted. "I am ná Bolan Thea." She spoke Vynshàrau Haárin laced with gesture that was almost bornsect in its complexity. "You wish an opponent?"

"I—" Rilas looked down at her stones. They had transitioned to yellow and green spirals, and she had only three stones left to align to complete the required arrangement when ná Bolan interrupted. Now, as she watched, the pattern altered to cross-hatching lines. She had been so close—

"I have lost you your game!" Ná Bolan crossed her right arm over her chest, a most formal gesture of apology.

"Such is not important." Rilas cast a final look at the stones before sweeping them off the table and into her cup. "I am ná Nahin Sela, and I do wish discourse. Since we departed Elyas Station, I have spoken to no other passengers." She looked about the games room, empty but for herself and ná Bolan. "One ship-cycle past, yet all still remain in their rooms." She handed the other female the cup, then smoothed the table covering so the stones would tumble cleanly and lay well.

"They pray. They send transmissions to the worldskein." Ná Bolan shook the cup and cast the stones. "Ní Tsecha Egri is dead, and they ponder that which comes after." The polished rounds scattered across the table surface, the first pattern developing almost immediately. Left-hand spirals, a difficult design to manipulate.

Ponder? Rilas watched her new opponent arrange the stones, hands moving with a quickness that rivaled her own. "They worry greatly, I most believe. Many considered ní Tsecha as their propitiator."

"I did not." Ná Bolan completed her arrangement just as the spirals altered direction "What status had he, the first Chief Propitiator to be made Haárin? He was anathema." She then used her handheld to record her points and her time. "NìaRauta Sànalàn is my propitiator."

Rilas fought the desire to bare her teeth as she collected the stones into her cup and shook them. So good after so long, to hear the words of a godly Haárin.

She cast her stones. X marks. The simplest design. She bared her teeth and arranged the pattern, hands moving as quickly as they had when she assembled her rifle. "I have won this round!" She activated her own handheld and entered her scores. "We shall play a series—"

"Ná Nahin?"

Rilas looked up to find a ship's security dominant standing before her.

"Glories of the ship's day to you." He bared his teeth. "You will accompany me, please, to the security workroom." He stepped back from the table, then paused, waiting.

"Detained?" Rilas leaned against the high seat the dominant had offered her. "There are issues with my documents? With the business I performed in Karistos?"

The dominant did not respond, but wrote a note on a piece of parchment with an inking stylus. As the other dominants on this Sìah Haárin cruiser, he dressed much as a humanish. Trousers and shirt of dark green, the uniform color of the ship. Around his neck, a strip of knotted cloth decorated with blue and green whorls. He wore his brown hair clipped short, which left visible the silver hoops that arrayed both earlobes from top to bottom.

Unseemly. But security just the same, which meant that she needed to answer all questions and appear cooperative at all times. Even the godly act of disputation would be forbidden her, since Haárin who worked too long with humanish saw such as an attempt to evade and obstruct rather than as the blessed discourse that it was.

Rilas tried to climb onto the seat, but one of its legs proved shorter than the other three, which sent it tipping to the side each time she set her weight upon it. *Ungodly.* The male sought to disquiet her with his silences and his broken furniture, this she knew as surely as she knew her robes and her rings. She had spent season after season training against such. It could not be unexpected.

As though he had heard her thoughts through the air, the dominant stopped writing. He set down the stylus, then picked a hand light from a tray of writing tools and shone it upon the parchment, setting the inks. Then he sat back, hands clasped before him on the desk. "When we arrive at Guernsey Station, you will present yourself to this office. From here, you will be escorted to the Haárin Trade Board offices located at the station."

"I ask again, ní—" Rilas checked the front of the male's shirt, then the top of his worktable, in search of a plate or disc bearing his name. She had seen such on the other ship dominants and suborns. Why did he not offer the same information? "Why am I to be detained? Are my documents not in order? Is there a question of my actions on Elyas?"

The male took a documents slipcase from the stack on the side of his desk, and removed the parchment contained within. "You are a broker of decorative tiles?"

"Yes, ní—" Rilas fought to straighten, to relax her throat and lighten her tone. "Yes. I am a tile broker."

"How long was your stay in Karistos?"

"Two Elyan days."

The male nodded, a maddening humanish gesture that could mean anything or nothing. "When we arrive at Guernsey Station, you will be met by ná Calas Pélan, who is security dominant for the station. She will advise you of whatever you are entitled to know. You will be housed in suitable rooms, and communications will be sent from ná Calas's dominant to yours conveying our sorrow at the disorder of this interruption." His hand paused in its movements. "Who is your dominant, ná Nahin, so that we may process the notification with godly haste?"

Rilas hesitated. Ná Nahin Sela was a tile broker of Rauta Shèràa, and thus had nothing to hide. She needed to behave as such. "My dominant is ní Kolesh Metán. His business rooms are within the Trade Board in Rauta Shèràa." For this, she and nìRau Cèel had planned. Just as every godly Haárin acknowledged an Haárin dominant, so did she, for each of the Haárin she had ever pretended to be. And just as she had played the part of many

Haárin, so had her dominant. The male owed his life and allegiance to nìRau Cèel, as she did. If he were ever contacted, he would respond as was appropriate to his skein and standing.

"We shall initiate contact with ní Kolesh." The male dragged the input board across the desk until it rested before him. "The Trade Board is well outfitted with rapid communications, thus we will seek to contact him immediately." Another worthless nod. "We shall address the skein dominant as well, and present our regrets over any delay."

"The skein dominant?" Rilas felt her heart quicken once more. "Such would be an interference."

"Such is the most formal of protocols, ná Nahin." The male's hands stilled in their labors. "I only seek to placate. To acknowledge your concerns and address them." He began inputting once more. "If reparations are due the skein of tilemasters, we of the security skein will make them, and truly."

Rilas watched the male work, and pressed a hand to her stomach, her roiling soul. *I could kill him before he knew I had moved.* And before she had reached her rooms, his skeinsharers would be on her, and all would be as lost. *But all will be as lost in any case, for the dominant of the tilemasters' skein will not know of ní Kolesh.* His name existed in the roll, but he had no formal presence as a tilemaster. *They would seek him and not find him.* "I would request that you delay contacting ní Kolesh until I have done so."

The male tilted his head to one side, but since he did not alter his posture or raise either hand, it meant only more nothing. "Why, ná Nahin?"

"Because there is discord between ní Kolesh and the tilemaster dominant, unto the edge of challenge, and I most fear that any interruption of business will aggravate this discord further." Rilas paused to breathe, and felt her heart slow. Yes, if one accepted order, the gods protected one, and granted one cleverness. "Such contact as you wish to make would compel either ní Kolesh or the dominant to offer challenge, and such is not seemly. I as a suborn should not be the one to provoke such. The provocation should originate between them."

The male sat back and lowered his hands to the desktop. "And if I notify ní Kolesh, he may take the news to the skein dominant himself, and the challenge, if it is offered, may be offered in a more orderly manner."

"Yes." Rilas drew herself most straight. "I am gratified that you understand."

"I understand why I am most content to no longer live within the worldskein." The male folded his hands one over the other and rested them upon his knee. "I believe that given the tension between ní Kolesh and his dominant, it would be more fitting if you contacted him yourself. That way, you could explain the circumstances most fully, and determine between you the best method to approach the skein dominant."

Rilas bared her teeth. Her heart beat as slowly as if she slept. Those who worshipped the beauty of Caith would always be assured a well-illuminated path. "Such a solution would be most gratefully accepted, and truly."

Rilas restrained herself as the communications suborn instructed her on the use of the headpiece and showed her more times than was necessary the order of activation of the various relays and feeds. She knew more of the workings of such communications than any suborn. *But a tile broker would not know of such matters.* Thus did she remain silent, and gesture gratitude when the suborn completed his useless teachings and departed the cubicle.

The security dominant so readily allowed me this. Rilas stood before the recording screen and prepared herself to speak. *Does he believe that I will say something of interest to him?* She fully expected that he would intercept her message, or perhaps have it relayed directly to his workrooms. *He thinks himself most as humanish.* Crafty. Devious. *Do you believe, you with no name, that you are the only idomeni who is this way?* One of the first lessons nìRau Cèel had taught her was how to adopt humanish ways, to defeat the enemy by becoming as they were.

Across the narrow cubicle, the screen indicators altered in countdown. Rilas stood straight, tilted her head to the right in regard, curved her right hand and brought it level to her chest.

"Ní Kolesh." She bared her teeth. "Glories of the day to you." She elevated the pitch of her voice. "With regret I tell you that I will not be able to attend our planned meetings at Phillipa Station. I will be detained at Guernsey Station for an unknown span of time. I am to be asked questions by ná Calas Pélan, security dominant of the Guernsey Haárin. I have not been told that which these questions concern." She stopped, held her breath and listened, even though the cubicle was enclosed, soundproofed so that no one outside could hear that which was spoken within.

"Such is all I can say, ní Kolesh, for such is all I know. May our ventures be blessed by Shiou in spite of the efforts of Caith to hamper our path. Blessings of future days grace you, and all who labor for you." With that, Rilas gestured farewell, and stepped out of range of the display. She had done what she could, which was more than could have been hoped. She had notified nìRau Cèel of where she traveled and who would detain her. She prayed to Caith that by the time she arrived at Guernsey Station, some order would have arrived from Shèrá releasing her from having to respond to ná Calas's questions. *But if such is not forthcoming ...* Another method of interference would suffice. She could think of several that would affect an older station such as Guernsey. Provided access to the proper materials, she could construct the devices herself.

Rilas pressed the cubicle door pad, waited for the door to open fully. Stepped out into the corridor and followed the path to the games room. She found ná Bolan Thea still seated in the same chair, executing a complex solo game with three sets of stones.

"Have you committed crimes, ná Nahin? Is that why security dominants demand to speak with you and take you away from your games?" The female bared her teeth. "Nahin the criminal. I shall warn everyone of you."

Rilas clenched one hand. Imagined Bolan's neck and the blow required to break it, then stopped herself. *Ná Bolan is a godly Haárin, and such is her way.* The combative, challenging way of idomeni. The way she, Imea nìaRauta Rilas, would have recognized had she not been so concerned with humanish-acting security dominants who did not comprehend the custom of nameplates.

"I am indeed a criminal." Rilas bared her teeth and sat, and prayed to Caith for a disaster to befall Guernsey Station.

As the ship-cycle passed, more and more Haárin ventured out of their cabins. Rilas remained among them, and behaved most as that which she was supposed to be. She studied business dispatches prior to mid-afternoon sacrament, participated in movement sessions in the gymnasium and in discussions in the ship's veranda. Through ná Bolan, she met others. They filled the games room and discussed ní Tsecha's death in between the clatter and toss of the stones.

It did not surprise Rilas overmuch when the male security dominant who had questioned her earlier entered the games room. Their ship was small. They would be bound to encounter one another. Even so, she felt relief when he did not acknowledge her and sat at another table. *Nahin the criminal*, ná Bolan announced, and she accepted the mocking with bared teeth. Cast her stones. Arranged her designs. Kept her scores.

Rilas won several rounds, and played until the corridors darkened, a sign of the ship-night. She left the loud ná Bolan and the others behind and returned to her rooms. Entered. Paused in the doorway and studied the worktable, the altar alcove, the laving room and bedroom beyond. Could detect no sign that someone had entered during her absence and searched her belongings, yet trusted the sense she had acquired over many such journeys and accepted that someone had. The male security dominant, possibly. One of his suborns, more likely.

Rilas walked through the rooms, one by one. Took note of objects and their locations and positions. *Twenty ship-cycles until Guernsey.* She prayed to Caith for the time to pass quickly, even as she knew what awaited her there, and realized that she might be praying for the lesser choice.

CHAPTER 21

"Kilian says Haárin to be questioned in connection with assassination."

Rilas read the title of the Guernsey newssheet once, then again. Then she studied the image of Kilian that had been placed next to the text, looking her in the eye as she would never have done if they stood together in the flesh.

Godless eyes. Anathema. The sickly green, pale as Oà, too light against Kilian's dark skin.

"Humanish or Haárin—it's all the same."

Rilas crouched before the image display, one hand fixed on the controls. She had obtained a copy of the newssheet as soon as it had been received by the ship relay, replayed it constantly, as every idomeni had done since it had first been released. Argued over it on the ship's veranda, in the games room, the movement room, as they had argued over the news of ní Tsecha's assassination, released only a short time before.

"Humanish or Haárin—it's all the same."

Morden nìRau Cèel's response had been swift, his godly aspect broadcast throughout the worldskein to the Commonwealth beyond. *The Kièrshia is anathema,* he had entoned, shoulders rounded and voice deepened. *Idomeni do not kill in such a secret way.*

But then the stories emerged of deaths that occurred within the circle as the result of godly challenge, of knives that had slipped and blood that had flowed too well.

Such is different, and truly. Rilas deactivated the display, watched Kilian's eyes darken to blackness. *Each slip of the blade is the will of the gods.* If a soul heard the call of the gods, its duty was to answer. Any action that assisted it upon its way served as part of that reply.

"All is anathema." Rilas paced. They would dock at Guernsey within half a ship-cycle, and still she had heard nothing from ní Kolesh, not even an acknowledgment of her message. *They have notified ná Calas, and I will not be questioned.* But if this was the case, why had not the nameless ship security dominant informed her? Why allow her to wait, and wonder?

She sensed the tension grow in her limbs and knot the core of her soul. Now was not the time for the games room, even though she had arranged to meet with ná Bolan. Now was not a time for the stones.

She removed her overrobe, trousers, shirt. Greyed blue and sand they were, colors of the gaming room and veranda, made of cloth which possessed a delicate sheen and a light hand. Walked to her storage chest and removed sand-shaded trousers and sleeveless shirt and put them on. Bound the fasteners. Knotted the ties. Heavier cloth, this, dull to the eye and mended many times.

Rilas looked down at her bare arms, gold-brown skin darkened by Shèráin sun and crosshatched by the pale ridges of old scars. Flexed her hands, watched the muscles work.

"Time for the blades." Wooden ones, most unfortunately. But such would have to suffice.

"She proclaimed such at the meeting house on Elyas." The male, a young Dahoumn, pale and blocky, executed a complex turn of wrist that caused his blade to spin as a fan. "She stood atop a stage, as humanish do, and proclaimed while all about her shouted and clapped their hands."

Rilas worked her blade in a solitary exercise, close enough to the Dahoumn to hear him, but far enough away to seem separate from his group. All were younger, pale, shorter Dahoumn and darker, taller Sìah, and most disordered. They did not work their blades in unison, and bumped and banged into one another repeatedly.

"After she proclaimed, humanish challenged Haárin, and forced them to lave the circle afterward, to clean away their blood," said another of the group, a Sìah female. "The walls as well . . . or walls and floor . . . or just the walls?"

"It's all the same," sounded a female voice. A humanish voice.

Kilian's voice.

Rilas flinched. Her hands dropped. The end of her blade caught on the edge of the floor pad, stopping her motion in mid-twist. Pain radiated up her right wrist and along her arm, a thin line of flame. Her hand spasmed and the wooden blade spun out of her grasp, through the air and into the midst of another group, striking an elder male in the face before clattering to the bare floor.

The male covered his nose with both hands even as the blood flowed through his fingers and down the front of his tunic. A few Haárin shouted, while one ran to the communication array and pressed the switch that summoned the ship's physician-priest.

Rilas turned to the group of youngish, who stared at the blooded elder, their blades at all angles. One began to laugh, until his neighbor elbowed him in the pit of his soul. Another, one of the females, had positioned herself behind the others, ducking so she could not be seen.

"What has happened?" Another of the elder male's group stepped between Rilas and the youngish. A male of middle years, Sìah or light-skinned Vynshàrau, breeder's fringe gathered in a knot and tied with a cord, arms so hacked with scarring there seemed no clear skin left. "Answer."

"She lost control of her blade." The young Dahoumn male pointed to Rilas. "Demand answers from her."

The male turned. "So?"

Rilas gripped her injured wrist and stared past the male to the Dahoumn. "One of them spoke in the Kièrshia's voice, and another laughed."

The male stepped around to the rear of the youngish gaggle, where the guilty female all but crouched as an animal to hide herself. "Do you find the Kièrshia's voice an amusement?" He gripped her by the wrist and pulled her upright. "She who accuses all idomeni of anathema? You imitate her?"

"I did not—" The female looked toward Rilas. "We did not mean—"

"Stop cowering!" The young Dahoumn faced the scarred male. "Ná Lia did nothing wrong. She—" He pointed at Rilas. "—she listened to private talk. The blood is her fault."

The doors opened and the physician-priest entered together with a suborn. They hurried to the elder male, who had been led off to the side of the room by others in his group and now sat on the floor, head tipped back to squelch the bleeding from his nose.

"You distracted her." The scarred male released ná Lia, then pushed her toward the rest of her group. "If you speak loudly enough to be heard, you will be heard, and others will act as they will when they hear you."

"That is for them. We shall still say that which we will, and laugh at that which we will." The young Dahoumn broke away from the rest and faced the scarred male, moving around him as though they stood within the circle. "We did not laugh at ná Kièrshia's voice. We laughed at the expression on her face when she heard it." He pointed again to Rilas, looking her in the eye as he did. "As though she had seen a demon. Such was how she appeared, and truly."

The scarred male looked toward Rilas.

Warrior skein. Rilas began to straighten, and forced herself still. Whatever the male may once have been, whatever honor he may have earned, he was now Haárin, and she would show submission to no Haárin.

"Ná Kièrshia is the cause of fear in some." The scarred male turned back to the Dahoumn. "She is anathema."

"All is anathema." The Dahoumn laughed. "Ní Tsecha is dead. What difference? He was anathema. Such was all we heard, that he was a shame on all idomeni. Now he is dead, and such is anathema as well, and all cry out at the sadness of it, the sadness of the death of one we called anathema." He picked up a discarded wooden blade and inscribed a circle in the air. "A humanish would tell you to make up your minds. He is Tsecha, or he is not. He is great, or he is not. We mourn and honor him, or revile and forget him. We hate him and all for which he stood, or we do not."

The scarred male kept the Dahoumn in his sights, turning with him. "NìRau Cèel has said—"

"Cèel is a hypocrite!" Ná Lia found her voice once more. "He exiled ní Tsecha, and made him Haárin. But now ní Tsecha is dead, and he calls him great."

"Great now that he is dead," the Dahoumn said. "Great now that he cannot write, or speak." He stopped his turning of his blade and stilled. "Great now that Cèel does not have to listen to him any longer."

All had gone quiet in the room. Even the physician-priest and her suborn had stilled to watch the two males circle one another. Meanwhile, the Dahoumn's friends had moved to one side of the room, the scarred male's to the other.

Rilas backed toward the far wall, away from both groups. The Dahoumn's arms showed pale and lightly scarred, as nothing compared to those of the other male. Such would prove an unseemly challenge, unbalanced and graceless.

The scarred male's shoulder rounded. "Why do you speak against nìRau Cèel? Humanish killed ní Tsecha. He did not."

"He wished to. He would have executed ní Tsecha if he ever returned to Shèrá. Some say—" The young Dahoumn began to circle again. "Some say that Cèel paid humanish to kill ní Tsecha. Thus could he condemn the killers even as he rejoiced that the killing had been done."

None moved. Even the elder male who bled over his shirt listened.

"Who are these 'some' who say this?" The scarred male's voice deepened in anger. "Who?"

"Many." The Dahoumn stilled once more. "Many say this."

"Such is—"

"Anathema?" The Dahoumn bared his teeth. "A humanish would say that if all is anathema, then nothing is."

The silence that followed was disturbed by the physician-priest, who aided the elder male to his feet and guided him to the door.

Rilas followed them, straightening and lifting her chin as though requesting the injured male's pardon. But as soon as she stepped into the corridor, she left them behind. Rounded the corner and—

—collided with ná Bolan, who stifled a cry of surprise.

"Ná Nahin?" The female curved her right arm in profound question. "What is this?"

"We must leave." Rilas continued down the corridor. Prayed the physician-priest would not come after her, or the scarred male, or any of the Dahoumn's idiot companions. "There will be a challenge fought, and it will be a mess. I do not wish to witness such."

"Shall we play the stones, then?"

"Yes." Rilas massaged her wrist. The joint felt hot to her touch. Tender. Not a break, but a sprain, or a tear of a tendon. She could provide an ice wrap herself, pray over it herself. She did not need to see the ship's physician-priest, who would ask her why she lowered her hands, why she let the blade drop. *Because I heard the Kièrshia's voice.*

And first the priest would laugh. Then she would ask, *Why do you fear ná Kièrshia?*

Because she knows.

But what does she know?

"Ná Nahin?"

Rilas felt the hand on her arm. "Ná Bolan."

"You are not well."

"I am most well, and truly."

Bolan removed her hand and gestured reluctant agreement, a tilt of head and sweep of arm. "We dock at Guernsey in a short time. Will you disembark?"

"Yes." Rilas closed her eyes, heard Caith's laugh. *I shall allow myself one round of the stones.* Then she would present herself to the security dominant, the male whose name she did not know, even after twenty ship-cycles and numerous encounters in corridors and in the games room. The male who had searched her rooms and found nothing. *He will give me good news.* He would tell her that she would not be questioned on Guernsey, that she did not even need to leave the ship. That she was free to travel on her way.

She paused as Bolan coded open the door to the games room. Followed her inside, and found the security dominant seated alone at a table, casting stones.

"Ná Nahin. Ná Bolan." He gestured to the empty chairs next to his own. "Join me in a game before we prepare to dock."

Rilas walked past the chair he pointed out and sat across from him. "You have received a message for me?"

"Yes, ná Nahin." The male bared his teeth, then handed her the cup of stones. "Your play."

The Haárin concourse of Guernsey Station had no gargoyles, no stained glass or transepts. Instead, there were white and grey walls and battered grey flooring, kiosks and shops and hallways as bright and crooked as the snow-coated branches of winter trees.

Rilas walked beside the security dominant. He had not allowed her to leave his presence since their meeting in the games room, arranging for one of the ship suborns to collect her possessions, and remaining with her throughout the approach and docking sequences.

"This way." He pointed down yet another corridor, this one marked with plaques covered in Sìah script. "The office of ná Calas is here—" He stopped as a rumble like thunder sounded, shuddering through walls and floor.

Then came the sirens, like the screeches for beasts.

"There has been an explosion." The dominant grabbed Rilas by the arm. "We must find a shelter and—"

The door of ná Calas's office opened and a female emerged. A most familiar female.

Rilas slowed, hands clenching even as her wrist ached.

"Ná Bolan Thea?" The security dominant gestured toward Bolan, a vague wave of the hand that meant nothing. "You have knowledge of ná Calas—" He stopped, then looked at Rilas, his lips moving, saying something . . .

A shadow moved in from the side. A male, dark-clad, his arm raised. The security dominant turned toward him, but too late. Brought up his arm, but not high enough to counter the blow. Fell where he stood, groaned and shuddered and stilled as the blood seeped from his battered skull and puddled around him.

Rilas watched his soul leave him. Then, slowly, she raised her eyes.

"NìaRauta Rilas." Ná Bolan spoke with a voice not hers. Gone was the querulous tone, the high pitch of the suborn, replaced by depth and strength and the chill of snow.

Rilas sensed the male at her back. "Why? I am going to him freely." He gripped her injured wrist, and she gasped.

Then Rilas felt a sting, a sensation of warmth travel up her arm. A cessation of pain. Tried to pull away and found she could not move at all. Looked to the female she had known as ná Bolan Thea, the female she had not known at all, as her knees weakened and her vision tunneled and her whisper roared in her ears. "Freely . . . I go . . . freely . . ."

CHAPTER 22

Jani opened her eyes and checked her bedside clock. *Six hours out. Guernsey Station, here we come.* She pushed off her bed cover, shivered as the chill air hit her, and dragged it back on. Waited for the sensation to leave, the light-headedness that came from too little sleep over too long a time. Waited a little longer, and knew she could wait forever for her head to clear and her limbs to feel like parts of her body again and not dead weight. Pushed the cover off again and sat up.

The entry buzzer twittered. She ignored it. It twittered again, a mechanical imitation of a songbird.

"Jan? Are you awake?"

Val? She shook her head, wondered if she still dreamed. Things had remained cool between them over the first half of the voyage, their sole interaction the odd greeting during inadvertent corridor encounters.

"I'd like to talk to you for a minute." Val gave up on the buzzer and switched to tapping on the door panel. "Jan?"

What could you possibly have to say to me? And did she want an answer to that question? *No.* Did she really think she could avoid it for long? *No.*

Did she long to hear another voice right now besides the one in her head? *Oh, hell.* She slapped the door pad on the bedside end table.

The panel swept aside and Val stuck his head in, looking first to his left, then to his right, as though he expected crossways traffic. "We missed you at breakfast." He stepped inside, a casual vision in blue and brown. "Jeez, this place is small." He stopped and looked around the one-room cabin, then paced the sitting area, which was separated from the sleeping area by a strip of carpet and wishful thinking. "My bathroom's bigger."

"I think Anais took charge of the assignments." Jani stretched her legs and grazed the edge of the carpet with her toes. "I'm probably lucky she didn't stick me in the engine room."

"Or an airlock." Val sat in the sole chair, a straight-backed thing with balky ergoworks. "This is bullshit—why didn't you ask for something else?" He grimaced as he tried to work into a comfortable position.

Jani looked around and shrugged. "I've lived in worse."

"Yes, but that's not your life anymore, is it?" Val drummed his fingers on the chair arm, then looked toward the corner near the bed, and the small desk that held a workstation and stacks of wafer folders. "Working?"

"Researching separatist groups. Going over dossiers." Jani stood and walked to the closet, dragging the bed cover with her and wrapping it around her shoulders. "Niall got me some information."

Val eyed her makeshift robe and shook his head. "Don't tell me—you can't adjust the temperature in here, either."

"OK, I won't tell you."

"That old bitch." Val swung a leg over the arm of his chair, shifting it back and forth to avoid kicking a nearby table. "Are they going to let us go wherever we want on that carrier? Like, all the way to the other end?"

Jani dragged out a set of coveralls, then tucked them back inside, opting instead for wrapshirt and trousers in dark blue. *Going to ride on a carrier.* Probably time to stop dressing like she actually had lived in a ship's engine room for three weeks. "I think we'll be limited to a transient VIP area, which, if distant memory serves, is usually one section of a single deck. Unless we're escorted. They don't want civilians wandering around, getting into trouble."

Val sighed. "I could use some trouble. Some nice, attractive trouble that didn't run my heart through a grinder." He laid his head back, watched her dress through half-closed eyes. "You know, one of the best things about owning my own ship is having the freedom to pick my travel companions." He looked away for a moment. "Barring the odd billet privilege." He frowned. Sniffed. "I think I'm paying for it now, because so help me Jesus, the absolute last people in the Commonwealth that I would choose to long-haul with are Anais, Yevgeny, and you know who." He groaned. "*God.* Anais has a cackle that could shatter crystal at fifty meters."

Jani finished tying the sash of her shirt, then stood on her toes so she could check herself in the half mirror. "I wouldn't know. She never laughs when I'm around."

"No, she doesn't, does she?" Val gave a mean little grin. "I think we'd fail every group dynamics evaluation on the books. Anais and Yevgeny pretty much talk to one another. You know who spends all his time either working in the Service area or showing off in the gym. John's like you, spending way too much time in his cabin. I always call it his tiger-in-a-cage mood, pacing and pissed as hell. I finally pulled it out of him a couple of days ago. Did you have to be quite so brutal?"

"He'll still have his work. Overall ownership changes, is all. Does that really matter?"

"Yes. A little. Maybe more than a little. He thinks it's payback for not telling you about Tsecha."

"Maybe he should stop thinking about himself so damned much."

"Yeah." Val massaged his temples. "Then there's you and Niall, two people I could long-haul with any time . . ." He studied the ceiling. "He's drinking. You know that?"

Fuck. Jani glanced at Val in the mirror. *Of course he can tell. It's his job.* "It's not as bad as it could be."

"How bad does it have to be?" Val folded his arms and nestled into the chair, as though he intended to nap. "He covers it pretty well, and his staff protects him when he doesn't. But it's going to get worse the closer we get to Shèrá, and on top of that he'll be on a carrier with his precious Roshi, which means he'll be under even more pressure." Again, the half-closed eyes, the deceptively casual observation. "You're no better off than he is, though in your case the problem isn't liquor. You're not sleeping well, though. Anyone can see that." He worked into a sitting position. "John was the one who mentioned it to me. He said that when he'd bring it up back in Thalassa, you'd brush him off. He thought maybe Meva was getting under your skin."

Jani folded her sleep shirt and stuffed it beneath her pillow, then sat down so she could put on her boots. "Did he send you here?"

"Would it matter if he did?" Val hesitated, then shook his head. "Not to worry. Mine is a solo effort." He sat forward, elbows on knees and hands clasped between, so friendly and expectant. "What you say here, stays here. You know that."

Do I? Jani rested a booted foot atop her bed and wiped away smudges with the corner of the sheet. "I'm fine."

Val watched her. Waited until she met his eye, then waited some more, his brightness fading as the realization settled. That she wouldn't tell him. That if he pushed her, she'd lie.

"Well . . ." He stood slowly. "It is good to be trusted by those you love."

"Likewise." Jani took what grim satisfaction she could in his blush, in the way he suddenly couldn't meet her eye.

"We had our reasons, Jan." He walked to the door, head down.

"You always did."

"Yeah, well—" The tweet of the entry buzzer cut Val off, and he struck the door pad with his fist.

Niall pushed past the panel before it opened completely. "There's been an explosion at Guernsey. One of the Commonwealth docks." He wore dress blue-greys, the shine of his badges and designators providing sharp contrast to the dullness of his skin and eyes. "It's bad."

Jani rose slowly, whispered the question she had grown to dread during her time in Rauta Shèràa. "How many?"

"One hundred twenty-six confirmed dead." Niall turned to leave, then hesitated. "And climbing."

Val left to track down John, who was arranging transport to the station to aid the medical team. The rest of them gathered in Niall's office, a converted conference room restocked with desks and workstations and alive with the bustle of staffers, their commander's desk serving as the hub.

"Service Station liaison believes it was a small pulse bomb." Niall called up a holo of the dock area schematic, which formed above his desk. "Structural damage was significant in the immediate area." He stuck a stylus in the middle of the image and inscribed a circle around an area that encompassed a large gangway some distance from the main concourse. "No breach, thank God. The sealer layer did its job."

"Looks well off the beaten path." Scriabin walked around the image, taking it in from every angle. "Why so many dead?"

"The starliner *Capria* had just docked. Emergency due to mechanical issues." Lucien pushed aside a stack of files and sat atop his desk. "Passengers were in the process of disembarking when the bomb exploded."

Jani lowered into a chair. "The gangway was full . . ."

"Yeah." Niall turned off the imager, and the schematic faded. "The station is in full shutdown. Instead of docking there, we will hook up directly with the *Ulanov*." He nodded toward Scriabin. "Luckily, your pilot has carrier experience. Otherwise we'd have had to ship one over who did."

"Minister Ulanova and I will need to port over to the station in any case." Scriabin paced. "We have people there. We need to ensure that supplies can get in, arrange transport for family members."

Niall nodded. "We can see to that as soon as station security gives us clearance. For now, we need to—"

The door opened and Anais Ulanova swept in. She wore somber brown and carried a rolled newssheet in one hand. "Horrible. Just horrible." She ignored Jani, shot a venomous glare at Lucien, then focused her attention on Niall and her nephew. "Could it have anything to do with this?" She unrolled the newssheet and laid it on Niall's desk.

Scriabin strode to his aunt's side. His brow arched as he read. " 'Kilian says Haárin to be questioned in connection with assassination.' "

Jani sat up straighter as all eyes fixed on her. "I never spoke to a reporter. I haven't given an interview in months." She stood and walked to the desk. Tried to read the article, only for Ulanova to wedge in front of her, blocking her.

The woman stabbed the sheet with a carmine-tipped finger. "It states that you gave a speech to your enclave informing them that ní Tsecha had been assassinated, and that several Haárin were being sought in connection with his death."

"I would like to read it without benefit of translation." Jani shouldered her aside, then checked the byline and the banner. "I don't know that reporter, and I've never spoken to anyone from the *Amsun Star*." She read each sentence once, then again, her heart tripping as the truth dawned. One of her Thalassans had talked. *I didn't tell them not to.* Because she hadn't thought it necessary, because she never spoke to a reporter if she could avoid it.

Scriabin's voice emerged tight, mounting anger laced with disbelief. "You informed your entire enclave that Haárin would be questioned in connection with Tsecha's assassination, and it never occurred to you that one of them might talk to a reporter?"

No. Jani looked across the desk at Niall, who blew out a long breath, then shook his head. "They had a right to know what happened. A right to know the truth. I was leaving them behind to face who knew what? Sanctions? Attacks? I had to tell them why. I couldn't let them find out from someone else."

"Goddamn it." Scriabin's face flared. "Relations with the worldskein are all but severed. Our border colonies are in danger, and some of us are risking our lives—"

"And I had an enclave to keep a lid on." Jani felt the anger rise, swamping out the fatigue and uncertainty. "Haárin hybrids getting into fistfights with humanish hybrids because a humanish killed Tsecha. Haárin and humanish who were friends ten minutes before."

"Strictly speaking . . ." Niall waited until he had everyone's attention. "The article isn't incorrect," he continued at lower volume. "We are talking to Haárin about Tsecha's assassination. Nowhere in that article does it state that we think an Haárin killed him."

"Don't be disingenuous, Colonel." Ulanova jerked her head toward Jani. "Thanks to her lack of judgment, we have this wrenching disaster to contend with."

"What has this article to do with the bombing?" Jani caught the glitter in Ulanova's eyes, saw the thin-lipped smile form. "You're saying they're related?"

"Of course they're related. You say that Haárin played a part in Tsecha's assassination—"

"That's not what I said."

"—and humanish are killed in revenge." Ulanova breathed hard, cheeks flushing. "Anyone with any intelligence can see that this is the case."

"You're saying the Guernsey Haárin are responsible?" Lucien avoided looking at his former patroness, concentrating instead on the state of his cuticles. "And they've been so peaceful to this point."

"This stupidity would drive anyone over the edge, no matter how peaceful they'd been to this point." Ulanova reclaimed the newssheet and rolled it into a tight tube. "First, Zhenya and I will go to the station. Observe the damage. See to our annexes." She turned to Jani, finally looking her in the face. It was all there, reflected in the woman's shining black eyes. The history between them, the hatred and the humiliation and the loss. "Then I will go to Hiroshi Mako and request that you be sent back to where you came from." She turned on her heel and walked out, head high, triumph radiating like an aura.

Scriabin waited until the door closed. "I'll do what I can." His crisp tone indicated that it wouldn't be much. "We'll talk more after we return from the station." He followed after his aunt, his posture bowed and his step slower, the brawler who had taken a hit from an unexpected quarter and couldn't shake it off.

Jani leaned against Niall's desk. Felt all eyes upon her, Niall's and Lucien's and the rest of the staff's. Struggled to find her voice. "They know it was a bomb?"

Lucien slid off his desk and walked to her. "They've found a few pieces."

"And you think my remarks triggered the attack?"

Niall swore under his breath. "Did you hear me say that?" He stepped around his desk and stopped in front of her. "Did you plant the bomb? Did you detonate it? Then you're not responsible. Don't let that bitch get to you."

Jani nodded. "I should go over."

"Why?" Lucien shrugged, ever the pragmatist. "What can you do?"

"I'm still a documents examiner." Jani patted the place on her hip where for years her scanpack had hung. "I think Guernsey Station has two, total, and they're probably going in five different directions about now." Long ago memories surfaced. The smells. The images. "We're always needed at times like this."

"Why? You—" Niall paled. "Oh, Jan, no."

"I have to." She stared him in the eye until he looked away.

Scriabin's pilot docked the *Madelaine* with the *Ulanov* with practiced ease. From the juncture point, Niall escorted Jani down tight winding corridors to the carrier shuttle bays, where medical teams and repair crews stood waiting for transport to the station.

"Station staff is overwhelmed in more departments than one." Niall patted the pocket containing his nicstick case, then eyed the NO IGNITION SOURCES sign and let his hand fall. "Are you sure you want to do this? Because we have dexxies of our own whom we can send over."

Jani turned her back on Niall and walked around the bay. Heard his muttered, "—and I may as well argue with a goddamned wall." Felt the stares of the Spacers as they studied her, recognized her, and started talking. She had taken time to change clothes, switching out the delicate tunic and trousers for coveralls in drab dark grey. Her old Service duffel hung from her shoulder, nudging her hip with every step. Inside were her scanpack, tools, and spare parts. A verified copy of her Academy certificate, just in case anyone questioned her.

Her shooter, just in case.

"Ma'am?"

Jani turned to find a baby-faced corporal with a recording board eyeing her expectantly. "Jani Kilian. I'm part of the Shèráin mission." *For the time being, at least.* "I'm a documents examiner, and I wondered if they needed help with close-outs at the station?"

Before the corporal could reply, one of the med techs piped up. "They do. I heard one of the doc techs say that they're falling way behind. The station dexxie was going to put out a call."

"Looks like you won yourself a seat on the next nonmedical shuttle, ma'am." The corporal glanced past Jani toward Niall, who hovered grim-faced like a doubt-filled father of the bride, then back at her board. "If you follow me over here, we'll scan you in."

Jani followed her to the ID scanner. Stood still for the retinal, ear, and palm scans, and hid a smile as the diplomatic sigil popped up on the display alongside her confirmation. *Thank you, Stash Markos.* She held onto her duffel and passed on through to the boarding chute into the shuttle, then turned in time to see Niall step around the scanner and hurry after her. "Diplomatic immunity works even better than scanproof compartments."

"You're armed, aren't you?"

"I'm sorry, Colonel?"

"Goddamn it." Niall followed her up the single aisle to a pair of empty seats. "What are you up to?"

"Nothing." Jani opted for the window view. "I wouldn't lie to you, Niall. Not now." She inserted her duffel into the grapple rack under her seat, then buckled herself in. "I know this isn't a good time, but when can we talk to Nahin Sela?"

"I knew you were going to ask that." Niall fastened his own seat harness, then pressed a hand to the back of his neck. "I told Pascal to use his charm and see if he can get through to the station liaison, but I think they'll tell us that they have enough on their plate for the moment."

"He's proving useful, isn't he?"

"I don't want to talk about it."

Around them, seats, grapples, and overhead racks filled. Then came a series of warning *pings*, followed by wave after wave of shudders as the boarding chute detached, the airlock sealed, and the hangar door swept open. Jani looked across the aisle to the starboard observation port and the view beyond, pitch-black tempered by a spray of stars. Felt the acid rise to the base of her throat and her stomach threaten rebellion as the shuttle directionals activated and the craft elevated then drifted to the side, freeing itself from its mother carrier and the bulk of her gravitational field.

Jani glanced at Niall, who sat with his head resting against his seatback, his eyes closed.

"I always like that floaty feeling when you first break away." He sighed. "Like sleep without the dreams."

"You can have it." Jani swallowed carefully. Breathed slowly. Looked out her portside observation port and saw only the gunmetal bronze surface of the carrier, fretted by seaming and welds and the odd bleached splash mark that developed when the destructive flash of the debris shield flared brightly enough to oxidize the surface coating.

"You ever pull carrier duty?"

Jani shook her head. "Never asked for it. The Academy degree pretty much guaranteed a slot at Rauta Shèràa Base." More recollections surfaced. The entire damn voyage was proving one long gantlet run down memory lane. "And I'd heard stories about carrier duty."

"The old Service." Niall grimaced. "I remember her well."

The shuttle began its swing around to the far side of the station, a maneuver that finally allowed Jani a clear view of the immensity that was the CSS *Viktor Ulanov*. Ten football fields in length and at least three in height, a sloping, featureless throwback to older style vessels that Service wits had christened "space whales." In the distance, the winking lights of her escort destroyers and caravelles, arrayed in uncloaked patrol like worker bees guarding their queen.

"Roshi's making a point by taking her into the worldskein." Niall leaned forward to take in the view, eyes alight with pride. "This is called a carrier group, Morden nìRau Cèel, and we've got thirty-three at home just like it."

"The idomeni have carrier groups, too." Jani sat back. Ships had never impressed her during her Service days, and the feeling hadn't changed with time. "Been years since I did close-outs. I'd hate to think that I can anticipate lots of practice."

They passed the undamaged side of the *Capria,* an ornate silver bird outfitted with useless but attractive turrets and masts. Every so often a Service hullwalker, welder in hand, would float into view before disappearing on the other side of the ship.

Then came the darkness of Guernsey Station itself, a kilometers-long grid that dwarfed even Service carriers.

"They're going to drop us off on the other side of the main concourse, where there was no damage." Niall settled back in his seat. "The hospital, all the waiting areas, they're all on that side as well." He licked his lips. "The morgue."

Minutes passed. Then came the clicks, hisses, and barely detectable bumps of docking. Another series of *pings,* followed by still silence. Then, as if on cue, everyone unsnapped their harnesses and gathered their belongings.

The first thing that struck Jani as she entered the main concourse was the quiet. The area had been evacuated after the blast, passengers, vendors, and other personnel shunted off to station annexes to wait out the emergency.

"It happened down there." Niall pointed to a gangway entry halfway down the concourse, which had been sealed off with flex paneling and a semicircle of emergency cones. Station security paced the area, pulse rifles lowered but ready to be brought into play at any time.

Jani looked down a nearby gangway, a long, bare tunnel capped at the far end by the ship juncture. "It was like dropping a grenade down a well, wasn't it?"

"Pretty much." Niall muttered under his breath. "It wasn't your fault, all right?" He nudged her elbow. "The paper pushers are all down here."

Jani followed Niall down a corridor that ran between lines of darkened shops and kiosks, then into a large room filled with desks, the only sounds the rustle of parchment and the occasional beep of a scanpack.

"I think you can take it from here." Niall waved her on into the room, then let the door close.

Jani walked to the nearest desk, where a woman in a green station uniform ran her scanpack across an identity card. "I thought you might need some help."

The woman looked up. Her brown eyes were dull, her dark skin ashy from the shock of too much, too fast.

Then she fixed on Jani's face and her jaw dropped. "Jani Kil—" She stood. "If you're here to take charge—" She motioned toward her chair.

Oh, please, no. Jani shook her head. "Just show me a stack."

"Oh." The woman stared at her desktop for a moment, then looked up. "Beah Lynn, Station Documentation."

Jani reached into her duffel and pulled out her scanpack case. "I'm traveling on the *Ulanov*. I heard you were shorthanded."

"Yes." Lynn led her to an empty desk in a far corner, glancing over her shoulder every few steps as though making sure she was still there.

Meanwhile, the stares from the surrounding desks. The buzz of voices.

"Jani Kilian—"

"Two of Six—"

"Academy—"

"Tsecha—"

"Knevçet Shèràa—"

"Here." Lynn pulled out Jani's chair, then transferred a stack of document slipcases from another desk. "These have all had prelim and collate. They just need to be closed."

Jani sat. Removed her scanpack from its case and ran a hand over the scuffed black surface, then touched the device's underside, activating it. Took the top slipcase from the stack and started to undo the clasp until she realized that Lynn still stood by the desk.

"I just want to say—" The woman rolled her eyes, struck her thigh with her fist. "Twenty-five years ago the Helier Express ran a series of stories about you and the other humans who attended the Academy. I saved them all, and I read them over and over." Her face lit, despite the fatigue and the hell that surrounded them. "But yours especially, because you were a colony kid, like me, and I thought that if you could make it—" Her eyes filled. "I became a dexxie because of you, and now you show up to help." One tear spilled, then another, and she turned and ran back to her desk.

Jani watched the woman until she sat and resumed her work. Then she undid the clasp of the slipcase. Removed the contents and spread them out on the desk. Identity cards. Three credit chits. She read the names, examined the faces. *Albee.* Mother and daughter. They'd each named the other as their emergency contacts.

Jani adjusted her scanpack settings, then ran the device over the cards, sending a burst of energy through the inset chips. Fried them, canceled them out so they couldn't be used, so that relatives could show them, along with the d-certs, as proof of demise.

D-certs. Death certificates. *And all the old terms come back into play . . .*

"You're really Jani Kilian?"

Jani glanced at the young man at the desk next to hers. "Yes."
"Wow."

. . . *as dust upon my tongue* . . .

Another slipcase. Thicker, this one. *The Denischevs, from Hortensia.* Father, mother, and two sons, ages fifteen and twelve.

Scan. Cancel the paper like the bomb canceled the lives it represented.

The Seligs, from Helier, Guernsey Colony. Husband and wife, ages eighty-four and seventy-eight.

The d'Abos of New Indies. A family of three, mother, mother, and daughter.

"You don't have to do this."

Jani looked up to find Val standing in front of her desk. He had dragged on a disposable coverall, probably to cover the bloodstains. "I have to do something." She took another slipcase from the stack. "And I've done it before. One of the duties they don't tell you about when you sign up for the scanpack and make the appointment to have your brain cells farmed." She sorted out the d'Abos' lives atop the desk. "How are you doing?"

Val twitched a shoulder. "'Bout what you'd expect." He pulled a dispo pack of nicsticks from his trouser pocket. Shook one out, then showed the pack to Jani. "The colonel will be glad to learn that I do occasionally buy my own." He bit the tip, took a long pull. "John told me to take a break."

"Is John taking a break?"

"You're kidding, right?" Val pulled over a chair from an empty desk and sat. "Word is that as the Guernsey-based emergency services arrive, we'll start backing off. Six-eight hours. Then off we go."

"Val?"

Jani and Val looked around to find John standing in the side entry to the room. Like Val, he wore a disposable coverall, only his didn't cover everything.

"Sorry. We need you again." John looked in Jani's direction. "What are you doing here?" His chill, dark voice. The voice he used for strangers, and those he knew whom he didn't like.

Jani pointed to the documents on the desk. "Help with close-outs."

"Hmm." John stepped aside so Val could walk past him into the corridor. "The next time you wonder why we don't tell you things, remember this day."

"Dammit, John." Val grabbed his arm and pulled him out of the room.

Jani stared at the door after it closed. Then she completed the close-out of the lives of the d'Abos, and moved on to the next slipcase. Then the next. The next.

"Jani?"

This time it was Lucien who stood over her desk, kitted out in fresh dress blue-greys, his brimmed lid tucked under his arm.

"Mako wants to see you."

CHAPTER 23

Admiral General Hiroshi Mako's office was located aboard the *Ulanov,* in a suite replete with galley, dining room, and a bar. The glossy top of his truewood desk was clean but for a comport, stylus stand, and holos of his wife and children, the paperwork the purview of the staffers who swept in and out with the silent dispatch of temple acolytes.

Mako himself stood in front of one of the observation ports that dotted one wall, a browned, bald stump of a man, arms folded, dress blue-grey tunic pulling across broad shoulders. He turned as Jani and Lucien entered, revealing a round, high-boned face that bore a few more lines, a few more shadows, than when Jani had last seen him in person over a year before.

You've aged since Chicago, Roshi. But then, hadn't they all?

"My sympathies on the loss of your friend." Mako's voice emerged a gravel growl, the roughness exacerbated by the ship's dry air. "He was . . . one of the great ones." He made as though to say more, but was interrupted by Niall, who emerged from the galley bearing two steaming cups.

"Would you like coffee, gel?" He handed one cup to Mako. "They've got everything back there but the coffee plantation itself."

"No, thanks." Jani chose a chair on the side of the room opposite Mako's desk. Sat on the edge, back straight, duffel at her feet. Lucien settled for a seat in a far corner, like the low man that he was, while Niall opted for a cushy lounger close to Mako.

The man himself walked around the desk and perched on the edge, setting his coffee untouched beside him. "Anais spent the better part of the morning apprising me of your culpability in the Guernsey matter." Mako tilted his head toward Niall. "My colonel has since expressed his opinion, which differs significantly." If he fought the urge to raise his voice, he hid it well. Instead he sounded tired, as though this was the latest disaster in a snakebit campaign. "You should've realized that what you said would leak out. A remark like that is just the sort of thing a reporter would latch onto to create controversy."

Jani felt the anger rise, clearing her head for a blessed moment. She hadn't been able to concentrate since leaving the station, her mind a muddle of emotion and half-formed thoughts. "I said it before. I'll say it again. They had to hear it from me. They needed enough time to prepare for any reaction. Any retaliation."

"I've messaged back to my team at Karistos to start digging." Niall sipped his coffee, then set it aside and dug for his 'sticks. "The fact that the article appeared in the *Amsun Star* is a red flag. I fully expect to learn that Exterior played a major role in funneling that remark to the press, at which point I will kick that bitch's bony ass." He exhaled a smoky sigh. "You made yourself one hell of an enemy, gel."

Jani looked to the corner where Lucien sat, and pondered the skills of those who always seemed to land on their feet. *But such is not my way.* She sketched a word on the leg of her coverall. Another. "Sensitive bunch, this group that carried out the bombing. They read that Haárin will be questioned in connection with Tsecha's assassination, and they get all shirty and kill hundreds of their own. When do you think they'll claim credit? All the groups I researched are very keen about claiming credit, but this group is different. What's taking them so long? Think they're saving it up for a threefer? One more tragedy and they win a brand-new skimmer?"

"Jani?" Niall stubbed out his 'stick and moved to the edge of his seat, ready to rise. "Are you all right?"

"Where's Nahin Sela?" Jani pointed to him. "You sent Lucien to find out about her."

Lucien stood. "I'm awaiting a call-back from the Guernsey Merchants Association. They seem to have a better relationship with the Haárin than we do." As if on cue, his handcom buzzed.

"Take it here, Captain." Mako's voice held the same brand of wary disgust that Niall's did when he spoke to Lucien, aversion to the man coupled with grudging acknowledgment of his talents. "We'd all like to know what they have to say."

Lucien activated the handcom. Listened for a moment. "Nahin Sela's disappeared. The ship security officer who was escorting her to the Haárin office is dead." He shook his head in response to the unspoken question. "The Haárin office is in a completely different section of the station. It was unaffected by the bombing." He paused to listen. "Three ships broke away before the Haárin closed their side of the station as a safety precaution. Two were larger passenger vessels that responded immediately when asked to submit passenger information. The third was a smaller courier-class vessel that ignored attempts at contact, cloaked, and vanished, presumably on its way to the GateWay."

"So let's shut the GateWay down." Niall glanced at a wall clock. "We have three station-hours to initiate."

Jani wrote another word on her knee. "The idomeni have a GateWay out here, too. Samvasta."

"It has a reputation for instability." Niall chuckled with a complete lack of humor. "Half the ships that enter it don't come out the other end."

"I heard those same stats twenty years ago." Jani stood and walked to the observation port. Looked out into the star-spattered dark. Imagined Nahin Sela, hunkered down in a cabin, awaiting the jump through a balky GateWay and wondering if she would punch through to the other side. *I certainly hope not.* "Beyond the wording in various treaties, do you have any reason to believe that Shèrá hasn't repaired it?"

"We do keep an eye out for those sorts of activities," Mako said dryly. "It's one of the reasons we're here." He tapped his comport. "Ask Vice Admiral General Vega to stop in when she has the chance."

The four of them looked at one another. Then Jani sat in front of a coffee table and inscribed across the top. Words. Numbers.

Niall opened the drawer of a side table and removed a stylus and a sheet of letter parchment. "Here, gel." He put the stylus between her fingers, then slipped the parchment beneath her hand.

"Only humanish assassinate." Jani pondered the stylus, a curving sweep of silver much like a Sìah blade. "Except when they don't." She wondered why she hadn't thought of it before. *Only humanish assassinate.* Just as only humanish ate in public, smoked, drank bitter lemon on the rocks. *We are all the same in this.* She'd said it herself, but grief and loss had prevented her from seeing the facts for what they were.

She looked at Lucien. "The sill provided the better view."

Lucien nodded, slowly at first, then faster as he figured out what she was talking about. "Yes, but standing allowed the assassin a greater ability to maneuver. Remember?" His voice came soft, light. A voice for animals, children, and absent-minded older relations. "The rubble on the sill wasn't disturbed."

"You said the dust was smeared."

". . . yes." Lucien nodded as slowly as he spoke. "Possibly they set something on it, a gear bag or a weatherall. Analysis of the scans of the area may indicate what exactly laid there."

"An idomeni who lay on that sill would feel the sharp edges of the rubble through their clothes. The mind-focusing properties of pain." *Focus*, she wrote on the parchment. "And they'd have the better view."

"An idomeni assassinated Tsecha?" The first flare of surprise entered Mako's voice. "An idomeni named, perhaps, Nahin Sela?" His tone sombered. "So the dock explosion—"

"Diversion. To keep us from getting our hands on her." Jani looked to Niall, who watched her with wide, worried eyes. "She didn't have to watch the monitors because she already knew what happened." Pieces slotted into place, one after the other. No need to force them. No need to change them in any way. Because this time they *fit*. "Because she drove what happened. She killed Tsecha."

"Jan?" Niall's voice came so gentle that Mako turned to stare at him. "That's a leap. I'm not saying you're wrong, because you know the idomeni better than any of us, but it's a major leap to take Sela's walk down the concourse and her disappearance now and extrapolate assassination."

"It's more than that." Jani set aside the stylus and parchment. "Wholeness of Soul. Tsecha had spoken out against it many times. It was the subject of his last treatise, which he published just before he died." She stood, returned to her place by the observation port. "It's a major tenet of the major idomeni religions. The idea that injury to a body also damages the soul that inhabits it, and that any sort of prolonged, grave illness or injury so endangers the soul that it is preferable to let the body die than to attempt to save the life." She closed her eyes, remembered that last argument in his workroom. They had argued so much, toward the end.

"Jan?" Once more, Niall's voice, bringing her back.

Jani opened her eyes, looked out to the black. "Tsecha had come to feel that the concept of Wholeness of Soul was no longer acceptable, that those propitiators and physician-priests who espoused it were anathema. He felt that the humanish practice of doing all possible to preserve life was the one idomeni should adopt." She studied her hands, the animandroid left and real right. One was nourished by rose-pink carrier, the other by blood. Other than that, they looked identical, felt and sensed the same. "A body can suffer horrendous injury, and the life can still be saved. I'm living proof of that. But the brain must remain relatively uninjured, because we haven't yet figured out a way to restore it, to rebuild it, in the way we can a limb, an organ. Nerves."

Niall sat back, the events of that day replayed in the way his shoulders sagged, in the pain in his eyes. "My God."

"Whoever killed Tsecha made sure that he couldn't be saved by destroying his brain. But they left the rest of his body uninjured, intact but for a punctured eardrum." Jani turned her back on the starscape, leaned against the wall, felt the chill through her coverall. "That brand of cruelty would only, in my opinion, have been practiced by one to whom the original principle meant a great deal. And who had come to hate Tsecha very much."

Mako passed a hand over his face. "Do you know what you're saying? Do you?" His comport beeped, and he struck it with his fist. "*What?*"

"Vice Admiral General Vega is here, sir," the disembodied voice meeped.

"Bring her in," Mako bit out. "You're saying Cèel had him killed." He twisted around to glare at Jani. "No one else hated him so much."

Jani nodded. "I know."

The door swept aside and one of the hot-and-cold-running aides escorted Alex Vega into the office. She was a tall, stocky Felician, as old as Mako and just as seasoned, brown skin a sharp contrast to the silvery braid that wound her head like a crown. The *Ulanova* group was hers, and if the presence of her supreme commander aboard her flagship unsettled her in any way, that upset didn't show in her calm brown eyes.

But she knew tension when she stepped in the middle of it. She stopped in the center of the room and regarded each of them in turn before fixing on Mako, who kicked any preamble to the curb and started in with the most important question of the moment.

"Is Samvasta GateWay operational?"

"No, sir." Vega's voice was mellow. "It's not."

Niall raised a hand. "Has Shèrá made any attempts to repair it, ma'am?"

"Oh, they've tried. We detect their soundings and send out cancellation waves. They have not been able to do more than the most preliminary surveys." Vega's tone altered from Felician caramel to vinegar. "Is someone going to tell me what the hell is going on?"

Mako gestured toward Jani. "Vice Admiral, I don't know if you've ever met Jani Kilian."

Vega focused on Jani with narrowed eyes. "Anais Ulanova does not have anything good to say about you. I'd normally consider that a recommendation, but she blames you for the Guernsey bombing."

"She's full of shit." Niall carried his coffee to the bar and tossed it into the sink.

Mako looked ceilingward. "I can bring you up to speed on the twists and turns later. At the moment, the most important issue is whether an idomeni courier can evade capture by bypassing Guernsey and punching through Samvasta GateWay."

"Only if they want take a substantial risk that they will not come out the other end." Vega's face reddened. It was clear that she wanted context and she wanted it yesterday, but she didn't dare blow up at Mako. "I will not send anyone to patrol that area. We lost two tracer pilots last month when they approached too closely just as the boundary destabilized without warning. They vanished. There was nothing left."

Niall added ice to half a glass of colorless liquid that Jani hoped was water. "We could stick Anais Ulanova in a drone and shove her into it, see what comes out the other end."

"That's enough, Colonel." Mako closed one hand into a fist. Opened it, then clenched it again. "Ms. Kilian believes that an Haárin named Nahin Sela assassinated ní Tsecha Egri at the behest of Oligarch Cèel. Sela was to have been held at the station for questioning, but during her transfer to the Haárin offices, Cèel's agents detonated the bomb as a diversion. While all attentions focused on the *Capria,* they killed Sela's security escort and took Sela aboard a courier, which vanished soon after breakaway. We wonder if they might attempt to punch through to the worldskein via Samvasta GateWay in order to avoid capture."

"So the idomeni have adopted the practice of selective elimination." Vega watched Jani all through the course of Mako's explanation. "All I will say is that they are taking the risk of their lives if they attempt to punch through at Samvasta."

"So what if the GateWay is only marginally functional?" Jani watched Niall drain half his drink in a single swallow, and knew it wasn't water. *Mako and Vega are too agitated to notice.* Unfortunately, there was someone else in the room who wasn't. She glanced at Lucien, a figure half in shadow, eyes fixed on Niall. "What if marginal is sufficient?" She heard her voice ring inside her head, and paused to breathe. "Nahin Sela has been ordered home by the fastest route possible. Her escort has no choice but to take the risk."

"The circumstantial evidence does seem to be piling up." Niall finished his drink, then set the glass in the sink. "What about Neason Ch'un?"

"Nahin Sela killed him, too. Why, I don't know. He saw something. He bothered her. He attacked her." Jani tried to inject warning in the look she gave Niall, but he regarded her blankly, all alarms missed or, more likely, ignored. "She screwed up. She didn't fade into the background, as killers are supposed to." She avoided looking at Lucien, who had returned to his corner, forgotten by everyone else. "She attracted attention."

"So Cèel sends his goons to bring her home, and they slaughter over three hundred humans as a cover." Mako slid off his desk and paced. "We have no proof. Niall is right, it's all circumstantial." He stopped in front of Jani, their past fractured relations as visible in his eyes as those with Anais Ulanova had been in hers. *Forget that now,* the look said. *Help me anyway.* "Can you give me proof?"

I don't need proof. I know. But courts needed proof, as did admirals general and cabinet ministers. So she answered in the only way she could, as much as she hated to say the words. "I don't know."

The VIP section's observation port proved an artful arrangement of twin spindle lifts that corkscrewed up the two sides of an enormous span of clear metalloceramic, then opened out onto a narrow catwalk that spanned the width of the pane.

Looks like about a two-story drop. Jani tore her attention away from the dimensions of the indoor balcony and looked toward the station. The damage to the *Capria* was more visible from this angle, shiny pink hull sealant smeared across the side of the ship like blown bubble gum.

She heard the observatory door open, footsteps. The sound of the left-side lift ascending. Looked toward the one-person capsule just as it opened and Lucien stepped out onto the catwalk. "What are you doing here?"

"I could ask you the same question." He stopped just beyond arm's reach and looked toward the *Capria*. "Does it help to stare at it?" He waited for her to answer, mumbled something in French when she didn't. "Pierce said Anais is full of shit. Why don't you believe him? Don't you trust him anymore?" He stared at her until he drew her eye. "I saw him take that drink in front of Vega. A dumb risk. He's not doing well, is he?"

"I'd say you'd been talking to Val, if you and Val were talking." Jani kicked at the balcony railing. *I need a map of this tub.* She had tried to corner Niall after the conclave in Mako's office disbanded, but he shook her off and she had tried to follow. *It took him one flight of stairs to lose me.* In a pulse-driven city with officers' clubs, bars, and liquor stores on most every deck. "He shouldn't have come. He should've stayed in Karistos."

"He couldn't. He has to turn the clock back twenty years and make it right—" Lucien tried to dodge, but before he could, Jani kicked his leg out from under him. He hit the balcony floor hard and she followed him down, planting her knees on his chest, pinning his shoulders, rendering his arms useless. He tried to kick out a leg and twist so he could throw her off, but every time he tried, she pushed down with her knees, immobilizing him.

After one last failed attempt, Lucien struck the floor with his fist. "Uncle." Then he laid back his head and smiled. "You scoot up a little bit, we could have some fun."

"While you're on this tub, you keep your mouth shut about Niall, and your two-bit psych eval to yourself." Jani pushed herself off him and scrambled to her feet, ready to kick hard if he came after her.

"I'm always the target." Lucien sat up. "You want to batter the world, but the only one you can put your hands on is me." He worked into a crouch and stood, then set about straightening skewed badges and brushing the creases from his tunic. "You'd kill to protect him, wouldn't you? He'd do the same for you. I think if he ever got his hands on Anais, he really would stuff her in a drone and send her down Samvasta GateWay." His voice held the childlike curiosity that it usually did when he pondered emotional connections. "What does that feel like?"

"You want a lesson in humanity, take a class. They've got a branch of Chicago Combined on this damned thing."

"I just find it fascinating is all. When you first met him, he gave you the creeps."

"I didn't know him." Jani edged down the railing, intent on

remaining just out of Lucien's reach. *I don't need this now. I really don't.* "Some relationships improve over time."

Lucien ignored her insult. "It's all gotten messy, hasn't it? Tsecha's death. This bombing. And you think you know what happened, but you can't prove any of it. And Mako needs proof, and unless you can give him something, he may just start thinking you're lying. He may even start believing those things Anais is saying about you, despite what his colonel tells him." He leaned easily on the rail. "And that's not even the worst of it. If Cao catches on about the secession deal, we just might see Family members jailed for the first time in memory. As for the non-Family members, who knows what might happen? Rebellious Service officers, for example." He looked over the side to the poured poly floor ten meters below. "This balcony isn't nearly as high as the one in Thalassa." He looked at Jani and his gaze sharpened. "The view's the same, though."

Jani tried to walk past Lucien to the left-side lift, but he stepped in front of her. She turned and headed for the other lift, but he circled her, blocking her again.

"I'm here." He edged closer. "I've been here for weeks."

Jani feinted to one side, then stepped back as he blocked her again. "A sympathetic ear."

"An ear. When did you ever give a damn for sympathy?" Lucien started to laugh. "You know what's funny? I've actually missed this. Arguing with you. What sane person would miss arguing with you?" He shook his head, and wiped his eyes.

Jani turned her back on him and looked out at the stars. Sometimes, she found it easier to argue with Lucien if she didn't look at him. *I don't love him.* No, but love and sympathy and other of the finer emotions had never defined what passed between them. "When did you start thinking of yourself as sane?" A cheap insult, but with some luck it would irritate him enough to drive him away.

She stared at the stars. Tried to count them. Waited for the sound of the lift door, the sign that she was finally alone. Waited for any sound at all. When the silence continued, she turned to find Lucien studying her.

No, that wasn't the word. His expression—rapt, grave—she'd seen it before. In the half-light, after he'd undressed her, run his hands over every part of her, made ready to do all those other things to her that he did so well . . .

"You never change." His voice emerged rough, as though he'd

just returned from the same memory. "And I keep coming back for more, again and again and again—" He moved in, resting his hands on her waist, pulling her closer without seeming to apply any pressure at all. Kissed her cheek, lips barely brushing her skin. Maneuvered her gently to the other side of the balcony, blocking her view of the *Capria,* because if she opened her eyes and saw it, she'd make him stop, and he couldn't have that.

So simple. Jani closed her eyes. Savored the growing ache between her legs as his lips moved across her neck, the trip of her heart as he fingered the front of her shirt and touched the topmost fastener. *Simple answers to simple questions.* Did she want him? *Yes.* Did she trust him? *Never.*

Did she want to forget, even for a little while?

Yes.

Could she afford to?

Jani opened her eyes. Took what was there, to remember later. The sense of his body as he pressed her against the railing, the hardness and the heat. The softest scents of male and musk. The crisp feel of Service cloth and the silken touch of hair that seemed lit from within.

"This is pretty much what you did with Val, isn't it?" She touched Lucien's cheek, stroking it until he raised his head. "The air of defeat. 'Here I am—why do I bother?' " She brushed a non-existent smudge from one orange collar tab. "Well's run a little dry, has it? You're starting to repeat yourself."

Lucien blinked. Then his eyes widened. *"He told you?"* He released her as through she burned. "That pathetic—"

"Not the details." Jani walked to the left side lift capsule and hit the door pad. "Anyone who's watched enough bad porn could fill in the details." She entered the tiny booth as soon as it opened. Hit the Down pad. A simple task, as long as she didn't look back. "You chose your path, Lucien. Deal with it."

She rode the lift down. Pushed out of the small capsule as soon as the door opened, like an animal freed from a cage. Felt Lucien's stare track her as she walked across the observatory and out the door.

She walked until she found a vend arcade. Bought a map of the *Ulanov* from a kiosk. Found a build-your-own-sandwich shop, inserted enough tokens to cover a double order, and poked through the vend coolers, assembling as she went. *Ham—cheddar—mustard—* She sprinkled a handful of peppercorns across her ham slices, then fixed them in place with a generous swathe of mustard. Spread pickles on both sandwiches, added tomato slices, and on Niall's a dollop of potato salad. Arranged the food on a couple of dispo plates, then piled them on a tray.

She consulted the map again. Stuck to stairways and primary corridors. Crossed from the VIP wing into Officer Country. Turned the corner onto the row of Transient Officer suites, and almost collided with Mako, who was headed in the opposite direction.

"Kilian." Mako looked at the tray and his eyes softened. "I think he ate lunch, but that was some time ago." He had changed into casuals and carried a battered gym bag. "I stopped by to see if he wanted to take a break, work out . . ." He blinked, leaned against the wall. "What is it?"

Jani tried not to look too closely at Mako. He stood more than a head shorter than she, and in his grey T-shirt and blue pull-on pants looked more like an old man headed out for a day of beach-combing then the supreme commander of the Commonwealth Service. "What do you think?"

Mako rubbed his bald scalp, shook his head. "I don't know how many times I told him, 'Niall, you saved the Service the cost of three courts-martial.' We'd have fried them anyway."

"They were Family."

"We'd have fried them anyway." Mako's eyes brightened with fight. "I'd have made sure." He glanced at Jani sidelong, as reluctant to confide in her as she was to listen to him. "I told him he didn't have to go on to Shèrá. Before you showed up with Pascal, I told him. The way he looked at me, as though I'd kicked the last skid out from under." He stared down at the floor. "Talk to him. Because he can't—" He pushed away from the wall. "He can't go on in the direction he's headed. Not here. Not now." He edged past her and disappeared around the corner.

Jani stood in place for a time. Finally studied the map again, and started down the corridor. Checked nameplates until she found N. PIERCE. Hit the entry buzzer. "Niall?" She waited, then hit the buzzer again. "I need to talk to you." She watched the red entry light, waited, waited. "Niall?"

Long moments passed. Then the light flipped to green.

Jani palmed into the cabin to find the lights dimmed. She closed her eyes, then opened them, hurrying their adjustment to the half-dark. Saw the shadow in the far corner, seated in a chair, obscured by smoke. "Have you been drinking?"

"Yeah, but like I told you, it doesn't help." Niall's voice emerged slurred. "We're leaving a cruiser behind as a show of force. Fort Helier is on alert. Guernsey ComPol are rounding up members of human separatist organizations. If what you say is right, it's all a waste of resources and manpower. I always like feeling useful." The tip of his 'stick glowed as he took a pull. "Is that a tray?"

"I made sandwiches." Jani held out the food like a child displaying a craft project. "Ham and cheese."

"You *cooked*?" Niall shook his head. "Constructed." His voice emerged hushed. "For me?"

"Do you want it or not?"

"I'd be . . . loath to eat it." Niall cocked his head. "Might have it bronzed."

"Fuck you, all right?" Jani walked to the table beside Niall's chair and plunked down the tray, coughing as the clove smoke raked her throat. "Eat." She took her plate, hied to the opposite side of the sitting room and fell onto the couch.

"You sound like my dear Roshi." Niall took the sandwich in hand and peeled back the top slice of bread. "I've never seen potato salad used as a filling before."

"My papa makes mashed potato sandwiches." Jani bit into her sandwich and immediately hit a peppercorn. "You fry up the mashed with butter and onion. Dice in some bacon." She savored the sinus-clearing capsaicin rush. "Grill the bread first, or it sogs up fast."

"I can imagine." Niall broke off a corner and bit carefully. "Thank you, gel." He chewed. Paused. "Been dreaming much?"

Jani mined another peppercorn from the depths. "A little."

"You know the drill. Tell me yours and I'll tell you mine."

Jani nodded. *First, there comes simple. Then there comes hard. And then there comes this.* "It's been the same one the past few nights. I walk into the Laumrau camp, pull back the flap of the first tent, and no one's inside." Sweat trickled down her back, and she blamed the pepper. "Then I turn around, and there they are. All twenty-six of them, shooters drawn." She laughed, a dead bark of a sound. "It's a short dream."

Niall set his plate aside. "Mine's old. It's the one where I'm just about ready to take out Ebben." His voice softened. "And she stops running, and turns, and points at me. 'Sergeant Pierce,' she says, 'a good Spacer only shoots the guilty.' So—" He exhaled with a shudder. "—I set aside the long-range I'm holding, and take out my sidearm, and activate it, and—" He held his hand to the side of his head, index finger extended. "—I—" His finger twitched.

Jani waited until Niall lowered his hand. "You haven't had that one for a while." Another peppercorn, because the burning made her feel alive. "Three more weeks of this crap."

Silence settled until the warning klaxon sounded, announcing thirty minutes until breakaway.

CHAPTER 24

Stillness. Stillness and warmth and the sound of running water.

The security dominant, whose name she still did not know, yelling at her, his words as shatterboxes in her head.

Quiet, and the sense that one would never move, ever again.

"She wakes, nìRau."

Rilas opened her eyes, then closed them against the glare of white that struck as the light of a sun. *Ceiling.* She clenched her hands, felt the rumple of cloth. *Bed.* Pushed up with her elbows. Tried to sit up—

The bed seemed to shudder, as a shuttle upon reentry.

Her soul screamed. She twisted to one side as the acid heat rose in her throat and freed itself, as she convulsed again and again.

"All will be well, nìaRauta."

She felt a hand on her shoulder, supporting her as she leaned over the purge receptacle. After she finished, she fell back onto the bed, felt a cool cloth move across her forehead, over her mouth. Heard prayers, the wishes of a physician-priest that her patient remain in the esteem of the gods.

She is not my priest. She did not recognize this female's voice, this touch. Even so, she thanked her. Drank from the cup she held to her lips, laid back as she bade. Accepted the frozen cylinder placed beneath her neck as the greatest of gifts.

"The sedative affects some idomeni in this way. Even treatment does not counter it. The gods forgive your unseemliness, Rilas."

Rilas raised her head. Blinked away the tears that had filled her eyes, and looked toward the figure at the far end of the room.

"Imea nìaRauta Rilas, survivor of Samvasta GateWay. The gods are with you, and truly, and would forsake me if I did not honor such courage. Thus have I come in person to welcome you home." Morden nìRau Cèel sat near the entry, in a chair so low he seemed to rest directly upon the floor. "In between meetings. So many meetings. And the arrival of the humanish. So many arrivals."

Rilas pushed so that she sat upright, even as the physician-priest struggled to push her back. "I was coming to you freely."

Cèel gestured apology. "Unfortunately, nìaRauta, others sought to interrupt your coming. Thus were we compelled to ensure that your journey home was not impeded."

"An escort, nìRau." Rilas shifted to and fro, struggling to see around the physician-priest, who stood at the foot of the bed and operated the levels and adjustments. "Such would have proved adequate." The edges of her vision blackened and she sagged back.

"You cannot sit up too far, or you will sicken again." The priest returned to her side and held her down, then rearranged cushions under her head. "I have raised the front of the bed as far as I will."

"Raise it higher."

"You are too ill, nìaRauta. Your reaction to the soma is too profound—"

"Raise it higher."

"Do as she bids, nìaRauta Ansu." Cèel stood, then arranged the sleeves of his overrobe. "She will not rest as you wish until I have told her that which she believes she needs to know. Such is as she is. This I know, and truly."

The physician-priest straightened, but whether she did so in supplication to Cèel or the gods, Rilas could not surmise. After a few moments she walked around to the foot of the bed and pressed the adjustments. The front of the bed rose, and Rilas motioned with her hand for it to continue.

"Enough." Ansu stopped the elevation at the quarter point. "Any higher and you will faint." She glanced back at Cèel, then gestured her leave-taking and departed.

Cèel walked across the room to the single narrow window,which had been barred on the outside. "Ansu is my own physician-priest. She believes and truly that she is bound to care for all Vynshàrau as she cares for me." He bared his teeth, then turned to observe the view. "The Haárin ship bearing Tsecha's reliquary arrives within the next two sun cycles. The Cabinet ship on which Kièrshia travels arrives soon after. I would prefer to blast it out of space rather than allow it to dock, but such would constitute an incident, and our hands must appear as clean." His voice emerged guttural, deepened by anger and the demand for obedience. "They will search for you, and they must not find you. You must remain here in this hospital until they depart."

Rilas raised a hand to her ear, then felt along her temple to her eye.

"I have your book, nìa. NìaRauta Ansu removed it as you slept." Cèel offered a posture of regard, tilting his head to the right, raising and curving his right hand against his chest. "I viewed Tsecha's collapse. I regret that I could not also view his death, but such is as it is." He turned to her. "You have earned the greatest esteem of all Vynshàrau. Of all idomeni." He once more gestured gratitude, then left the window and walked to the entry. "Now I must take leave of you. You will be cared for here until the ungodly depart." He paused and bared his teeth. "Or are expelled, when we convince them that the words of the Kièrshia are as nothing and that only humanish assassinate." He walked to the door and placed his hand upon the pad.

Rilas struggled to boost herself up on her elbows, stopping to swallow each time her soul rebelled. "NìRau?"

The door had already swept aside—Cèel put out a hand to stop the panel from closing. "Nìa?" His voice once more emerged deep, a sign of his impatience.

"I was returning to you." Rilas eased back against her cushions. "There was no need for this. No need to humiliate yourself by witnessing my illness. No need to—" She did not say it aloud. Such was ungodly, and as suborn, it was not her place to say it. *No need to humiliate me.* An Haárin thought. Such was her dismay that the memory of living as one corrupted her mind.

Cèel stood silent. Then he stepped through the entry. "They would have captured you, nìa. Such could not be allowed." He let go of the panel and it swept closed.

Ansu visited Rilas several times over the course of the next cycle. She oversaw the preparation of her sacraments, escorted her to and from the altar room. When she arrived after mid-afternoon sacrament and asked if Rilas wished a walk in the hospital gardens, she met no argument, for Rilas did not believe herself able to refuse.

They walked in silence for a time. Despite her unease, Rilas allowed herself to enjoy the heat of the Shèráin sun, lost to her for so long. She strained for any noise in an effort to determine her location. Voices and traffic meant the City Center. The rhythmic echoes of mallets against anvils meant Temple, where metallurgist-priests forged the ceremonial blades.

She sniffed the air. Salt tang meant they were near the bay, while faint sulfur and ammonia marked the blessed green-houses—

"You are so quiet, nìaRauta Rilas." Ansu looked her very nearly in the eye, as though she conversed with an esteemed friend.

"I am relishing the sun, nìaRauta Ansu." Rilas bared her teeth, then turned her head so Ansu could not see her face. *She studies me.* She felt a quickening in her soul. *She reports to nìRau Cèel of me.*

"I met ní Tsecha Egri only a single time, many seasons ago." Ansu folded her arms and tucked them inside her overrobe sleeves. "NìRau Cèel had appointed him ambassador to the Commonwealth, and I was to offer instruction to his physician-priest prior to their departure for Earth. He insisted upon attending our discussions, which was most unseemly." The priest's shoulders rounded in memory. "He corrected me, several times. I suspect he partook of humanish foods, so much did he know of their effect on idomeni."

"He was anathema." Rilas stopped before a *chala* shrub and bent low to one of the fragrant white blooms. "He lived with humanish, and died on one of their worlds, bereft of the esteem of the gods or of any godly idomeni. His fate was most deserved, and truly."

"There is talk that the half-humanish will release his soul here. Such is not a thing I care to witness." Ansu lowered to a bench and smoothed her hands over her sand-hued overrobe. "NìaRauta Sànalàn should officiate at such a ceremony. As Chief Propitiator, she intercedes for all Haárin. Even the godless ones." She fell into silence, and continued to pass her hand over her over-robe even as the cloth lay smooth as parchment.

Rilas straightened and walked to a flowering tree. Blessed *vrel*, its flowers as brilliant red as fresh blood. *NìaRauta Ansu, you who considers all Vynshàrau yours to care for, why do you spend so much time caring for me? Why do you stay with me, sit with me, talk to me of Tsecha?* She bent close to the bloom, taking what pleasure she could in its beauty. *Am I your only patient but for nìRau Cèel? Have you no other duties to see to?*

"Tell me of your journeys, nìaRauta." Ansu raised her hands and heightened the pitch of her voice in wonder. "NìRau Cèel has told me that you have traveled to many worlds for him."

Rilas stepped back from the tree and turned to the female, who sat with her back to her, hands in her lap, her neck fully exposed. Clenched her hand, then let it relax. "Indeed, nìaRauta Ansu, I have traveled." And she described some of her journeys to the priest, because she had nothing better to do. And because she believed, and truly, that she had no choice.

Alone in her room at night, Rilas thought too much of the Haárin security dominant whose name she did not know.

She had watched death before, both that which she brought on and that brought on by others. Killed before with her hands, many others besides the idiot humanish, felt bodies shudder and go limp as they released their hold on their souls and became waste to burn or bury. But she never thought of those others. Never saw their faces in dreams. Never heard their voices in her head when all about had gone quiet.

Yet now she continued to think too much of the Haárin security dominant whose name she did not know. Recalled that last godless look of his, directly in her eyes. Saw his lips move, and pondered the words he had spoken. English. Of all languages, why an ungodly humanish one?

It had taken her some time to work out that which he had said. She had resorted to writing out the sounds phonetically, matching them with the few humanish words she knew until she identified the language.

Realized that he had spoken English to her because he did not want ná Bolan and her suborn to understand.

She looked down at the paper she held, scrap parchment recovered from a trash pile and now covered with her script.

Hee. Whel. Keel. U.

Hewel keelu.

He well kill—

And then, as though an illumin had activated, she understood, and wrote those final words.

He. Will. Kill. You.

Even now Rilas wondered if she had misheard him, if he had said something else. If he had even spoken at all, and the soma had addled her memories.

But at night, in the silence, she heard him, his words as clear as if he spoke to her in the hospital garden.

He will kill you.

She had not thought of those words until her second night in the hospital. The library contained nothing of interest, no newssheets or transmissions. The Haárin ship bearing Tsecha's reliquary would arrive the next day, but at the hospital no one knew of anything. Rilas's questions to suborns met with disclaimers and denials, and Ansu claimed no interest. Thus was she left to imagine the carved wooden box, the bound scroll it contained, the godless spirit that called it as home.

Then, later, as she lay in her strange bed and pondered the darkness, she imagined other things. Tugged at the edges of her bed cover, suddenly chill despite the blessed warmth.

He will kill you.

"The Kièrshia had asked for the Guernsey Station Haárin to stop me." Thus had she begged for help from her dominant, who in turn had gone for aid to his dominant. To Cèel.

But ná Bolan Thea joined me soon after departure from Elyas Station. Which meant that the female had been sent by nìRau Cèel to follow her to Elyas, that she had watched for her return to the station, and bought billet on the appropriate ship.

Rilas lay still. "NìRau Cèel had placed spies, as he always has." Her dominant, who had taught her to question as no suborn ever had. Who had taught her the worth of untruths, of speaking one thing and planning another. Who had taught her the value of suspicion.

He did not ask what happened at Guernsey. He did ask of the humanish death. He did not ask what I had done to draw the interest of the Elyan Haárin. He had not asked her to explain anything.

Words of his returned to her. Words he had spoken long ago, when she asked him of another of his suborns who had not returned home after completing a task. *Do I ask this blade why it cuts? No. I use it, and I set it aside when I no longer need it.*

And Rilas lay in the quiet dark and pondered her suspicions and knew. That the Haárin whose name she did not know had known who she was and who had sent her. That he had known that which she had done. And that he had known also what awaited the blade after it had performed its owner's bidding, a knowledge that had come to the blade much too late.

He will kill you.

She lay in the darkness, and imagined.

CHAPTER 25

"Let's run through this one more time." Niall pinched the bridge of his nose. "Meva walks down the aisle first, ahead of the reliquary." He sat across a breakroom table from Jani, untouched vend alcove coffee at his elbow. "But you won't walk with her?"

"I told you before, I have no standing with Rauta Shèràa Temple." Jani had plucked a lemon from the fruit bowl and started to peel it, piling the bits of rind on the table in front of her. "Meva and I have been messaging back and forth about this for the last two weeks—where were you?"

"Studying station plans. Working out routes. Ensuring you don't get killed anywhere between the docks and the embassy. Minor details." Niall rubbed bleary eyes. "So you're just going to let Meva leapfrog you? Tsecha considered you his suborn, not her. She has no business escorting his reliquary."

"The more important issue is Tsecha's status. He merits every honor possible, and he won't receive them if I'm seen anywhere near that procession. Besides, it would reflect badly on Feyó, and she needs all the boost she can get right now."

"Ah-hah." Niall took a packet of crackers from a dispenser and peeled it open. "Feyó and Meva did see your interview-that-wasn't. I wondered what the reaction to that would be."

It was good, and truly, priest-in-training, that you were not present when ná Feyó read your words. "It didn't go over well." Jani pried out a section of the fruit and popped it into her mouth. Felician lemon, green as emerald and sour enough to bring tears to a hybrid eye. "Meva had to explain repeatedly that questioning didn't equal accusation. She said Feyó accepted her reasoning, eventually.

But given all the tensions, we felt that shunting me to one side during the official ceremonies was the best option." Another wedge. A cough to add to the tears. "It seemed the best way to make up for John's and Yevgeny's delay in telling Feyó that it was assassination. You can't allow her to lose face within the worldskein if you expect her support for Outer Circle secession."

"Your circumspection is commendable." Niall took a cracker from the packet, but instead of eating it, he broke it into bits, then laid the bits out on the tabletop and moved them around like game pieces. "It's also out of character, which worries me no end."

Jani ignored him, hunting through the spice dispenser until she found the pepper. "After Tsecha's soul is released, Meva technically becomes the propitiator and can walk behind the reliquary when it's transported to its final interment in the Temple catacombs." She sprinkled pepper on the lime and took a taste, savoring the added bite. "I would like to see that, but there's no way they'd let me down there."

"Who gets the honor of letting the old bird out of his cage?"

"It's all Meva." Jani pulled off another lemon section. Sprinkled pepper. Chewed. Swallowed. Wiped her eyes. "It's the least awkward solution. Temple feels that the honor of a former Chief Propitiator will thus be maintained, and Tsecha's soul will be able to proceed to the First Star without further impedance."

"If they wanted to maintain honor, they shouldn't have kicked Tsecha out of the club in the first place." Niall continued to rearrange cracker pieces. "I'm not just arguing for the sake of arguing. In a reasonable world, you would walk in front of his reliquary. You would officiate at the release of his soul."

"In a reasonable world, he'd still be alive." Jani returned the pepper to its slot and hunted for a new taste. *Ginger? Onion salt?* "Meva told me that Feyó told her that she still hears his voice." A sprinkle of ginger on another section of lemon. More tears. "I need to let it be. It's not the fight I want to fight now."

"You do understand that hearing you preach caution makes the hairs on the back of my neck stand up?" Niall swept cracker remains into the tableside trash receptacle, then freed a 'stick. "Know what I think? I think you're laying low. You don't want to attract undue attention while you hunt for Nahin Sela." He blew a smoke ring, then watched it until it dissipated. "I'm not saying I don't believe you. But we've looked. For three weeks we looked for any sign, any hint, any trace of evidence. Then we messaged ahead to embassy security and had them look."

"They were most thorough, I'm sure." Jani flicked a piece of lemon peel into the trash receptacle to join Niall's crackers.

"The request came from Roshi. Damned right they were thorough." Niall took of sip of his coffee and grimaced. "Take it from this old Victorian—if Cèel has one-tenth the brains I think he has, Nahin Sela will never be found. She died when her ship tried to punch through Samvasta, or she's sleeping the big sleep at the bottom of Rauta Shèràa harbor. If Cèel felt merciful—excuse me whilst I laugh—she's at some idomeni version of a resort doing whatever the hell it is that idomeni do for fun. But wherever she is, we can't get her, because there is a very powerful and ruthless male whose status as Oligarch depends on her continued absence." He stood and walked to the sink, cup in hand. "Galling as it is to admit, I think the bastard won this round." He poured the coffee down the drain, let the water run. "You ready?"

Jani didn't have to ask what he referred to. *Ready to enter Rauta Shèràa Station again? See the city from the shuttle windows? Walk out of the shuttleport and feel the heat and smell the flowers and the bay? Ready to stare your past in the face and remember?* "I found images of Rauta Shèràa in the library. Started slow, and worked my way up. I got to revisit all my old haunts. The old bazaar. The walkways along the river. Amazing how little has changed. I bet I could still trace my old route from the human-ish enclave to the Academy and not get lost." She wrapped the lemon remains in a dispo napkin and tossed the wad into the tableside receptacle to join the ghosts of Niall's crackers. "I'm as ready as I'll ever be. You?"

"Glad I've had enough to keep me busy is all I can say." Niall leaned against the counter. His face had grown greyer since they'd departed Guernsey, his cheeks more sunken. His uniforms hung. Over the last three weeks, he had smoked too much, eaten and slept too little. But he hadn't taken a drink since the night of the *Capria* bombing, a struggle that had left its mark in the form of haunted eyes and a shortened temper.

"So." He drew up straight. "We disembark *after* Meva and the reliquary, after we give the crowd that's come to greet Tsecha's wooden box a chance to clear out. Shuttle to the surface, where skimmers await. On to the embassy enclave, where we hook up with everyone else. You're wearing your shooter vest?"

Jani tugged down the front of her grey wrapshirt, revealing the silvery lacework beneath.

Niall nodded. "Embassy security's providing the bulk of the

ground coverage. They have a decent relationship with the Station Haárin, if not the bornsect Council. They seem to know their collective ass from a hole in the ground."

"Praise, indeed." Jani tried to draw a smile, and managed, a little. "I'll be fine."

"Yeah." Niall reached into his pocket. "I want you to plug this in." He pulled out a small metal flat that looked like a smaller version of his nicstick case. "It's an ear bug." He flipped up the top and shook out a small, milky disc. "We'll be able to remain in touch at all times. You'll also be able to hear all the chatter, know what's going on."

"I've seen these before." Jani took the bug from Niall, then walked to the sink. "Got anything to plug up the other ear?" She activated the tap and wet the disc, then massaged it between her fingers until it softened and expanded.

Niall drew a jittered breath. "Don't think that hasn't crossed my mind."

"Cèel isn't interested in killing me." Jani inserted the bug into her right ear, shivering as she felt it expand and fill the canal. A momentary muffling of sound, then a return to clarity. "He excised his particular thorn."

"Proof, gel." Niall motioned toward the door. "Can't take him down without proof." He waited for Jani to draw alongside, and they walked into the corridor just as the approach klaxon sounded.

"One hour to go. I'll walk you to your cabin, then go on to the bridge." Niall's step slowed. " 'And so we return to that place of war. To that place that summoned our blood.' To damned Shèrá."

"I've been waiting for a quotation." Jani fought to keep her voice light, even as her chest tightened. "They've been thin upon the ground of late."

"Listen to you." Niall smiled. "Henry the Fifth. One of my favorites. Especially the part where he rallied his men before the Battle of Agincourt. They were outnumbered, exhausted, that morning of St. Crispan's Day." His expression turned grave. " 'In peace there's nothing so becomes a man as modest stillness and humility. But when the blast of war blows in our ears, then imitate the action of the tiger. Stiffen the sinews. Summon up the blood.' " He looked at Jani, beautiful eyes dark with the memories of what they'd seen twenty years before. " 'Once more into the breach, dear friend. Once more.' "

* * *

Jani took one last turn around her spacious sitting room as she waited for the *Madelaine* to dock. This leg of the journey had passed more easily than she feared. Only the odd mealtime had proved a challenge, between John's and Anais's determination to ignore her existence and Lucien's refusal to follow their example. This time around, Val had interceded in the matter of cabin assignments, snagging her a two-bedroom suite complete with working thermostat, as well as an office. The ability to access secure networks and Cabinet-class libraries and archives had allowed her to pass the time in productive seclusion. She had searched the records of shipping companies and research facilities in areas of the Commonwealth with a history of idomeni infiltration. The Outer Circle. The Jewelers' Loop. Hunted through manifests and invoices and directories, on the lookout for the materials that might have been used to manufacture the weaponized prionic, and for scientists who might have constructed it.

Proof, gel. Niall's words rattled in her head. The haystack needle. The one-in-a-billion shot. *If I had more time . . .* She told herself that, even as she knew. Even as she feared.

. . . the bottom of Rauta Shèràa harbor . . .

"But that's too good for her." Jani sat in a lounger, and waited for that mildest of bumps that would tell her the *Madelaine* had docked at Rauta Shèràa Station.

She yawned for the first time in days. She had managed to sleep, even as the dreams came. Convinced herself that any night during which she didn't die counted as a good one, and so managed to find some rest about half the time. Sent message central transmit communications to Dieter at Commerce expense, and viewed the replies until she could recite them by heart. *A few more fights . . . brought in Dathim's friends . . . the training is going much as you'd expect.* Dieter's skills at saying everything and nothing with the same words came into play repeatedly. She tried to read the truth in his eyes, in the way he'd lower his head as he spoke, as though exhausted. Trying to deduce, even as she dreaded what she might learn.

Nothing in the newssheets, at least. No unrest in Karistos. Some problems in Meteora, its smaller sister city to the south, but those proved to be related to the local ComPol's mishandling of a political corruption investigation, not the aftershocks related to Tsecha's death.

It's like reading tea leaves. Trying to divine truth over great distance with little concrete information. To compensate, the

imagination ran roughshod, dragged the rest of the mind to places
it didn't want to go—

"*Jani?*"

She flinched. Slumped and swore at the ceiling, her heart
pounding. *Dammit, Niall.* She touched her ear, activating the bug.
"*What do you want?*"

"*Could you please come to the bridge.*" Not a question, but a
veiled command, delivered in a voice gone tight enough to string
a violin.

Jani slapped the door pad. The panel opened to reveal a vision
in dress desertweights, brimmed lid tucked beneath his arm.

"There have been developments." Lucien stepped to one side,
eyes fixed straight ahead, and waited for her to precede him down
the corridor.

"The station stopped all shuttle flights at midnight, Rauta Shèràa
time." Niall hesitated, then shook his head as the feed from his ear
bug claimed his attention.

Jani heard the same string of chatter, saw from the distant look
in Lucien's eyes that he received it as well.

Felt the cold sweat bloom and trickle.

"An update for we the deaf would be nice," Scriabin snapped.
He wore tunic and trousers in Commerce dark green, an unfortunate contrast to his reddening face.

"Tsecha's welcoming committee is currently estimated at a
quarter million inside the station proper." Niall paused again.
"Could be three hundred thousand. The ones who couldn't make it
here are lining the Rauta Shèràa streets. Estimates there have
topped the two million mark, but I understand that number is
swelling as I speak." Another of his aides whispered something in
his open ear, and his expression darkened. "Two point five million, and still climbing."

"They came to see him home." Jani smiled, felt a swell of
pride nudge aside the fear. "Even though Cèel tried to marginalize
him. Even though Temple declared him anathema and tore his
writings to shreds."

"I wouldn't read too much into it." Ulanova entered the bridge,
a flicker of black-garbed flame, her usual uniform of ministry burgundy set aside in deference to idomeni religious protocols.
"Idomeni see things as they are. Whether for or against Tsecha, they
would turn out, simply to watch." She surveyed the narrow,
instrument-lined room, gaze sliding past Jani and pausing on Lucien

before settling on her nephew. "The embassy has sent an escort to clear our way through the mess, surely? There's no need for us to remain on board for hours to come."

"I want to see it." Jani turned to the bridge's small monitor, which currently showed a view of the gangway, populated by a quartet of embassy security guards. "Can we see it on the port?" She nodded toward the semicircle of clear metalloceramic that served as the bridge's window.

"Why can't we watch in person?"

Everyone turned to find Val standing in the entryway.

"It's been ages since I passed through the place, but there have to be areas at one end of the concourse or the other where we can stand and not get in anyone's way." He glanced at Jani, looking away before she could grin, the eternal coconspirator.

"I would like to watch as well." Scriabin fielded his aunt's glare. "It's history, Tyotya. I want to be able to tell my children that I saw it firsthand."

"We are in the human section of the concourse." Niall shot a glare at Val that should have dropped him on the spot. "We would have to move to the outlet in the idomeni section, along with all those poor souls who have flown up here for the sole purpose of protecting you. I don't believe that standing in full view of a small city's worth of idomeni is the best course of action for a group of humans—" He redirected his glower at Jani. "—or one hybrid in particular to take, given the circumstances and the prevailing mood."

Ulanova favored Niall with one of the few smiles she'd allowed over the course of the voyage. "I agree, Colonel. I believe—"

"I'd like to watch, too." John stepped inside, casting an edgy glance in Jani's direction before looking away. He wore her favorite daysuit, the pale blue-grey that matched his eyes. "If we're just going to stare at a display, well, we could've done that in Thalassa."

"*Yes.*" Niall fit three weeks of ramping tension into a single word. "You could have."

"You're outvoted, Niall." Jani heard the twitter in her ear, felt her heart skip. *Three hundred fifty thousand.*

"No. I'm in charge of security. My vote trumps everyone's." Niall muttered a curse as the same number fed into his ear. "Look, I liked him, too. But we could be looking at a riot here."

"I'll hide behind someone." Jani read Niall's eyes, the pleading and the question. *Are you that eager to walk out there? To take that first step?* No, she wasn't. But what choice did she have? "Let's go."

Niall led them to the exit, muttering all the while, every angered inflection broadcast into Jani's ear. *"I didn't know you knew those words,"* she whispered, and watched his face flare.

Then Lucien squirted ahead while Niall moved behind. Shortcut code streamed into Jani's ear, names and locations and positions and conditions, so quickly that she couldn't identify the individual words. The inner door slid aside, then the outer door, and with as much formality as a stroll down the Thalassan beach, they walked out onto the gangway.

CHAPTER 26

"My God." John stopped at the point where the gangway opened out onto the human concourse.

"Nothing's changed." Val drew up beside him. "Not a thing."

Jani wiped her hands on her trousers as the shiver of nerves and fear and anticipation washed over. Glanced at Niall to find him fixed in place, as shaken as the rest of them.

"Damned place always was a beauty." He spoke softly, as though to himself, before switching back to security jargon.

"Yes." Jani nodded. Compared to the baroque excesses of Elyas and the jury-rigged clutter of Guernsey, Rauta Shèràa Station was as airy and elegant a public thoroughfare as ever existed. Sand-colored walls curved upward, carved at the peak to form a lattice like interlocking fingers from which skeletal metal chandeliers hung at regular intervals. The walls themselves had been equipped with illumination insets that provided most of the lighting, and made the space glow like a windowed room on a sunny day. In niches along the walls came the only shots of color, arabesque panels in green, blue, and worked metal.

Lucien's soft French crept into Jani's ear, as though he lay beside her in bed. *"It's like a cathedral without the pews or the altar. No snack kiosks. No shops. No holos of ministers or the celebrity of the moment."*

"You've never been here?"

"No."

"It affects newcomers that way." And the not-so-newcomers, as well.

They stepped out as one and started down the causeway. Lucien remained in front, Niall to the rear. *"—like herding kiddies through the dinosaur exhibit—"* Jani picked out his voice amid the stream. *"Keep 'em moving and don't let them touch anything."*

Few humanish populated the place, since without the shops and eateries, there were no magnets, no reasons to hang around. They soon reached the end, which abutted an even larger cathedral that was the main concourse, near the spot where Tsecha's reliquary would emerge. Val glanced at his timepiece, then stood on tiptoe and checked out the crowd. "Can't we move out a little more?"

"Perhaps you can." John shook his head. "I'll have to make do with the sidelines. Hybrids have no rank here. I crouch near the front, I'll get hammered for commanding status I don't have. It only looks like a scrum out there. There's strict organization according to skein, sect, and degree of outcast."

"Have you ever noticed that idomeni . . . smell?" Lucien sniffed, then grimaced. *"I never noticed it before. It's weird. Faint, but highly annoying. Sickly sweet, like dead flowers."* He eyed Jani sidelong. *"We won't discuss the heat. We're lucky that cooling cells in desert-weights are standard now."*

"I don't recall inquiring after your comfort." Jani tensed as a murmur rippled through the concourse, all heads turning toward the far end.

Val stepped over to them. "I just overheard Niall talking to one of his staff. Meva has just disembarked." He looked crisp and cool despite the unhumanish heat, as did his pale yellow daysuit, which also must have come equipped with cooling cells, given his lack of apparent discomfort. He remained at Jani's elbow and ignored Lucien, who for his part didn't seem to notice.

Jani edged as far out into the concourse as she dared. The place was about two hundred meters long, and filled from wall to wall with idomeni but for a narrow aisle that cut through their center. She looked behind her, saw Scriabin standing a few meters back. Ulanova leaned on his arm, as fixed on the unfurling scene as any of them.

Jani turned back toward the concourse just as something in the air . . . changed. She felt the charge, the tension. *The priest has come home.* Her eyes filled, tears spilling even as she tried to blink them away.

After a few moments a familiar figure became visible through the crowd. Meva, dressed as neatly and conservatively as Jani had ever seen in pale tan trousers, shirt, and propitiator's overrobe.

Her waist-length hair, which she normally wore in a messy knot, had been braided and looped into a breeder's fringe as weighty as the wigs of ancient Egyptian figures. She walked slowly, her back straight as a plumb line, her head high. She'd encounter Haárin first, some dressed in jewel tones, others in palest earths and pastels. Farther along, she'd meet the bornsects who had come to pay their respects, but here, she met those whom Tsecha had led, those whom he had instructed, inspired. If she spotted Jani, she gave no sign, keeping her eyes fixed straight ahead as she passed by and continued down the concourse.

"How can so many beings stay so damned quiet?" Niall, his voice in Jani's ear as hushed as a child's.

Jani watched Meva until another change in the air caused her to look back from whence the female had come. At first she saw nothing. Then, through the crowd, it became visible, a box of plain, polished wood that floated through the air, a meter or so above the floor.

"You never mentioned pallbearers, did you, gel?" Niall's voice again. Questioning child.

"No, I didn't." Jani watched as the reliquary veered toward the middle of the concourse as though guided by an invisible hand, then continued its haunting progression. As it passed the midway point, one of the Haárin standing at the front of the crowd raised both arms above her head in a posture of abject supplication. A few rows behind, another Haárin raised his arms.

Then another.

Another.

Finally, the rest of the idomeni, Haárin and bornsect, raised their arms in one upward sweep, the whisper of cloth the only sound as arms brushed and sleeves fell back, revealing traceworks of challenge scars. They stood, still and silent, as the reliquary continued on its way, a shadowed square, dark and dead amid the lightness and life.

Jani looked at John to find him standing somber, arms at his sides. He eyed her sidelong, his face reflecting the same question she asked herself. *What do we do, except watch? How do we show how we felt?*

John nodded. Then, moving in unison, they straightened, lifting their arms above their heads as the idomeni had. Val stared. Lucien simply watched.

"Dammit—you're not supposed to attract attention. You're supposed to—" Niall's voice cut off as Jani plucked the bug from her

ear and shoved it in her pocket, then raised her arm again. A few Haárin glanced in her direction, but most watched the reliquary until it vanished from view. Then they slowly lowered their arms.

Jani lowered her arms as well, and waited for the crowd to disperse, to follow the reliquary, to walk to their shuttles.

But they did none of those things. Instead, they remained where they stood, and looked once more toward the far end of the concourse. Toward her.

The silence weighed, heavy as a grieving heart. The idomeni stood still, and quiet, and waited.

"You took it out, didn't you?"

Jani turned to find Niall at her shoulder.

He touched his ear, then looked past her toward the assembled. "Fucking hell. Not a one has budged." He glared at Jani. *"Dammit."*

"You must get us out of here, Colonel." No more smiles as Ulanova shook off Scriabin's restraining hand and dogged Niall's elbow. "We'll be overrun."

"They're waiting for you." John's voice, quiet as shadow.

Jani looked him in the eye for the first time since they had departed Guernsey. Felt his surprise. His uncertainty. "I know."

Niall pointed to his ear bug. "Station Haárin are asking whether you intend to join the procession. The place is at a standstill and they have incoming craft that may need to be diverted if things don't shake loose soon."

"If she walks out there now, she declares herself ní Tsecha Egri's successor." Ulanova raised her own supplicant hand to the heavens, then let it fall. "In spite of her origins. In spite of the fact that she possesses no standing within Temple or the Haárin hierarchy. That would be a supreme display of arrogance, even for her."

Scriabin, silent to that point, walked over to Jani. "They could attack you. If they did, we might not be able to get to you in time."

"I don't think they'd do that." Jani tugged at the front of her shirt, then passed a straightening hand over it. "I think they're just waiting for me to make up my mind."

"So you are forced by circumstance to declare yourself Tsecha's successor," Ulanova bit out. "How convenient for you."

Jani took the ear bug from her pocket and reinserted it. "If anyone challenged me, I'd have to fight." She looked at Niall. "We didn't work this out ahead of time, but I'd like you to be my second if that happens."

Niall's eyes softened despite his irritation. "You know my answer, gel. What would I have to do?"

"Guard the edge of the circle to make sure I don't step outside it. Declare the challenge at an end if I'm too injured to continue."

Niall nodded. Swallowed hard. "We'll be close around you. We do have Haárin security in the crowd. Overhead scan. Interference patterning."

"Got anything that will stop a half-meter short sword?" Jani patted his arm. "It will be their call. How they perceive me, whether as Tsecha's suborn or . . . something else." She turned, and walked toward the concourse. Sensed a different sort of ripple radiate through the crowd as she approached, one that produced the occasional whitecap.

Jani tried to walk normally, even as the soles of her feet tingled and her knees threatened to buckle. She caught a whiff of the aroma Lucien described, the flower-sweat of idomeni packed shoulder-to-shoulder as far as her eye could see. Felt their heat as she walked the narrow gantlet, the full-face stares of the bolder Haárin.

"Keep going, gel. I've got your back. You're twenty meters in."

One hundred eighty to go. A lifetime in a few minutes. Jani imagined Tsecha's reliquary in front of her, leading the way. Touched the stones of her rings, drew strength from the chill hardness. Met the eyes of an elder female who bared her teeth, and bared her own in return. Slowed as an Haárin male stepped out of the crowd and strode toward her. Stopped as he reached beneath his overrobe and pulled out a blade as long as his forearm and brought it around in a long, slow arc.

Jani continued forward, reached out, gripped his wrist with her left hand, the hilt of the blade in her right, and twisted. Held the freed blade above her head—

"Let me the hell go!"

—then turned to find Niall standing stricken a few strides to the rear, a station Haárin hanging onto his arm. "I'm fine, Niall." Then she turned back to the male and handed him back his blade as the crowd surged forward and closed in behind her, bearing her along like a wave.

"What the hell was that?" Niall's voice rang in her head, as shaken as ever she'd heard it. *"What in bloody hell—"*

Lucien's voice broke in. *"I think it may have been the Haárin equivalent of asking for an autograph."*

"You think so?" Niall's sneer could have curdled milk. *"Well, fuck that—"*

Jani plucked the bug from her ear again. The crowd altered the farther along she walked, the brightly colored garb of the more militant Haárin giving way to the subdued coloration of the conservatives.

Then, near the end of the concourse, palest colors only, the braided fringe of the breeder the only hairstyle to be seen. *Born-sect.* Lighter Oà and Sìah, darker Denas and Pathen.

"Glories of this strangest of days to you, Kièrshia!" A male voice, speaking lightly accented High Sìah. But the words came from a Pathen male, who stepped forward and held out his hand to Jani. He was shorter and broader than Cèel, than any Vynshàrau. His skin was the yellowed black of old bronze, his shirt, trousers, and overrobe sun-yellow slashed with white. "And to the one you bring home to his rest."

Aden nìRau Wuntoi. Jani stopped, stood up straight, prayed her High Sìah was up to the challenge. "Glories to you as well, nìRau Wuntoi." She felt the pressure from behind as idomeni crowded inside her humanish comfort zone, the bones grind as Wuntoi gripped her hand in his.

"Favored of ní Tsecha, who believes and truly that his own Haárin killed him." Wuntoi bared his teeth. "Did you fear to meet his fate when you walked out into this place?"

The bracing bluntness of idomeni. Jani waited until Wuntoi released her hand, until the silence stretched to snapping and she knew she had his attention. "Have idomeni grown so fond of secret killing that I must worry, nìRau?"

Wuntoi raised his right hand, curving it in question. "No godly idomeni believes in such. You would have nothing to worry of from one of them." He cast her a glancing look in the face, his brown-on-brown eyes as chill as Lucien's. "From an ungodly, you would need to worry, as all idomeni would need to worry, and truly." With that, he stepped back into the crowd, and was swallowed up by his suborns.

Jani felt a push in the small of her back and started walking again. Parsed Wuntoi's words over and over, damned her sketchy High Sìah and wondered if she had heard properly. *He thinks it's possible an idomeni killed Tsecha. He accepts the idea.* Her heart hammered as she reached the end of the concourse and the station Haárin closed in, separating her from the all-enveloping welcoming committee and delivering her to a hidden alcove, where an enraged Niall waited, bracketed by Lucien and Scriabin.

Jani held up her hands. "No blood. No chance of injury." *Except when Wuntoi shook my hand.* "Cultural differences, Niall."

"Is that what we're calling it now?" Niall started to pace, then stopped and stood, glare fixed on some unlucky point in the distance. "No more crowds. No more knives for fun. And you will put that bug in your ear and leave it there—do you understand?"

"Wuntoi greeted you." Scriabin's eyes held surprise and a sharpness akin to envy. "The Pathen dominant. What does it mean?"

"I think it means that he accepts the possibility that an idomeni had Tsecha killed. He referred to an ungodly idomeni whom we all need to worry about. Was he speaking in general about the unknown idomeni who killed Tsecha, or was he just trying to turn us all against Cèel?" Jani leaned against the alcove entry, longed for nothing more than a comfortable seat on a shuttle, a chance to breathe. "I don't know where he learned humanish doublespeak, but he's damned good at it."

"I wonder if Cèel knows his feeling, or if it will take him by surprise?" Scriabin pointed down, in the general direction of Shèrá. "I doubt seriously that he will be expecting it."

"Assuming that's the case." Niall relaxed a little, and even managed a grin. "Cèel is going to start shitting little green apples any time now."

Scriabin's lip twitched. "He's made of fairly stern stuff, Colonel."

"Then it'll hurt that much more." Niall took Jani's elbow and steered her toward a walkway that led them back into the humanish concourse. "Let's go. Our shuttle received expedited clearance, which I swear comes courtesy of your new friend Wuntoi. Everyone else has boarded."

"Welcome back to Shèrá, Niall," Jani said under her breath.

"Maybe." Niall shook his head. "I may not understand cultural differences, but I know a power struggle when I see one. Your new friend drew a line in the sand, gel, and you're it."

Jani eased out of Niall's grip as they reentered the humanish concourse. Shivered, and blamed the coolness of the air.

CHAPTER 27

Jani walked out of Rauta Shèràa shuttleport's humanish section and gasped as though someone had punched her in the stomach. It was just past the height of summer, and the heat was as she remembered, a palpable oppression that seemed to close in on all sides, a challenge even to her hybrid tolerance. The sky, cloudless and milky blue, played home to the errant drift of seabirds and the more focused streakings of the swallow and hatchlike birds that called the city home and built nests in eaves and gutters. In the distance she could see the same spires and towers, the domes of the Trade Board, Council, and Temple.

The air smells the same. Walk anywhere in Rauta Shèràa, and you'd smell flowers. Near the port, the blooms of choice had always been *camalas*, fist-sized clusters of pink-trimmed white trumpets with a scent that always reminded Jani of cinnamon. She walked over to one of the shrubs, which had likely greeted her during her first arrival, twenty-five years before, and sniffed. *Still cinnamon.* A little sharper than she recalled, and maybe her hybridization was to blame.

The shuttleport itself, a cottage version of the orbiting station, also looked much as it ever had. She'd walked its corridors as a callow teenager, a Spacer and diplomat, a fleeing war criminal. *Now I'm back to diplomat.* Technically. She knew some who would argue the designation, herself included.

"What do you think, gel?" Niall drew up next to her. He held his nicstick case in one hand, ready to light up as soon as he entered the refuge of one of the embassy triple-lengths that abutted the curb. "Stuff of nightmares?"

"When I first came here, I thought it was one of the most beautiful cities I'd ever seen." Jani watched as Scriabin and Ulanova slipped into a skimmer bearing the ambassadorial crest on the door. They were followed closely by John and Val, who boarded a vehicle branded with the familiar caduceus. "Then reality started chipping away."

"The only things that struck me were the heat, and that I couldn't smoke outside the enclave." Niall nodded toward a Service blue skimmer. "Roshi got here a day ahead." He guided Jani toward the vehicle as though afraid she'd bolt.

Jani stepped into the passenger cabin, shivering as the chill, dry air washed over her. Sat on the edge of the bench seat and let her eyes adjust to the comparative darkness.

"Glories of this strangest of days. I fear Wuntoi is a master of understatement." Mako regarded her from the opposite bench.

"Understatement of the year." Major General Callum Burkett, commander of the Service Diplomatic Corps, snorted a laugh. "We've been in damage control mode ever since that damned article of yours reached us. Then we watched the arrival, which will henceforth be capitalized in all reports and formal précis. Morale did a one eighty within minutes. That little thing with the sword got a nice round of applause." He glared at Jani from his seat in the opposite corner of the cabin. "Is it ever easy with you?"

"Hi, Callum." Jani smiled. "How's Jeanina?"

"My lady wife is just fine, thanks, and don't change the damned subject." Burkett was the image of the middle-aged officer, tall, rangy, and sharp-featured, a darker tan and older eyes the only outward signs of time's passage. He and Mako wore the same uniform as did Niall, dress desertweights replete with cooling cells and special seaming to permit ventilation. "If your plan is to keep Cèel off balance, you're doing a helluva job. If your plan is to keep the rest of us off balance, stop it right now."

Conversation ceased as the front passenger gullwing opened and a familiar figure slipped in next to the driver. "All luggage has been scanned and loaded, sir." Lucien just had time to glance over his shoulder at Jani before the darkened privacy barrier slid into place.

The skimmer pulled away from the curb, then gradually accelerated, driving Jani back against her seat. She took in the view through her window, the wide avenues of the central city, the blockish buildings of white and tan stone, walkways filled with crowds of bornsect and Haárin.

"The reliquary just arrived at the Haárin enclave." Burkett emitted a grumbling sigh. "He was one of the most irritating beings I ever had the misfortune to meet, and I wish I could have told him how much I—" He turned his face to the window. Swallowed hard. "You had to like him, didn't you? You couldn't help yourself."

"Someone could," Mako muttered. After that they fell silent, the only sound to reach them the announcement by their driver as they approached the gates of the humanish enclave.

Burkett poured himself coffee from a large upright brewer, then returned to the couch. "We expected Cèel to be challenged by Wuntoi sometime in the last month or two, but Tsecha's death caught the Pathen completely off guard, as it did all of us."

After entering the humanish enclave, they had been taken immediately to the embassy, a four-story expanse of tan stone that dominated the enclave's central cul-de-sac, which like the other buildings in the place had been constructed according to idomeni protocols. Only the triple-wide entryway broke the smoothness of the facade. Windows were reserved for the rear views, which looked out over a series of gardens laced with artificial streams and surrounded by high brick walls. The feeling was one of enclosure, of shuttering away, which couldn't have been a coincidence given Cèel's opinion of humanish.

Jani sipped coffee. After their arrival, they had been deposited in one of the larger sitting rooms, there to wait for the others in their group. The decor had been chosen by someone who shared Anais Ulanova's taste in furnishings: brocade-upholstered couches and chairs, dark woods, and silk and velvet-covered walls. No reds or burgundies, since those shades would have conflicted with idomeni religious prerogative. But there were plenty of other rich tones to make up for the omission, jewel shades of blue, green, and purple, with a gold mine's worth of gilt thrown in to provide contrast. *Winter colors.* The sight of them combined with the humanish room temperature to make Jani shiver all the more, as though they'd brought with them the stiff winds and dry, cold air of a Chicago winter.

"Wuntoi is biding his time now." Mako had eschewed coffee and, despite the early hour, gone straight to the liquor cabinet and the vodka. "Too much news tumbled in too quickly. First the death, then the news of assassination and the rage at humanish when the news proved true." He sat sprawled in a corner lounge chair like a disgruntled bear and stared into his frosted glass. "Then came your article, and the fallout, both expected and . . . not so." He regarded Jani with the same sharp wonderment that Scriabin had at the station. "None of us believed the idomeni would have ever accepted the possibility that one of their own could have done the deed. Not a one."

"Tsecha's influence." Burkett sat back, eyes fixed on nothing. "I sensed the strength of it increasing with every passing day, especially among the Haárin." He glanced down at his cup, then frowned and set it aside. "But the Haárin don't have the power around here—that's Cèel and the Council and Temple hardliners, and they're hammering on the rest to dissolve diplomatic relations with us, recall the Haárin from their humanish enclaves, and seal their borders." He rose and walked to the liquor cabinet, pulled another frosted glass from the tiny cooler and filled it to the brim with vodka. "Wuntoi would love to accuse Cèel of planning Tsecha's assassination, but first he needs proof, and human-style criminal investigation methods are in their infancy here. Service Investigative has reported that they've fielded a few hesitant probings, but nothing has come of them, and when we try to reach out, the idomeni pull back, lock down." He raised his glass, studied it for a time, then sipped. "Which means that, unfortunately, we are forced to sit, and wait."

Silence claimed them. After a time, Jani shifted in her seat as the stares shifted to her. "How is Cèel responding to the undecideds?"

"With some old-fashioned threats." Mako tossed down the last of his vodka. "He's said that he will win any civil war—the Vynshàrau are the most populous sect in this region, numbering twelve million or more, and as head of the warrior skein, Cèel commands a fighting force of over a million, not including Haárin. He'll treat those who fought him as he treated the Laum years ago. Pathen, Oà, Sìah. Every sect that questioned him would be wiped out. It would make the Night of the Blade look like a playground melee. He'd decimate his people, and call it the will of the gods."

Jani looked to the door and drummed her fingers on the arm of the couch. "So what's our ambassador's opinion of all this?"

"Dear Ava Galina." Mako sneered. "In over her head and sinking fast. Takes her direction from Cao, who so far is doing her usual fine job of ignoring the obvious."

"So now she's closeted with Scriabin, who may be trustworthy, and Ulanova, who damned well isn't. What are they discussing?

Escape plans?" Jani looked to Niall, who had taken a seat in the far corner as soon as they arrived and had remained still and silent ever since. "Do you have escape plans?"

"Coordination with Fort du Lac and Phillipa Station. We have combat shuttles squirreled away down the road, on what passes for our base, and the *Ulanov* twiddling its thumbs just beyond Shèráin space. We would bypass Rauta Shèràa Station entirely, of course." Niall straightened, his air of gloomy introspection dissipating now that he had a definite problem to focus on. "Given the quality of Shèrá's orbital defense array, which is unfortunately damned good, and assuming Cèel's normal level of vindictiveness, I'd say we'd be lucky to evac ten percent of the enclave."

As that bit of news settled over the room like a dark cloud, the door opened and Scriabin lumbered in. "You all made it here—good. I gather from the general air of despondency that you've been apprised of the situation." He walked to the liquor cabinet and became the third customer for the vodka. "Ava had little to add. No official statement from Cèel concerning your arrival, but he supposedly called in the Haárin dominants for an emergency conclave as soon as the images hit the displays." He grinned at Jani. "The dominants who were here, at any rate. Most of them were at the station, welcoming you." He leaned against the cabinet and raised his glass to her. "So, Cèel is rocked back on his heels for the first time in a long while, and to that I say, *Nazdrovya*." He gulped the vodka, then hefted the empty glass, eyes fixed on the fireplace on the other end of the room.

Jani set aside her coffee and wished she were still humanish enough for liquor to have the desired effect. "I'd have Service Investigative talk to ní Galas, Feyó's security dominant. Station and enclave Haárin are much more advanced than the locals when it comes to criminal investigation, and they've had over a month to investigate the assassination."

"I filled in Callum concerning the missing Nahin Sela," Mako offered. "He believes that the Rauta Shèràa Haárin enclave investigators, however backward, are withholding information."

Burkett's face darkened. "It would certainly shed a great deal of light on some of the oddness that we've seen these last few weeks. If they suspect that Nahin Sela is being hidden somewhere in Rauta Shèràa . . ."

"It's their humiliation. If one of theirs killed Tsecha, they want to solve it themselves." Jani stood, tense muscles protesting every movement. "If I could beg your indulgence, I would like an hour or so to settle in. I'm guessing the day's schedule is pretty well packed."

"We're all within a stone's throw of one another, in any case." Burkett downed the balance of his vodka, then set the glass upside down on the table. "We'll talk to Feyó's investigator and go from there." He looked to Jani and blew out a sigh. "One hour at a time. That's what we're down to."

"Maybe I should develop a taste for vodka." Jani acknowledged the scattered weak laughter with a short bow. Only Niall, who knew her best of all, eyed her unsmiling, with the wary stare of a man who knew that somewhere there was a shoe teetering on the brink.

By the time Jani reached her suite, a three-room corner expanse with views of the gardens, her luggage had been deposited and was in the process of being unpacked by a pair of officious aides. She grabbed her duffel before either of them could put their hands on it and headed down the hallway in search of the nearest stairwell.

"Hello."

Jani froze in mid-stride at the sound of the unfortunately all-too-familiar voice, then slowly turned.

Lucien had arrived at the embassy the same time she had. Yet judging from the crispness of his dress desertweights and the fresh-scrubbed shine on his face, he'd already showered, changed uniforms, and performed whatever other ablutions served to eliminate every trace of long-haul fatigue. *When Cèel bombs the enclave, he'll die with his mirror-finish boots on.* "You're staying here?" She looked past him down the hall and tried to divine from which room he might have emerged. "I thought you had to stay at the base."

"No room. It's just a dink place—provides embassy security and some firepower, and that's about it. Between Mako's people and Pierce's crew, they're hanging from the rafters." Lucien shrugged. "Such are the sacrifices we make when called upon."

Jani felt the heat move up her neck as his innocent look sharpened and altered into something focused and . . . not so innocent. She turned, started back down the hall. "I have to go—"

"You're all everyone's talking about. Your entrance. Your unspoken announcement to one and all that you're taking up where Tsecha left off." Lucien hurried past her, then stepped in front of her, cutting her off. "They're replaying the images over and over and over—"

"Until it backfires. Then I'll be on everyone's shit list again." Jani tried to elbow past him, but he grabbed her by the shoulders and pushed her against the wall.

"Does that mean I'll finally have some company?" Lucien leaned in until he pressed the length of his body against hers. "Someone to talk to? Have dinner with? Someone to—" He abandoned the preamble and kissed her hard, bruising her mouth as his hands burned their own path along her buttocks and up her back before finally moving forward and settling on her breasts, cupping and massaging and teasing—

Jani tried to push him away, but each touch, each sensation, unlocked memory and need and desire. Craving. To quench a thirst long denied, ease the ever-growing tension and allay the fear and soothe the quickening ache between her legs. *Simple.* Take that one simple path, if only for a little while. "I don't have time." She tried to shift away from him, but he'd laced his legs through hers and pinned her against the wall and all she could feel were his lips and hands and the press of his erection through his uniform and her pounding heart and the slow trickle of sweat down her back. "I bet they have imagers in the corridors."

"Not in the private wing—the residents would riot." Lucien paused, his breathing rough, his hands stilling, hovering, a devil's promise on hold. "Your room?"

"Aides unpacking the luggage."

"I've got Facilities working on the shower." Lucien turned the handle of the nearest door, prying open the panel and releasing Jani just long enough to peek inside. "Oh, look. Housekeepers' closet." He arched an eyebrow. "Blankets. Pillows." He took her hand and led her through the gap, then pushed the panel closed and wedged the inside handle in the locked position with a long-handled scrubbing brush.

"You've done this before." Jani leaned against a narrow worktable.

"I've done everything before." Lucien slipped the duffel off her shoulder and tossed it in the corner. Pulled her shirt out of her trousers and opened the fasteners, peeling open the front of her bra along the way and applying a quick lick-and-tease to her nipples before undoing her trousers and sliding them down.

Jani reached for his tunic, but he pushed her hands away and undid it himself, slipping it off and laying it carefully across a shelf. His T-shirt, he pulled off more quickly, and it stayed where it landed.

"I don't think this table will hold—" Before Jani could argue load capacity, Lucien swept a shelf's worth of pillows to the floor and lowered her onto them. Kissed her again while his hands found their way everywhere, excited her everywhere, brought her to the edge before easing off ever so slightly. Then with a flick of hand and a twist of hip, he undid his trousers and slipped inside her, moving, then stopping, then moving more quickly and stopping once more, the same ebb and flow again and again until he couldn't stop himself anymore and he buried his head in her neck and whispered things to her that he hadn't said since Chicago and called her things he'd never called her before and she wrapped herself around him and raked her nails across the small of his back and rode his sharp gasps and choked moans and matched them with her own.

Then held him as he slumped against her and relaxed in a way only he could, loose-limbed as a cat after a surfeit of cream.

Her breathing slowed, eventually. The ability to form sentences returned. "If the housekeeper comes in here for towels, they're going to get a hell of a shock."

Lucien laughed, a deep, warm sound that wrapped around Jani like the pillows. "You think they haven't learned to knock before entering a room in this place?" He slid off her onto his side. "You haven't worked in many government buildings, have you?"

"Not with you." Jani scrutinized the ceiling for a time, then looked at Lucien to find him studying her in turn, head cradled on his arm, eyes half closed.

"Six weeks." His voice emerged tight. "Wasted. And why? We could have—and it isn't like you and Shroud were still even—" He rolled over on his back. "Who the hell knows?" He muttered something under his breath, then closed his eyes.

"You could sleep in here, couldn't you?" Jani sat up. Tried to stand until her trousers hobbled her and she fell on her ass and finally lay back and yanked them up.

"What are you doing?" Lucien sat up, a vision of randy dishevelment amid the white-on-white toss of pillows.

"I have to get out of here." She recovered her bra and shirt from the floor and put them on.

"You just—" Lucien stood, pulling up his trousers in one easy motion, a man who had never been hobbled by his clothes in his life. "Wait a minute." He collected the rest of his uniform and dressed. "Dammit."

"I need to get to the Haárin enclave." Jani tried to remove the brush that held the door closed, yanking on it twice before Lucien nudged her aside and removed it with a twist of his wrist. "I need to talk to Meva or Dathim or Galas or somebody."

"Do you trust the security of comport communications around here?" Lucien didn't wait for her to shake her head. "Then you have to leave the enclave, and you can only leave the enclave in an authorized vehicle driven by a licensed member of the embassy staff." He smiled and waved his hand in her face. "Hello. Me, again."

CHAPTER 28

Jani waited in an alley beside the embassy building while Lucien signed out a skimmer. She had returned to her room to collect her overrobe in case she needed it, but instead of donning it, she rolled it up and stuck it in her duffel. She didn't want to be recognized now. She didn't want to be followed. She just wanted to find out what, if anything, Galas had discovered about Nahin Sela.

A sedate four-door in Service blue-grey appeared at the end of the alley. Lucien disembarked and walked around to the passenger side to see to Jani's door, then used the exercise as an excuse to kiss her neck.

"Do you know where we're going?" He inserted himself into the cabin and steered onto the enclave access road, then tapped a blank display in the middle of the dashboard. "If I can avoid using the mapping system, that's one less way they can track us."

"I remember where the Haárin enclave used to be." Jani felt her heart trip as they floated through the gates, the skimmer shuddering as it switched from the humanish to idomeni skimtrack system. "From what I've seen, they rebuilt the city exactly has it had been before the war. I should be able to find it."

They drifted through the streets. Jani recognized old landmarks, buildings she had used as guides when she first arrived at the Academy and hadn't known enough Laumrau or Vynshà to understand the street designators.

"Where's the Academy?" Lucien maneuvered into the slower lane so he could sightsee.

"We won't pass that—it's about ten kilometers north of here." Jani felt her throat tighten, and struggled to will the sensation away.

It looks the same . . . all the same. The parks and the art-filled niches in the walls of buildings otherwise so featureless they looked like molds a child had made with wet sand and a bucket. "First you'll pass the Council dome, then the Temple dome. Then there's the Haárin enclave. Then you pass all the dominant temples for the gods. Shiou's is the largest, followed by Caith's, which is what you'd expect. Then there's a riverwalk, and on the other side of that—" She fell silent. She'd had nightmares, yes, and hadn't wanted to return to this place. What she hadn't expected was that part of her would have . . . missed it all, the crowded streets and the sand-hued monotone and the flowers and the heat and the distant smell of the bay.

"It's a little like Thalassa." Lucien had slipped into absorption mode, where he watched and memorized and said as little as possible as things burned into his brain. "Thalassa's brighter, and there's that undercurrent of Karistos attitude, but still." He sat back, still on point but a little more relaxed. "I know why Tsecha liked Thalassa so much."

"Yeah." Jani fixed her attention on the view. They'd just passed the street leading to Caith's temple, a squat, ugly edifice with a dome of tarnished silver. Sedate clothing and breeder's fringes gave way to the occasional sheared head or burst of rebellious color, the entire scene clicking into place when an all-too-familiar figure emerged from the crowd.

"Pull over." Jani waited until Lucien edged out of moving traffic, then pushed up her gullwing and waved. "Dathim!"

Dathim strode toward the skimmer. "Hah—I came to see you as well." He pulled up the rear door and piled into the backseat.

Jani turned back to face him. "Are you sure you want to be seen with me?"

"What difference?" Dathim folded his arms and sat ramrod straight, the top of his clipped scalp grazing the cabin headliner. "Cèel watches us and listens to us and what difference? Hell with him." He looked out the window, then bared his teeth. "We go to the river and talk there. In the open where all can see."

"So that's the Academy?" Lucien stood atop a stone bench and gazed across the river toward the congested scattering of white buildings large and small that stretched from the main avenue down to the bay. "It's smaller than I thought it would be."

"It's about the size of a ministry compound." Jani looked at the place where she'd spent four of the more harrowing years of her life. "One of the smaller ministries." She stepped up next to Lucien.

"The library is the largest building—you can see the gold dome. The rest are classrooms, a few labs. The scanpack brain farming is performed at Temple because it's a medical procedure, and all those labs are staffed by physician-priests."

"Humans don't attend anymore?"

"No. There were a few classes after ours, but then the war came—"

"Your overrobe—where is it?"

Jani turned to find Dathim glaring at her.

"You should wear it." He folded his arms. "He died for it, and you traveled here because of it, and you should wear it."

Jani looked out over the riverwalk. The time for midday sacrament approached, and most idomeni had retired to their altar rooms, leaving the usually crowded walkways sparsely populated. "I didn't want to be recognized."

"Then you should not have followed him. You should not have come here. You should not have walked behind the reliquary." Dathim grabbed her duffel from beneath the bench and held it out to her. "Meva is outraged. She will yell at you when she sees you again. Put it on."

"You're a bully, ní Dathim Naré." Jani yanked open the duffel fasteners and removed the overrobe, shook it out and pulled it on. "Now we better get out of here."

"Now we must talk." Dathim sat down on the end of the bench, hands on knees, like the town chatterbox. "Ní Galas does not trust his secure communications at the enclave, either. He told ná Meva that it would be much the same as if he went to Council and spoke to Cèel directly."

Jani leapt down to the ground and perched on the rim of a planter. "Ní Galas has been busy?"

"Ní Galas has been to the Trade Board. He showed the images of Nahin Sela to all he met." Dathim gestured disgust. "They are all godly idomeni who do not look others in the face. They had never heard of Nahin Sela, and did not recognize the hair or the clothes, so they could not say if they knew her." He held up his index finger and pointed at Jani. "But there was one female. A bornsect. She did not know of Nahin Sela, but she did know of Imea nìaRauta Rilas." He lowered his voice, a concession that said all anyone needed to know about the quality of the information. "Rilas is a member of Cèel's household. She has been thus for many years. The female said that she is absent much, and spoke sometimes of travel."

Jani pushed away from the planter and stared at the river. "Galas will not be permitted to speak to Rilas."

"A fact which he knows." Dathim lowered his voice even more. "Meva has petitioned Cèel for permission to request that another bornsect speak to Rilas. Wuntoi, or another of the sect dominants."

Jani turned slowly. "Meva has already asked Cèel—" She fell silent when she looked past Dathim to the sloping lawns beyond.

"Oh, shit." Lucien stepped down from the bench and headed along the river to the nearby charge lot. "I'll get the skimmer."

They weren't a large crowd of Haárin, a few hundred or so. But judging by appearances, they were the gamiest, all shorn hair and garish colors on the males, horsetails or loose hair on the females, some of whom wore long skirts instead of all-pervasive trousers.

So quiet. Like the crowds in the station. *What do they want me to say?* Did they expect her to preach, like some of the ministers her papa listened to when he entered one of his "loud religion" phases? *Sermon by the River.* She swallowed a nervous laugh. *I don't even believe in your gods.* What could she say to them that they would want to hear?

The Haárin remained standing, because she was the propitiator and the level of their heads had to remain above hers as a show of respect.

Out of the corner of her eye, Jani saw Lucien maneuver the skimmer up to the top edge of the slope. A dash across a short stretch of lawn, a few quick strides, and she'd be free.

Instead, she crossed her ankles and lowered to the ground. Slipped into Vynshàrau Haárin, because that's what most of them were.

"Ní Tsecha missed Rauta Shèràa. Humanish have a term—homesickness—a longing for the places where one lived as a youngish, where one grew up. He used to tell me stories . . ."

"They were just stories." The embassy security guard grinned. "The one she told about Tsecha when he was young and studying at the Temple school and made this confetti bomb—ohmigod—" She finally took note of the less than enthused audience reaction, and fell silent.

"The Haárin were orderly in the extreme, sir." The second guard shook his head, disbelief stripping the years from his face. "They just followed us to the van, and one of them opened the door for her, and another held out his arm so she could climb in. I mean, Christ on a cracker, if Cèel calls that a riot, I'd hate to see—"

"Thank you, Sergeant—that will be all." Niall waited until the pair filed out before planting his elbows on the desk and burying his face in his hands. "If I were to ask you what you were thinking, would I want to hear the answer?"

Jani sat across from him. She'd removed her overrobe and hung it in her closet, then showered and changed into the more embassy-appropriate dinner attire of a severe black trouser suit. "They expected me to say something, and I didn't know what else to talk about."

"You shouldn't have been out there in the first place." Ulanova sat against the far wall next to her nephew, who sat with arms folded and his head down. "Of all the self-aggrandizing, egomaniacal, inflammatory—" She fell silent and pressed a hand to her forehead.

Lucien, who sat off to one side, well away from the center of the action, raised his hand. "In my opinion, sir, ní Dathim planned for this to happen." He spoke softly, his voice steady, determined to soldier on whether anyone listened or not. "He shamed Jani into putting on her overrobe, even though she expressly informed him that she did not want to be recognized. We felt that since the time for midday sacrament was near, no idomeni would be out on the river. The local hardcore Haárin, however, have apparently stopped following prescribed meal times, a fact we had no way of knowing."

Niall plucked a stylus from the desktop holder and tapped it against the blotter. "You shouldn't have been out there, period. As matters stand, Cèel is threatening to pull all driving privileges for embassy personnel—"

"Ní Galas took Nahin Sela's image to the Trade Board." Jani spoke quickly, trying to fit it all in before anyone interrupted. "One of the bornsect females recognized her as a bornsect named Imea nìaRauta Rilas, a member of Cèel's household."

Niall's tapping stopped. "Why didn't you tell me this sooner?"

"Meva plans to petition Cèel to allow another of the bornsect dominants to talk to Rilas." Jani met Niall's tired eye. "That crack you made about the bottom of the bay just might come to pass."

"What about the bottom of the bay?" Scriabin lifted his head.

"Niall is of the opinion that if Cèel hasn't already killed Rilas, he plans to do so soon. When the threat of exposure is sufficient." Jani avoided Niall's eye even as she cast credit his way. He'd freed a 'stick, and now sat glaring at her through a haze of smoke, like the villainous interrogator in a cheap holodrama. "Meva's petition to allow another bornsect dominant to speak with her might be enough to force his hand."

"And then we lose the only being who can testify to Cèel's culpability?" Scriabin sat up, fingers drumming on knees. "Is it too late to ask Meva to withdraw her petition?"

"This is Meva we're talking about." Niall's voice emerged desert dry. "She's a handful even by idomeni standards, and we have no diplomatic bludgeon with which to compel her to cease and desist."

"Meva can be a pain in the ass." Jani ignored Scriabin's just audible, "Pot. Kettle. Black," and Niall's arched brow. "But the concepts of trial and conspiracy and culpability don't apply here. Cèel would never stand trial as we know it. The only penalty for a crime like assassination is the same we've seen before with the Laum—another sect ascends to *rau*, and the sect that had been in power is obliterated. That blanket condemnation doesn't apply here. We're only interested in Cèel. We're blazing a new trail."

"Is this your way of telling us to trust Meva?" Niall's voice took on an avuncular lilt, as it sometimes did when they spoke in private. "You don't like her, but you trust her?"

"The two aren't always mutually exclusive." Jani took a deep breath. "Why don't we ask her to meet with us so we can discuss this?"

Meva was contacted. She proved very eager to arrange a meeting, as there were several things on her private agenda that she felt needed an airing.

"Priest-in-training, you call yourself. *Hah.* You do not even wear your overrobe. The greatest ceremony in which a priest can participate, the transport of a soul. And you do not even wear your overrobe!" Meva had taken charge of the chair in front of Niall's desk. She still wore the same conservative clothing, including overrobe, that she had during the procession, but the overall effect had acquired a rumpled aspect. Some hair had escaped the tight braiding of her breeder's fringe, sticking out at odd angles. A few of the beads that decorated the braid ends had gone missing as well.

She looks like she got caught in a wind tunnel. Jani stood against the near wall, arms folded. Imagined finding Meva trapped in such a device and hitting the activation pad herself. "I didn't want to attract attention." She ignored Ulanova's mutter.

"You are a priest, *priest*. We are that which we are. To hide such is not even anathema. It is simply stupid." Meva sat back and fixed her attention on Scriabin, who had abandoned the seat next to his aunt for a chair next to Niall's desk. "As for my petition, why should I withdraw it? I wish to speak with Rilas. If I cannot do so, a bornsect dominant may do so in my stead. Aden nìRau Wuntoi proved most agreeable to my request, and truly."

"Well, he would, wouldn't he?" Scriabin picked his nails, which over the intervening hours had crossed the border from neat to ragged edged. "It's in his interest to keep Cèel off balance."

"It is in all our interests to keep Cèel off balance, and truly, Minister."

"Yes, but at the same time, ná Meva, it is still taken for granted that a human assassinated ní Tsecha. If Rilas vanishes, never to be found, humans lose their last best chance to prove that one of theirs did not commit that crime." Scriabin's face darkened, as though the conversation dredged up images of that day. As though they replayed in his mind. As though he wanted them to stop and knew they never would. "No one will know the truth."

Meva's expression softened, a little. She sat up straighter, her voice lightening. "The gods know, Minister."

Jani read the answer to that in Scriabin's eyes. *Your gods aren't our gods, Meva.* They didn't affect elections. Didn't quell colonial unrest, or allay the suspicions of Haárin who had lost docks and goods and ships to bombings, followed by their dearest priest.

Then there's the Capria. Meva's gods didn't affect a damned thing where that was concerned.

"Tomorrow, much will be decided." Meva bared her teeth. "Kièrshia will confront Cèel with Tsecha's assassination. She may demand of him then that we be allowed to question Rilas."

Jani fielded the expressions of alarm that focused on her. "That is why I came along, remember? To officially inform Cèel that Tsecha had been assassinated."

"That was when we felt no doubt whatsoever that a humanish had committed the crime." Scriabin picked his nails with renewed vigor. "Now we have doubt, and given our delicate position here, we're not really in the position where we can accuse our host of planning the murder of his most vocal critic."

"Why not?" Meva didn't raise her right hand to chest height and curve it, but let her voice carry the question. "Off balance was the term you used, Minister. To keep Cèel off balance is the only way to drive forward that which is to be."

Scriabin and Niall glanced at one another, a library's worth of enclave evacuation plans transferred in one look, their likely failure in the next. "I think that tomorrow," Scriabin said, eyes still on Niall, "we make our appearance. We swallow whatever insults, whatever threats, Cèel flings at us. And we bide our time, and continue the search for nìaRauta Rilas, for any evidence that Cèel planned Tsecha's assassination. When we have the facts, then, and only then, do we move." He finally looked at Meva. "Do I have your pledge, ná Meva, that you will not do anything to escalate the tensions between Cèel and the Commonwealth?"

Everyone held their breath as Meva sat silent, meeting Scriabin's concern with a bland gaze and an air that Jani remembered all too well.

I could talk to Tsecha until I couldn't talk anymore. And he would still do what he planned, because he was right and she was wrong and any discussion of the matter was simply an irritating way to pass time. *I told him that his treatises would anger Cèel.* The signal time in her life when she would have enjoyed being wrong.

"I will do nothing to irritate Cèel, Minister," Meva said finally.

Niall nodded. Scriabin closed his eyes. Even Ulanova reacted, her shoulders sagging as though tension seeped away.

Then Jani looked to the back of the room, where Lucien sat. Once more in the shadow. Once more, apparently forgotten. He stared back, eyes narrowed, bullshit detector cranked up to the most sensitive setting. *Perhaps they believe her,* the look seemed to say. *I sure as hell don't.*

Meva stood. "Now that you have forced pledges from me, I must return to the enclave. Early evening sacrament approaches, and I believe and truly that there might be cake." She ignored the assorted farewells and thank-yous, her eyes meeting Jani's as she turned and walked to the door.

"I'll walk you to your skimmer, ná Meva." Jani pushed off the wall and followed after her. "So you can yell at me some more."

"I can never yell at you enough, ná Kièrshia." Meva waited in the doorway for Jani to catch her up, and together they walked down the embassy corridor to the entry.

"You lied to Scriabin." Jani lowered her voice as one of the guards emerged from her office to open the door for them.

"I told him that which I will do, which is nothing." Meva shrugged. "You will do that which you will do. Whether it is that which we discussed in Thalassa, or something else which I do not know, you will do it."

As they approached Meva's skimmer, the driver-side gullwing swept up and Dathim emerged. "Did you yell at her for forgetting her overrobe, Meva?"

"Yes, Dathim. But I do not know, and truly, whether it mattered. Whether it had any effect." Meva stood aside while Dathim raised her door, then pushed away his hand as he attempted to help her into the cabin. "Tomorrow, Kièrshia."

"Tomorrow," Dathim echoed as he slammed the door, then circled the vehicle and inserted his formidable frame into the driver's cockpit.

"Enjoy your cake." Jani raised a hand in farewell, and received a flicker of hazard lights in reply. Turned, and found Niall standing at the top of the steps, watching her.

"Well, that was interesting." He sat on the top step and dug out his 'sticks. "Think Scriabin made any inroads?"

"She said she wouldn't do anything to upset Cèel. I think we're stuck with taking her at her word." Jani sat down beside him. Dusk was just beginning to fall, the undersides of the clouds purpling and the sky fading. *Rauta Shèràa sunsets.* She'd enjoyed them at one time, when they didn't carry with them the promise of worse days ahead.

"How are you doing?" Niall leaned back on his elbows, 'stick dangling from his lips, releasing puffs of smoke with each word.

I have never felt more lost, more helpless. More restless. I have never come closer to regretting my life. Jani whittled the words down to a shrug. "I was about to ask you the same question."

Niall sat up straight and wiped off the elbows of his tunic. "Have you been to the base?" He waited until she shook her head. "It's completely different in appearance—new buildings, new skimtrack layout. But the square meterage is the same, so if you remember where things used to be, you can still . . . figure out where . . ." He pinched the end of the 'stick, then broke it in half. "There's a certain area I avoid, let's put it that way. Otherwise, it's all just bunky." He flipped the halves one by one into a nearby planter. "You?"

"I haven't tried to sleep yet." Jani watched a trio of swallow-like birds flit silently across the skimway and vanish into the trees. "I feel as though it all happened yesterday, that I've only been gone a moment." She savored the weaker warmth of late afternoon sun. "I don't know what's going to happen."

"Pretty standard with you, isn't it, gel?" Niall tried to grin and failed. "We're as ready as we can be. Now all we can do is wait. Always the fun part."

"Yeah." Jani stood, swept grit from the seat of her trousers. "You going to the reception?"

"Wouldn't miss it." Niall stood, stretched. "Probably be the last party we have around here for a while."

Rilas tried to sleep, but the words of Ansu's suborn returned, again and again—

And then she proceeded through the concourse, nìaRauta, after ní Tsecha's reliquary . . . and so many waited for her . . . and she spoke by the river of ní Tsecha . . . and the Haárin listened, and laughed . . .

—and again and again.

It seemed as though she had spent an entire season in this room, in this bed, but when she stopped to count the number of sacraments, the times Ansu had visited, she realized that only two sun cycles had passed. *They have drugged me.* She suspected such after the first cycle had passed, when she slept longer than she ever had. Until after sunrise the next day, which was something she never did.

They will keep me here until the humanish leave. Even though she would have pledged to nìRau Cèel to remain silent, to leave Rauta Shèràa, to travel to the islands of the Dahoumn and remain there until she grew most old.

I came to you freely.

But such did not seem to matter to nìRau Cèel, because the anathema was here, and the Haárin followed her, and listened when she spoke of the outcast Tsecha.

Rilas opened her eyes to find Ansu standing over her.

"You are awake, nìaRauta?" The physician-priest stepped back from the bed and crossed an arm over her chest in alarm.

"You are surprised at such, Ansu?" Rilas sensed the female's dismay at such casual address. "You are most as your most esteemed patient, Ansu. You greatly prefer the formalities."

"Such are godly behaviors, Imea nìaRauta Rilas." Ansu stressed the full form of Rilas's name as a form of scolding. "We should all strive to follow such at all times." She lowered the rail on one side of the bed just as the door opened and a suborn entered pushing a skimchair. "Now, we shall go outside for a short while, because it is a godly day, and truly." Ansu took Rilas by the arm and pulled her until she sat up. "The warmth will enliven you."

The withholding of your drugs would enliven me. Rilas tasted the unseemly sourness that spread over her tongue and wondered what Ansu had given her. Not soma, for she did not feel ill in the pit of her soul. Instead there was exhaustion, and the inability to concentrate, and a weakness in her limbs. She tried to sit up, to move onto the chair as Ansu bade. But her knees buckled and her heart fluttered and even the suborn wondered at her growing weakness as he pushed her chair onto the veranda, and the clear sky, and the godly sun.

"You shall drink this, nìaRauta Rilas." Ansu poured liquid from a flask she carried into a small cup. "It is a Sìah concoction which will enliven you, and truly."

"Thanks to the gods for such, nìaRauta Ansu." Rilas watched as Ansu's shoulders lost their slight curve of displeasure, and knew what she had to do from this point on. Speak as one who would cooperate, even as she behaved as she had to in order to regain her strength and save her life.

Rilas held the cup to her lips, allowed the barest touch of pale brown liquid to skin. Then she waited until Ansu had turned her back and tipped the cup, spilling the liquid to the ground.

—

CHAPTER 29

Mako tipped the last of the wine into his glass, then crooked his finger at the steward, who removed the empty bottle and set another, already opened, in its place. No decanting. No sniffing or pondering the bouquet or the origin of the grapes. The first order of the evening was to get just drunk enough, and Hiroshi Mako was already halfway to goal.

Guests sat at a scattering of tables that had been set out in the garden. John and Val arrived together, but adjourned to opposite sides, Val sitting with Ulanova and her coterie and John opting for the Service table at which Niall, Burkett, and Mako held court. Lucien, who had been sitting there, rose as soon as John sat down, and walked from table to table, chatting and cracking socially acceptable jokes while looking for a place to land.

Jani watched it all shake out from her suite window. Wished she had the option of a good drunk. A night with Lucien in an actual bed. A chance to forget. The tension permeated the air like the scent of the bay, infiltrated her every thought. *What do you expect me to do, Meva?* What could she do to make things better? How could she keep from making things worse? *And Meva's not helping. "Do that which you do."* Which was what, exactly? Breathe? Yell? Shoot someone?

Jani watched the dinner seating settle out. Watched Mako empty the latest bottle into John's glass, then call for another.

Offered a prayer to Ganesh, checked herself one last time in the mirror, and headed downstairs.

* * *

"Jani, get over here!"

Jani abandoned the tiny two-chair table in a darkened corner near the stone wall and braved the walk through the gantlet to join an old friend beneath the trees.

"It's so good to see you!" Brigadier General Frances Hals threw her arms around her and hugged her hard enough to hurt, then pushed her down into the chair next to her. "Cal Burkett has locked me and my staff in the embassy basement for the duration. We're prepping paper for treaties and agreements, and hoping like hell that some of them get signed." She was a short, compact woman of middle years, dark of hair and medium complected, a New Indiesian who had worked her way up the documents ranks to become Service Diplomatic's strong right hand.

"He didn't tell me you were here." Jani pointed to the star adorning the collar of the woman's white tunic. "About time."

Frances touched the designator and her face lit. "Thanks." Then her expression clouded. "I'm surprised that poor man can still remember his name, truth be told. This place is a pressure cooker." She looked to her other dinner partner, and some of the animation returned. "Captain Pascal was giving me his eyewitness account of what happened at the riverwalk. My God."

Guess you finally found a place to land. Jani shot Lucien a *shut up* look, which he fielded with an arched brow and a *Who, me?* shrug. "It was an experience." She gave the wine bottle a last look of longing before taking a lemon wedge from the appetizer tray and squeezing it into her iced water, and was trying to think of something innocuous to talk about when a blocky shadow fell across their table.

"Is there room for another?" Scriabin sat before anyone could reply. "To spend one meal not discussing politics would seem like a month's vacation at this point, wouldn't it?" The ground rules thus set, he proceeded to hold forth on everything from wine to olives to the best places in Chicago to buy blintzes and handmade shirts, with occasional interjections from Lucien and encouraging noises from Frances.

Wait staff served and cleared, served and cleared. A salad. Soup. Some sort of fish. All struck Jani's hybrid palate as bland in the extreme, but she ate because she had to and because the company was good and she could feel herself relax even as the night wore on and the next day drew nearer.

Then someone suggested music, and someone else rolled out a synth box, and soon the strains of some band or other sounded.

Then Val took over, pushing tables out of the way and pulling a feebly protesting Ulanova onto the floor. A few more couples followed. Word spread, and soon people wandered over from the base and the working part of the embassy, drawn by the open bar and the music and the chance to let off steam that had been building for months.

"Ma'am?" Lucien stood and offered Frances his best recruiting poster smile. "Care to take a turn?"

Frances drank him in, her eyes alight with the effects of the wine and appreciation of blinding male beauty. "Don't ever tell my husband," she whispered to Jani as she took Lucien's hand and followed him onto the floor.

Scriabin watched them for a time and shook his head. "He is an utter waste of talent and training, but I don't know a minister in Chicago who wouldn't kill for ten percent of his charm." He turned back to Jani, arms folded across his barrel chest. "I know you better than you think, you know." He sat back, crossed his legs ankle to knee. "I remember the uproar when my uncle Acton learned that his boy Evan had dropped the family standard and hooked up with a colonial girlfriend. There the dear scion was, in the alien wilds of Rauta Shèràa, ignoring all attempts at communication. Acton had already earmarked my cousin Alyssa for him, and you did not cross Acton van Reuter once he'd made up his mind." Grey eyes dulled. "My mother tried to play peacemaker. 'Let the boy have his fun,' she said. I think that deep down, she knew what Evan was, and she didn't want him for Alyssa. Not that Alyssa was any prize, but even she didn't deserve Evan. But mother's efforts came to naught, to the regret of many." He picked up a knife and speared a wedge of cheese from the dessert platter. "I'm sorry for all that happened. I would have paid a great deal for the opportunity to see you take on the old Hawk."

Jani looked around the garden. The noise level had ramped up, taken on an edge. Laughter had grown too shrill. There would be at least one fistfight before it ended. Affairs broken and begun. She'd attended enough parties with Evan to know the signs, had even thrown a few herself under his guidance. *He lived for this.* Oblivion achieved in noise and seen through the bottom of a glass. Then came Knevçet Shèràa, and that final, brutal cleaving. "I'm sorry that the eradication of the Twelfth Rover Corps and the deaths of a score of good Spacers came between you and this entertainment."

Scriabin stilled, knife held upright and cheese beneath his

nose for an assessing sniff. Then he grinned, and bit. "See? That quality of moral anger, tossed out as an afterthought. I'd have paid much. Not sure if you would've won, mind. At least not in the long run. Not many did who possessed a ghost of a conscience." He chewed thoughtfully, then speared a slice of apple and commenced the same examination he'd given the cheese. "Did you love Evan?"

Jani looked to the Rauta Shèràa sky for respite, but the light from the party lanterns overwhelmed the stars. "Worse than that. I trusted him."

Scriabin winced. "I am sorry." He set the apple aside, put down the knife. "You will have to forgive my aunt her outbursts. She senses this is her last chance to regain former glory, and she sees it slipping away."

Jani looked past Scriabin to the dance floor, where Ulanova still partnered with Val. She smiled brightly at his every joke and comment, but every so often her gaze would drift to Lucien and sharpen. "Did you volunteer to act as her keeper, or did you draw the short straw at a Family meeting?"

Scriabin ignored the question, shifting his chair so he could watch Mako and Niall, who still sat with John and talked, expressions serious and tones low. "Roshi is worried about what tomorrow may bring, as are we all. You have my word that if the worst happens, I will do all in my power to protect Thalassa."

"Can you do anything for Niall?" Jani watched Niall shake his head at something John said. They could have been arguing politics, or opera, or interpretations of *Hamlet.* "They'd call it treason. They'd execute him."

"What do you think are my chances of dragging him from Roshi's side, if it comes to that?" Scriabin sighed. "I would do my best for them all, but they would have to help." He allowed a knowing grin. "Besides, Hiroshi Mako is many things, but suicidal isn't one of them." He rose just as Lucien and Frances returned to the table. "Until tomorrow, ná Jani. Ná Kièrshia. She who tells stories to Haárin by the river." He bowed to Jani and Frances in turn, ignored Lucien, and strode back inside the embassy.

"I think that's supposed to be a hint." Frances glanced at her timepiece and sighed. "When the ministers start decamping, that's the sign that a career-minded officer needs to take to her bed."

"Or someone's bed, at any rate." Lucien didn't sully the remark with a nudge or a wink. He simply left it to hang in the air, to be ignored or picked up as the listener saw fit. "I need to get going as well. Guess who pulled desk officer duty? Three guesses. First two don't count." He bowed to Frances, then leaned down and kissed Jani with all the gentle, patient promise he had set aside earlier in the day.

"God help me, Jani Kilian." Frances watched Lucien walk across the floor and disappear into the embassy maw. "How do you keep your head straight with him around?"

Jani felt a tingle along the side of her face, and looked toward Mako's table to find John watching her. "Sometimes I don't."

"Do tell." Frances checked her timepiece again. "And after all this is over, you will tell. When we have some time to breathe."

Jani hesitated. Then she stood and hugged Frances tightly. "Thank you."

Frances sniffed. "We all do what we have to, girl." Her voice emerged husky, and she covered it with a cough. "Get a good night's sleep."

After Frances left, Jani sat down again, tired and worried, yet loath to leave the music and the sounds of other people having fun. She turned over her unused wineglass and filled it. Took a long drink, tasted the bland sourness of watery grape juice, and pushed the rest aside.

"John said that he has to work on something that would give hybrids a chance to get in on the fun."

Jani smiled as Val sat down next to her. "Hello."

"I've been hearing the most amazing stories about you." Val studied her, then shook his head. "Or perhaps I shouldn't be amazed anymore." He wore one of her favorite evening suits, a rich forest shade that brought out the green in his eyes.

"Those stories may not seem so amazing after tomorrow." Jani took a sip of lemon water to strip the wine taste from her tongue. "We'll see."

Val watched her for a time, then looked toward the dance floor. "Niall said that this party has a Last Days of Empire edge to it. Mako told him to pull his head out of his ass for five minutes and loosen up, but he was three sheets to the wind at that point. I don't think he meant it."

"Did Niall have anything to drink?"

"Not a drop." Val made a point of studying his hands. "How are you?"

"Business as usual. Everyone's pick for Diplomat of the Year." Jani looked to the dancers again to find John intertwined with a lissome redhead in civilian wear. *And so it goes.* "You?"

A breeze sent the lanterns rocking. As Val watched his business partner dance, the light played across his face, accenting the lines and hollows. "He's sorry, you know." He picked up a fork and dragged it across the table, leaving grooves in the cloth. "He wishes he could take it back, what he said at Guernsey Station, but he doesn't know how."

"And so he has Valentin Parini, his eternal apologist, stop by to feel things out while he feels up the embassy staff." Jani laughed a little too long, then forced herself quiet. "It's over, Val. Your services as peacemaker are no longer required. Let it be."

Val shifted as though he sat on a tack. "I'm sorry." He looked toward the floor again, and fixed on a sharp lieutenant with black hair and a crooked smile.

"I can look after myself, you know." Jani smiled as Val blushed. "Go have fun." She squeezed his hand as he kissed her cheek, then left her to go hunting.

Ulanova had long since departed. Val laid claim to his lieutenant and escorted him to Mako's table, the panicked expression on the young man's face a sight for the ages.

Jani sat, and listened to the laughter and the shouts and the music, to the growing disquiet that pushed all else aside. Then she rose and went on a hunt of her own.

Jani followed Ulanova's aide into a sitting room. Left to her own devices, she paced the perimeter, studying the framed paintings and wondering why the peach silk walls didn't make her feel warmer. Paced some more. Studied more brush strokes and compared the quality of frame gilding. She expected Ulanova to make her wait, and wasn't disappointed. She was well into her fourth detailed examination of a Russian provincial landscape when she heard the door open.

"What do you want?" Ulanova remained in the entry, one hand gripping the jamb. She had exchanged her severe trouser suit for a flowing crimson skirt and white wrapshirt, and had freshened her hair and makeup.

If we were still in Chicago, I'd guess dinner on Gaetan's patio. Or the opera, or some other formal occasion. Of which there were damn few to be had in the humanish enclave in Rauta Shèràa. "I don't want to talk to you any more than you want to listen to me, so I'll be brief. If you back out of this and leave them to twist, I will dredge up every crime you ever committed, every misstep you ever took, and hang you with them."

Ulanova's face flushed. "You have nothing."

"Only experience." Jani smiled. "And a very good source of information." She hesitated as she wondered if she could possibly be wrong, and then realized that it had been as obvious as the sky overhead. "Could I please talk to the desk officer, ma'am?" she asked in her best imitation of a new recruit. "I understand he's here."

Ulanova stared. Then the first flicker of triumph brightened her eyes and she smiled. "Darling?" When nothing happened, her voice took on an edge. "I don't think there's any point, I really don't."

Another moment of stillness. Then Lucien emerged from the next room. He'd loosened his tunic collar and held a glass of wine.

Jani started to laugh. *Like a cat, from house to house to house—* She forced herself calm. "I'd like to talk to him, please."

Ulanova headed for the security call pad. "Go to hell."

"Excellency." Jani held out a hand. Heard her papa's Celtic lilt in her voice and wondered how she'd managed to dredge it up. "Even the condemned get a final wish granted."

Ulanova stopped and stared, mistrust and puzzlement warring on the narrow battleground of her face. Then she smiled again, because that was what her kind did when they felt they'd won. "Ten minutes, darling." She waved a heavily ringed hand in Lucien's general direction and swept into the adjoining room.

"Got that, darling?" Jani walked up to Lucien and clapped her hands under his nose, took what pleasure she could in his flinch. "Ten minutes." She backed away before she caught a glass of wine in her face. "How did she foist you off on Mako? That's what I want to know."

"Mako trusts Scriabin to keep her in line." Lucien's voice emerged low and tight. "Taking me on was part of the deal they devised to shut her up."

Jani leaned against a chair. Fatigue had caught up with her, and her knees felt weak. Or maybe it was just self-disgust, and growing anger too great to control. "What she does to Niall, I do to you. If he's arrested, I'll see you're arrested. If he's condemned, I'll do all I can to ensure that you take his place."

Lucien stared into his glass, then set it down on a table so hard that it splashed. "You're bluffing."

"You think I wouldn't trade you for Niall?" Jani saw his eyes narrow and knew that he'd guessed her answer.

"You don't have anything negotiable." Lucien shook his head. "No information to offer in exchange."

"But you told me so much when we lived in Chicago." Jani shrugged. "When I had time on my hands, I even confirmed some of it."

Lucien took a lid off a candy dish, then set it back in place with a clatter. "I do have safeguards in place."

"To use against me?" Jani caught the slight twitch of his head. "Oh, you don't, do you? You actually trusted me. That's sweet. Maybe you really do love me after all." She jerked her chin toward the adjoining room, where no doubt Ulanova listened with clenched teeth. "Your girlfriend's waiting. Time to drop those well-tailored trousers and earn your keep." She headed for the door. Heard the footsteps behind her and tried to dodge, but Lucien was younger and faster and pissed off to boot. He grabbed her arm and spun her around, ducking out of the way as she swung her fist, then pushing her against the wall with all the force he hadn't spent on her earlier.

Jani made ready to propel off the wall. Brought her fist up once more. Felt the idomeni in her whisper for blood. Then her eyes met Lucien's and she saw how his shone. How bright his face, like a young boy's, his breathing hard and fast.

He took a step toward her, then hesitated. "I can be out of here in an hour." His voice had dropped to a whisper. "Two at the most."

As though someone flipped a switch, Jani felt her own heart slow, her head clear. "You've always played both sides." She straightened her skewed tunic. "You always told me that you did me more good than harm, that you were my insider, but it was all just talk. You were just covering your ass. Shoring up your fallback. Making sure you'd have a soft place to land no matter what happened. No matter who won. You never risked anything you couldn't afford to lose. People, idomeni, humanish, and hybrid are in danger for their lives now. Risking everything to change worlds. You don't deserve to breathe the same air." She walked to the door, twisted the handle so the workings screeched, and shouldered through the gap into the corridor.

"Is that supposed to hurt me? Make me regret my wasted life?" Lucien followed her into the hall. "I'm not an idiot! Do you hear me? I'm not one of your damned fools!"

Jani pushed past the door into the stairwell, down the stairs and through a safety door into the night. Music still sounded from the garden. Voices and laughter. Noise. Nothing but noise.

CHAPTER 30

Rilas knew that Cèel had ordered Ansu to kill her. Three times that day, Ansu had brought her the same drink as before, the pale brown brew that was supposed to enliven her. She assumed that she should still pretend to feel tired, that such would be Ansu's excuse to drug her further. *Then when I am too lethargic, they will drown me, or send me downstairs.* A natural death. An accident.

They should have sent another such as me to perform this task. It was an insult to treat the one who had killed Tsecha in such a way as this. Rilas could hear Caith's laughter in the night as she pondered the injustice.

"Glories of this night to you, nìaRauta Rilas." Ansu entered the room bearing the tray that held the pale brown poison. "I trust you enjoyed your time outside and you are no longer as tired?"

"You ask me the same thing each time you visit, Ansu, and each time my answer is the same." Rilas raised an arm, let it fall. "I still am most tired. I am this way because you seek to poison me."

"Poison?" Ansu set down the tray on a table, took the top off the decanter and poured. "No, nìaRauta, this is a tea brewed from blessed leaves . . ."

Rilas slipped out of the bed. Ansu thought her drugged, and would not expect rapid movement. Would not expect her to behave as she had been trained. She crept across the floor, bare feet silent on the tile. Closed in behind Ansu. Raised her hand, then brought it down where neck met shoulder, as she had with the humanish male.

Ansu fell just as hard. Twitched a little more. Died just as quickly.

Rilas stripped off the physician-priest's clothing, working quickly in case bladder or bowels released and soiled them. Overrobe first, the most important thing, followed by shirt and trousers. Boots.

That unseemly task completed, she dragged Ansu's body to the bed and hoisted it atop. Covered it, making sure to turn her face from the door and tuck the covering high enough to obscure all aspects of her appearance.

Rilas then straightened the overrobe, picked up the tray and departed the room. Few idomeni walked the corridor, and none regarded her in any way. She set the tray upon a rack designed for such things and walked to the entry. Her heart beat harder as the door opened and she passed outside, felt the blessed night air in her face.

I will go to the Trade Board. She kept many things in her workroom there. Things given her by Cèel, and other things that he would not expect her to have.

The streets between the hospital and the Trade Board were much as they always were, filled with merchants and brokers, even in the middle of the night. None noticed her, for which she gave thanks, as the coarser Haárin traders were known for stopping physician-priests in the street and requesting remedies for various ailments.

She entered the Trade Board, passed from corridor to stairway to corridor, ever upward until she reached the last ring of workrooms at the base of the dome. She had never told anyone of this place. The door operated by a simple touchlock that was not connected to the board array, which meant that no one knew when she entered or departed. She had originally taken the workroom in order to practice secrecy, the possession of knowledge known to her and her alone. As the time passed and she grew more familiar with the concept, she began to store things in the room as well. Weapons. Documents. Clothing. Remains from previous tasks that she had been ordered to destroy but had not.

She kept them as secrets instead.

Rilas unlocked the door. Opened it and activated the illumination to a low level. Stepped over boxes and crates until she came to that which she sought.

The projectile rifle, similar to the one that she had used to assassinate Tsecha, lay in pieces. She assembled it quickly, then removed the packet of ammunition from the bottom of the crate and inserted one cartridge into place. Took the secondary from its container and activated it, confirming that it communicated with the sight mech.

Then she set the weapons aside and lay on the floor. When morning came, she would show Cèel how wrong he had been to mistrust her. How ungodly it was to have treated her as he did.

I did as you bade. She closed her eyes. *I would have come to you freely.* Now such did not matter. Whether he wished her to or not, she would come to him all the same.

They gathered in the embassy drive at the base time of oh-eight, which on this day fell approximately one hour after early morning sacrament.

Jani smoothed the front of her overrobe, a needless exercise that spoke to nerves more than wrinkled cloth.

"Good morning." Scriabin left Lucien and Ulanova by their triple-length and strode over to her, his the clear-eyed gaze of a Family politician who had learned long ago how to pace himself. "Slept well, I trust?"

"Well enough." Jani turned her back on Lucien and forced a smile.

"We've heard word of a little bit of a dust-up around Temple, but it isn't expected to interfere with the conclave." Scriabin pulled out a set of sunshields from a small slingbag and donned them. "We will leave in ten minutes or so."

"I guess that means all our drivers can still drive?" Niall drew alongside Jani and glared at her over the top of his sunshields. "You haven't delivered any more sermons, have you?"

"It wasn't a sermon." Jani thought she sounded calm enough, but Niall and Scriabin shot each other looks that she read as easily as though she could see their eyes through the shields.

"We'll be going in Roshi's skim. I'll leave my shooter there since I can't carry it into the damned place." Niall started toward the starred triple-length, beckoning Jani to follow. "Everything OK, gel?" he asked when they moved out of Scriabin's earshot.

Jani looked to the sky, still streaked with early morning cloud. "The time is out of joint."

"Oh bloody hell. When you start tossing the quotations around, it's all over but the last rites." Niall pulled a case out of his trouser pocket. "Here." He handed Jani a new ear bug. "Because I have a feeling that you lost the last one."

"Can't use it." Jani tried to hand it back to him. "I need water to prep it."

"Fountain right over there." Niall led her to a small grassy side yard where a brass dish burbled merrily away. "If you have trouble inserting it, I'll be happy to find you a plunger." He stood silent guard as she prepped and inserted the bug, then whistled a verse of the Service anthem as he led her to Roshi's skimmer.

The cavalcade departed the embassy, sweeping through the enclave at speed, then slowing to a grind as they merged with the inevitability of well-ordered idomeni traffic. By the time they reached the entry to the Council enclave, Feyó and Meva had already arrived. They stood next to their skimmer, bracketed by Dathim and Galas.

"Something has happened." Feyó looked toward the Council entrance, where a greater than normal number of brown-garbed security guards had arrayed themselves. "But no one will tell us. Security dominants only stare when we speak to them. It is most unseemly."

Meva turned and started toward the Council entry's triple-wide doorway, beckoning for Jani walk with her. "Feyó told me that she again saw ní Tsecha during sleep. He bared his teeth. I wish I could have such dreams. Such a sight I used to see each day and did not think of it. Now I think of it constantly, and wish I could see it again." She quickened her step so she could walk next to Jani, a blip in the steady state of idomeni hierarchical protocols. "I viewed images of you speaking of him to the Haárin. Such was a good thing, and truly." She touched the sleeve of Jani's overrobe. "Do you know that which you will say?"

Jani shook her head. "No idea."

Meva bared her teeth. "Good. If you do not know, then Cèel cannot possibly guess, which means he cannot prepare."

They continued along the walkway, up the steps and through the entry, side by side.

Rilas awoke. Removed Ansu's clothing and donned the rough garb of a building worker, wrapping the braids of her breeder's fringe in a length of cloth and binding them to her head so she would look as a shorn-headed Haárin. Packed the ammunition and the secondary in a worker's slingbag, then broke down the rifle and packed that as well. Opened the workroom door and looked both ways. She heard nothing, saw no one. The workrooms at the base of the dome were not of the best, and not many used them. She was alone, of that she felt most sure.

She walked down the corridor to the stairway and down, down

and down to the street. Busy as always in the morning, both born-sect and Haárin, workers and brokers and merchants, entering and leaving. She blended with them, as she had been taught.

A pair of brown-garbed security suborns walked past her. She thought nothing of such—Council and Temple lay near and many security labored there.

Then she saw another pair, and another, and knew. That Ansu's body had been found and Cèel now searched for her. She bared her teeth at the thought. *You did not wish to see me, nìRau, but now you wish to see me a great deal.*

She walked as a tired worker, her gait plodding, and headed north toward the Haárin enclave. She saw fewer security suborns as she neared the place, which she expected. Haárin took charge of their own. They also did not work well with Cèel's security, who demanded much and provided little. She doubted, and truly, that they knew anything of the search for her.

She approached the enclave entry. Walked past the gate sentry, who did not look up as she passed. Down the first lane of houses, in search of one that was empty.

A small house, with a window that faced the bay.

All she needed was a window. The secondary would do the rest.

She set the bag upon the floor. Assembled the rifle and inserted the ammunition cartridge. Activated the secondary and loosed it, watched it flit upward until it vanished. Activated the sight mech and waited for the blinking green indicating that the two had inter-faced.

Rested the rifle barrel within the window corner. Looked through the sight mech and saw the Council grounds.

Click

The line of windows that faced the gardens.

Click

Through the windows, into the Council chamber beyond.

Rilas curled around the rifle. Held it close.

Waited.

Jani entered the Council chamber. It was a multistoried space, the masonry cut by windows on the side facing the bay, tiered seating lining the other three walls.

Tsecha brought me here once. He had still been bornsect in that time before the war, had still used his born name of Nema. How that name had sounded along the corridors when the other

Council members realized that the propitiator of the Vynshà had brought one of his humanish inside the blessed space.

At least it was not Temple, one of the councilors had said. That fact hadn't helped.

Jani matched the room she remembered with the room she stood in now. The same pale sand walls and tiled floors, the Sìah chandeliers and artwork of all the major bornsects. The bombs had missed it, a miracle, given the battering the Vynshà inflicted on the city before they entered it on that last night. The night the Laum lost the right to call themselves "rau." The night eighty-five percent of their bornsect population died. The Night of the Blade.

"It is most as it was," Meva said as she paused next to her. "Most as I recall." She stared out the window at the bay, then followed Feyó to the seating.

Jani looked to the entry on the other side of the chamber. First would come the line of suborns, lowliest first. Then the dominant aides, followed by the Sub-Oligarch and the Speaker to Colonies. Then would come Cèel.

Jani's heart tripped and slowed as the first of the suborns filed through the entry and the councilors walked to their seats and the humanish groups broke up and scattered to their preassigned positions. She walked toward the tiered seats where the propitiators gathered. *I accused his killers. I walked behind his reliquary.* Wore his rings, and his robe. Held his soul. *I have the right.*

Jani felt the stares, heard the questioning mutters, as she stepped over the lowest, highest rated, tier and on to the second. She triangulated according to her relationship with Tsecha, the size of Thalassa, and the status due to her Vynshàrau blood. The number of times she had fought in the circle. Given all that, the fourth row seemed fair. Three rows lower than Meva, who watched her silently. Not presuming much, but not giving anything away, either. Pushing just enough, as was her way.

"Kilian?"

Jani sat, then looked down toward the floor to find a flustered-looking Scriabin trying to lean over the seats to talk to her without falling over any agitated priests.

"What the . . . ?" He almost placed his hand over his mouth, but stopped in time and put it behind his back instead. "What are you doing?"

"This is my place, Your Excellency." Jani spread out her over-robe as she saw a few other propitiators had done, expanding her personal space a little more. "Given all I've done and what I am, it is an appropriate place, and truly." She bared her teeth. "Go sit down." She flicked a finger in the direction of Ulanova and the others, who stood in the middle of the floor and looked on in alarm.

"Do you know what the hell you're doing?" Scriabin's face reddened. "Do you?"

"I do that which I do, Your Excellency. I am that which I am." Jani folded her hands in her lap and turned her attention to the entry in time to see the Speaker to Colonies enter. "Go sit down."

"What the hell are you doing, gel?" Niall's voice in her ear.

Jani didn't reply, didn't hunt for Niall's face among the many. She ignored his intrusion as she ignored Scriabin's continued bids to get her attention, and waited.

Morden nìRau Cèel had always cut an imposing figure. A dour warrior who stood over two meters tall, dark as Vynshàrau but with the green eyes of Sìah. He had led the Vynshà armies and their Haárin cohorts during the final stages of the War of Vynshàrau Ascension, had spent the last weeks of that war in the hills that ringed Rauta Shèràa. First he'd directed the bombings that shattered half the city. Then, on that last night, he had ordered the Haárin to swarm over what remained, blades in hand, and slaughter the Laum who remained.

Such is what they do, what they had done for thousands of years. Such is how idomeni wage war. And the humanish side of Jani still reeled from the memory. Of the lines of Laum, standing in line as for bread or billets, their shirts open, waiting for the sword.

Cèel walked directly to his low seat in the front row of the Vynshàrau section, crossed his ankles and lowered to the floor. His status thus announced, he finally looked around the chamber. His gaze settled first on Feyó, who had taken a seat in another tier with other Sìah Haárin, then on Meva. He gestured to her, baring his teeth when she curved her shoulders in reply.

Then he looked toward the humanish seats, which had been scattered throughout the chamber with no rhyme or reason that Jani could discern.

Two reasons I can think of for that. She fussed with an overrobe cuff. *One is symbolic—dilute the hated humanish.* The other made tactical sense—split the enemy. Prevent them from conferring, comparing notes. Offering one another moral support. She watched Cèel as he continued to scan the seats, once, then again, then again. As though he searched for someone. His gaze moved over the propitiators' tiers and he stilled. Cocked his head.

Then his shoulders curved as though they cramped, and the voice that made John's sound like air through a tin whistle boomed.

"You dare! Anathema! Half-humanish thing!" High Vynshàrau, replete with gesture, curve of hand and twist of arm and neck, the click and clatter of translator headsets being jammed into place serving as background music.

Jani glanced at the headset that hung from a hook on the seat in front of her. Realized she didn't need it. The Vynshàrau sounded as Acadian French to her ears, a language of dreams, basic as breathing. *"I am that which I am and I sit where I will."* She pitched her voice low as a show of aggravation and lack of respect, but didn't curve her shoulders just yet. *"I killed Laumrau as they took sacrament, contaminated godly ceremony with humanish action. Humanish filth."* Her heart beat strong and her limbs felt as the air as rage that had built since Tsecha's death took hold. *"But I was humanish then. Such was my excuse."* She bared her teeth. *"What was yours, Morden nìRau Cèel? For killing ní Tsecha Egri as he stood upon a road, forsaking godly challenge and the cleansing act of war? What excuse had you to kill him secretly, in such a way that sickens even humanish?"* Finally, she let her shoulders curve, until her back twisted so she could barely see over the priest who sat in front of her. *"If I am anathema, what are you?"*

The inside of the Council chamber played across the sight mech. Rilas fixed on the edge of the dark head, the curve of neck that she knew as well as her own. Then Cèel moved back, beyond the scope of the secondary, the view blocked by a section of brick.

Rilas twitched the settings on the sight mech, forcing the secondary higher until it cleared the section of wall. If she had planned better, she would have stolen a hair from Cèel's head, a drop of his blood, and typed the secondary to him so it would sense him as the one made for Tsecha had sensed its target. *If I had planned . . . if I had known.* But she could not have known. Betrayal was, Cèel had taught her, a humanish failing.

She twitched the setting again. Again.

Cèel rose, his back a crippling curve, and started across the floor toward Jani.

"You think if you rise, you lose standing?" Jani stood, straightening her spine as much as she could. *"I can stand before you and still call you what you are."* She stepped over the bench,

then down to the next, then down to the floor as Cèel scrabbled toward her.

Rilas fixed on the dark head. Held her breath.
Pressed the charge-through.

Jani heard. A muffled bang, as though a bird struck a window.
Glass, clattering to the floor. A splash of blood.
A beat of silence. Then the humanish screams, the idomeni cries.
Security dominants surrounded Cèel, who pressed a hand to his face, blood seeping between his fingers. Humanish security herded their charges away from windows and idomeni leapt down from the tiered seats.
"Jan!" Niall ran to her. "Get over—" He grabbed her wrist and pulled her to the side near the main entry, where Scriabin and the others stood clustered.
"Who do you think fired that shot?" Jani tried to pull out of his grip, but he had her like a manacle and all she could do was follow.
Galas stood talking with Burkett, his hand locked around Feyó's wrist just as Niall's was around Jani's.
"Galas said that there was an unusual amount of activity on the Council security frequencies earlier this morning." Niall continued to herd Jani toward the wall. "He tried to eavesdrop, but he was blocked. Tried to tap an old source, but all he could get was that there was an accident at the Temple hospital. A physician-priest died in an accident."
"Who sends out hot and cold running security guards because of accidents? They were stacked two deep in front of the entry when we arrived." Jani gripped Niall's fingers with her free hand and tried to pry them open. "Look at Cèel."
Niall turned just as the male pulled a security dominant to one side, started talking in a manner stripped of gesture. "Jan, he's just been through an assassination attempt—"
"Those aren't the moves of an Oligarch who's just been shot at and is taking instruction from his security team. Those are the moves of a ringleader directing the show."
"He's a warrior, for chrissake."
"He knows who shot at him, and he's pretty sure where she is, and he's telling his security dominants where to find her." Jani tried to bend her arm to break Niall's hold, but he countered that

move as well. "They kept Rilas at the Temple hospital. She escaped. She killed a physician-priest in the process." She sensed others move close to her. Only Ulanova hung back, her bitterness like armor. "They know where she is and they're going to track her down and lock her up or kill her. We need to get to her first."

"Well where the hell is she?" Niall looked to the heavens. "In this whole damned city, where in hell?"

"She feels a closeness to Caith," said Galas, who now grappled with a squirming Meva. "Such was what the others on the ship stated when they were questioned at Guernsey."

"Caith's temple is north of here, the same direction as the shot came from." Jani smiled. "I know where it is."

"I'll take you." Lucien turned away from a grasping Ulanova and maneuvered next to Jani.

"We'll take her." Niall looked toward the main entry. "If they'll fuckin' let us out of here."

They moved toward the main entry, found it blocked by Haárin and humanish and the guards who'd herded them there.

"There's a side door." Jani reversed and hurried up a narrow corridor that ran alongside the chamber. "Tsecha and I once escaped through it when some councilors took exception to my presence."

"Can't imagine why that would have happened." Niall stepped in front of her. "I'm going first, just in case."

Jani fell in behind him. On the way, they passed a wall decorated, as most were in the place, with sets of blades, foursomes and pairs, arranged in squares or crossed like X's.

Jani took one of the shorter blades from its hook and slipped it into her belt, then followed Niall out the door.

CHAPTER 31

Rilas dropped the rifle, left it where it fell. Grabbed her bag. Ran. Out of the house, into the street. She had never missed a target. Never.

The blessed sun—she felt its heat, even as it failed to warm. Her heart pounded and her hands felt as though she had washed them in snow. *He will kill me now.* Cèel knew she had killed Ansu, knew she sought to kill him.

She slowed as she came upon Haárin. Rough clothes, as bright in color as birds and insects. Ungodly. They watched her pass, eyes on her face. She turned away.

But not in time.

"You!" An elder male strode after her. *"Tileworker!"* He waved for her to approach, a humanish gesture that made no sense, relayed no mood or status of request. He could ask her anything. She would not know what to expect until he did so.

"My friend and I—" He waved toward another male, who sat on a chair on front of a house, and bared his teeth when she looked toward him. "—we have a wager. I say that all tileworkers use hand-axes instead of short picks. He says otherwise. We are stopping every tileworker we see to ask them, axe or pick."

Rilas forced a humanish shrug. "Hand-axe," she said, and turned to go.

"No." The elder male stepped in front of her, blocking her path. "You must show us."

They claimed a compact two-door from one of the embassy drivers. Stopped by Roshi's skimmer so Niall and Lucien could recover their weapons, and sped through the Council gate just as it closed. Jani drove because she knew the city best.

"Where are you going?" Niall flinched as they coursed down an alley that allowed only a hand span's clearance on either side.

"Caith's temple." She zipped along a tight roundabout, causing the skimmer to tip up on its side and drawing mutters from the rear of the vehicle.

"You'll lose contact with the skimtrack." Lucien braced his hands on the cabin wall and his seat. "This isn't a damned sports skimmer."

"I spotted at least twenty-five security folk headed into the Trade Board as we passed." Niall ignited a 'stick. "Do they think she shot at Cèel from there?"

"I doubt it." Jani slowed as the alleys grew even narrower, the buildings closer together, blocking the sun and making it seem at times as through she drove through a tunnel. "Her Nahin Sela identity was based there. I'm guessing that others were, too. Cèel is going to bottle up anyone who can identify her and shake loose as many records and other physical evidence as he can."

"So where does that leave us?" Niall sat forward, checking each alley and dead end. "If he destroys all evidence and captures the killer, what have we got?" He turned to her. "What are you going to do?"

Jani saw the tarnished silver dome in the distance, the temple of Caith. Kept driving, and said nothing. Touched her right ear, activated the ear bug, and heard the Vynshàrau spill into her head. "Cèel's security is using one of your streams."

Niall touched his ear. His brow arched. "They must think Rilas has the ability to eavesdrop on all of theirs, so they hijacked one of ours." He frowned. "You understand what they're saying?"

Jani nodded. "They think the shot came from the Haárin enclave." She paused, smiled. "They're headed toward Caith's temple. They're going to capture her there."

Niall unfastened the top of his shooter holster. "Let's go."

Rilas stood with her hand on the opening of her slingbag.

"You must show us—axe or pick." The elder male edged to one side or the other each time Rilas tried to walk around him. "You could say anything."

"Why would I do such? It is not godly."

"Hah. She speaks as a bornsect." The other male bared his teeth again. "The bornsect tilemasters use picks."

"Are you a bornsect?" The elder male tugged on Rilas's sleeve. "In clothes such as this? In an Haárin enclave?" He laughed, a guttural hacking sound.

"I do not have to show you what I use." Rilas pulled away as the elder male sought to grab her sleeve again. Broke into a run when he sought to chase her, and heard their jeering as she turned off that street and onto another.

Cèel knows where I run to. Rilas knew that bornsect security waited outside the Haárin enclave, that they patrolled the streets around the temples. She reached into the bag, gripped a shooter, held it fast.

Past the meeting house, the workrooms, the schools for the youngish. She drew near the enclave gate and quickened her pace.

"It's so goddamned dark here." Niall looked out at the claustrophobic press, the tarnished metalwork and dark woods and streets with barely enough room for one being to pass another. "Who lives here?"

"Those who serve Caith. Propitiators. Trainees. Temple maintenance." Jani eased the skimmer into an alley.

"This is not a search." Lucien watched the scene outside his skimmer window and shook his head. "They aren't cordoning off the streets. They aren't going house to house."

"I see bodies scurrying across rooftops." Jani pointed to a figure that vanished in the shadow of an overhang. "They're herding her as unobtrusively as they can. They know where she's going. We just need to get there first." She powered down the vehicle and opened her door.

"What are you doing?" Niall looked around. "This isn't Caith's temple."

"I need to slip through the net." Jani lifted the overrobe's draped shawl collar over her head like a hood, hiding her short hair and obscuring her face.

"Dammit, Jan." Niall pushed open his door and struggled out. "You can't meet her like this. She's desperate and she's armed." He circled around the front of the vehicle. "Jan?" He stopped, turned in one direction, then the other. "What the fuck—"

Jani backpedaled down an alley narrow as a knife slice, listened to the garbled mix of Vynshàrau and Niall's voice through the ear bug. Heard Lucien, and realized he wore a bug as well. *And he understands Vynshàrau.* But not as well as she did.

"*She ducked down that alley.*" Lucien's voice held resignation, anger. "*We'll never find her now.*"

"*We should've stopped her.*" Niall's voice now. "*Dammit.*" Sounds of him getting into the skimmer, slamming down the gullwing so hard that the sound echoed.

Jani crept down the alley. Found another. Another. Candlewax and wood oils. The damp that found a home in the dark and the shadow. She smelled them all, remembered them all. From a quarter century before, when Tsecha had brought them here, the six humanish he had chosen above all.

Caith is a damned thing, but she serves some purpose, for you cannot have order without its opposite. But for Caith, blessed Shiou would have no reason to be. They had all called him *inshah* then, and hung on his every word.

She stopped at the end of an alley that opened onto a wider road. Across the road, a blackened building with a double door entry, topped by a tarnished silver dome.

In the distance, faint sounds. The hum and whine of skimmers. The never-ending Vynshàrau pouring into her head.

Running feet. Growing nearer.

Jani reached into her pocket, closed her hand around the hilt of the blade, and waited.

Caith called to her. Rilas heard her voice in the pound of blood in her ears, the pain in her knees, her weakness. She ran through alleys, walkways, avoiding the larger streets down which the security skimmers coursed.

She could see the blackened temple dome, the most blessed of sights. Quickened her pace even as she knew her heart would burst. They would keep her here, protect her here.

Then from the corner of her eye, she saw. A propitiator, head covered, emerge from an alley and walk across the narrow street toward the entry.

"*Inshah!*" Rilas forced the cry even as the strain tore her lungs. "*Inshah—ha'alan elas!*" Teacher—wait for me.

The priest slowed but did not stop. Rilas ran to her. Reached out to grab her overrobe, to bid her to stop, to raise her arms before her and beg for protection.

"*Inshah! Ha'alan elas! Inshah!*"

The propitiator turned, too quickly. Rilas caught sight of the pale eye. In the way of the fighter, she looked down at the propitiator's hand, and saw the darkness where none should have been.

Tried to stop. But could not.

Felt the blade—and saw—the face—

Jani braced and staggered back as Rilas barreled into her. Felt the blade go in, and jammed it deeper. In and up, toward the heart. The female's eyes widened even as they clouded. Her lips moved even as blood trickled from the corner of her mouth.

"On your Way, you will pass a shade that awaits the soul of the greatest idomeni." Jani felt wet warmth down the front of her overrobe as Rilas slumped forward and her blood flowed. "And when you pass it you will say, ní Tsecha Egri, I am Imea nìaRauta Rilas, who killed you." She gripped the back of Rilas's headcloth and yanked her head up, stared into the snake-boned face, the dulling eyes. "Because every murdered being deserves to see the face of the one who killed them. Such is orderly." Her eyes burned and her voice keened through a tightening throat. "So says the priest." The female's body slumped again, and Jani felt her last breath leave.

"Let her fall."

Jani looked up to find Lucien standing a few strides away. Behind him, Niall, still running.

"Let her fall." Lucien took a step forward, then pointed to the ground. "She's dead. Let her drop."

Jani pushed Rilas off her shoulder. The female fell back, her weight and the angle of her collapse yanking the blade from Jani's hand.

She felt their eyes on her. Niall, sad, resigned. Lucien—

I know what you want. You want to watch them die.

—the professional—

You want to look into their eyes and watch the light go out.

—shaking his head in disgust, then walking to the body and commencing an odd search, feeling her hair, her ears, down the back of her neck. "There's nothing here. Her book is gone. They must have removed it after they captured her."

While Lucien searched the body, Niall picked through the slingbag. "There's enough firepower in here to blow out a wall— why the hell didn't she use it?"

"She thought she'd entered refuge." Lucien stood, then pulled a dispo cloth from his trouser pocket and wiped his hands. "Perhaps she didn't think she needed it."

"More fool her." Niall continued his search. "What do they look like?"

Lucien held up his hand, thumb and forefinger five or so centimeters apart. "Like an imager, but a little larger. It's more sensitive, more complex. Adjustable."

"Anything like this?" Jani pulled the bug from her ear. It splayed across her hand, soft and cool and clear, like something from the sea.

Lucien shook his head. "Not really."

"Will it do in a pinch?" Jani closed her hand to keep the bug from drying out. "From a distance, will he be able to tell?"

Before Lucien could answer, Niall pointed toward the far end of the street, now blocked by a cluster of skimmers. Security guards emerged and walked toward them, shooters raised. "Cavalry finally arrived."

Jani ignored them, bending to Rilas's body and pulling at the blade. It didn't budge at first—she grasped the hilt harder, almost lost her hold because of the blood, pulled again. A muffled *click* sounded as the blade came free, broken, a third of its length left behind.

"What has hap—" The security dominant stopped when he saw the knife, the blood, the overrobe.

"You will take me back." Jani wiped the blade upon the sleeve of her overrobe, then returned it to her pocket. Stepped around the body, past Niall and Lucien, to the end of the alley and the waiting skimmers.

The Council guards opened the gate to them, the entry, then flowed in after them and closed and barred the doors.

Jani entered the chamber. Saw that they all watched her. Scriabin, so pale. Ulanova, uncertain. Burkett. Frances. They stood against one wall with the other humanish, spectators at another civilization's turn of fate.

The crowd parted until no one stood between Jani and Cèel. He stood at the far end of the room with the other Vynshàrau, had fallen silent upon Jani's arrival. Between them, worked into the floor with squares of faded red stone and tile, a circle about five meters in diameter. A circle in which an idomeni fought both as Nema and as Tsecha. A circle that had once been stained by his blood.

Jani pulled her ear bug from her pocket and raised it above her head, shifting her hand so the light struck it, so Cèel could see it.

Cèel stood rigid, eyes fixed on some spot at her feet. Then, slow as a rising sun, he raised his head and fixed on the bug.

"In the name of my teacher, whom you killed, I challenge you." Jani could barely hear her own words for the roaring in her head, wondered if Cèel heard them at all.

Then she saw him nod once.

The sense of the idomeni changed then, from on edge and uncertain to sure and precise, as actors in a familiar play. Bornsect and Haárin fanned out and moved to seats assigned based on skein and standing, leaving humanish to mill about like sheep in a pen until Feyó and Galas took them in hand and led them to appropriate places.

"Jan." Niall moved in beside her. "I keep you in the circle and I declare the fight ended if you can't go on." He wiped a hand over a face gone grey. "Dammit, is this—"

"Kièrshia?"

Jani turned to find Dathim standing behind her, Meva at his side.

"He will kill you." Dathim spoke as softly as ever he had. "He is of the warrior skein. He is larger, stronger, faster, and more skilled. He had fought in the circle many times." He stepped forward. "I will fight him. I will—"

"It's not your fight, Dathim."

"I was his suborn as well as you!"

"I was his student. He was my teacher." Jani slipped off her bloody overrobe, handed it to Niall. "If he kills me, use it. Break him with it." She turned toward the circle. Blood sang in her ears. Sweat tingled her scalp. She sensed the room as brighter, thought for a moment that the illumination had intensified. *No—this is how it feels to fight as Haárin.* An augielike focus. A sharpening of the senses.

He will kill you.

"Then I will see his face." She started to walk toward the circle, found her way blocked by a male bornsect. Taller than Cèel, and even more scarred. She stared him in the face, and he looked to the side, revealing a gnarl of an ear, half of it sliced away. He pushed a tray of blades at her and pointed to the one she should take, the one that Cèel as the challenged had chosen. A curved Sìah, a sleek crescent with a barbed tip. She picked it up, then walked past him and stepped inside the circle.

Cèel waited on the other side. The scarred male took his place behind him, whispered in his ear.

Jani saw a propitiator out of the corner of her eye, gesturing prayers and invocations against demons. Sànalàn, Tsecha's sub-orn, who betrayed him.

Keep your prayers. She said her own. To Ganesh. Remover of obstacles. *Guide my hand, Lord.*

She crouched as Dathim had taught her, bent forward at the waist, one leg ahead of the other, arms outstretched to take the hacks of her opponent's blade. Then she tucked her arms in a little to protect her sides, her ribs, and stood on the balls of her feet so she could move more quickly. As if it would help.

He will kill you.

Knife fights never lasted long, especially mismatches.

Cèel moved in first. A short stab that nicked Jani's left wrist, sent rose-pink carrier dripping to the floor. She stepped in it as she tried to parry, felt her boots slide.

Another quick move by Cèel. Another hack, to her right arm this time.

Jani brought up her blade as Cèel backed off, caught his right wrist, sent the blood spraying to the tile. Heard no cries from the assembled. No cheers. Because this was not that sort challenge. Because sometimes knives slipped, and all knew that this would be one of those times.

Another circling. Another thrust parried. Another. Another.

Then Cèel stepped in. Brought his blade arm around just as Jani brought her knife up. Struck her wrist hard, metal on skin and nerve and bone.

Jani's hand flew open as pain sang up her arm. The blade flashed flame as it tumbled through the air.

Cèel closed in. Gripped her around the waist with his free hand as though they danced. Jani brought up her knee to strike him in the groin, but he lifted her like a doll, shifted her so she struck his thigh instead. She looked him in the face to find he looked in hers as well, eyes like new grass frozen in ice. Then he bared his teeth—

—and sound receded—time—each heartbeat a year—

—and drove in the blade—

—warmth flowing through her skin—spreading—pressure— no pain—her heart—heart—

"*Nìa!*"

—looked past Cèel—outside the circle—saw a figure—shorn head—bared teeth—

"*Nìa, you must—*"

I must.

Her hand brushed her pocket—she felt the hardness of the broken blade—drew it out just as Cèel released her and stepped back and—

—she stepped forward—brought up the knife—sliced down—sliced back—

Heard Cèel howl. Felt his blood splash over her. Watched him fall back, hand clutching his thigh, blood flowing like a river, spreading across the circle.

Looked down. Saw one knife in her hand. Saw the other, in her gut.

"*Nìa!*"

Yes, inshah?

Stepped forward into the tunneling black—

That is most stupid, nìa, and I want to hear no more.

Inshah?

Yes, nìa?

Someday you'll be the death of me.

CHAPTER 32

Breathing . . . breathing . . .

Pain.

Jani opened one eye, then closed it as the room light battered her. Heard movement off to the side. "Hmm . . ."

"Jani." A deep voice. A voice of bedsides and cloudy nights. "Don't try to move."

"No—" She paused to summon saliva and lick her lips. "—prollem." She raised a hand that weighed at least a hundred kilos and rested it atop her chest. ". . . Heavy."

"Yes." John lifted her hand and placed it back atop the bed, squeezing it before releasing it. "Cèel stabbed you in the abdomen. The blade curved up—he nicked your left lung, and your heart." A pause. Sounds of shaky breathing. "You're healing now."

"I got him . . . too . . ." Jani nodded. Tried to nod. "What . . . happen . . . ?"

"Not now. Get some sleep."

Sounds of a chair being dragged across the floor. The creak of old ergoworks.

Jani pried one eye open, then the other, saw a shape backlit by the glare of a bedside lamp.

"Let me adjust this—" Niall ramped down the brightness, then leaned close. "Shroud doesn't know I'm here, so I need to make it fast." He looked at her stomach, the padding of sensors and bandages, and winced. "He said that you're far from a hundred percent, so you weaken fast and can't catch your breath and feel like an elephant's sitting on your chest."

Jani held up two fingers.

"Two elephants." Niall grinned. "Has anyone talked to you? About the fight?"

Jani tried to shake her head, stopping when the room spun. "Cèel—stabbed me. I stabbed—him. It was—a tie."

Niall's breath caught. "One of the news services got it all. Don't know how they snuck a relay past bornsect security, but they did. The gel who imaged it spent the next hour in the can throwing up everything down to her shoes, but—she did good. It's a bloody damned thing to watch—the son of a bitch grinned like a skull right before he—" He pressed a hand to his mouth, then slowly lowered it.

Jani reached out, touched Niall's arm with the tip of her finger. "I hit him—" She paused to breathe. "—too."

"Yes, yes." Niall glanced back toward the door as he took her hand and patted it to try to settle her down. "The thing is, Jan, you . . . hit him in the groin, his femoral artery and—" He squeezed her hand. "—he bled out in the circle. In a minute, he bled, and it was—" Another shaky breath. "He's dead, Jan. Cèel's dead."

"I would just like to state for the record that this is bullshit." Val held Jani around the shoulders, propping her upright until the bed headrest rose up to meet her. "It's only been two days. We told you that she needed at least a week."

"Doctor, if this wasn't so important, we wouldn't intrude." Scriabin sat at the foot of the bed. He wore full diplomatic rig, Commerce green tunic bearing every medal and award he'd ever received. "Hurt much?"

"Only when I laugh." Jani tried to sit up higher, and stopped when the elephants began to tap dance across her rib cage. "Judging from the expressions on your faces, I doubt we'll be doing much of that, so I'm—probably safe."

"Niall admitted that he told you." Mako shook his head. "He thought someone should have told you in the operating room. He thought you'd be able to hear, and it would cheer you up." He clucked his tongue. "My Niall . . . can be the bloodiest of bastards."

"Which is why he'll be your Niall until the stars go out." Jani brushed off Mako's glower. "So I went into the circle with a second knife." She touched her thigh where her trouser pocket would have been, where the blade would have rested. "I remember pulling out a knife. I remember stabbing him. Nothing particularly lucid."

"I can't say I'm surprised." Val sat on the end of the bed, opposite Scriabin. "I wasn't particularly lucid afterward, and all I did was watch."

"Did Council lodge a protest?" Jani looked from one face to the next, sensed the need to speak combined with the reluctance to say what needed saying. "It wasn't exactly a fair fight, was it?"

"No, it wasn't."

Everyone turned to the door.

John filled the entry like a pale guardian, his medwhites rumpled, his face a mask. He glared at Mako and Scriabin, but saved his sharpest look for Val, who started to grumble an explanation before deciding silence the better course.

Then John looked at Jani, and his expression warmed, a little. "Cèel was the better, more experienced fighter. He did not enter the circle in the spirit of challenge, but with every intention of killing you. Everyone who witnessed that fight knew that."

Jani detected the jittery undertone in the so-familiar bass. "How much did you see?"

"Everything." John hesitated, then walked to one of the analyzers that ringed her bedside and studied the readout. "Niall contacted us as soon as you offered challenge. We saw . . . everything."

Jani waited as the silence stretched. "Are you going to tell me what else happened, or do I have to bribe an orderly to snag a copy of the image?"

"I would wait a few years to look at that, if I were you." John remained fixed on the readout. "Cèel's physician-priest wasn't there. We found out later that Rilas had killed her during her escape from the Temple hospital. There were other physician-priests present, but half a minute or more passed while they shook out their hierarchical underwear, and that was a half a minute or more that they didn't have. Our best trauma people would have had their work cut out for them. You couldn't have struck a better spot if you'd aimed." He shot her a look filled with wonder and the barest hint of cold-blooded admiration. "Then they started on the prayers. I think I recall someone cutting away Cèel's trouser leg to look at the wound, but I confess that my attentions were fixed elsewhere by that point."

Jani watched as the physician who had pieced her together from char and ashes, who had brought her back from the brink any number of times, returned to his pondering of readouts. "John, did they . . . ?"

"Do I think they let him die?" John raised his head, his eyes bright. "Good God, is there any doubt?" He jerked his chin toward Val, who nodded. "They went through a few of the motions, but they didn't do a damned thing that mattered."

Scriabin cleared his throat. "Well, there was the issue of Wholeness of Soul—"

"As convenient an excuse as any. If pressed, I'm sure Temple can justify every move they made. And every move they didn't." John laughed. "He went too far. The other sects wanted him out without matters getting too messy. Saw an opportunity, and made the most of it. Assassination by medical negligence. The history scrolls of the idomeni are no doubt filled."

Jani looked from John to Val and back to John. For all their professional disdain and outrage, there was one point they continued to skirt. "Could you have helped?"

The silence radiated like cracks in old glass. Man and hybrid looked at one another, decades of closeness whittling down hours of discussion to the arch of an eyebrow, the twitch of a lip.

"You weren't much better off, you know. We had our hands full." Val looked at the floor and shrugged. "They wouldn't have let us near him anyway."

"Besides, it's not as though he'd have thanked us. Saved by a humanish and a hybrid—I'm sure if you'd have set out the choice before him, he'd have chosen death." John turned back to the analyzers and concentrated on touchpad entries. "But it's a moot point. As Val said, we had our hands full with you."

The room seemed to chill as the truth revealed itself in the humanish manner. In veiled looks and words left unsaid. In the arch of an eyebrow and the twitch of a lip. *Yes, we could have tried, but we didn't. Because you came first. Because we saw the look on his face when he drove in the knife. Because he had Tsecha killed. Because the bastard deserved it.*

Mako walked to a side table and poured himself water from a carafe. "Remind me to never get on your bad side, Shroud." He lifted the glass in Val's direction. "That goes for you, too, Parini." He drank, his stricken expression broadcasting that he would have preferred vodka and even that might not have helped.

Jani waited until the shockwaves settled to the occasional ripple. "So what happened after they carted away the bodies?"

"A firestorm." Scriabin stood and paced. "The Pathen strong-armed a Council vote with a speed I didn't believe possible outside of Chicago. Aden nìRau Wuntoi is the new Oligarch. The Pathen have ascended to *rau*."

"I didn't think a bornsect could ascend to *rau* on a vote." Val moved to the window and perched on the sill. "What happened to the civil war part?"

"Peaceful transfer of power isn't the norm, but it has happened." Jani picked her muzzy brain for appropriate bits of idomeni history. "The sect that ascends needs to have built one hell of a consensus, but we knew the Pathenrau had been working on that for a while."

"After Council refused to allow Cèel's suborn the right to ascend, they kicked all Vynshà out of Council and Temple." Scriabin stood and paced at the foot of the bed. "Some of the Temple dominants are arguing that Cèel's planning of Tsecha's assassination was so profoundly antithetical to all that is idomeni that it taints all Vynshà." He slowed. Stilled. "And that all Vynshà must pay."

"Pay how?" Jani heard the dread in her voice. "How are they supposed to pay?" But she knew the answer. One night twenty years before, she had witnessed the answer. *The sin of one is the sin of all—*

Then her gut clenched and she doubled over, slumping to her side as the spasms started and her heart skipped.

"I'm going to have to ask you all to leave." John turned her over on her back, fingers flicking over the sensors. "*Now.*"

It was a still night, the moon obscured by cloud—
Jani sat in the hospital's small garden and watched the fish in the ornamental pool, the melodramatic phrasing of the *Colonial Times* playing in her mind's ear like the narration it was. The story had begun with the last days of the War of Vynshàrau Ascension. The reporter had mined every accessible archive and even a couple that technically should have been out of bounds.

Bornsect tradition held that all members of a sect shared in the decisions of their dominants. Therefore, when it became evident that Laumrau dominants had conspired with members of the Commonwealth government and Service to imprison humanish in the hospital-shrine located at Knevçet Shèràa and to subject them to mind control experimentation, the sin of the few became the shame of the many, and the many accepted that the sin was theirs as well.

"And since all the Laum sinned, all the Laum paid." Jani worked to her feet, one eye on the relays that studded her right arm and transmitted her vital signs back to the handhelds that John and Val carried with them at all times. "I think there are a few isolated settlements left. A few Laum left alive to pass along the tale, and the warnings."

"Teaching idomeni history to the fish?"

Jani turned to find Lucien standing in the garden entry.

"I wanted to visit earlier, but Val warned me off." He walked in, brimmed lid tucked under his arm. "I figured my best bet would be to sneak in and take my chances." He stopped just beyond reach. "It's sheer insanity outside these walls, you realize that? Vynshà are gathering in the streets and Wuntoi is ready to send out the Haárin to bottle them up."

Jani lowered back into the chair. "No one tells me anything. Scriabin and Mako were here yesterday, but John ordered them out after—" She patted her chest just over her heart. "They're going to slaughter the Vynshà. It'll make the Night of the Blade look like a skirmish."

Lucien took a seat on a nearby bench. "What did you expect?" He picked up a branch that had fallen from one of the dwarf weeping willows and poked the water, sending the fish scurrying for shelter. "That's how they've operated for thousands of years. It's insane. A dominant commits a crime, and the entire sect gets thrown over the side. If humans did that, we never would have lasted long enough to make it out of the caves." He hit the surface hard enough to make a splash, then tossed the branch into the water and watched it bob and float.

Jani watched him out of the corner of her eye. *Duplicitous bastard.* Yet here he was, the only one who seemed willing to tell her what went on beyond the hospital gates. "What's the official Commonwealth position?"

"That it's an internal idomeni matter."

"Like hell it is." Jani heard her cardiomonitor emit a warning *beep*, and breathed slowly until it settled. "What happens to the Vynshà Haárin?"

"That's still being discussed." For the first time, Lucien seemed anxious, clenching his hands and shifting restlessly. "Dathim's under a sort of house arrest until they decide."

"What do you mean, 'sort of'?"

"I think they were afraid to come out and tell him." A quick smile, which soon vanished. "They finally settled on having Meva suggest to him that he should remain within the confines of the enclave. She's technically under house arrest as well. Feyó is trying to intercede for them, but she isn't having much luck." Lucien clapped the tips of his fingers together. "They'd kill Dathim and Meva because they're Vynshà, even though they're Haárin?" He made a drifting gesture with one hand. "If you'd kept your mouth shut and let me handle it, none of this would have happened. Rilas just would have disappeared."

"You couldn't have gotten to Cèel."

"He rode in a skimmer on occasion, didn't he? Idomeni tech isn't all that different." Lucien sat back, smoothing his hands over his thighs, then dragging his brimmed lid onto his lap and tracing a thumbnail over the gold braid. "That's what they're all saying. That you had to get in everyone's face. Again. You had to broadcast. Again. Everyone knew you were coming. Everyone knew what to expect. You said things that should have been kept quiet. You did things that upset people. And now everyone's stuck. Because it's all out in the open, they have to act in certain ways. Instead of an easy transfer of power to a Vynshà who would have been more amenable, millions are going to die. Because you couldn't keep your damned mouth shut." His hands stilled. "That's the difference between you and me. I do the job, and I know how to keep my distance. I don't get involved. I don't get emotional." He paused, eyes fixed on the fish, which had begun to emerge from beneath stones and logs and swim about again. "I just do it."

"Does anyone bother to consider that Tsecha wouldn't want this?" Jani paused to breathe as her heart monitor once more beeped a warning. "He was Vynshà. They're his people. Do you think if he were alive now he'd let this happen?"

"He's dead." Lucien shrugged. "What he'd think doesn't matter."

"So it's come to that already?"

"Ani is saying that history is repeating. You did the same thing at Knevçet Shèràa. Drew down fire. You killed Rikart Neumann, and because you did that, Acton van Reuter had to act, had to order Evan to take care of you. You force people to do things they don't want to do because you don't know when to lay low. When to lay off." Lucien tugged at his lid's gold braid too hard, ripping it away from the brim. He swore under his breath and massaged the cording with his thumb, trying to work it back into place. "You always have to push."

"You've made your point."

"Have I? Is it really getting through?"

Jani watched him set his lid back on the bench beside him, then lean forward again, hands flexing. "Lucien?"

He raised his head and looked at her. His eyes glittered like the stones that lined the bottom of the pond, dark and cold and devoid of life. *"What?"*

Jani sighed as she felt the last piece in a long running puzzle slip into place. *I always knew it would come to this.* Always knew that someday, the man who had spent his life playing all sides of the game would eventually make a choice. "Speaking hypothetically, of course, because it's all I can do to get up out of this chair. But if I were to attempt to run out of this garden right now, I wouldn't make it to the entry, would I?"

"Ani prefers Feyó." Lucien fixed on the fish again. "Feyó knows something of how humans operate, but she's not an expert. Ani thinks she'll have an easier time manipulating her if you're not around." He smiled, shook his head. "No, that's not all of it. Ani hates you and wants you dead."

Jani nodded. Odd, that she didn't feel scared. That she didn't feel angry or betrayed. That she didn't feel the least urge to fight for her life. *I'll be able to apologize to Tsecha in person for destroying his people.* And to the d'Abos, and the Seligs, and the other passengers of the *Capria*. As for the pain or the sensations, well, she'd died often enough to have felt them all at least once. The only thing she had yet to experience was that last letting go, and odds were that it would slip right past without her realizing. *Paying forward for the millions.* Yes, it was right. Yes, it was just. Insufficient repayment, but all she had to offer. All she had to give.

"I've risked everything I ever wanted, everything I ever earned." Lucien picked up a stone and hurled it into the midst of the fish, sending them darting back to the rocks as water splashed. "And every goddamned time, I'd have to stand there and listen as you told me that whatever I did, it wasn't enough. Not enough risk. Not enough blood. You're not running for your life this week, so you can't be serious. What the hell else do you want from me?"

"Not a thing." Jani shook her head. "Not anymore."

Lucien bulled on with no indication that he'd heard. "I can't be what you want me to be—I'm not made that way. I can't say what you want me to say. I can't feel what you want me to feel." His voice dropped to a whisper. "I don't love you."

"I should have realized when you told me all about assassins who needed to get close to their victims that you were trying to tell me something. If I made a list of all our encounters since Elyas, I would guess that each one was an opportunity you let slip. The clinch on the catwalk—that was your best shot, I think. Overcome by guilt over the *Capria,* bit of a push and over the railing she went. Clear case of suicide. No wonder Anais seemed so upset each time she saw me. I wasn't supposed to survive the journey here, was I?" Jani took as deep a breath as she dared, then slid to the edge of the chair. "Well, you'll do the job good and proper now, and you'll be set for life. Ani will never question you again. Hell, she'll probably write you into her will." Using the chair arms for support, she worked to her feet. Then she undid the collar of her pajama top and pushed back the collar of her robe, exposing the area around her neck.

Lucien straightened. "What are you doing?"

"Would it be easier if I turned my back?" Jani turned to face the garden entry, then reached up and tapped the place where her neck and shoulder met. "I've done this before, so watch where I'm pointing. Edge of your hand, right here." She lowered her hands and clasped them in front of her, then stilled. Strange how she'd never felt so calm. She had no trouble keeping the cardiomonitor silent. "I'll keep looking straight ahead. The sun's in just the right position—I won't even see your shadow. One hard shot, Lucien. All that stands between you and everything you ever wanted." *And between me and everything I deserve.*

Nothing, for long seconds. Then she heard him rise, the crunch of the soles of his polished tie-tops against the stone rim of the pond. Sensed him close in, as she always could, and shut her eyes.

Felt him grip her shoulders and ease her around to face him. Opened her eyes as first he pulled her pajama top closed, then straightened the collar of her robe. He didn't look her in the face. He barely looked at her at all.

Then, his ministrations completed, he rested his hands on her shoulders for a scant moment, before letting them slide away. "Happy now?" He stood before her, head bowed, then circled around her and started toward the other end of the garden.

"You—" Jani inhaled. This time her heart skipped, stuttered. The edges of her sightline blackened and her knees buckled.

Lucien caught her before she hit the ground, and lowered with her. Held her, drew her closer, and pressed his lips to the place were her neck and shoulder met.

"So you're going to kill me after all." Jani heard the cardiomonitor start to skitter. "You've just settled on your weapon of choice."

"I learned from an expert." Lucien's arms tightened as he hugged her closer.

"Damned fool."

"No argument there."

"Let her go."

Jani saw John push through the garden gate, Val at his heels. She sagged against Lucien, felt the hybrid lawn prickle through her pajamas. "He's not doing anything."

"There's something wrong with her." Lucien released her and scuttled backward as Val and John linked arms beneath Jani's legs and behind her back and hoisted her up. "She's not her usual self."

"If you had a twelve centimeter gash in your gut courtesy of a Sìah barbed blade and a hole in your heart that didn't want to close, you wouldn't be your usual self either." John glared at Lucien as he and Val maneuvered Jani back to her chair and lowered her into it. "Perhaps you'd like to experience the sensation firsthand?"

"John." Jani laid her head back. "Shut up."

"Jani, you can't afford—"

"Just shut—" She grabbed the front of his medcoat and shook as hard as she could. "—up."

"That sounds more like—" Lucien fell silent as both John and Val turned on him.

Jani looked past her twin guardians to her singular—what was he? Ally? Lover? Never a friend. *Just . . . Lucien.* "Do you have a skimmer?"

Lucien nodded. "I can get one."

Jani slapped the sides of her chair, then jerked her thumb at the garden gate. "I have to go to the enclave and get Dathim and Meva out."

"You're not going anywhere," John said as he checked the various analyzers on the chair.

"I'm going to the enclave to get Dathim and Meva." Jani stared at the side of John's face until he finally looked at her. "Then I want to talk to Wuntoi."

"He's been advised not to talk to you." Lucien stood off to one side, hands behind his back.

"Then we're going to have to persuade him otherwise." Jani tugged on John's sleeve. "John."

"You're in no condition." Val picked up the standard while his colleague fussed with a balky readout.

"Just give me something to get me through."

John's head came up, eyes blazing. *"That's not how I work."*

"Just get me through the next twelve hours. If I can't get something started by then . . ." Jani took John's hand and squeezed. Felt the initial resistance, the slow softening.

His eyes brimmed. "You were all I cared about."

"I know. That was the problem, wasn't it?" Jani leaned close enough to kiss. "Whatever it takes. Please."

CHAPTER 33

"The dominant's name is ná Dena Lau." Scriabin read the name off his handheld display, and did a decent job of pronunciation. "Ava always found her quite reasonable, but now that she has a possible death sentence in her future, all bets are off. Word is that if she cooperates with Wuntoi, he'll exile her enclave instead of killing them."

Jani pondered the view through the skimmer window. City Center appeared much as it always had, the walkways filled with both bornsect and Haárin, all proceeding in an apparently orderly manner.

"Jan?"

Jani touched her ear. "I'm here."

"I'm with Galas . . ." Niall paused, said something to the Haárin male. *"We're north of the Temples, near the site of your Sermon on the Park Bench. Lots of Haárin gathered here, and more streaming in from the surrounding streets."*

Jani looked to the north, past the domes and spires of the City Center. Imagined Niall guiding the small two-seater along the river, Galas riding shotgun. "Any Pathenrau security?"

"A few. No warriors, though. Galas said that he heard they were calling up a few brigade equivalents from the southern encampments in preparation for—"

Jani waited. Tapped her ear a few times. "Niall?"

"In preparation for the slaughter." A shaky sigh. *"Jesus Christ, there are kids out here. Youngish. Some of them can't even walk yet."* Another pause. *"We're going to get started here. Feyó's crew has shown up. What's your timing?"*

Jani checked the view. "Coming up on the enclave now." She tapped the bug, shutting it down. She didn't want a stream of Niall-speak interrupting her, distracting her. She still felt tired, despite the stimulant John had reluctantly given her. *As for the wound . . .* She reached beneath her shirt and touched the bandage, a mass of sensor wrap and healing accelerants that sent out signals, she felt sure, to anyone with a handheld who wanted to know the state of her heart.

"You all right?"

Jani looked over at Val, who watched her from the other end of the seat. "I'm fine."

"Then why do you keep touching it?"

"Just to drive you crazy."

"Already there." Val entered a notation in his handheld. "Bobbing along like a ping-pong ball in your wake."

"I know the feeling, Doc." Scriabin looked up from his handheld and gazed out the window. "She makes Tyotya Ani seem meek and retiring."

"You can both shut up any time now." Jani scooted to the edge of her seat as the embassy double-length floated to the curb. The driver's side gullwing swung up, releasing a uniformed Lucien, who hurried around to her side of the vehicle and opened the door.

Jani emerged, taking Lucien's offered hand and holding on tight because she needed the support. Continued to lean on him as she slowly straightened while trying to ignore the pull of bandages and healing tissue. Her propitiator's overrobe, a clean backup she'd salvaged from the depths of her luggage, unfurled to her knees.

A crowd gathered, Haárin and bornsect both, ripples of hushed speech propagating as she walked to the enclave entry. *I don't look too bad for someone who died three days ago, do I?* She squeezed Lucien's hand, and he released her and stepped to the side, far enough away so that she appeared fully ambulatory, but close enough to catch her in case the unthinkable happened and she collapsed.

She reached the gate just as ná Dena emerged, a middle-aged female wearing the headwrap and rough clothes of a laborer.

"Glories, Kièrshia." Dena spoke Low Vynshà Haárin, a language stripped of gesture. She looked Jani in the eye as well, her Vynshà gold laced with amber and streaks of brown. "I know why you are here. I can do nothing. NìRau Wuntoi compels. I must obey. Ní Dathim and ná Meva must remain until all is decided."

Jani started to speak, then stopped as cold sweat broke out and flecks of light shimmered in her sightline. *Not now, goddamn it.* She bent forward at the waist. Hunched her shoulders. Prayed as she never prayed before that Dena would interpret her posture as growing rage, not an attempt by a weak half-humanish to remain standing by any means possible.

Saw the brown-streaked gold flicker, and knew her prayer had been answered, at least for the moment. "Blood trade, Dena. You hold them for Wuntoi, he lets your enclave leave Shèrá. But if you leave, and Vynshà here die, all will know you betrayed. All will know, because I will tell them." She heard Lucien shift his feet, and knew he understood enough of what she said to glean the threat. *Too harsh? Too bad.*

Dena's shoulders started to curve. "Tell what you will, to who you will. NìRau Wuntoi said that they were of ní Tsecha, and ní Tsecha died."

"So?" Jani parsed Wuntoi's words, searching for the slant he'd given them, the meaning that would have convinced Dena to imprison her own.

Then it hit her like a blow. Her heart stuttered. *"He told you they helped kill ní Tsecha?"* She drew up straight without thinking, looked to the sky, felt the pain across her midriff like the swipe of claws. "They both lived here once." She rounded her shoulders again, stepping away from Lucien as he edged closer. "You knew them."

Dena nodded. "I know of Meva." The harmonics of irritation in her voice indicated that she had known Meva all too well.

"You know she studied ní Tsecha's writings, that she followed him."

"Yes, ná Kièrshia, but—"

"You know ní Dathim, the tilemaster?"

"All know ní Dathim." This time the tone was softer, kinder.

"You say this. Yet you believe that this ní Dathim who you know would participate in secret killing? That ná Meva, who one can hear through walls, would do so as well? Ní Dathim would face you in the circle and strike you down—" Jani poked Dena in the chest hard enough to jostle her. "—and ná Meva would talk you to death, but she would never strike in secret."

"NìRau Wuntoi will slaughter us as we did the Laum." Dena's eyes darkened. Yes, she was of an age. She may have witnessed. She may have even participated.

"Wuntoi will slaughter—no one." Jani stopped to breathe.

"Give them to me now, and I will guard you as I guard them. I will guard all Vynshà as I guard them."

Dena looked to the street, the idomeni who crowded from three sides. "NìRau Wuntoi will hear you," she said in halting English. "But will he listen?"

Jani nodded. That was the sticking point, the one thing in all this that she could work for, but not guarantee. "If I can't save you, I'll die with you. This I swear, on Tsecha's soul."

Dena stood quiet, her eyes fixed on nothing. Then she gestured to her suborn, a hulking male who gestured affirmation, then reentered the enclave. A few minutes later he emerged, Dathim and Meva in tow.

Meva grabbed Jani's sleeve and made as if to speak, but Jani shook her off. "Get into the skimmer," she said in Sìah Haárin. "Before they change their minds." The two followed Lucien to the vehicle, piling into the rear seat while Jani walked toward the crowd. They pushed forward as she approached, a few raising their arms above their heads in displays of abject respect.

"I have taken ní Dathim Naré and ná Meva Tan." Jani spoke High Vynshà, every word replete with change in posture and gesture. "They were ní Tsecha's, as was I. Now they are mine. I care for that which is mine." She paused, until the tension ramped and it seemed as though the air itself would shatter under the stress. "Line the streets from Council to the river, where I met some of you four days past. Do this in the time after mid-afternoon sacrament. I will await you there." With that, she turned and swept back to the skimmer. Waved off Lucien's offered arm, maintaining her show of strength until he closed her gullwing after her. Then she slumped forward, arms crossed over her stomach, while Val knelt on the skimmer floor in front of her, handscanner at the ready.

"John is going to have a fit when he sees these numbers." He checked her vitals, then dragged a slingbag from beneath the seat. "What was that all about? A meeting by the river? Who are you expecting?" He pulled out an injector already loaded with a cartridge, pushed up Jani's right sleeve and pressed the device to her skin. "You can't take much more of this, you know? If John doesn't come up with the right protein soon, we're going to have to open you up again."

Meva and Dathim sat on the opposite bench seat, crowding Scriabin on both sides. Dathim watched the medical ministrations with the skeptical eye of an owner who wondered if his horse would make it through the race. "The Vynshà will not die as did the Laum." His voice was a rumble. "They will take as many with them as they can."

"No one will have to die. Not even me." *I hope.* Jani sagged against the seat as whatever Val dosed her with took effect. "Now here's what I need you all to do . . ."

The skimmer pulled away from the curb, its progress slowed to a walking pace by the idomeni who crowded in from every side, touching the vehicle as it drifted past, like a talisman.

By the time they reached the river, Niall, along with Feyó's crew, had completed their end of the project. The awning they'd erected on the edge of the river proved a drab thing in dark grey, which Jani suspected had been creatively reappropriated from Rauta Shèràa Base stores by a certain colonel of her acquaintance.

"Afternoon, gel." Niall strode beneath the awning, clipwrench still in hand. He tossed the tool aside and helped Val and Scriabin maneuver a skimchair out of the skimmer boot, eyeing Jani all the while. "You've looked better, you know."

"I've felt better." Jani sat in the chair as soon as Val activated it. "Is she here?"

Niall stepped back outside and motioned to someone standing alongside the awning. "Your turn."

A shadow moved along the fabric wall. Then a small face framed with dark brown curls peeked around edge of the poly-cloth.

"Come on in, gel. She only bites if you bite first." Niall gripped the young woman's sleeve and tugged her inside. "This is Bailey Schiff, an enterprising stringer for ChanNet, who has already imaged one event of the century and is ready to move on to bigger things."

"It's good to—" The young woman held out a hand to Jani, her eyes widening. "—meet. You."

"Thank you for agreeing to this." Jani gave Schiff's hand a squeeze, because the young woman looked like she needed it. "If this goes according to plan, you won't have to do anything." *We won't think about what will happen if it doesn't.* "All you'll have to do is stand near my chair."

"And an exclusive interview after it's over," piped Schiff, her nervousness evaporating like morning dew in the Rauta Shèràa sun.

"And an exclusive interview after it's over." Jani turned her chair around and motioned to Lucien. "You should get going."

"Are you sure he'll be there?" Lucien's voice emerged tight, his business-as-usual facade showing its first crack. "You never contacted him. You never asked for a meeting."

"If he looks out the window, he can see what's going on." Jani heard a rise of voices, looked out to the river to see that the crowd had doubled in size in the few minutes since their arrival. "He'll be there."

"From your mouth . . ." Lucien lapsed into French as he returned to the skimmer and got in.

Jani watched him pull away. Saw Meva's face in the rear window and raised a hand. Felt a flicker of relief when the female bared her teeth and waved back.

"Ava received a communication this morning." Scriabin grabbed a folding stool from a stack and shook it open. "Li Cao is still insisting that this is an idomeni matter."

"I'm sure she has her reasons." Jani edged her chair behind the draped fold of the awning, then rolled up her sleeve so Val could give her another injection.

"If you pull this off . . ." He shook his head and concentrated on positioning the injector.

Jani winced as the injector pinched, sighed as the drug warmth wandered up her arm. Watched the street that stretched from the enclave to the river, already obscured by the idomeni who gathered there. "Did you bring it?"

Val sighed. "It's right here." He reached into his slingbag, pulled out the plastic hospital dispo bag and handed it to her.

"He's coming." Niall appeared at the front of the awning. "Pascal picked him up at the front of the Council building. He drove him as far as the enclave, then let him off. Dathim and Meva are leading him here."

"Through the crowds?" Jani smiled.

Niall touched his ear, listened for a moment, then nodded. "It's just like it was in the station. They've closed in on both sides—there's barely enough room for him to pass."

"Well, time to get ready for company." Jani shifted her weight so the chair tipped forward and stood.

Niall gaped.

It had taken Val the better part of the day to find the clothes Jani had worn the day she killed Rilas and Cèel. They had been bundled into a biohazard bag during her presurgical prep and avoided the incinerator through sheer happenstance. Permanent bends and ripples had been created in the shirt and the front of the trousers by Jani's and Cèel's dried blood. The overrobe, streaked with Rilas's blood, had fared a little better, but still looked like something that had been used to wrap a butchered animal.

"Jani?" Scriabin licked his lips. He'd watched her remove the garments from the bag and put them on, and still hadn't recovered. "Do you think it wise to greet a new Oligarch while wearing clothes soaked in his predecessor's blood?"

Jani bared her teeth. "Welcome to Shèrá, Your Excellency."

Jani walked out from under the awning and across the river walkway to the end of the avenue. As she did, idomeni closed in on both sides, both bornsect and Haárin, Vynshà and Sìah and Oà, as well as the odd Pathenrau rebel, gold-bronze faces like shots of night amid their lighter-skinned brethren.

Aden nìRau Wuntoi walked toward her, shoulders curved in anger, Dathim and Meva serving as escort, the crowd closing in behind him and bearing him along. He slowed when he registered Jani standing at the end of the walkway, slowed even more when he saw the clothes she wore.

When they reached the end of the walkway, Dathim and Meva turned as sharply as Spacer recruits, coming to a halt beside Jani. That left Wuntoi standing by himself, an arm's length distant, idomeni pressing around him from three sides.

"The reason?" His English was unaccented. He had been working toward Pathenrau ascendance for a long time.

"One should always look into the faces of those you would kill." Jani turned and pointed toward the awning-covered enclosure. "Now we shall go, and talk of them." She waited for Dathim and Meva to walk ahead, then fell in behind them, allowing Wuntoi his place of precedence bringing up the rear. *With the Vynshà hard on his tail.* She held back her grin without much trouble. She still felt the tightness around her chest, the weakness and cold sweats. Val had rigged a cardiopack over her heart that would inject the appropriate drugs and proteins in case it misbehaved, and had hidden in the backseat of the double-length, a mere twenty-five meter dash away in case of medical crisis.

They entered the enclosure. Everyone rose, Scriabin immediately surrendering the stool, which was of the proper height and style for an Oligarch. Wuntoi smoothed his overrobe around him and sat, a lifetime's practice with bornsect furniture allowing him the balance to situate himself with nary an unseemly wobble. He looked around the sheltered space, then settled in, gesturing dismissively toward Jani's skimchair. "You sit in that chair because you are weak."

"Physically?" Jani shrugged, ignoring the pull of her incision and the heft and drag of the cardiopack. "Mentally is another matter, and unless you wish to challenge me, it is the mental with which you will have to deal."

"A second knife." Wuntoi looked toward the crowds, who had encircled the enclosure as closely as Feyó's security would allow and now sat on the lawns and watched them. "Unseemly."

"So is attempted murder within the circle. But knives have always been known to slip, and idomeni often die who are not meant to." Jani replayed scattered moments in her mind. The moment when Cèel knocked away her blade. When he drew her in like a lover and rammed his own knife into her gut up to the hilt.

"I am here at your bidding, because you were favored by ní Tsecha. And because you are weakened, and I pitied you." Wuntoi fixed his gaze at a point over Jani's shoulder, on the border between disrespect and regard. "What do you want?"

Jani caught Niall's eye as he clenched his fists and arched her brow. *Calm down, Colonel.* Wuntoi was making a show of putting her in her place, but buried between his lines lay a certain inevitable conclusion. *He didn't have to come here.* He could have ignored her invitation-that-wasn't. Left her with a hatchery's worth of egg on her face, surrounded by idomeni who would wait and wait until they finally realized that ní Tsecha's toxin had provided them nothing worth waiting for. *You don't want to accede to the dictates of Temple, Aden nìRau Wuntoi. You don't want to slaughter the Vynshà.* All she had to do was provide him a way out that allowed him to fend off his propitiators, and she'd have an ally for life.

All she had to do . . .

"I know, and truly, why you wish to speak with me." Wuntoi shot the cuffs of his overrobe. "Temple has dictated that which they wish me to do. The sin of Morden nìRau Cèel is too great to be set aside. It must be shared by all Vynshà. As they all partake of the shame, so must they all pay the cost of it." He pointed to Jani. "You comprehend such. You, who helped damn the Laum."

Jani nodded, struggled to ignore the ache in her chest. "I will never forget the Night of the Blade." The escape from the consulate hospital basement, the dash through the streets to the shuttleport, and the realization that something horrible was unfolding before her eyes. "Ní Dathim Naré fought for Morden nìRau Cèel then. He was one of the Haárin who came down from the hills and rendered the justice of the gods upon the Laum."

Hearing his name, Dathim turned to them, raising a hand in greeting and baring his teeth.

Jani ignored him. "Thinking back, I wonder at the decision. The vast majority of the Laumrau had no knowledge of their dominants' collusion with humanish, or of that which occurred at Knevçet Shèràa." She inhaled, smelled heavy bay air and imagined it light and hot and desert dry. "Do I believe that a laborer here in Rauta Shèràa shared the guilt of the dominants who planned, the warriors who surrounded the hospital and would have killed me and my suborns if I had not killed them first?" She shook her head. "I do not. I argued of this with ní Tsecha, as I argued with him of many things. When he died, he had repudiated the concept of Wholeness of Soul, a tenet of major idomeni faiths. I have no doubt that if he had lived, he would have repudiated the slaughter of the Laum as well."

"You have no doubt." Wuntoi rocked his head back and forth, the panspecies *sez you* gesture. "But you do not *know*."

Jani pointed to the crowd seated on the lawn outside. "They are here because of their esteem for him. Because even though he is dead, they believe that he can deliver them. That his wisdom will find voice here, and change minds." She sat back, ignoring the flutter in her chest. "Forget that there are also Sìah out there, and Oà, who supported Pathenrau in their ascension. Forget that there are also Pathenrau, who see fit to disagree with the decisions of their dominants." She breathed in, breathed out. A glorious thing and truly, to breathe. "The Vynshà who are out there now did not wish to see ní Tsecha dead, and they should not be made to pay for the crimes of those who did."

Wuntoi remained silent. His slouch had straightened somewhat. He didn't seem quite as angry as he had when he'd arrived. Maybe she was getting through. Maybe . . .

"Prime Minister Li Cao and her suborns are content to allow idomeni to decide this matter." Wuntoi folded his arms, and looked for all the world like a negative image of Evgeny Scriabin. "Why do you butt in?"

Jani glanced at Scriabin, who seemed fixated on the state of his fingernails. "It is in Li Cao's interest to trade with the worldskein. It is in Li Cao's interest to encourage worldskein support for the Outer Circle colonies, so that she can hold back her own material support and expend it in other ways." She felt Scriabin's stare burn a hole in her cheek, and ignored it. "It is not necessarily in Li Cao's interest for the worldskein to be united and strong, and a worldskein that has just slaughtered millions of its own and lost tens if not hundreds of thousands more in the resulting rebellion against this slaughter, is not united. It is not strong."

Wuntoi fixed his bronze glare on Scriabin, whose face had reddened to sunstroke levels. "Humanish do not care. If they have nice tilework, and trueleather, and Sìah metal sculpture, they will not care about the history of those who produce such."

"Maybe." Jani gestured to Schiff, who paled and swallowed hard, but managed not to faint. "Yet they will record. They will transmit. They will remember." She bared her teeth. "Now, when most humanish think of idomeni, they think of ní Tsecha, who looked them in the eye when he spoke with them, and made them laugh, and behaved in ways they understood. If the slaughter goes ahead as planned, ní Tsecha will be forgotten, and when humanish think of idomeni, they will think of blood in the streets and the hacked bodies of youngish, and Rauta Shèràa will come to mean anathema. Humanish will move on, together with hybrid and Haárin, and bornsect will be left behind to fester in a pit of your own making."

"You say this to me?" Wuntoi waved his finger under Jani's nose. "You are sitting there in clothes that are stiff with the blood of those you killed."

"Vengeance. Self-defense." Jani once again pointed to the crowds on the lawn. "Slaughter." She shrugged, lowering her arms slowly as her sightline darkened. "It's a fine line, granted, and not always logical. But you cross it, and humanish will be a long time forgetting." She sensed Niall next to her, staring straight ahead, temper at the boil. *Sorry, Niall.* If a stronger worldskein made his job harder, it wasn't her problem. She was not of the Commonwealth anymore.

Wuntoi pushed a handful of braided fringe behind an ear ringed with gold studs. "And your solution to the Vynshà problem is?"

"They were his. Now they're mine." Jani held out her hands to the crowd. "Give them to me. Declare them Haárin, as a sign of your ascension. Declare them what you will. But give Tsecha's people to one who was also of Tsecha, and release them."

Silence fell, so profound that Jani could hear the breeze rustle the awning flaps. Then Scriabin cleared his throat. "That's fifteen million bornsect and over three million Haárin."

Jani shrugged. "He doesn't want them." She twitched a thumb at Wuntoi. "He would kill them. I am of Tsecha, as they are." She bared her teeth again. "I have died several times, and they are as dead. The dead leading the dead. It makes perfect sense."

Wuntoi regarded her with narrowed eyes. "They would need to leave this place and go to another."

Jani nodded. "And they will need places in which to live, and work to do and food to eat when they get to wherever they're going. The transit systems of two civilizations should be able to handle the load. We have experts to work out the logistics. We have builders and food experts. It will not be an instantaneous transition—it may take years. But it can be done."

Wuntoi cocked his head, as though considering. "You, as the dominant of a small enclave of most strange hybrids, are empowered to negotiate this agreement?"

"As dominant of Thalassa, I am acknowledged to be a Head of State by the Outer Circle colonies." She nodded toward Scriabin, who groaned softly. "If you doubt, propose such to Feyó, who will see her Outer Circle enclaves quintuple in size. Propose it to your suborns, who will eliminate Vynshà from their lives without blood. Propose it to Temple, and hear their screams—" That drew the equivalent of a nasty grin from Wuntoi. "—and if it serves, they will negotiate it, and come to the same conclusions, and you will have the diplomatic imprimatur you seek."

Wuntoi sat quietly. Then he looked up at Jani and bared his teeth. "To hear the screams of Temple would be a good thing, and truly." He stood. His shoulders held no curve.

Jani worked to her feet a little more slowly. Val's cardiopack had done *something*. The weight on her chest had lessened, and she felt tired rather than weak. "Humanish say that if a decision does not anger someone, it's the wrong decision."

"Do we really say that?" Niall managed to keep most of the sarcasm out of his voice.

"It is a good thing to say." Wuntoi seemed a different male than the one who had entered the enclosure a quarter hour before. His eyes had brightened. His voice sounded higher as the anger leached away. "I look forward to using it often, and truly." He nodded once to Jani, then walked out of the enclosure as the idomeni scrambled to their feet and parted for him once more.

Scriabin pressed a hand to the back of his neck. "Li Cao is going to have a stroke when we tell her this. She won't allow it."

"Then delay the final treaty signings, and make damn sure you win the next election." Jani patted his shoulder on the way out of the enclosure. "It's the best solution."

Scriabin followed after her. "It tips the population balance of the Outer Circle toward idomeni."

"If it's a good place, more humanish will come." Jani felt a looseness across her upper back, which was the only indication of how much it had ached previously. "What other decision could there be?" She started down the incline toward the double-length, where Val stood waiting.

"You know, I think I've figured it out."

Jani stopped and turned to find Niall standing at the top of the rise, lit 'stick in hand.

"On the first day of Creation, a Kilian cried out, 'It's dark in here—someone take care of it!' And then there was light." He doffed his lid and flipped it up in the air. "It's the only possible explanation!"

CHAPTER 34

Val's medical magic held. By the time Jani arrived at the embassy to see what diplomatic pitfalls and pushbacks awaited, it had once more donned its party finery. The mood seemed more subdued, however, as technical types in ill-fitting daysuits and uniforms bearing the white trouser stripes of the Sideline Service sat around tables with handhelds and trackboards and shook their heads in between trips to the open bar.

Mako met her at the opening to the garden, drink in hand. Whiskey, by the look of it, with no ice worth noting. "You realize you've set in motion a nightmare that will cause the logistics experts of two systems to awake screaming in the night for years to come?"

Jani shrugged. "It's good to spread the nightmares around."

"Hmm." Mako sipped his drink, then stared into his glass. "For someone who's just upended two governments and increased her own power and influence exponentially, you don't seem very happy."

Jani walked with him to an empty table near the stone wall. "It was his dream, this blending together. And he didn't live to see it."

Mako studied her for a time, then moved on to the sweeping tree branches that brushed to the ground. "I got to know ní Tsecha a little before he left Chicago. Niall always called him 'that wily old bird.' " He sat down and pondered his drink. "You reach a certain level in government, in the Service, you assume that . . . some might prefer if you did not exist. You don't dwell on it—you'd go mad if you did. It just crosses your mind occasionally that the day you're currently living might be your last."

Jani didn't say anything, even as the thought that she had earned membership in a very select club settled in her stomach to lie there and burn.

"He expected it, I think. The attempt, at least. No one could have written what he did, made the enemies he made, and not expected to have someone endeavor to extract the ultimate price." Mako rubbed the edge of the table with one thick finger. His hand was a battering ram, broad and brown and heavy-knuckled, the hand of a man who could handle any opponent face-to-face. Which was why he now concerned himself with the opponent that had been schooled in the use of sight mechs and long-ranges and explosives.

"He prepared as well as he could have, I think." Mako's voice grew tempered. "Feyó is sound. Not as much of a risk taker as she used to be, but she has managed to bring the conservatives to her side without losing the firebrands like Dathim and Meva, and that says something. There were those he influenced, the common idomeni, Haárin and bornsect both. The humans like Scriabin, who admired him." He looked out over the garden. "And then, in case all that failed, he had his second knife." He glanced up at Jani, then rose and headed for a table beneath the trees, where Cal Burkett had already opened the second bottle.

Jani sat in the chair Mako had vacated and watched the party. She had cleaned up with Val's aid, and changed into a dark blue wrapshirt and trousers that hid all her medical attachments and helped her blend in with the shadows. She gestured to a passing waiter and ordered iced water with bitter lemon. Sat back, and breathed, and closed her eyes.

"He told me, 'Meva, if anything happens to me, you must take her there.'"

Jani's eyes snapped open. Her heart skipped. "Dammit, Meva."

The female bared her teeth. She stood in front of the table, still dressed in her propitiator's overrobe, the object of stares from every part of the garden. "'You must take her to Shèrá,'" she continued as she sat across the table from Jani, "'because if anything ever happens to me, it will be from Shèrá.'" She picked up the tiny coffee service and poked through the sweetener packets, occasionally holding one up to the sun to examine it more closely. "'You must allow her to do that which she does, even if such maddens you. Even if such drives you to challenge her yourself.'" She set down the service with a clatter. "And I wished to, most certainly. When you accused Haárin of his death, I wanted to meet you at Guernsey and fight you in the middle of the concourse."

"I didn't accuse the Haárin . . ." Jani waved a hand, let it go, surrendered to the futility of trying to explain reality to those who preferred their altered truth. "I don't know how you talked Feyó into going along after she found out."

"I persuaded her."

"You bullied her. You're a bully, Meva."

"Pot. Kettle. Black." Meva bared her teeth. Sat back, hands folded in her lap, and watched the party, which gradually returned to its previous volume and activity levels once everyone adjusted to the propitiator in their midst.

Then the waiter arrived with Jani's bitter lemon. He set it down, then looked at Meva.

"That." She pointed to Jani's drink. "Galas thinks much of it," she added, as the young man headed back to the bar, aplomb itself but for the occasional backward glance.

Jani waited until he returned with Meva's drink. Waited longer, until the music and dancing started and she knew no one else could hear. "Dathim told me what you said to Tsecha about me." She breathed in until her chest ached. "You're right. I'm not a priest."

Meva nodded, eventually. Poked at the ice cubes with her straw. "This, I know. So did Tsecha, in the end. He saw that you did not study. He knew that you did not believe." She paused to sip. "But then he realized that which you were. You are the bringer of pain and change." She held out her glass to Jani. "Do that which you do. Leave the gods to me."

Jani hesitated. Then the token dropped, and she clinked her glass against Meva's, took a sip to seal the toast. "I think I saw him. After Cèel stabbed me. He was standing outside the circle. I heard him say, 'Nìa.' And he bared his teeth."

"He reminds you. His soul waits for release." The first hint of shadow crossed Meva's face, and she grew more subdued. "He asks you to do so."

"I thought you would do that."

"He would wish you to do so, I think."

"At Temple?" Jani shook her head. "Temple tried to push Wuntoi into slaughtering the Vynshà. It doesn't seem the right place." She paused, raked through all the Vynshà theology that she'd struggled to remember and now tumbled about her brain as though it had always been there. As though she had always known it. "Can I ask you . . . ?" She spread out a napkin and asked the waiter for a stylus, and talked while Meva listened. Until the music ramped up and the laughter and talking grew louder. Until Meva tucked the napkin into her overrobe, said that she needed to speak to those at Temple whom she trusted, and left.

Val came eventually, with John in tow, but the undercurrent of tension made conversation too painful to pursue. Lucien missed out due to the fact that this time he actually had pulled desk officer duty. No one mentioned Anais or regretted her absence.

As night fell, Jani pleaded fatigue and left, but instead of retiring to her suite, she departed the embassy and headed for the base. Stopped at the gate, asked if Colonel Pierce was on site, and received the surprising news that she had been cleared. That she was expected. That she would know where he was.

She found Niall sitting on a bench that had been set in a patch of lawn next to an office annex. The bench fell under the building's shadow and the lighting was poor. She would have walked past the spot if she hadn't seen the telltale pinpoint glow, stark as the reflection off a predator's eye.

"It actually does cool off at night." She sat near the end of the bench, an arm's length away. Close enough, but not too. "I remembered that it did, but then I wondered if it was just memory playing tricks." She quieted, let the silence settle. Her job wasn't to talk, but to sit, wait, listen. To be there.

"Haven't had time to think about this much over the past few days. Every time I turned around, you were getting yourself killed or pulling some diplomatic rabbit out of a hat. I suppose I should thank you for the distraction." Niall took a last pull on his 'stick, then rolled the gold-striped cylinder between his fingers. "It happened over there." He pointed to a place about twenty meters distant, the current resting place for a cluster of skimmer charge-stations. "Those stations weren't there, of course. Nothing was. Just a piece of open land in between the buildings." He sniffed. His face was in shadow, and maybe it was a good thing. "I wonder if anyone knows what happened there? Someone. One of the old-timers."

Jani looked toward the spot and imagined a night twenty years before. The darkness shattered by bombs and artillery. The shouts. The panic. And in the middle of it all, a twenty-one-year-old sergeant, sent to perform a very special task. "How do you feel?"

Niall laughed, a single, humorless jerk of his shoulders. "I really shouldn't bother to eat decent food until after we pull out of here." He leaned forward, elbows on knees, and continued to work the spent 'stick. "But the offices are open at all hours now, thanks to you. Always a bathroom handy. A can to kneel before."

Jani studied his profile, details muted by the half-light. Sharp nose and line of jaw, set off by his brimmed lid. *He could take it off.* Yes, they were outdoors, but they were seated, and, technically at least, having a conversation. *But he won't do it.* He was an officer in the Commonwealth Service, with a tradition to uphold. Standards to maintain. An ideal to live up to.

"Go ahead and say it." Niall glanced at her, then faced front once more. "When you're this quiet for this long, I can just about hear the hum of machinery."

"That's the animandroid." Jani raised her left arm, then let it fall. Twitched her left leg. "Bad joke."

"You're allowed, gel." Niall sighed. "After the day you've had, you're allowed a lot."

Jani pondered for a time. Then she tapped him on the shoulder and pointed to his spent 'stick. "Got any extras?"

Niall stared. "Parini will bloody kill me."

"If it weren't for me, he wouldn't have anything to do around here but dance and pick up unsuspecting lieutenants." Jani held out her hand. "C'mon."

Niall scrabbled into his trouser pocket and pulled out his case. "When was the last time you smoked?"

"Years." Jani took a 'stick, crunched the tip, then paused to wipe a tiny fleck of the bulb material from her tongue. "I don't remember—can you swallow this stuff?"

"It's safe." Niall grinned as he pulled out one for himself and bit down. "Years ago, if the pieces were big enough, we'd have spitting contests." He shook his head. "I've said it before, gel. Just when I think you can't surprise me anymore."

"Drinking's a waste of time. I want to see if nicotine still has any effect."

"First Doc, then you." Niall paused to take a deep drag, then blew out a quartet of rings. "Gonna work on Meva next."

Jani eyed the 'stick warily, then took a drag. Her throat closed as the fragrant smoke flowed into her mouth, and she coughed. She bent double to take the pressure off her chest. Her eyes teared.

"Jesus wept—don't try to pull like me! I've been at it since the days o' me youth." Niall took the 'stick from her and tapped her between her shoulder blades until she quieted. "Baby puffs, until you work up to it."

"Thanks."

"What I'm here for."

Jani took back the 'stick and tried again. The merest sampling. "Taste's a little like the way *vrel* blossom smells." She dabbed her eyes with her sleeve, then stilled and watched the smoke stream upward until the night breeze took hold and scattered it. "If you had to do it again, now, how would you secure them?"

Niall sat back, one arm crossed over his stomach, the other straight, the 'stick dangling from his hand. "I'd have demanded more people. One guard per, and two to back them up in case friends decided to come to the rescue." His eyes narrowed as he considered the problem. "Armored skimvan right here near the building. None of this escorting through the base shit." Pause to inhale. "If I could coax a medico to come along, I'd just drug 'em and stack them in the van. Wouldn't even give them the chance to see one another, to get excited."

Jani nodded. "And if you had been put in that situation a year or two earlier?" She waited for him to speak, and knew it would be some time before he did. *Because he knows the answer.* "I think you'd have shot them without a second thought." She took another puff, and tasted the *vrel* blossom. "You were once a remorseless bastard, Niall Pierce, untempered by finer feeling or much of a moral sense. It wasn't that you lacked those things. They were there, and always had been. They were just . . . dormant. You lived a life in which you couldn't afford them, so you set them aside." She lowered her voice as a brace of file-laden clerks trotted past. "Then you met Mako, and somehow he instilled in you the notion that there was still a modicum of honor left to be mined from that calloused orphan heart. You learned that you could be part of something bigger than yourself, and that realization hit you like a sockful of rocks. All those sensibilities that you'd set aside awakened and roiled to the surface."

Niall sat still, eyes fixed straight ahead. Breathing a little quick, a little shallow. Might have been nicotine. Or memory.

Jani kept her voice level, soft. "The problem is, you need tools to deal with bigger than yourself, and you hadn't acquired them yet. So, when the shit hit the fan, you fell back on the bastard because that was still your default. It was the man you still were, to some extent. But then, as time passed, you changed. You became a better man, the man you wish you had been twenty years before." Her throat tightened, and she blamed the smoke. "One of the best I've ever known. But I've told you that before." She watched a wad of paper skitter down the walkway, coaxed by the breeze. "The bill's been paid, Niall, with hard-earned coin. Give yourself a break."

For a time it seemed as though he hadn't heard. Then came the voice, from twenty years away. "They keep me posted, like old friends. I hear Ebben scream like she did when she saw the others die and realized she was next. I see the look on her face when I aimed the long-range at her. I feel the pounding of my heart, the certainty that if I let her get away, she'd flee to her friends, save herself by giving Roshi and the rest of us away." He doffed his lid, scratched his head, set it back on. "I relive it all as if it was yesterday."

"And you likely always will." Jani pressed a hand to her mended stomach. No pain, only pressure, as through someone had placed a foot on her diaphragm and pressed down. "If you hadn't changed, you wouldn't see them. They'll always be there to remind you of how far you've come."

Niall stared straight ahead, a still image captured in a moment of tension. Not a twitch, not even the flicker of an eyelid, broke the stasis.

Then, after a few moments, movement, his nostrils narrowing as he snorted. "You really believe that?" He stood, straightening the line of his tunic with his free hand. "I've heard lines of bull from the psychs before, but I think you just won the prize." He edged away from her, one slow step after another, toward the charge-station array. "What's your default?"

Jani stood and walked after him, slowing every so often as her heart skipped. "There's a reason why we're friends."

"You? A remorseless bastard?" Niall glanced back at her, then shook his head. "You were born with the tools. If Ebben and the others had bolted on you, you'd never have—" He stopped in front of the charge-stations, reduced to shadowed shape by the darkness. "You never panicked in your life."

"How do you know?"

"Because you'd have told me. Sometime, during one of our bull sessions, you'd have dropped a hint." Niall touched the corner of one of the stations, then pulled back as though it burned. "What do you see, now that you're here? What do you remember?" His voice came soft, but there was an undercurrent. A plea for parity, for a weakness she could share.

Jani sniffed the Rauta Shèràa night air, tinged with dampness and city smells. Not baked. Not light. Not as clean as the desert. "It's like in the dreams. The openings to the Laumrau tents close like a self-sealing envelope, and the flaps make a ripping sound if you yank them apart too quickly. The tent material itself looks flimsy, like rotted silk, but it's stronger than it looks." She stared down at the 'stick in her hand, dose ring still indicating three-quarters full. Felt a tap on her arm, saw Niall's extended hand, and passed it off with a grateful nod. "When I reached the first tent, I tried shooting through it. But it was coated with barrier—don't ask me why I didn't assume it would be coated with barrier, I just didn't—and the charge dissipated across the surface." She moved her feet. Knew she stood on cement, yet felt sand instead. Shifting sand. "I panicked then. I knew whoever was inside had heard the shooter. That those in the surrounding tents heard it as well." Her heart tripped, and she blamed nicotine, the injury. "I had resigned myself to death when I walked down the dune toward the encampment, but part of me wasn't ready to go. I grabbed the edge of the flap and yanked it back—" She tried to mime the motion until the grip of her incision stopped her. "—heard that ripping sound. A female sat at her altar table. She looked up when she heard me. Set down her fork. And just stared." Her hand came up, fingers closing around a nonexistent weapon. "She never moved, not even when she saw the shooter." She turned to Niall to find him watching her wide-eyed, 'stick stalled halfway to his mouth. "I know they heard me. They had to have—"

Niall let his arm drop. "What?"

"It was like fish in a barrel." Jani felt sweat bead on her temple and brushed it away. "Why didn't one of them try to stop me? There were twenty-six of them and one of me. They must have heard. They must have known what was going on. And rather than commit sacrilege by interrupting their sacrament, they remained in their tents, and let me slaughter them." She walked to the nearest charge station and leaned against it. "I wonder sometimes whether they wanted to die. Whether the enormity of their sins had borne down upon them, and they decided en masse that death was better than going on as they were."

"Suicide by homicide?" Niall paced a tight circle. "I think that's a stretch, but I'm human. We've a tradition of fighting to live." His voice had lightened now that they'd moved on to her nightmare. "I think they froze. They didn't expect a human to come into their camp and attack them, and when they heard it happening, they didn't take it for what it was." He snorted again. "Death by culture clash. The history pages are filled. I blame the bornsect mind-set. Damned lockstep thinking. If they'd had even one Dathim Naré in that encampment, you'd have been dead before you reached the first tent." He spun on his heel to face her and shook a finger under her nose. "Don't try to slap a coward label on yourself, Jani Kilian, because I won't let you. If just one of them had woken the hell up and realized what was happening, you wouldn't be standing here now questioning yourself. The potential for death was there." He shook his head in disgust. "Fish in a barrel, my ass."

Jani smiled. "That's our job, I guess. Prop up one another every so often. Shake some sense."

"You were here for me tonight. I'll be there for you tomorrow." Niall held his head high as he started again to pace, touching one of the stations each time he passed. Then he stopped and his shoulders sagged. "It won't ever go away?"

"I don't think so."

"Ah, well." Niall took a step closer. The light from a safety illumin fell across his face, revealing the greyness, the sheen of sweat. "Maybe it's worth it, if only to watch you try to smoke." He smiled. Walked to one of the charge-stations and leaned against it. "So what's next for the team? Release the old bird's soul at Temple? Allow him his rest?"

"In a few days." Jani leaned against another of the stations, savored the machine warmth. "Meva and I are planning something."

"Why does that phrase strike fear in my heart?" Niall looked around for a moment, then gestured to her. "Come on, gel. I'll walk you back. Some of us need our sleep."

CHAPTER 35

"They've been ferrying idomeni out there since the ceremony was announced early yesterday. Last estimates were upward of two million. Could be two and a half to three by the time we get out there. The logistics are staggering." Niall took a swallow of coffee, then smacked his lips. "You've been taking lessons from Shroud. This stuff really could wake the dead."

"Flattery will get you a refill." Val topped off Niall's mug, then hovered over Jani, carafe at the ready. "What's wrong with it?"

Jani set down her still full cup. Breakfast in the kitchen of Val's guesthouse had commenced a few minutes before, after hurried awakenings and conferencing with ministers and admirals general and quick showers. "Stomach's a little knotty." She jerked her chin at Niall. "He's trying to scare me."

"Don't get me hopes up, gel. It'll go to me head and there'll be no dealing with me." Niall moved from caffeine to sugar and carbohydrates, spreading a slice of toast with marmalade, then folding it over and dunking it in his coffee. "They've also set up displays in Temple and major squares. Other cities. Worldskeinwide transmission. We won't even talk about the Commonwealth networks."

"Good. *Don't*." Jani took a lemon wedge from a plate of garnishes and bit into it.

Val stifled a yawn, then sat next to Jani and eyed her with professional calculation gone a bit bleary around the edges. "You know how John and I feel about this?"

"I know." Jani took up her fork and picked over her food, forcing down some fried meat, some scrambled eggs. Protein seemed the best bet, given what her day held in store. "But Meva and I talked about it. Then she discussed it with some of the propitiators she knew at Temple, and they concluded that while there's no real precedent, it's theologically sound." She smashed an overcrisp rasher of bacon into bits, then set down her fork. "He and I talked about it once, for some reason I can't remember. If I ever went back, what could I do in order to . . . restore balance?" She held out her right hand and studied her redstone ring. The one Tsecha had given her when she graduated the Academy. The one that hadn't fit until she'd begun to hybridize and her fingers thinned.

"We could've delayed this, you know." Niall's verve ebbed, replaced by his more usual coiled spring wariness. "I could've taken you out there beforehand, let you see the place. Get a sense of it."

"It wouldn't have helped." Jani pushed away from the table and stood, her propitiator's robe falling around her knees, the red-slashed sleeves settling past her wrists. "I could visit it beforehand a hundred times, and it wouldn't help." She sniffed, smelled clear air and heat instead of coffee and toast, then looked down at Niall to find him studying her, eyes a little too shiny for comfort.

"We'd better—" He looked away, cleared his throat. "We've got a long ride ahead of us. We'd better leave." He picked up his brimmed lid from its resting place on the spare chair and put it on, squaring the angle as always by running his thumbs and forefingers along the edge of the brim. "I'll wait by the skimmer." He strode out the kitchen door without a backward glance, a rough-edged vision in tan and white.

"He does get emotional, our Niall. Especially where you're concerned." Val took a last swallow of coffee, then pushed back his chair and rose with obvious reluctance. "I visited Knevçet Shèràa once. You were still in induced coma, and John and I weren't sure—" He inhaled shakily. "I wanted to see the place for myself. I'd heard rumors enough, and I wanted to see." As though in deference to the upcoming ceremony, he had donned a daysuit in dark cream, the jacket's lapels a fair match for an overrobe's shawl collar. "I couldn't get within ten kilometers of the place. The Vynshà had taken over that area, and they'd installed perimeter patrols. A gate with armed sentries."

"Tsecha wasn't sure when they razed the hospital. He didn't think it happened until after he'd been put under house arrest, but no one would tell him anything and he could never find the records of the destruction." Jani saw Tsecha in her mind's eye, overrobe billowing as he paced around her and ranted over Temple perfidy. "He always felt that they should have kept it open, as a reminder." She heard his voice in her head, the sibilant rise and fall, only to have it silenced when Val touched her arm.

"Let's go." He linked his arm with hers and walked with her into the morning.

"They'll kill you if you go out there, Captain. You know they will."
"They're at sacrament, Borgie. They don't even have any guards posted."
"What are you going to do?"
"Just go back inside. Wait until I return. Then we'll go from there."

"No need for you to get out." Niall steered the skimmer into the embassy drive. "We just need to join up with the ministerial cavalcade so that we all leave at the same time." He tapped the dashboard input, then studied the display. "Then it's on to the enclave—Feyó's skimmer is waiting just inside the gate. It will pull in behind and follow us to the destination, of course. *Protocol*." He drawled the word as though it were a particularly foul descriptor.

"Knevçet Shèràa." Jani caught his gaze in the rearview. "You can say it, Niall. It's all right."

"I know that." Niall reddened, as he did whenever he was caught being delicate. He then disembarked to talk to Ulanova's driver, which left the vehicle unguarded.

Jani turned to Val. "Do you think—" She was interrupted by a rap on the window, and lowered it.

"Hello." Lucien looked in, stepping back a little as soon as he spotted Val.

Jani ignored Val's mutter. "You driving, as well?"

"Mako and Burkett. The cabin barrier will go up as soon as we set out, and I'll be left with my own thoughts for company." Lucien looked back toward the Service triple-length, near which the two men and various aides had already gathered. "I better go." He reached in and took hold of Jani's hand. "*Bonne chance*." He brought it to his lips and kissed it hard, then trotted back to his post.

"Some of us have all the luck." Val sniffed. "I don't hold grudges. Please don't give it a second thought."

Jani surveyed the yard and spotted Scriabin standing by his own triple-length, talking to an aide. "I have some unfinished business to attend to." She felt Val's hand close over her own, a not so subtle attempt at restraint. "I'll just be a minute." She shook off his hold, pushing up the gullwing and exiting the skimmer.

Scriabin actually brightened when he saw Jani approach. "Good morning! I hope that you're—"

"A word, please." Jani ignored his proffered hand, saw the light in his eyes flicker.

"Zhenya?"

Jani and Scriabin both turned just as Anais Ulanova emerged from the passenger cabin of Scriabin's skimmer.

"We'll be leaving in a few minutes." She glared at Jani, but this time her hatred was tempered by uncertainty. Fear. A hint of panic. "There is something I wish to discuss with you on the way to the ceremony." She focused on her nephew, her voice ripe with conciliatory lilt. "It may take some time."

Scriabin studied his aunt for a few moments, then shook his head. "Oh, Ani." He pressed a hand to his forehead, then wiped it down his face. "What have you done now?" He looked past her to the center of the drive, and swore.

Jani followed Scriabin's glower. To her complete lack of surprise, she saw Lucien standing beside Mako's skimmer, watching them. Once again, hours of discussion whittled down to words left unspoken, to scant expressions. To Lucien's bland disregard as he met Ulanova's pleading eye, and the warm smile when he looked at Jani. To the way Ulanova's face paled as the realization hit home that her lover had betrayed her.

"I'll be a few minutes." Scriabin shot his cuffs. "I need to speak with ná Kièrshia now." No "Tyotya." No patient smile of Familial duty. Only the dead voice and cold eye of a man who had reached his limit.

Ulanova held out a hand to him. "Zhenya, I—"

"Get in the skimmer."

Ulanova flinched. Then she lowered her hand and, with a last sullen scowl at Jani, did as she was told.

Scriabin waited until an aide slammed the skimmer door closed. "I don't want to hear what you have to tell me, do I?" Weariness had replaced anger now, his normally powerful voice emerging weak. Defeated.

"I'll be brief." Jani led him to the small side yard, where the small fountain burbled just loudly enough. "The time wasn't right before to discuss this. It isn't any better now, but the way things are going, there may not be a good time for months." She picked up a handful of gravel from a hammered bowl and started flicking the stones one at a time into the water. "Anais sent Lucien to Elyas to kill me." She surprised herself with her casual tone. *Nothing to see here—move along. Happens every day.* "She convinced Mako that he and I were still close, that he'd make a useful . . . maybe 'spy' is too harsh a word. Maybe 'pair of eyes' will suffice." She flicked stones into the water with the beat of her words. *Plink— plink—plink—* "But the fact was, she felt Feyó more amenable and preferred the idea of having her in charge of Thalassa. My dominance would garner her nothing. She knew I didn't trust her. Knew that if I had anything to say, she'd wind up on the sidelines."

Scriabin stood rigid, and stared at the stone wall in front of him. "If you heard this from Pascal—"

"He has this habit of telling me the truth." Jani tossed another pebble. *Plink.* "A choice between believing him or your *tyotya* is no choice at all." She recalled Mako's words. *You reach a certain level . . . you assume that some might prefer if you did not exist.*

"I don't—" Scriabin pulled a handkerchief from inside his sleeve and wiped his forehead. "I will do a little digging on my own, if you don't mind. Some things one must confirm for oneself, however much one trusts the messenger." He shook out the embroidered cloth, then folded it into a neat square. "I may . . . talk to Pascal, just to gather a few details." He glanced at Jani sidelong, his discomfort coating him like his sweat. "In any event, she won't . . . she won't bother you again."

"No. She won't." Jani tossed the last few pebbles into the water. "I should mention that Thalassa plans to nationalize John's share of Neoclona. It'll settle the question of ownership once and for all, and the income should help finance our expansion."

"I daresay." Scriabin paused to lick his lips. "I expect you would like assurance of my and Minister Ulanova's support for this, election win or not." He sighed heavily. He knew blackmail when he heard it, and who to thank for the privilege.

"I want the takeover to happen, and Chicago to stay out of the way." Jani brushed off her hands. "Financial support would be appreciated as well, as a show of good faith." *Because there's a GateWay to be considered, and millions of new colonists, and the security of one-quarter of your remaining Commonwealth.* A new Oligarch, eager to mend fences with disenfranchised Haárin. She didn't say any of that aloud, of course, because she knew she didn't have to. Scriabin was an old hand—he could do the math in his head.

"We should get going." Jani left him by the water and returned to her skimmer, where she found Niall waiting.

He pulled open her door. Offered her his hand for support.

"Took a little break to stretch our legs and read someone the Riot Act, did we?"

"However did you guess?" Jani brushed off Val's questioning stare. "Let's go."

Her blood flowed down her arm, as warm as the wind, and she sopped it with strips of shop cloth that she'd worked into a braid. Then she tied the braid to a stake and drove the stake into the ground. According to an ancient Vynshà ritual, she had just taken her soul from her body and pinned it in place. Preserved it from whatever desperate act her now godless body intended to perform.

"I've never seen the streets this empty." Val stared out his window, shook his head. "Not even during the last bombing forays." He glanced at Jani. "I won't ask if you're nervous."

"It's not like I'm giving a speech." She tried to smile, but the effort made her face ache. "I'm numb." Her heart thudded as the entry to the Haárin enclave came into view and Feyó's skimmer appeared at the gate.

"What does he think of all this?" Val glanced toward the sky. "Wherever he is, in whatever form. What might he be thinking?"

"That it all ended up pretty much like he predicted it would." Jani watched one of Meva's suborns close the doors to a skimvan, and knew it contained the reliquary. "That he won."

Val lay his head back and stared through the curved window at the cloudless sky. "You could be right."

Jani turned to track the van as they passed it, as it floated out onto the road and slowly accelerated after them, like a shark chasing down its prey.

You won, inshah. She imagined a loud laugh, a loose-limbed walk and shining auric eyes.

Rauta Shèràa diminished as cities always did, from center to various sections and quarters to the outskirts, until it receded, shortened, faded into the horizon behind them. Thirty minutes passed, and the land rolled and roughened, stone in white and brown and coral pink dotted with grey-green scrub. An hour passed, and even that fell away, until all that remained were the outcroppings and the dunes and the high blue milky sky.

So where are the crowds? Jani was about to rib Niall that his sources had miscalculated by a factor of ten or more when they passed over a rocky ridge and into the shallow bowl that held the sands of light's weeping. She saw them then, seemingly as numerous as grains of sand, held back from the center of the bowl by low barriers and patrols of mixed humanish and idomeni security. A sea of faces—the true meaning of that hackneyed phrase was driven home with a hammer as in every direction she looked idomeni filled her view.

Then there were the skimmers, the vans and trucks and arrays and holocams.

"Oh my God." Val sat up straight, hand scrabbling along the seat to link with hers.

"Told you." Niall eyed her in his rearview as he halted the skimmer on the rim.

Jani nodded. Her mouth had gone as dry as the land surrounding them, her muscles clenched so tight that it hurt to move.

Niall exited the skimmer, setting his lid and straightening his tunic as he walked back to Jani's door and opened it. "Need a hand, gel?" he asked, and offered her his.

Jani gave Val's hand a last squeeze and let it go even as she reached out and took Niall's and held it fast. Stepped out onto desolation that had not changed over the course of twenty years, breathed the light, dry air that smelled the same, felt the heat that drilled her to the hybrid bone.

She looked off to her right, toward the site where the hospital had stood. Every block and tile had been knocked down and carted away years before, sunken into burial sites all over Shèrá, leaving only the telltale flatness that spoke of mechanical leveling and foundations and the incursion of civilization into a place not meant to contain it.

Jani imagined the outlines of walls, three stories high and devoid of windows, a flat roof. Remembered nightfall, that first chill in the air, and the warmth of her blood as it ran down her arm.

"Jan?" Niall leaned close. "You're wearing the bug. Anything goes wrong, just call."

"I'm all right." She let go of his hand, reached beneath her overrobe to the sheath on her belt. Slid out the short blade that Meva had sent her the previous day and started down the slope. Did her best to shut out the faces and the cams and the weighted silence, the faint whistle of wind and occasional cry of a bird the only discernable sounds. *How can so many bodies make so little noise?* No one spoke. Overrobes and sleeves fluttered, the only movement in the vast ring of mortality.

As she neared the bottom, she pressed the point of the blade to her right sleeve and slashed downward, the cloth renting with a sharp ripping sound, like the opening of a tent flap. She slowed, then stopped as she reached the foot of the slope. Off to the right, twenty or so meters distant, stood Meva, bracketed by Dathim and Feyó. Behind them, upon a small altar stone, rested the reliquary.

She started walking again. Four strides. A fifth. Then she stopped, raised her arm so the cloth tumbled back to the elbow, revealing her bare forearm. Drew the blade across her skin, then waved her arm in a sweeping arc, spraying her blood.

That first, wasted shot. The opening of the tent. Wide, staring eyes.
The second shot.
One—
Another tent. No wasted shot this time.
—two—
The next tent, and the next.
—three—four—

. . . another cut, another spray of blood. Another. Another. Too many times to track. Too many times.

—fifteen—sixteen—seventeen—
She tried to pray at first, impose order upon the random path she walked. Then realized that order had no place here.

One Thalassan day, her soul cloth vanished. She hunted for it, couldn't find it. Ran to Tsecha's house to tell him, only to find that he had taken it, or sent someone to take it. He had untied the knotting and shaken loose the braids. I have returned your soul to you, nìa, he told her.

And she returned theirs to them.
—twenty-four—twenty-five—
Twenty-six.

"That part's over." Niall's voice, in her ear.

"As much as it can ever be." Jani looked toward the network skimmers. "Hope they got it all."

"You're almost through it, gel. Just a few minutes more." Niall

paused, cleared his throat. *"Give the old bird a nod from me when he goes."*

"What do we do now, Cap?"

"Place me under arrest, Sergeant Burgoyne. I've broken treaty law. You have to arrest me."

"No, you did it to save us—"

"If you don't arrest me, they'll think you were involved. Borgie—listen to me. You didn't know what I was planning—that's what you'll tell them because it's the truth. You didn't know, and when I told you what I had done, you did your duty and placed me under arrest."

"Captain—"

"I did what I had to. Now it's your turn."

Jani stood over the last place. The last. Her right arm had numbed. She felt stiffness where blood had dried, the sting of the breeze across open wounds. But no pain. Not yet.

She sheathed the blade. Turned to the right and walked. Her head felt afloat, her knees wobbly. There was a hollow where her heart had been.

She fixed on Meva, who stood still as statuary, arms folded and hands tucked into the sleeves of her overrobe. As she drew closer, the female stepped to one side, allowing her a clear path to the reliquary.

Jani stopped before the altar. Lifted the reliquary lid. It seemed heavier than it had in Thalassa, hard-edged and unwieldy. She brought in her elbows and braced them against her sides for support, hefting the lid like an overladen tray and setting it down on the left side of the reliquary. As her hands slid along the edge, some roughness caught her finger, the one bearing the redstone ring. She felt the sliver slide in, the sting when she pushed the lid farther up the table and applied pressure to the wound. *Making sure I stay conscious, are you?* Her lip twitched as she fought the urge to grin. *Always the considerate one.*

She moved away from the lid and stood before the open reliquary. "Hello, old friend." She reached into the box and took hold of the scroll, clutching it hard with her left hand to compensate for the weakness in her right. "The place has been cleaned for you. Their souls have been healed." Her hands remained dry and steady, and she thanked her old teacher as she lifted the scroll and set it on the altar. "Follow them home," she said as she opened the cover, then turned each page. Felt something brush her cheek, and knew it was the breeze, but decided that for today she would imagine it as something else.

I understand more than you believe, nìa.
    "Yes, nìRau. I think you did."

Jani braced her hands against the altar. "The stone is so nice and warm."

Meva moved in beside her and placed her hand against the stone as well. "I find it cool." She touched Jani's right hand, then took Jani's arm and led her up the incline. "You feel most as yourself, ná Kièrshia?"

"I feel most as someone who's going to pass out if she doesn't sit down soon." Jani fielded Meva's look of horror. "Don't worry— I won't faint in front of the worldskein. I will maintain my presence and my godly composure." She breathed, felt her heart skip, saw golden flecks invade her field of vision. "Stay away," she said to John as he started to walk toward her. "Not until I get inside the skimmer." She looked toward the crowds, who had not yet begun to disperse, and offered a slight hand wave to the nearest reporter, who waved back. Slid into the skimmer as soon as Niall flipped up the gullwing, then gripped the edge of her seat as John and Val piled in after her and the weight imbalance caused the vehicle to shudder and buck like a small boat in a storm.

"When I watched you draw that blade down your sleeve and make the first cut, I thought to myself, 'Hot damn, she nicked her brachial artery. John and I will be running down to get her in two, three minutes.'" Val pushed up her right sleeve and swallowed hard. "I assume you're going to want these to scar?"

"You assume correctly." Jani felt some remnant of tension leach away as Val and John eased her onto her back. John then dragged a seat cushion out of its holder and tucked it under her knees while Val attached a transfuser pack to the crook of her right arm.

Niall immediately began the tricky exercise of maneuvering the triple-length through the dispersing crowds. "'Then will he strip his sleeves and show his scars, and say, "These wounds I had on Crispin's day." Old men forget: yet all shall be forgot, but he'll remember with advantages what feats he did that day.' Henry the Fifth again." He paused. Started to speak, stopped, then tried again. "Is she all right?"

"She will be as soon as we get her blood volume back up." Val grumbled under his breath. "Did you have to bleed quite this much?"

"She did what she had to." John pressed a scanner lead to her shirt just over her heart. "It was . . . the most starkly beautiful thing I have ever seen."

"Scared the hell out of me." Val adjusted the transfuser settings, then fell back onto the seat opposite. "Hundreds of thousands of idomeni, and none of them so much as whispering."

Jani closed her eyes. Felt the vehicle hum run along her spine. Drifted in and out of sleep. Dreamed of the reliquary. Dreamed she saw Tsecha, walking across the sand toward her, overrobe billowing behind him. Dreamed she heard John's voice, Niall's response.

Felt the skimmer slow, then stop, and realized that she wasn't dreaming at all.

"I'll only be a minute." John said as he placed his hand on her brow.

Jani opened her eyes just as he pushed up the gullwing and exited the skimmer. "Is this where I think it is?"

"Yeah." Val sat on the edge of his seat. Then he sighed, wiped his eyes, and followed his partner outside.

"Network vans are going to be coming through any minute. I told him he needed to make it fast." Niall sat back, pulled out his case. Soon the clove aroma drifted through the cabin. "Should've figured he'd want to see this place. It's his Knevçet Shèràa, after all."

Jani sat up. Moved her arms, her legs. *No stars in front of my eyes.* Walking might prove another matter entirely, but she wouldn't know until she tried.

"Can't sit still, can you?" Niall shook his head. "They might want to be alone, you know? They might just need some time."

Jani looked through the open door to the scene beyond. John pacing back and forth, Val standing off to one side, his hand over his mouth. No shrine on this site. No marker or fencing or designation of any kind.

"It was a turning point for me, too," Jani said as she disembarked. "I used to wonder what this place looked like." She walked carefully, slowing as the hollow sensation in her chest returned. "I thought about coming here once, when you and Val went to a meeting at the consulate." She came to a halt an arm's reach from John, who had stopped pacing and now stared down at the ground. "Eamon even left the place unlocked, probably hoping that I'd bolt. But I couldn't find a skimmer."

John didn't respond at first. Then he crouched, worked his hand into the sandy ground, gone from dune to semi-arid as they drew near Rauta Shèràa again. "Here." He let the ground trickle through his fingers, then made a sweeping motion with one arm. "Wreckage scattered for kilometers. Remains. We'd pick up some blackened bit the size of a finger and didn't know if we were looking at tissue or a charred piece of transport until we scanned it." He cleaned his hand on the leg of his trousers and slowly straightened. "Then we found—" He stopped. Swallowed. "We'd watched idomeni die for months. We weren't allowed to help. We weren't allowed to save . . . so many. I lost count. Then we found you, and decided—" He turned to look at her, eyes bright as the sun that blistered above them. "—and decided that we would save you, and that no one would stop us." He laughed. "Law of unintended consequences. If I knew then what I knew now . . ." He fixed on her for a long moment. ". . . I'd still do it. I wouldn't change—" He turned away. "My decision, to add to all the others that we made, and lived with, and paid for."

They stood in silence, each a prisoner of their own memories. Then Val stirred.

"We're getting the high sign." He jerked a thumb toward the skimmer, which Niall had converted into a holiday display of blinking warning lights. "The network vans are headed this way. We better get going."

Jani waited for John, then slipped her arm through his. They walked back to the skimmer side by side, at peace, at least for now. Got in and headed back to the city.

CHAPTER 36

". . . and the first two thousand houses have been completed in phase one of the new western section." Dieter made a notation on his recording board. "That makes ten thousand in the past three months."

Jani nodded. Outside the library window a pair of seabirds swooped at one another, their squawks audible even through the filtering glass. *Are they fighting or mating?* She watched them circle one another, the tips of their wings seeming to touch. *Is there a difference?*

Then she sensed a ripple in the silence, and looked across the table to find her suborn eyeing her expectantly. "That's a lot."

"Yes, it is." Dieter set down the board, then tucked the stylus behind his ear. "A less preoccupied person might even be impressed."

Jani smiled. One thing she'd missed during her time away was Dieter's gentle chiding. *And now I've had a lifetime's worth in the past few months.* "I'm sorry. It's a marvelous achievement."

Dieter sighed, then started gathering up his files. "If you don't want the blow by blow details, just say so. I can save them for the monthly reports."

"When did we start doing monthly reports?"

"Last month, when the first funding arrived from Chicago to help cover phase two of the western expansion along with the far southern expansion near Meteora. Prime Minister Scriabin is an old Commerce hand. He likes reports with tables and charts and whatnot."

Jani tried to hand Dieter a file, but she had taken it out of order, and he frowned and set it aside. "Doesn't he trust us?"

"He simply wants an accounting." Dieter piled the first armful of documents onto the trundle that followed him everywhere like a loyal, overlarge dog. "He's entitled. He's a major underwriter of what is likely the largest resettlement project ever undertaken."

"The Commonwealth push into the colonies was bigger."

"You're going to argue now?" Dieter returned to the desk for a second armful. "The Vynshà migration involves fewer individuals, yes, but also a much shorter time frame." To the trundle, then back to the desk again. "And we're looking after things like infrastructure and such, which was more than Mother Commonwealth ever did for our great-great-however-many-grandfolk." The last armful. "This exodus will be handled properly."

By committee. With monthly reports. Jani sighed. "The teams are in place. We have departments now, instead of someone in a corner desk with a workstation and a good memory. All humming along."

Dieter stopped. Cocked his head. "What's wrong?"

"I don't know." Jani walked to the window and searched for the birds, but they'd moved on to another part of the sky. "Meteora? Didn't they have a corruption problem there?"

". . . Yes." Dieter wedged the trundle between two chairs to keep it from drifting, then joined her at the window. "We haven't done much there yet. A team of engineers and architects traveled down last week to look over the proposed site for the first enclave." He slid the window aside and stepped out onto the balcony. "It's not as beautiful as Thalassa, in my opinion. Greyer. Greener, perhaps. Mountainous."

"It's cold." Jani pushed up the sleeves of her pullover and held out her arms to the summer sun. "I remember someone saying it's cold."

"That was me, sometime last month." Dieter stared at her scarred forearms and shook his head. "Sounded a bit like your homeworld. Acadia. Land of a Thousand Storms."

Acadia. She'd considered going home, for a little while. But while her parents would want to see her, she wasn't sure anyone else did. *Half Haárin. Cat eyes.* And those would be the kinder names. *Maybe later.* When she could tell Declan and Jamira Shah Kilian that she didn't care, and mean it. *Not now.*

Dieter waved a hand in front of her face. "Jani, are you—"

"Why is Meteora on the list of sites?" She opened her eyes wide and tried to look attentive.

"Governor Markos thought that the presence of some businesslike, physically intimidating Haárin might push out some of the more hardcore humanish criminal element. And some Oà expressed an interest in settling down there. Makes sense. It's more their climate."

"Oà?" Jani looked toward the once bare cliffs of Thalassa, now coated with houses like an overiced cake. "I didn't know—" She glanced at Dieter and shrugged. "Maybe I did."

Dieter contemplated her for a time, then shook his head. "Poor Captain Kilian. You'd have gone barking mad on a peacetime base. Or driven your commander likewise." He left her to return to his trundle. "Problems don't need to be life and death to be important. There is still much to be done here."

Jani remained on the balcony. Heard the library door close. Dragged a chair over to the railing, sat and propped up her feet. Because she was ná Kièrshia, Dominant of Thalassa, and had nothing to do until her next meeting.

"Sit down, Jani." Rudo Sikara ushered her into the office he kept in the business area of the Main House. "You are looking well." He looked dapper in charcoal grey, a red rose pinned to his lapel. "I met with Doctor Shroud yesterday, at the Karistos office. I told him I'd be seeing you." He sat at his polished bloodwood desk, bare but for a stylus stand and a trueleather blotter. "He sends his regards."

Jani nodded. She hadn't seen John since their return to Elyas. He had decamped immediately to oversee the expansion of the Thalassan medical facility in Karistos. When he did return to see patients, she spent the day in Karistos. She knew the ache would subside eventually, supplanted by a loss of trust on both sides that cut to the bone. "When next you see him, likewise."

Sikara nodded. Would have shuffled papers if there had been any on his desk to shuffle. "What did you wish to see me about?"

Jani leaned forward, elbows on desk, chin cradled in one hand. "Speaking as a longtime resident of Karistos, what can you tell me about Meteora?"

Sikara's beetle brows arched. "An unfortunate history. Rough sort of place. Smuggling, that sort of thing." He grinned, shifted in his seat. "I began my career there."

"Do tell." Jani took out a paper notebook and stylus, because she knew she would probably need to take notes, and in any case thought better with paper in her hand.

A few days later she stood at the walkway railing outside the library and inhaled the aromas of mid-afternoon sacrament.

"Veena made tandoori chicken." Dieter leaned beside her, his eyes on the mealtime bustle. "I would gladly crawl across the courtyard on broken glass for Veena's tandoori chicken."

Jani nodded. "It reminds me of my mother's."

Dieter stood quietly, fingering the cuff of his shirt. "When are you leaving for Meteora?"

Jani smiled. Did she really think her esteemed suborn wouldn't be able to figure it out? "Today." She watched the bustle in the courtyard below. Knew she'd miss it, even as she knew she needed to go. "Not for long. A few months, maybe. Change of scenery will do me good."

"The term is 'adrenaline addict.' " Dieter sniffed. "Who will I show my monthly updates to?"

"You can send them to me." Jani grabbed the railing and leaned back, enjoyed the sensation of a healed knife wound that no longer pulled or ached. "I'll initial them and send them back."

Dieter rolled his eyes. Quieted again. Started to speak, then hesitated. "Was it that bad?"

Jani considered her answer, because Dieter deserved a careful reply. "It's better now." The dreams had stopped, for the most part. Physically, she was as healthy as ever. Emotionally, she'd heal.

"It's different here now." Dieter's eyes glistened, until he blinked the shine away.

"It always will be." Jani's chest tightened, and she blamed the aftereffects of the wound that didn't bother her anymore. "And it's a good place. The best place. But Meva's propitiator now, and you're in your element with the organization. There's nothing left for me to do but sign off on others' work."

Dieter blew out a breath. "Best let Colonel Pierce know where you're going."

"I will." Jani stood still for a time, and took a last, long look. Then she patted Dieter on the shoulder and left him standing at the railing. Down a flight of stairs to her bed-sit, the small room she had moved into when she left John. Opened her closet and grabbed her duffel from the top shelf, still heavy with stuff from the voyage to Rauta Shèràa. Coveralls. Boots. Small clothes. *Jani's Noah bag,* Lucien had once called it. *Two of everything in case of disaster.*

What have you been up to, Lucien? I haven't seen you since we got back. Probably toying with her as he had with Val, declaring his interest, then holding back to see if she cared. *Eternal gamesman.* She checked the scanproof compartment beneath the duffel's fake bottom, which contained her scanpack and shooter.

Tools. IDs in a number of names. Because she liked to keep in practice, and because you never knew.

She closed the room. Locked it, because she knew she would return. Took the stairs to the courtyard. Waved to Dieter on her way to the entry, and felt his stare serve as escort as she walked out the door.

The garage proved empty, for which she was grateful. She opted for an older, nondescript blue four-door because no one would miss it and it wouldn't attract attention. Popped the gull-wing, tossed her bag onto the passenger seat, and inserted herself into the cabin. Pressed the charge-through, edged out of the parking slot, activated a music band—

—and stopped.

"OK." Jani pressed the charge-through again. The vehicle shuddered, moved forward a few meters, and stopped again.

"Way to make a break for it, Kilian." Jani popped the hood, then got out and examined the multicolored array of boards and battery casings. "Where the hell do you start?"

"Problem?"

Jani turned to the entry. Saw the rangy figure, backlit by outdoor brightness. Felt her heart stutter, and called it surprise. "What are you doing here?"

Lucien shrugged. "I haven't seen you since we got back." He wore civvies, white T-shirt and tan pull-ons. Trainers. "Just thought I'd, you know, stop by and see how things are going." He stepped up to the skimmer and pondered its innards. "What are you doing?"

Jani flipped up the top of a compartment cover, then closed it. "I'm trying to fix this thing."

"What's wrong with it?"

"It won't go."

A corner of Lucien's mouth twitched. "That narrows it down." He walked outside to his skimmer, a sleeker two-door the same coffee brown as his eyes. Opened the boot and drew out a large slingbag. "Would you like me to have a look?" Without waiting for an answer, he dropped the bag in front of the balky vehicle, crouched down and started rummaging. "I may have something here that can help." He drew out a scuffed grey oval about the size of a scanpack.

Jani caught a glimpse of the bag's contents before he closed the top. Other ovals. Squares and canisters. A lumpy polycloth roll tied with cord. "Are all those things what I think they are?"

"Just tools." Lucien placed the oval against the large flat-sided case that held the skimmer's brain. The device adhered. Hummed. Then dull blue light fluttered across the surface before settling down to a steady throb.

Lucien disconnected the oval and read the script that scrolled across the surface. "It's dumping your code. It's not that it doesn't recognize your permission to drive it, it's that it forgets. So you'll be able to reinitialize and start it, but as soon as you try to make a change that requires your code, like a Net setting or somesuch, it will have forgotten that you're allowed to drive it and shut down."

Jani shrugged. "So I won't try to reset anything."

"It's not that simple. You don't know the cause. Pinhole leak in the battery housing. Bad board." Lucien powered down the device and tossed it back into his bag. "The code-dumping is a symptom, not your main problem. Even if you don't touch anything, the skimmer could still stall out and leave you stranded between here and wherever you're going." He crouched down, concentrated on closing the bag. "Where are you going?"

Jani watched him fuss with the closures, drawing out the task, giving her plenty of silence to fill. "Just wanted to take a ride into Karistos."

"To see John?" Lucien stood, all perky helpfulness. "I can take you." He nudged the bag out of the way with his foot, then started to push the malfunctioning skimmer back into its slot. Looked through the open gullwing into the cabin. "Don't forget your—" He eased the skimmer to a stop and stared at her.

I should've put it in the boot. Jani shoved her hands in her pockets and tried to avoid looking at him.

"You're leaving?" Lucien moved away from the vehicle and into her sightline, leaving her little choice. "Where are you going?"

I should lie. But she didn't want to. "Meteora. The site of our southern expansion." She walked to the skimmer, tried to open the passenger door—

"It dumped—"

"My code." Walked around to the driver's side and dragged out her duffel.

"For how long?" Lucien finished pushing the skimmer back into place, then shut the door.

"For as long as I need." Jani slung her bag over her shoulder and examined the other skimmers. "I'm surplus to requirements here. Everything's clicking along." She leaned against a charge-station. "I need to go someplace that isn't. Clicking along. Yevgeny likes reports with tables and charts and whatnot. I thought I could go in search of some whatnot."

"I can drive you there." Lucien hoisted his bag, then stood there looking like a star athlete in search of a gym. "I have time."

"You taking some leave?" Jani tried to remember the last time Lucien had more than a day's leave when she lived in Chicago, and found she couldn't. "For how long?"

"As long as I want." Lucien's voice went as dead as it had in the clinic garden. "It's been a busy few months. After Zhenya won the election, deals were made. Ani resigns her ministry in payback for trying to have you killed, shuts up and smiles and takes the ornamental position doled out by her nephew. Along the way, certain embarrassing issues get shoved under the rug." He waved. "Like me." He looked around the garage, brow furrowed, as though he couldn't wrap his mind around his predicament. "I was strongly advised to resign my commission. They didn't have to ask me twice." A shrug. "I'm out."

"You'll go back to Chicago?"

"I was also advised to avoid Chicago for the foreseeable future." Lucien laughed. "You always warned me that something like this would happen." He settled his gaze on her, and his smile faded. "Would you mind a little company?"

Jani pressed her hand to her stomach. Felt the thread of a scar just below her ribs, where Cèel had driven his knife. "It's not a glittery place. Not like Karistos. It sure as hell isn't Chicago."

"You'll be there." Lucien took a step toward her. Another. "Things never remain boring for long when you're around." The smile returned. "Which is why you need me. To get between you and all those people who would prefer that you didn't shake things up quite so much." He jerked his chin toward his vehicle. "And my skimmer goes, and I can cook, and I have many other uses, not all of which you're familiar with."

"Be still my heart." Jani looked at his skimmer and shook her head. "It's too nice. It'll attract attention."

Lucien walked up to her, took hold of her duffel and slipped it off her shoulder. "It's fast. In case you've forgotten, there have been moments in our past when fast came in handy." He carried the bag to his skimmer and tossed it into the boot, then followed with his. "Let's go. We can make it there in time for dinner." He slammed the lid closed, walked around to the passenger side, popped the gullwing and waited.

No. Jani watched him, as expectant as a groom at the altar. *Not again.* Even though he had his uses. Even though she could look at him forever. *Even though . . .* He didn't even love her. He admitted it. *And I don't love him.* But she and John had loved one another. *And look how that worked out.*

She stared at Lucien until she caught the flicker in his eyes, the realization that she just might say no. Then she took one step. Another. Walked to the passenger side, let him help her in, sat quietly as he closed the door and circled around to the driver's side.

"It's green there," Jani said as Lucien pulled down his gull-wing and pressed the skimmer charge-through. "Green and mountainous and cool."

"That'll be good, for a change." Lucien steered around the garage and across the Main House yard, down the cliff road to the beach. Then the vehicle shuddered and they were out over the water, whitecaps lapping and seabirds swooping low.

Jani looked at the beach in her rearview and saw figures walking along the water's edge. Meva. Dathim. A few other Thalassans. She lowered her window, stuck her hand out and waved. Meva watched for a moment. Realized who it was and waved back, punching Dathim in the arm until he and the rest of the group started waving as well.

Jani kept waving as they grew smaller and smaller. Until they were bright specks In the distance. Until they were gone.

SFBC 50th
ANNIVERSARY COLLECTION

Year One (2003): The 1950s

1 *The Door Into Summer*, Robert A. Heinlein
2 *The Space Merchants*, Frederik Pohl & C.M. Kornbluth
3 *The City and the Stars*, Arthur C. Clarke
4 *Three Hearts and Three Lions*, Poul Anderson
5 *City*, Clifford D. Simak
6 *Under Pressure*, Frank Herbert
7 *The End of Eternity*, Isaac Asimov
8 *The Stars My Destination*, Alfred Bester

Year Two (2004): The 1960s

9 *To Your Scattered Bodies Go*, Philip José Farmer
10 *Norstrilia*, Cordwainer Smith
11 *The Man in the High Castle*, Philip K. Dick
12 *The Dream Master*, Roger Zelazny
13 *Stand on Zanzibar*, John Brunner
14 *A Canticle for Leibowitz*, Walter M. Miller, Jr.
15 *The Left Hand of Darkness*, Ursula K. LeGuin
16 *Rite of Passage*, Alexei Panshin

Year Three (2005): The 1970s

17 *Rendezvous with Rama*, Arthur C. Clarke
18 *Gloriana*, Michael Moorcock
19 *The Forever War*, Joe Haldeman
20 *Her Smoke Rose Up Forever*, James Tiptree, Jr.
21 *Wild Seed*, Octavia E. Butler
22 *The Snow Queen*, Joan D. Vinge
23 *The Mote in God's Eye*, Larry Niven & Jerry Pournelle
24 *Deathbird Stories*. Harlan Ellison

Year Four (2006): The 1980s

25 *Ender's Game*, Orson Scott Card
26 *The Anubis Gates*, Tim Powers
27 *Blood Music*, Greg Bear
28 *Mythago Wood*, Robert Holdstock
29 *Courtship Rite*, Donald Kingsbury
30 *Good Omens*, Neil Gaiman and Terry Pratchett
31 *Schismatrix Plus*, Bruce Sterling
32 *Startide Rising*, David Brin

Year Five (2007): The 1990s

33 *Snow Crash*, Nael Stephenson
34 *Rats and Gargoyles*, Mary Gentle
35 *Memory*, Lois McMaster Bujold
36 *Only Begotten Daughter*, James Morrow
37 *Doomsday Book*, Connie Willis
38 *Steel Beach*, John Varley
39 *The Iron Dragon's Daughter*, Michael Swanwick
40 *A Fire Upon the Deep*, Vernor Vinge